I0760630

Janet McNulty

Book 3 in the Enchained Trilogy

This is a work of fiction. The names, characters, places, and incidents within are the products of the author's imagination or are used fictitiously, and any resemblance to actual persons, living or dead, business establishments, events, or location is entirely coincidental. The publisher does not have any control over and does not assume any responsibility for author or third-party websites or their content.

ISBN-10: 1-941488-98-6 (MMP Publishing)
ISBN-13: 978-1-941488-98-0

Library of Congress Control Number: 2023908466

Printed in the United States of America

First Edition

Making sacrifices to do what is right is not easy, and sometimes comes at a heavy cost, as Noni learned. This book is dedicated to those who do it anyway. The world would prefer that we watch our programs, waste time on the internet, play mindless video games, and remain unaware of what is happening in the world around us. And while we are blissfully ignorant, everything changes and we find ourselves wondering why and how it happened and unsure of what to do afterward. The world wants us fighting among ourselves over the littlest thing, because as long as we are divided, we are distracted. This is what the world wants. This is what created Noni's world. But like Noni, we need to push against the mold society uses to shape us and realize that, in the end, we are all people with the same hopes and dreams, and that there is far more that unites us, then divides us.

This book is for those who, like Noni, sacrifice to do what is right and help those around them. You don't have to go to the extremes she did. Sometimes, all it takes is a kind word, a simple act of kindness, or a smile.

Trigger Warning

If you are offended by any of the topics or themes contained in this book, rest assured, no one gives a shit.

Grow a pair.

Or close the book.

N27461

Contents

Chapter 1	Rain	1
Chapter 2	The Aerodrome	13
Chapter 3	Obey	30
Chapter 4	Kumi's Warning	43
Chapter 5	A Funeral	63
Chapter 6	Faya's Scorn	70
Chapter 7	Another Visit	78
Chapter 8	A Challenge Made	86
Chapter 9	Preparation	114
Chapter 10	Prey	129
Chapter 11	Kition	161
Chapter 12	Perce	180
Chapter 13	A Wider World	198
Chapter 14	Arel's Long Arm	215
Chapter 15	North	233
Chapter 16	Discovery	251
Chapter 17	Predator	259
Chapter 18	Sullenness	274
Chapter 19	Githinji	293
Chapter 20	A Request	311
Chapter 21	Snared	318
Chapter 22	Survival	341
Chapter 23	Mercy	351
Chapter 24	Sacrifice	363
Chapter 25	Forgiveness	377

Chapter 26	New Faces	384
Chapter 27	New Surroundings	396
Chapter 28	Retribution	410
Chapter 29	Unexpected Turn	440
Chapter 30	Reckoning	456
Chapter 31	A Lie Exposed	489
Chapter 32	Arel's Protector	515
Chapter 33	A Final Farewell	539
Chapter 34	Noni's Peace	542

N27461
ENTOMBED

Chapter 1

Rain

Rain pours from the sky in a gentle beat, having never stopped after the night Mandi was arrested—the night she lied for me—as I stand at attention with my fellow arbiters, hands clasped behind my back, staring straight ahead at the gigantic viewscreen in the square of the eastern sector. Row after row of uniformed bodies, all in black, stand upright, ready to accept what is in store for us today, what none of us are allowed to escape: a public execution and a warning. Raindrops splash in the puddles surrounding me, sending up small bits of water as they strike the pavement, making my boots look like charred islands in a sea of murky water.

Moving my eyes, I try to glimpse the other arbiters standing in formation in the square as rain drips from the edge of my cap—we only wear them on special occasions—and look at all of them as they stare straight ahead, never flinching, never taking their eyes off the dark viewscreen before all of us, remaining poised, like perfect statues. Commander Vye stands on the edge of the line, keeping herself at attention, refusing to move a single muscle, like her counterparts, except—her mouth twitches, the tiniest movement of a muscle most would never notice, unless they searched for it. My eyes continue to move up and down the line of arbiters, observing who is present and who is not, and as I continue to look up and down the rows, I realize Renal is missing. Not all arbiters will be in the square to witness the executions; some must still patrol the streets to keep order and to make certain Arel's will is obeyed, but it's odd Renal would be assigned to such duties when he has always been at Commander Vye's side for events like what we are all about to witness at this moment.

A drop of rain taps my nose and runs down its ridge to the very tip where it clings to it, hanging in the air for a moment, before letting go and plummeting to the paved ground where it splashes, and I almost hear the miniscule splash in the deadened silence of the square. No citizens or plebeians are out today. They are not allowed, and any who leave their home will be executed. Word about an arbiter disobeying their duty and turning their back on Arel's authority gets around fast, but when it is two arbiters, swift action must be taken to ensure it does not happen again, lest people get ideas. Arel is never to be challenged.

I spot Molers three rows ahead of me, and the anger I had the night of Mandi's arrest flares up, boiling within me, causing my rib to ache where he had kicked me that night, but my desire to attack him, to rip him apart, squashes any residual pain I have. My fists clench, ready to obey my will; all I need to do is give them the command, and in response, my right foot shifts as I abandon reason, but before I can go further, the viewscreen flashes to life as a bright white light stretches across it before Kumi's face fills it from edge to edge.

"People of Arel," he says in a somber tone, doing everything he can to sound saddened and betrayed, but underneath that sullen demeanor lies a caged rage, "this is a tragic time for us, and it saddens me to have to bring this news to you—"

The camera pans out, revealing Tapiwa standing behind Kumi, and for a moment, I wonder who is the one in charge between the two of them. Kumi always gives the speeches, is always the face in front of the camera, but Tapiwa always stands behind him, watching his every move, listening to his every word, like she is now. Her plum-colored lips move as though she is repeating Kumi's words, but the coldness in her eyes gives a different impression: she isn't repeating his words, but hoping he remembers what he is to say—the real power behind the throne.

"—but two of our own—arbiters, no less—have betrayed us, betrayed our trust! They used their position to disobey the laws that are in place, laws that are there to protect us all from the cruel world outside our walls, and to protect us from the threats within our walls. This betrayal cannot go unpunished. They swore to obey and to protect Arel, but instead of serving our collective community, they chose to give in to their individual desire and abandoned us all in the process. Their selfishness has caused us pain, suffering, and irreparable harm to our way of life!"

I flinch as Kumi's tone goes from somber to wrathful.

"In the days before Arel, we were ruled by the fair-skinned and treated as oxen, but we rose up and defeated our masters, setting up this city, Arel, as a testament of our hard-won freedom! We have achieved equality, where no one hungers, no one wants for anything, and where no one is jobless. We all do our part for the good of Arel, as we all must, and the sacrifices of so many to bring about our collective freedom has been spat upon by these two traitors! They have turned their backs on you!"

A few grumblings rise among my fellow arbiters as Kumi's words bring out their anger, and the same demon comes to life within me, but it isn't Mandi or Amal it wants to devour. Commander Vye clears her throat, silencing them. We are arbiters. Emotions are our downfall. Flickering lights within grime encrusted windows attract my attention as I realize that even though people are to remain locked in their homes during this time, they are also required to watch the executions as well, and curiosity always forces people to act when they are forbidden to. Such is the way of Arel.

"These protectors of our society, of our ways, helped people sneak to the outside world where they could embolden our enemies! We are one! If even one person abandons us, it puts our society in danger and mitigates our shared struggle. One individual, straying from our cohesiveness, will give Kition what it needs to wipe us off the face of the earth! Alone, a person falls, but together, as a collective, we are strong and we will prevail, which is why the treachery of the two who will be brought before you cannot be allowed to stand!"

"Why?"

The quiet voice echoes over the plaza from the loudspeakers as it comes from one of the concubines standing behind Kumi. Both Tapiwa and Kumi turn toward the girl as she tries to sink into the shadows, hoping her braids will hide her, but what must have been intended as an internal, private thought had been released for all to hear. Within seconds, arbiters appear and drag the girl off the stage, clamping a hand over her mouth so that even her screams will be silenced.

"The infection spreads! It is time for the people of Arel to remember their place and what is at stake if noncompliance becomes the norm. Have you all forgotten the wars? The period of starvation? The chaos that followed when we refused to give up our selfish desire for individuality? Strength in…"

"Our kind!" The voices around me echo, reverberating off the exterior brick walls of the buildings surrounding us, and I imagine the people within their residences repeating the mantra of Arel with enthusiasm, but while their lips move, mine remain still.

"Strength in—"

"—numbers!"

"Strength over—"

"—weakness!"

Still, my lips do not move. Something deep within tells me I should repeat the words, that I must repeat the words like I have done countless times throughout my life, but another part of me wonders if I am more than what I have been trained to be, if I can be more than what my superiors told me I would ever be. Are greater numbers better than one? And what is our kind, a people that demands obedience at all times where nonconformity is punishable by death? I shove these thoughts away. I cannot have them. They are what caused me to get Mandi arrested in the first place. They are the reason Mandi now faces execution. They are the reason so many I have tried to help in the past have perished, and by my hand. I...

"Weakness is—" Kumi shouts into the microphone.

"—failure!"

The shouts of the others surrounding me drown my thoughts and beat through my chest, urging me to join, but I cannot.

"Failure is—"

"—death!"

A wisp of movement catches my attention and I turn my head, not wanting to disrupt the formation or bring unwanted attention to myself, to get a better glance at what seems out of place. A lone man stands inside an alley, tucked inside the shadows, obscuring him from prying eyes, but I make out the faint shape of his form through the veil of rain falling to the ground. For a moment, I believe we have locked eyes, that he has been watching me, and that uneasy feeling that overtook me the day the mysterious voice convinced passengers on a railcar to attack me overwhelms me again. Is he watching me? Before I can determine what this stranger is doing out in the rain, observing a bunch of arbiters standing in formation, he disappears, fading into the background as though he was never there.

"Bring out the prisoners!" Kumi demands.

The camera pans from Kumi to a copper door with Arel's

insignia on it as it opens, releasing a low screeching sound as two forms are dragged out of the darkness within and forced to step into the drizzling rain. They have been stripped of their arbiter uniforms and forced to wear what look like gray sacks with holes cut out for their arms, legs, and their heads. My eyes glue themselves to the viewscreen as Mandi walks with her head held high, proud to be executed for what she believes in; or she is too stubborn to show fear in front of her executioners because fear is a quality arbiters are not allowed to possess. Behind her, Amal pulls away from the arbiters leading him to the two poles at the end of the pathway, screaming as he tries to get away, insisting he is innocent. More arbiters appear and place a muzzle over his mouth, silencing him as they haul him to the two poles, while he kicks his feet in fear.

"Look upon them!" shouts Kumi. "Look upon their treacherous faces! See how the coward tries to run. These are the ones who put our collective safety at risk! They are the ones who decided their personal desires were more important than you!"

A series of boos and hisses rise among the crowd, filling the courtyard at the presidential palace where Kumi speaks, followed by rotted vegetables flying through the air, and I find myself wondering if those had been handed out for this occasion. Arel prides itself on order, and rotted vegetables go against that order. Bits of moldy cabbage strike Mandi in the face, but she never flinches as she is tied to the metallic pole, while Amal continues to struggle before being subdued with a strike to the head.

"These two are to die here today," continues Kumi, "but we are merciful, and they are to be given a chance to speak any last words. To ask for forgiveness."

Mandi laughs in response. Her laughter silences the gathered crowd as all eyes turn toward her.

"Forgiveness?" she says, her voice strong despite the black and blue marks that litter her face or how her swollen lip tries to impede her ability to speak. "You don't know the meaning of the word. You speak of treachery, but neglect to mention that you and your sister committed the first act of treachery when you murdered your father with poison! And we all know that the real power is the one in your bed every night." Mandi glances at Tapiwa, whose smug expression transforms into rage. "The real treachery occurred when we abandoned reason for madness. Tell me, Kumi, how much longer do you think you have before the one behind you has no further use for you? How much longer do you—"

Tapiwa swipes the air with her arm, signaling to the executioner to pull the lever controlling the flow of electricity to the poles Mandi and Amal are tied to, and Mandi's voice stops the moment her muscles seize from the current coursing through her. I want to tear my eyes away from the scene, but know that if I do, my loyalty will be questioned. So, I remain rigid, like I am supposed to, and clench my teeth together, doing my best to show no emotion as Mandi's face contorts in pain before her head hangs limp, telling me that she is no more. An arbiter stalks up to her, checking her pulse before moving to Amal and doing the same. He turns to Tapiwa and nods.

Mandi was right. Kumi is not the one in charge.

The acrid smell of burning brick and wood tickles my nose. Like a puppet on a string, I put my nose in the air, sniffing with intent as I search for the source of the odor, turning my head as needed, until I spot a trail of smoke twisting as it rises into the air. This is different from the constant thick, black smoke that rises from the crematoriums every day. This fades in and out as though someone is trying to put it out, or it is too afraid to make itself known, but it grows stronger with each second that passes, meaning that it is a different sort of fire.

Alarms blare throughout the square, spurring everyone into action. Arbiters disperse, running in every direction as they race to their duty stations, while Commander Vye shouts orders at certain arbiters, and I find myself trapped in the ordered chaos, trying to force my way through it.

"Noni!"

I turn in response to my name and see Commander Vye waving at me to follow her. Other arbiters move in different directions, as I push two people out of my way and squeeze past my fellow arbiters, sprinting over to Commander Vye, whose impatience grows the longer I delay. Someone bumps into me, almost knocking me over, but I catch my balance and hurry to the edge of the plaza, not caring if I shove others to the ground.

"Noni," Commander Vye says as I reach her, "you know the place Molers took you. Take five and head there now!"

I pause. I remember that place of filth where children are forced to give the elite members of Arelian society certain pleasures.

"What are you waiting for?" screams Commander Vye. "Go!"

I grab five arbiters rushing past me on the shoulder and motion for them to follow me, and Commander Vye's stern gaze orders them to obey.

More fire alarms blare throughout the city as we rush through the streets, darting down alleys in an effort to get there faster, while shutters close and people remain locked inside, not wanting to be out among the pandemonium and knowing what will happen to them if they are. We reach the narrow entrance to a side street, and I stop for a moment, remembering the man who lay there after Molers had shot him, how his unfeeling stare chilled me to the bone, and the rage I felt from his execution. A small cough yanks me back to the present and I take off with the five arbiters behind me, all of them unaware of where we are headed. My feet fly over broken pavestone after broken pavestone as I rush to the brothel's location while rain splashes around us and the brick walls surrounding us turn darker and more sinister.

"Watch out!" yells one of the arbiters with me.

A fire engine races down the narrow passageway, scraping the sides of the brick walls enveloping us as it charges toward the fire, sending sparks into the air. We dive into doorways, pressing ourselves against them as it surges past us, squealing as it goes and the wind from its passage whips rain into my face, stinging my skin. My racing heart refuses to be calmed as I step back into the narrow street and share the same look of relief with the arbiters accompanying me; each one of us knows we just escaped death, and no one would have mourned our passing. We are expendable.

Taking a deep breath to steady my nerves, I continue to the place Molers had taken me in what now seems like a lifetime ago. They follow me. Together, we race through the narrow brick-lined passageway as a thunderous roar grows around us the closer we get to the fire. The water soaking my clothes sizzles from a rise in temperature. We pop out of the narrow street and stop as the fire before us rages in a fury as though it desires nothing more than to destroy this stain upon our society. Men stretch hoses from their trucks and point them at the fire in an attempt to put out the blaze, but their efforts seem fruitless as the flames grow stronger while the rain turns into a light drizzle, almost as though it wants the building to perish. I agree with the rain. Let it burn.

"You there!" shouts one of the firemen. "Help us with this!"

The six of us hurry toward him as he struggles with his hose. We each pick it up and stretch it out, pointing it at the blaze, and help him steady it as another turns on the water. Nothing happens. Searching for the problem, I find where it has twisted and formed a kink and grab the arbiter closest to me to help untwist it.

"Look out!"

Before we can reach the knot in the hose, a third of the roof collapses and crashes to the ground, sending sparks, charred wood, and ash in our direction before it swirls in an angry fervor around us, stifling our ability to breathe. Another beam plummets to the ground, pelting me with embers, and I dive out of the way in an effort to avoid it. Coughing, I push myself to my elbows and turn toward the building as more of its supports crumble as the fire consumes them, and that's when I remember: the children—there were children in there!

I rush for the fire, pushing all rational thought aside as I remember the innocent souls who had been forced to work in that place, knowing that no one will have bothered to save them; but before I can take a second step, a strong arm wraps around my stomach and yanks me back, preventing me from putting my life in peril. The arm whirls me around so that I face the man it belongs to. Renal? Where did he come from? And why is his chin swollen?

"Help me with this!" he shouts at me and another arbiter.

I abandon my curiosity about Renal and hurry after him to the hose with a knot in it, and together, we unwind it, straightening it out, while another arbiter stretches the hose and points the nozzle at the burning building.

"Now!" shouts Renal at a man controlling the water valve to the pipes that run underneath the city.

The man twists the valve and water bursts from the nozzle, spraying the flames before us as others with water hoses join in, coating the burning building in a shower of cool liquid while the drizzling rain ceases. The fires grow smaller until they are no more, leaving us with smoldering ruins. As the smoke clears, I stare at the charred ruins before me as bits and pieces break away and clack on the ground amidst a low rumble of thunder in the distance and fear going in there, afraid of what I will find.

Commander Vye arrives on the scene and charges up to Renal, while a crew assembles to investigate the carnage further. "Is it done?" she asks him in a low whisper.

He replies by inclining his head in affirmation, while I take a closer look at his hands and notice the blood on his knuckles and the slight tear in his uniform. My eyes dart to his jaw, spotting a bruise forming around a tiny cut that could only have come from a punch to the face. Feeling my eyes upon him, Renal scowls at me and I jerk my gaze away, attracting the attention of Commander Vye.

"Noni!"

"Ma'am?" I reply, trying my best to sound casual.

"You and your arbiters will help clean this up."

"Yes, ma'am," I reply.

I motion for the five arbiters that I had picked earlier to follow me into the remains of the building, taking one last look at Renal's bloodied knuckles as my mind concludes what happened here. A board breaks underneath my boot as I step inside what is left of the brothel, while soot covers my palm as I hold onto anything I can to steady myself. Silence reigns while a smoky fog envelops me, cutting me off from those searching the charred remains with me, while my stomach leaps from the fear of what I will find, but instead of the burnt bodies of children, I see only those who imprisoned them. In slow motion, body after body of the brothel's guards are uncovered, each bearing the marks of having been in a fight, each lying in a crumpled heap as the place perished around them. One has a slash across his neck, while another's hangs at an odd angle, telling me it is broken. An arbiter beside me brushes soot away from a teenage girl's face, and for a moment, I feel pity for her, until I spot the baton in her hands and my mind flashes back to the day Molers brought me here to prove a point, the moment I saw this same girl shuffling the children into the main room for me to look over should I be interested in being entertained, and my pity turns to satisfaction that she met with justice for her actions.

A clawed hand reaches out of the ash heap, and I kneel down, clearing away the debris, revealing the arm and the person it is attached to: the proprietor. I remember him, and the disgust I felt at his words and actions as he mocked me in front of Molers. His wide eyes should fill me with some sort of sorrow at his death, but it doesn't. I am pleased he is gone, killed from the knife sticking out of his chest.

"It's a wonder the other buildings did not catch fire," says one of the firemen investigating the building.

"These walls," replies another, "were reinforced to protect this place should one of the other buildings catch fire. Who knew it would do the opposite?"

The voice of one of the arbiters with me attracts my attention. "It looks like they were all in some sort of fight."

Curious, I ease my way to another burned corpse, and though most of it is unrecognizable, some of the skin remains untouched by fire, but the bloodied bruises are unmistakable. I lift the hand of another, examining the marks on the knuckles, similar to Renal's, and a conclusion forms in my mind as a memory washes over me. I once asked him what he would do to a place like this if he could. He told me that he would burn it to the ground, and as I glance from one body to the next, I realize that one thing is missing in this place: the children that had been forced to work here. They are nowhere to be found. Someone helped them escape.

"Arbiter Noni," asks one of the arbiters with me, "what are your orders?"

I stare at him, wondering why he has asked me that before realizing that when Commander Vye had instructed me to pick five arbiters and come here, she had placed me in command of them.

"Bag them," I say, referring to the bodies that litter this place.

He salutes and hurries off to tell the others, leaving me alone in the burnt building with bits of water dripping from the charred wood that still stands, while a few firemen search for a cause to the fire, but they needn't look. One man stands out in my mind as the sole reason for this incident: Renal.

Chapter 2

The Aerodrome

Strands of hair dance around my face as sweat drips down the sides of my temple, caressing my skin as I ram my fist into the red punching bag hanging before me. The quad is empty this early in the morning. I prefer it that way. Bits of gold and red appear in the sky, lighting the top edges of the wall and draping it with droplets of color as it brightens with each passing second. Dawn approaches. My breaths come in rapid gasps, syncing with my fists as I jab the bag and watch it jerk away before it swings back toward me in a pathetic attempt to fight back. I spin around and jab my elbow into the hardened surface, not caring about the bit of pain that tingles up my arm.

Renal's face fills my mind as I recall his bloodied knuckles and how he tried to hide them when he caught me staring at them. Another jab shifts the punching bag to the right while I dance around it. What happened to the children there? Where are they? I remember the day I asked him about the brothel and the words I was never meant to hear.

That place deserves to burn.

That is what he told me. That is what he has done. I'm sure of it. The brothel is little more than a few charred remains, broken boards, and burst pipes, wallowing in the odor of smoldering refuse, and in secret, I am pleased about its demise.

I raise my left knee and ram it into the punching bag before practicing a counter-strike. The ability to fight hand to hand is as important as physical prowess, and I have allowed my skills to become rusty. My eyes narrow as the bag swings back toward me, threatening me with its size as the wind catches it and whips it, but I am ready as I brace myself, digging my heels into the dry grass while pulling my fist back. With all the strength I can muster, I thrust my fist forward, plowing it into the bag, causing one of the chains holding it to pop loose.

"You should learn to control that anger," says a voice behind me.

"Yes, commander," I reply, turning around to find Commander Vye standing there as though she has been here the entire time watching me.

"Get changed," she orders me. "We've been summoned to the aerodrome."

What? Only the most skilled of arbiters are ever allowed into the aerodrome. One must be part of the elite, unless there is another reason for this summons.

"Why?" I ask, and the question is out of my mouth before my brain has a chance to stop it.

Commander Vye's hawk-like gaze pierces through me, informing me that I have overstepped my bounds and am close to enduring another punishment. "What was that, arbiter?"

"There is no excuse for my insolence, ma'am," I say. "It's just... I am not worthy to go to the aerodrome."

"I'm sure you meant that we are not worthy," says Commander Vye; the tone in her voice tells me that she does not buy my pathetic excuse. "Our presence is requested. That should satisfy your curiosity."

By requested, she means demanded. There are no requests in Arel, only orders and obedience; dissent is met with swift punishment.

"Permission to speak freely," I say.

"Granted."

"May I ask who has requested us to make an appearance?"

Commander Vye's lips form a thin line, but her voice remains calm. "President Tapiwa. You keep making an impression upon her."

Why would President Tapiwa want Commander Vye and me to visit the aerodrome? Is she trying to make a point like she did when she ordered us to visit the crematorium?

"Why are you still standing here?" Commander Vye demands, spurring me from my musings.

I salute her and run off, ripping the tape from my hands, dropping it on the grass when I reach the door, and race through the sitting area to the stairs and charge up them. The door to my room slides open as I reach it, and I waste no time pulling my sweat-soaked shirt off as I rummage through my closet for a clean one and yank it over my head, wishing that I could have showered first, but Commander Vye's orders are clear: be quick. I check my pants as I search for a uniform jacket. They seem clean enough and will have to do. After I zip up my jacket, I rush for the door, but pause when I pass the mirror as my untidy hair grabs my attention. With a few quick swipes of my hands, I twist my long hair and wrap it around itself, redoing my bun, until every strand it in its place. Satisfied, I hurry through the door and down the stairs to the foyer before stopping cold.

Gwen and Sheila stand with Commander Vye with frightened looks on their faces.

"Commander..." I begin, but she cuts me off.

"We've all been requested."

Sheila looks at me, but I shake my head, hoping she understands that there is nothing I can do. The decision has been made and we are stuck with it. I feel Commander Vye's eyes on me, waiting for me to do as I am expected, so I stroll to the yellowed door covering the entrance to the manor, and it opens before me, allowing the bright sun to strike me in the face as I enter into its graces, only to be stopped by a surprise once again: a transport awaits us with its doors open.

"There is no rail that goes to the aerodrome," Commander Vye says, answering my unspoken question.

I step toward it and get in, taking my place in the back seat, while she sits in the front. Sheila and Gwen crawl in on the other side, taking their place on the floor, as their station dictates, and I move my feet over to the edge of the footwell to give them more room, hoping that Commander Vye does not notice. The doors close and the transport moves as the driver puts it in gear, taking us away from the gated driveway of the manor, and I watch as the building fades in the distance, looking pathetic and uncared for, while Sheila and Gwen huddle in the footwells, wondering why they are with us. They are not the only ones wanting to know the reason for their accompaniment on this errand.

The transport works its way through the streets of the eastern sector, bypassing the dwindling crowds of people—if you can call them that as more restrictions on our movements have been put in place—and ignoring the trolley's sharp bell as we pass over the tracks in front of it, heading for the northern sector. Like I have done on several occasions, I watch as the dilapidated buildings of the eastern sector change into pristine structures of glass and steel, with windows that possess no cracks or chips and are so clean that dirt does not dare cling to it. They tower over us, making me feel smaller than an insect as we wind our way through their maze, heading to the upper levels of the city. The whine of a railcar screeches around us as it passes above us, resembling a centipede made of rainbow glass, instead of a form of transportation meant to help Arelian citizens move throughout the city and keep us connected; but as I peer into the windows, I notice that very few are on it, unlike the times I have ridden it where it overflowed to the point where people forced their way on and off, not caring who got in their way, so long as they moved in the end.

We turn down a road I do not know and the windows darken, as though someone has blacked them out. Panicked, I press my face against the glass, wondering why I can no longer see through it before realizing that we will crash if the driver cannot either. I whip my head forward, but Commander Vye remains rigid as though nothing has changed, and that is when I notice it: the driver wears dark glasses, but unlike any I have seen before. As the transport turns to the left, before banking to the right, I realize that these are specialized glasses that allow him to see through the now blackened windows.

"The location of the aerodrome is protected," says Commander Vye, and judging by the warning in her voice, I know that I am to sit back and remain still. I settle back into my seat and try to give an encouraging grin to Sheila as she glances up at me with frightened eyes, while Gwen's head remains buried in her soiled knees.

The transport slows.

My head jerks up as the windows change, allowing me to see through them again, and my mouth drops open as a giant overhang towers above us, stretching upward until it forms a pointed arch, reminding me of the letter A, and as my eyes scan the off-white stone, I spot the three s's on the right side of a horizontal beam, finishing what is supposed to be the insignia of Arel. We pass underneath the beam and disappear into the interior of a massive building designed to hold aircraft. The transport pulls to a stop and the doors unlock, telling me that I must get out. I do. Echoing sounds strike my ears as I step out of the transport and place my feet on solid, yet smooth, concrete that has texture to it to provide traction and prevent my boots from sliding as I stand up. Arbiters in flight suits hurry past, ignoring us as though we are of little importance, and perhaps we are, since, compared to them, we are little more than insects: annoying and unwanted.

Two arbiters march up to us, and I stand at attention. "Identify yourselves!"

Commander Vye speaks first. "Commander Vye. Serial number V21923."

One scans the back of her neck, nodding as her identity is confirmed before turning toward me.

"Arbiter Noni," I say. "Serial number N27461."

He scans the tattoo on the back of my neck, the one I received upon birth, and nods, confirming my identity.

"Noni," says a sticky-sweet, familiar voice as Tapiwa approaches us with Kumi walking beside her, and he gives her a small, affectionate pat on her behind—thus giving credence to the rumors of their unusual, yet close, relationship—and anger flashes in her brown eyes before dissipating, not wanting to spoil the charade, "how good of you to come."

"As always," I reply, doing my best to hide my confusion at the request of our presence here, "refusing you is most unwise."

She smiles at me, showing me her teeth—each one makes me wonder if they are made of actual pearls—through her plum-colored lips, warning us all that it is best not to challenge her.

"Commander," Tapiwa says in a more formal tone, nodding in Commander Vye's direction.

"Madam President," my commander replies.

"This is Commander Ramis," Tapiwa introduces us to a stoic man who appears from nowhere and stands with his feet shoulder-width apart and his hands clasped behind his back. "He will be showing us around today."

"Madam President. Mr. President," says Commander Ramis, addressing them both.

Once again, I find myself believing that Kumi is little more than a pawn.

"If you'll follow me," Commander Ramis says.

I glance at Commander Vye, wondering why we are here, and judging by the expression on her face, though she does her best to conceal it, she is just as mystified, but one stern look from her forces me to do as I am told. We trail behind Commander Ramis and the two presidents with Gwen and Sheila in tow, their heads bowed, as is their place. I want to comfort them, to tell them that it will be okay, but I dare not as such an act is considered a sign of weakness.

Why are they here? Why are any of us here?

Intuition tells me that something is not right, but I cannot place a finger on it and have no choice but to follow Commander Ramis as he leads us from the entrance and into a dim, half-moon-shaped corridor that stretches before us in what seems to be a never-ending series of domed lights providing enough light to see the polished concrete beneath our feet. The copper paneled walls, each with a series of striations that make it appear to be moving, even if I stand still, curve above us, until they converge at the white lights above, stifling any noise contained within the passageway. Commander Ramis' swift pace hurries us through the corridor until we reach another door that unlocks and opens as we arrive so as not to inconvenience us. I steal a quick glance at Gwen and Sheila, but Commander Vye clears her throat, causing me to quicken my pace, and I charge through the doorway with the rest of my party almost gasping as a burst of sunlight hits me when I exit the darkened tunnel.

"Welcome," says Commander Ramis, "to the Arelian aerodrome!"

I crane my head back, taking in the massive skylight above us that allows the sun to fill the entire area with its rays, allowing us to see all the aircraft contained within the massive hangar, each stored in a specific spot with hoses running to and from them, pumping fuel while arbiters dart about with tablets, checking flight lists and inventory, and making certain that each craft is ready to fly at a moment's notice. I have only seen them soaring above me when they dropped their bombs to stop a riot, but seeing them up close causes me to have a new appreciation of the engineering that makes their existence possible. A cloud moves in front of the sun, causing its light to dim and brighten, sending a rippling effect over the shiny exterior of each of the aircraft, as though it is a delicate dance that must not be interrupted.

A few arbiters look up from their tasks as we stroll through the hangar, but bury their noses back into their work when they see Tapiwa and Kumi, concealing any curiosity they might have about our presence here. I watch as they check the internal systems of each craft, while others clean them, ensuring that their mirror-like surface remains that way, so as to show the power and might of Arel. As my eyes dart from one craft to another, a mixture of pride, trepidation, and anger fills me when I remember the riots in the streets of Arel some months ago and how the aircraft here were used to put it down; or how the riot in the mines was ended with the same aircraft before me, and how I almost lost Chase because of it.

"Your plebeians can remain here," says Commander Ramis.

We stop. I whip my head around to look, first at them, before staring at Commander Ramis. Leave them here? Why?

"Sir," I begin, but Commander Vye cuts me off.

"Wait over there," she tells Sheila and Gwen, pointing to a series of storage crates that are nestled next to an unoccupied cart.

They bow in obedience and do as they are told, while I bite my tongue to keep it silent.

"Continue, Commander," says Commander Vye.

Commander Ramis leads us further into the aerodrome, having walked among the aircraft there and allowing us a better look at them as though he is showing off his most prized possessions. "We have over one hundred aircraft stored here, each able to fly the greatest distance in the shortest amount of time. They are able to hold about twenty-five one-thousand-pound bombs. I'm sure you have witnessed their glory in the past."

Witnessed? I was in the middle of it.

"The aircraft you see here will allow us to win the war against Kition and to preserve the stability and greatness of Arel." With each passing word, Commander Ramis raises his arms and his voice as though to advance his point, allowing his words to reverberate off the walls and echo around us, causing chills to strike my back as each one hits my ears.

Once satisfied that his dramatic flair had its effect on us, he turns and heads even further into the aerodrome with all of us in tow. "If you'll all follow me."

We do.

Air wrenches, voices, and the engines of go-carts surround us as we hurry after Commander Ramis while he takes us to a set of stairs on the far end, leading to a balcony with a wall of glass behind it as shapes move about within. Once we reach the metal-grated steps, he hurries up them, motioning for us to follow. I lag behind as everyone stomps up the steps to the metallic balcony above, eyeing the mirror-like supports as they stretch from the ground to the balcony, making the space underneath appear to be a tiny shelter hidden away from the bustling activity surrounding it, but Commander Vye clears her throat, causing me to quit daydreaming. The view from the dais takes my breath away as I lean on the rail, looking out at all the aircraft before me as the sun shines upon them through the massive skylight, forming tiny rainbows and bright auras that blind any who dare to look straight into them. Pride fills me, knowing that this is all because of Arel, until I remember what they have been used for in the past: Arelian citizens are the only ones I have witnessed suffer under such might.

"Shall we?" Commander Ramis says to us as he holds the door to what must be the command center open for us, and we all pass through.

Screens with lines and dots fill the room around us as arbiters wearing headsets speak into their mouthpieces, communicating with someone on the other end. Others wander the room with tablets in their hands as they mark them with a stylus. A few glance in our direction, but upon seeing Commander Ramis and Tapiwa, they turn back to their work.

"This is our command center," says Commander Ramis.

I study the radar screens surrounding me, mesmerized by their colors, knowing that each one denotes a specific area.

"Here is where all our missions are led from. Our pilots may fly the aircraft, but the real skill comes from here, in this room. Each person you see here monitors various areas of Arel and the wilderness surrounding us and determines where our craft must be sent to subdue any threats."

I spot a screen with pictures of familiar buildings surrounded by blackened dust, recognizing it as the mines, and my mind is thrust back there to the night of the unrest and the bombs that had been unleashed, killing any unfortunate enough to get in their way. A slow anger rises within me, but I pinch my wrist to remind myself that this is not the place, or the time. I must remain in control.

"You can see why Arel is the envy of everyone," boasts Commander Ramis.

"The aircraft you have here," says Kumi, stumbling as he walks, making me wonder if he has indulged in certain pleasures, "is magnificent. Though, as stunning as the view is from up here, it would be a shame to not witness their real might up close."

"You are correct, Mr. President," replies Commander Ramis. "Please," he says to the rest of us, "explore for yourselves and learn why Arel is feared by all."

Confusion strikes me for a moment as Commander Ramis folds his hands behind his back and allows us to wander away on our own. Such an act seems odd in a place that is supposed to have some of the tightest security, but I pick up my feet and allow them to take me where they will as the others drift apart, including Commander Vye, and I find her lack of interest in my whereabouts odd. I head out of the command center and down the stairs, moving in the direction where Sheila and Gwen should be before rethinking my actions, knowing how it will look if I choose to concern myself with two plebeians who are deemed expendable. Turning, I move toward a lone craft that is kept apart from the main part of the hangar, wondering why it is by itself. Unlike the others that have a more silver sheen to them, this particular aircraft possesses a black hue that is matted, absorbing the sun's rays instead of reflecting them, as though it is designed to blend in rather than stand out.

An arbiter folds a hose nearby. She glances up at me before returning to her task, treating me as nothing more than a mere annoyance that is best left alone. Perhaps that is her orders and the command given to all here.

"Excuse me," I say to her, "why is this one different from the others?"

The arbiter finishes wrapping the hose and stalks away, refusing to acknowledge my presence. Bewildered, I stare after her, wondering why she will not answer my simple question.

"Stealth," says a voice, and I whirl around, startled by its sudden appearance. Kumi stands behind me, alone. Looking around, I do not see the others and find myself regretting having gone off by myself, making me susceptible to being singled out by one of the presidents of Arel. I have never seen Kumi, unless he was by Tapiwa's side, and have never seen him speak to anyone alone before.

"Stealth?" I ask.

"Yes," replies Kumi as he approaches me with a hungry look in his eyes, causing me to clench my fists, even though the punishment for challenging a member of the presidential palace is most severe, making the crematoriums a welcomed end, "the ability to move around unseen and unheard."

"I know what stealth means, Mr. President," I reply, keeping my voice even, and somewhat respectful.

"Of course, you do," he says, closing the distance between us as I move back, until I am against the giant tire that is half my height. "As an arbiter, you have been trained to be stealthy."

"So, what is the purpose of this craft?" I ask.

"What do you think it is for?"

"To strike Kition without warning and to help us win the war against them," I say, repeating what I have been forced to believe while at the training facility.

"Ah," says Kumi with a laugh, in an unsuccessful attempt to conceal his sarcasm, "Kition. Our greatest enemy."

He circles around me, causing the hair on my skin to crawl with unease, not because of what he may do to me should I anger him, but because of the way he speaks the name of Arel's greatest foe, and as I think back to my lessons from the training facility, it seems that Kition always attacked when unrest within the city brewed. The timing was… convenient, but…

No! It can't be!

"Kition. Kition. Kition," says Kumi, as though singing a song, not a cheerful melody, but one of doom and deceit. He reaches up to touch my cheek, but I grab his wrist and yank it down, twisting it as I do, not caring what the consequences will be.

"I am not one of your concubines," I say.

All of Arel knows that the presidential palace holds a harem of plebeians that are used for the entertainment of both the presidents, but no one dares speak of it, knowing full well what will become of them and those they care for. It is rumored that some arbiters, those who fail in their duty to Arel, have been sent there as a warning for the rest of us.

Kumi laughs, entertained by my refusal to fawn over him. "Isn't it amazing how people believe anything you tell them? Kition will destroy us. Insurrectionists are among us and will destroy our way of life. Barbarians attack our walls and will kill us all if they get inside. And fear… fear reigns supreme!"

Kumi circles around me, whispering his words, while I wonder about his intentions, or if he has lost his mind, when I notice a tin box the size of a golf ball in his hand and wonder if it contains tablets intended to alter one's state of mind. Drug use is forbidden in Arel, but like all forbidden acts, people do it anyway, especially those at the top of society.

"Sir…" I say, but Kumi ignores me.

"Sometimes, the real enemy is the one staring back at you," Kumi finishes, when a harsh cough jerks him to attention. He steps to the side, revealing Tapiwa, who was not there a moment ago. Her sharp gaze pierces through me, causing me to shrink underneath it, and the jovialness she had earlier has been replaced by silent, controlled rage.

"I believe your consumptions of the day have made you too free with your tongue," she says to him.

"Sister," he greets her, but his carefree nature disappears.

"Leave," orders Tapiwa.

Kumi walks away, and as he passes her, she whispers, "Get better control of yourself."

She turns her attention to me. "It appears that my brother's condition has caused him to say some things."

"I would not know, ma'am."

"And just what would you not know?" Tapiwa closes the distance between us, a dangerous edge to her voice that causes sweat to pool underneath the collar of my uniform jacket.

"I was unaware that he was unwell," I say, trying to find the right words to appease her. "I would have sought you out sooner if I had."

"His condition has been questionable of late," she says, but her voice still conveys that she is dissatisfied with my answer.

"I should go, ma'am," I say.

"And what did he say to you?"

"I do not listen to the rantings of an ill man," I reply, wishing something—anything—would happen to free me of Tapiwa's cold confrontation.

In answer to my silent plea, a scream echoes around us, spurring me into action, and I run away from Tapiwa's interrogation, heading for the noise to find Gwen on the floor with Sheila shielding her from the arbiters surrounding them as they toss bits of metal scraps at them. One arbiter in particular stalks up behind Sheila as she cowers on the floor with her arms around Gwen, while Gwen buries her face into her shoulder, and raises a crowbar, ready to strike. My mind races, searching for a way to stop this. I cannot let Gwen and Sheila be beaten or traumatized by this mob of bullies. She draws closer. Looking all around, I search for anything I can use to stop the arbiter before she finishes what she has set out to do. I spot another arbiter with a bolt in his hand and wrench it from his grasp—he protests, but I knock him to the ground—and chuck it at the arbiter approaching Sheila from behind, knocking the crowbar from her grasp.

The cheering and laughing stops as ringing silence surrounds us as all eyes turn toward me with a mixture of surprise and hatred for what I have done. I glare back at them, daring all of them to do something, knowing that I have no chance of defending myself against them, but fear attracts predators faster than honey attracts ants, and I refuse to show any of them my weaknesses, though I am afraid I may have shown them one.

"Challenging a plebeian is easy," I say, allowing my voice to fill the area as it bounces off the aerodrome walls and dances around us, "but challenging a worthy opponent requires more courage. Or are you too weak to attempt it?"

The other arbiters back away from us, forming a circle, hungering for a fight that they will be able to spend their nights talking about, while Sheila pushes Gwen away from everyone. Her fearful eyes tear at me, but I have made my challenge and must now see it through. The arbiter picks the crowbar off the concrete floor and grins at me as she steps to the side, pacing while calculating her first strike. For a moment, I wonder how she is able to get away with walking around in her undershirt while the top part of her jumpsuit is tied around her waist, but force the question from my mind. Now is not the time.

As we circle one another, eyeing each other and waiting for the other to strike, Commander Ramis, Commander Vye, and Tapiwa appear, but none of them intervene. I made a challenge, and it must be fulfilled.

The arbiter swings the crowbar in circles as she contemplates her first move, making me wonder if she intends to fight at all. She charges me, tightening her grip on the crowbar, and flings it at my head, but I dodge out of the way, ducking low as she rushes past me and almost slams into the gathered crowd watching our spectacle as though it is mere sport. She turns to face me, her murderous eyes focusing on me as she sizes me up and forms her plan to take me down, while sweat reflects off her toned muscles, telling me that she is a formidable opponent, but so am I. She swings her crowbar and I dodge in time to miss being struck as it whooshes through the air near my right ear, sending chills down my back, despite the sweat pooling between the fabric of my jacket and my skin. Again, she charges me. I drop to one knee, twisting as I do so, and thrust my left elbow back until it collides with her stomach, before turning again and ramming my fist into her mouth.

She staggers back while I jump to my feet. Her venomous eyes dig into mine as she wipes the blood trickling from the side of her mouth. Enraged, she rushes for me with her crowbar raised. I dodge again, but realize too late that it was a feigned attack, and before I can react, her elbow digs into the middle of my back, causing me to rear upward, exposing my stomach for the crowbar as she strikes me with it. A sharp cough escapes my lips from the force of her strike as my stomach feels as though 100 fists crashed into it, and as I hunch over in pain, a metal rod rams into the side of my head, forcing me to fall to the ground. The iciness of the concrete seeps through my clothes as I lie there, dazed while the world spins before me as I try to regain my focus, but a boot in my middle ceases such an effort, and I fall back to the ground.

Taunting footsteps and laughter drown my senses. I will myself to focus, to ignore the pain in my stomach and in my head as bits of blood drip from my temple and onto the gray concrete beneath me. Pressing the heels of my hands into the ground, I force my shaky arms to lift me up when I notice a shadow moving for me, and I throw myself backward in time to avoid another kick. The arbiter screams in rage as she stomps the ground in an effort to end me, but I roll away, avoiding each blow, until I reach the crowd watching us. Each of her steps pound the ground as she heads for me, but I sit back on my heels, ready for her next move. She makes it.

I jump forward, catching her around the middle and force her to the ground. Within seconds, I am on her, and I punch her with one hand while my other goes for the crowbar. She throws me off her and jumps to her feet, while I squat on the ground. Leering over me, I watch as her chest rises and falls while she raises her crowbar once again. I leap at her, but instead of going for her stomach, I aim for her left knee and plow into it with all my weight and feel it bend backward from the force of my impact. Her anguished yells of intense pain tell me that I hit my mark, and she crumples to the ground, unable to support her weight any longer as her leg sits at an odd angle. Wasting no time, I lunge for the crowbar and rip it from her grasp before placing it on her throat and pressing downward, cutting off her ability to breathe.

"Yield," I whisper to her.

She flails her arms, but I have the upper hand.

"Yield!"

She nods.

I release her and stand up, chucking the crowbar away, well out of reach, and the arbiter sits up, but stops moving the moment she tries to put weight on her leg.

The clacking of heels approach us, moving in a slow rhythm as though contemplating their next course of action, and I turn my head to see Tapiwa stepping forward.

"Well," she says, clapping her hands together, "that was entertaining."

No one moves or dares to speak as she bends low, pretending to help the arbiter I have defeated.

"Weakness," she says to the arbiter, "is failure."

We all watch her, unsure of her intentions.

"And failure"—a knife appears from underneath her long sleeve, and Tapiwa sticks it beneath the arbiter's rib cage, jerking it upward, ensuring her demise—"is death."

Tapiwa stands up, allowing the arbiter to lie on the ground in a pool of her own blood as her eyes stare straight ahead, void of life, and stalks away, pausing as she passes me. "That was enlightening," she says as she passes by. "Don't you think?"

Silence is my answer. I do not know what to say as I steal a glance at Sheila and Gwen, who both huddle in the shadow of an aircraft, wishing this nightmare would end, and I share their sentiment.

Tapiwa moseys away with a pleased grin on her face as she disappears into the shadows.

I look at Commander Vye for guidance, but she has none to provide as she tries to hide the same worried expression on her face and gestures for me to follow her, while Sheila and Gwen trail behind. No one bothers us as we walk through the aerodrome to the same doors we had entered earlier as they all go back to their assigned duties, as though a dead body in the middle of the hangar is a common occurrence, while dread engulfs my entire being.

Chapter 3

Obey

Lines of people stand before me, each spaced three feet apart as they stretch out from the booths that have been set up for this occasion: massive vaccination. Arbiters surround each line, ready to put down any who resist or prove to be troublesome. I watch as a fair-skinned man rolls his sleeve down after receiving his injection and notice the mark burned into it: the mark of a freed plebeian. On occasion, a plebeian will be emancipated as a sign of good will, that Arel is merciful, but in the end, and as Chase pointed out to me once, none of us are free: it is an illusion, and today solidifies this fact. In Arel, all citizens and plebeians are to receive a mandatory health check every five years where we are vaccinated against all diseases, or so we are told, but our mandatory wellness check was last year. Why is this one four years early? Any who do not comply with the wellness checks face swift punishment. Dissent is never allowed. All must submit to the will of Arel and her appointed leadership or perish, and it is my sworn duty to ensure that obedience is maintained, a duty I have questioned of late and shirked on occasion. Sometimes, I just want to be left alone. I shake such thoughts from my mind as they go against Arelian teaching and everything I have been taught at the training facility, and may lead to my death.

"Your duty is not to question, but to obey and enforce," I remember an instructor telling me and my fellow recruits while at the training facility.

The slow-moving lines before me remind me of the lines of formation that my fellow recruits and I were forced to stand in as instructors whipped us into shape. I remember one particular day. It was my 14th year as a recruit and we had been ordered to line up in formation in the courtyard. Someone had committed a carnal sin in Arel; he dared to question his role. We all stood at attention, hoping to not be called upon and made an example of, and I recall the relief flooding through me when the instructor called another's name.

"Grier!" the voice of the instructor had roared. "Step forward!"

A lone recruit stepped away from the rest of us, standing alone on the charcoal bricks of the courtyard with his black uniform making him look more like a shadow upon the pavement than a person.

"This recruit," the instructor had yelled while pointing at him, "dared to question an assignment! He dared to question the will of Arel! What is our sworn duty?"

"The obedience and protection of Arel, sir!" we had all shouted in unison.

"And what is the punishment for disobedience?"

"Death, sir!" we had shouted in unison again.

I had watched as Grier stood alone among his fellow recruits, alone among a sea of accusatory stares as everyone remained relieved that they were not on the receiving end of what was about to happen.

"Faya!"

The echoing of Faya's name off the buildings around us chilled me to the core. We were friends at the training facility, and she had been my only friend. Friendships—relationships of any kind—are discouraged, but they happen anyway, and Faya and I were inseparable at the training facility. Fear gripped me as I watched her step forward, and I remember the frightened look on her face as she stood opposite Grier.

"This recruit has also questioned the will of Arel!" the instructor had shouted. "What is the punishment for such disobedience?"

"Death!" the voices around me raged, but mine was not among them.

"But Arel is merciful," the instructor had continued as he paced in front of us, and my throat had seized up as an invisible clamp seemed to have been placed around it, almost like a collar. "Only one will suffer today and the other will be forgiven. You"—he pointed at all of us—"will decide which one receives mercy."

The instructor had pulled a knife from under his sleeve, and before I could stop myself, a single word, sharp and deafening, escaped my lips.

"No!"

The instructor stopped at my single command and turned toward me. I remember wanting to shrink under his piercing gaze, but had forced myself to remain rigid and strong. Weakness is never tolerated in Arel.

"Noni," he had called to me, "step forward."

I never moved.

Infuriated, the instructor seized me around the neck and dragged me out of the lines of formation and away from my fellow recruits, dumping me in the middle of the courtyard between Faya and Grier.

"It seems that Noni has volunteered to make the choice for you—to demonstrate the might and mercy of Arel!"

The knife clattered on the pavement in front of me when he tossed it.

"Make your choice."

A sickening feeling had overwhelmed me at that moment as the realization of what the instructor had demanded I do wafted over me: I had to choose who lived and who died. I refused to make the choice, and upon my hesitancy, the instructor pounced on me, gripping me by the chin and forcing my ear near his mouth.

"Weakness is failure," his hot, sticky breath whispered into my ear, "and failure is death." He pushed me to the ground and my hands landed near the knife, brushing the pointed end of its sharp blade.

"Choose!"

Faya's eyes met mine and her unspoken fear of death filled me as well, and my selfish desire to not lose anyone I cared about made the decision for me as I picked myself up, facing the instructor, before raising my left hand and pointing at Grier.

"What are you waiting for?" he had asked.

I looked at the knife as I understood the full extent of my instructor's command. It wasn't enough for me to choose who lived and who died; I had to carry out the act myself. They forced us to kill animals at the training facility so as to desensitize us toward the very notion of taking a life, but this was different; this time, I had to murder another human being, and failure to do so meant my own demise. As I hesitated, the instructor seized Faya, putting her in a headlock and squeezed his arm tight around her throat as his eyes bore into mine, while Faya's panicked ones pleaded with me to do what was commanded of me. I picked up the knife.

Grier, knowing what came next, turned to run, but the other recruits broke formation and blocked his escape, forcing him to face what Arel had deemed just punishment for daring to have an opposing thought in his mind. He dashed from one direction to another as I approached with the knife in my right hand, and each time, recruits blocked him. I gripped the dagger tighter as I approached, while sweat formed around its smooth hilt, threatening to cause me to drop it, and steeled myself for what I must do, or Faya and I would both perish for my lack of commitment to my duty as a future arbiter. Knowing his fate had been sealed,

Grier stopped trying to flee and faced me, and without a word, I plunged the knife into him, ramming it deeper and deeper until blood spurted from his wound, covering my arm in its warm substance, and as I pulled the knife out, I looked at my arm and my face's reflection in Grier's blood. His hand gripped mine, forcing my gaze to meet his and to look at the relieved expression on his face as though, in the end, he had been glad to be leaving this place, even if the finality of it meant that his brief existence had ended. In the end: death meant freedom.

Anger filled me in that moment, and as I stand in line, once again, waiting to be called, the memory of that anger fills me to the core of my being. I had allowed that same rage to dictate my next move that day as I had turned on the instructor, screaming in fury when I flung the knife at him, but he dodged, throwing Faya aside, and I had missed my mark. Within seconds, he was on me, and despite my training, I was no match for him as he threw me to the ground, forcing me to look up at him from the flat of my back, and the last thing I remember from that day is the sole of his boot coming straight for me.

"Arbiter!" the medical officer calls to me for the fourth time, yanking me from what had been a long-forgotten memory, forcing me back into the present, to this moment of once again doing as I am commanded, of obeying what none are to question.

I steal a quick glance over those who are lined up like me and spot Chase, and a bit of fear takes hold of me as I remember how the last time all of Arel was forced to line up like this for their mandatory vaccines, his sister had become ill, how none cared that another plebeian might die, and the drastic steps I took to get him the medicine he needed for her. It seems like such a long time ago, but it was only a year ago.

"Arbiter!"

Annoyed by the irate voice of the medical officer, I stalk up to him, my black uniform contrasting against his white one, and pull up my sleeve, exposing my arm while another scans the tattoo on the back of my neck, confirming my identity. He sticks a needle into me, pressing the plunger before removing it, and I pull my sleeve back down, straightening it so that my uniform remains unwrinkled before walking away. As I do, I glance back at Chase and hope that he remains unharmed as he is shuffled back into a transport by the arbiters around him to be taken back to the manor.

One man tries to run away and heads straight for me. The reflexive action of my training forces my arm to stretch out and catch the man by the collar of his red uniform, thrusting him back in line to get what we all must, and before I have a chance to second guess my actions, Commander Vye's voice calls my name.

"Noni," she waves me over to her.

I release the man as other arbiters move closer to him to ensure that he does not attempt another escape.

"Commander?" I say as I approach Commander Vye.

"A few citizens have not reported for their health check. We are to go get them."

Health check, wellness check—these are the names for the mandatory vaccinations. During this time, some are given a complete physical, but most of us just line up to get what we are ordered to.

"Yes, ma'am," I reply, knowing that I have been ordered to accompany her.

A transport pulls up, stopping next to us. Without waiting to be instructed, I open the door to the back seat and get inside, while Commander Vye gets in the front. It seems odd to be taking a transport to round up a few people who refused to show up for their "health check", but as I start to voice my concern, I shut my mouth, remembering that questioning anything in Arel can be fatal, and the gnawing feeling that this is more than a simple matter of ensuring compliance festers in the pit of my stomach. Ramshackle buildings (crumbling pieces of brick falling away from the exterior walls, a slanted balcony that looks like it will fall at some point, and the rotted paneling of windows demonstrate the sum of how people within the eastern sector live) pass by my window as we drive past, going to a part of the eastern sector that I have only been to on a few occasions. We turn down a side street and the shadows of the buildings stretch over us, blocking the sun and the high clouds that look more like a thin, gray veil doing its best to shield the sky from the inhabitants below. The transport slows to a stop. Commander Vye gets out, and I follow her.

She creeps down a narrow street—too narrow for the transport—with me behind her as we approach the entrance to an abandoned looking residence; its concrete steps form a frown as it seems to mourn for the corners that have broken away as cracks zigzag throughout them, causing more of the steps to break off from the least bit of pressure, while the support columns for the awning over them leans as it breaks apart in the middle, reminding me of how the eastern sector is left to suffer while other parts of Arel, the wealthier and influential parts, are well-maintained. No matter how many attacks Arel suffers, the area with the presidential palace, council chambers, and the economic powerhouse will always be rebuilt, but the eastern sector is where the dregs of society are sent and forgotten, and suffers the most from rebellion, which is why it is said that whoever can control the eastern sector is the most powerful in Arel. So far, none have succeeded. I push these musings from my mind as other arbiters in body armor and with weapons approach the front of the building, making no noise, and notice a wisp of smoke escaping a small hole in a cracked window that someone had tried to plug with a stained rag.

"You will take the lead on this," Commander Vye whispers to me.

Now Commander Vye's insistence on having me accompany her makes sense. She could have gotten any arbiter, a more experienced arbiter, but she chose me, and I cannot help but think that it is because of what happened at the aerodrome: I had showed sympathy for two plebeians.

"Comman—" I cut myself off, noting the hardened expression on my commander's face.

She has given her command and obedience is demanded. If I fail here, it will mean swift punishment, and a possible trip to the crematoriums; its fires are visible to all in Arel at all times as a warning. This is a test, and it is about more than my ability to carry out my duties—it's to judge whether I will fulfill them without question.

"Yes, commander," I reply as I eye the arbiters that surround us.

Commander Vye steps back, allowing me to take control of the situation as the other arbiters look to me to issue orders.

I eye the building before me, and a plan forms in my mind. One of the hinges of the door sits askew, meaning that it is loose and the screws stripped. This will make ramming it open easy, but it may still provide enough warning to the people inside, allowing them to escape.

"Arbiter," I say to the arbiter closest to me, "do you have any tear gas or flash bombs?"

He nods.

"Pick another to assist you. Upon my command, you each will throw in a flash bomb and a can of tear gas."

He runs off and chooses another to help him, as ordered.

"You"—I point at another arbiter—"get your battering ram and wait by the front door. The rest of you, prepare to enter upon my command."

They all line up in their positions, awaiting my orders. I steal one last glance at Commander Vye, who takes a step backward, letting me know that this is my command, and another test.

A jovial noise escapes from the hole in the cracked window, piquing my curiosity, and for the tiniest moment, I allow myself to entertain it, and I listen to the laughter and sounds of people enjoying themselves, until a cough from Commander Vye brings me back to the present and what is expected of me. I take my position, whipping out my baton as I do so, while the others await my instructions. I raise my hand with slow deliberation as my heart beats faster from the anticipation of what comes next and drop it.

Two sets of tear gas and flash bombs burst through the glass into the building, followed by a tremendous banging sound and a flash of light, while the tear gas fills the area with its smoke. The arbiter by the door strikes it with his battering ram, forcing the door off its hinges as it swings inward, allowing the others to go inside, and they rush in screaming at the occupants to get down before dragging them out.

"Run!" screams a woman from inside.

One manages to flee and charges into the street, looking all around him as he tries to figure out a way to escape. An arbiter hurries out after him. The man runs toward me, his red uniform contrasting against the soiled brick walls of the buildings surrounding us, almost like a bloodstain, a reminder of what this world offers to any unfortunate enough to live in it. Instinct takes over, formed from 18 years of indoctrination at the training facility, and I throw my baton out, catching him in the middle, causing him to double over as he takes in a sharp breath. Before he can recover, I bring my baton up and ram it into his back, forcing him to his knees. He glances up at me, and once again, my training takes over, and I raise my baton for a third time.

"No!" screams a woman as an arbiter drags her outside, the same woman I heard earlier.

I turn my head to get a better look. She's a plebeian!

Both the plebeian woman and the man in the red uniform look at each other as they share a silent gaze of longing for one another, worried about the other's fate more than their own, and the nature of their relationship is made clear.

I pause. The two of them remind me of Chase and the forbidden nature of our relationship—a forbidden love. Associating with anyone outside of your caste is forbidden. Arbiters associate with arbiters, engineers with other engineers, waterworks with other waterworks, and so on; and to associate with plebeians beyond the role of master and slave is a most severe crime with a fitting punishment. Offenses like this do happen, but Arel always cracks down on them, and as I study those before me, I realize that this was never about missing a "health check", but about Arelians associating outside of their class and forming forbidden friendships, thus violating the caste system, and about my increased sympathy for plebeians, and one in particular. This is a test all right, and a warning.

As the seconds tick by, I realize that I have been standing in the street, leering over this man with my baton raised—a statue in time—but Commander Vye's hawk-like gaze forces me to make a decision. If I show mercy, I will be taken away and they both will die. If I am merciless, one or both may die, but I will survive. I think of Chase, Sheila, and Gwen. Who will protect them if I am arrested for failing to perform my duties as an arbiter in this place at this particular moment?

Just like in the munitions factory, just like the tribunals from before, I am once again being commanded to show my commitment to Arel by proving that I am as ruthless as the rest of them. Failure means death, or worse. I bring my baton down, striking the man in the face. When he looks at me again, a red stripe stretches in a diagonal line from his forehead, down the middle of his broken nose, and to his chin.

Arbiters force the others out of the building: another plebeian and two more Arelian citizens, one in a blue uniform and the other in green.

"For failing to show up for your wellness check, you all are to be reprimanded," I say, pacing before them.

Another arbiter appears with a case full of syringes, while the remaining arbiters grab hold of the dissidents, ensuring that they do not run. One by one, each of them receive an injection. The man with the case approaches the one on the ground, but before he reaches him, the others scream in agony as their mouths foam and they drop to the ground, writhing in pain before going still. The man in the red uniform breaks free and races for the plebeian woman as she continues to cough and struggle for air, and he lifts her with gentle hands as he brushes her hair back with his dark fingers, whispering to her before her body goes limp and her vacant eyes stare through him.

"Stop!" I command the one with the syringes.

I cannot allow another to die in such a senseless way. All of this, every bit of it, is wrong. As I watch the man in the red uniform cradle the woman he loved, I realize that neither of them cared about the fact they had been born in a different caste: all that mattered to them was their love for each other, the bond that they had formed making appearance and class immaterial. They were two people who wanted to be together, and left alone, but Arel forbids such notions.

The man holding the box with the last syringe gives me a quizzical look, but I ignore him and turn toward Commander Vye, hoping she will listen.

"He's an engineer," I say to her. "We need his expertise."

"He violated the law," Commander Vye replies.

"Might I suggest reeducation? If that fails, the crematoriums."

The man in the red uniform looks at me, pleading with me to give him the syringe, as though that would be more of a mercy than my attempt to spare his life. Memories of the plebeian girl in the council chambers flood my mind as her face, which begged for the same, fills me. I granted her wish then, and even now, a part of me wants to grant this man his, but I am tired of killing people because they refuse to believe the way Arel dictates they should. Having your own thoughts is not a crime. Still, a part of me believes that forcing this man to live will torment him for the rest of his days, but before I have a chance to change my mind, Commander Vye speaks.

"Very well. Your judgement is sound."

Arbiters seize the man, ripping him away from his beloved, ignoring his howls of anguish as he is forced to leave her pale body on the cold pavement, a white blotch among grit and grime. Before they pass by me, the man spits on me, coating my black uniform with a shiny bit of saliva, and the hatred within his eyes unnerves me, forcing me to question my actions, and what I believed to be compassion, making me wish I had spoken sooner when questioning my first course of action. Perhaps allowing him to die would have been more merciful. As they haul him away, I remain rigid, immobile, and uncertain about my actions.

"Noni," Commander Vye says, pulling me from my spell. She motions for me to go inside where the dissidents had been.

Knowing I will not get out of this, I salute her and head for the door with two arbiters following me, keeping my gaze straight ahead so that I do not have to look into the dead faces of those who had been living moments before, but whose corpses are now left as a warning because of me. The moment I step through the shattered doorway, a sticky sweet smell mingled with the odor of burnt grass strikes my nose, and my throat clenches as it gags from the smell, but I refuse to give in to the impulse to cough; I refuse to show weakness. Torn couches sit on the sides of the room, their once vibrant yellow color more of a dull brown. A table, cracked and with a broken leg, is in the center of the room, coated in ash and trays that hold burning bits of grass rolled in special paper. Illicit drugs. That is what they were doing as they laughed and talked, unaware that we were outside. I know what I must do, and what the punishment for not following through will be.

"Burn it," I say to the arbiter closest to me before I step back outside into the muggy air, hoping to feel some sort of relief, but it is denied to me.

Commander Vye still stands in the middle of the abandoned street.

"Are there any more orders?" I ask her.

She shakes her head and starts to walk away, but I stop her.

"Have you ever asked yourself," I say as fire erupts within the building behind me, "if what we do is wrong? If they deserved this?"

She glances at the bodies on the ground before answering. "Do not convince yourself that what you did to that engineer today was merciful. I've been watching you, Noni, and I'm not the only one. If the aerodrome was not warning enough, then let today serve as one, and rid yourself of this newfound compassion before it gets you killed, or before far worse happens. It will cost you in the end."

"They were just people—individuals—who wanted to live their lives. Do we all not want that?"

Commander Vye's face hardens. "There are no individuals in Arel. You are what Arel says you are. Your identity is what Arel says it is, and for you, that is an arbiter."

She stalks away, making light sounds on the broken pavement, leaving me alone in the street while the fire burns every trace of nonconformity behind me as a warning of what happens when one goes against the dictates of Arel.

Chapter 4

Kumi's Warning

My head lays on Chase's chest, listening to the steady beating of his heart as he sleeps with his arm around me. I had snuck down to the plebeian quarters last night, unable to sleep in my own bed after all that has happened, and though he protested at first, knowing what the punishment would be if someone caught us, he later relented and held me, until we fell asleep. The boards above us creak, alerting me to the fact that morning has come, and I need to get to my room and change before reporting for duty, though I do not wish to leave the warmth of his embrace. Chase grunts when I slide out from under his arm and sit up, glancing at Gwen as she slumbers on the other cot with her blanket wrapped around her as its frayed edges hang in the air, while her hair spreads out on the pillow, hiding her face, reminding me of the night I had first run into her. The board creaks again as hard stomps sound above me, and I jump up, having wasted too much time.

"It can't be morning yet," Chase says as he stirs.

"It is," I reply, standing, trying to straighten out my tangled hair before giving up on it.

"Morning comes too quickly," he says, and Gwen stirs.

I put my finger over my mouth, and he quiets his voice, even though they will both need to be up soon to start their duties. Plebeians are expected to report to their tasks early and to do them with pride and cheerfulness, even while being beaten, but as I think about all the horrors Gwen has had to endure in her short life, I want her to get as much rest as possible.

"I know," I whisper.

"I wish we could run away," he says.

"And go where?" I ask. "Between the outposts and the barbarians, we would never make it."

"What about the ones you helped escape?"

I stare at the floorboards, blackened from years of grime and the formation of mold from the constant dampness that plagues this place as I think about the ones I helped escape in the past, Sigal's family being the first, and I wonder if any of them ever survived once outside the wall. Arel may be harsh, but so is the world beyond the wall.

"I don't... I have a difficult time believing any of them have lasted very long out there."

"Then why do you help them?"

Why? That is a question I ask myself each day, and the answer is always the same.

"Because certain death would have met them here. Out there, they have a chance, and it was a choice they made. What right did I have to tell them that they couldn't try? To be honest, I don't know if I am helping anyone or making things worse."

Tears well in my eyes as I remember the pregnant woman I had failed to help escape, and I feel the weight of her body once more as the memory of her dying in my arms haunts me once again. Chase's muscular arm wraps around me, comforting me, like he has done for so many nights. "You cannot blame yourself for every horrible thing that happens."

"Can't I? Some of it is my fault."

"Not all of it." He wipes a single tear that drops on my cheek and lifts my chin so that I stare into his gray eyes. "If you want to keep helping people get outside the city, I will be here, and if you ever decide that you want to leave, I will be here. We'll get Gwen and Shelia and take our chances, together."

I nestle my head into his broad shoulder, relishing the warmth of his body, wishing that we could stay like this forever, but the commotion above us reminds me of who I am and where we are.

"I need to go. Stay safe while I am gone."

Chase grabs my hand as I walk away and holds onto it for a moment as he looks into my eyes, and I know the unspoken message he has for me. He has said it so many times: do what you have to to survive.

"I will," I tell him.

As I leave the room, he goes to Gwen and shakes her awake with a gentle hand, whispering to her that it is time to get up. I tiptoe down the hallway, taking a quick peek in Sheila's room, only to find that she has already gone upstairs, which I should have done much earlier. I hop on the first step of the stairway, avoiding the small pool of brown water before it, and hurry up them, keeping my movements light so as not to cause much noise. My hand slips from the dampness coating the rusted railing, and the soft clack of a screw that has come loose and popped out of its hold, hitting the floor, reminds me of another bit of repair work that will never be completed. Such is the norm in the eastern sector. Once at the top, I open the door a couple of inches and peek out, making certain that no one is in the hallway before darting out and to the stairwell leading to the second floor. I hurry up them, dashing into my room before anyone sees me.

A soft whimpering sound prickles my ears, causing me to turn away from the door and to the shape hunkering beneath my bed.

"Sheila?" I say.

She doesn't come out.

"Sheila!" I rush to the bed and pull her out from underneath it, wiping the tears from her red and blotchy face as she looks up at me.

"He's going to kill me!" she screams.

"Who?"

"The Master Arbiter."

Molers. The rage from the night Mandi was taken away simmers, until it reaches a boiling point, but I close my eyes, refusing to give in to its demands. Now is not the time.

I help Sheila up and seat her on the bed, hugging her as I do so, trying to comfort her and let her know that everything will be all right. "Tell me what happened."

"I was supposed to serve breakfast today, but as I brought a plate of eggs out, I bumped into him and spilled egg all over him. He..."

She doesn't need to finish as I turn her face, studying the bruise forming on her chin, knowing what happened. Molers punished her. It doesn't take much to anger him, and his retributions are swift.

"He threatened to send me to the crematoriums."

The crematoriums. Their fires always burn, day and night, never ceasing, always devouring, ravenous for more bodies. Any who are sent there are never seen again. The lucky ones feed the fires; the unlucky ones manage them.

"Where is the little bitch?" roars Molers in the hallway as his boots stomp on the floor, sending angry hollow sounds throughout the manor that echo around us.

Sheila shrinks. There isn't much I can do to protect her. He will search every room until he finds her, but I must do something.

Molers comes nearer, yelling as he goes.

"Sheila," I say to her, "there is one way I may be able to get him to leave you alone for now, and it's going to hurt, but know that I don't mean it."

She looks at me with tear-filled eyes.

"Do you..."

"Yes."

Thinking as fast as I can, I look around my room for anything that might—my boots! I have an extra pair laying on the floor, scuffed, and unclean, having never made it into my closet. I grab them and wave her over to the door.

"Are you ready?" I ask her, wishing I had another option, and she nods.

Molers reaches my room as I open the door and throw Sheila through it, willing myself to cut myself off from my emotions and to remain expressionless as she hits the wall, while hoping that I haven't thrown her too hard, but the act must be believable.

"You little—I told you to clean my boots"—I wave my boots in the air, allowing Molers to see the mud still caked to the soles—"and this is what I get! Look at them!"

I throw the boots at her, with enough force for them to land near her, but not harm her.

"I want them cleaned and shined until I can see my face in them!" I shout, hoping my ruse works, but the doubtful expression on Molers' face tells me that he only half buys it.

Knowing that I need to do more to convince him that she has angered me, I approach Sheila and tower over her as she looks up with a horrified expression, acting in the manner in which I have been taught, in the manner I exhibited while still at the training facility when I believed that all plebeians were meant to serve and not to be seen as people. Steeling myself, I raise my hand and bring it down upon her, leaving a bright red mark on her cheek, swallowing as she yelps in an effort to not break down while she cowers on the floor, clutching her face and the fresh mark I have put there.

"Now go," I hiss at her, frightened by the sound of my own voice. "It will be the worse for you if they aren't cleaned by this afternoon."

Sheila snatches the boots and scrambles to her feet, rushing down the stairs and to the laundry, where I hope she is able to avoid Molers for the rest of the day, while I remain rooted to the floor, mustering what strength I have to not show any sympathy for her.

Arbiters are not supposed to have sympathy or empathy. Emotions are for the weak; that is what my instructors taught me, and for the moment, I wonder if they were right as my lip quivers, but I mustn't allow anyone to see it, least of all Molers.

He walks up beside me.

"Is there anything I can do for you, Master Arbiter?" I say, keeping my voice even.

"A bit harsh for some scuffed boots," he says in a mocking voice.

It is a test to see how I will react. Molers never thinks any admonishment is harsh; he believes they are never cruel enough. I turn my head, staring him in the eyes, keeping my face as emotionless as I can before speaking.

"Weakness is failure and failure is death."

Smirking, Molers leaves, and any heads that had poked out of their rooms to witness the commotion disappear as he does so.

Alone at last, I grip the corridor wall for support as the tears burst free, desiring to be contained no longer, as the guilt for what I did to Sheila overwhelms me, caging me with its condemnation. I may have had to do it to save her for now, but it does not make me feel any better, nor does it eliminate the guilt. A door opening jerks me from my self-loathing, and I wipe the tears from my face as I hurry back inside my room before another can see me, and as I pass through the door, I spot Chase at the end of the hallway covered in shadow—how much did he witness?—watching me with concern, but I cannot look at him right now: my shame is too great.

I rip my shirt and undershirt off and put on clean ones, dumping the old ones in the laundry, but before I let go, I hold them a moment as I ponder what just happened and my most recent actions. Did I do the right thing? Will Sheila forgive me? I release the clothing. Knowing I need to get downstairs soon, I pull on a fresh pair of uniform pants before snatching a clean jacket from my closet, smoothing the wrinkles that try to form in habitual fashion, before putting my long hair into a tight bun as required by regulations. Once the last bobby pin is secured, my hands fall to my side in slow motion as I study my appearance in the mirror, silhouetted by the red glow of the morning sun forcing its way through the window and into my room. I look every bit the arbiter I should be, except for my eyes: brown like my skin and where they were once full of pride, arrogance, and excitement, now sadness, guilt, and confusion fill them. My hand reaches up and touches the place where the tattoo is (an N with my serial number contained within it) the one given to me upon birth, denoting my assigned station within Arel. This is not who I wish to be. Not anymore. I am supposed to protect, not harm, and it seems I have been forced to do the latter more than the former.

I leave my reflection in the mirror, the reflection of a young woman I no longer know, and hurry out of my room and down the stairs to the main floor of the manor, stomping on the step that creaks, not caring if it alerts others to my presence. I spot a plate full of hard-boiled eggs on the table in the dining room and rush in there to snatch a couple, not caring if I seem rude, and shove them in my mouth, eating them as fast as I can. Good thing too, because at that moment, Commander Vye's voice echoes down the hallway from her office and to my ears.

"Noni!"

Swallowing the last of my meager breakfast, I stroll to my commander's office, doing my best to maintain a professional appearance and to not let on that her sudden command of my presence unsettles me. I pass the doorway leading into the kitchen and notice Molers hovering over a tray with a plate of food on it, sprinkling some sort of dust-like substance over it, but before I have time to wonder about it, my name echoes through the manor a second time, and I hurry to Commander Vye's office. I enter the familiar room, noting the reports stacked in a neat pile in a corner of her desk, the pens lined in a neat row before the reports, and the absence of dust—not even the slightest speck of it can be seen on the shiny, metallic surface—as she sits in her chair, straight-backed and rigid, watching me with her hawk-like gaze that had filled me with anxiety upon my first day here.

"Commander," I say.

"I hear that there was a disturbance upstairs earlier."

Molers. My fists clench as my thoughts turn toward him, but I take a deep breath and relax. Now is not the time.

"Just a plebeian forgetting her place," I reply, knowing the charade I must keep.

"Master Arbiter Molers..."

"With all due respect, ma'am, Molers wants your job, and he doesn't like me much."

Commander Vye's eyes narrow as she glares at me. I have overstepped my bounds, once again. I know it, but I tire of the constant questioning of my loyalty. Have I not proven myself?

A soft knock raps the door.

"Enter," says Commander Vye.

A plebeian enters with a tray containing a plate of food—the same one I had spotted earlier in the kitchen with Molers—a glass of water, a napkin, and utensils, and places it in front of her before leaving without a word.

My mind springs me back to a few minutes earlier. What was Molers doing in the kitchen? Dread washes over me as the sense that something is not right prickles my mind, and as Commander Vye readies her fork, I dive for the tray and shove it off the table, contents and all, allowing all of it to clatter to the floor, covering it in eggs, fruit, and cauliflower, while the water splashes the stained wall.

"What is..."

"Forgive me, commander," I plead with her, cutting her off, "but I don't think you should eat that."

"Noni, you must learn..."

"I saw Molers alone with it earlier."

Silence envelops the room upon my words as the irate expression on Commander Vye's face softens and she realizes the implication within my words.

"Please, commander," I continue, "think about it. Molers managed to get himself assigned here to the eastern sector after years of being denied. Any who can command the eastern sector may be able to advance further, and may even have the chance of being named Admiral and placed in charge of the guards at the presidential palace. His ambition knows no bounds. The only person standing between him and his goal is you."

Commander Vye ponders my words before speaking. "I know that there is no love lost between you two, and his reputation at the training facility is well-known."

She eyes the cauliflower on the floor, alone as though it was sacrificed for another's end.

"Your presence has been requested at the hospice here in the eastern sector," Commander Vye says, changing the subject. "You will report there immediately."

"Commander..." I begin.

"You're dismissed!"

"Yes, commander." I salute her, but before I can leave, she stops me.

"One other thing: I'm not the only one here with enemies."

Her warning unnerves me as I open the door, stopping when I see Molers outside. Was he waiting there for the moment when I call for help?

"Master Arbiter," says Commander Vye, noticing his presence, "is there something I can do for you?"

He glances at the overturned tray and its contents littering the floor, while the water seeps through the wooden floorboards. "No, commander," he growls.

The disappointed look on his face betrays his true intentions.

"Then get a plebeian to clean this mess up," replies Commander Vye. "Noni, you have your orders."

I salute her again before turning to Molers and saluting him, as is expected when meeting a higher-ranking officer, and head for the front entrance, glancing back as Molers stalks off, doing his best to contain his rage over his failed attempt at poisoning my commander. I cannot help but smile at his misfortune.

Within minutes, I am at the trolley tracks, having run out of the manor and down the driveway to the street. Enough time has been lost, and I do not wish to be punished for wasting more. The bell of the trolley alerts me to its presence, and as it hurries past, I jump on, not waiting for it to stop, and take my place near the front, ignoring the eyes that watch me, except something is different about them. In the past, people turned their glances away the moment they noticed my arbiter uniform, but today, they keep their gazes upon me. I glare at all of them, not wanting to show weakness as weakness invites trouble, but I am alarmed by this. Something has changed in Arel, and the sense that this change puts my life in a precarious position fills me with a sense of dread. I meet the stares with an unwavering gaze, one all arbiters are taught to have, but only a few turn away, while the rest remain fixed on me, and as I glance from one set of eyes to the next, the voice from the loudspeaker of the railcar repeats its words in my mind.

To my relief, the trolley approaches my stop and I jump off, glad to be out of there. As I walk the last two blocks to my destination, I keep a wary eye on the people passing me, noting how some avert their gaze, while others do not, similar to my experience on the trolley, pausing as I reach the walk to the hospice, when a lone figure standing on the other side of the street—half in shadow and half in sunlight—catches my attention. I recognize him as the same man I saw during Mandi's execution, and can feel his eyes on me like I did that day. I start for him, but stop when my wristband chirps, reminding me of my orders, forcing my reluctant feet to turn back to the hospice and continue onward. The white building of the medical center glows gold in the sunlight as I approach the bleached columns with the hospice insignia on it, stopping when I see the two guards stationed in front of the semi-transparent, silver doors. They were not here the first time I entered this place.

"Identify yourself," they demand.

"Arbiter Noni. Serial Number N27461. I was summoned here."

Before the guard can respond, the doors to the medical center slide open and Doctor Sahir rushes out.

"Arbiter Noni," he greets me, "it's a pleasure seeing you again. Please follow me."

I do, wondering about his amicable manner. When I was last here, he was pleasant, but all business.

"It is good of you to come."

"I was told my presence had been requested."

Doctor Sahir stops. "You don't know?"

The quizzical look on my face must have answered his question because he starts talking once again.

"President Tapiwa wished for you to be here."

Tapiwa. She has been requesting my presence a lot these days, and I have not figured out the reason behind it.

"Please," Doctor Sahir says, holding his arm out, motioning me to allow him to lead me through the facility.

I follow him down a hallway, its immaculate white walls blinding me as they work in conjunction with the copper floor to reflect the sun's light that spills through the oval skylights above us. Doctors, nurses, and technicians pass us as we hurry to the other end of the hospice where the room of glass is, but before we reach it, Doctor Sahir veers to the right, heading down another corridor with amber lights reflecting off the pristine walls, while plebeians clean them so that they remain spotless. Doctor Sahir's boots clack on the tiles, and I remark at how they bear no scuff marks or signs of wear and tear, just like his white uniform, wondering how he keeps them that clean before remembering that the plebeians are the reason.

As we reach the end of the hallway, the amber glow of the wall lights dims, overpowered by the intense brightness of the sun as we enter another hallway with crystal glass for its exterior wall, allowing us to see the interior of the atrium, and as I look up at the walls of glass above me, I spot the bay window Doctor Sahir had shown me on my first visit. I press my face against the cool glass, trying to take in as much as I can, marveling at how perfect this place looks, despite the fact that a portion of it is still under repair from one of the barbarian attacks. As we walk past the atrium and the glass hallway, I spot a figure that doesn't seem to belong in this place, and my pace slows so that I can get a better look at him: Luther. I stare at him, wondering why he is here, though I conclude that it does not seem to be because of health issues as he talks to a group of engineers; their red uniforms stick out against the white walls behind the panes of glass, making quite the sight as medical staff rush by in their white uniforms, while I stand alone in black.

"Arbiter Noni," Doctor Sahir calls to me, "the elevators are this way."

I peel myself away from the glass and my curiosity about Luther's presence.

"I thought the elevators were on the other end," I say, remembering the elevators I was brought to on my first visit here.

Doctor Sahir chuckles. "We have more than one elevator, and these"—he presses a button once we reach them and a soft, green light scans his thumbprint—"go to a more secluded area."

The elevator dings as the copper doors open, allowing us through. I step inside and Doctor Sahir presses the lone button on the panel next to the doors, and once again, a light scans his thumbprint. The doors close. The smoothness of the elevator's movements tricks me into thinking that we have not gone anywhere at all, even though it takes us upward to one of the many floors above us.

"Noni," Doctor Sahir's voice changes to one of concern and a warning, "be careful of what you say when we reach our floor."

My brows scrunch together in confusion. Why is he telling me this? A quick glance around reveals no camera, meaning that only certain individuals are allowed in this elevator—the sort that do not wish to have their activities recorded.

"What troubles you?" I ask.

"Just watch yourself."

An unnatural heat rises around me, making me sweat underneath my uniform, causing the material to cling to me as Doctor Sahir's indirect warning unnerves me. I want to ask him why he is doing this and what has happened, but time is short, and soon we will reach our destination. A part of me wonders if he has helped me before, and I think back to the time I forced myself to be hospitalized here so that I could get the medicine I needed for Gwen's illness. Was he the one who gave it to me? At first, I believed that it had been Natalie, but I could be wrong.

"Doctor," I begin, "did you..."

A soft ding warns us that we have reached our floor and the doors open, revealing a private room with one way in and one way out: the elevator. Doctor Sahir steps through the doors and into a massive chamber with me following behind, frustrated at having been interrupted, but perhaps it is for the best. Fogged glass surrounds us as we head to a bed with a lone occupant and a figure standing next to it on the other side of the room, walking past a plush couch and chestnut tables. Movement catches my attention, and I realize that we are not alone; palace guards hide in the shadows, blending in with the background, ready to strike should any threat arise. Alerted to our presence, the figure by the bed turns around.

"Noni," says Tapiwa in a silky voice—her golden gown ripples with each movement, making the lavender embroidery appear to come alive—and her faux pleasantness causes me to be wary of her, "I'm glad you came."

I nod my head, even though I had no choice in the matter.

"I would have sent one of them down to get you"—Tapiwa points at one of the guards in the room—"but Doctor Sahir insisted on bringing you himself."

"Considering your brother's sudden illness, I needed to make certain that she would not introduce any additional complications. A quick health check was called for, for your brother's safety."

"Of course," Tapiwa replies, and I notice a tightness to her voice, as though she is feigning concern over the state of her brother's health. "And?"

"She is a true testament to the perfect health of our arbiters," says Doctor Sahir.

I take a closer look at Kumi, whose once dark face now looks ashen and is covered in sweat as his eyes try hard to focus on those around him. Not long ago, I saw him in the aerodrome and he was healthy, if a little intoxicated, but this sudden turn for the worse seems off, as well as his presence here. The presidential palace has its own hospice and there are better medical facilities within Arel, so why is Kumi here? Why am I here?

"Tell me," says Tapiwa, "how are things in the eastern sector?"

"Unchanged," I reply with caution. "There is increased unrest, but if you want a full report, shouldn't you talk with my commander?"

"I have heard disturbing news about your commander," says Tapiwa. "There has been a report filed about her inability to contain the unrest as though she wishes not to."

A report? Tapiwa does not seem the type to read arbiter reports. Why would she bother with it unless... unless she believes that the ones who initiated the bombings and recent attacks on the people originated here in the eastern sector and that Commander Vye might have something to do with it.

Incensed at such an allegation against my commander, and having an inkling as to whom made that report, my mouth speaks before my brain can contain it. "Madam President, Commander Vye has always served Arel and executes her duties with precision. She makes certain that the arbiters under her command fulfill their oath to protect Arel, and any who do not are met with swift punishment. I have never witnessed her act in a manner that would convey an ounce of betrayal. As for that report, it might interest you to know that Master Arbiter Molers has his own ambitions and does everything for his own ends."

Doctor Sahir steps behind Tapiwa and shakes his head at me, warning me to contain myself, but my anger at being used and tested outweighs my common sense and my sense of self preservation.

"I never said it was him who sent the report," says Tapiwa.

"You haven't denied it either," I reply.

Tapiwa bursts with laughter, but it sounds hollow. "I knew I liked you, Noni. Such a bold one, but even temerity overstays its welcome."

Kumi squirms in the bed and Doctor Sahir checks his vitals. "Madam President," he says, "I must speak with you alone."

I watch as the doctor leads Tapiwa away—the light shines upon the gold threads in her hair, making it look more like a crown—and explains her brother's situation to her, and judging by the movement of his arms, it isn't good, yet her face remains emotionless, as though she does not care, or is pleased.

Kumi's sweaty hand clamps around my wrist, forcing me to face him, but before I can pull free of his grasp, his lips move, but his voice is inaudible. I glance at Tapiwa, making certain that she remains unaware of Kumi's actions before I bend low to hear what he has to say.

"Beware of my sister," he whispers to me, his voice strained and hoarse. "Nothing is as it seems. Kition isn't... poison... our father."

He takes in a sharp breath.

"She likes her toys," he continues, "and when their usefulness is spent, they are tossed aside."

His hand tightens around my wrist, using the last of his strength.

"Theater... it's all... trust no... one."

He releases my wrist when she turns around and I bolt upright, pretending to have been standing at attention the entire time as she rushes back to the bed, glaring at me.

"Did he speak to you?" she demands.

"No, ma'am," I reply.

She studies me, unsure of whether I speak the truth or not, but very aware of how she must keep up appearances.

"Permission to speak freely," I say to her, and she nods. "Why am I here? With the growing unrest, I belong out there protecting the people of Arel."

"Of course," she replies. "Doctor Sahir will show you out."

Knowing not to argue, Doctor Sahir inclines his head to her and ushers me to the elevator, and I obey, realizing that it is time for me to leave, but finding the ease of which she agreed with my desire to leave odd. As we head for the door, a plebeian appears from the shadows with a pitcher full of water and runs into me, knocking me backwards as she spills the clear liquid on my front. I look around me, feeling Tapiwa's eyes on me, watching what I do next and knowing what I am expected to do. The sense that this is a setup plagues me, but I mustn't falter now. I glance at the plebeian girl—she looks to be the same age as Gwen or Sheila—and the frightened eyes that stare up at me, waiting for my outburst of anger at her mistake. Silence rings in my ears as all of them watch me, waiting to see what my reaction will be and the real reason for me being called here dawns on me: Tapiwa wants to know just how deep my sympathy for the plebeians goes.

I raise my hand, swallowing back my emotions, and backhand the plebeian, allowing the sound of my hand meeting the girl's face to fill the room.

"Stupid girl," I mutter, hoping my voice does not crack, and walk away, entering the elevator as the doors slide open for me, with Doctor Sahir by my side. Before the doors close, I direct my gaze at Tapiwa and notice the victorious smirk on her face.

Once the elevator stops, Doctor Sahir leads me through the hospice and to the entrance in silence as there is nothing he can say that will undo my actions, or make me feel better about them. As we stroll through the facility, personnel glance in our direction, noting our presence, before going back to their tasks and ignoring us, as though we are little more than a speck of dust on the floor. The shapes move on the other side of the semi-transparent, silver doors coming into full view as the doors slide open for me once we reach the entrance.

"Noni,"—Doctor Sahir places a gentle hand on my shoulder—"I'm sorry about your instructor."

The kindness in his voice disarms me and almost makes me lose the rigid demeanor I adopted on the way out, but I cannot breakdown here.

"How is Natalie?" I ask, trying to regain my composure and change the subject.

"She'll be fine."

I smile at the doctor and step out into the sunlight, breathing in a deep lungful of air, glad to be out of that place, and still wondering what the full extent of Tapiwa's plans are. Luther stands outside with the group of engineers, discussing the exterior of the building, and I decide to go over there to hear what he has to say when I notice the same man that had watched me enter the facility still standing in the same spot, having never moved. I start for him, wondering why he is there, when a series of harsh coughs force me to notice another man approaching the far side of the building, which is odd because most who need of medical care would go through the main entrance. Puzzled by his behavior, I watch as he approaches the far corner, unable to contain his cough, and as his hands reach into his pocket, the flap of his jacket pulls away, revealing a strange looking vest. Something is not right.

"Hey!" I shout at him.

He refuses to acknowledge my presence and increases his pace.

"Hey!"

Luther looks at me before glancing at the man, and that is when I realize that the vest is a bomb.

"Get out!" I scream at everyone while running for the man with the vest. "Get out of here now!"

Before I can take another step, a loud blast deafens my ears as a tremendous force lifts me from my feet and throws me backward, until I crash onto the pavement as debris lands on top of me, causing me to black out for a moment.

"Noni!"

I know the voice that calls my name, but it sounds distant, muddled by the ringing within my ears. Hands move a piece of steel off me.

"Noni! Noni, wake up!"

The same hands remove more of the metallic debris that covers me, but my disoriented mind refuses to focus.

"NONI!" screams the same voice as a hand slaps my face, not hard, but enough to force me to open my eyes, and I lay my head back as Luther's face comes into focus.

"We need to quit meeting like this," I joke, followed by a series of coughs as I choke on the dust hovering in the air, while bits of glass clink on the pavement, forming a ring around us.

"Can you move?" he asks me, showing a concern for me that he has never exhibited before.

I try to sit up as I force my mind to concentrate, glad that sounds penetrate my ears, growing louder as they do and the ringing dissipates.

"Are you okay?" I ask.

"Me? Never better," he replies as he helps me to my feet.

I scan the chaos around me and spot the same man that had watched me enter the hospice and I take off after him, stumbling at first as I struggle to maintain my balance, but I push through, and with each step, my mind becomes sharper, zeroing in on the man. If he has something to do with this, I intend to find out. He runs.

I chase after him, but falter and am forced to cling to a nearby rail to maintain my balance, but as the man disappears further into the distance, my resolve to catch him strengthens, and I rise to my full height before taking off after him again.

"Noni!" Luther shouts after me.

I ignore him. If this man knows anything about this bombing, I must find out. I charge after him, hurrying down the walk and into the streets where onlookers gather to marvel at the hole in the only remaining medical facility within the eastern sector. My pace slows as I shove my way through the gathered crowd, and instead of clearing a path for me like most have in the past after seeing my arbiter uniform, they remain frozen, refusing to allow me passage. One snatches my arm. Out of impulse, I punch him in the face, forcing him to let me go and to step out of my way. Once through, I race down the street, ignoring the commotion around me, and my focus on the man is so great, that I never notice the ledge of the sidewalk I approach. My foot catches it and gravity takes hold, causing me to crash onto the pavement, tearing the left sleeve of my jacket as I land.

The man stands yards away. He turns back, and when he realizes that I have not given up pursuit, he darts down a narrow walk. Rising to my knees, I force myself to get up, even though I teeter on the verge of passing out, and continue after him on legs that feel more like rubber than anything else. I turn down the same street I last saw him on, and reach a dead end, but there is no sign of him. As I study the area, wondering where the man went, a metal bar slams into my back, pushing me to my knees. I turn in time to see the man swing the metal bar at me again and raise my arms, blocking it, but as I attempt to take it from him, he flings me into a stone wall, knocking the breath out of me, and I fall to the ground.

My dazed mind refuses to work, but I will it to concentrate enough to roll out of the way of his foot as he tries to kick me. I stagger to my feet, swaying from the exertion. Seeing my weakness, the man smiles, his dark skin making him look wraithlike in the shadows, telling me that he believes he has won. He charges for me. I dodge, allowing him to slam into the wall behind me before twisting around and wrapping my arm around his neck. The man spins in circles before jumping backwards, slamming me into the same wall… once… twice… The third time, my choke hold loosens and he flings me off him. Before I can recover, the toe of his boot rams into my abdomen, causing me to cough. I try to get up. A fist rams into the side of my face, forcing me back to the ground. Coughing some more, I, once again, try to get up, but a hand seizes my hair, ripping my head back so that I can look into the merciless eyes of my opponent. I am beaten. I know it. He knows it. Leering, he raises his fist for the final blow, but just when I think it is over, a metal bar appears from nowhere and catches the man in the face, causing him to release me. He turns to confront his new foe and receives a second blow to the face, causing him to crumple to the ground.

"Noni!" Luther bends over me with concern on his face, dropping the metal bar and placing both his hands on my cheeks to stop me from moving around and to help me become more alert as I teeter on the verge of unconsciousness. "Noni, look at me!"

I stop squirming upon the concerned tone of his voice. He has never displayed this emotion to me before, and it surprises me, causing me to look into those intelligent eyes of his.

"The man," I whisper.

Luther glances at the man lying on the ground and shakes his head. "I'm afraid he took another way out."

I jerk my head in the direction of the man's body and realize that he is dead as foaming bubbles escape his lips. Cyanide. Somehow, he had been poisoned, or… My mind refuses to finish the thought, afraid of entering the dark place such thinking goes for fear of it being true.

"We need to get you out of here," Luther says, hauling me to my feet, and I lean on him, unable to stand on my own.

As Luther leads me away from the body in the street, I steal one last glance at it, afraid to think the thought that tickles the back of my mind when the loudspeakers throughout the city come to life, bearing a terrible announcement.

"Citizens of Arel, President Kumi is dead!"

Dead? My mind hurts from the thoughts racing through it. Kumi's warning to me, Tapiwa's interest in what he told me, the bomb—something is not right, but before I can dwell on this further, darkness overtakes me, and my head lolls to the side as Luther carries me away.

Chapter 5

A Funeral

A sea of people stretches out before me (each segregated according to the color of their uniform, and those without a uniform are in a specific area of the courtyard below, and no plebeians are allowed) as I stand upon the balcony of the presidential palace, the same balcony where I received the Arelian Medal of Honor for my acts of heroism when the wall had been attacked over a year ago. The oval-shaped supports reflect the yellow rays of the sun as it pokes out from the swarming clouds above us, and I marvel as the light outlines the carvings of laurel leaves and eucalyptus flowers upon them. No shouts or cheers greet me like they did when I received my honor. Any murmurs throughout the crowd are drowned by the expectation of a lugubrious mood as guards patrol the courtyard, each wearing a helmet so that no one can see their face, while others remain poised on the tops of the towers around us, ready to put down any who dare to disrupt this occasion. I glance to my right at the still figures of Commander Vye and Renal, while wondering why I am here, and the sinking feeling that Kumi's warning has become reality worries me.

A silver coffin with Kumi's face engraved upon its sides sits in the middle of the square with the Arelian flag draped over, and velvet rope surrounds it with a guard placed at each corner, ensuring that no one tries to touch it. I stare at it, wondering what Kumi had tried to tell me and what had led to his sudden and mysterious demise. He wasn't old—early forties—and had not been ill, except for that time when I saw him in the hospice. I think back to that day he spoke to me at the aerodrome and how he had acted strange. He never acted that way during the execution of Mandi and Amal. I had assumed that it was because he indulged in illicit luxuries, but is it possible that he was being poisoned? Whatever the truth is, it is about to be buried and become a faded memory of something that happened long ago, and the only record of it will be what is approved by Tapiwa and the council.

Two weeks have passed since the bombing of the medical facility in the eastern sector, but it still lives in my memory as though it has just happened, and in the memories of the citizens of Arel. Luther had taken me back to the hospice, where Doctor Sahir wasted no time getting me into triage, ordering Natalie to keep a close eye on me, as though worried that something might happen, as though I might be a target. Two days I spent in the medical center until being released, after which, Commander Vye kept me stationed at the manor with Renal shadowing me, though Chase still managed to sneak into my room to check on me, until she received word that Tapiwa requested my presence at Kumi's funeral.

Tapiwa. What is her game? It is said that she refused to bury her brother at first and has spent the last two weeks lamenting his passing, until one of her aides talked sense into her, but as I glance at her erect posture and emotionless face, I wonder if the stories are true, or were told to make her seem more human. I push such thoughts from my mind; they will only get me and those I care about killed. The story of her being distraught over her brother's death must be believed, yet I have difficulty doing that.

A hush falls over the crowd as Tapiwa walks to the microphone, her slow steps making her appear to float as the train of her floor-length, ramie overcoat—black, like her skin, with the Arelian insignia embroidered in silver from hem to collar—trails behind her, allowing everyone to see the charcoal-colored pantsuit she wears with its V-neck stopping at the top of her breasts as the lace trim provides a semblance of elegance on such a mournful occasion. She pauses for dramatic effect as she stares out over the silenced crowd, wetting her rose-colored lips, having chosen a different shade of rouge from what I am used to seeing on her, before speaking.

"People of Arel," she says as a camera hovers in front of her, broadcasting this entire moment to the entire city, "a darkness has overtaken our great city. My brother Kumi is dead—killed by extremists who despise our ordered and just way of life! This was not just an attack on me, but on you!"

She points at the crowd with a fingernail the color of midnight as a way of instilling fear within them as soft thunder rolls in the distance while the clouds above us thicken, blocking out the sun, but only a few react the way she intends. Frustration covers her face, but she disguises it before any have a chance to think about it as she continues.

"The explosive device that took my brother's life was delivered by a plebeian!"

No, it wasn't.

I jerk my head in Tapiwa's direction, biting my tongue as she rewrites the narrative about what had happened. It wasn't a plebeian that attacked the hospice, but an Arelian citizen, and it is possible that he was part of the growing rebellion within Arel.

"It is clear," Tapiwa continues, "that we have been too lenient with them. For too long, the fair-skinned mistreated us, and ever since we freed ourselves from their subjugation of us, they have sought to undermine the justice and freedom that we seek to maintain! Therefore, as of this moment, all freed plebeians will be forced back into servitude, as is their place, until they atone for their unjust ways. Only then, will we achieve true justice. Only then can we heal the wounds of the past!"

The past is whatever Arel says it is at any given moment, and it changes from time to time to suit the needs of the council, to the point where very few, if any, know the truth.

"True justice?" shouts a man, mirroring my own thoughts. "This isn't justice!"

Within seconds, guards yank the man from the crowd and execute him in the square for all to see, causing all those present to remain still, frozen by the fear of what will happen to them if they question Tapiwa's words. Angered, I start to move, but Commander Vye places a viselike grip on my shoulder, holding me back, forcing me to remain where I am as though it is a nonverbal reminder that I cannot do anything for him now.

"Therefore, let the fair-skinned beg for our forgiveness—for our mercy!"

Guards move out from in front of a platform within the courtyard. I didn't notice it before, and it looks as though it has been built for this occasion. Lined up in rows of six are plebeians of various ages, ranging from 11 to 60. All of them stand still, unflinching as the guards surround them, pointing their weapons at them, but their frightened eyes give them away, and without being told, as though this had all been planned, they speak as one.

"We apologize for our existence! We apologize for our abhorrent nature! We apologize for the sins of the past! Forgive our impurity! Show us mercy!"

"The stain of the fair-skinned has infected us all, and because of this, my brother has paid the ultimate price!" Tapiwa looks over the crowd, her eyes devoid of any essence of humanity as she revels in her power over the lives of others. "And so shall they!"

The guards open fire on the plebeians, executing them in front of us all, and as the storm of gunfire pounds my ears, I start to move, but Commander Vye seizes my wrist and jerks me back, refusing to let go until I acquiesce to her demands and realize there is nothing I can do to save them. The only pity they receive are the tears welling within my eyes and blurring my vision as I try to hold them back, knowing what will become of me and my commander if I give in to their demands to be freed. When the gunfire ends, all that remains of the plebeians—once living human beings—are a mass of bodies smeared red with the fresh spillage of blood—their blood.

"Starting now," continues Tapiwa, "a new curfew is in effect. Only those who are essential will be allowed to leave their homes. You will only associate with those within your class. Any caught breaking these rules will be considered a traitor to our stability and treated as such. Our collective safety depends upon each of us sacrificing for the collective good.

"Today starts a new day in Arel! A day of justice! A day of liberty!"

A crack of thunder bursts above us, deafening my ears for the moment, as though it is an ominous sign of what is to come, like nature herself is angered by Tapiwa's actions.

"We will bring the traitors who killed my brother to justice, and only then will we have peace! Strength in—"

"—our kind."

The anemic voices responding to the start of the Arelian mantra incenses Tapiwa, proving that either she doesn't have the charm of her brother, and the loyalty of those around her, or that many within Arel no longer believe in its quest for dominance and control as it keeps us divided, separated from one another so that we never see each other as individual people and as equals.

The guards on the towers point their weapons at the crowd.

Tapiwa begins again. "Strength in—"

"—our kind!" the crowd shouts with forced enthusiasm.

"Strength in—"

"—numbers!"

"Strength over—"

"—weakness!"

"Weakness is—"

"—failure!"

"Failure is—"

"—death!"

Tapiwa stares out at the crowd with her frigid gaze, assessing them and the depth of their loyalty to her before turning and stalking away, with the train of her overcoat flapping in the wind.

Unable to contain myself any longer, I turn toward my commander. "None of this is true! It wasn't a plebeian, but a—"

Commander Vye's hand slaps me across the mouth, forcing me to take a step back as the words trying to come out get trapped in my throat, afraid to be spoken. Having heard me, a guard approaches us with his weapon raised, but Renal steps between him and us, ready to stop him if he must. The guard pauses.

"Is there a problem?" Renal demands in a low, but firm, voice, and once again, I wonder if he is a marshal.

The guard turns and leaves.

"Keep your mouth shut!" Commander Vye hisses in my ear.

"Commander, I was—"

"Whatever Tapiwa or the council say happened"—Commander Vye snatches my arm, squeezing it so tight that the circulation stops—"is what happened, understand?"

A note of fear fills her voice, something I have never heard before or even thought her capable of. Commander Vye is scared, but not for herself. What am I not being told?

"Yes, commander," I whisper.

She releases my arm.

"Commander," I say, having one question that needs to be answered, "why were we summoned here?"

"You were summoned," she replies, "but I refused to allow you to come here alone."

Just me?

"But why was I summoned here?" I ask.

She glances at Renal who nods his head, as though giving her permission to answer my question.

"Tapiwa wanted all those who had earned the Arelian Medal of Honor present," Commander Vye says, "or so she said."

"Where are the others?" I ask.

There were at least four other arbiters who earned that medal; they received their commendation on the same day I did.

"Out of all the ones who have received such an honor, you are the only one left alive. The others met unfortunate and untimely deaths."

My mind reels from the news, unable to process it, while wanting to know what happened to the others to cause their deaths, and the sinking feeling that their deaths had been orchestrated fills the pit of my stomach. My eyes take in Tapiwa as she leaves the balcony, and for a brief moment, she glances in my direction with a devious smile upon her lips, and as I watch her leave, Kumi's warning plays itself in the back of my mind.

Chapter 6

Faya's Scorn

The sparse sounds of the plaza permeate my ears as few people dart about—thanks to Tapiwa's new order that only essential personnel be allowed outside their homes—going about their business as I sit at a table to an outdoor café, picking at a piece of broccoli with my fork, missing the usual crowd that would be here at this time. The empty tables add to my loneliness. With each passerby, from the few that are allowed outside, I notice that my uniform does not instill the fear that it once did, not that I ever liked the fact that people were afraid of me in the past, but it proved handy on occasion. What concerns me most is not that people feel brave around arbiters, but the looks of hatred they direct toward me, and after having witnessed the way some arbiters flaunt their power, I understand why, though it does not make me any less anxious about it.

Once again, that uncomfortable feeling of being watched creeps over me, making me want to run, but I refuse to give in to the paranoia or to give the person satisfaction. Keeping my head still, I glance around while pretending to take a sip of my water, missing the days that Sigal's café was still open and how he always slipped me some juice or pie, even though he was not supposed to. I spot him. Standing in the shade of the food store is a man doing his best to not be noticed by the other arbiters patrolling the streets, but his gaze remains fixed on me. Who is he? Does he work for Tapiwa? She does not need to send others to spy on me incognito; she can use my fellow arbiters, and such is the norm. He must work for someone else, but whom?

I put my glass down and start to stand up when a familiar voice stops me.

"Sitting down on the job, are you?" says Faya with a little sarcasm as she approaches me.

I remain in my seat, after stealing a look at the man, but he has disappeared, much to my disappointment.

"Faya," I say, trying to choose my words with care; the last time we spoke, it did not end well, "what brings you to the eastern sector?"

"Business."

This new formal air of hers warns me to be wary of her. Faya has never acted this way toward me before, but something is different.

"It's good to see you," I say, hoping to rekindle that friendship we had shared while at the training facility. "How is Joel?"

"He was sent on assignment outside the wall," Faya replies, her voice tight as though she is trying hard to not show emotion, but anger mixed with grief creep through anyway. "There wasn't much left of him when he was found."

What? Joel was high up within the arbiter hierarchy. Why would he be sent outside the wall on an assignment that is done by a lower ranking arbiter, or one that was being punished, unless... This explains Faya's coldness toward me. She blames me for his fate, and she might be right: it may be my fault.

"Faya, I'm..." I begin, but she cuts me off.

"You had received the Arelian Medal of Honor, one of the

highest honors within Arel. You were given a chance to join the palace guard. He risked everything for you by making that recommendation, and he did it because..."

Faya cuts off her words, choking back a well of tears and sadness that threatens to break free, and I realize that Joel only made that endorsement because she had asked him to, to help me, and now he is dead, and she blames me.

"Faya, I wish I could bring him back for you."

"You only had to do one thing!"

"Much has happened since then."

"Yes, the capturing of two traitors. You always did have to play the hero."

"Now, wait just a minute," I say, growing angry over her accusations. I can make allowances for her heartache, but to accuse me of always doing wrong is going too far. "How many times would you have died at the training facility if it were not for me? Faya, I have always..."

"I never asked you to help me!"

Taken aback, her words pierce me deeper than any knife ever could as I stare at her. It may be grief speaking, but it may be something more than that. "Then I won't, anymore."

I stand up.

"Noni..." squelched emotion starts to break through the hardened façade of hers, but is stopped when a voice we both despise surprises us.

"Are you two cats fighting?"

Grelyn. Both Faya and I abandon our dispute and put our passions aside as we turn toward a common enemy. Back at the training facility, Grelyn always harassed Faya, and I always stepped in and became one of her targets as well. Upon receiving my commission, I had hoped to never see her again, but as luck would have it, Grelyn keeps showing up in my life at the most inopportune times.

"What are you doing here?" I demand as she looks me up and down with those unnatural blue eyes of hers that stick out against her black skin. "Were you not assigned to one of the outposts?"

"I was," Grelyn replies, "but it seems that recent events have convinced the council that my talents are needed here."

Her ability to see in the dark will prove useful now that Tapiwa has issued stricter lockdown measures, and a sinking feeling of which sector she has been assigned to fills what is left of the hollow in my stomach.

Faya snorts.

"My condolences," Grelyn says, but sarcasm fills her voice.

Faya clenches her fists, but I grab her wrist, preventing her from acting upon impulse: it will only cause more trouble, trouble that I know she wishes to avoid.

"Secrets in Arel have a way of revealing themselves," Grelyn says to the both of us, and a part of me wonders if this is a warning.

"You're right, Grelyn," I say. "They do. Should I reveal yours? How is Trevors doing? Have you heard from him lately?"

Grelyn's cocky manner vanishes as a cloud of rage covers her face and she turns toward me, ready to defend the one thing she cares about most, but before she can act upon impulse, Chase appears from nowhere, interrupting us.

"Arbiter Noni," he says, "Commander Vye wishes to see you."

Incensed at being interrupted, Grelyn raises her fist to strike Chase, but I seize it.

"You know the law," I growl at her. "No plebeian is to be punished for carrying out their orders."

Grelyn's fury at being stopped calculates whether it is worth starting a fight here in the middle of the square and enduring the consequences that will follow, or letting it go, for the moment.

"It never stopped you before," she hisses.

I know what she refers to. There was a time when I struck plebeians for entertainment and had no remorse for such actions, but that was before my assignment to the eastern sector, before I witnessed how even citizens fear the arbiters, and before I met Sheila, Chase, and Gwen.

"If you wish to challenge me, say the word," I tell her, "and you can explain to Commander Vye why I am late."

Grelyn rips her arm from my grasp and drops it by her side before storming away.

I take one last look at Faya, but even though we both share the same sentiments toward Grelyn, nothing has changed her current ire toward me, and nothing I say will help the situation, so I remain silent and walk off with Chase, hoping that Faya will find a way to forgive me for Joel's death.

I hurry through the streets of the eastern sector, making my way to the manor, when Chase pulls me to the side and in between two buildings.

"What are you doing?" I demand. "If I'm late, Commander Vye will..."

"Do nothing," Chase says.

"What?"

Chase looks around before speaking. "I made it up. Commander Vye sent me on an errand. That's why I was in the plaza. You looked like you needed help, so I intervened."

I don't know whether I should be mad at him for putting his own safety at risk for me or flattered that he cared. As he looks at me with those gray eyes, I embrace him, holding him close as my initial anger toward him turns into gratitude and worry.

"You cannot take risks for me," I tell him.

He places a gentle hand on my cheek. "You take them every day for me, for Gwen, and Sheila."

"Do what you have to, to survive, remember?" I say to him. If anything happened to him...

"Without you, there is no survival."

"What about Gwen? She needs you."

Chase drops his chin, staring down at his feet, guilt ridden at having forgotten his sister. "She's growing like a weed," he says. "Soon she'll be considered old enough for other duties besides cleaning."

The worry in his voice mirrors the same concern I have for

Sheila. She and Gwen are close in age, and both will reach what is considered the age of maturity for girls within a few years, even less time for Sheila, after which their usefulness will be evaluated, and if they are deemed to be of good stock, they will be sent to a maternity ward to be breeders.

I place my fingers under his chin—the bit of stubble there pricks my skin—and lift it so that his eyes stare into mine. "We'll figure something out."

He smiles and holds me close, but I push him away before anyone has a chance to spot us, knowing what the punishment will be if we are caught.

"You need to go back," I say.

He relents, squeezing my hand one more time before peering around the corner and darting off, heading back to the manor.

Relieved to be alone for a moment, I slump against the brick siding of the building, allowing the pock-marked exterior to press into my back as I empty my lungs in an effort to rid myself of the queasiness within my stomach as unease takes root there. A shadow moves in the corner of my eye, and I turn my head, spotting Luther as he goes to a fruit stand—one of the few allowed to be open after Tapiwa's newest decree—and picks up an orange, inspecting it before placing it back on the pile. Remembering Mandi's last words and the day of Kumi's death, I walk over to him. I need answers, and he might have them.

"Papers," I say to him the moment I reach him, hoping he goes along with my ruse.

Luther looks at me, unsurprised about my presence, and holds up his wristband instead of making a scene. I scan it and the mark on the back of his neck, noting how he has permission to come and go around Arel as he pleases. His expertise in engineering must have something to do with that.

"You," I say, turning to the man in charge of the fruit stand,."Papers."

He holds up his wristband and inclines his head so I can see his mark as well, and I scan them both.

"It says here that you were supposed to have closed up five minutes ago."

A bead of sweat appears on the man's temple. "I'm sorry, ma'am. He was here and it would be rude to lock up before he has left."

"You know the penalty for breaking the law," I say.

"Please, ma'am," the man pleads, "please show mercy. I am only here to earn back what was lost." He snaps his mouth shut the moment he says that.

"Explain," I say.

"Last week, my credits were depleted because I… I made a mistake."

"What sort of mistake?" I ask, growing curious.

"I forgot my place. It was a momentary thing and I regret it. I really do."

As the man tells me his story, his shaky demeanor makes sense. He must have committed some sort of transgression that resulted in losing all his credits. Every citizen of Arel is given a certain number of credits each month to use to buy food, goods, or pay for housing, but if a person steps out of line, says one thing that can be considered treasonous, they may find all their credits taken from them as a warning to others. Sometimes, Arel prefers fear and humiliation over reeducation and execution when it comes to maintaining order. The individual's struggle to earn Arel's mercy warns others just how hard their life can be if they get ideas that Arel finds abhorrent. I do not wish to make this man's life more difficult, but I must talk to Luther and maintain appearances.

"I might be willing to overlook this," I say, "for the price of your freshest oranges."

The man hands me one from the pile, the same one Luther had handled a moment ago.

"Do you call that fresh?" I knock the orange out of his hands; my deception must be believed.

"I have more," quivers the man.

"Where?"

He points at a lone building nestled into the city block full of brick that towers over us all several yards away.

"Then go get them," I say.

The man bows and runs off.

Knowing I only have moments, I round on Luther after making certain no one watches us, and say, "I need to speak with you in private."

"As I recall," replies Luther, "you know where I live."

"Will you be there?"

"Come after dark."

I turn away from him as the man returns with a small basket of oranges, and their citrusy, sweet aroma fill my nostrils, making my stomach grumble as it desires to feast on them, while he holds them out to me. I snatch the basket from his hands.

"Conclude your business," I say to him and Luther, maintaining my role as arbiter, hoping that the man believes every bit of it, but the thought of taking his fruit from him disgusts me. I look at the basket, counting the five oranges within it, and place two of them back on the pile with care. "You can keep these."

Luther grabs an orange and allows the man to scan his wristband, thus deducting the appropriate number of credits from his account, and bows to me before walking away.

I take one last look at the man before leaving and head back to the manor. I have three treats to deliver and an appointment to keep tonight.

Chapter 7

Another Visit

Chase munches on one of the oranges I brought back to the manor from the fruit stand as we wait for Luther to answer his door, hoping that he does so soon before anyone notices our presence. For the second time in a row, Chase insisted on coming with me to see Luther, but I do not mind; I like the company. He puts the last piece of the orange in his mouth, and I smile, pleased that he enjoys it. When I had gotten back to the manor, I found Sheila in the foyer and gave her the oranges, pleased that the bruises on her face had healed. She knew what to do with the treats.

The door opens and Luther's eye appears, inspecting us and making certain that we are alone before ushering us inside. The familiar setting of a musty couch positioned in the middle of the room with a few papers—Luther always used old, regular paper instead of the thin screens that look and feel like paper, but were miniature computers—while a single lamp rests in a corner, shedding a faint yellow light on everything as little bits of dust float before it. I head for the table near the door to the kitchen, the same table I had sat at while stitching myself up after having gotten hurt while trying to sneak some people out of the city. Before I can sit down in the metal chair, that seems to be a little off-balance, Luther directs me to the couch, and judging by the pattern of faded fabric versus non-faded, it appears the couch is used to hold books more than for sitting.

"I see that you came with your bodyguard," mutters Luther.

I glare at him. I am capable of taking care of myself.

"It was a joke," Luther adds, and I soften my expression.

"I see that you have a few less books than normal," I say.

"Your friends have a little something to do with that," Luther replies. "You didn't come here for a social visit, so get on with it."

Always straight to the point. Taking a page out of his book, I jump to the reason for my visit. Time is not my friend, and I do not wish to waste it.

"You watched the execution," I say.

"Who didn't?" replies Luther with sarcasm. "It's not as though anyone had a choice."

"Mandi—the woman—spoke about the first treachery. What did she mean?" I say, realizing that Luther would not know who Mandi was.

Luther releases a long, slow exhale, debating whether to tell me what I want to know or talk me out of it. "Some secrets are best left that way."

"Are they? Perhaps they need to come out. Tapiwa was quick to silence Mandi when she talked about her father."

"Of course, she was. The death of our presidents', or I should say the president's, father was both convenient and untimely."

"Explain," I say.

Luther leans back, rubbing the graying stubble on his chin as he considers his words, and whether it is wise to tell us or not, though he has already told us much in the past, and he did allow us in his home.

"There is a lot that is kept hidden," Luther begins, "and Arel's media, if you can call them that, make certain that you only hear what is considered 'approved' news. Any history that they do not want the people to know is covered up and forgotten. Soon, any who might remember past events are either convinced that they do not remember it accurately, or are gotten rid of, and I bet you know how."

The crematoriums. Always burning. Always ravenous for more flesh to feast upon. The fires burn day and night, and the smoke is always visible, reminding all of us in Arel where we will end up in the end—some sooner than others.

"Arel loves to play mind games on its people, and the death of Tapiwa's father is one of them," Luther continues.

"So, what happened?" asks Chase, intrigued.

"President Chimalsi was the father of both Kumi and Tapiwa. He was a strong man—a proud man. Chimalsi was not like his father before him or his grandfather. He could be a hard man, but he was different; he had different ideas. Arel rules by force and carries out its edicts with an iron fist—this you know—but Chimalsi believed that governance should be done with examples of great leadership, not by brute force. After his father died, Chimalsi assumed the presidency, as was expected. He married a woman who shared his ideas on allowing the people of Arel greater freedom. He produced two children.

"Under Chimalsi, the idea of freeing a plebeian came to fruition. It was unheard of before then. The council was not happy. There were other things Chimalsi did. He wanted to end the class system that Arel has. He wanted people to be allowed to choose their own path in life. And with each change he tried to make, the council remained steadfast in blocking him. It was at this time that Chimalsi's wife died a mysterious death, and his grief was great."

"What happened?" I ask.

"Chimalsi's duties as president did not leave him much time for his children, and so, he hired a governess, and she was as dark-hearted as they come. She and Tapiwa grew close, and it is rumored that she encouraged the unnatural nature of Tapiwa and Kumi's relationship.

"Well, the years passed as they always do. Chimalsi was able to get a few of his reforms through, but most were blocked by the council, but when it became evident that age was catching up with him, he knew he had to name a successor, and here is where Chimalsi broke with tradition on a scale most of the Arelian elite refused to forgive, most of all, his own daughter. Fearing what his children had become, especially one, Chimalsi refused to name a successor, but decreed that there would be an election held where the citizens and plebeians of Arel would decide whom would take up his mantle. The council fumed, but one person above all was the most furious: Tapiwa.

"She is not as charming as her brother, nor as charismatic, and feared that she would lose. Kumi always had a way of charming those around him, but Tapiwa only instills fear. But the election would not only be between them because Chimalsi also decreed that anyone could seek the position.

"Chimalsi was found dead the next morning. The doctors said that his heart gave out while he slept, yet he was healthier than most. Before his body was cold, Tapiwa used the unnatural attraction Kumi had for her to manipulate him, and before the day was over, the council declared them both to be the Presidents of Arel, and by presidential decree, all of Chimalsi's reforms were ended. Any who disagreed or who still respected her father were rounded up and sent to the crematoriums, or worse. The fires burned so bright for the next several days that it was as though we had a second sun."

Chase and I look at each other, unsure of how much of this story is true, but I have no reason to not believe Luther; he has never lied to me. He has scorned me on occasion, but it is not his words that capture my attention; it's the tone of his voice—sorrowful, reminiscent, almost as though he is remembering a time from long ago, a time from his own past.

"Luther," I ask, trying to be delicate, "why are you in the eastern sector?"

Luther is an engineer. Most engineers are assigned to the southern or northern sector. A few, the younger ones, are assigned to the eastern sector, but most get out within a few years, and the nagging feeling that Luther was sent here from another sector as a penalty for previous offenses refuses to leave; it is a suspicion that I have had since our first meeting.

"How perceptive of you," Luther replies in his usual crass manner, to which I have become accustomed to. "I did not think that arbiters were so intuitive after all vestige of humanity was beaten out of them."

"You're being punished," Chase interjects.

Luther releases a long sigh, weighing whether it is worth telling us the truth about his past or shoving us out the door. My curiosity hopes he chooses the former.

"Your powers of perception are correct, though rummaging through my things probably helped you to come to your conclusions."

I avert my eyes, remembering the night I led a raid on Luther's residence, and how I helped him escape punishment for sedition.

"I was not always here," Luther continues. "I was once in the executive district where I worked as an architect and an engineer. I had received my commission a few years prior to Chimalsi's death, but had already proven myself indispensable and had received a temporary assignment to the presidential palace. I was there the day of his death. I remember Tapiwa shedding no tears over her father's demise, whereas Kumi was distraught. He loved his father. Tapiwa comforted him, but it seemed forced and with a hint of disgust, but she had appearances to maintain and a goal to achieve. I witnessed it all, and after Tapiwa, through Kumi, made her decree, I was told to forget all that I had seen, that my own eyes never saw it in the first place, and that what I remembered was little more than false history as all record of Chimalsi was destroyed and forever buried.

"Tapiwa had wanted me disposed of, but this was one of the

few times the council disagreed with her. You see, I had redesigned the aerodrome and some of the systems used there, and only I had the specifications because I deleted the documentation, the specs—everything. It's all up here"—Luthor points to his head—"and, thus far, no new engineer has been able to recreate what I designed almost three decades ago."

"So, that is why you were sent here," Chase comments.

"I was sent here as punishment and where I could be watched. The council allowed me to come here with my wife, and we were allowed to adopt a girl, and though I was happy to have my family, I saw it for what it was: a means for Arel to control me. While my wife and daughter lived, I was willing to do anything to protect them, including keeping my mouth shut and continuing to build whatever they wished, and that included black fire."

"What?" The word is out of my mouth before I have a chance to stop it.

"Yes, Noni, I created it," says Luther. "In my youth, I wanted to create something that would change the world. In my effort to create better weapons to protect the people of Arel, I researched the properties of Greek fire and tweaked it, and thus, black fire was born. Arel saw it for what it was, weaponized it, and has used it to terrorize those she sees as the biggest threat to her power."

"The barbarians," I whisper.

"No," Luther corrects me. "The people. Entities like Arel do not fear outsiders; they see them as resources that can be used and abused until their usefulness is spent. Entities like Arel fear their own people. They fear what you might become if you were to realize that you don't need them. Arel used black fire to clear out entire sections of the city—of people they deemed a threat to their power. I watched as people who wanted to be able to choose their own futures burned in the never-ending flames."

"But wouldn't the city have burned for years?" I ask.

Luther shakes his head. "The flames always extinguish themselves within hours, but any unfortunate enough to be touched by them meets a far worse fate."

"What happened to the governess?" asks Chase.

"She disappeared the same day Chimalsi died," Luther replies. "She taught Tapiwa a little too well."

"The day at the hospital," I say as my mind races with all it has learned, "what were you doing there?"

Luther chuckles as though he remembered a bad joke.

"I was summoned. Told that my skills were needed to repair the hospice within the eastern sector. A refusal is never accepted, so, naturally, I agreed. I do find it interesting that I happened to be right where the bomb went off. It is also interesting that, though Kumi's room was not touched by the explosion, he managed to die because of it."

"You believe…" I begin.

"I believe that someone was trying to tie up loose ends," replies Luther. "My wife and daughter are dead, and I believe someone realized her mistake."

I think back to that day, to the explosion and all the people who were hurt. I was only there because Tapiwa had requested my presence. Am I a loose end? Chase squeezes my hand to comfort me and I return the gesture, glad to have him here, unsure of what I would do without him.

"It is late," says Luther.

Taking the hint, Chase and I stand up and go to the door, opening it an inch to make certain no one is outside so that we can sneak away.

"I never thanked you," I say, turning back to Luther before I leave, "for saving my life."

"I did it to curry favor with the powers that be within Arel; saving an arbiter's life always looks good."

Unsure of whether to believe his cold remark or not, I scowl at him in disbelief.

"I had a quiet existence until you showed up at my door," Luther continues. "Now be gone, the both of you, and let an old man get some much-needed rest!"

Luther shoves us out the door and slams it in our faces, leaving me to wonder if I should be insulted or amused.

"I think he likes you," Chase jokes.

Grinning, I give him an affectionate smack on the shoulder before heading for the hole in the fence. We need to get back to the manor before our absence is noticed.

Chapter 8

A Challenge Made

The Kevlar vest weighs my shoulders down as I put it on, strapping it to my torso so that it fits snug and does not move before putting on arm and leg protectors, remembering the last time I was here getting ready for my duty assignment on the wall. Trix had been here and had threatened Sheila, so, I tossed her over the wall to the wild dogs below and never looked back as they tore her apart. Now, I dress alone for my latest assignment, wondering why I have been posted on the wall tonight. Perhaps it is my rotation.

Once dressed, I scan my wristband and the wall slides open, allowing me to look upon a whole array of weaponry: rifles, knives, and hand grenades. I snatch a knife and tie it around my waist, tucking it under the back of my vest so that it is not visible, comforted by the sheathed blade nestled back there, ready for when I need it. The door to the armory opens and another arbiter walks in, but I ignore him as I choose the semi-automatic rifle I wish to use while on duty and reach for one, inspecting its barrel and its magazine for any defects. All weapons are to be cleaned before being put back in the armory, but sometimes something gets missed or a person gets lazy. As I start to sling the strap over my shoulder, a hand seizes it and rips it away from me before shoving a different rifle into my hands.

"You're to use this," says the same arbiter that had walked in.

I inspect the weapon, confused as to why I have been denied the ability to choose my own, and pull the magazine out, making certain that it is full, before looking at the man with a quizzical expression.

"Is there a problem?" he says to me.

The arbiter outranks me, so I am not in a position to question his decision, and now is not the time to challenge someone.

"No, sir," I say, taking the rifle and slinging it over my shoulder before heading for the door.

"Arbiter!" he yells at me. "Your helmet."

I snatch the helmet he holds out to me, chastising myself for forgetting it, and step outside, leaving him behind in a room full of enough weapons to wage a small war.

The low hanging sun's light causes me to squint as I walk into it, heading for the nearest stairwell. Before I place my foot on the first stone step, the arbiter from the armory steps outside and whistles at me, indicating that I should follow him. Unsure of what this is all about, I do as I am expected and allow him to lead me to another stairwell to the top of the wall. He waits for me to go inside the enclosed space and its dark interior, devoid of all light and any essence of life, and the sweltering atmosphere stabs my lungs as each breath I take feels as though my chest is filling with water vapor. The fear of being trapped in a tight space strikes me, and though claustrophobia is not an ailment I suffer from, this stairwell makes me want to succumb to it as I climb upward, accompanied by another arbiter who seems more interested in my actions than in his duties, causing the ominous feeling that something isn't right to waft over me and wrap its tentacles of dread tight around my chest so that each breath is a struggle. Each step leads to more and, for a moment,

I wonder if I will reach the end, though logic tells me I will: I've been up these before. Fresh cool air cups my face, giving me relief as orange sunlight embraces my walnut-colored skin, freeing me from the terror that grips me.

"This way," says the arbiter as he walks toward the W within the wall.

I pause. I thought I had been assigned elsewhere.

"Is there a problem?" he demands.

"No, sir."

Thinking it strange that my orders seemed to have changed all the sudden, I keep my thoughts to myself and trail after him, knowing that I am subject to whatever a commanding officer decides. I follow him across a walkway going from the inner to the outer wall, taking a quick glance at the snarling dogs below as they hunger for a meal, never satisfied as they are kept in a semi-starved state so that they will devour any unfortunate enough to fall into their midst.

As I watch the dogs fight among themselves while they watch us with the hope that we will fall, a memory slaps me in the face: one I had buried long ago and hoped to never revisit. I remember the day my instructors at the training facility forced us to watch a pack of wild dogs eat someone, and how little time it took. Recruits are taught to not feel emotion, empathy, or sympathy; they are taught to ignore pain. Pain, sympathy—it is all weakness, and weakness is failure. During my sixth year as a recruit, the instructors lined us up in the courtyard, forcing us to surround a cage with three wild dogs in it, snarling and snapping at each other and any who dared look at them, and I remember the perturbation I felt as one of them kept its ravenous eyes on me as though I was nothing more than its prey, only to have that terror replaced with worry as a plebeian stood on a platform with two arbiters, one on each side, above the cage—all of it built for that occasion.

"Sympathy is for the weak!" shouted the instructor at us that day. "Empathy is for the weak! Emotion is weakness! Compassion is weakness! The only thing you should feel is anger and hatred for your enemy! They deserve your wrath! The only love you should feel is for Arel: it deserves your undying loyalty and complete devotion!"

The instructor had looked around, studying the young faces before him before continuing, and I hear his voice in my mind now, like I heard him then.

"Do you feel sympathy for him?" He pointed at the plebeian forced to stand on the edge of a platform.

"No!" we had all shouted back.

"Nor should you. He is of the fair-skinned. He is your enemy! Beneath you! He deserves only your scorn as he serves you, and if he fails in his duties..."

As the instructor's voice trailed off, an arbiter pushed the plebeian man into the cage with the dogs, and his agonized screams as they tore him apart sent chills down my back, while blood pooled on the ground, forcing me to turn away. The instructor noticed.

"Recruit!"

All eyes had turned toward me.

"Step forward!"

I did, afraid of what was to come.

"Climb to the top of that platform."

I never moved.

"Climb!" The instructor had kicked me as a way to motivate me to do as I was told.

I ran to the steps leading to the platform and climbed up them as the dogs watched me with fresh blood covering their snouts. Once at the top, I had looked around me, frightened that I would be the dogs' next meal, but as I waited for what I feared was inevitable, a plebeian woman screamed in protest as arbiters dragged her across the stone courtyard and to the platform, forcing her up the steps and past me, until she stood at the edge, while the dogs growled and barked at the commotion.

"Perhaps a more personal touch is needed," the instructor had said.

I studied the plebeian woman before me and gasped. To this day, I do not know how they knew, or if the event had been planned from the beginning as a way of making a point to us all, but the woman they had brought out was a plebeian woman who had been the closest thing to a mother I have ever had. When I suffered beatings, she tended my wounds, dressing them and singing a lullaby as she did. When childhood nightmares plagued my dreams, she had snuck into my room, careful not to wake my bunkmates, and comforted me, humming the same lullaby, but such affection between plebeians and citizens, arbiters most of all, is forbidden. So, there she stood at the edge of the platform, her eyes softening when she saw me and my horrified expression.

"Push her," the instructor said to me.

I didn't move. I couldn't as I stared at her while her dull blonde hair, greasy from having not been allowed to wash it in weeks, trailed in the wind, while a slight smile turned her lips, not a nervous smile, but a comforting one as though to tell me that it would be okay.

"Push her," the instructor said again, "or I'll cut off your legs and you'll watch as the dogs eat them!"

The plebeian woman—I never learned her name—took my hand and placed it in the middle of her chest. "It's okay," she had whispered to me, brushing a strand of hair that had escaped my ponytail from my eyes before placing her palm on my cheek as I shook, dreading what would happen next, while her blue eyes—not bright like Grelyn's, but natural, soft like twilight—looked into mine.

"It's okay," she had said.

"Now!" The instructor's voice echoed around us as she moved her foot backward and stepped off the platform, while her fingers tore the edge of my sleeve as she fell to the dogs below.

I had tried to turn away, tried to not look at it and pretend that none of it was real, but one of the arbiters on the platform with us seized my arm, wrenching it behind my back, while his other hand grasped my chin and forced me to watch as the dogs tore into her, and her screams stabbed my eardrums and burned themselves into the eternal pit of my memory. After two agonizing minutes, one of the dogs had clamped its jaws around her throat, silencing her forever as scraps of her bloodied shirt drifted in the wind to be carted across the crimson pools staining the blackened brick of the courtyard. Once silence reigned again, the arbiter had tossed me off the platform, allowing me to crash onto the ground below.

Two purposeful steps clacked on the ground as the instructor had approached me and leered over me, hoping I had learned my lesson. "Plebeians are not like us," he had said. "They are a scourge in this world."

"They are a scourge," my voice trembled as I repeated his statement.

"They must learn their place," he had said.

"They must learn their place," I repeated.

"Arel is my mother. Arel is my father."

"Arel is my mother," my weak voice repeated. "Arel is my father."

"My loyalty is to Arel."

"My loyalty is to Arel."

"All else is weakness. Weakness is failure and failure is—"

"—death."

The instructor eyed me before dismissing me. "Now get back in line!"

I had picked myself up and scurried away, retaking my place, while glancing one last time at the dogs in the cage and what was left of the woman. I never once thanked her for her kindness.

"Arbiter!"

The outranking arbiter's sharp voice rips me from the past and a memory I had long since buried and hoped to never experience again, and I finish crossing the walkway, following him through a maze of blackened brick, the remnants of previous attacks and the use of black fire, as he leads me to my station on the outer wall.

"Arbiter," he yells at another arbiter when we arrive in the center of the outer wall, overlooking the grassy field beyond, "what are you doing here?"

A lone arbiter stands guard on the wall, and the feeling that he is not supposed to be here fills my mind, making me wonder if I am supposed to be here by myself. On most occasions, arbiters on the wall are in groups of two or three, never alone, but something seems off about tonight. The lone arbiter takes off his helmet and turns around.

Renal? What is he doing here?

Before I have time to ponder this development, Renal holds up his wristband, allowing the arbiter with me to scan it, and his face sours when he sees the results.

"Very well," he says. The arbiter turns toward me. "You'll be here all night. Stay alert."

He stalks off, leaving me alone with Renal, who turns back toward the grassy plain and the trees beyond without a single word to me and puts his helmet back on. Confused, but thankful to have his company, even if we do not speak to one another, I secure my helmet and face the tangled trees beyond as the sun dips below the blackish-purple horizon, plunging us into darkness, while the shadows of the trees lengthen until they touch the wall before vanishing. A serene calm surrounds us as we remain at our post, poised and ever watchful, and a part of me hopes that tonight will be different from my first night upon the wall. No noise interrupts the night, except for the chirping of a single cricket as it calls out so that anyone who hears it will know that it is here, and that it exists. I take a quick glance at Renal, wondering why he is here; the arbiter that scanned his bracelet did not seem pleased about his presence.

I scan the horizon as best I can, but the moonless night makes it impossible to see anything, making me wonder why those on the wall are not assigned helmets with night vision, or are only some allowed such gear? The more I think about what we are allowed to use, the more I wonder about this wall and if its true purpose is to keep people in, not out.

Still nothing. Good.

Bored, my hand reaches for the charred stone of the wall, but I stop it when I remember that black fire might have touched it. Though the fire will burn out, sometimes its effects can still be felt and burn your skin, and it is best not to risk it, as I learned soon after arriving in the eastern sector.

A muffled cough sounds nearby, forcing me to glance in its direction at the arbiter who made it as he tries to pretend that he hadn't coughed at all. I do not blame him. Illness is a sign of weakness. I turn away from him to allow him the illusion that no one heard his discretion.

As the minutes turn into hours, my mind wanders, thinking back on all that has happened since I received my commission as angst fills it, forcing me to consider horrendous scenarios that may never happen, before morphing into wild fantasies of me and Chase running away with Gwen and Sheila by our side. I shake my head, willing my mind to focus on my task. Danger could be seconds away and my unfocussed state will get me killed. Once again, I scan the horizon, but see nothing, only the stars above me as the veil of darkness dangles before me, hindering my ability to do my duty and protect the people of Arel from the unknown beyond the wall.

The smallest of sounds penetrate my internal dialogue as I scold myself for allowing my mind to think about trivialities instead of focusing on my task, almost like pebbles flying through the air and coming a little too close for comfort, but not enough to cause alarm. I turn my head in the direction of the noise and look at the arbiter that had coughed earlier, but he staggers as he clutches his neck, the one vulnerability left unprotected by our armor, before toppling over the edge of the wall. I duck down, using the wall as protection as I peer over its edge, seeing faint shapes move out of the corner of my eye, but when I try to focus on them, they disappear.

"Renal!" I hiss, pointing at the grass below as a rock, coated in oil and set aflame, flies from the trees and for the wall, pelting the brick exterior as sparks shoot in every direction.

The alarm!

I run from my post, charging across the wall to where the alarm is, and drop to my knees, sliding the last few feet as another flaming rock soars above me, striking the inner wall and spraying me with embers. Once I reach the alarm, I activate it, allowing it to fill the once still air with its warning. Thinned-soled shoes hit the walkway behind me. I spin around, finding a barbarian standing there. How did he get over the wall so fast? Were they already here? He raises a hatchet and charges for me. I yank my rifle from my shoulder and point it at him, comforted by the power it brings me, and squeeze the trigger, forcing the barbarian to stop midstride as he expects to be shot. Nothing. I squeeze the trigger a couple more times, but each time, the rifle refuses to fire: my weapon is jammed. The barbarian grins at his luck.

Furious at having been given a faulty rifle, I flip it around, grasping its barrel, and swing it as hard as I can, catching the barbarian in the side before dodging out of the way of his hatchet as he swipes at me, and its blade rips my sleeve. He charges again, raising his hatchet for a killing strike, but before I can react, gloved hands seize both my arms, pinning them to my sides, forcing me to stay in place. I lift both my feet at the same time, kicking the barbarian in the chest, forcing him to teeter backward, and dive forward, causing whomever had grabbed me from behind to fly over my back and crash onto the ground in front of me.

Another arbiter? Why would a fellow arbiter attack me instead of help me during an attack?

The arbiter moves for his weapon, and I cast all questions aside, choosing self-preservation over momentary curiosity. I jump for my rifle and swing it at the arbiter, hitting him in the head before blocking an attack by the barbarian; his hatchet slides across the barrel of my weapon, creating a series of sparks that are carried away by the breeze, until I relax my muscles, causing the barbarian to lose his balance as I ram the butt of my rifle into his side, forcing him over the wall and to the dogs below, and they pounce on him within seconds. With the barbarian gone, I turn to face the arbiter, but he points his pistol at me and fires, catching me in the middle of my chest, and though my body armor stops the bullet from penetrating my body, its impact forces me to the ground as the wind is knocked out of me. Struggling to catch my breath, I lay on my back as my chest feels as though it has been struck by a boulder and look up, helpless, unable to do anything as the arbiter that had attacked me leers over me, his weapon pointed at my head, preparing to finish me. My eyes remain glued to him as I am determined to meet my end with courage if this is to be my last moment in this world. Without warning, Renal seizes the man's weapon hand, ramming his fist into the crook of the arbiter's elbow, forcing his arm to bend, before twisting it, until his pistol faces him. It goes off. The arbiter drops to the ground as Renal remains standing with the pistol in his hand.

He stares at me—fiery flashes of light cover the reflective surface of his helmet—and for a moment, I wonder if he is going to kill me as he seems to suffer from an internal struggle, before he raises his pistol and fires at two barbarians approaching me from behind. Clutching my chest, and wincing with every move I make, I force myself to sit up. Renal holds his hand out to me. I take it, and he hauls me to my feet before giving me the pistol, and though the weapon is light, it feels like a great weight within my hand as I grapple with the notion that a nameless arbiter tried to kill me without reason, but I haven't time to think about it.

A barbarian slams into Renal. Before I have time to help him, another grabs my shoulder and jerks me backward. I wrap my fingers around his thumb and yank it back, breaking it. He removes his hand. Whirling around, I raise my pistol and fire, blowing a hole in his head. He drops to the ground. Renal! I twist back around to help Renal, only to find him with the barbarian in a choke hold, squeezing as hard as he can until the man goes limp and he drops him to the ground.

The slow grumble of an engine attracts my attention, and I

almost gasp when I see what the barbarians have as they aim a machine gun fastened to the top of a transport at the wall. Renal and I drop to the ground as a flurry of bullets pelt the barrier, sending shards of stone and metal in every direction as they burrow deep within the structure, while more gunfire soars over us, striking any foolish enough to be in its path, and the fresh corpses of arbiters surround me as I cover my head. Something lands in front of me, clinking on the ground.

"Grenade!" I yell, jumping to my feet and leaping across the opening between the outer and inner wall as the grenade goes off, propelling me forward.

I slam into the edge of the inner wall, but fail to grasp its ledge and plummet to the ground below, where the esurient dogs await another meal. My stomach lurches into my mouth as panic overtakes me, while my fingers tear at the stone, desperate for something—for anything—to grab hold of. I touch metal. Instinct forces me to seize it, and my body jerks to a halt with my feet dangling inches out of the dogs' reach as they jump for me with saliva dripping from their fangs, hungering for the taste of my flesh, while bits of wall rain down upon me, pelting me and coating me in dust. I need to get out of here. Pressing my feet against the wall, I try to hoist myself up and reach for a protruding brick, but I slip and drop back down, and the metal bar dips, threatening to drop me. I squeeze my only lifeline to the point where the ridges of the metal rod dig deep into my skin, causing my hands to sting. Sweat fills the space between my skin and the metallic rod, and I start to slide off. With each passing second, the dogs below jump for me, and the thought of being eaten alive causes my mind to freeze as their powerful jaws snap at me.

"Noni!"

Renal stands above me, having taken off his helmet, and throws me a rope. I reach for it, but miss. He tosses it again as my hands slip another inch and my feet dangle even lower, forcing me to lift them up to avoid being grabbed by the wild dogs. The rope hits the wall, but I fail to grab it. Renal chucks the rope at me a third time. Knowing that if I miss it again, I will perish. I summon my courage and lift my feet, planting them against the wall, and push myself upward as I reach for the rope and manage to wrap my fingers around the line. Momentary pain grips me as my body slams into the brick of the outer wall, but I ignore it as I climb upward, while Renal pulls me up. He reaches down. I grasp his hand, thankful to be away from the dogs.

The blade of a curved sword strikes the ground near my head. I roll to the side and onto my stomach as my new attacker raises his sword high in the air. Before he can bring it down upon me, I lunge for him, ramming my head into his stomach, and wrap my arms around his middle as we crash to the ground. Rolling, I keep my arms wrapped tight around him, refusing to let go as I bring him to Renal, who grabs him and throws him off me. He hits the edge of the wall and drops to the dogs below, and his screams fill the night as they tear him apart.

I look up and see a barbarian at one of the flamethrowers, spewing black fire on the arbiters along the wall. The ink-like flames flare up, devouring everything in its path, while people wail in agony as their flesh melts away from their bodies, and rage wells up within me as they run and squirm in an effort to make the torture cease. I point out the barbarian to Renal.

"Can you get me over there?" I ask.

He gathers up the rope and spots a walkway going between the inner and outer wall and urges me to follow him. I do, dodging intruders and arbiters and shoving them out of my way until we reach the walkway. Renal wraps one end of the rope around the narrow walkway, while I tie the other end around my waist. We look at each other for a moment, and I nod in answer to his unspoken question as he grips his part of the rope as tight as he can. I jump off the walkway. Gravity takes its hold, and I plunge downward, until the rope pulls tight, jerking my body to a sudden, momentary stop that only lasts a second as I swing forward and toward the flamethrower. Air rushes past me, whistling in my ears as I swing for the edge of the wall below the flamethrower. I grab the wall's edge and hoist myself upward, untying the rope around my waist.

I charge the barbarian at the flamethrower. He sees me and swings the flamethrower in my direction, but I dart out of the way, rolling across the ground before scrambling to my feet. As he struggles to point the flamethrower back in my direction, I rush toward him and drop to the ground, sliding across the pebbles that tear into my legs, until I pass underneath its barrel. Wasting no time, I ram the heel of my foot into the man's knee, dislocating it. He drops to the ground. I roll out from underneath the flamethrower and plow into him, knocking him on his back. As he struggles to get up, I grip his head and bash it into the concrete three times until he stops struggling, before jumping to my feet and taking my position at the flamethrower, turning it toward the barbarian and coating him in black fire. He writhes in agony as his anguished cries fill my ears before he topples over the edge of the wall and to the invaders below, lighting many of them on fire, and as they try to flee, they spread the black flames to others.

I point the flamethrower over the open field and pause, remembering the last time I had done so and how, when my actions were replayed at my commendation ceremony, I looked inhuman, devoid of emotion as I slaughtered others in the name of Arel. Time slows around me as I weigh my actions and the cost to my soul, but the more I consider it, the more I realize that the ones attacking the wall intend to harm all within Arel, and if I do nothing, if I remain immobilized by the fear of losing what vestige of humanity I have left, I'll sentence innocent people within the city to a fate worse than death. I do what I must and spew the flames of black fire over the open field, like I had done before, blocking the terrified screams from my mind as the flames rip across the grassland in front of the wall, transforming it into uninhabitable, smoldering ash.

A mortar shell slams into the wall below me. Its blast rips me away from the flamethrower and propels me backward as a mixture of stone, ash, and pebbles envelop me. I crash onto the ground, unable to stop as I roll toward the edge of the wall, but before I drop downward, a hand grasps my arm and stops me, pulling me back up. Strong arms haul me back onto the top of the wall and away from the edge. When I look into the face of my savior, I find Renal; he had somehow managed to reach me in time, but before I can thank him, a man charges us with an iron rod in his hand, releasing an earsplitting battle cry and heading straight for me. Renal pushes me out of the way and tackles the man, twisting as he wraps his legs around the attacker's torso before grabbing his arm and wrenching it backward, breaking it. As the man succumbs to pain, Renal rips the iron bar away from him and jabs it in his neck. A small mark sticks out on the man's forearm. Curious, and giving into it, I take a closer look: he was a freed plebeian. This is not the first time I encountered a freed plebeian attacking the wall with barbarians. Something falls out of his hand. I pick it up. It is a picture of me.

"You need to..."

The whine of our aircraft drowns Renal's words as they swoop low over the ground and drop bombs, but the explosives land both on the wall and on the grassland beyond, almost as though they do not care if arbiters die. Renal pushes me toward a tower, and together, we race against the clock as we try to reach some level of safety as the bombs detonate around us, pelting us with fire and stone projectiles. I bring my hands up to cover my face. As more explosive hit the ground, I increase my speed and dive through the opening to a tower, slamming into its far wall as Renal covers me with his own body as a way of protecting me, while the bursting bombs deafen me and rubble falls around us. All hell breaks loose as the bombs continue to drop, while Renal and I hope that the tower we hide in remains intact, until...

Silence.

Renal releases me and we crawl out of the tower to find a wall being held together by a few rods and stone, while a mass of bodies stretch out before us on the grassy plain below, and an overturned transport with a machine gun blown in half. The attack has finished. I glance up as the Arelian fleet flies away—some of the aircraft goes back to the aerodrome, while others do not, making me wonder why—unconcerned about the carnage left in its wake. Arbiters and barbarians lie together, strewn about, all sharing the same fate, while others crawl out from under the wreckage and look around, dazed.

"Noni," Renal says to me, shaking me to get my attention, "you need to leave."

His words do not register as I look beyond him and the flames that burn bright, sending bulbous clouds of smoke into the star-filled sky above. The manor is on fire.

Chase!

I tear myself away from Renal and charge for what is left of one of the stairwells.

"Noni!"

I do not listen. All I can think about are the three people I left behind at the manor, and the fire that may now kill them.

"NONI!"

Renal's desperate voice fades as I hurry down the stairwell, stopping when I realize the bottom last four steps are missing. I jump to the ground below, landing on my hands and knees and ignoring the rock that digs into my leg. My only focus is the manor. I leap to my feet and charge down the streets, not caring about the alarms or the sounds of the medical transports as they hurry for the wall. I must reach them. The city flies by, blurred by my desperation to get to the manor as quick as possible, and I pay little attention to the people leaving their homes to see what the commotion is all about, even when they try to ask me questions about what they should do. I can only think about Chase, about Gwen, and about Sheila. What if…

No! I will not think about that. They must be alive and unharmed.

One man staggers up to me, speaking gibberish as his fear inhibits his ability to talk, and I push him away from me.

"Stay in your home!" I tell him, not bothering to stop as I race through the plaza and dart down the street that will take me to the manor, while the massive screens throughout the city flash to life and a woman's face—tight curls dusted in gold glitter dangle about midway down her temple, accentuating her chestnut skin—appears on the screen, giving a report about the latest attack on the wall, and images of the event rotate behind her.

I ignore it as my eyes focus on a plume of smoke rising behind a building when a corner of its roof falls. I increase my pace and dart down an alley before coming out on the street leading to the manor. Once I reach the driveway, I pause, staring at the massive flames that engulf the manor, the place I call home, the only home I've known after leaving the training facility. As fire consumes it, helplessness overwhelms me, and I remain frozen to the ground, unable to act until an arbiter jumps from a second story window, screaming in agony as her body becomes a human torch.

Chase!

I charge for the massive inferno, not caring if I get too close as the heat from the flames sears my skin through the fabric of my jacket. Commander Vye's voice hits my ears as she directs arbiters to specific areas of the manor (some are sent to get hoses, while others break open the valves to the underground water pipes to connect the hoses to), but in my haste, I do not stop to listen to her as my mind concerns itself with three specific people. As I run to the building, my feet crunch on the grass, dried out by the heat of the flames as they stretch higher and higher, covering the outside of the manor itself, hungering for more, and without thinking, I hurry to the front entrance. The door slides open upon my approach, but the sudden introduction of air causes the fire contained within to burst outward, breaking the door and creating a force that knocks me off my feet.

"Chase!" I scream, getting to my knees, but the roar of the flames drowns my voice.

No response.

Arbiters and plebeians run in circles around me, ignoring me as I remain on the ground, searching every soot-covered face I see, but none of them are who I am searching for.

"Sheila!" I scream as loud as I can, but my voice fails to go beyond the thundering fire as it burns brighter. I jump to my feet and run like a madman, whipping my head in every direction, hoping to see one of them, but it turns into despair as my search remains unfulfilled.

"Why would they attack us?" an arbiter asks Commander Vye, but I do not pay much attention to him or her harsh response, forcing him to shut his mouth as I continue looking for either Chase, Sheila, or Gwen.

"Chase!" I shout, coughing on the smoke that fills the area around the manor. "Gwen!"

Still no answer. My stomach sinks as my heart beats faster in my chest, while the notion that they may all be dead fills me with dread and a sense of being alone in a world built upon cruelty. A girl limps away from the fire, clutching her arm. Thinking that it might be Gwen or Sheila, I run to her and turn her toward me so I can see her face, only to be met with bitter disappointment, but I cannot leave her here. I grab the nearest arbiter and shove her toward him.

"Take her to a medical transport," I say, not caring if he outranks me or not. "Now!" I yell at him when he fails to move.

"Sheila!" I scream again, growing more desperate as seconds drag by, mocking my efforts at finding the ones I care most about and rejoicing in my misery.

"Noni!"

I stop.

"Sheila?"

"Noni!" the voice shouts at me as a shadow approaches, her pale skin and clothes coated in ash, and I squint to try and get a better look at the figure as the light of the fires toy with the idea of letting me see who it is that calls my name.

"Sheila!" I shout, running to her and embracing her, squeezing her so tight that she coughs, but I don't care; I don't want to let her go. She is alive, and she is safe. She wraps her scrawny arms around me, and we hold onto one another, glad that the other is okay.

"Your face," she says, noticing a bruise forming; I hadn't felt it until now.

"It's fine," I tell her. "Where's Chase?"

Sheila's face falls, and I lift her chin so she will look at me. "He went to find Gwen. After he helped me get out, he couldn't find her and..."

"Sheila, where are they?" I ask as a minacious feeling swathes me.

Sheila points at the emblazoned manor. "In there."

No! They can't be! They...

Resolve takes control of my mind and body as I stand up and face the burning building, determined to not lose Chase or allow him to lose his sister. They're alive still. They have to be. I scan the area around me, looking for anything I can use as a shield against the flames and spot a piece of siding. It will have to do.

"Find someplace safe and wait for me," I say to Sheila, giving her a final hug.

She grabs my wrist as I start for the fire and I pause, turning back to her, my heart aching over the worry and fear on her face.

"I'll be back," I tell her, trying to comfort her and give her a light kiss on her forehead, the way I imagine a parent would give to their child. "I promise."

She lets go.

I face my foe, holding the siding like a shield and charge a window that is more smoke than flames, crashing through it, landing on the hard floor of the manor as shattered glass circles me. Thick smoke smothers my lungs, destroying my ability to breathe, forcing me to bury my face into my sleeve in a futile attempt to filter it out as I look around, despite the particles hovering in the air that sting my eyes. Coughing, I force myself to stand up, keeping the bit of siding in front of me as I navigate my way from the... Where am I?

My elbow bumps into a bookcase. The recreational center. Having gotten my bearings, I make my way to the hallway.

"Chase!" I shout, but I cannot hear my own voice over the roar of the fire.

Where would they be? I force my mind to remember Gwen's responsibilities for the night so as to get a better idea of where to look. She had kitchen duty, and once plebeians are finished in the kitchen at the end of the day, they're allowed to go to bed. The basement! She would have gone there after finishing her tasks.

Fire reaches out for me as I work my way through the hallway and to the basement door, sending searing tendrils of flames toward me in an attempt to grab hold of me and imprison me in its hellish blaze. Something creaks beside me and shifts. I dodge out of the way as a piece of the wall crumbles and falls straight for me, sending up a cloud of glowing embers and ash, smothering me in its toxic fumes and causing me to choke as I try to inhale, while the piece of siding slips from my grasp and flies into the inferno. If hell is real, this place at this moment would be it. I do not hold religious beliefs; they are forbidden and taught to us to be nothing more than mere superstition from a more primitive age, since serving the will of Arel is supposed to be the center of our existence, but as the thunderous roar of the raging fire pounds my ears, causing my head to feel as though it is trapped in an ever-tightening clamp while my veins pump blood as fast as they can, the fanciful notion of a god protecting me is the only comfort I will find here. Let me find them. Even if they are... I need to know.

Another panel of the wall drops in front of me, sending a plume of smoke and ash into my face, blinding me as my eyes water in an inefficacious attempt to clean themselves of the debris, while my throat seizes as I cough in rapid succession, trying to expel the contaminated air from my lungs. Flames crawl up what is left of the walls and stretch out on the ceiling above me as it consumes everything in its path, but despite my need to keep moving, I cannot as my body is racked by incessant coughing, until vomit mixed with spittle bursts from my mouth and lands on a few paint chips laying on the charred floor, oblivious to the chaos surrounding it. For a split second, I remember the paint chips swept into a pile on my first day here and how I had stepped on them, spreading them across the floor, not caring that I had added to the work of the plebeian girl holding a broom. That girl was Sheila and she waits for me to return to her with Chase and Gwen.

Ironing my will, I stand up, covering my head to protect it from the heat that singes my skin and causes a few blisters to appear as it cooks, and I kick the fallen piece of wall out of my way, determined to reach the basement, and where I hope to find both Chase and Gwen.

"Chase!" I scream again as loud as I can. "Gwen!"

I reach the basement door and it sits off-kilter as the fire has eaten away one of its hinges. Perfect. I step to the side of the door and kick it over and over, harder and harder, and the more it dangles at a precarious angle, the more I slam the sole of my boot into it, until it pops free and crashes into what's left of the smoldering floor.

"CHASE!"

I delve into the smoky darkness, covering my mouth in a feeble attempt to filter out the smoke pollution as I hurry down the steps, while being somewhat cautious. I do not know how stable they are. A step breaks away underneath my weight, and I cling to the rail, ignoring the pain as the metal burns through my jacket and my skin as I try to not tumble downward. Bright orange seeps through the floor above me, warning me that my time grows short. I need to find them—now!

I jump to the next step, using the rail as a way of stabilizing myself as I hurry down into the darkness beyond, broken only by a single lamp on the wall, whose murky light morphs into gray shadow as the clouds of smoke multiply. The light bursts when I reach the bottom of the steps, sending bits of glass my way, and I raise my arm while turning away to protect myself from its fury.

"CHASE!" I shout into the darkness as my voice grows hoarse and breaks from the smoke that coats it.

Please answer. Please!

"Noni?" the familiar sound of my name coming from his lips causes my heart to skip for a moment from this elation as my pleas are answered. He's alive! "Noni!"

"Chase, where are you?"

"Over here!"

I follow the sound of his voice, running my hands down the splintered wall, not caring about the slivers of wood that catch in my fingers and dig into my skin, following the sound of his voice as I navigate my way toward him. More orange pokes through the floorboards above, shedding a portentous light upon me as I hurry toward him.

"Chase?"

"Keep coming!" he yells. "Follow my voice!"

I do. The more I go toward it, the clearer it becomes, and soon, the roar of the fire disappears as all I hear—all I want to hear—is Chase's voice.

I hurry through the hallway, which resembles an oven more than a corridor as the intense heat from the fires above me swarms the area, causing my skin to blister underneath my jacket, but I shove the pain aside, keeping my mind zeroed in on Chase's voice.

"Chase!"

"You're almost here!"

I pick up the pace, dodging to the right as a piece of the ceiling crashes on the floor next to me, avoiding a fiery death by an inch, but I refuse to let it deter me from my mission. A silhouette sits before me, more like an onyx shadow amidst a smoky fog of impending doom as he kneels on the ground, blocked by a fallen beam and a mass of debris from reaching his goal.

"Chase," I whisper as I hug him, glad to hold him again and know that he is alive. "Where's Gwen?"

In answer to my question, he points past the beam, and I see a small pale face, blackened by ash and soot, peering back at us as fear fills her eyes the more the ceiling above us creaks and burning bits of wood drop around us.

I study the fallen plank and spot a place where she may be able to squeeze through.

"Gwen, can you fit through this?" I ask.

She huddles in a corner, hugging her knees, paralyzed by fear.

"Gwen," I say in a gentle voice, "I need you to be brave."

She shakes her head; fear has overwhelmed her, trapping her the way it traps us all.

A low groan echoes above us as the wooden panels begin to buckle. They won't hold for much longer, and we don't have much time before this entire place collapses.

"We need to go," I say.

"I won't leave her," Chases protests, referring to his sister.

"You won't have to," I tell him, placing a gentle hand on his cheek.

I study the small opening. Gwen will fit, and I may be able to as well. I dive for it, but my armor catches on the splintered wood and holds me back.

"I tried to get through, but it's too small," says Chase.

Not for me. I rip off my body armor and shove it into Chase's hands, trying not to choke on the smoke that burns the back of my throat and clogs my airway, refusing to give in to its demands that I succumb to its will.

"Use this to lift that beam," I tell him, pointing at the joist, "and I'll go get her."

Nodding, Chase grabs the armor and uses it to protect his hands from the smoldering wood as he lifts it enough for me to squeeze through.

I crawl through the hole, flinching as smoldering embers attack my face in an attempt to stop me, but I refuse to give in: this fire will not defeat me. As I wriggle my way through, a plank of wood snatches my jacket and tears through it, scraping my stomach and causing a few droplets of blood to fall, but I ignore the pain, knowing what will become of us all if I fail: failure is not an option because, right here, right now, it is certain death for us all. I burst free from the hole and hurry to Gwen as she continues to huddle in a corner.

"Gwen," I say to her, "we need to go."

She pulls away from me and buries her face in her knees.

"Gwen, come on!"

She refuses to budge.

Enflamed bits of wood drop from above, touching my jacket and setting it ablaze. As Gwen screams, I rip my jacket off, throwing it to the floor and stomp on it until the flames are out before going over to her. Panic—I see it in her eyes—has imprisoned her, but if it continues to do so, we all will die; so, I do the only thing I can think of; I do what my instructors did to me. I grab her mop of hair, pulling her head back, exposing her face and slap her across the cheek as hard as I can. Shocked back into reality, Gwen stares at me, accusing me with her eyes of harming her, but I seize the few seconds I have of her attention.

"Get ahold of yourself!" I shout at her. "Your brother is over there! Do you want him to die because of your fear?"

I haul her out of the corner and push her toward the hole in the collapsed debris.

"Go!" I yell at her as I shove her through the small opening before pushing my own way through.

Once through, Chase seizes his sister, giving her the biggest hug he can before pushing her down the hallway as paneling from the wall burst free of their hold and crash into the other side of the corridor, while the pipes behind them explode from the water within turning into steam. She screams. Refusing to stop, Chase picks her up and carries her as we run for the stairs, but as we reach them, its supports buckle and topple to the floor, sending thick spirals of smoldering ash into the air that swirls around us, causing us to heave. I spin around, doing my best to look for another way out as my eyes sting from the smoke, tearing up to the point where everything is a blur, forcing me to wipe them with the back of my soot-covered hand in a useless attempt to clear them.

"This way!" Chase shouts, heading down a narrow space that I never realized was here.

He turns and steps sideways through it, wheezing as he carries Gwen, whose frightened screams drown the thunder of the fire above us and the blazing pieces of plaster that crash around us. I follow him, trusting him. More steam erupts from a pipe, blasting through the wall and almost hitting me in the head. Startled, I yelp, but try to squash it so as not to alarm Chase or frighten Gwen any more that she already is. We burst free of the narrow space and into a small room with a window near the top of the ceiling. It isn't big, but it may be large enough for us to crawl through. Before we have time to appreciate our luck, the narrow passageway caves in and piles of burning debris block any escape, sealing us inside and forcing us toward the only remaining exit: the window. I study the medium-sized, rectangular window as the light of the fire dances upon it, intensifying at periodic moments before diminishing, only to reignite as a way of mocking our efforts to escape its fury and its judgement, but I refuse to let Chase or Gwen die here.

I spot a plank. Seizing it, and not caring if it burns my hands, I wrench it free of the fallen rubble, hacking as a cloud of sparks billow around me, surrounding me with their constant reminder of our predicament, and I rush to the window, ramming the plank into it. The glass cracks. Pulling it back, I slam the plank into it again and again, until the glass shatters, after which, I run it along the edges of the window, clearing it of razor-edged shards that threaten to cut any who dare cross their path. My boots crunch the fallen glass as I reach my hands out to Chase.

"Give her to me," I say.

He hesitates for a moment, wondering what my plan is.

"I'll take her while you crawl through the window first."

He hands me Gwen, who squeaks as the flames grow more intense, and I turn my back toward them to protect her from their wrath as Chase hoists himself through the basement window, having to squirm to fit through. Once freed, he turns around and reaches through the opening for Gwen. I hand her to him, and he yanks her through the opening. My turn. I place my hands on the edges of the window and start to jump up to it when a beam breaks free of its hold and crashes to the floor, hurling me backward and blocking my only way out.

"Noni!" Chase screams.

He thrusts his hand through a tiny opening, ignoring the flames that burn his skin, and I take it, grasping it as tight as I can, not wanting to let go, but knowing I have to, or we will both perish.

"Leave me," I tell him, choking back tears at the thought of forcing him into this position.

"No," he protests.

"Go!" I yell at him. "Take care of them. Please."

As tears stream from my eyes, I let go of his hand and drop back to the floor as the fires stretch out further, encircling me, and my lungs burn from the smoke and the heat, unable to take much more. Angry, I scream, releasing my frustration at the fire and the universe for forcing me into this position, knowing that I would never leave someone I cared about behind to die, knowing that I would give my life for theirs, and for stripping me of any chance of happiness.

Fire. It burns. It stings. And it will now be my grave.

Accepting my fate, I curl up on the floor, refusing to fight, refusing to challenge it, surrendering to its demands. They are safe. That is all that matters.

My eyes close.

Water… I hear water hitting the beam that blocks the window and the flames dissipate before someone kicks at it over and over again, refusing to give up, until he has broken a path through.

"Noni!"

Chase's distant voice circles around me, urging me to come back.

"NONI!"

I open my eyes and see Chase in the window with his hand—the skin blistered and peeling from being scorched—out to me, having created an opening. Summoning my strength, I push myself to my feet, coughing from the exertion and run to him, jumping over the fallen beam and grabbing his hand, gripping it as tight as I can as he jerks me through the window. We roll across the grass, away from the manor as the support structures crumple and break away, succumbing to the rapacious fire's demands. Before I can stop myself, I kiss Chase, thankful for his tenacity and willingness to save us all, and not caring if anyone sees us or about Arel's rules regarding class. He is a plebeian and I am an arbiter, but all that matters to me is that he is a man and I am a woman, and we risked our own lives to save the other.

A terrified scream pulls us apart.

Sheila!

I look over in the direction of the scream and see Sheila cowering on the ground as Molers kicks her, and rage overtakes me, springing me into action.

"Take care of her," I tell Chase, pointing at Gwen before jumping to my feet and running for Molers.

I plow into him as he raises his foot for another kick and knock him to the ground. Determined to stop him, I roll onto all fours and lunge for him before he has a chance to grasp what has happened, ramming my fist into his face, following it with an elbow to the back of his neck.

"Noni!" I hear Commander Vye's voice, but ignore her as the choler within me controls me.

Molers throws me off him and punches me in the jaw, stunning me for a moment. I watch as he pulls his fist back again, but before I can react, Chase tackles him, pulling him off me, but he is no match for Molers. Molers twists around and grips Chase by the neck, ready to break it, and I'm too far away to stop him; so, I do the only thing I can think of to save the man I love.

"I challenge you to the Rite of Conquest!" I shout, loud enough for everyone gathered to hear.

Molers stops.

All movement stops, except for Renal—he must have arrived while I was in the house—who forces his way through the crowd, taking his place by Commander Vye's side, only to stare at me with a mournful look on his face.

"I challenge you to the Rite of Conquest," I say again, knowing that once the challenge has been made, it cannot be undone.

A sardonic smile creeps across Molers' face as he releases Chase. "The price?"

"They go free," I say, referring to all three: Chase, Sheila, and Gwen, but those around me believe I am only talking about Chase and Sheila, since they do not see Gwen. Either way, I am taking a huge gamble.

"Only one may be freed."

"Her," I say, pointing at Sheila, who stares at me with tear-filled eyes.

"Perhaps we'll let the fates decide," says Molers.

"And what is your price?" I demand. A challenger is allowed to demand a reward if victorious, but the rite allows the one being challenged to request a reward as well.

"Your servitude."

The way the words come out of Molers' mouth sends chills up my spine, but I remain rigid, unwilling to give him the satisfaction of seeing me afraid.

"Do you accept my challenge?" I demand, sounding braver than I feel.

Molers' eyes dart between me, Chase, and Sheila, and I know that he has learned my secret: that I care for them, but before silence can rein much longer, Renal steps in.

"Master Arbiter, the challenge has been made. What is your choice?"

Molers doesn't have to accept my challenge to the Rite of Conquest. Anyone can refuse a challenger, but to do so marks them as a coward, and cowards go to the crematorium. Molers knows this.

"I accept," he says.

Renal turns toward Commander Vye, awaiting her command.

"Very well," she says, disguising her concern for my actions, but knowing there is nothing she can do about it. "Take them away."

I steal one last look at Chase before a black bag is rammed over my head, and my hands are put in restraints as I am led to my fate.

Chapter 9

Preparation

The cold metal table I lay on seeps through the thin polyester gown I was forced to put on when I arrived at the training facility. I don't know why they brought me back here—I haven't seen it since I received my commission—but perhaps they had nowhere to take me that would be protected from outsiders. I start to sit up, but the arbiter in the room with me jerks his eyes in my direction, causing me to change my mind and lay back down, calculating whether I should take him out, but foresight warns me that there are at least two more arbiters outside the door. Once an arbiter issues the challenge to the Rite of Conquest, and once it is accepted, all precautions are taken to ensure that neither party backs out.

The Rite of Conquest is a right bestowed upon arbiters as a way for them to earn renown and prestige, but it is also used as a way to rid one of an enemy. During the rite, both arbiters are given a tracker, in addition to the wristband they already wear, and are dumped in the wilderness beyond the wall with a single drone to record their actions, and no tools—they must hunt one another and survive the elements like primitives. Only one is allowed to return, and if I win, I will accomplish two goals: no more Molers and prominence within Arelian society, giving me more freedom. The rite itself has been initiated five times in the past: only one is known to have survived it, and I challenged him, though his victory has been marred by rumors that he was never the true champion, but that his opponent was, and is a man who remains a mystery to this day.

White rectangles stretch across the ceiling, causing me to squint as I stare at the bright light they release, illuminating the mirror-like walls of the medical wing, making them appear more white than silver. I twitch my arm, admiring the perfect reflection in the walls and chuckle when the arbiter with me flinches, ready to act should I make an undesirable move. Growing impatient, I drum my fingers on the table, not liking that the gown I wear is the only thing between my naked body and the frigid table—arbiters stripped me of my clothes the moment I arrived.

The door slides open and in walks a medical officer, his white uniform almost blinding me, and he heads straight for me with a tablet in his hand, scrolling through charts. Without saying a word, he grabs the sphygmomanometer instrument and wraps the cuff around my bicep to measure my blood pressure. Silence ensues between us as he continues with the examination, putting all the information in his tablet. Minutes pass as he moves from one thing to the next, taking my temperature, taking my pulse, measuring my heartbeat, checking my pupils, checking my ears, and checking my esophageal muscle.

"You are a fine specimen of Arel," he says, breaking the tense silence, and heat rises around the back of my neck as something does not feel right.

Hands grab me under my arms, pinning me to the table as the arbiter in the room holds onto me, having snuck up behind me while my attention remained focused on the medical officer.

"It's not often that we have access to such a fine specimen," says the medical officer, pressing his hands between my thighs and opening them.

I twist at the waist, freeing one of my legs from him and kick the medical officer in the face, forcing him to stumble back as he clutches his nose and blood oozes between his fingers. Before he can react, I bring my knee over my head and ram it into the arbiter's face. His grip loosens. I roll off the medical table, allowing my bare feet to plop on the frigid tile floor as I prepare myself for an attack. The arbiter lunges at me. In a flash of motion, I scoot the table between us, catching him in the stomach, before grabbing his head and ramming it into the metallic surface. While he buckles over, stunned, I hurry to the medical officer and slam him into the wall, snatching him by the back of his head and shoving his face into the wall as many times as I can, until the arbiter whips out his electrified baton and sticks me with it. Electricity courses through my body, causing my muscles to seize, but I will them to move and snatch the baton from him, striking him in the face with it.

More arbiters enter the room. I stun one with the baton, but two of them tackle me, and I crash onto the tile floor, gasping as the wind is knocked out of me, while another arbiter pries the weapon from my grasp before turning it on me. Another one kicks me in the stomach. I reach for the ankle of one, but a fist plows into my face, stopping me. My body writhes in agony as five different electrified batons send jolts of pain through me, preventing me from being able to defend myself or plan a counterattack.

"What is the meaning of this!"

The pain stops. Wheezing, I hack up a mixture of mucus and spittle as I try to regain my breath and bearings as the torment of the electrical shock still permeates my body.

Commander Vye stands in the room, her gaze piercing through all present as she demands answers, but no one speaks. She stalks up to one of the arbiters in the room, her nose only inches from his face.

"Well?"

He says nothing.

"Have you no tongue?" Commander Vye demands. "Perhaps I should cut it out!"

"It was just a bit of fun," he says.

Commander Vye's lips form a thin line as she raises her fist and punches the arbiter in the face, knocking him to the floor. "How is that for a bit of fun?"

One of the arbiters shifts and Commander Vye rounds on him. "You wish to try something, mister?"

He backs down.

"He just wanted to admire a fine specimen," the arbiter who had been in the room with me from the beginning says, pointing at the medical officer.

Commander Vye walks up to the arbiter. "Admire. And where were you? Was it not your job to ensure that no harm came to the challenger of the Rite of Conquest? Perhaps I should send you someplace where you will be 'admired'. You disgust me."

None of the arbiters dare meet her gaze, afraid of the punishment they may be forced to endure for incurring her wrath, and just like when I first met her, I find myself wanting to be like her: to be able to command obedience with a single look.

"Dismissed!" she yells at them, and they all leave.

Commander Vye approaches the medical officer. "So," she says, "you wanted to admire a specimen?"

The man backs away, fearing what she plans to do, but he is no match for her.

She wraps her fingers around his throat and slams him into the wall. "Well, take a good look! And the next time you wish to admire one of my arbiters, I will cut off the only thing that makes you a man and feed it to you!"

In a flurry of movement, she stretches out his arm and places her other hand behind his shoulder, breaking his collarbone and ignoring his cries of anguish as she throws him out of the room.

"Get up," Commander Vye tells me as I remain on the floor. "Don't let them see weakness."

Weak prey emboldens the predator. This is what we are taught, and it's true. Still reeling from the shocks of electricity, I grasp the table in the room and haul myself to my feet, doing my best to stand tall and proud. Satisfied, Commander Vye goes into the corridor, returning with a small, black bundle in her hands and dumps it at my feet, allowing the articles of clothing to scatter.

"Put those on," she says.

I scoop up the clothes and place them on the medical table before stripping off my gown, allowing the harsh light to make my skin appear more blue than its normal dark tone, unconcerned that my commander stands in the room with me. There is no privacy among arbiters. In the training facility, we learn to not care if others see us naked. I put on the underwear and bra first before slipping the undershirt on, followed by a uniform shirt and the tight-fitting pants that show every curve of my legs and the toned muscles that form them. After I finish lacing up my boots, Commander Vye leaves the room, and I follow behind, not waiting for her orders.

She heads down a long corridor with walls that light up as she moves, illuminating our path, while I take in their barren nature—no art, no texture, not even a sign of paneling—and wonder where she is taking me, and why. Our boots tap the coffee-colored, porcelain tiled floor, making soft sounds as we hurry through the hallway, with me skipping to keep up with my commander's fast pace. My mind races as she hurries along without bothering to speak or see if I am following; she knows me well. As I study the walls around me, none of it looks familiar. This is not a part of the training facility I know; though, when I was a recruit, there was a wing that all recruits were forbidden to enter; the punishment for doing so was severe.

During my seventh year as a recruit, one of the older ones decided to break into the forbidden wing of the facility by shorting the electronic locks. He was caught within minutes and the commandant had all of us line up according to year in the courtyard to witness the consequence of disobedience. I will never forget his screams as they hacked off his arm possessing the hand that still held the wire he had replaced, using a blunt axe, and waved it in front of us as blood dripped onto the black stones while he suffered the most agonizing moment of his life before they executed him. His head landed next to my left foot when he fell. As this memory fills my mind, I wonder if I am now in the forbidden wing, only to have that question answered when we pass a small window looking out at a courtyard below—a place I got to know well in the first 18 years of my life. I pause before it, staring out at the recruits lined up in formation, repeating the Arelian mantra.

"Strength in—"

"—our kind!"

"Noni!" Commander Vye's voice breaks my reverie, and I pull myself away from the window and follow her through a set of double doors as they open, breaking the Arelian insignia that is carved into them in the center, allowing us to enter a massive training room.

Recessed lights illumine the room before me, shining fluorescent beams onto the ropes, pulleys, weights, ladders, and balance beams. I step into the chamber, awed by all the equipment, and wonder why we were forbidden to enter this part of the training facility, when a fist plows into the side of my head, knocking me sideways and to the floor.

"Always be aware of your surroundings!" Commander Vye's voice echoes around me as she stands over me with her fists raised.

Angered, and feeling betrayed by her actions, I jump up and charge her, but she swerves out of the way and jabs the heel of her hand into my back, forcing me to the floor again.

"Use your head!"

Why is she doing this?

I lunge for her, but she expects it and steps out of the way, allowing me to crash stomach first on the floor, and my chin stings as it hits the hard tile.

"Stop acting like a sixth-year recruit!" she yells at me.

My pride hurt, and growing more infuriated by the second as she makes a fool of me, I rise to my feet and glare at her and her mocking stance. I feign a punch, and as she goes to block it, I bring up my other fist, catching her in the chin, but it never phases her. She swings a fist at me, and I block it as she brings her knee up into my stomach. Gasping from the sudden pain, I refuse to show weakness, and reach for her thigh, gripping it, thinking I have the advantage as she hops on one foot, but Commander Vye twists and drops to one knee, forcing me to loosen my grip before she seizes me by the shoulders and pushes me into the floor with her arm in the back of my neck.

"Molers will not be so kind," she whispers into my ear. "He has trained you. He knows your weaknesses. He knows your style."

She lets me up.

"Stop relying on your physical strength and use your head!" Commander Vye says.

She throws a punch. I duck, dodging it, and ram my shoulder into her side, knocking her off-balance, but before I can put her down, a steel rod strikes me in the chest, throwing me backward and to the floor. When I look up, Renal stands in the room—I never noticed his presence—with the rod by his side.

"Pay attention to your surroundings!" Commander Vye screams at me in frustration.

Feeling stupid—we are taught early on to have situational awareness, but I allowed myself to believe that the commander and I were alone in this room—I face both her and Renal, calculating my next move while considering theirs. We eye each other, circling one another as we gauge the other, wondering who will make the first move. Renal lunges, but I drop to the floor, swinging my foot around and knocking his out from under him. As he stumbles, I round on Commander Vye, kicking her in the chest, but before I can turn back to Renal, he hits me in the back with the pole and

I fall to the floor. He rushes me, but I jump up and grab the bar. Commander Vye approaches. Eyeing the room, I spot a rope nearby and the balance beam between it and us. I only have seconds.

I drop to the floor, landing on my back, and fling Renal over me, until he crashes onto the tile. Commander Vye rushes me. I roll across the floor underneath the balance beam and closer to the rope, before springing to my feet and catching her leg as she kicks at me, twisting at the same time, enabling myself to fling her into the hanging rope. It tangles around her, and I spring on her, wrapping it around her hands and feet so that she is unable to move. Once done, I turn back to Renal, running for him and jumping over the balance beam before scooping up the pole. He dodges my first attack, but I roll over the balance beam with the bar in my hands and bring it down upon him, and before he has time to recover, I use the rod to sweep him off his feet, forcing him to the ground, and jump on his back, pointing the end of the pole at his neck.

"Please tell me you did not make this easy on me," I taunt him.

He smiles, and without warning, he throws me off him, snatches the rod from my hands and pins me to the floor. "Never become overconfident," he says before releasing me.

"Better," Commander Vye says. "You're good, Noni, but up until now, you have only faced people who are not trained like you. Molers is different. He has three times your years of training, knowledge, and experience. He shows no mercy and feels no compassion."

In that moment, a part of me wonders if Commander Vye knows my secret, but if she does, she never reveals it.

"Now untie me," she says.

I do.

The doors open as arbiters storm in and surround us.

"Commander," one of them says to her, "you have been charged with attacking a medical officer. You are to be…"

His words trail off when Renal steps between him and Commander Vye. "I attacked him."

The arbiter's mouth opens, closes, and opens again. "Lieutenant, I..."

"Take me in if you wish," says Renal.

"But the commander is..."

"To be let go."

"I have my orders, sir," the arbiter says with trepidation.

Renal stalks over to where more metal rods are and picks one up, holding it by his left side while the one he took from me hangs by his right, ready to strike if necessary. "Who here thinks he can challenge me?"

Each of the arbiters look to one another, unsure of what to do, and as I watch the scene unfold before me, I ponder whether Renal is something more than a Lieutenant within the corps, perhaps more than a marshal, but whenever I pry into his backstory, I'm met with roadblocks, and I do not dare challenge him.

One foolish arbiter charges him, but Renal sidesteps and kicks the man in the calf, breaking it to the point where the bone reveals itself. As the man cries in agony, Renal silences him before facing the rest. Two more come at him. In one swift movement, Renal jabs one in the throat, hits the other in the groin, swings the rod, and rams it in the back of the neck of the first, forcing him to the floor, before disabling the second. Movement catches my attention, and I turn in time to see an arbiter come for me, but before I can react, Renal throws the pole at the man, striking him in the shoulder and pounces on him, ramming his forearm into the man's throat, causing him to fall backward and lie on the barren tiles, unmoving.

He rounds on the last remaining arbiter. "Tell the one who sent you, to quit sending first-years to accomplish what he is too much of a coward to do himself."

Renal's eyes focus in the distance at a far point within the corridor beyond, and I follow his gaze, noticing Molers watching the entire proceeding before skulking off into the shadows. Why is it he is not under guard like I am?

The remaining arbiter runs away.

"Come," Commander Vye says to me, and I do as ordered. She pauses by Renal and whispers, "Meet us at her room."

Renal nods and drops the rods before disappearing, but before I can contemplate where he is headed, Commander Vye snaps her fingers, forcing me back into the reality of my situation, and I trail after her, matching her brisk pace as she walks through a maze of hallways, until we come to a slate-colored door. She touches a pad and it opens, allowing us inside a small room with a bed in the corner—its pressed, charcoal blanket stretched in a way where not one wrinkle is present—and a table with two chairs in the center. The uninviting floor—blacker than my hair—makes me believe that it will be cold to the touch, but I haven't the luxury of critiquing my accommodations, considering where I will be taken soon.

"Commander," I say, "what's going on?"

"You made a challenge," she replies.

"Why am I under constant guard and Master Arbiter Molers isn't?"

Commander Vye lets out a sigh, debating if she should tell me, or let me continue to brood over questions I will never learn the answers to.

"Haven't you wondered why he was at the dinner of your medal of honor ceremony?"

Yes. I have thought about that several times, and each answer I come up with is more sinister than the previous.

"Will I make it through this?"

"That is up to you, Noni. It does appear, however, that our standing president wishes to use this challenge of yours for her entertainment, while the tribunal sees it as a training lesson for future recruits. Either way, you have attracted the attention of people best avoided.

"Molers is well-trained. He is very skilled. He has made it through this before. He will hunt you and he will kill you. Stay sharp. Stay alert. Molers will not be the only one hunting you."

Not the only one hunting me?

"What..."

A single knock on the door stops my words in my throat.

"Enter," Commander Vye says and in walks a plebeian with a tray of food, and she places it on the only table in the room before leaving without uttering a single word.

"Commander..." I start again, but a harsh knock rattles the door, stopping me.

Commander Vye opens it, and I see Renal's face as I peer around her to satisfy my curiosity. "Don't tell her," Commander Vye whispers to him, and judging by the somber tone of her voice, it seems that she does not want me to know the news Renal gave her. Before I can consider it any further, Chase enters the room and Renal steps aside, taking up his post outside the door, while Commander Vye steps out, leaving the door ajar.

"Chase!" I say, not caring if she or Renal hear me; they must already know my secret.

He puts his hand over my lips, forcing me to contain my enthusiasm at seeing him as he looks around, his eyes nervous.

"Chase," I say in a lower voice, "what is it?"

"I don't know," he replies. "They got me out of that detention center and brought me here, and I keep thinking that there has to be a more disturbing reason for it."

"Hey," I say, putting my hand on his cheek, and he holds it there for a moment, "it'll be okay."

The aroma of steamed green beans and meatloaf permeate my nostrils, causing my stomach to grumble and reminding me that it has been a while since I've eaten, and before I know it, my hand reaches for one of the beans, but Chase stops it. Curious, I watch as he takes a piece of the meatloaf and a single green bean and nibbles on it before pouring a glass of water and taking a sip, while Commander Vye's watchful eyes take it all in. After a few minutes pass, he pushes the food toward me.

"You don't think..." I begin.

"I believe that you need to be extra careful."

I take a bite of green bean and offer him some, but he turns it down.

"You need it more than I do," he says.

"Chase..."

"Eat."

I place a bite full of meatloaf in my mouth, doing as Chase asks, wishing he would quit looking at me as though I was about to die, though, I share his sentiment.

"Have you seen Sheila?"

He shakes his head. "They split us up soon after taking you. I haven't seen her since, and no one will tell me anything. I'm a plebeian."

My face falls as worry takes over my mind with the uncertainty of what has happened to her, while all I can do is hope she is safe and will remain safe until I return.

"Noni," he says, "promise that you will do what you need to, to survive."

"Chase…"

"Promise me."

"I will."

He presses his forehead against mine when Commander Vye enters the room.

"Time to go," she says in her usual business-like tone.

Reluctance dictates Chase's movements as he heads to the door, but Commander Vye's impatient clearing of her throat speeds him up as he goes into the hallway.

"Commander," I say, "I'm sorry for putting you in this position. I know my impulsive actions of late reflect on you, and…"

Commander Vye closes the distance between us, and her expression softens as she cuts me off. "Your actions only reflect on you. I told you once that I saw a lot of myself in you. I was wrong. You are far better. When the rite begins, trust no one, and do as Renal tells you."

She moves to the door, but pauses and turns toward me.

"Get some sleep. You'll need it."

The door hisses as it closes behind her with a quiet thud, leaving me alone in silence with an empty food tray as exhaustion wraps its tendrils around me, urging me to retire for the night. I move to the bed and sit on the hard mattress, stretching out on it, falling asleep before my head rests on the feather pillow.

The door opens and heavy boots stomp on the tile floor as arbiters rush for me and ram a black bag over my head and jab me in the thigh with a needle, injecting me with a tracker—a good place to put it because, if I try to remove it, I'll impede my ability to walk—before yanking me off the bed and dragging me out the door. Groggy, and wondering how long I have slept, I try to move my feet in an effort to keep up with their brisk pace and to avoid having the edges of my boots drag across the floor, but my legs refuse to obey me, causing me to stumble. In response, one of the arbiters jerks my arm as a way to convince me to stand up and keep up, even though I have no clue where I am being taken.

"I'll take her," says Renal—I recognize his voice—and my head flops forward when we stop.

"Sir," says one, "we have orders to…"

"I said," Renal growls at them, "that I will take her." When the arbiters surrounding me continue to hesitate, Renal speaks again. "Tell them you are following my orders."

The arbiters hand me over to him, refusing to say another word, and he takes my arm and leads me down the hallway, until we pause before a door that swooshes open, allowing a rush of air to blow past us before we step through. I want to ask him why others are afraid to challenge him, but know that this is not the time, nor will he answer. My foot bumps something as a metallic sound echoes around me when Renal steps forward, and it takes me a moment to realize that there are stairs in front of me. I lift my foot higher, missing the edge of the step, and walk in an awkward fashion the further up the stairwell we go as the air becomes more and more stifling.

"Head north," he whispers to me through the black canvass over my head, while tying a leather strap around my waist before covering it with my shirt. "You won't be alone out there, but you may find allies."

We reach the top of the steps and another door slides open, allowing the sounds of the outside world, mixed with the whooping sound of helicopter blades, to swarm over us and pound my ears, making me wince from its sudden impact.

"Stay focused," Renal says to me before we are stopped by another arbiter. "Room three and look beneath the floorboards."

"I'll take her from here," says another arbiter.

Renal hesitates a moment before releasing me and allowing the other to take my arm, but before I can take another step, he stops the other arbiter, saying, "If she does not arrive at her destination point in the same manner in which I have given her to you, I will find you."

The arbiter says nothing, leaving me to imagine the expression on his face, but the careful manner in which he guides me to the helicopter leads me to believe that he is more scared of Renal than of his own superiors. He shoves me inside the aircraft, and I land on my stomach, before rolling onto my back and sitting up as we lift into the air. I want to take the bag off my head, but every time I try, hands shove it back on. The spinning blades fill my ears as they sound more like gigantic hammers hitting hollows within the ground as we rise high into the air, before banking to the right. I allow my body to move with the craft as it veers in different directions before settling on a constant path, while my mind races with one possible scenario after another for where I will be dumped.

After losing track of time and any sense of direction, the helicopter slows before lowering itself. My heart beats faster as the knowledge of what lies ahead causes my nerves to fire overwhelming impulses throughout my body, causing my hands to tingle and my breathing to quicken in anticipation of the inevitable. I try to calm myself, but it proves useless as hands ram into the middle of my back, shoving me out of the craft, allowing me to land with a harsh thud on the hardened earth, and my lungs empty themselves from the impact. The helicopter flies away, growing more and more distant with each second, telling me that I am alone in a wilderness I do not know.

I rip the bag off my head, sucking in fresh air, filling my lungs until they can hold no more before exhaling. Something pokes me in my lower back. Feeling back there, my fingers brush over the leather strap Renal had given me and the two knives it holds, while I scan the area around me with its overgrown brush and the unknown dangers it contains. The whine of a drone draws my attention. Of course. Arel wants all my movements recorded so that it can be used in future training exercises, but the softball-sized device annoys me, and I don't want to make the life of those watching me any easier, so I scoop up a nearby branch and hit the drone with it, forcing it into the protruding knob of a tree trunk, breaking it. Pleased, I drop the branch and look up, studying the position of the sun in relation to my surroundings and orienting myself until I face north.

Time for the hunt.

Chapter 10

Prey

Sweltering heat encloses around me as I trudge through the entangled mass of trees in this jungle, while the sun beats down upon the canopy, turning it into more of an oven than a place of relief from its fiery embrace, making the slight chill of the morning appear to be more of a distant memory, rather than something that happened a few hours ago. A rounded frond drapes in front of me, and it pricks me with its pointed end as I move it out of my way in an attempt to keep going. Renal said to go north. I have no idea why, but I refuse to believe that it was done in an attempt to trick me: he has never done that before.

A thousand tiny pinpricks stab my calf as fire ants hurry up my boot, going under my pant leg and up my bare skin, biting me with their pinchers and jabbing me with their stingers. Frustrated with my own stupidity—I had stepped on an ant colony without realizing it—I jump away, waving my foot around, before pulling up my pant leg and smacking the ants off me. Once I free myself of the swarm of angry insects, I hurry away from that area, jogging through the thick brush in an effort to get away before sitting on a log and examining my leg, frowning at all the red welts forming and wincing from the lingering burns of the multiple bites. I tear off the sleeve of my uniform jacket and dig into the dirt, delving under the first layer to the cool moist soil below and scoop some up, wrapping it in my sleeve, and place it on the insect bites, allowing the coolness of my makeshift compress to numb the pain and reveling in the momentary relief.

A low growl sounds behind me. Chills sprint down my back from the sudden ominous feeling that wells up within me, causing me to sweat as my muscles prepare to flee from the danger that has presented itself. I turn my head with caution, until I face the latest threat to my life. A wild cat—long ago, they had a name, and most refer to them as dangerous predators that do not deserve one, but I once heard a man use the word puma to describe one—crouches on the ground, baring its fangs at me as its whiskers bend backward from its continual soft growls, warning me that I must pay the price for wandering into its territory. My heart quickens as my body prepares to respond.

I drop my homemade compress and leap to my feet, but before I can take two steps, the animal tackles me, forcing me to the ground. I roll onto my back and push my chin to my chest so as to protect my throat, while trying to stop it from slashing me with its claws. It hisses and roars in frustration as I squirm underneath it, trying to push it off. My hand brushes a rock. I snatch it and slam it into the wild cat's head, forcing it to coil back, giving me the opportunity to scramble away and run. Branches and leaves crunch underneath my heavy boots as I charge through the wilderness at full speed, hoping to put as much distance between me and the cat as a harsh yowl warns me that it still considers me its prey. I run faster. Branches and leaves stretch out to stop me as though entertained and wanting to see what will happen if I am caught in the wild cat's claws. My feet fly over the ground as I hurry. A log lays in my path, threatening to stop me. Knowing that the wild cat is still behind me, I lift my feet and jump over the log, stumbling as I land on a pile of stones obscured from view by a carpet of dead leaves, and I cringe when tiny slivers pierce the skin of my hands as they catch my fall. The wild cat crashes through the wilderness behind me. Ignoring the agony within my hands, I leap to my feet and charge through the trees as I hurry through the bush, hoping to either get away or that the cat will give up its pursuit. I lose on both counts. It draws closer, and with each step I take, I feel the wild cat's presence and know that I must think of something.

Light increases as the trees thin out. Emboldened, I run faster, pushing myself to my limit as my chest heaves from the increased exertion. The trees thin out even more, revealing a drop off, and I am headed straight for it. I cannot stop. I cannot turn around. There is nowhere for me to go. The wild cat is on my heels, clawing at my legs, and for a moment, I believe I will fall and become its meal when a high-pitched whine hits my ears as a softball-sized drone appears to replace the one I broke earlier. The animal pauses, distracted by the drone. I use the momentary interference to look around for a means of escape, spotting one: a vine wrapped around a tree protruding from the slope of the drop off hangs low enough for my purposes. The cat smacks once at the drone before turning its attention back to me.

I run.

Sweat pours down my face as I charge for the hanging vine with both the cat and the drone right behind me, focusing my attention on it. I reach the edge and jump through the air, grabbing the vine and swinging away from the cat as it tries to lunge for me, but it misses and falls down the slope, disappearing into the brush below. My relief is short-lived as the vine snaps and I drop to the ground beneath me and tumble down the slope, unable to stop myself, until I reach the bottom and land with a sharp thud. I do not move as I try to catch my breath and allow my head to stop spinning. Once my equilibrium returns, a painful cry jerks me awake, and I turn my head in its direction to see the wild cat lying on the ground with a stick stuck in its leg as blood trickles from the wound, while a vine remains tangled around its foot, and the fear I had earlier morphs into sympathy as it struggles to get up but falls.

I stand up and start to walk away, but pause, struggling with leaving it there and being comforted that it will no longer be able to harm me and helping it; the more I consider it, compassion dictates my next move. The wild cat looks at me with distrust in its eyes as I step toward it and kneel down by its hind leg, reaching for the vine around its foot as a low growl emanates from its lips. I hesitate, keeping my eyes on it as it keeps its gaze on me.

"I'm trying to help you," I say to it in a gentle voice.

The growl softens.

With care, I pry the vine away from the wild cat's foot, while the drone hovers around me, recording my actions, and I imagine what those watching are thinking: I should have left it to die or killed it for food. Once freed, the cat and I stare at one another, gauging the other's move, before my hands reach for the stick protruding from the animal's leg. The cat jerks when I grasp it. Keeping my eyes on it, I rip the stick out, and it swipes at me with the pads of its paw but does not touch me. Now, I need to dress the wound, but if infection sets in, the animal will die. A soft buzzing prickles my ears, and I smile when I spot a bee's nest within the rotted trunk of a tree that looks like it had been struck by lightning at one time.

I pick up a thin, long branch that had fallen to the ground and move toward the nest, being careful to keep my movements slow and steady so as not to alarm the bees as they fly around me. Steeling my nerves and forcing myself to not react when they buzz my ear, I ease the branch into the nest at a glob of honey near the top. Once the edge of the branch is coated in the sticky substance, I pull it out of the hive and tiptoe away, until I am a safe distance from it. I use my finger to pick honey off the end of the branch and rub it on the open wound of the wild cat's leg, being as gentle as I can, but it remains still, as though it knows what the honey is for. I examine my handiwork, realizing I need something to keep it covered, so I rip the other sleeve of my jacket off and wrap it around the leg, covering the small hole, and tie it with a loose knot so that it will fall off at some point. The cat sniffs the dressing as I step back.

"Perhaps we can come to an understanding," I say to it.

The wild cat stands up and stalks over to me, sniffing me and taking in my scent before snorting and wandering off.

"I think I'll call you puma," I say as it leaves.

It disappears into the brush.

The drone circles around me, being nothing more than an annoyance. Once again, I reach down and find a stone, and when it floats to my hand to investigate, I seize it and smash it with the rock. Rustling catches my attention. I move toward it with care, pulling back the branches of a bush, where I find a small rabbit with its neck broken, as though it has just been killed, and when I glance up, the wild cat's snout vanishes into the shadows, and I smile, knowing that we have come to an agreement.

I study the rabbit and pull out a knife from the belt that Renal had given me to dress the animal, but once done, I realize that I need to cook it somehow. A fire will produce smoke and light, which will attract attention, and I do not wish to make it any easier for Molers to find me. I push the toe of my boot into the ground and find that it is soft enough for me to dig. Tiny pebbles dig into my knees as I kneel down and tear into the ground with my hands, forming a tiny bowl to place the fire in, and I create a small ventilation tunnel to feed it air. To prevent cave in, I line the sides with small stones, which will also allow the fire to burn hotter so the meat will cook faster.

I need fuel.

As the sun moves across the sky, I search for dry twigs that are small enough to place in the hole I have made and pick up some dry grass as well, but only what I need to light a fire. Once everything is placed in the hole, I use one of the knives Renal gave me and scrape it across a dry rock to create enough sparks to light a fire. A little flame pops up. Before it can disappear, I breathe on it, providing it the oxygen it needs to grow, and it does. Pleased, I snatch a long stick and sharpen the end to create a spear and place the pieces of the rabbit on it. My stomach gurgles as the aroma of cooked meat fills the air, reminding me of how hungry I am, and it takes all my willpower to not check my meal every few seconds to see if it is done, but once it is, I devour it, and nothing is left once I'm finished.

With my stomach satiated, my eyelids droop as the need for sleep overtakes me, forbidding me to rebel against its demands. I know I cannot stay awake forever and will need to sleep, but I do not want to be exposed. I move away from the fire and into the brush behind me, but not before placing a few pebbles in a line marking the way north, and pile it over me as a way to keep warm during the night, but also for camouflage in case anyone finds me. The fire can burn itself out as the last smoldering remains glow before going dark.

A sharp snap causes my eyes to spring open as I jerk awake. Darkness surrounds me, meaning I have slept long enough for the sun to disappear beneath the horizon. Another tiny sound permeates my ears, but it is miniscule, almost as though someone is trying to not be heard. At full alert, I slink out from underneath the brush I had piled on me and crawl behind a tree as two figures with assault rifles and night vision goggles stand between me and the fire, which is now nothing but icy charcoal. One bends down and touches it, confirming that it is cold before signaling to his partner to spread out. Cursing the tracker within my leg which led them here, but thankful that it only leads them to the general area of my location, I crawl across the ground, going further into the trees and bushes, hoping to remain unseen as I try to think of a way out of here.

Careful footsteps approach as I press myself against the gnarled trunk of a tree, pulling the knives out of my belt, ready to defend myself. A leg appears beside me. I spring from my place of hiding and ram one of my knives into the throat of the arbiter searching for me, while using my other knife to cut the shoulder strap of his weapon, freeing it from him. He drops to the ground. I snatch the night vision goggles and put them on, but they go dark the moment I do. Dammit! They are biometric and will only work for the arbiter whose DNA was programmed into the goggles. Tossing them aside, I grab the rifle and realize that it is also biometric.

Cursing, I start to move away from the body when gunfire breaks the night's peace, forcing me to dodge behind another tree trunk as bullets fly past me with the rifle still in my grip. More bullets rip into the tree I hunker behind as my mind races for what to do. My hands find a rock, and I toss it to the side as far away from me as I can. The arbiter jerks in that direction, releasing a hailstorm of bullets as I sneak around the tree and approach him from behind, raising the rifle and bashing the butt of it into his head. While he is stunned, I jab him in the stomach with the barrel of the rifle before bringing it up and hitting him in the chin. His head flops forward, exposing the back of his neck, allowing me to strike him again and forcing him to the ground where he lies still.

The click of a weapon stops me. Scolding myself for believing that the two arbiters I saw were the only ones here, I turn, making certain to keep my movements slow so as not to force the hand of the one with his weapon pointed at me. We stare at one another, though all I see is a faint outline of his shape, while his night vision goggles allow him to see me as though it is daylight. He points at the rifle in my hand. I drop it. It's useless to me anyway. A low growl echoes from behind him. As the realization that we are not alone dawns on him, he turns around to find the wild cat that had chased me earlier crouched behind him, preparing to strike as its lips curl back, and it hisses at him. The animal pounces on the arbiter, knocking him to the ground as his squeals of fear are silenced when the animal's fangs clamp down on the man's throat before he is dragged away into the underbrush.

I hurry to the fire pit I had dug, looking for the line of rocks placed there before I fell asleep. Found them. Once I am reassured which direction is north, I check to make sure my knives are secure and leave, knowing that I cannot stay here a moment longer as it is evident that Molers is not the only one hunting me.

My feet ease themselves to the ground as I try to make no noise while skulking through the dense forest surrounding me. I do not know who else may be out here hunting me, and my intuition tells me that the three I encountered are only the beginning. This cannot be part of the challenge, at least not the ones I have heard about, unless it always was and no one said anything, but something tells me that Molers is not being hunted like I am. Is the purpose of all this to wear me down before I face Molers out here? Is he just sitting in some room watching all this, enjoying luxuries, while I struggle to find my way in this wilderness? Anger courses through me at the thought of him lying on a sofa, eating delectable treats, while I satisfy myself with a scrawny rabbit. I shake the "what if" scenarios from my mind. I do not know where Molers is or how he fares out here, but this sort of thinking will not help me survive the situation I am in now. Renal told me to head north. So, I shall.

Mellow silence reigns through the night, broken only by the soft chirping of a cricket when I step too close, or the humid breeze that brushes the leaves of the tree, letting me know that its presence is always around me. I welcome the comforting sounds as I wander in a strange place, while doing my best to peek through the holes within the canopy to see the position of the stars. On occasion, I spot the north star, only to have it blocked a moment later as though the jungle itself plays games with me. The further I go, the more the branches tangle among themselves, forming barriers, while vines and leaves twist around each other, forming natural locks to an impassable gate. I shove an overhanging branch out of my way as I climb over protruding roots that seem to stretch up in an effort to trip me and impede my progress.

The slow trickle of a stream alerts me to the possibility of fresh water being nearby, and my throat clenches, reminding me that I have not drunk anything for a few hours at least. Desperate to satisfy my thirst, and to prevent dehydration, I hurry toward the sound, but moss wraps itself around my foot, forcing me to stop. I try pulling it free, but the vegetation holds tight, refusing to let me go, almost as though it has its own plans, and the more I pull, the more it clings, until…

My foot pops free, but the sudden release causes me to lose my balance and fall backward, and when I hit the ground, it gives way beneath me, allowing gravity to pull me into the earth as I fall into complete darkness, until I slam into a solid surface with bits of timber and dirt raining down upon me, surrounding me in clouds of dust and disturbed mildew. Hacking, I roll onto my stomach, wincing from the bruise that will now form on the left side of my back, and look up, peering into the blackness around me, before picking up a splintered piece of wood that seems to have rotted through. I seem to be in a cavern, but the shape of the walls and the ceiling are too square and unnatural as though they had been carved out by machinery and designed that way.

I'm not in a cave. I'm in an abandoned mine.

Dust hangs in the air, never moving, never ceasing as it waits for me to inhale it, making me cough as it sticks to the back of my throat and forms a gritty blanket that blocks my airway. My hand reaches out for something to use to help me lift myself to my feet, nd finds a support that had broken in two and leans outward, away from the sides of the tunnel. Darkness. That s all I see. Glancing up at the hole I have just fallen through, I try to jump for it, hoping that I can climb back through it, but it is too far above me and there is nothing but lose dirt for me to grab, causing my hands to slip and me to fall back downward. I need another way out, but which way do I go? If I pick the wrong direction, I will end up going deeper in the mine, and to my death. I rub the sole of my boot across the ground, feeling a slight incline and decide to head uphill, hoping that it will lead me to the mine's entrance and out of this place.

Each slow step proves awkward as I walk, doing my best to not trip as the bleakness of the tunnel surrounds me, providing no light for which to see, forcing me to rely on the tunnel walls for guidance. Pebbles fall behind me, clacking on the ground, and the harsh echoes make it sound as though I am surrounded by an army of exploding mortar shells as they break the silence, forcing me to whip around, but I find nothing. With no other choice, I continue heading forward toward what I hope will be my salvation from this place. Dirt crumbles away from where my fingers touch the tunnel walls, while my feet slide across the ground in my efforts to feel my way around. A supporting timber breaks in my grip as I place my hand on it, almost causing me to fall over from the sudden pull, and I slam into the rocky ground, gasping as I find myself looking down into a never-ending abyss of pure black, while dirt and pebbles fall away from me only to disappear into nothingness.

This chasm must be why the mine was abandoned. They must have dug too close to a fault line. Years ago, talk spread throughout Arel about an earthquake that destroyed one of our most precious sources for resources. Is the very place I find myself in now the mine those rumors spoke of? Whether it is or isn't, is of little concern as I remember that I must get out, or risk dying down here. I need to know the distance to the other side. My foot hits a piece of metal and I scoop it up and throw it, listening as it clinks when it lands, telling me that I don't have far to jump. Taking a deep breath, and hoping I have guessed well, I take a few steps back from the edge of the chasm before running toward it and taking a literal leap of faith. My feet hit something metallic and uneven as I land on the other side, causing me to fall over, but my hands fly out and find something solid to cling to, preventing me from hitting the ground, and relief washes over me as I realize that I have made it, for now.

I feel the metallic edge of the item that saved me and am able to make out the faint line of an empty cart situated on a rail that has been cleaved in two. Steadying myself on my feet, I use the cart to support myself as I continue on before being forced to let it go so that I can restart my trek in the mines as I try to picture the people who would have been here digging for whatever resource had been discovered and deemed valuable. My feet stumble as I step on broken timbers making up what is left of the track, while soft silt shifts beneath me, giving me the sensation of walking on a boat as I stretch my hands out to feel my way through. Something catches on my foot, and as I try to yank it free, I lose my balance and tumble to the ground, landing hard as the silt compacts beneath me, and my hip bursts in sudden pain that takes its time subsiding as I slam into the metallic rail. Looking around for the source of my sudden fall, I spot a skeleton still dressed in coveralls that look more like dusty rags than clothing, its arms stretched out as though whoever it was had been trying to crawl to safety. Startled, I jump, scooting on my bottom in an effort to get away from it, and back into more skeletal remains sitting on the ground as though the people they used to be had grown tired. The feeling that I need to get out claws at me, and I leap to my feet, ready to run, but stop when I see more remains. This isn't just an abandoned mine; it's a tomb.

I don't know why all these remains are here, but I have no desire to become one of them. I turn to hurry away when a wall of fur stops me. Unsure of what it is, I touch it, wondering why there seems to be wiry fur in front of me when a growl warns me that my obstacle is alive, and as I take a few steps back, I realize that it is a bear whose slumber I have disturbed. I run, not caring that I have no idea where I am going, even as I trip over fallen timbers or scattered tools, abandoned here like those people. I need to get out. I have to get out. My breathing comes in gasps as I panic and try to keep my distance between me and the bear. An opening appears and I veer toward it, charging down another shaft of the mine, hoping it leads to an exit, but it's a dead end. Turning back, I hurry to the main part of the tunnel and duck as a massive paw comes for me, while the bear howls in anger at having missed. I spot a piece of timber hanging at a precarious angle and pull at it, freeing it from its hold, and throw it behind me. The bear puts its paw on it, but it shifts under the animal's weight, causing the bear to fall face forward as I continue running away.

The sound of metal upon metal stops me as it echoes all around me, growing louder the farther down the tunnel it goes. It happens again. Coincidence or not, I head for it, hoping that it leads me to a way out. As I hurry toward it, I stumble upon another shaft diverging from the main part of the tunnel and sprint down it, following the sounds of metal upon metal, hoping that my intuition is correct. The roar of the bear spurs me onward as it comes nearer. If I am wrong…

I push such thoughts out of my mind as I race down the mining shaft, past more human remains, abandoned equipment, and another cart that is still full of dirt and unrefined ore. The clang happens again, telling me I am close. Quickening my pace, I charge down the tunnel, not daring to stop, and refusing to slow down, even when my foot catches on a broken bit of rail, threatening to make me fall, but I catch myself and continue onward. I stop. Fallen debris blocks my path, but as I peer at it, I notice a small opening and a bit of air brushes my skin. There must be a ventilation shaft here allowing air inside.

The bear's howl warns me that I have little time. I dive for the small opening, pushing my way through, despite the tight squeeze. The beating claws of 400 pounds of bear charging straight for me fills my ears, causing me to panic as I wriggle my way through the barricade, until I come out the other side and roll across the ground as the bear crashes into it. Some of the wood splinters and dirt falls from above, coating the top of my head as the animal reaches through it in an attempt to get me, snarling as it does. Knowing I cannot stay here, I feel around for the breeze I had felt earlier, hoping it will lead me out of here when I touch it. Cool air brushes my fingertips, and I follow the zephyr, allowing it to lead me to a part of the tunnel wall covered by fallen timbers.

This must be it.

The bear snarls and claws at the debris preventing it from catching me, but the more it charges it, the more it threatens to break away. I must get out of here. Splintered wood pricks my palms as I grasp the fallen timber blocking the ventilation shaft and toss it aside, revealing a hole, stretching upward at 45-degree angle. A tremendous crack punctures the air around me, warning me that the bear is almost through. Pulling out my knives, I dive into the opening and ram the blades into the hardened dirt, crawling upward as fast as I can as the bear enters my little conclave and shoves its snout into the hole, pushing against the sides of the entrance. I move faster, ignoring the rock that cuts into my knees as they scrape across the ground, while pebbles fall toward me, sneaking underneath my shirt, scraping and scratching my skin as they go. My foot slips and I slide back a few inches, sending small clumps of soil downward, hitting the bear in the nose. Disgusted, it gives up and turns away, but I push myself onward, refusing to quit or to die in this cramped space of rock and clay. Claustrophobia threatens to overtake me as the seconds tick by, counting my time in this channel, while the moist vapor from my breath engulfs my face, causing dust to cling to it, forming a mask.

Light shines up ahead. Invigorated, I push myself further with my legs, while the blades of my knife release soft metallic thumps each time they strike the loam. More dirt rains down upon me, causing me to cough as it gets in my mouth and my eyes to sting as it strikes them, but I will the discomfort away, focusing on my goal: to reach the surface of the earth. The further up I go, the brighter the light ahead of me becomes, urging me onward, beckoning me to come to it, and I obey, wanting to get out of here. Almost there. Just a little bit further.

My head bursts out of the hole, and I take in a sharp breath, reveling in the sweet aroma of freedom, glad to be out of the suffocating mine. With a giant tug, I haul myself out of the abandoned mine's ventilation shaft and lie on the ground, catching my breath when I spot it: a single flask made from animal skin lays on the ground within arm's reach as though it had been placed there for me to find. I pick it up, studying it, wondering who placed it there and if the noise I heard leading me to my salvation had been intentional, but the more I ponder it, the more my parched throat demands the water contained within the flask to wash away the dust that coats it. My hands tear off the top to the flagon, and I lean back, tipping it into my mouth, relieved to have something to drink, but before I can quench my thirst, the barrel of a gun appears at my head, and for the first time, I realize that the light I saw never came from the sun—the sky is still dark with a thin line of brownish-red on the horizon—but from a transport.

"It seems like a little mole has just crawled out of its hole."

I know that voice and had hoped to never hear it again. Lowering the flask, I look into Commandant Paq's vengeful eyes, aware that I will be made to pay for what happened the last time I saw him.

"Welcome back," he says, before the butt of a rifle strikes me in the face, stunning me, allowing the arbiters with him to strip me of my knives and tie my hands, while securing the other end of the rope to the fender of the transport. "I hope you don't mind walking."

The driver of the transport puts it in gear, pulling the rope taut and jerking me forward as my feet stumble in an effort to keep up and not fall on my face, while the five arbiters with Commandant Paq laugh and mock me each time my legs almost buckle beneath me. My legs walk in a disjointed fashion as they are forced to stretch out or take small steps, depending on whether the driver of the vehicle hits the gas or not, all in an effort to keep me from being able to plan any sort of escape, while the exhaust swarms over me, choking me and making my nose and throat burn from the polluted air, much to the entertainment of others.

"Where did you get this?" Commandant Paq demands, snatching the flask from me after noticing it for the first time and holding it out to me.

I spit in his face, and he backhands me in response, leaving a red welt on my cheek, but I refuse to look away or tear up, despite the stinging pain that nestles into my skin, not wanting to give him the satisfaction of seeing me in even the slightest bit of discomfort.

"Where did you get this?" he demands again.

"I found it," I reply.

A doubtful expression crosses his face as he wrestles between believing me or accusing me of lying. Commandant Paq pulls a baton from his belt and rams it into my stomach, causing me to double over, and as I do, the transport forces me to the ground and drags me a few feet, allowing the uneven ground to scrape my legs and tear at my pants, exposing bits of my skin to the sharp pebbles that slice it. Laughter emanates from the arbiters around me as they treat me as nothing more than a mere spectacle meant for their entertainment.

"I'll ask you one more time: where did you get this?"

My face remains stoic as I refuse to answer. I have no idea who left it there, and I have no desire to allow Commandant Paq any sort of victory over me.

He prepares to strike me again when someone steps forward and stops him.

"When you are done having your bit of fun, you might want to remember that she was to be returned unharmed."

Grelyn? Of course, she is here. She can, in the literal sense, see in the dark, so it makes sense for her to be here, helping Commandant Paq hunt for me, but it seems that he is not doing this of his own volition: someone gave him orders.

"Perhaps I should remind you who is in charge here," Commandant Paq approaches her, holding his baton to her neck, but she never flinches, while her eyes send daggers at him, wishing him harm, reminding me how I had once thought that she would have preferred to have been under his tutelage as they are a lot alike: it seems I was wrong. Though there is no love lost between us, I do admire Grelyn's fortitude and métier. I do not know what happened between them, but Grelyn's face exhibits nothing but malice toward him.

"Maybe I should remind you of the same," she says, her unnatural blue eyes boring into the commandant's as the laughter surrounding us dissipates when the other arbiters realize that a power struggle is on full display in front of them.

A drone hovers low, circling all of us and broadcasting everything it captures to whomever watches. Even the transport stops as all eyes remain on the power struggle before us.

Commandant Paq lowers his baton and places it back in its holder, while never taking his eyes off Grelyn as sunlight spills from the horizon and covers both of them in a burnt orange glow, making their dark skin tone appear more reddish than the approved color of Arel, while they continue to glare at one another, challenging the other.

"If you are that concerned, then you can babysit her," Commandant Paq says, stalking off. "Move out!"

The rope binding my wrists pulls taut once again as the transport continues, forcing me to follow and remain on my feet or be dragged behind; I prefer the former. The tires kick up dust in my face, and though my natural inclination is to cough so as not to inhale it, I refuse, allowing my throat to clench tight as I struggle to breathe, but I cannot show weakness here: I must not. Sometimes, I think I see movement in the trees surrounding us as we trek down the rocky road, with me stumbling on occasion when the driver of the transport chooses to hit the accelerator for a moment to ensure I remain awake, but despite my efforts to get a closer look, I am unable to make out anything other than wilderness. The quick flicker of movement behind brush could be an animal, but something tells me it's not.

Who did leave me the flask of water? Did the same individual know about the mine and the way out? Was it him who banged on the remains of the metal side of the ventilation shaft to lead me out of the darkness and back into the light?

I sneak a peek at Grelyn, but her gaze remains ahead, not daring to glance in my direction as her eyes focus on the farthest reaches of the road for any dangers that may present themselves. I study the others that walk beside me, trying to decide if it is worth daring an escape, but their guard is up, and I am certain that they expect me to make some attempt at freeing myself. To test my suspicions, I tug on the rope around my wrists, hoping to loosen it, but Grelyn rounds on me, stopping me.

"Do that again, and I will bind your feet," she growls at me.

"Why are you here, Grelyn?" I demand.

"I was ordered here."

I snort in disbelief. She may have been ordered here, but she might have volunteered as well, hoping to receive command of an outpost. It is said that any who can command the eastern sector will have their choice of assignments, but the same is true for any who can command an outpost. Outposts are separated from Arel, and though they receive the occasional supplies, they must rely on the leadership of their commandant for survival.

"This is not the way," I say.

"Silence."

"I challenged Molers, not all of Arel. What is all this? Who am I being brought to?"

"I said, quiet."

"Does Molers not have the courage to hunt me himself?"

"It's not what you think."

"Then what is going on here? This is not the Rite of Conquest, and you know it!"

"I told you once, that there is more happening here than you know."

"I should think, that of all people, you would want me to finish this. I remember what Molers almost did to Trevors."

Her cheeks tighten, telling me that I have struck a nerve. At the training facility, Trevors challenged Molers to a fight, and Molers almost disfigured him, which would have resulted in his expulsion from the corps: his death; and it wasn't the first time Molers almost murdered Trevors.

"Have you ever thought about leaving?" I say after a few moments of silence pass between us. I do not know why I asked her that question, but a part of me wonders why she and Trevors never tried to sneak out of the city. "You both are smart, strong—you could survive out here and build a life together, instead of hiding in secret."

"Shut up!" she hisses at me, placing the blade of her knife to my throat.

"Go ahead," I say to her, keeping my gaze locked on hers.

She lowers her dagger.

Onward we walk, with me towed by a transport as the ultimate humiliation, while a drone hovers nearby, capturing everything, and I find myself wondering who is watching, and why. As my mind races from one thought to the next (Chase and Shelia in a cold, dark cell; Gwen sick with worry about her brother; Commander Vye under constant surveillance because of me; and Renal's ability to instill fear in others due to his mysterious past), the sun passes overhead, brightening as it goes, and as its light touches upon the dust within the air, the sky turns more brown than blue. Wisps of pale gray clouds float above us, dulling the sun's intense rays for a moment, before allowing it to show itself in full force, while the transport continues to pump exhaust into my face, forcing me to endure its pollution, despite the natural inclination to cough, while different scenarios of a daring escape play through my mind: the next as dumb as the previous. There are too many arbiters, and what I need is a distraction.

One of the wheels of the transport bounces as it hits a pothole, causing the vehicle to jostle before it reaches even ground again. I look behind me and notice a few potholes—not as large as the one the transport has just hit—but perhaps there are more, and perhaps they are much larger. The driver steers the wheel to avoid another hole in the road and a plan takes shape in my mind. I veer to the side, away from Grelyn, before wandering back to the middle of the road, noticing how the head of the driver turns to watch me in the rearview mirror, but I also notice that the end of the rope tied to the transport has frayed from rubbing against the rough surface of the bumper. Perfect. Once again, I step sideways, going to my right, before zig-zagging back across the road and continue my side-to-side movements, hoping to keep the driver's attention focused on me, while the friction of the rope rubbing against uneven metal will weaken its hold. Grelyn's gaze settles on me as she wonders what I am doing, but before she can put it together, the front wheel of the transport plops in a hole the size of a deer, trapping the vehicle.

When Grelyn jerks her head in the direction of the transport as the others gather around the front wheel to assess the damage, I push her into the rear bumper and yank at the rope. It breaks free. With no time to untie my hands, I run, heading toward the tree line as Grelyn recovers from my attack. She charges after me. Alerted to my escape attempt, the others follow as I dive behind the trees and continue uphill. If I can reach the crest, perhaps I can escape. I charge up the hill, climbing as best I can, but its steep incline proves to be more cumbersome than I had first thought, causing me to sink to my knees, but I push myself onward, desperate to get away. An arbiter closes in on me, but a small rock hits him in the face, causing him to fall backward and roll down the hill. With no time to consider who threw it, I continue climbing up the hill as my legs burn from the effort before the rope around my wrists pulls tight, yanking me off my feet. Its other end has wrapped itself around a bush.

Desperate, I struggle with my bonds, trying to get my hands free of its constraints so that I can get away. Arbiters close in, but more rocks fly from behind me, catching them in the face, forcing some to seek cover, but not Grelyn. Her malicious eyes dig into mine as she focuses on me, angered that I have embarrassed her. While I struggle with the rope, she uses her hands and legs to climb upward, at a speed I never knew was possible, but before I can consider my options, a low growl emanates behind me. Not wanting to know what is there, but knowing I cannot avoid it, I turn my head, keeping my movements slow and calm, and see a wild dog, its ribs poking through its hide, looking at me as though I am its next meal.

It lunges for me. I stretch out the rope that is still tied around my wrists, and fall backward as its teeth sink into it while it bites and snarls in an effort to get to me as saliva drips from its blackened fangs and onto my shirt. I throw it off me, and it lands on its side before springing to its feet. An arbiter rushes for me, but the wild dog attacks him, gripping his arm with its jaws and yanks him down to the ground before going for his throat. Another dog jumps for me.

"They hunt in packs!" yells Commandant Paq as more wild dogs charge over the hill for us.

One seizes me around the shoulder and drags me away as I kick my feet and reach out for anything to hold onto, but my bound hands make it impossible. I grasp a rock and bash it into the head of the animal, pleased when it yelps in pain and lets me go. As I roll onto my stomach and look up, the dog and I eye each other for a moment and its growl warns me that I haven't a chance. No matter what move I make, it's faster. It leaps for me but falls to the ground as a single round enters its eye and its brain. Glancing up, I see a man dressed in black camouflage situated on the top of the hill with a rifle raised, but before I can ponder a guess as to who he is, he disappears; the only thing I know for certain is that he is no arbiter.

Gunfire reigns around me as my captors kill the pack of wild dogs that have found us, and within moments, they disperse. Glancing back down the hill, I spot Grelyn as she heads for me. I need to go. I hoist myself to my feet and charge up the hill with Grelyn right behind me, determined to not let me escape: I must be too valuable of a prize for whomever wants me. My pulse throbs in my neck as I charge up the hill, breathing in rapid succession to provide the necessary oxygen to my body as it exerts itself. I'm almost there. Just a few more steps. My foot steps on loose rock that breaks away beneath me, causing me to tumble to the ground. I sit up and see another arbiter coming for me with his weapon raised. Frantic, I claw my way upward, but Grelyn pounces upon me, dragging me backward and rolling me onto my back. For a split second, I am able to steal a glance between the arbiter preparing to fire at me and her before the bottom of her boot slams into my face, stunning me, forcing me to teeter upon unconsciousness as I am dragged down the hill and back to the transport, and before my world goes black, I hear Commandant Paq scolding Grelyn.

"Your incompetence allowed her to escape!" screams Commandant Paq.

Grelyn opens her mouth to retort but is cut off.

"You will carry her."

Rough hands scoop me up, and I grunt when her shoulder presses into my stomach, while the world around me phases in and out of focus before I pass out. My head bobs back and forth, bumping into the firm muscular back of Grelyn as she carries me over her shoulder, waiting for me to regain consciousness, while the evening sun causes the trees surrounding us to form elongated shadows on the dusty road before us. My head throbs from the motion of being carted like nothing more than a sack of potatoes, and as I start to become aware of the world around me, the driver of the transport revs the engine, jolting me awake, informing me that they freed the wheel while I was passed out.

"Good," Grelyn says, dropping me. "You're awake."

I crash onto the ground, and frown as now both my head and my bottom throb. Ignoring the discomfort, I force myself to my feet, while the other arbiters around me chortle, amused by my misfortune.

"How much further?" I ask.

"Until we get there," Grelyn snaps.

"What outpost are we going to? We're not headed to Commandant Paq's, yet he seems to be the one in charge here, unless he is nothing more than an errand boy, and you are little more than his obedient plebeian."

Grelyn's fists tighten, and I smile, knowing that I have touched a nerve.

"We're going to the same place where you spent time healing up after you suffered a broken leg."

The third outpost. I remember that place. The arbiters there did not act like sloven fools, nor were they ruled with an iron fist like in the outpost that Commandant Paq commanded, but were disciplined and treated in a fair manner.

"It will be nice to see Commandant Jensen again," I say.

"Commandant Jensen is no longer there. It seems that someone found evidence of her smuggling plebeians out of Arel."

What? Commandant Jensen was not the type to violate the law in such a fashion, and as I think back to my time there, and the fight Grelyn and I had, a dreadful suspicion creeps in on me.

"You," I hiss.

"I told you once, Noni, that there is much that happens outside of Arel, and you would have done well to have listened to me."

"You didn't act alone, and you would have expected to have been paid a high price for such an act." I glance at Commandant Paq as he berates another arbiter for getting mud on his boots. "What deal did you strike with the Devil for which you will never receive payment?"

Grelyn's scowl darkens, but I continue pushing.

"The outposts do offer a bit of freedom from the watchful eyes of Arel, the sort that would allow a forbidden relationship to flourish, but it seems that someone reneged on his part of the deal," I continue.

Whether Grelyn had struck a deal with Commandant Paq is unproven, but considering her animosity toward him, it is possible that he promised to help her and betrayed her. I can use that to my advantage.

"The wilderness is dangerous," I say, "and many never survive." I glance at Commandant Paq. "All I ask is that I be allowed to complete the rite and my silence shall remain. As an arbiter, I deserve that much."

Grelyn faces me, measuring me, trying to determine if I can be trusted.

"I have never told anyone your secrets," I say.

"We'll stop here for the night!" Commandant Paq shouts and everyone stops. "Grelyn, make yourself useful and start a fire."

Incensed, she stalks off, while another arbiter secures me to the trunk of a tree, forcing me to sit in a pile of half-dried excrement left by some animal, but I keep my mouth shut; provoking them is not prudent right now. Left alone, I scan the area, noting the cliffside and the tops of the trees that poke over its edge. Only 11 arbiters remain, not including Grelyn or Commandant Paq. I press my mind to formulate a plan, but no matter how I work it out, any attempt to flee will result in my death; so, I nestle into the trunk of the tree as the sun dips below the horizon, allowing the shadow of night to wash over us as it grows darker by the minute to where the only light left is the fire that Grelyn starts.

Laughter spills from those gathered by the fire as they chew on a few rations while pointing at me and telling jokes at my expense. I ignore them after taking note that only six sit around the campfire; there is no sign of Grelyn, Commandant Paq, or the other three. Tugging at the rope, I rub it against the base of the tree to see how well it might fray, but the fibers hold firm, refusing me the least bit of reprieve, while a drone hovers nearby, buzzing around my head and being more of an annoyance than a fly that refuses to go away. I swat at it, but it backs away, out of arm's reach, before circling around me again, making me wonder who watches the feed on the other end.

More roars of laughter escape those by the fire, making me cringe at all the noise they make; none of them established a sentry—a rookie mistake, but something I can exploit as long as they remain distracted by their own entertainment. The drone hovers near my head again, and the whining of its propellers make my ears cringe, angering me to the point where I snatch it out of the air and pin it between the trunk of the tree and a rock, making certain that its camera faces away from me. It vibrates as it tries to free itself, but to my satisfaction, it remains stuck. I wring my hands, stretching them apart every so often so as to try and work them free.

"What's that?" says one of the arbiters by the fire, drawing my attention.

"Stop your squawking!" says another.

"Something hit me," the first one continues, but the others laugh.

Curious, I watch as the dancing flames illuminate their dark faces while they chew on their rations, hoping to see what it is that made the one arbiter squeal, and as I turn back to the rope around my hands, something drops from the air at an arch and lands in the dirt next to another.

"There it is again," says the same arbiter that had spoken the first time. He scoops something off his shoulder and holds it out for all to see. "It's a date."

The others ignore him and his concerns, but as they do so, more dates fall from above, pelting them and the ground nearby, while something small and dark flies through the sky. More movement scurries through the still oval-shaped leaves of the trees, remaining hidden from prying eyes, until the time is right. A sense that someone watches us surrounds me, telling me that this is my chance to escape, and while the arbiters by the fire argue among themselves, I pull against the rope around my wrists, intent on breaking free; I only need a few more...

Loud squawks fill the night air as a hoard of bats swarm from above, circling the arbiters by the fire, blocking out the yellow-orange glow as they cling to them and bite at them in an attempt to get the sticky substance of the dates from their uniforms. As the rodent-sized animals swoop from above, the arbiters around the blaze jump to their feet, yelling and screaming in terror, while tiny fangs and claws dig into their skin, forcing them to ignore me. With one hard tug, the rope around my wrists snaps, freeing me, and I leap from the ground and charge into the dense trees, ignoring the overhanging fronds that slap me in the face in an attempt to slow me down.

"Shut up! All of you!" Commandant Paq appears from the shadows, furious at the level of noise on such a calm night, silencing the arbiters as the bats dissipate. "You all are acting like recruits! Where is your sentry?"

No one answers.

"I want a perimeter set up," Commandant Paq says, "and keep your eyes—she's escaped!"

Commandant Paq's words echoes throughout the wilderness, following me as I charge through the brush, dodging fallen branches and low hanging leaves in an attempt to get away. As shouts and yells follow me, I stop, reconsidering my options. They will expect me to run without thinking, and if I do, the noise generated will alert them to my location: I need to do the unexpected. Listening, I note the position of my pursuers as they crash through the dense trees, crushing leaves and dried sticks as they conduct a sweep, and if I know arbiters, they will do it according to a specific pattern.

Backtracking, I step into the footprints my boots have already made, being careful not to make noise and to keep my nerves at bay, while beams of light float across the area in an attempt to find me, until I am even with a tree. I judge the distance between me and it as I prepare to jump for its trunk. I have to get this right. I jump sideways and twist in the air so that I face the tree, gripping the knots on its trunk when I slam into it. Voices settle nearby. Hurrying, I climb upward, but my sweaty hands slip, causing me to slide down a few inches. Undeterred, I crawl up the trunk, until I reach the branches, and hoist myself onto one, steadying my breathing as I crouch, looking downward, shielded from view by the intertwined blotches of green, red, and brown as the edges of the leaves tickle my skin in an effort to convince me to react. I remain still, waiting, and watching.

An arbiter screeches several yards away, as though someone has attacked him, but whom? I force the question from my mind. Now isn't the time.

The steady crunching of dried brush alerts me to another's presence, and I watch the faint outline of a figure move beneath me with caution, as though he does not want to be heard, but I know he's there. Poised on my branch, I wait with the patience of a predator, salivating over the thought of a fresh kill as the arbiter moves until he is below me. I jump from my branch and land atop him, forcing him to the ground as his weapon skitters across the earth as he loses his grip. He kicks at me, catching me in the chest and forcing me to take a step back as the wind is knocked out of me, but I refuse to give in to the pain and pounce on him again, catching him around the knees and pull his feet out from under him. Stunned, he lies still for a moment, but his slowed reaction gives me the edge I need, and I jump on his chest and ram my fist into his throat, until I feel my knuckles crush his windpipe. He clutches at his throat, and as he suffocates, I reach for his weapon, seizing it, and beat him in the head with it, until blood pools on the ground.

Another arbiter approaches. I raise the semi-automatic rifle and prepare to fire, but nothing happens, and after checking it, I realize that this one also requires a biometric signature just like the ones from the first group of arbiters that ambushed me. I place the hand of the dead arbiter on it, and for a moment, my elation fills me when a faint green light appears, but the moment my handprint registers, a red light flashes and the weapon locks itself. Only the arbiter assigned to the weapon can use it; if any other person touches it, it freezes, becoming useless. This is how Arel has made certain I will have no advantages out here in the wild. The only way for me to use this weapon is for me to have the arbiter's hands in constant contact with it. Cursing my terrible luck, I dip behind some brush, listening to the purposeful steps of another arbiter as he hunts me, picturing in my mind his whereabouts as I plan my own trap. He's close. Remaining statuesque, I listen as the arbiter creeps closer to me while still clutching the rifle, careful to not make too much noise as he searches for his prey, but tonight, I am the predator.

Another yell for help, coming from behind me, startles the man—a moment passes where, once again, I wonder who has attacked whom—and he turns to face the noise, only to see me. I plow the rifle into the man's stomach before flipping it and ramming the butt of the gun into his face. He staggers back. I pull the barrel free of its hold, giving me two makeshift batons, and swing both at his shoulder. He blocks and slams the heel of his hand into my collar bone, forcing me to take a step back. Using his advantage, he raises his weapon and prepares to fire, but I charge him, bringing one makeshift club down from above and the other from below, catching the barrel of his rifle in between and twist, freeing his weapons from his hands. He kicks at me, but I raise my weapons and block, stepping back each time he attacks, never letting him near enough to touch me. He rushes me, but I dodge and jump at him, catching his head between my weapons and I twist them, breaking his neck. He crumples to the ground—bits of leaves fly away when he lands—with his vacant eyes staring upward at the canopy above us.

A twig snaps. I toss the lower part of the rifle away from me toward the arbiter that approaches. He turns when it thumps on the ground, and I jump between the narrow opening of two trees situated close together, catching him in the side and forcing him to tumble to the ground. Before he can react, I grab his left forearm and yank it at an odd angle while pressing against his shoulder, until I feel it pull free from its socket. He yowls in pain, but I plunge the barrel of the weapon I took apart into his throat, silencing him for good.

Another surprised yelp alerts me that I am not alone hunting these arbiters, but before I can react, a fist strikes me on the right side of my jaw, knocking me to the ground. Dazed, I look up to find Commandant Paq standing over me. He swings his right foot back, mustering all the momentum he can as he kicks me in the middle and lifts me a few inches off the ground. Gagging, bits of stomach acid free itself from the confines of my stomach and escape my mouth, dropping onto the ground beneath me, coating a leaf with browned and decayed edges.

"You little bitch!" he roars at me as I try to crawl away, but he stops me with a kick to my right side, causing me to squeal. "You thought you would be allowed to conduct the Rite of Conquest unhindered? Molers won the last one. You are just an ant, one I am about to crush."

"By cheating," I spit at him.

Commandant Paq kicks me again, sending me rolling across the ground. "I should have ended you that day of the hunt."

"How is your outpost?" I say between fits of coughing. I have no idea what became of Commandant Paq after Commander Vye and I left the outpost he was in charge of, but judging by his reaction to my question, the outcome must not have been ideal. I spot a fallen branch the diameter of my arm, and a plan forms in my mind. "What did the council say when they learned that an arbiter fresh from the training facility beat the Bell and overcame your challenge?"

My snide remarks anger him even more and he kicks at me in a fury, and I allow him to take his anger out on me, while inching my way closer to the branch with every swing of his foot. I reach for the branch. Commandant Paq screams in a rage as he prepares to kick me again, but I seize the branch and hold it between me and him, catching him in the shin. He lunges for me, but I dive between his legs and strike him in the other shin. Enraged, he pulls out his baton and swings it at me. I roll out of the way. He swings again, but I bring up the branch in front of me and our weapons clack as they meet. I twist the branch, tearing the baton away from his grasp, but he counterattacks by grabbing my shoulders and pushing me downward as he brings his knee up, ramming it between my breasts, before plunging the sole of his boot into my ribcage, forcing me away from him. I fall backward, crashing onto the ground with a grunt. Something plops on the ground beside me, just within reach: a hatchet.

Commandant Paq stomps toward me, ready to finish me off. I lie on the ground, waiting for the right moment to strike, letting him believe that I have given up. His boots draw closer as he rushes for me, reaching for his pistol. Just a few more steps. As he reaches me, but before his pistol is free, I snatch the hatchet by the handle and leap upward as I swing it at him, striking him in the jugular. Shocked, his eyes widen in disbelief as he attempts to plug the hole

I have left in his neck, while warm blood spurts from it and all over him, dripping from his elbow to his hip and down his leg to the soil beneath his feet. He drops to his knees, his face saying everything, asking how it could end like this for him before he falls face forward into the brush littering the ground.

I study the hatchet in my hand, noting its rudimentary craftsmanship, but though unrefined in construction, it is effective. An idea crosses my mind. Knowing that the drone is still where I left it, I bend down and hack at the back of Commandant Paq's neck until his head is freed from his body. I clean the hatchet by rubbing its blade across the earth before trekking back to the tree where I had been tied to, noting that no sounds reach my ears as silence falls upon the wilderness around me while I walk among the remains of those who had captured me: they are all dead, but not by my hand, and the kill is precise as though it came from someone who is well-trained, someone who once went to the training facility. I reach the tree and pull the drone that is still trapped between the trunk and a rock free, turning it so that it can see Commandant Paq's severed head.

"You've sent your goons to hunt me. Now do it yourself! Or are you not arbiter enough to complete my challenge?" I lean in closer, so that whomever watches can get a good look at me. "I'm coming for you."

I throw the drone onto the ground and pick up a rock to smash it, until it is nothing but wires and a broken outer shell before tossing Commandant Paq's head aside.

"You'll want this."

I whirl around, ready to meet my next threat, but stop when I see Grelyn holding the belt with the two knives that Renal had given me. Cautious, I take it from her and tie it around my waist before putting the hatchet in it as well. If she had wanted me dead, she had ample opportunity to kill me.

"You're right about one thing," Grelyn says to me, "this is not the arbiter way."

The low rumble of an engine approaches.

"You should go before they get here," says Grelyn.

"What about you?"

"Don't worry about me. Your legend will grow even more after tonight. Just do me one favor."

I give her a quizzical look, having never known Grelyn to offer me any sort of help or ask for it in return.

"When you find Molers, kill him."

I intend to.

Before I can respond, headlights appear through the trees and Grelyn slips away, disappearing into the darkness as though she was never here. Damn her and her ability to see in the dark. It makes her impossible to find.

"There she is!" shouts an arbiter on a transport with a machine gun attached to it.

Time to go.

Scanning the area around me, the edges of the transport's headlights caress the tops of trees yards away, illuminating them in a faint light. I must be near a cliff. I run for the edge of the cliff, jumping over a fallen log as bullets pelt the ground around me, splintering the trunks of trees and severing branches from their hold, but I refuse to slow down or look back. As I reach the ledge, the gunfire stops as someone pulls the trigger man from his seat, and I leap into the air, allowing momentum and gravity to dictate my fate.

Wood snaps and cracks as I slam into the first layer of branches, closing my eyes and holding one arm in front of my face to try and protect it from the splinters flying around me as I fall. Pain seizes my left side as I crash into another branch with a knob that digs into me worse than any knife might have, and as I continue to plummet to the earth below, my body turns, forcing the soft spot of my torso to take the next impact. With each branch I hit, the slower I fall, until I reach the bottom layer of the entwined branches and burst free of the confines of the trees and their thick canopy.

Instead of hitting solid ground, I plunge into water, and the current of the river carries me away, twisting and turning me until I am so disoriented that I have lost my sense of direction. Foaming water forces its way into my mouth, causing me to cough and spit while trying to breathe at the same time, making me choke even more as the rapids decide where I will go. I try to swim to the shore, but each stroke causes excruciating pain to surge up my left side from the bottom of my rib cage to my armpit, causing me to freeze, which results in my head dipping beneath the surface of the river. As I try to think of a plan, a thundering roar engulfs my ears, warning me of another danger: I am heading for a waterfall. Desperate, I look around as water splashes around me, obscuring my view of the shore and the trees near the bank, until I spot one growing out of the side of a cliff, the same cliff that borders the waterfall, and a vine hangs from it. This is my only chance. I think back to the sewage tunnel and how, as recruits, we would slide down the metal tube, allowing the water to carry us until we reached a drop-off, and our only salvation was a low hanging ladder, and missing it resulted in death. This is like that, but on a grander scale.

I use my arms to line myself up with the vine as the river pushes me toward the waterfall, and its roar intensifies until I hear nothing but the rush of falling water. As the water careens over the edge, it propels me into the air, and for a moment, I feel weightless, before gravity takes hold and I start to drop. I reach for the vine as it dangles in the air and wrap my fingers around it the moment I touch it, and it pulls tight as it tries to support my weight, stopping my fall. My relief is short-lived as the vine snaps and I plummet to the river below, disappearing into the vaporous clouds that form as the falling water crashes into the river. The current pulls me under, forcing me to hold onto what air is left in my lungs, before shooting me downriver and away from the falls. Seconds pass as I remain submerged, though they feel like hours, before I emerge from the water and my head tears through the thin veil of the surface, allowing me to take in a lungful of air. The further downriver I go, the slower the current becomes as the white rapids dissipate, and despite the weakness in my arms and legs, I force them to move me toward the riverbank where I crawl out, not caring that dry sand coats my uniform as I lay on my stomach, breathing deep as my wet hair flops around my head, covering my face.

A bird chirps nearby, convincing me to look up at the faint red glow, with a tinge of orange, on the horizon, and I gasp in disbelief. Before me lies the ruined wall of a massive city, but instead of buildings that shine and reflect the coming sunrise, the glass is broken or dulled by decades of grime; but what shocks me is not the ruined nature of the city itself, but the insignia on the crumbling archway hanging over a road that used to lead one through a grand entranceway. I have found Arel's archenemy. I have found Kition.

Chapter 11

Kition

As the sun's light intensifies, sweeping over the earth and shrouding it with a burnt orange glow that morphs into a lighter shade the higher above the horizon it gets, I stare at the archway and the titanium plates peeling away from the supports, dulled by years of dust that has formed its own outer layer, disbelieving where I am. I cannot stay here. I force my legs to stand up, and I wobble through the archway as they struggle to support me, looking up at the underside and the words printed there, though some letters are missing.

Hope Is My Guide; Liberty My Dream.

My eyes remain focused on the words as I continue down the main road and its crumbled pavement, almost tripping over the tall tufts of grass that grow through the cracks, breaking what once was one long road into misshapen sections of asphalt. A titanium plate drops from the archway, crashing on the ground as I walk, breaking the eerie silence surrounding me, warning me of what I will find, but I ignore it and continue my trek through Kition. This must be what Grelyn warned me about at the last outpost. She must have found this place during one of her patrols and learned one of Arel's darkest secrets: Kition, our most hated enemy, no longer exists, and from the looks of it, it seems that they have not been around for several decades or more. As I pass an obelisk-shaped building that stretches up forty stories, with its top forming a spire that goes even higher, I remember the barbarians that always attack the wall and how their weapons bear the insignia of Kition, but if this is what is left of Kition, where are they getting the weapons? Unless…

I refuse to consider it, even though it must be true, but I cannot fathom that the very people charged with protecting Arel would supply its own enemies with weapons and let them attack us. As my mind wrestles with what it does not want to believe, I place one foot in front of the other, continuing through the ruins, stumbling as my foot settles upon uneven ground, while I make my way toward what appears to be a fallen railcar track with holly bushes growing through its bars as their branches wrap around the metal, claiming it as their own, blocking my path. Undeterred, I push the branches of the bushes out of my way, ignoring the tiny thorns that press into my skin, and force my way through them, disregarding the snags on my clothing as I reemerge on the other side, only to stop the moment I do.

A hole within the city balloons before me as ash and dust are all that remains of the skyscraper that used to be here, but it's not the vaporized building that horrifies me: it's the skulls of what used to be people. I take a step back, but jump when my foot crushes a femur bone, and the more I try to not trample the remains surrounding me, the more I lose my balance, until I crash onto the ground and stare into the empty eye sockets of what used to be a person. To my right are two more skeletal remains: one large, one small, with the larger one holding onto the smaller one as though it was a mother trying in vain to comfort her child, knowing that the inevitable had come for them both, and for a moment, I imagine the fear she must have felt as she tried to put on the façade of bravery for her child. Unable to help myself, I reach out to touch the remains, not wanting to believe my own eyes—afraid to believe them—and as the tip of my index finger touches one of the arms, they both disintegrate, turning into dust, only to be blown away by the breeze as nature does its best to sweep away this tragedy; but it is already ingrained within my mind, and my memory. Distraught, I scramble to my feet and run, stomping on any bones that get in my way as I push past ivy snaking its way up the rusted poles of street lights and stretching across to form its own barrier, not caring about the leaves that stick in my hair. I cannot stop. I have to get away from this mass grave. My feet fly over the skeletons littering the ground, slipping on them, threatening to give way underneath me, until…

A small bit of light catches my attention, and I stop. Mesmerized, I approach a door that still has its glass, while the one next to it possesses nothing, and wipe the grime from it, brushing the gritty substance from my hands as I stare at my reflection—my unrecognizable face with its bruises and cuts and the dark circles under my eyes, reminding me of the forlorn faces from the mines—and the remains of a city behind me with the tops of its buildings caved in, eroded from neglect and decay, while the residents remain in the open, denied the decency of a proper burial. The more I study my reflection, the more I realize that I have been lied to—all of Arel has been lied to—by the very people who swore an oath to protect and defend us. We have been betrayed. My whole life is a lie.

As the words repeat over and over in my mind, my stunned silence steeps until it boils, transforming into a rage that has been imprisoned for far too long, and the more it brews, the more it yearns to break free of its chains—the very chains I have been trapped in my entire life, even if I never knew it—until it controls my actions, compelling me to lift my right foot and kick the glass out of the window, shattering it and allowing it to pool around me as the shards tinkle on the broken pavement, coating the tops of my boots, turning the tarnished black exterior into glittering dust.

I move on. With each step, my rage grows. With each step, my heart aches for a people I never knew. Each skeleton turns into the face of someone from Arel, whether it is someone I was forced to execute for the crime of wanting to live his own life, the woman who died in my arms in the minefield, the infant I murdered, or the only ones I care about: Shelia, Chase, Gwen, and even Luther, Renal, and Commander Vye. Each skull reminds me of them, and the more I trample on what is left of a long-forgotten civilization, whose memory only lives on with the tainted tales of Arel, the more I imagine them lying here. A tremendous crash sounds behind me, sending echoes that grow in intensity before fading away as a support beam falls, causing the structure it held to crumble away and smash into the ground, sending up plumes of dust that billow in the wind, forming swirls of white particles that thin out the higher into the sky they go, until nothing remains. Bits of dust sweep across the expanse before me, carried by the wind, and stick in the back of my throat when I inhale, reminding me of my thirst and how I have not had any water for hours.

As though something in the universe heard my silent plea for a drink, a single drop of water falls from an exposed pipe and into an open well—its cover had gone missing long ago—and splashes in the liquid within, sending a welcome sound to my ears. I head for it, desperate to quench my thirst, knowing I will die without water and stop the moment I reach the well. Bending over its edge, I peer into the murky darkness below and the film on top of what I had hoped would be my salvation, but the more I study it, the more I question whether I should touch it. My need for water wins the debate, and I reach down, dipping my cupped hand into the questionable liquid and past the bits of leaves and dust particles that float on the surface before pulling it out and bringing it to my mouth. I spit it out. The water is foul, made so by the destruction surrounding it. Frustrated, I stand back up and search my surroundings, hoping to see some source of fresh water, but conclude that I need to go back to the river.

I turn around, dreading the trek back to the raging river that almost drowned me, but I have little choice if I want something fresh to drink that won't poison me. Taking ginger steps so as not to disturb the remains surrounding me, I head back to the overgrowth of thorn bushes and to the road that led me here, but before I get too far, movement catches my attention, and I stop, jerking me head upward to get a better glance at what may be danger. I see it again, a wisp of movement as a person disappears. Knowing that I cannot remain here, exposed to whomever is also in this cursed place, I sprint to an outdoor staircase, which looks more like a fire escape than a means of getting to the upper floors, but its lower half has broken off and rests on the ground as nothing more than a crumpled heap of molten metal, damaged from a force more powerful that anything I am aware of. I try jumping for it, but it is too high. Desperate to get to the top, I spin around on my feet, hoping to find anything that I can use to climb up with when I spot a downspout three feet from the stairs. It will have to do.

I jump for it, gripping it as tight as I can as I straddle it and press my feet against the smooth, glass-like exterior of the four-story building and inch my way upward. Images appear on the side of the wall—there must be a residual power source somewhere—advertising a product I had never heard of before, as though it mocks my efforts to climb upward while making me appear to be no more than an ant, but they are broken and garbled, as though the power fueling it decreases at an exponential rate, until it goes black, never to be seen again. My foot slips on the smooth surface, causing me to fall a few feet as I cling to the downspout before stopping, and my feet dangle in the air, beating against the exterior of the structure, leaving marks within the layers of dust that cakes it. Relieved, I resume climbing the downspout a second time, hoisting myself up as

I inch my way upward, not bothering to look down the higher I go, keeping my focus on the lower step of the staircase. Almost there. My exhausted arms scream at me to stop, but I refuse their pleas, not wanting to give up and admit defeat: defeat is weakness. The lower step is almost within reach. While hanging onto the downspout with my left hand, I reach for the staircase with my right, frustrated when the tips of my fingers brush the concrete step.

Climbing higher, I press the soles of my boots against the wall, bending my knees as much as I can before leaping from the downspout and to the staircase. My upper body slams into the step, causing me to yelp from the pain as my legs dangle in the air. Using what strength I have, I haul myself onto the lower step, but it gives way under my weight as the rusted metal bolts break apart, and I drop to the ground below. Desperate, I throw my hand out, reaching for anything I can grab hold of, and grasp the railing as the step falls to the ground, leaving me hanging, swinging in the wind as I second guess my actions, but I cannot turn back now. I grab the rail with my other hand and yank myself upward, until I can crawl onto one of the steps, breathing a sigh of relief when I do as I sit upon it, resting for a moment. With no other choice, I stand up on the stairs, using the rails to keep my balance as they sway, telling me that whatever connects them to the side of the building has weakened and could give way, and hurry up them, until I reach the top and step over a ledge onto the roof.

I spot the figure I had seen earlier. It runs. I chase after it. The person bolts across the roof, moving faster than I believed he could, and jumps across an opening to the roof of a nearby building. I do the same, keeping pace with the stranger, hoping to catch him and to get some answers about this place. He reaches the end of the roof, jumping to another that looks more like a triangle, and scrambles to its peak before running across it on the narrow platform that is there. Refusing to stop, I leap across to the roof, but misjudge the distance and slam into its edge, but before I can crash to the ground below, I grab a spoke sticking out of its edge and haul myself onto it. I allow myself a few moments of relief before crawling up the steep side of the roof, continuing my pursuit. My sweaty hands slip on the smooth exterior, threatening to force me to tumble to the street beneath me and be skewered on the sharp tip of a lamppost as it leans to the side. Pressing my palms and feet into the roof, I crawl up it and to the platform that goes across its upper peak. The lone figure looks back at me. Frightened, he bolts and runs to the other side, but his foot slips and he tumbles over the side of the roof, but I dive for him, refusing to allow my only chance to learn some answers slip away, and grab his hand before he falls too far, while seizing an iron rod poking out of the roof to keep from falling myself.

"Let me go, you Arelian filth!"

He's not a man at all, but a woman. Surprised by this, I relax my grip and almost drop her, but my curiosity convinces me to keep my hold on her.

"Let me help you," I say.

"Why?" she spits. "So you can do to me what your kind did to this place?"

"What?"

I don't understand. Kition was always the aggressor, or so I have been told, but maybe that was also a lie.

"Let me help you," I say.

"I'll not be your prisoner! That is what your people do. Come in the middle of the night and arm any willing to carry out your cause, before raiding the settlements around here for whatever you deem valuable."

"I'm not like them," I plead with her.

The woman scoffs at me. "You Arelians murdered my brother and my father in front of me over twenty years ago, before murdering my husband and my child years later. You're all the same!"

She releases her grip on my wrist so that gravity pulls her from my grasp.

"Don't!"

It's too late. Her hand pops free of mine and she plummets to the ground below, bouncing on the roof before she crashes on the broken pavement, becoming nothing more than a faint memory that will soon be erased.

The metal rod breaks away, causing me to fall, and I tumble down the steep, metallic side of the roof, tucking my head and arms in, turning myself into a ball as I do in an effort to protect myself. When I reach the ledge, I thrust my hands out and grab hold of it, but it only slows me for a moment as the momentum of my fall breaks my grasp, and I continue to the ground below. Something pliable wraps around my body as I fall, slowing my descent, and I realize that I have landed in an awning, but the decayed material gives way, forcing me to continue downward. For a brief moment, I believe this is the end, but fate has something else in store. My body slams into a grate—made brittle from rot and decay—that breaks apart from the impact, allowing me to disappear into darkness, until I crash into water. Stunned, I do not move at first, until the desire to breathe forces me to, and I kick my way to the surface, breaking free, gulping for air, wondering how I am alive, and where I am.

Darkness surrounds me, mixed with the tender sounds of dripping water echoing off the steel walls surrounding me as droplets fall from above and plop into the filmy liquid encasing me, beckoning me to surrender to its will. For a brief moment, I consider it, tired as I am from the constant beratement of those around me, the constant tests and questioning of my loyalty, and being forced to witness the death and destruction of so many innocents, but before I delve too deep into the pit of self-induced despair, I think of Sheila and Chase sitting in a cold cell, all alone, and frightened; I think of Gwen sick with worry about her brother and wondering if she will be alone for the rest of her days. Their faces drive me; their forced suffering compels me to remain afloat and to search for a way out of this place. Defeat is weakness, weakness is failure, and failure is death, but not for me—for them.

Treading water, I look around, hoping to find any sign of a way out, but the pitch blackness makes it difficult as the only light I have spills through the hole I created when I crashed down here. With no better ideas, I swim until I find a barrier, and once I do, I place my hand on its cool surface, ignoring the slime that coats my palm as it peels away and sticks to me, forming a line between my hand and the wall itself. As I follow the wall surrounding me, hoping to discover a way out, I picture in my mind what it looks like, envisioning a dome-like structure made of heavy steel, and sealed to contain the water within, believing that I must have fallen into an underground aqueduct. Over time, the water has become stagnant and turned rancid, making me want to retch from the acrid fumes this place releases. Something slithers past me, causing me to jump and splash water, catching myself in the face and getting some in my mouth. I spit it out, but the foul taste remains. As the snake moves into the beam of sunlight, I notice its flat and slender head and realize that it is harmless, not that I want to stay here much longer with it as my only companion.

Wasting no time, I bob in the water as I circle the perimeter of my surroundings, not liking the slime that coats my skin and clings to me worse than static electricity to hair, until I find something that does not match the rest of the area. Instead of hitting a barrier, like my foot had for the last several minutes, it hits nothing. Taking a deep breath, I plunge beneath the surface and find a doorway, leading to a tunnel. This must be the way out, or at the very least, my only hope of getting out of here. I pop my head through the surface again, preparing myself for what I must do next: swim through the tunnel. Memories of the time Chase and I were trapped in a tunnel and almost drowned fill my mind, causing my heart to race from the anticipation of what will happen if I fail, but the reality of my situation forces me to push aside my fears and do what I must.

I suck in a lungful of air, dive beneath the surface and swim for the tunnel, pushing my way past a fallen pipe as big around as a 200-year old tree, until I reach a door. It's sealed shut, but I need to open it. Desperate, I feel every inch of the door with my hands as the darkness encloses around me, taunting me, and making me feel more isolated, before I touch it: the wheel that controls the opening mechanism for the door. I tug on it. Nothing. Cursing my bad luck—my lungs scream at me to go back, to allow them to be free again—I pull on the wheel as hard as I can, but it refuses to budge. Bubbles escape from my lips as my lungs refuse to hold onto the air contained within them any longer, and my head hurts and spins from the need for oxygen. I swim out of the tunnel and hurry to the surface, expelling the air within my lungs the moment my head pops free from the filmy water. Gasping, I let out a frustrated scream, angered that I cannot catch a break. At every turn, I face an obstruction, and I have grown tired of it.

The faces of Chase, Sheila, and Gwen float through my mind, reminding me of what I must do and of whom I am doing this for. I will not stay here. I will not die here. Gulping more air, I plunge below the water and kick my feet, propelling myself through the murky substance and into the tunnel, passing over the fallen pipe, until I reach the door, where I grab hold of it and yank. It still refuses to budge, but I refuse to quit. I pull on it again, and again, refusing to be beaten, refusing to be overcome, and in one last desperate attempt to move the wheel, I plant my feet on the door, bracing myself, before tugging so hard that I fear I will rip my own arms off.

It moves. Not by much. Perhaps it only budged a half an inch, but it's something: it is hope. Once again, my lungs demand that I free them of the air they hold, and I jettison myself back through the tunnel and to the surface, where I breathe as deep as I can before delving beneath the water a third time. I reach the door and pull on the wheel until my lungs demand release and go back to the surface, repeating the process over and over again (swimming through the tunnel, pulling on the wheel, and swimming back to the surface), and each time, the wheel turns a little bit more. My exhausted muscles plead with me to rest, but resting means drowning, so I force them to obey my will, to carry me through the water and pull on the door. I do not know how much time passes, but a quick glance at the sunlight spilling into this metallic cavern tells me that an hour or more must have gone by as it has shifted position.

Heavy breaths escape my mouth when I surface the last time, but I am close; I know it. Sucking in another lungful of air, I dive once again and swim through the tunnel, past the pipe, until I reach the door, wrapping my fingers around the wheel and pulling at it with all my might, screaming in frustration as it turns at such a slow pace, that the unwelcomed thought of being trapped in this place enters my mind, until…

The latch breaks free and the door opens.

The pressure of the water forces the door to burst free of its hold and it flies away from me, allowing the water contained behind it to pour forth, and it does, taking me with it. My body is thrown through the opening and into another tunnel as the force of the water takes me with it, and I twist and turn so many times that I have no clue which way is up or down, or where I am as disorientation takes hold of me, while a great pressure rams into me and forces me to go down its predetermined path. My ears ache from the roar of the water rushing past me, causing my head to pound as the pressure builds to a point where no amount of relief will save me.

I need to breathe. Pain grips my left shoulder as my body slams into the side of the metallic tube, and I bounce off it only to crash into the other side as the water carries me, whipping me around as though I am little more than a rag doll meant to be abused. When I believe this nightmare will never end, I shoot out of a massive pipe and into the open air and sunlight before plunging downward with the waterfall. The rigid surface of the water below feels more like a wall of brick when I break through it and continue downward, far beneath the surface, before floating back to the top, and when my head bursts through the surface of the brown water, I gasp for air, choking as bits of water goes down my throat. I look around, relieved to be outside in the sunlight again and realize that the underground aqueduct system gave way to a canal that worms its way through the center of Kition. Tired, I allow the current to carry me until I reach a ledge. I grab onto it and heave myself out of the water, lying flat on my back, staring up at the sky and the thin film of clouds above me, enjoying the sensation of air filling my lungs, only to leave it moments later so as to start the process again, but my moment of serenity is short-lived, killed by the familiar whine of another drone that has found me as it mingles with a menacing growl.

Turning my head to the side, I spot the bared teeth of a wild dog inches from my face as yellow saliva drips from is fangs, pooling on the dust coated asphalt as it stares at me with a hungry look in its eyes. I turn over onto my stomach, placing my hand into the silt with slow precision, doing my best to not goad it into an attack as the wind swirls around me, transforming from a small wisp of air into a constant force as though it is trying to warn me of impending doom, but I ignore its pleas, keeping my attention focused on the animal before me. Its low growls vibrate in my ears as it watches me, gauging my movements and deciding whether I am prey or predator, or worth the trouble at all. The incessant whining of the drone unravels what patience I have left, but I refuse to give in to its distraction as I keep my eyes on the dog while it continues to bristle and growl at me, waiting for me to make the first move. I force myself into a crouched position, ready to spring into action as I reach back to the hatchet within my belt, freeing it from its hold, while never taking my gaze off the wild dog. I cannot outrun it, but I can fight. Death will take one of us today, and it will not be me.

The annoying drone brushes too close to the wild dog's ear, causing it to jerk away before leaping for me. I dive to the side, somersaulting on the hard surface of the canal bank as I try to put some space between me and the animal, but it is quick, and spins around to face me, and before I can react, it is on me, snapping its jaws and barking loud enough to wake the ghosts that reside here.

I flop on my back—my hatchet flies from my grasp—placing my left arm between me and the dog in an effort to protect myself. Its sharp teeth sink into my flesh, and I cry out from the sudden sharp and burning pain that courses through it as blood drips from it and onto my clothing. It releases me, but only for a second before going for my throat. Once again, I thrust my arm out, holding it off as its fangs draw too close to my face, and its hot breath leaves a film of odorous vapor on my chin, making me want to gag. I reach for the hatchet. It's too far. The drone circles around us, capturing every moment and broadcasting it back to whomever watches on the other end. Are they taking bets? Are they concerned for me or hoping for my demise? Is this nothing more than mindless entertainment for them as they pretend that it is a training video that will be shown to future recruits? Or is it a way for them to measure my resolve and my skills?

I refocus on my predicament as the dog presses into me, desperate to kill its prey, while I try in vain to reach my weapon. I go for the knife in my belt, but as I move, the dog jumps at me again, forcing me to hold it off with both hands. I punch it in the snout and it yelps, jumping back, while the drone hovers close by, irking me to no end. I snatch the drone out of the air as the dog leaps for me with its jaws open and ram the softball-sized sphere into its mouth, stopping it. It jerks back, whipping its head side to side as I spring to my feet and dive for the hatchet, snatching it as the dog charges me again. I roll onto my back, flinging the hatchet at it, and strike the dog in its face. It jumps back, but I refuse to let it go, and attack again and again, hacking away at the animal's neck and face until it drops to the ground and lays unmoving in a pool of its own blood. I slump on the ground, pressing my knees into the silt that moves around me in the wind, forming tiny waves, while holding my bloodied hatchet before me, staring at the poor animal and remembering how I had shown mercy to the puma, but none to this dog. It may have been about to kill me, but it should not have ended like this: it did not need to end like this. The more I dwell on it, the more enraged I become. I throw my head back and let out an enraged howl at the darkening sky above me as thick, charcoal gray clouds form overhead, warning me of even more danger, but once again, the ever-present drone, now scuffed from teeth marks, hovers around me, taunting me. I whip my hatchet through the air and knock it to the ground, pleased when sparks escape from it before its light goes out.

Before I have a chance to relish in my small victory, more growls reverberate from behind me, forcing me to turn around and come face to face with four more wild dogs, each one looking at me with a ravenous hunger in their eyes. I rise to my feet, slow and steady, while eyeing each of them as they pace before me, snarling and snapping their jaws at me as I reach for one of the knives in my belt, holding it and the hatchet in front of me, ready to fend off my new quarry as they size me up. Seconds pass as we eye one another, waiting for one of us to make the first move, but before any can, lightning flashes above us, followed by a crack of thunder so loud, that it drowns all else. One of the dogs sniffs the air before running off with a worried whine, followed by the others, leaving me alone on the bank of the canal next to the corpse of the dog I had killed moments before.

The feeling of danger wafts over me as I glance up at the black sky above me—it's not even noon—and turn in a circle, watching as flash after flash of lightning streaks overhead, lighting up the ruined city surrounding me, making the shadows of the crumbling buildings around me appear more wraithlike as thunder snaps around me, causing my chest to vibrate. I put my weapons away and search for a place of safety, finding nothing as I stand exposed on the edge of the canal. The hairs on my arms stand up as a charge of electricity fills the area around me, warning me to move, and I jump away as lightning strikes the remains of a tower 50 yards away, sending a shower of sparks and metal shards my way. I need to get out of here.

I run, not caring what direction I go in, as the wind rises up around me, whipping around me, threatening to carry me away as its wrath beats down upon me. The sound of glass attacking the ground hits my ears as the rain starts, beating the roads, buildings, and me with its fury as the droplets pelt my skin, sending the sensation of a thousand stings coursing through me, and the more drenched I become, the more frigid my skin becomes, causing the rain to morph into tiny needles digging into me, until numbness takes over. A blast of wind slams into me, knocking me off balance and causing me to stumble as I run in a vain attempt to escape this onslaught of nature herself, but she isn't done with me: she is just getting started.

I continue my charge through Kition, jumping over fallen debris as the wind swirls the rain around me, illuminated by the constant lightning strikes that flash with such severity that it causes me to have motion sickness, but I cannot stop. I need shelter. Lightning. Thunder. Rain. All three attack me, treating me as nothing more than a tiny ant in their world, as a pest that must be eradicated. My feet pound the uneven ground, slipping in the water that rises around my ankles, threatening to carry me away, but I refuse to stop.

I dive through an opening where a window had once been, but find no relief from the rage around me as I find myself in a roofless room with a wall missing, allowing the rain to continue to pelt me. As the thunder continues its incessant booming, I hunker in a corner with my hands covering my ears in a futile attempt to protect them from the deafening noise as flash after flash of lightning light up the area around me, making it look as though it's daylight, unable to stop a scream from escaping my lips. Bits of the dilapidated wall fly away, a few at first, before big chunks of it lift away, carried away by the forceful winds whipping around me, almost knocking me over, despite my crouched position, and before I know it, the wall is gone before…

Silence.

The wind stops.

The rain stops.

The howling stops.

Confused, I look up at the sky above me and the swirling clouds as they grow bigger from their constant movement, getting ready to release their wrath on any unfortunate enough to be nearby: me. Unease fills me as I watch the mesmerizing scene before me, hypnotized by the seeming intelligence of the clouds above me as they prepare to finish what they have started, unable to move as I continue to watch something I have never seen before. Never before have I appreciated the beauty of anything; such admiration is forbidden in Arel, and most of all among the arbiters, but if this is to be my final moment, I want to admire something about this world, even if it is devastating.

The rain starts again. Soft at first, and from a distance, but it grows louder as it rushes for me, appearing to be a moving wall that closes in each second until it reaches me. Pain grips the top of my shoulder, causing me to flinch as I realize that the rain is not rain, but hail the size of pebbles before growing to the size of stones, and before I can register the danger I am in, the wind whisks around me, picking up any debris it can and circles me, tearing apart the final bit of the crumbling building I am in, telling me that the worse is yet to come, while a whirring roar, the likes of which I have never heard before, pounds my ears, making me think that my eardrums will burst from the intensity of the chaos.

I bolt from my position as a transport crashes into the ground where I once was, running through the chaotic atmosphere, covering my head in a futile attempt to protect myself from the downpour of stones made from ice, doing my best to ignore the burning pain each time one strikes me. Without warning, a force of wind slams into my side, propelling me into the air and forcing me to fly a few feet before crashing into the dirt, skidding on the ground as my shoulder takes the brunt of the impact and shards of glass and metallic slivers dig themselves into my exposed skin, causing blood to pour down my arm only to be whisked away by the storm as the hail morphs into rain once more.

Looking up, I see a swirling, black funnel made from dirt, bits of the buildings that once made up the city of Kition, and rain, making its way through the metropolis, searching for me. I run. My mind races in a desperate attempt to discern what to do, but deep down, I know that there is no escape from this as it heads toward me, taking out power lines, glass towers, and railways, devouring them all in a vain attempt to quench its incessant hunger. Unable to see where I am going—the rain is so thick that I cannot see my hand in front of my face—I charge through the remains of Kition, tripping over cracks in the road and entire trees that have been ripped from the ground and placed in front of me, as though the storm mocks my efforts to escape it. A lamp pole dives for me—a missile hurtling toward its target—and I dive to the ground in time to avoid its lethal blow, rolling through the mud as the momentum of my movement mixes with the wind, propelling me onward in an attempt to discombobulate me, but I refuse to be beaten, to give in.

Jumping to my feet, I charge through the chaos, hoping to find a place of relative safety to wait out the storm, but everywhere I turn, the storm cuts me off, mocking my efforts, taunting me in my fruitless attempt to survive, but each time I think of quitting, or giving up, I think of Sheila and Chase sitting in the detention facility and its macabre environment. I fall to the ground, plunging face first into the pooling brown water around me and the slime mixed in with it as my foot steps into a pothole, and it grabs onto it, seizing it, refusing to allow me to flee, and agony grips my ankle as I twist it, spraining it. Grimacing from the pain, I roll onto my back in time to watch as the decayed railway above me frees itself from its confines and charges straight for me. I roll out of the way, covering myself, before it crashes into the ground, sending bits of metal everywhere, splashing into the water surrounding me, showering me with its rage.

I push myself to my feet as the swirling mass of earth mixed with wind heads for me, destroying everything in its path in an attempt to get to me, but stop as an invisible wall, formed by the zephyr, impedes my progress, refusing to allow me passage, holding me prisoner and forcing me into helplessness as I watch the funnel come for me. Determined to not have it end like this, I push my way forward, leaning into the wind as it attempts to stop me, inching my way through the maelstrom. A dark shape lies ahead, or so it seems, and on the off-chance that it may be a place of safety, I head for it. Leaves mixed with rain pummel me, slicing my exposed skin with their razor edges, transformed into misshapen knives that do the bidding of nature, but I ignore the stinging torment, refusing to give up. Chase never gave up on me. Sheila risked her life for me on countless occasions. I owe them my resolve. I must overcome my current predicament. The funnel draws nearer as I walk perpendicular to it, heading for the darkened rectangle before me that takes on the appearance of a door the closer I get to it.

Rain pelts me, stinging my eyes as I continue to the door—it swings in the wind as the storm tries to tear it from its hinges, but it holds firm—eyeing the columns in front of it and hoping that I will reach it in time. The rage of the funnel pulls at me, demanding that I allow it to take me away and drop me someplace far from here, but I refuse, and as I feel my feet lift into the air, I leap for one of the columns, clinging to it, glad that its once smooth exterior has been roughened by time, giving my slippery palms something to hang onto. Terrified screams escape my lips—a part of me admonishes myself for giving in to this fear—fear is weakness—but I push it aside as the funnel closes in on its chosen victim—as a suctioning force pulls my legs into the air, desperate to get me to release my hold on the column, but I dig my fingers into it, not caring if they bleed or if my nails are ripped out.

I reach for the door handle, but am too far. Cursing, I stretch my arm out, desperate to grab hold of the door as the fingers on my other hand slip, threatening to lose their hold on the column. I readjust my grip and reach for the door again, while rain stabs my face, and the wind howls around me, ridiculing at me with each flash of lightening, making the thunder sound more like roaring laughter at my pathetic effort to survive. Almost there. My grip on the column weakens and nature's invisible hands seize my body, but before they can rip me away, a hand juts out of the darkened doorway, seizing my wrist, and I cling to it as it pulls me inside and the door slams shut behind us, thrusting us into screeching silence.

Chapter 12

Perce

My head spins for a moment as I grapple with what has happened, but I haven't time to ponder it as a masculine voice orders me to move.

"This way," it says.

As my eyes adjust to the darkness, I realize that I am in a stairwell with steps going upward and downward, which is where the voice comes from.

"Now!"

I push myself to my feet, clinging to the broken rail of the stairs, hoping that it will support me as my rubbery legs carry me downward, descending into the never-ending darkness and the mysteries concealed there. Whenever I falter or slow down, the same voice urges me to keep going, and I do, knowing that I have no other option. Minutes pass as we continue downward, until we reach the last step and enter some sort of chamber.

"We should be safe here," says the voice, and he throws things into a pile, and despite my attempt to see what it is, all I make out are outlines in the inky darkness, but it sounds as though furniture being tossed about.

A flame erupts, forming a pinpoint of light that hurts my eyes for a moment as it grows stronger, before starting a fire that engulfs the pile of debris that the stranger has created, allowing me to see that it was chairs and broken bits of wood.

"Here"—the stranger guides me to the flames, forcing me to sit next to them—"warm yourself before you catch cold."

As the fire illuminates his face, my brows scrunch together from recognition: I have seen him before—he was the one who helped Chase and me when we were lost in the wilderness.

"I know you," I whisper.

He sits opposite me. "I didn't think you would."

"What are you doing here?" I demand, my guard up.

"Most people thank the person who saves their life."

"You didn't answer my question."

He puts down his rifle and quiver of arrows. "I was hunting when I saw an Arelian aircraft fly overhead. Fearing for my people, I followed it and realized that something was different when I saw it dump you in the wilds."

"You're the one who's been following me," I say, putting it together.

He nods.

"Why? Why didn't you show yourself to me earlier?"

"You did put a knife to my throat the first time we met."

"I also took it away," I quip, as the warmth of the fire drives away the cold that has enveloped my skin.

He chuckles before tossing me a pouch. "Are you hungry?"

I open the pouch, finding dried dates, figs, and nuts in it, and shove a handful into my mouth as my stomach reminds me that it has been quite a while since I fed it last. "Why were you following me?" I ask.

"I have heard rumors that Arel likes to dump their people in the wilderness as some sort of test of their ability to survive."

"It's the Rite of Conquest," I say. "An arbiter can challenge another to the Rite of Conquest, in which the two are taken to unknown locations and expected to survive the elements, as well as hunt the other, after which, they fight to the death."

"What is the reward?"

"Freedom."

"But not for you," he says, noting the solemn note in my voice. "You're doing this for someone else."

I remain silent, but my silence confirms his suspicions.

"It seems that you are the one being hunted rather than doing the hunting."

I remain silent as the fire reflects off his brown eyes and makes the coarse hair on his brown fingers appear more like dark creatures crawling up them. Yes, I am being hunted, and this entire experience has not gone the way I thought it would; it seems that changes have been made to the Rite of Conquest, but what and why, I do not know.

I notice the sniper's rifle sitting next to him. "You know how to use that?"

He grins at my question. "My father taught me."

Something crashes above us, startling me, and I look up, afraid of what I might find, but my companion remains still, and for the first time, I notice the stash of firewood, canisters that must contain water or food, and something tucked away in a corner that looks like a sleeping pallet.

"We're safe here," he says, trying to calm my fears.

"This isn't the first time you have stayed here, is it?"

"No," he replies. "My father showed me this place when I was a child. He used to take me hunting with him, and there were times when a storm would spring up, much like this one, and he brought me here to wait until it passed. I've been staying here ever since, when necessary."

"And no one else knows of this place?"

"No. Most won't come here. They believe this place is cursed."

"But I saw a woman here," I say.

"I said most won't, but there are those who, on occasion, risk coming here in search of supplies."

The light dances upon his unwrinkled face, meaning he hasn't reached the age of 30 yet, and as I study it, trying to read him and discern his motives, I conclude that this man has none: a rare honest individual in a dishonest world.

"So, who are you doing this for?" he asks.

"One is a girl. She hasn't reached womanhood yet, but will soon, and as a plebeian, her prospects after that are grim. She'll either become a breeder, be sent to a pleasure house, or become a citizen's personal companion, until her body is used up and she is sent to do more menial tasks."

He scowls at my statement, knowing what I mean as I say it with little feeling. Such is the way of my world.

"She doesn't deserve it."

"Do any of them?"

"No," I whisper. "Her name is Sheila. I want her to have the ability to decide her own life, and if I succeed in this Rite of Conquest, she will."

"And the other?"

"You already met him. You helped me save him as he dangled from a cliff."

"I will help you," he says.

"I could betray you in the end."

He smiles, but I do not know if he is grinning at me or my words. "I don't think you will. I'll take you to my clan. They might be able to provide some assistance, though, they don't like Arelians much."

"Then, why would they help me?"

"They won't. But most of my things are there, some of which may prove useful to you."

"And why would they let you help me?"

"We have helped the occasional Arelian escape in the past. Either way, you don't have much choice."

"It's a bad idea," I say.

"Why?"

"I have a tracker in my leg. If a drone gets close enough, it will pick up on it."

He gets up and rummages around his things until he pulls out what looks to be a leather breastplate, but heavy and made of thick material, and he tosses it to me.

"Tie this around your leg. It should make it more difficult to find you."

Examining it, I discover that sewn within the material are thin metallic plates, but pliable and nonrestrictive; it should dull the strength of the signal from my tracker. I wrap it around my leg and tie it off, hoping that it works, knowing that I haven't much choice.

"You just carry one of these around?" I ask.

"I told you: you're not the first Arelian I've met. You should rest. The storm won't pass until morning, and it's not safe to wander the wilds at night."

"I never caught your name."

"I never caught yours."

"Noni."

"Perce."

I stretch out in front of the fire, relishing in its warmth and looking forward to some sleep, exhausted from the day's events, and rest my head on my arm, falling asleep before my eyes close.

I don't know how long I slept, but when Perce wakes me, it feels as though I had only just closed my eyes, but I sit up, ignoring my tiredness, wishing I could sleep some more, or lay here, but I know that if I do, Chase and Sheila will suffer for it. I am an arbiter. I am strong. I must complete what I have started.

Perce puts out the fire and grabs what supplies he needs before leading us up the stairs and to the doorway he pulled me through when he saved me from the storm. He unlocks it and pulls it open, revealing a world of destruction as the morning sunlight touches us, allowing us to see what the storm left behind. If I thought the massive towers and structures looked pitiful before, nothing compares to the trail of carnage stretching out before us as a path of flattened buildings forces its way through what was once the city of Kition.

"It seems the storm left some things standing," says Perce, pointing at a structure about four stories high. "We need a better view."

He runs off, hopping over fallen debris with deftness, not letting any of the fallen lamp posts, beams, and sheets of metal mixed with shattered glass and insulation slow him down. Not wanting to be outdone, and still needing his help, I follow him, hoping that I have not misplaced my trust. The wind whistles through what is left of the city as glass structures form a jagged mountain range of what was once a manmade splendor, but is now little more that steel skeletons with dark hollows where full panes of glass once were. My feet sink into remnants of paneling and insulation, grayed from the chaos enveloping it, as tufts of fibrous material brush across the ground, rolling over the torn edges of paneling and what was once a staircase, but is more like a hill of broken concrete, shattered as though it had turned brittle from the harsh environment it was destined to be in, and stops next to my boot. I pick it up, studying it as I twirl it in my fingers, trying to envision what it must have been or what great structure it was once a part of, and as I look at the bits of fiber sticking into the air in a mishmash fashion, I try to picture the city of Kition in all its splendor, before ruin and decay claimed it as their own.

"What are you doing?" Perce asks me.

I look at him and his brown skin—some of it his natural skin tone, some of it damage from long hours spent in the sun—and his questioning eyes as they drill into mine, wondering why I am standing here in the middle of a dead city and the aftermath of a storm.

A part of me wonders if I can trust him before my mind remembers that twice he could have harmed me, but chose not to: the day he saved both me and Chase, and yesterday during the storm. No, if he had wanted me dead, he could have left me out here to perish with the funnel cloud.

"What happened here?" I ask.

"The inevitable," replies Perce. "What always happens. Rot."

My brows scrunch together in confusion.

"What do you know of Kition?" asks Perce.

"They are selfish, greedy, caring only about their individual natures and pursuit for wealth and not for the plight of others, putting their individual desires ahead of the common good and our collective society," I repeat what has been drilled into my mind since the day of my birth. "They are the enemy of Arel."

Those last words are slow to leave my mouth and mixed with doubt.

Perce does not judge my quickness to repeat what I have been programmed to believe as his face softens from pity. "Yes, Kition was the enemy of Arel," he says, "and Arel was its enemy, but it failed to realize it before it was too late."

"You knew this place?"

"No. I've heard tales of it from the older ones in my village as they retell the stories that their elders told them. They described Kition as a robust city full of people from every background—people who managed to live together in a cohesive society, despite their differences. And how they prospered. Their railcars flew over the rails without ever having to touch them! Every bit of technology you can imagine began here. And the food—there was so much of it that no one starved! They talked. They laughed. They got along. These streets used to be filled with people. Then came Arel, desperate, starving, willing to do anything to survive. So, Kition opened their doors to them and traded with them, unaware that as they did so, they sealed their own fate. Arel stole technological secrets from Kition and used Kition's good will to build their own city into what you live in today. Arel took, while Kition gave. And one day, the bombs fell, bombs Arel created after stealing Kition's secrets, while taking advantage of their kindness."

"Why destroy them?" I ask, though I needn't bother, since a part of me already guesses the answer.

"If Kition ever wised up to what Arel was doing, they could have destroyed them in one fell swoop. Arel beat them to it."

"How do I know you speak the truth?" I ask.

"How do you know Arel told you the truth?"

I already know that they had lied.

"Here," Perce says, pointing at a jagged wall, indicating that we should climb it.

He holds out his hand to help me, but I charge forward, unused to such a notion, and grip the protruding bricks of a wall that looks like it will fall apart at any moment, hoisting myself upward. Smiling, Perce follows behind me. My muscles scream at me to stop climbing, having never recuperated after the last few days of surviving a new harsh environment, but I ignore them, not wanting to stay on the ground, surrounded by the remains of what used to be a city, and exposed to any who might still be hunting me; getting to higher ground is wise, and I intend to succeed. Bits of brick cut into my tired fingers as I grip notches, holes, or knobs, while pressing my feet against the side of the wall so that my legs support some of my weight. As I climb, sweat coats my hands, making my grip slip, causing me to almost fall, but Perce reaches out and catches my arm before I do, allowing me to reposition myself and continue the climb.

The sun, whose warmth I appreciated at first, turns into a nuisance, and its heat reflects off the brick, turning it into a cooking iron that roasts my skin and makes me wish it was cooler, but I push such a notion aside, not wanting to show weakness in front of this barbarian—though he does not seem like some others I have met—and let him believe that I cannot complete a simple task.

A sharp sting grips my elbow as it scrapes against the roughened exterior of the building, tearing away the top layer of skin, but I ignore it, knowing that I have almost reached a set of stairs that lead the rest of the way up. Glancing back, I see Perce as he climbs with ease; either that, or he is doing his best to not show weakness in front of me, and I still wonder why he helps me. Almost there. Just a couple more feet. The bar to the first step looms above me, and I throw my hand up to it, gripping it as tight as I can, and pull myself up, but as I do so, my grip falters. Time moves in slow motion for a moment as gravity wraps its fingers around me and pulls me to the ground, and the only thought in my mind as I fall is that I have failed both Sheila and Chase. Without warning, a hand grabs my arm, and my body jerks to a halt as I slam into the wall and shove my hand into a hole, using it as a handhold, only to look up and see Perce staring at me, making certain that my grip on the wall is secure before letting go. Undeterred, though frustrated at my failure, I continue onward, scaling the wall for a second time and ignoring the sharp edges, created by the wind and the sand it carries, as they dig into my exposed skin and tear into my clothing.

We both reach the lowest step, breathing a sigh of relief, and hike up the remainder of the wobbling staircase, taking the steps two at a time. A bracket securing it pops free of its hold and the staircase lurches, causing us to pause as we look at each other, sharing the same thought: these stairs will not hold for much longer. Wasting no time, we charge up the steps as another bracket breaks free and clatters on the ground below, holding onto the rail as the staircase leans away from the building. With each step we take, a bracket releases the staircase and desperation pushes us onward as we near the top ledge of the roof. I jump at the ledge, grabbing onto its worn edges and haul myself over it, until my feet stand firm on the roof. Perce does the same, and after his foot leaves the staircase, it drops to the ground, creating a deafening noise as it crashes, sending bits of metal in every direction, adding to the decay of this place.

"That's unfortunate," he says as he eyes the destruction.

I raise an eyebrow at his understatement of the situation, wondering how we are supposed to get down from here, but he does not notice and walks to the other side of the roof, going around a giant hole, spanning about half of it, with care. I follow suit, edging my way sideways along the ledge as I avoid falling through the opening.

"About five miles in that direction is my home," says Perce.

"What was that?" says a voice from below, and both Perce and I hunker behind the ledge of the roof, hoping that we remain unseen.

We both peek over it and see two arbiters: one scouring the ruins below for the source of the noise he heard, for the staircase that had fallen because of us, and the other leaning against a rusted pole, unconcerned about his partner's apprehension.

"Probably just something falling over," replies the other in a bored tone.

"I heard something crash over here," says the other.

"Look around you! This whole place is falling apart! Come on."

The second arbiter stalks off, mumbling to himself, while the first one scans the area one last time before leaving.

Before we have time to be thankful for our luck, the roar of a transport engine reaches our ears as a cloud of dust forms in the distance, trailing behind a vehicle as it pulls up to a set of three transports already parked nearby. Two arbiters get out when it stops, and I realize that not everyone standing near the transports is an arbiter; some are barbarians. Intrigued, I watch as the two recent arrivals converse with one of the barbarians and some form of payment exchanges hands before the backs of the transports open and crate after crate of Arelian weapons are dumped on the ground. I blink several times, not wanting to believe what is before my eyes: Arelian arbiters are giving Arelian weapons to the very barbarians that keep attacking us. Righteous anger boils within me, and I start to stand up, wanting to put a stop to this travesty, but Perce yanks me back down.

"What are you doing?" he demands.

"They're giving weapon to our enemies!" I hiss.

Pity softens Perce's features. "You don't know, do you?"

"Know what?"

"This is the way it is. Those barbarians are from a different clan; they are more warlike and bloodthirsty, but they also hunger for wealth and power. Arel has been giving them weapons for a long time, and in exchange, they are to attack your city."

The attacks. The constant state of fear of another occurring. The convenient timing. It all makes sense. The biggest enemy of Arel, the biggest threat to Arel is Arel itself and its leadership. It was all an illusion to keep the people contained and forever imprisoned in a system that saw them as nothing more than resources to be used until nothing is left. I lean against the ledge of the roof, not wanting to believe what I have witnessed as my mind grapples with the truth that has been laid out before me.

"But not all of them are barbarians," I say, remembering the freed plebeian from the first night I was to stand guard on the wall, and in answer to my suspicions, another transport pulls up, and when it stops, both plebeians and Arelians get out. Some look at their feet, while others stare into the eyes of the arbiters and barbarians surrounding them.

"I've watched on many occasions as they bring people from your city and dress them like the other clans," Perce says as I watch arbiters give the new arrivals the garb of the barbarians and weapons.

"Kill without mercy!" says the commanding arbiter. "If you survive the night, you will earn your freedom."

Were these people ones who had been found guilty of a crime and hope to use this as a way to erase that stain from their record?

"They are never given their freedom," Perce says to me in a hushed tone. "The ones from your city who survive are executed by the clan hired to attack the city."

"How do you know all this?" I ask.

"I never believed it when my father told me about it, until the day I witnessed it for myself."

Perce motions for us to leave, and I know we have stayed here too long, but before we have time to move an inch, someone spots us.

"Up there!" shouts an arbiter.

Cursing, I jump to my feet with Perce right behind me, and we charge across what is left of the roof we are on, making our way to the neighboring one, and without thinking, I jump across the narrow space, hoping that the structure will hold. My feet crumple beneath me as I land, and I crash onto my side, but I haven't time to register the sharp pain in my shoulder when I land. Shots fill the empty air around us, pelting the roof as I crawl to a ledge and hide behind its remains, while my mind races for a solution to my current predicament. Perce's feet plop on the concrete roof beside me and he dives to the ground to avoid being hit.

"Any ideas?" I ask.

He looks around. "If we can get to the tall grass over there, we might be able to lose them long enough to get to the trees."

His plan sounds good, but there are too many of them. We need to even the odds, and I spot a way to do that as an arbiter with a belt of explosives dives behind the corner of a building. Before I can voice my plan, a bullet whizzes past us and puts a hole in the wall of the neighboring building. Sniper. Curses run through my mind as I reconsider my options. Light catches me in the eye, causing me to avert my eyes, until I see a piece of reflective paneling laying nearby, and as I study it, I consider the roof beyond it and how a lamppost—its lamp is missing, but the pole still stands—is within reach from its edge. I need to know where the sniper is. I grab some rubble and throw it, and a shot strikes it. Got him.

"Can you get to the tower over there" I ask Perce, "and take out that sniper?"

He nods.

"When I say, head for it."

Bracing myself for what I must do, I take a deep breath to calm my nerves and push the thought that this could be my last moments aside—failure is not an option—before jumping to my feet. I snatch the reflective paneling and hold it, catching the sunlight and blinding any in its path as I race for the edge of the roof, jumping as I reach it and land on the neighboring gable and its beam running across it, continuing onward without slowing my pace. Gunfire strikes the tiles beneath my feet as I charge across with the reflective paneling held up like a shield protecting my right side. When I reach the edge, I throw the panel away and leap for the pole, sliding down it to the bottom, and before any arbiters or barbarians can find me, I dart away and into another structure, disappearing into its decayed darkness.

Mildewed dust fills the air around me as I run through a hallway, stumbling over a broken chair, shoving drywall and pink insulation (grayed from mold and dust and tangled in a mesh of stripped wires hanging from the exposed ceiling) out of my way in an effort to find an exit, as the sounds of gunfire and shouts from those searching for me echo through the ruins and to my ears. I barge through a door, causing it to fall off its rotted hinges, and crash onto the floor when I spot what used to be a window. A barbarian creeps past with his weapon raised as he searches for me. I jump through the opening, tackling him, and we roll across the ground as dust coats our clothes. He tries to get up, but I wrap my feet around his ankle, forcing him to fall back down before ramming my fist into his face three times in rapid succession.

Once subdued, I take his weapon and scramble away, hunkering behind a crumbling wall with only its bottom quarter still somewhat intact as bits of it fall away and drop on my chest. Footsteps alert me to the presence of another. Peeking around the wall, I spot an arbiter as he walks with deft precision while looking around, and I press my back into the wall, waiting for him to pass. I leap from my position and place the middle of my weapon around his throat, pulling back as hard as I can before twisting it. He stops moving. I haul his corpse behind the wall and pull some rubble over it to conceal it before darting off.

The remains of a sunroom—I assume it was once a sunroom as I look at the exposed metal rods that stretch up and form an arch over me, rusted from years of neglect and a constant bombardment of the elements, but no glass remains, except for a few stained green shards—stand between me and a group of five arbiters and barbarians working together to hunt me and Perce. The thought of it disgusts me as I grapple with the notion that Arel has spent years hiring barbarians to attack the wall, all so they could keep the people in line with a constant bombardment of fear—fear of the outside world. I see Perce charging for the tower. They will see him! Knowing that if I do nothing, he will be killed, I stand up, exposing my position and aim the weapon I took from the barbarian and fire, killing all five.

Sniper fire strikes one of the rods next to me, sending shrapnel in my face, slicing my cheek. I turn away and drop to the ground, crawling for safety, as more sniper fire pelts the ground around me. A burning sensation overwhelms my left calf as a bullet strikes it, causing blood to soak my pant leg. Desperate, I scramble across the ground underneath a piece of broken concrete that provides cover from the sniper, and roll onto my back to inspect my leg. It looks as though it pierced the muscle and went all the way through: a clean exit. I rip a piece of my shirt off and tie it around my leg to stem the bleeding as more gunfire pummels my small place of refuge, breaking it apart to where there will be nothing left if I do not leave. An explosive device clomps on the ground as it rolls into my sanctuary, stopping at my hip.

Shit!

I charge out of there, diving behind another broken down wall, as the device detonates, and its blast picks me up, hurling me across the rubble before allowing me to crash onto the ground, knocking the wind out of me as I land on my side and feel bits of rock and metal dig into me. Stunned, I do not move, while my rational mind screams at me to get up, but the pain coursing through me compels me to remain still. I wriggle my fingers and move my arms as I try to sit up and ignore the wave of nausea that overtakes me. A shadow looms over me. Looking up, I find myself staring into the eyes of a barbarian as he points a blade at my throat, ready to end my life. I do not flinch as I harden my face, refusing to give him the satisfaction of seeing fear. Before he can carry out his plan, a bullet rams through him, splattering me with his blood, and he drops to the broken pavement, which looks more like a tiered garden of weeds, beneath us. I glance at the tower. Perce must have succeeded in subduing the sniper.

I haul myself to my feet and head for the tree line, stumbling as I go, as my legs refuse to obey my commands. Someone charges from the side. I rip the knives out of my belt and stab him in the hand as he swings at me, before plunging the other knife through the bottom of his chin, but as he drops to the ground, the weight of his body takes me with him, causing me to fall to the ground and wince as pain seizes my calf. Still dazed from the explosion, my efforts to stand back up prove useless as I collapse on the ground again, wishing my mind would focus. A black boot appears before my eyes, allowing me to see my reflection in its polished surface. I tear my blade from the dead man's chin and ram it into the boot, using the screams of the one it belongs to as a target as I jump up and throw my second knife, catching my opponent in the chest and removing the blade before he hits the uneven ground.

A distant whistle catches my attention. Turning toward it, I spot Perce as he points to a cleared path leading straight to the trees beyond the city. I head for it. My legs flop on the ground as I move, while my calf scolds me for forcing it to support my weight, but I haven't a choice, and I lean against a pole for support to regain my footing and will my body to move. I will not die here. Noise attracts my attention, and I look ahead, seeing a sea of barbarians and arbiters between me and the tree line, hoping to block my path and stop me. I think of Chase and Shelia depending on me to succeed.

Failure is weakness.

Weakness is death.

I push the pain in my calf aside, ignoring it as I was taught to do at the training facility, as I focus on my goal, on what is most important, gripping my knives so that the hilts leave imprints in my palms, as I put one foot in front of the other, slow at first, before engaging in a full sprint. The first obstacle jumps in front of me, but I duck as he swings, dodging his fist before twisting and plunging both blades into his stomach, and continuing on without bothering to acknowledge his agonizing death. Wind sails through my hair as I charge forward, dropping to one knee when another attempts to block my path, slicing his inner thigh with one of my knives and his Achilles tendon with my other. As he drops to the ground in a rage, I silence him for good and do not register the body that drops beside me, killed by sniper fire coming from Perce.

My rage drives me as I plow through the barbarians and arbiters before me, cutting, slicing, and stabbing as I go, not caring about the blood that coats my face and arms as they fall around me. One comes up behind me. I twist around and plunge a knife into the side of his neck and pull him close, using him as a shield, while another unloads his weapon in him, hoping to hit me. When the magazine empties, I drop the dead man and stalk up to the other as he struggles to change the magazine to his weapon, but his frightened hands falter, causing him to drop it as I leer over him and finish him.

The trees are not far. My calf yearns for relief, but I refuse to allow it any, and though my steps are uneven because of it, I run as fast as I can to my salvation in this chaotic mess. An arbiter rams into me, knocking me to the ground. Before I can react, he lifts my head and knees me in the face, causing my nose to bleed, and warm blood drips from it, pooling in the red dirt as I shake, and my world goes in and out of focus, but I must remain conscious. I cannot fail now. The arbiter kicks me again, but I rear up and block it before rolling to the side to avoid another blow. Still dazed, I watch as he comes for me once more, and I block the first two attacks, but his third strikes me in the face, causing me to fall back to the ground. He paces around me, relishing this moment as I struggle to get up, but I refuse to lay here and allow him an easy victory, so I push myself to my feet, despite the pain in my calf and the blood that oozes from it, and hold my knives out to the side, waiting. He leaps for me, but I dodge to the side, avoiding his blow. He swings again, followed by a kick, and both times, I dodge out of the way and cross my arms before me, blocking another attack. Frustrated, he pulls back before running at me again. My eyes turn to slits as I focus on his movements, guessing what the next one will be, and before he reaches me, I duck out of the way, whirl around him, and stab him between the shoulder blades before running my other knife across his throat.

A battle cry forces me to turn around, only to watch as a barbarian with three stripes of black paint stretching across his face (one on his forehead, another across his nose, and the third covering his chin) charges for me, but drops to the ground, killed by a single shot from Perce, standing in the distance. We lock eyes a moment before I race for the tree line once more. An arbiter and a barbarian jump out at me, but I dispatch them with ease, refusing to slow my pace. Another leaps for me, but I duck downward, turning in a half circle, before cutting him down and continuing onward, until I have left Kition and reach the trees, exhausted and ready to collapse. Leaning against a tree, I check the bandage around my calf, wincing as a thousand needles mixed with fire charge up it, chastising me for forcing it to support my weight. A drone hovers next to me and I eye it for a moment, unsure if it had managed to find me or was here with the arbiters in Kition. The tip of my knife sends a hollow thump into the air as I ram it through the drone and into the trunk of the tree before removing it, allowing the drone to drop into the grass and leaves, sending sparks in every direction.

Footsteps sound behind me, and I whirl around with one of my knives raised before realizing that it is Perce. Relieved by his presence, my body takes it as a sign to shut down and my legs buckle beneath me, but I never touch the ground as Perce catches me. The sensation of being picked up and carried is the last thing that registers in my mind as my eyes close and the world fades.

Chapter 13

A Wider World

The tinkling of glass shards—not piercing or ear splitting, but pleasant, almost musical—pierce through my slumber, forcing me to wake and open my tired eyes so that the light from the morning sun can seep through. A moment passes before my vision clears and the remnants of sleep fade away, though my body still feels exhausted as a sharp ache seizes the entirety of my lower back the moment I try to move, causing me to release a small yelp of pain. A hand, feminine, but dried out from years of washing, pushes me back down on the bed as a way of telling me to not move, and as I lay there, every memory of my time in the wilds fills my mind as all my wounds make themselves known once more as a way of chastising me for my poor choices. The tinkling of glass catches my attention again, and I glance in its direction, finding a wind chime made from the shards of colored glass, but smoothed out so that the edges no longer cut any who dare touch it, and shaped in a pleasing array of ovals and spirals that provide a soothing melody when the breeze caresses it.

Despite the wishes of the woman with me, I force myself to sit up and ignore my muscles as they scream at me for daring to move when all they desire is rest. Once up, I lift the faded, homemade blanket—its once vibrant red now grayed from years of washing—with frayed ends to get a better look at my calf, but the same hand grips my wrist, stopping me. Unsure of who this woman is, but knowing I am in no position to argue as my body reminds me of the ordeal it has been through, I release the blanket and lie back down.

"Morning, Amber," says a familiar voice, and I turn my head to see Perce entering the room. "How is your patient today?"

"She doesn't listen," the woman complains, speaking in front of me for the first time.

Perce smiles, but whether he is smiling because he has experienced my impetuous attitude or because he knows something about this Amber that I do not, I cannot say; I am left there in the middle of an unspoken conversation as little more than an observer.

"How long?" I say, forcing them to acknowledge me. "How long have I been here?"

"Three days," replies Perce.

Three days? I've been out that long?

"Amber thought it best to keep you sedated."

"Why?" I look at the woman. "Do you think I am that much of a danger?"

"We don't often allow Arelians here," Amber says to me. "The governor will want to see her," she says to Perce, whose face takes on a sour look.

I start to get up once again, not wanting to see anyone. Chase and Sheila need me, and Gwen needs her brother. The longer I stay here, the more they suffer.

"Stay put, girl!" Amber scolds me. "You're not going anywhere on that leg anytime soon."

Perce steps away for a moment and comes back with a wheelchair, and I frown the moment I see it and his expectation for me to get in it.

"I will walk," I say, not liking the idea of being pushed around in such a contraption; it's a sign of weakness.

"Not on that leg you won't," he says.

"I can't stay here," I say, almost pleading with him to let me go.

"You are not well enough to leave."

I glare at the wheelchair and the bare parts of the seat where the cracked leather has peeled away.

"Would you like me to put you in it?"

Scowling at Perce, and the very notion of him manhandling me, I lift myself up, ignoring the stabbing pain in my calf and the pins and needles in my back muscles as they refuse to obey my will, and place myself in the wheelchair, almost falling into it at the last second. Once seated, I look at my thigh and the casing that is still strapped around it, tightening it as needed to ensure it does not fall away.

"So far," he says to me, "no Arelians have been spotted nearby."

He wheels me out the door and into the late morning sunlight and a world of boisterous sounds of merchants selling their wares and potential clients haggling over the price, lining the paved streets, though some are in need of repair, while structures overlook them and the activity that fills them. Exotic spices fill my nostrils as we pass one such merchant, and I look at the mounds of powder forming a colorful array on his table as reds, orange, and yellow all blend together, creating a kind of abstract painting, marveling at this display as Arel never allowed anything like it to exist.

He pushes me past another merchant with linen folded in a neat pile (the lightest of pinks, blues, greens, and a pale yellow, and the boldest of red, purple, brown, and a deep shade of orange that would put any fruit bearing its name to shame) and tied with ribbons, all waiting to be purchased and turned into garments. Unable to contain myself, I reach out and touch one, reveling in its softness and the silky feel of it, having never worn anything so exquisite in my life. Arbiter clothes, though sleek, are made from basic materials and as inexpensive as possible, for if an arbiter dies, why bury him in such finery? Only those on the topmost tier of Arelian society are allowed such expensive wares, but here, it is on sale for any to buy if they have the money to purchase it. The man at the stall gives me a wary look, either annoyed that I have soiled his merchandise, or uncertain of my motives as my arbiter clothing gives me away.

"What do you have for me today?" Perce asks the man, diverting his attention from me to him.

"Perce," the man greets him with respect and reaches for an already made garment: a sleek coat that stretches past the waist and settles at the base of the hip, with sleeves that look to be snug, yet loose enough to allow movement, and bluer than the sky.

Perce takes it and twirls it around, examining it before handing it back to the man.

"Not bad," he says, "but I was speaking about the lady."

Lady? No one has ever called me that before. I am an arbiter. Expendable. Not once have I ever been considered a lady, or a person of any value.

"Have you not seen the state of her coat?" Perce says to the merchant.

I look at my sleeveless arms, remembering how I ripped the sleeves from my jacket during my time in the wilds and realize how pitiful I must appear to everyone here.

The merchant brings out another jacket, tailored for a more feminine physique, but still bulky, and hands it too me. I try it on, but the heavy material weighs me down, making me feel as though I am anchored to the ground. Perce notices my distaste and agrees.

"Come, come, man. Have you anything more fitting? Something lighter, yet functional?"

The merchant stares at Perce, unsure as to why he helps me, or cares about my manner of dress.

"If you have nothing of better quality, I will go to someone else," Perce says.

"No!" the man blurts out, afraid of losing a sale. "Wait!"

He digs through his trunks of already made clothing and pulls out a jacket blacker than my hair, but with material that reflects the light around us, but matted so as not to be overpowering, but it is the red trim lining the collar and the edges of the sleeves that intrigue me. The man hands it to me, and I put it on, tying the belt so that it is snug against my waist. The satin lining caresses my skin, allowing me a taste of luxury, while the exterior makes me look like more than an arbiter: a person of substance. The snugness is not too tight but will allow me freedom of movement when I find Molers, but its warmth wards off the chill in the air, reminding me of the changing season.

Perce looks pleased. "We'll take it. How much?"

The merchant's brows scrunch together, almost as though his mind debates telling the truth, or marking up the price to take advantage of my limited knowledge of this place, but Perce's steady gaze settles the matter.

"Seventy."

Perce hands over coins and the merchant gives him a bill of sale.

"Come again," the merchant says as Perce wheels me away and we continue down the street as people wander about, and for the first time, I do not feel like an oddity. In Arel, people always steer clear of arbiters, afraid of what we might do and of the authority that we have, but here, people ignore me, except for the occasional curious onlooker or hate-filled stare from those who recognize my uniform pants and must have had unpleasant dealings with Arelians in the past, but they don't dare do anything with Perce by my side, which makes me wonder: who is he to these people? Many nod in his direction or address him with a respectful greeting, and he returns them in kind.

As we continue our trek through the city, a commotion catches my attention, and I turn my head toward a small dwelling where two men attempt to shove an overlarge couch through a medium-sized doorway. The arms of the couch rip as they push it through, causing one to swear, but they manage to get it outside, and as they carry it down a set of stairs, a long-haired, brown cat, with bits of black fur dotting its coat, offset by its white paws, jumps on the back of the sofa and settles on the pillowed top, as though it is a throne, and watches the world with a grin, causing me to smile as well.

Perce pushes me underneath a giant archway that looks to be centuries old, yet new at the same time from fresh coats of white paint covering repairs that had been made, and as we pass under it, it's as though we've transitioned into a different world, one that is both ancient and newborn. A horn beeps as a white bus, its underside darkened from grime, rolls by, warning people to get out of its way before stopping to allow passengers to depart, while others rush forward to get aboard, dropping coins into a container as payment for passage. The driver closes the door before honking the horn again as it rolls away to its next station, and as my eyes follow its path, I notice a rail two stories above the ground—not as elaborate or elegant as Arel's, but functional—with a shuttle speeding past as small shapes of people fill its tinted windows.

Perce must have noticed me staring at it in disbelief because he breaks the silence, and my awe, saying, "We are not all savages."

His statement reminds me of the barbarian Commandant Paq had forced me to hunt and how I had spared his life after realizing that he was no different than me, and how he believed that all Arelians were savages in the same way Arel believes the same about all barbarians.

"Neither are all Arelians," I say.

The smell of water enters my nose—not stagnant or musty like the aqueducts underneath Kition, but fresh and clean, reminding me of a spring rain—as we approach a series of walkways that cross a canal system and a set of stairs leading down to it. Perce steers me toward a ramp with a crack running up its middle, past a group of people examining it and taking measurements as though preparing to repair it in the near future, and takes me to a ferry as a man in an oversized fur beaver skin coat calls for passengers. He guides my wheelchair down the path with expert skill, never losing his footing, nor getting out of breath from the exertion as I watch people rush past us, some going to the ferry and others away from it, ignoring us, except to greet my guide, causing me to wonder for the second time who and what he is to these people. Perce is no mere wanderer of the wilds.

"Tickets!" the ferryman says in a gruff voice as his beard (brown with flecks of white) beats against his chest in the wind, but steps aside when Perce flashes a pass at him. "Your pardon, sir."

"No worries," Perce replies in a respectful tone.

He wheels me onto the ferry and toward a doorway, leading to the interior of the boat with benches at each window for passengers to sit and admire the view, but I've no desire to be inside a glass box.

"Please," I say, stopping him, "can we stay outdoors?"

Perce answers with an amicable grin and steers me away from the doorway and up a ramp to the boat deck where others, like myself, wish to remain outside, finding the perfect spot on the bow. A bell rings three times, sending sharp, yet pleasant, musical notes to my ears, causing me to look up and find a silver, domed-shaped bell high above us, so shiny that it must have been polished, and the ferry raises its anchor and moves forward to the other side of the wide canal, allowing me a better view of Perce's city and its granite buildings that must have been carved by skilled sculptors who wished to bring a bit of elegance to a harsh world. Walkways stretch out above us as we pass along the water, filled with people, as though forming a bridge between two worlds, allowing individuals to go where they will. I start to stand up, but falter as my leg rebels against being used so soon. Perce reaches a hand out to help me, but I hold mine up stopping him. I must do this on my own. Forcing my injured leg to cooperate, I steady myself and shuffle to the rail, placing my hands on its copper exterior, tarnished a dull green due to the constant bombardment of water and the natural elements, and look up, taking in as much of the view as I can.

"Welcome," Perce says behind me as a flock of pigeons fly over the tops of the buildings with the golden sun as their backdrop, almost like an ancient painting on canvas, "to Croatia."

I feel like a child as I gaze at the spires reaching for the sky as they tower over smaller structures, each with their own architectural design as the city stretches onward with no end that I can see. I watch as a woman pokes her head out a window several stories up and reaches for a line holding fresh laundry and removes the dried pieces. She glances in my direction, though I do not know if she sees me or is watching the ferry as it passes below her. Water laps against the boat, splashing the hull and spraying the air with fresh water droplets that coat my face as I take in all that surrounds me, marveling at how the people here managed to build all this, while Perce watches me with amusement.

"How did you build all this?" I ask.

"We didn't," Perce replies. "Much of what you see has always been here. Some of what you see we may have added, but much of it is far older."

Silence passes between us before he breaks it.

"Are you thirsty?"

"What?"

"Are you thirsty?"

"Why are you so nice to me?"

"I told you: my father said that we should help those who need it and deserve it."

He walks away, leaving me to admire the odd beauty of what he calls Croatia. Though not as pristine, streamlined, or elegant as Arel, this place has a different kind of beauty, one that is more genuine as people gossip among themselves and laugh, unafraid of saying something that might be considered seditious. The ferry floats past a building that looks to be nothing but a series of steps leading to nowhere with sunken holes within it, forming oval-shaped windows, while the entranceway is marked by an overhang watching over it. Curious as to why it was constructed this way, I keep my eyes fixed on it and on the people treading atop it with reverence, informing me that this is no ordinary building, but a place of worship perhaps.

"Arelian filth!" says a harsh voice behind me, and I turn around in time for a man accompanied by two others to spit on my new jacket. My fist clenches as I measure them and calculate the best course of action, but before any of us can make a move, Perce appears with a small cup of water in his hand.

"Is there a problem?" he says, his voice devoid of friendliness.

"Perce," says the one who spat on me—it seems my host is known by many in this place—taking a step back and changing his harsh tone to one of worry, "do you know who she is?"

"My guest," replies Perce.

"But..."

"And you've soiled her jacket."

Perce's eyes narrow and his tone issues an unspoken command that the others pick up on, and the one who spat on me pulls a handkerchief out of his pocket and walks up to me, but before he can clean off his spittle, I catch his wrist and tear the cloth from his grip. After wiping my jacket clean, I place the dirtied handkerchief in the man's palm. He takes it without a word as Perce watches the proceedings.

"It's just as well you showed up," the man said before walking away, but Perce stops him.

"You suffer from the illusion that I saved her from you, when in fact, I saved you from her." He closes the distance between them. "Never mistreat a guest of mine again."

The man bows his head and leaves with his companions, while I ponder the scene before me.

"Here"—Perce places the cup of water in my hand—"you should stay hydrated."

"Who are you?" I ask after taking a sip of the refreshing liquid. "And what are you to them?"

"Merely a citizen of this city," he replies, evading my question.

"Don't toy with me or play me for a fool. Back in Kition, you took our enemies out from that tower as though you had done it before. How?"

"I have some skill with firearms—"

"That take years to develop."

"You should finish your water," Perce says. "We're almost there."

"What aren't you telling me?"

Perce remains silent, allowing my question to go unanswered and to hang in the air, as though it is some foul odor that he wishes to avoid, leaving me with little choice but to finish my water before settling back down in the wheelchair. A child's laughter catches my attention, and I glance at it to watch two children, a boy and a girl, kick a ball between them as they play in front of the two adults with them, whom I assume are their parents. All have smiles on their faces, enjoying their moment of fun, while I look on, uninvited, reminded of what has been denied to me my entire life, but not just to me, to all of Arel. The boy strikes the ball with a harsh kick and it hits the girl in the head by accident, causing her to cry and run to her mother, who stretches her arms out and comforts her, while the father explains to the boy why he should not have done what he did, and a well of emotions opens up within me as I remember the days of pain I experienced at the training facility with no one there willing to provide even the smallest amount of comfort. I have never known a mother's embrace or a father's wisdom, or even the sort of comfort that Chase tries to provide his sister so as to spare her the harsh reality of their existence; I have only known punishment for disobedience and Arel's wrath for daring to question its dictates.

A memory seeks me out, one I buried long ago. In my seventh year, Faya and I had snuck out of our rooms and met up with two other recruits and a plebeian to kick a ball around for pleasure, making up our own game as we went, enjoying a moment of fun. We laughed and giggled, and for an hour, we forgot where we were and how we were expected to act before being interrupted by instructors who had noticed our disobedience and dealt swift punishment upon us. They struck each of us with a baton, and any who cried in pain received another blow, and we all suffered ten lashes as a reminder of our insolence. Faya and I tended each other's wounds that night, but we never spoke to the other two recruits or plebeian again, nor did we dare play a game after that.

The ferry reaches its destination, and the ferryman yells a command or two at his crew as they throw a line to another standing on the dock, who ties it around a post, securing it and holding the boat steady. People line up to depart, and Perce wheels me into the line as we follow the crowd down the ramp and onto the dock, before veering away from the crowd. He takes me to the center of his city and a street overflowing with people, some hurrying to get to their destination, while others amble along, taking their time and enjoying this one moment of their existence, while spaced throughout the crowd are vendors, selling their wares to any passerby. The savory smell of one such vendor causes my stomach to grumble as it reminds me of how long it has been since I last ate anything, and I glance at the bread-like items lined in neat rows on a woman's cart as they rest under a heat lamp. Perce notices my interest and purchases one, handing it to me with a grin. I stare at it, unsure of what to do with it.

"Go ahead," he says, motioning for me to eat, "we call it a pretzel."

I take a bite, reveling in the soft, chewy texture of the pretzel as my mouth waters from the salt crystals touching my tongue, and a small bit of saliva dribbles from the corner of my lips, causing me to wipe it away with the back of my hand.

Perce laughs from my bit of embarrassment.

"I cannot repay you for this," I say.

"You are my guest," he replies. "It would be rude of me to expect repayment."

"How did you build this place? In Arel, we are taught that barbarians are primitive and live in tents."

"Some of the other clans do," Perce says. "Their advancements are rudimentary, but here in Croatia, we are lucky. We have engineers and architects, but much of what you see was built before us. We merely live here and maintain it and live in relative peace, though sometimes, the destructive ways of others find us."

Perce pauses as we pass a mound of rubble, and I notice the scorch marks of fire having ravaged through there after the initial destruction.

"What happened?" I ask.

"Some of the other clans are jealous of our prosperity and wish to have it for themselves, and Arel always seeks to demonstrate its might to the world."

Perce steers me down another road that leads to a courtyard with a massive quad full of trimmed topiaries and rose bushes, each a different color, lining the edges of the quad, until it reaches a massive building with four pentagonal-shaped columns supporting an archway that covers the entranceway. We pass beneath the archway and through the entrance into a foyer with artwork I have never seen before, some depicting a major battle with people dressed in unusual clothing, and one of a man with his hand on a book, and wearing buckled shoes and knee-length breaches, accepting some great honor being bestowed upon him. The contrast between this artwork and that of Arel's is unmistakable, because in Arel, all art is to honor the two presidents, and now they will only honor Tapiwa.

"What do these paintings mean?" I ask, unable to peel my eyes away from them.

"We do not know," Perce admits. "These came with the structures my people found when they came here long ago. We simply maintain them. I like to believe that these tell a story of accomplishment and humility."

We pass by a stone within the walls with the number 1789 on it.

"And that?" I ask, pointing at it.

"Don't know. It was here as well. Much of the knowledge of the past has been lost, but we try to preserve what we can, even if we do not fully understand it."

He wheels me over to an elevator, and we get inside the dark interior with its sides painted brown, instead of constructed from reflective siding like the ones in Arel. Still, I marvel at the fact that they even have one, and Perce seems able to understand my unspoken thoughts.

"As I've said, we are not all savages."

The doors open and he wheels me down a corridor with a faded green carpet with bits of white speckled within it, stretching the length of the floor, illumed by a few lamps dotting the walls, though some of them remain dark and in need of repair. As we traverse the length of the hallway, I notice a man with a mark on his arm, the mark of one who tried to escape Arel, but was caught, tinkering with the wires of an unlit lamp. We lock eyes for a moment, before he turns away, making me wonder what he thinks of me: an arbiter in a wheelchair. Somehow, he had managed to escape and came here. He finishes putting the lamp back together as we pass by and it turns on, shining its light on blue wallpaper, dulled from years of neglect.

"He's from Arel," I say to Perce once we are past.

"Yes," Perce replies, "many from Arel have come here seeking a new life."

My mind turns to Sigal and his family. What became of them after I helped them leave? Did they come here? A part of me hopes that they did, but I suspect that their fate will forever be a mystery to me.

"We're here."

Perce stops before a domed doorway and opens it, allowing me to see inside a chamber with chairs situated within it, all facing the same direction, and all forming a semi-circle around one seat at the front, each with a person sitting in it. All eyes turn toward me as Perce wheels me in and heads to the front of the room, where a woman with gray curls framing her face sits, and her hardened expression reminds me of Commander Vye. She stands up to face me as her colorless lips, cracked and dry, form a thin line within her pale face, marked by a couple of age spots near the chin.

"So, the rumors are true," says someone within the chamber, but the woman holds her hand up and silences him.

"Perce," says the woman, "on time as usual."

My fists clench, ready to defend myself from this room of on-lookers who all look upon me as a stain upon their world, but Perce places a gentle hand on my shoulder, causing me to relax, but my eyes stay focused upon those within the room as I take note of the exits and the number surrounding me.

"What is your name?" demands another within the room.

"Ask me nicely and I might tell you," I hiss, not liking the man's tone.

The woman at the front holds up her hand, forcing the man to close his mouth.

"We already know that you come from Arel and that you are one of their arbiters. The least you can do is give us your name."

I remain silent.

"Very well," says the woman. "My name is Susan. Perce has brought you here because it is not often that an arbiter falls within our ranks. In fact, you are the second one to not try and kill us all, and according to Perce, you spared his life, when you could have easily taken it."

"Noni." I say, giving my name.

"What brings you to our city?"

"Him," I say, pointing at Perce.

"Let me clarify," says Susan, "why are you outside your city's walls?"

I consider not answering at all, or telling a lie, but they will see through it.

"It is called the Right of Conquest. I and one other are dumped in the wilderness, where we must hunt each other and survive off the land."

"And when you find the other?" she asks.

"Only one survives," I reply.

I look at the faces staring at me, mulling over the truthfulness of my words. "I must go back out there."

"Why?" asks one within the room.

"Because I am not finished. Because I have not won," I say.

"Preposterous!" says a man with a mole underneath his right eye, standing up from his seat. "You can't possibly believe all this!"

"There are rumors that Arelians do this sort of thing," replies another.

The man with the mole scoffs at the other's words.

"She speaks the truth," Perce says in my defense. "I watched as she was dumped in the wilds."

"And I am to believe you?" says the man with the mole. "We all know your affinity for them and who your father was. Make no mistake, the only reason why you are allowed here is because your mother was her daughter," he says, pointing at Susan, "half-breed."

Perce clenches his fist, but Susan's voice stops him from following through on his intentions.

"Enough! Such language will not be used here, and you will show my grandson respect. Has he not proven himself?"

"It appears he prefers wandering in the wilds, and the company of Arelians, than the civility of our city," says the man with the mole. "Have we not suffered enough from them? Why are we entertaining her?"

"She has shown no harm to any of us," says a woman.

"The question is: what do we do with her?" another in the room speaks.

A series of voices echo around me as they debate my future, while my anger builds at their insistence of acting as though I am nothing more than an object to them.

"Death!"

"Don't be ridiculous! We are better than them!"

"Imprisonment!"

"Exile!"

"No! Mercy is the better way. She has shown no aggression here."

"Not today," says the man with the mole, "but violence is all they know."

"Perce's father was different," says another.

The man with the mole laughs. "Arelians are all the same. Look at her. Look at her eyes! They are the eyes of a killer! Are we to let her remain, gathering secrets on us so that she can report it back to her superiors? Have we not suffered enough? She should be dealt with in the only way they understand. She should—"

The man's words catch in his throat when I pry a loose piece of metal out of the wheelchair and chuck it at him, silencing him before forcing myself to stand on my unsteady legs.

"Enough! All of you!" I shout. "I am tired of my future being debated and decided for me as though I have no mind of my own—as though I am not even here! I am not some tool to be used and abused until my usefulness is spent! I am not a plebeian, and none of you are my masters! I will not sit here and listen to you speak of me as though I am worth no more than an insect! I am a human being—an individual with wants, desires, and heartache—and I will decide my fate! Not you! Not any of you!"

I turn toward Susan.

"If you want me to leave your city, I will. I've no desire to stay, anyway."

"May I ask why?" she says with sincerity.

"My business in the wilds is unfinished," I reply, thinking of Molers, before my mind turns to Chase, Gwen, and Sheila, "and its conclusion determines the fate of three people I care about who are still trapped in Arel."

"You cannot leave"—Susan holds her hand up when I start to protest—"at least, not until you have healed. How far do you think you will get on that leg?"

"I've faced worse."

"All in agreement?" says Susan.

A series of "ayes" echo around me, outnumbering any opposing votes, confirming that I am to stay until my leg has mended.

Perce helps me back into my wheelchair and steers me out of the chamber and back into the dull hallway with its broken lamps and faded carpet.

"Your father was Arelian," I say to him.

"Yes," he replies.

"He was a sniper, wasn't he?" I say.

"Yes. He left Arel. Never spoke why. My mother always had an affinity for the wilds and found him half dead out there. She nursed him back to health, and he devoted himself to her ever since. When I was born, many here wanted to shun us all. They wanted to know how she could love a killer, and saw me as nothing more than a half-breed: not Croatian, not Arelian, not anyone. To ensure my survival, my father taught me all that he knew: how to survive in the wilds and how to hit your mark from five hundred yards. As I grew older, he and my mother taught me that, if you earn the respect of others, they will not care who you are, and over time, many forgot why we were shunned in the first place and spoke to us again."

"Where are they, your parents?"

"Both are dead. Illness took my mother. Grief took my father, proving to me that Arelians are capable of love; they can change."

"I'm sorry," I say.

"What about you?"

"Arelians do not have parents. We are taken at birth and sent to our designated assignment where we are trained, from birth, to be only that. I was made an arbiter. The Martial Diplomatic Corps is all I've ever known, but that is no longer who I am. I want to leave Arel, and I want to take the ones I care for with me. That is why I must win the Right of Conquest."

"Then I will see to it that you are well enough to do so."

No other words are spoken between us as Perce leads me back outside and into an unknown world. No other words are needed. His promise is enough.

Chapter 14

Arel's Long Arm

The sharp edge of a rounded, triangular shaped leaf drooping low from the tree that houses it pricks my cheek as one of its almost invisible spikes touches my skin, while I remain still, hidden by the foliage surrounding me, tinged brown from the changing season, with a bow in my hands, watching a lone boar push its nose into the dirt. Fifteen days have passed since Perce brought me to his home—fifteen days since I was last hunted by my own people, making me wonder why they have left me alone, or if something else had happened to prevent them from finding me. My calf feels more like its old self, and I wished to test it out, ensuring that my leg had lost none of its strength. Unwilling to let me go out alone, Perce insisted on coming with me, and when I refused, he teased that I was afraid he might be better at hunting than me, and with my pride stung, I charged him with choosing the challenge, and so he did: armed only with a bow, the first to kill the boar wins. I smile to myself as I remain still, studying my prey; I have been trained in a multitude of weaponry, including a bow and arrow.

The wind shifts, causing strands of my hair to tickle my face as it toys with me, telling me that I am now upwind. Cursing my luck, I remain still as I watch the boar lift its nose into the air and sniffs. It catches my scent. As it gallops off into the underbrush, I spring from my place of concealment and sprint through the wilderness, trying my best to remain silent as I leap over a leafy branch that had fallen away from its tree, brushing the ground with its shriveled leaves. I see the boar. It continues to gallop through the trees and bushes, evading me, aware of my pursuit. I pick up the pace as it dives through thorned bushes, knowing I will try to avoid them. My feet slide in the dirt as I come to a halt and look around for another path, spotting two trees that had grown close together, but managed to leave a small gap between them big enough for someone my size to squeeze through. I hurry toward the gap, twisting sideways so as to fit through it, and race through the wilderness, veering as needed to chase down the boar.

There it is! I stop and raise my bow, taking aim before firing. Missed!

As my arrow strikes the trunk of a tree, the boar changes direction again. I charge after it, spreading my legs as far as they will go to increase my stride and my speed as I run past trees and foliage, avoiding the protruding roots and tangled vines that all threaten to end my hunt. A vine wraps itself around me, causing me to slow my pace, but I tear at it, ripping it from its hold, refusing to allow it to stop me as I toss it aside. As I continue onward, I realize that I have lost the animal and pause to listen. Seconds pass as nothing happens, until the boar bursts through a bush, almost knocking me over as it charges past. Spinning on the balls of my feet, I press them into the ground before darting off after it, unconcerned about the amount of noise my crashing through the brush creates as snapping twigs and the crunching of dried leaves fill the air around me. I fire a second time and miss.

Angered at how my skill seems to have lessened from lack of use and training, I turn and continue charging through the wilderness, running parallel to the boar's trajectory, hoping to cut it off. Its feet pound the ground as it grunts from the exertion of its escape, while I increase my speed, turn, and run up the trunk of a fallen tree before leaping from its tip and landing on the ground in front of my prey. I stand up, raise my bow, and take aim, releasing the air from within my lungs as I focus on the wild animal running straight for me. I release the arrow. It sails through the air, hitting its mark, and the boar drops to the ground, sliding across the dirt, until it reaches my feet. I reach down to retrieve my arrow when I notice another sticking out of the animal and Perce steps out into the open.

"The kill is mine," I say, not liking the fact that I might have been beaten.

"How do you know my arrow didn't strike the beast first?" he asks, toying with me.

"How do you know it did?" I reply. "Where did you come from?"

"I was waiting here."

I glare at him.

"I knew that the boar's den is near here, and it always runs back to its home when frightened. I'd been tracking it for a while."

"You cheated."

"Or, I used preexisting knowledge to achieve my goal."

"Semantics."

Perce yanks his arrow out of the animal. "I'll give you half my earnings, if that will make you feel better."

"You sell the meat?"

"I sell it to the butcher, who sells the meat in his shop."

Perce stops speaking and the smug look on his face disappears when he glances at the breastplate that has been wrapped around my thigh. One of the straps broke free during my pursuit of the boar and dangles from my leg. I pull it back up and secure it around my thigh, hoping that it hasn't been off long enough to allow anyone from Arel to find me, but moments later, my fears are proven valid.

Something snaps, filling the area around us, as an arbiter in full body armor steps out from behind a tree, pointing his weapon at us. I raise my bow and fire an arrow at him, striking him in the neck. Another jumps out from his place of hiding and Perce fires an arrow at him, but it bounces off his armor as he raises his weapon and aims. Before the arbiter fires, I tackle Perce and shove him into the trees, taking cover as gunfire strikes the foliage around us, chipping off bits of bark and showering us in a storm of falling splinters. I motion for him to go in a certain direction, while I go in the other, hoping to outflank the arbiter firing at us. Understanding my motives, we split up.

I creep through the woods, ducking behind brush and tree trunks in an effort to remain hidden, while the arbiter stalks around, pacing the area, hunting for me. His boots crush anything unfortunate enough to be beneath them while images of the trees dot the mirrored surface of his helmet, and I skulk through the brush, taking care to not make a sound as I circle around him until his back is to me. Using myself as bait, I jump out into the open and whistle, forcing the arbiter to spin around, and I imagine the pleased grin on his face when he sees me, but before he can squeeze the trigger, Perce bursts from the trees and swings his bow at the man, striking him in the back of the neck. The man tumbles over, and Perce fires two arrows into his neck, stopping his movements.

"How many more do you think are out there?" he says.

I shake my head. "I'm surprised they only sent two. Usually…"

My voice trails off as two aircraft fly overhead, and the sound of their engines fill our ears as we watch them head for Perce's home in dismay. Arel not only found me, but also intends to make an example of those who helped me.

I charge through the trees, shoving dangling branches out of my path; their broad leaves try to slow me down and prevent me from reaching my goal as I chase after the aircraft, following their flight path on foot, dreading what I will find. My right foot lands on an upturned root that has rotted through, breaking it into pieces, mirroring what will soon be left of Perce's home. I do not know what I will do when I arrive; I only know that I cannot sit back and allow more innocents to die because of me. Distant screams seep through the dense wilderness and to my ears, propelling me onward as I increase my speed to the point where I almost trip because I am moving too fast. Thorny bushes lie in my path. Refusing to slow down, I jump at a low hanging vine, grab it, and swing myself over the natural barricade, landing on one knee before jumping up and continuing as the sounds of people crying out in pain grow stronger, before I burst from the line of trees and into the open, where I pause. Perce's city, his home, burns as Arelian arbiters, dressed in body armor and armed with flame throwers, set the area ablaze.

Leaving my common sense behind, I plunge into the foray and raise my bow as I take aim at one arbiter before firing. My arrow hits its mark and fuel canisters burst, covering the arbiter as the fire spreads over her body, and she flails about as the flames consume her until she drops to the ground. Another arbiter spews fire as people flee its wrath, hoping to escape, only to be caught and devoured by it. Once again, I raise my bow and fire. The arbiter grips his neck as my arrow pierces it—the weakest point in all Arelian body armor—and he grips it as blood squirts between his fingers before collapsing to the ground. I rush for him and tear at the straps of the flamethrower wrapped around his shoulders, trying to free it from his dead weight. A click sounds behind me. Cursing my forgetfulness to make certain no one snuck up behind me, I turn my head and look at my reflection in the helmet of an arbiter leering over me with a pistol pointed at my head, but before either of us can react, a hatchet soars through the air and nestles into the arbiter's head. He drops to the ground as I finish freeing the flamethrower from the other, while Perce appears beside me and rips his hatchet free.

"Help me with this," I say as I tug at the protective gear of the arbiter with the flamethrower, and he does.

I put the protective gear on and pick up the flamethrower, but nothing happens when I squeeze the trigger. Upon further inspection, I realize that it also has a biometric sensor on it, preventing anyone but the arbiter assigned to it from using it. I examine the dead arbiter's hands. Of course. The gloves he wears are made from specialized material that is thin enough for the sensors to read his fingerprints, while providing some protection from the heat of the flamethrower itself. More screams reach my ears as black smoke fills the area and fire rages through the streets of the city. Getting an idea, I snatch the hatchet from Perce and hack off the index finger of the right hand of the dead arbiter before handing it back to him.

"Save any you can," I tell him.

"What are you doing?" he stops me.

"What I have to."

Gripping the severed finger, I lift the flamethrower and take aim at the arbiters before me as they burn their way through the city, and press the trigger. It works. The biometric sensors read the print of the severed finger and fire bursts from the nozzle, streaking across the cityscape, coating any unfortunate enough to be in its path. More screams reach my ears as people try to flee the onslaught, and I hug the flamethrower close as I charge through the city and up a flight of stone steps, blackened from ash and scorching flames, hurrying down a walkway as the panicked cries of helpless people grow louder, stopping when I see four arbiters with flamethrowers spraying people with their fiery inferno, not caring who dies or who lives: they only care about their orders. I take aim and squeeze the trigger, bracing myself as fire shoots from the nozzle of my flamethrower, covering the four arbiters in front of me. Three of them drop their weapons and fall to the ground, writhing in agony as fire consumes them, hiding their bodies from the world, but the fourth manages to turn around and face me. Despite the pain he must be in, he aims his flamethrower at me and fires, forcing me to dive behind a brick wall for cover, hunkering behind it as fire rages around it, trying to get to me, searing my skin with its intense heat before ceasing.

Cautious, I peer around the wall and crawl out from behind it as I realize that the one arbiter now lies on the ground. Curious, I move over to him, noticing that half of his head is missing after being struck by the bullet from a sniper's rifle. Perce. Once again, he has saved my life. I glance around, looking for him, knowing that I will not find him: a good sniper is never seen, and you do not know he is there until after you are dead.

I charge down a series of steps and to a lower part of the city, helping any who need it as they try to escape, telling them to get out and head for the trees. A man yells for help. I rush for him.

"My leg," he says to me.

I look back at his leg. It's caught in some wire. Boots clomp the pavement behind me. Turning around, I spot an arbiter and raise my flamethrower, squeezing the trigger, but nothing happens. I'm out of fuel. The arbiter smiles, pleased that I am defenseless, as she draws closer, raising her saber. Though not standard issue, some arbiters carry sabers, preferring them over more modern weapons. She swings it at me, but I bring up the flamethrower, blocking her attack. Undeterred, she swings again, forcing me to block a second time. Annoyed, I keep my eyes on her as she paces in front of me, looking at me as though I am nothing more than an ant to be stomped on and eradicated for the crime of existing. Something gleams in the shadowed sunlight, and I watch as she unsheathes a second saber and swipes the air with both of them, displaying her skill. She charges, raising her sabers, and brings them down on me, while I raise my flamethrower to block, and my knees buckle from the force of her attack. She brings one saber down to try and strike my leg, but I twist the nozzle of the flamethrower to stop her, while keeping the other blade from reaching my face, and before she can react, I let go and ram my shoulder into her chest, pushing her back and startling her.

Once again, she paces before me, dragging the tips of her sabers through the ash on the pavement with a smirk on her face, sizing me up, and realizing that I will not be that easy to put down. She rushes for me, thrusting one of her sabers forward, forcing me to dodge to the side to avoid her attack, while with her other blade, she slices one of the straps of the fuel canister on my back, and it drops to the side as it swings from the one strap that is still intact. She swings at me again, and I drop the nozzle of the flamethrower before seizing the fuel canister and thrusting it outward, stopping her blades from striking me in the chest. She charges again, and again I thrust the canister outward, blocking her attack, while jumping at her at the same time and forcing her to fall backward onto the ground, dropping her sabers; they skitter across the ground, sending sharp tones in the air that mingle with the screams and explosions surrounding us.

Enraged, she scrambles for me, but my feet get caught in the hose attaching the nozzle and the fuel canister, causing me to lose my balance, making it easier for her to knock me down as she tackles my legs. I swing the fuel canister at her, striking her in the shoulder, receiving a fist to my face in response. I bring the fuel canister up again, attempting to hit her in the head, but she blocks, knocking it from my hands and sending it flying away, and as I try to think of my next move, she jams her elbow into my chest before scrambling away for her weapons. I snatch her foot. She slams her other into my face, forcing me to release her.

Dazed, I glance up as a single Arelian aircraft flies overhead, heading for the central part of the city, while the rumble of an armored transport reaches my ears. The glint of steel snaps me out of my fog as my opponent brings the blade of her saber down upon me, and I roll out of the way before it sinks into my neck, and as she raises her weapon again, I ram my foot into her ankle, causing it to buckle beneath her. I spot the other saber. As she struggles to get up, I hurry for it, but she predicts my actions and swings her blade at me, forcing me to dive beneath it and roll across the ground, until I reach my goal. Elation fills me when my fingers wrap around the small bumps on the hilt of the weapon, and I bring it up in time to block another attack.

I stare into her narrowed eyes as they convey her unspoken desire for me to die. I throw her off me. We stand up, circling each other, glaring at one another, knowing that only one will leave here today, and I have no intention of letting it be her. She charges, but her injured ankle makes her falter, allowing me the opportunity to dodge her strike, twist around, and swipe my blade across her outer thigh. She staggers back. I ready my stance, holding my saber in front of me, ready for her next attack. She does not disappoint. She rushes for me. I block, but she feigns her attack, tricking me, and before I realize it, she swipes her blade beneath my shoulder, and the stinging pain of having been sliced rushes up my arm. She charges again, forcing me to skip backwards as I block attack after attack, until I trip over a rock and fall to the ground, but before I can get up, she rams her knee into my face. Stunned, I slump over as I kneel on the hard pavement, surrounded by chaos.

Dirt crunches behind me as she takes a step for me. In an instant, I twist around, throwing myself on my back, and hold the saber in my hands straight in the air as it plunges into her diaphragm, stopping her final attack. Her eyes widen in shock and disbelief before closing, never to open again. I throw her to the ground, wiping the blade clean on her uniform, and rise to my full height as a wall of fire stretches across the center of the city. The whine of a drone prickles my ears. I glance at it, unsurprised by its presence—Arel loves recording their moments of victory—and slam it into the ground with my saber, breaking it.

I turn back to the man who is trapped, hurrying toward him. He struggles against the wire entangling his leg, and the more he pulls at it, the more it digs into his skin. I motion for him to hold still as I slip the blade of the saber between his skin and the wire, cutting it. Once freed, he hurries to his feet and thanks me.

"Get out of here," I tell him. "Get to the trees and take any you can with you!"

He thanks me again and runs off, disappearing behind a veil of gray smoke.

Something whizzes past me, forcing me to turn around in time to watch as an arbiter is thrown from his feet due to the impact of a high caliber round. Another runs for me. I dodge the attack, slicing his leg with my saber before punching him in the face, using the hilt of the blade to add to the impact. A sniper's bullet strikes a sign not far from me, diverting my attention to the armored transports with .50 caliber machine guns mounted on them, rolling into the city. I dart off, heading for cover, wondering where Perce was when the female arbiter attacked me, unless he had to change his vantage point because of the attacks by the Arelian aircraft. I haven't time to think about that now as I watch the armored transports approach.

A group of armed people from the city run up, forming two lines—the front line drops to their knees, while the rear remains standing—and takes aim at the arbiters manning the guns upon the armored transports and fire. When one arbiter falls, another takes his place, while an Arelian aircraft dips low and heads toward them, and a sinking feeling fills my stomach as I know what comes next.

"Get down!" I yell at them.

They scramble for cover as a barrage of bullets rain down upon them: some escape, while others are torn apart and bits of their flesh litter the pavement before me, forming rivers of bright red blood. Someone whistles at me, and as I turn toward it, a man tosses me a semi-automatic rifle.

"We need to take out those gunners," I say to him, pointing at the armored transports with the mounted machine guns.

"How?" he asks.

Perce. With his skills, he could pick them off one by one, but how do I get his attention? As I consider my options, I settle upon the stupidest idea imaginable, but it may be my only option, and

I jump out into the open, waving my arms and pointing at the armored transports before diving back behind cover.

"Are you crazy?" the man shouts at me as a few rounds miss me.

I laugh.

A hailstorm of bullets ravages the wall I and others hide behind before stopping all the sudden. Peeking around the corner, I spot the body of the arbiter that had manned the machine gun. Another jumps up to take his place but falls before he reaches it. Either Perce saw my stunt, or he shared my thoughts.

I watch the armored transports continue to move toward the center of the city and get an idea. "Take two men and head in that direction," I say to the man. "You two"—I point at two others—"come with me!"

"What..."

"We're outflanking them."

Understanding me, the man taps two people on the shoulder and motions for them to follow him. Once gone, I look at the two I ordered with me, and they nod their head, indicating that they are with me, for the moment. We dart out of our hiding place and skid across the pavement in front of the transport until we reach the other side of the opening and dash behind cover again. Wasting no time, we burst out, running parallel to the transports as we head for their sides, diving behind cover to avoid detection as explosions ricochet throughout the city, causing bits of glass and debris to crash around us, coating us, but we refuse to stop. I motion for them to pause, and they do as I watch the armored vehicles continue moving forward, unaware of our presence.

"Go!" I hiss, and we dash through the rubble, before ducking behind cover again.

I crane my neck to get a good look, pleased that we are now behind one of the transports, where its weakest point is. A sniper's bullet strikes an arbiter manning the gun on one of the transports.

"Now!" I yell.

We jump out and take aim at the transport in front of us, releasing a barrage of gunfire, until the arbiter operating the mounted machine gun drops over the side and onto the ground. One of those with me falls over with a hole in her back.

"Sniper!" I scream as I dive behind the remains of a wall.

Dammit! I should have known that they would have brought their own sniper. I try peeking over the wall, but a bullet striking the edge of it near my face forces me to drop back down behind it. Looking around, I realize that the other that had accompanied me did not make it as I spot his body in the middle of the street, but any sympathy for his demise vanishes as the distant whine of an aircraft approaches, preparing to release its own terror upon the city. Trapped between enemy aircraft and a sniper's rifle, my mind races for a solution. More gunfire pelts the wall, and I crawl on my stomach to get away as I look for a better solution, while bits of concrete pelt the ground around me, while the razor edges of broken glass cut into my palms and poke through the sleeves of my jacket, leaving marks on my elbows.

I hear water.

The canal! I'm not far from it. The aircraft draws closer, preparing to drop its bomb on my location, forcing me to increase my speed. Knowing that I have little choice, I jump to my feet and run for the canal as bullets pelt the area around me before ceasing, almost as though something made it stop, but I haven't time to think about it as I focus my attention on reaching the canal before the aircraft reaches me. I stretch out my legs, forcing them to move as fast as they can, and ignore the burning pain in them as they threaten to cease, while the aircraft's engines grow louder until their roar pounds my eardrums to the point when I hear nothing else, not even my own pulse thudding in my neck. Almost there. It drops its bomb. Sucking air into my lungs, I command them to hold onto it as I make a final sprint to the canal and leap off the edge, crashing into the water below, allowing myself to sink as a wall of fire explodes over the water, engulfing any unlucky enough to get in its way. My lungs beg me for relief, but I hold onto the air already contained within them, willing them to obey me as I swim underneath the flames, kicking as hard as I can to propel myself through the water as my movements send rhythmic, yet muffled, sounds to my ears, until I look up and see nothing above me. Once in the clear, I kick for the surface and gasp as my head bursts through and the desperation of my lungs win out. Burning embers float around me, dancing in the breeze as they circle around in a sort of waltz with the drifting smoke, now gray instead of white, that forms a cage around me before settling on the water's surface.

I swim to the edge of the canal and try to pull myself out, but my hands slip on the smooth rocks (sanded and shaped to give it character) that form its edge. I thrust my hand up again, but it slips a second time. Desperate to get out—I cannot stay here—I splash about, searching for any sort of opening that will allow one to escape the canal, when a hand enters my peripheral vision. Curious, I glance at the face it belongs to and almost sink beneath the surface from shock: Sigal stares back at me. I take his hand and he yanks me out of the water and onto the bank of the canal.

"Never thought I'd see you again," he says to me.

"How..." I begin, forgetting the raging war around us as my mind tries to grapple with the fact that he stands before me; I haven't seen him since the day I helped him and his family escape.

"That is a long story," he says. "We need to get you out of here."

He starts to help me up as water drips from my clothing, pooling around me and mixing with the blood of those who have fallen, but I stop him the moment the sound of an Arelian aircraft reaches my ears: it's turning for another pass, and if we do not destroy it, it will end us all. My mind races for a solution, knowing that the weapons in Sigal's and my current possession will not be enough. We need...

The rumbling of an armored transport vibrates the ground, and

I jerk my head in its direction, spotting one not far from us, unaware of our position, as it eases its way through the city, searching for targets.

"I need to get to that transport," I say.

"What?"

"If you take out their strongest weapons, they will leave."

Arel always searches for the weakest and easiest targets, but if we prove too troublesome, they will fall back to regroup, buying time. But this does not look like a mission of conquest, but one of terror: weaken your enemy so that they cannot attack you, but let them live with their shame as they rebuild, so that you can rob them again.

Sigal hands me a pistol, and I take it.

"Take out their transports," I say before darting off.

I keep my eyes focused on the transport as I run for it, avoiding the bullets that rage around me, using the smoke that hangs in the air, forming a barrier of its own, for cover as I race down the walkway past people desperate to escape the terror before them. I shove my way through them, pushing them to the side as I hurry for the transport, knowing that every second counts as the aircraft banks and turns around for another pass. I reach the end of the walkway and enter a small opening where an arbiter with a flamethrower stands ready. My feet slide on the pavement as I come to a halt and dash to my left, diving behind a fresh pile of rubble for cover as flames spew from the nozzle of the flamethrower, threatening to cook me as though I am nothing more than a chicken meant for the roasting pot. The aircraft draws nearer as the transport continues. I'm not far from it. The fires cease. Seizing my chance, I throw myself from my place of hiding, landing on my side and fire, striking the arbiter in the head.

Springing to my feet, I sprint for the transport, not caring as my foot splashes in a puddle near the dead arbiter's head, my mind focused on my mission to stop this terror. I hoist myself over a low bar sticking out of the ground, as I charge for the transport, attacking it from behind. It moves slow and steady through the streets, unable to go much faster as it avoids the fallen sides of buildings, burst pipes, and piles of rubble that once made up a beautiful and habitable city. Picking up the pace, I run up the side of the transport and rip the driver's door open, surprising the arbiter within, but before he can react, I grab his arm and yank him out of the vehicle and onto the broken pavement. I jump off and lean in to punch him, but he grabs my wrist and flings me against the side of the transport as it slows to a crawl before stopping. His hands go for my throat, but I bring my arm up, blocking him, before ramming my elbow into his face. He staggers back two steps, but regains his senses in time to stop me from kicking him in the middle and grabs my leg, lifting me off the ground as he flings me to the side.

Sharp pain grips my side when I land, but I thrust it aside, forcing myself to ignore it, as my training taught me to do, and sit up in time to block him when he tries to kick me, and as I hang on to his foot, I twist it, exposing the back of his knee, and jam my elbow into it, forcing him to the ground. He tries to get up, but I tackle him and backhand him with my pistol before shooting him. He drops to the ground, but I haven't time to think about it as I charge for the transport and jump at it, crawling up its side and to the nest where an arbiter mans the mounted machine gun.

As I reach the top, the arbiter seizes me, awaiting my arrival, and slams me into the machine gun itself, stunning me for a moment. His fist flies for me, but I manage to block it and deliver a blow of my own, receiving a kick in the chest in response. He throws me to the side and I almost fall off, but manage to grab hold of a handhold, but before I can stand back up, the arbiter kicks me in the stomach. Gasping for air, I pull out my pistol, but he seizes my wrist and slams my hand into the metal roof of the transport, trying to force me to release it, but I cling to it, knowing that if I let it go, it will be my end. I raise my leg and ram my knee into his side, causing him to falter, giving me time to pull myself to my hands and knees. He lunges for me, but I thrust my leg out and kick him in the stomach, causing him to stumble backward, until he falls over the side of the transport. As he tries to get up, I aim my pistol and fire, pleased when he falls back down and doesn't move.

The Arelian aircraft is almost here. Its engines grow louder, thundering off the sides of the buildings, causing them to rattle and my chest to vibrate as it approaches, ready to drop another incendiary device that will create another wall of fire. I leap into the machine gun nest and ready it, taking aim at the aircraft as it heads straight for me. I hold my ground. When my sights are lined up, I fire, releasing a hailstorm of bullets that target the aircraft before me, watching as it pummels the cockpit and the wings, pleased when smoke escapes from its engines and it drops to the ground, crashing into the pavement, taking out entire sides of buildings, benches, and lamp posts as it tears into the concrete heading for me.

Abandoning the transport, I run the moment I land on the ground, hurrying for the balconied area that serves as an overlook of the city. The aircraft slides across the ground, approaching fast, sending a plume of dust and debris into the air that covers me as I run away from it, desperate to escape as its engines surround me with their roar, drowning out all else. I refuse to slow down. The balcony nears. I increase my pace. As the aircraft crashes into the armored transport, creating a cloud of fire and shrapnel, I reach the overlook and jump over the railing, leaping for the banner flying near it, and grab the rope. It snaps. Gravity takes its hold as I drop to the ground and swing while clinging to the rope. The glint of metal catches my attention, and I realize that I am headed for a lamppost. The timing must be perfect. Wind blasts my face, causing my eyes to tear as I swing downward toward the lamppost, counting the seconds, until taking a literal leap of faith as I let go of the banner's rope and reach out for the lamppost. I slam into it, but instead of allowing it to stun me, I wrap my arms around it and slide downward, but before I can reach the bottom, an artillery shell strikes it base, and the next thing I know, I'm falling before the hard surface of water breaks my descent. Then, nothing.

How many moments pass remains a mystery, but I hear a distant, yet familiar, voice calling my name, urging me to open my eyes and wake up as water drips from my hair and my clothes, pooling around me once more. I hear my name again, more insistent than before. I want to sleep, to remain unconscious, but thoughts of Chase and Shelia force my eyes to flutter open, and as the world around me comes into focus, I realize that it is Perce's voice urging me to wake up.

"Easy now," he says as I start to sit up.

"The attack..." I begin.

"Over," Perce replies. "We took out their transports, and once that aircraft crashed, they retreated."

A pistol sits by my side. Is it mine, or someone else's? I cannot remember, but reach out and pick it up anyway, checking its chamber: it is mine now.

Angry shouts reach my ears, and Perce helps me stand up, allowing me to lean on him as we walk over to the commotion. We hobble down an alley—what's left of it—and come out in a small courtyard with a line of arbiters on their knees and a pipe sticking out of its center, shooting water into the air, and the harsh sound of it splashing onto the paved stones add to the terse atmosphere as people argue over what to do with the prisoners. Some wish to execute them, while others believe a more humane approach is needed, but I do not care about their wishes as I spot the commanding officer, the marks on his uniform giving him away. I push myself away from Perce and step over to the commanding officer, holding my side as I do, while my pistol bumps against my outer thigh. Hushed silence falls over the gathered crowd as eyes turn away from one another to watch me, and I spot Sigal among them, but I do not care. A drone appears, hovering around me as I move toward the commander. Good. I want Arel to see this. I stop before the commanding officer and he glares at me with venomous eyes, daring me to challenge him, to give him an excuse to fight me and earn his honor back, but I refuse his unspoken request.

"You are in command here," I say; it's a statement, not a question.

He spits at me and a wad of mucus lands on my knee, coating it with its slimy substance.

I aim my pistol at him. "Being captured by the enemy is a sign of weakness," I say to him, repeating a line from one of my instructors at the training facility.

He says nothing.

"Weakness is failure," I continue, "and failure is death."

I squeeze the trigger and never flinch as a hole is blown into his head and he crumples over in a pool of his own blood and brain matter.

I turn my attention to the drone hovering nearby, aim, and fire, pleased when it clatters on the wet pavement, sending sparks into the air.

Molers will understand my message: I'm waiting for him.

Chapter 15

North

The pack on my bed stares at me, mocking me as I stuff it with supplies, hoping that they will be enough to get me through the next three or four days, unsure of how much longer I will be out here in the wilds, or if Molers will even make an appearance. I cannot stay here, that much is certain. Sunlight spills through the small circular window, framed by a wood molding with a floral pattern carved into it, not bold, but somewhat faint, forcing one to search for it as though searching for the answers to a mystery, but the sun exposes its secrets as it lights the room, despite the layer of grime on the glass that tries to block its comforting warmth. Perce had asked me to stay four days to ensure that I am healed and able to travel; I gave him one. I will never be able to repay his kindness, or the fact that he is the only one who will miss my presence.

I finish stuffing some oranges into the pack, pausing for a moment as I remember the time Chase and I snuck out and went to the plebeian quarters of the city, and how I handed one plebeian an orange, and how his skeletal hand took it with caution and gratitude.

Tears well in my eyes, blurring my vision, as I think about Chase and how he is locked in a cold, dark cell, waiting for me to finish this. Such thoughts morph into resolve, and I ram the oranges into the pack before closing it, slinging it over my shoulder before hurrying out of the room, only to be stopped by an outstretched hand holding a small bundle.

"Sigal?" I say, confused by his presence.

"I know how much you liked my pies," he replies with a grin.

I take the small bundle and unwrap it with care, revealing a single slice of fresh baked pecan pie and revel in its aroma of caramelized sugar and roasted pecans.

"How did…"

"Of all the things," Sigal says, "my kitchen was one of the few things left untouched."

"Your family, are they…"

"They're fine."

Relief floods over me, glad that Sigal does not have to suffer their loss.

He hands me another bundle. "You'll need this."

"I can't…"

"I used to think that all arbiters were cruel, mindless, and always subservient to Arel's will. Then, one night, a young arbiter helped me and my family escape, despite the risk to her own life. I never thanked her."

"I think she knows," I say. "Thank you."

I place the bundle in my pack and stop before heading outside.

"Did you ever find Trilya?"

Sigal chuckles. "We may have to build it."

I place a gentle hand on his forearm, wishing I had been more cordial toward him back in Arel, that I tried to get to know him as someone other than the owner of a café that served delicious and delectable food.

"Good-bye, Sigal."

"This is not good-bye," he says to me, "just a temporary parting."

I strap the pack to my back and walk along the rustic, wooden floorboards of the home I have been allowed to stay in during my time in Perce's city, noting that they had just been swept. As I step outside, I try to think of where I should go, which direction I should head in, not knowing Molers' exact location, assuming he was even dumped in the wilds like I was, but the snorting of a horse stops my wonderings as I look up to see two of them saddled and ready to go, with Perce holding onto the reigns.

"What's this?" I ask.

"You do know what a horse is," Perce teases.

I roll my eyes. "Of course, I know what a horse is, but what is all this?"

"The wilds have some of the toughest terrain, leaving two options if you want to get someplace without using the roads: on foot or by horse. Since you need to travel at a fast pace, the horse is your better option."

Sigal steps outside and stops when he sees the horses, admiring them both and the way the sun's light accentuates their well-formed muscles.

"I only need one," I say to Perce.

"I'm coming with you," Perce replies.

He cuts me off before I can protest.

"The area you are traversing through is rough and difficult to navigate, even for someone who has been through it before."

"But that would be cheating," I say. "The Rite of Conquest is something I must win on my own."

"From what I have observed, your opponent isn't playing by the rules."

Perce has me there: Molers has not been abiding by the rules since this entire thing began. I have been hunted by other arbiters, something that is not part of the Rite of Conquest, and as far as I am aware, Molers hasn't been forced to survive in the wilds like I have.

"I call it evening the playing field," Perce continues.

Hating to admit it, I amble over to one of the horses and touch its muzzle, admiring the way the splotches of white mingle with the brown fur, forming a geometrical design that is no one's equal. The animal snorts and pushes its muzzle into my palm as I stroke it.

"She likes you," says Sigal.

"Her name is Bessy," Perce tells me.

"Bessy?" I raise an eyebrow.

Perce shrugs his shoulders. "She's a good horse and will never lead you astray, and is very protective of her rider. She'll treat you well."

"I ride alone," I say.

Perce mounts his horse. "Of course, you do, and I'm coming with you."

"Some would say that that is the opposite of riding alone," Sigal mutters under his breath.

"For a little way. I understand that you must finish this alone, in the end," Perce says. "Where are you headed?"

I think about the question for a moment, unsure of where to go or where I will find Molers, but perhaps, I need to let him find me. I remember Renal's advice: head north.

"North," I say.

Perce's face tightens, but he does not question me.

"All you do is put your left foot in that stirrup there..." Perce begins, but before he can finish, I place my foot in the stirrup, lift myself up, and settle into the saddle.

Sigal laughs. "She's an arbiter, son. There isn't much she can't do."

I smile. Most arbiters are not accomplished horse riders, but some are. While at the training facility, an instructor convinced the council to allow him to teach some recruits horseback riding. I was considered too young, but snuck into the class anyway, and on my tenth time being caught, the instructor relented and allowed me to stay. I tried to get Faya to join, but she wanted nothing to do with it. For two years, we trained with horses until the council decided to end the class.

"Thank you," I tell Sigal.

He approaches me before speaking. "If you need my help, send me word, and I will come."

"You don't..."

"I owe you everything. If it wasn't for you, my family would be dead."

"In Arel, devotion to family is considered weakness, but now..."

"Weakness is failure; failure is death: this is the mantra you arbiters are taught, but, perhaps, you should give yourself a new one," says Sigal.

"What?"

"He told me about why you have chosen to initiate the Rite of Conquest," Sigal says, pointing at Perce. "Arel would want you to believe that your devotion to the ones you care for is weakness, but that is not how I see it. I see it as a strength."

"So, what would your mantra be?" I ask.

"You possess a strength inside that most only dream of, and such strength is power, and it is life. Failure leads to introspection, which leads to strength, and strength is life."

"A cook, turned philosopher," I tease him.

"It does leave one time to be alone with their thoughts," Sigal says.

"Tell your family good-bye for me," I say.

"I will tell them that you said hello. You can say good-bye to them in person."

I tug at the reins and bump the horse with my heel to start her trotting before breaking her into a full gallop as I race through the mangled streets of the city, leaping over charred remains of a transport that is now missing its mounted gun, with Perce right behind me as we burst through what is left of the front gate, wasting no time: Chase and Sheila are waiting for me to end this. The hooves of the horses pound the hardened ground, while pebbles skitter to the side as we race down an open road, sending a trail of dust into the sky that mingles with a dust devil as the wind carries it away from us. I pull back on the reins, allowing Perce to take the lead, and he guides his horse off the road and into the thick woods lining them. I follow him. At first, I tug at the reins to direct my horse through the intertwined trees that form a wall of deadened leaves void of color and spiked branches that claw at the clothing of any who stray too near, but soon learn that Bessy knows her way as she steps over fallen branches threatening to trip unsuspecting travelers and forges a path through brambles without receiving a single scratch. The horses slow to a walk as they navigate around suffocating brush and moss-covered boulders that are waist high and appear to crawl out of the ground in an effort to seek refuge in the faint sunlight that spills through the tiny cracks within the leafy canopy. I watch as a brown rabbit cleans its ears before darting off to avoid our presence and spot the tip of a fox's tail as it skulks away, angered at our interruption of his meal, and a part of me smiles, glad to have spared the rabbit a terrible fate that day.

Perce steers his horse toward an incline, making soft clomps on the leaf-colored ground as it ambles up the hill where the trees thin out, allowing more sunlight to poke through. My horse snorts as I urge her to follow, but she does not protest too much as she starts up the hill, carrying me underneath dull leaves devoid of color, except for the few that have a hint of red or orange, but not vibrant as one would expect when the seasons start to change, and not the bright green that I am used to seeing. I reach up and touch one, pinching it between my thumb and forefinger, and it breaks free of the tree's hold, allowing me to hold it for a minute as I admire the veins running through it, but it crumbles and is carried away by the breeze, reminding me that life is as fleeting out here as it is back in Arel. I glance at the gnarled trunk of the tree and notice sap oozing down its rotted bark, almost as though it is bleeding to death and no creature, not even the ants, wants any part of it.

"The trees here are sick," Perce says, interrupting my musings.

"Do you know why?"

He shakes his head. "Some say that Arel poisoned this land so that none would be able to survive here."

"The wildlife seems to do okay."

"They've adapted, as did we."

We? How long have Perce's people lived here in these parts of the wildlands, and how long have they had to stave off attacks by Arel? The answer to my questions never come as Perce kicks his horse and hurries to the crest of the hill, and I follow after, him, not wanting to be left behind.

"There," he says, pointing at a clearing where trees and grass refuse to grow, leaving behind barren rock, some of which form spikes stretching upward to the sky as though they hope to touch it.

"We go through there," he says.

"What is it?" I ask.

"A labyrinth. Watch yourself, though. Those rocks will skewer anyone who falls on them, but there is a path through there."

"How did you learn of this path?" There is no chance that Perce happens to know a way through a maze of rock by accident.

"I would have died otherwise," Perce replies, not answering my question. "Are you certain you must go north?"

"Yes." Renal told me to, and I've no reason to believe he would lead me astray.

"That is interesting."

"Why?"

"There is an abandoned Arelian outpost just north of here. It hasn't been used in over twenty-five years. Very few know of its existence. Fewer still are alive to tell anyone about it."

"What happened to those stationed at that outpost?" I ask as a sinking feeling fills the pit of my stomach, warning me that I already know the answer.

Perce looks me in the eye before speaking. "They were slaughtered."

"By whom?"

"Another clan, more ruthless and cruel than anything you will have ever met. They attacked the outpost, and though the Arelians there made a valiant stand, after three days of constant siege, the barbarians broke through the front gates. They took no prisoners."

"Three days? Did they not send for help?"

"They did," replies Perce, "but Arel never responded."

"You said that your father left Arel, but it wasn't the city he left, was it?"

"He was one that survived that day. Some called him a coward. Others said that he was prudent. He told me that the barbarians broke through while he held a fellow arbiter in his hands, and she perished as they swarmed the outpost. He knew it was over, so he played dead, until he could escape."

I look out at the labyrinth of rock.

"The question is: who told you?"

I think back to Renal's insistence that I head north, at how he is able to bend the rules, at how other arbiters make certain to not anger him, and at how Molers always backs down in his presence. Renal may be a marshal, but he is also so much more.

"Another survivor," I say as I tug at the reins and urge my horse to continue down the slope and toward the labyrinth.

Granite spires greet us as we enter the labyrinth—some as tall as buildings, while others are the height of a man or shorter, but each with a sharp point that will skewer any unfortunate enough to fall upon them—but it is not their spear-like points that disturb me most: it's the silence. Nothing greets my ears, not even the whisper of the wind as I guide my horse into the valley of rocky spires (no crickets, cicadas, or even the buzzing of flies), just eerie silence—not even a whistling in my ears—as though life has been extinguished here, leaving nothing more than a graveyard of stone, devoid of any semblance of joy. Pure silence. My anxiety rises as the lack of sounds permeates every fiber of my being, reminding me that I have entered a place forbidden to all. Even the sunlight is not welcomed here as gray soil absorbs it, refusing to allow it to illuminate our path and provide the smallest amount of comfort, choosing instead to plunge us into a shadowed world of mystique and foreboding.

The hooves of the horses clomp on the rocky ground, sending tiny pebbles clacking down a small slope as we ease our way through the rocky spires. Perce leads us through a narrow passageway before veering to the right, only to make an immediate left afterward. I follow, keeping my grip tight on the reins of my horse, wondering how he knows where to go as my sense of direction left me the moment we entered this forsaken place. He makes another left, and I steer my horse, matching his movements, until…

He stops. Curious, I open my mouth to say something, but stop when Perce jumps to the ground and kneels before one of the spires, brushing away some of the blackened silt, exposing a small spot of green, and I stare at it, mesmerized by the single speck of color in this place.

"How…" I begin, but Perce cuts me off.

"There is a river that flows beneath here, and where it flows is where patches of moss grow, but the wind always covers it as though it wishes to conceal the labyrinth's secrets." He looks at me with a grin. "We're following the river. This is what my father discovered when he came through here all those years ago, even if it was an accident."

An underground river. That explains it. Bessy sidesteps, agitated by the silence of the labyrinth, and my leg bumps into one of the spires, allowing its razor edges to tear through my pants and into my leg, drawing a trickle of blood. I wince from the sting, but wipe away the droplets of blood, choosing to ignore its discomfort and refusing to show weakness in front of Perce.

"Careful," he reminds me, "these rocks will impale any who fall upon them."

He leaps back on his horse and steers it further into the maze of silence with me trailing behind, wishing that my time in this place ends soon.

Anxiety builds within me with each passing second as our horses follow our orders and carry us through the maze of lifeless rock while the echo of complete silence wears on me, weighing on my mind and forcing me to consider that I may never hear the sounds of nature again. I am not used to this. Even Arel had its usual sounds: the trolley, the people hurrying to their predetermined destinations, an arbiter's whistle, and the railcar—all familiar, and all in a place where life exists; outside the city are the sounds of crickets, the wind through the tall grass, and the growl of the puma; but here, there is nothing, and the more I am surrounded by this nothingness, the more I wonder if I have died and been denied peace in the afterlife. My horse snorts and my ears welcome it as it breaks the monotony of the eerie stillness that plagues this place. Perce continues checking for the moss and directs me as though he is not bothered by the lack of life here, or perhaps he is better at ignoring its pervasiveness, but it wears on my nerves, making me wish that something would happen and remind me that I breathe.

Clouds settle on the horizon, making an already dreary place seem even darker and more foreboding. A low rumble echoes across the land, funneled by the spires and to my ears, telling me that the universe heard my internal thoughts and has granted my wish, but not in the way I intended. Another roll of thunder passes over the land and to my ears as a distant flash of light brightens the horizon for a second before disappearing. A storm is coming.

"Not again," I whisper to myself as I remember the last one.

Perce pauses his horse and studies the horizon and the impending storm. "We need to move. If it rains, this entire place will flood and drown us both!"

He kicks his horse, encouraging it to move faster through the morass as he makes turn after turn, making me wonder if his hurried movements will force us to become lost as I follow him, hugging my horse in an effort to keep up. The storm draws nearer, approaching fast as it covers the land with its wrath, until it is upon us. Lightning strikes the top of a spire, breaking its tip and sending boulders down upon us as they plummet to the ground and pummel anything that get in their way and split into multiple pieces—small projectiles that shoot in every direction in search of an unsuspecting target—as they strike the ground.

My horse jumps and threatens to stop as rocks crash around me, but I press my heels into her side, urging her to keep going, or we will both perish. The sky flashes to life in a dizzying fashion as darkness turns to light over and over again, never allowing my eyes to adjust or my mind to confirm the time of day, until darkness looms again as the clouds grow thicker and bulkier, until… silence.

I pause for a moment, trying to understand this latest development, while pure instinct warns me to move, to seek shelter because the worst is yet to come, and the longer I listen to the stillness within the air, the sounds of ice striking metal reaches me—soft at first, followed by a dark curtain that draws nearer, until its earsplitting noise threatens to burst my head open as a downpour engulfs me, drenching my clothes and transforming them into heavy weights.

Lightning strikes another spire, sending sparks and rock in a 360-degree radius, frightening my horse and forcing me to cling to the reins as I push her to run after Perce. Blinding rain stings my face as we hurry through the labyrinth of rock, twisting and turning and hoping that we are not lost as I can no longer see Perce through the rain's thick curtain as it continues to pummel the ground, causing water to pool around the horse's ankles and panic to settle in. Two bolts of lightning strike the spire next to us, showering us with more rock and electricity, causing my horse to rear up on her hind legs in fear, and despite my efforts to calm her, she flings me off her back, and I crash onto the ground, wincing as the sharp edges of rock dig through my jacket and into my skin. By the time I regain my sense, my horse is gone.

"Bessy!" I yell, though I know it is pointless.

Fear dictates her movements and she has run off, seeking safety. Water covers my legs as I sit on the ground with lightning stretching across the sky above me. Knowing that I cannot stay here, I jump to my feet and run in the direction I last saw Perce, hoping to find him, but as I charge through the maze in a frantic search for my only salvation in this desolate place, I realize that he is nowhere to be found, and I am lost.

"Perce!" I scream, but receive no response.

Water reaches my calves as the deluge continues, promising to flood the entire area and drown me with it as I slosh around in the water, desperate to find my way out of this place, turning in circles, wondering where I am and how I am to get out when I stop. A few yards away from me is a small patch of green, revealed when the water washed away some of the soil. Water splashes around me as I hurry toward it and reach down to touch its semi-silky texture. Moss. What was it Perce had said about the moss? It grows where the river flows beneath. As though to help me along, the dark clouds part, allowing the sun to poke through for a few seconds, telling me which direction is north, before being forced back into its prison.

Invigorated, I charge through the labyrinth, darting around the razor edges of the spires as I force my way through the water as it comes up past my knees, growing higher by the second. I plunge into the water and rub away some of the rock, revealing a small patch of moss. Good. I am on the right track. As my legs grow sluggish in the water, I force them to carry me through it, determined to get out of this maze before it drowns me. I kick away another pile of rock, unveiling more moss. My vigor renewed, I trudge onward, plowing my way through the water, but as it rises, my efforts become more strained, and it becomes more difficult to wade through the current that threatens to drag me under. My foot snags on something and I fall face first into the murky water, gasping as some of it goes down my throat and chokes me as I splash around, desperate to escape it, but unable to as it continues to rise from the unending rain.

A hand appears. Like before, I reach for it and grab it, holding tight as it heaves me out of the water and onto a horse behind Perce. I wrap my arms around his waist as he steers his horse through the maze and the rising flood, and it plows its way through the water as though it has done this numerous times. Whenever the horse hesitates, Perce urges it onward with gentle words and it charges forward, ignoring the water as it reaches its stomach. Minutes pass, but to me, it is an eternity, as we force our way against the current and to the embankment, and elation fills me the moment we start uphill, only to evaporate as I realize the climb we must make. Once we reach the bank, Perce jumps off the horse, and I do the same, before he slaps its behind and sends it running off.

"What are you—"

"The horse will take care of itself!" he shouts back at me. "Climb!"

I dig my heels into the sludge around me as I push my way up the steep hill, forced to crawl on all fours as the mud turns into oozing slime that is slicker than ice and buries my legs beneath its obscurity, threatening to swallow me whole and make me part of its domain. My knees sink further into the muck, but I ignore it and reach into it with my hands, pulling myself upward as tiny rivers of mucilaginous water flow past me and into the raging flood water below. A quick glance at Perce tells me that he struggles as much as I do, but refuses to quit, just like me. My foot slips and my leg shoots out from underneath me, causing me to drop into the slippery mud and slide downward as I try to grab something—anything—to stop my descent, and before I plunge into the water below, I manage to grasp the edge of a boulder, stopping my fall.

Rain pelts my dangling legs as I hang in the air, catching my breath, while the swirling water below me conceals the tops of the spires and beckons me to let go and allow it to feast, but I think of Chase and Sheila and my grip tightens as I haul myself up and back onto the side of the slick hill, pressing my feet into the boulder as I heave my way upward, while slime oozes over me, impeding my efforts, but I refuse to allow it to defeat me. For every foot I climb, I lose four inches as the mud slides beneath me and some of it drops into the water below, their tiny splashes eaten by the current. Perce has reached the top. It isn't far. My muscles strain under my weight as I haul myself through the muck, defying gravity, and inch my way closer to the top, trying not to think about the distance I need to go as I keep my mind focused on my reason for being here, my only reason for succeeding, until…

Perce seizes my hand once I am within reach and hauls me the rest of the way up, and we both roll onto our backs, glad to be out of the labyrinth and away from the floodwater. A horse's snort jerks me to attention, and I bolt upright, finding both horses standing behind us.

"I told you they would take care of themselves," Perce says.

Bessy ambles up to me and nudges my shoulder with her cold, wet nose as if to apologize for abandoning me in the maze.

"You're forgiven, girl," I whisper to her, glad that she is unharmed.

"There is a cave near here," Perce says as he stands up and goes to his horse, inspecting the straps to the saddle, making certain that they are secure.

I force myself to stand up, pushing the thought of how horrendous a sight I must be as mud drops from the tips of my hair and plops on the soggy ground next to my heels as though it is clay waiting to be formed into a piece of pottery. Bessy nudges me again, and I pet her muzzle before taking the reins and walking her along the ridge of the hill that seems to be more of an island as water rages on both sides, forging its own path and carving out its place in the world, while Perce takes the lead.

Water streams down my face, forming snakelike paths in the mud that covers it, while the rain washes the rest away from my skin and my clothes, bathing me in its frigid waters, before allowing me to emerge clean and looking more like myself. The sky grows darker, making me wonder how long we were in the labyrinth, as the rain slows to a trickle and its white noise morphs into a series of soft drops that caress the leaves above us, creating its own melody as we pass underneath as though to encourage us to keep going, despite our wearied state and desire to rest. Bessy snorts, releasing a cloud of vapor in the cold air, and I rub the side of her neck to comfort her as we walk along the ridge—silhouettes in the dusk, searching for relief from the unpredictability and wrath of the wilds.

"This way," Perce says, as he points to what looks like a black hole in the side of a cliff; its edges remind me of the time Chase and I were lost in the wilds and were forced to climb a rocky face like this to survive, and of the time I first met Perce as he helped me save Chase from certain death.

He has never led me astray, so I follow him to this shadowed hole as he vanishes behind a curtain of dangling vines that sway in the chilled wind, stepping through them as though entering a new world. The closer I get to the dark shape, the more it takes on the appearance of a cave, a place of refuge from the weather, and from possible enemies lurking in the woods. As I continue my trek after Perce, I check the leather strap, with lead plates sewn into it, around my thigh, ensuring that it is still secure and blocking the signal from my tracker; though, this storm will make tracking me difficult. I smile at the thought. Perfect.

Once we reach the opening to the cave, Perce ushers me inside, and I do as he bids, taking Bessy with me as I feel the side of the cavern and navigate my way in the darkness. Something flops behind me, forcing me to spin around and watch as Perce drops a blind of sorts, made from vines and broad leaves braided together to form a camouflage and conceal the entrance. He's been here before. He steps though the cavern with ease, going to a firepit that had been dug out, filling it with dried wood and starting a fire, confirming my suspicions. As the flames spring to life, the molded lines (soft and curving as they run from the ceiling to ground, almost like tiny roadways within the black rock) within the cavern walls showcase themselves in the dancing orange flames, giving the place some character and making it seem more homier than one would believe possible.

"This is your camp," I say as Perce tosses me a pouch filled with jerky and dried dates.

"I have many camps," he replies, pulling hay from a storage bin for the horses to munch on.

"You don't spend much time in your city," I say.

Perce nestles by the fire opposite me and chews on a dried fig.

"No. I prefer the wilds. Out here, no one judges you because of your parentage or your appearance. All you need out here are your wits, your courage, and fortitude. The wilds reward those who respect it."

"Doesn't your grandmother miss you?" I ask.

"I'm sure she does," Perce says with sadness. "I'm certain she is worried about me now, but she knows that I become restless when I am home. She tried to make a home for me when my parents... But I will never be accepted. My father was Arelian, whose skin was darker than the night, and my mother's matched the snow, so I am called half-breed."

"Are you sure they are all like that and it's not your perception of them? Arbiters are not loved in Arel, and for good reason. And though most treat me as though I am nothing more than a machine trained to kill, a few have seen me for more than that, not as the arbiter, but as Noni."

I think back to Sigal; he never treated me as some mindless drone trained to execute any who challenge Arel's rule, but as an individual.

Perce laughs. "My father used to say the same. He never cared about the whispers behind his back. He loved my mother and he loved me; we were world enough for him."

"What happened?" I ask, sensing a note of sadness when Perce talks about his family.

"He died, protecting me."

"You said he died of grief."

"In a way that's true, but it's not the whole truth."

"You don't need to..." I begin, wishing I could take my question back, knowing that I should not have pried, but Perce cuts me off.

"During my sixteenth year, we had all gone out of the city to enjoy a beautiful day. My father loved roaming the wilds and wanted to show the both of us the most beautiful place he had found: a waterfall that seemed to change colors as the sun shone upon it. My mother had been ill and he thought this would be good for her. We made a day of it and had a picnic. It was one of the best times of my life. On the way home, we ran into Arelians on patrol. I don't know why they were so far away from Arel. Perhaps they were searching for defectors. They shot my mother. She died before she hit the ground. And we ran. My father shoved me into some foliage.

"'Stay here, boy,' he told me. I protested, but he clocked me on the chin before running off."

"He led them away from me, and in the end, they caught up with him, and I heard the shots. I don't know how long I stayed in the brush before crawling out. I found my mother first, and closed her eyes so she could sleep. I found my father three hundred yards away with the bodies of three arbiters. He put up a good fight, but in the end, it wasn't enough. I closed his eyes so that he could also sleep.

"I made my way back home and my grandmother had their bodies brought back and given a proper burial, and though she tried to make a home for me, I feel more at home out here."

I stay silent. There is nothing I can say, no comfort I can add. He has more cause than some to despise Arelians, and to despise arbiters like me.

"You may think that I should not help you, but my father would believe otherwise. Because of my father, I know that not all Arelians are alike. You are not like those who murdered my parents. I watched you spare the barbarian's life that day and challenge your superior's actions when he killed him. I watched you save the plebeian's life, and not just because you needed his help to survive. And I listened as you told him your name, allowing him to use it, something no arbiter would do. My father taught me that we are also to help those who need it, if we can, but that we are to help those who still have a small bit of their humanity left. You, by your actions, demonstrated that you do."

"You were there?" I sputter in disbelief.

"I was hunting and hid when I heard the commotion."

I think back to the day my convoy was attacked by barbarians, and how, despite being outnumbered, a few of the barbarians around me fell, and not by arbiters' weapons. That was him? It seems that I have a guardian out here in the wilderness.

"You should sleep."

"What about you?" I ask.

"I'll be fine." Perce pulls out a blanket and hands it to me.

I take it, remarking at how a handspun blanket feels so soft in my hands, and wrap it around myself.

"I'll keep watch."

"Don't you ever sleep?"

Perce grins before disappearing through the cave's entrance, leaving me alone with the warmth of the fire as his story fills my mind, making me wonder if we are all interconnected in some way. The fire crackles as I stretch out on the floor, glad to be out of the rain, and before I know it, my eyes close and the world fades from existence.

Chapter 16

Discovery

A musical chirp of a finch breaks its way through my slumber, forcing me to groan as I roll onto my back and open my eyes to find the golden-crested bird perched on a tiny ledge within the cave as its song echoes off the walls, unconcerned about my desire for more sleep. I peer at it, wondering how it had gotten inside, or why it chose this moment to make its presence known. I sit up, knowing that it is time for me to wake and I won't get much more sleep with my tiny companion singing as though it had no care in the world.

"You can stop that now," I tell it. "I'm up."

"And it's about time, too," says Perce, startling me; I did not know he was in the cave with me.

"What time is it?"

"A couple hours past dawn."

The bird's chirps continue, adding background music to our conversation.

"Incessant little guy, isn't he?" I say.

Perce chuckles and walks over to the tiny finch, placing his hand out for the bird to jump into, and it does. "Sometimes, the world wants to remind you that there is still some beauty left in it, despite the ugliness you suffer."

He kneels next to me and holds his hand with the bird in it out, allowing me to pet it, and I do, until the finch jumps onto my finger before giving one last chirp and flying off, disappearing outside the entrance and into the sunlight.

I stand up, folding the blanket and placing it aside in a neat pile before stepping outside where Bessy stands saddled and ready to go.

"I packed your horse for you," Perce says, "with enough provisions to get you through the next two days. This is where I leave you."

I check the saddle bags and notice something familiar within them: a hatchet, the same one that had been tossed to me when I faced Commandant Paq. I pull it out and hold it up.

"Take it. You need it more than me."

"I can't. It's…"

"I promised that I will help you save them," Perce interrupts, "and I hold to that. I leave you now because this is your fight, and it is what you want."

I place the hatchet back in the bag. A part of me does not want Perce to leave—I have gotten used to his company—but if he does not, the arbiters chasing me will kill him; and the only way to free Sheila and Chase is if I, and I alone, kill Molers.

"Take this"—Perce hands me a flare gun, but not just any flare gun; this one shoots a flare, invisible to the naked eye, that can only be seen with specialized spyglasses—"use it, and I will come."

I take the flare gun, rubbing my thumb over the Arelian design. "I guess I don't need to ask how you got one of these."

"You know the eastern side of the reservoir of Arel. If you need me, use it there."

"I don't know how to thank you."

"You get them safe. That will be thanks enough for me."

The finch from earlier flies up to us, flapping its tiny wings before nestling on a branch above us, chirping away as though to give its own bouts of encouragement.

With nothing else to say, I place my foot in the stirrup and lift myself onto my horse, setting her into a soft gallop as I steer her northward and we disappear through the brush and the trees, leaving Perce behind, but deep within the crevasses of my mind, I know I will see him again, and something tells me that I will not be alone out here.

The day passes as we amble through the forested wilds, with Bessy sliding on the soft earth a few times, as I keep an eye on the position of the sun, ensuring that we head north as Renal commanded, with me retightening the leather breastplate around my thigh to keep it in place, until the time is right for removing it. Quiet passes as we navigate our way; the only noise comes from small critters as they disappear behind brush in an effort to remain unseen as we wander through their territory, but I welcome the calmness as a much-needed respite from all the chaos the wilds and Arel have thrown at me. Planning and strategy fill my mind as the sun passes over us; even when I find Molers, he will not be alone, of that I am certain.

As night falls, we stop. It is not wise to move through the wilderness in the dark. I refuse to make a fire as I do not wish to attract attention, knowing that I will have to brave the chill of the night air, something I have been forced to do on countless occasions at the training facility as a way to build toughness. As I grab blankets from one of the saddlebags, I spot something that I hadn't noticed before: a bow with a quiver of arrows and a rifle—parting gifts from Perce. Amused, and thankful, I leave them be as I place a blanket over Bessy and wrap the other around myself before glancing up at the moon and the wisps of clouds that drift in front of it, waiting for the dawn to come.

Golden light warms my face—I must have fallen asleep—and I open my eyes to a peaceful morning, oblivious to the challenges I have faced and what I am about to do. Bessy nuzzles her nose into my shoulder as though to ensure I am awake, and I pet her muzzle, reassuring her before getting up to fold the blankets and stuff them back into the saddlebag, and climb into the saddle. As she trots along, content to be on the move, I munch on some dried apricot from one the pouches Perce had left me with, lost in my own musings about what I will do next when Bessy stops on the edges of the trees, overlooking a compound of charred and ruined structures that appear to have suffered a terrible attack, but one long ago, as vines wrap themselves around the exposed beams and the trunks of trees that sprung up within what used to be a human dwelling, claiming it for their own.

I have found the abandoned outpost.

Wondering why Renal would send me here, I guide my horse down the small hill and into the clearing leading us to the former Arelian outpost, unsure of what I will find. Like in the labyrinth, silence greets me, and the closer I get, the more unnerved I am by it as the feeling that I am about to walk into a graveyard wafts over me, filling me with dread. I enter through what is left of the gate—a single sheet of metal hangs from loose hinges, swaying in the breeze with a soft creak—and Bessy's hooves stomp on the rusted, metallic shards, now covered in coarse dirt, that remain as the only evidence that a gate had once been here. Passing through the gate is more of a formality, as the wall surrounding the compounds has portions of it missing, looking more like a slice of Swiss cheese than a wall, providing little protection from anything. Chunks of plaster fall away from the exterior of the wall as though to emphasize its continuing decay as I ride past.

I pause. Human remains litter the compound as a sea of skulls, femurs, and ribcages still clothed in their arbiter uniforms cover the ground, each one having suffered a terrible death, and each posed as though they had tried to make a valiant last stand. Death. It seems to follow me, and I think back to Kition and the horrors that greeted me there. I try to be careful as I urge Bessy to continue, not wanting to desecrate what is the final resting place of people who died for their city, even if their own city chose to erase their existence and their deeds. Or, perhaps they were trying to survive, but fate denied them that. Some of the remains turned brittle from the harshness of the world and transformed into dust, mingling with the dirt itself, and some remained intact, allowing critters to live in them. As though sensing my desire to respect the dead, Bessy walks with care and her hooves never touch the skeletal remains of what was once an arbiter doing his duty, only to pay the ultimate price. A spider crawls out of the eye socket of a half-buried skull and scuttles over its top, disappearing into the shadows, and as I observe the destruction around me, I wonder if this is what will become of me—if this is what becomes of us all. I shake the thoughts from my mind. I have a mission, and failure is not an option.

We continue our steady trek past what had once been pristine buildings that had been painted white so as to showcase the cleanliness that Arel demands, but are now nothing more than blackened ruins, charred from fiery explosives that punched holes into the walls, exposing the interior to the elements and allowing all within to rust from the humidity or be buried by the dust blown in by the wind. I steer my horse onward, stomping through fallen plaster that now mixes with the brown soil, though it is more of a paste due to the recent rain, passing another structure that has a tree forcing its way through the wall until it becomes a part of it as its giant leaves stretch out, covering the crumbling roof as though to shield it from the sun. A frond drapes downward, forming an arching overhang as its tip points toward the ground, its vibrant green the only sign of life in this desolate place.

A tattered tarp billows in the breeze, catching my attention, and I dismount in order to inspect it further. The moment I touch it, it disintegrates, allowing the particles to be carried by the wind and exposing its secret treasure: steel spikes with razor-sharp barbs along its side. There are not many left, so the barbarians that attacked this outpost had the foresight to take some of them, but there is enough for my purposes. I pick one up, being careful not to pierce my skin from the sharp edges, studying it. Rust has settled in, but they will still work.

"What do you think, girl?" I say to Bessy.

She snorts in response.

"I agree."

The time has come for me to determine the meeting between me and Molers.

I place the spike back with the others and stroll through the remains of the outpost for the arbiters' quarters, only they have numbers on the rooms. Every outpost is arranged the same way with the same layout. I find the quarters and grasp the sliding doors—they hang ajar but appear to be stuck in their position—ignoring the yellow fungus that squishes beneath my fingers as I force it open so that I can squeeze through. Murky darkness greets me as I cough from the stale air, filled with the spores of the black mold encasing the baseboards and snaking its way up the walls, filling in the vacancies left by the fallen plaster. Covering my mouth with my sleeve, I make my way to room three. The door remains shut, not that I am surprised, considering that there is no power. Raising my foot, I jut my heel out and kick the frail door until it cracks and breaks open, allowing me to pass through into a room with no source of light, except for a tiny hole within the window, blackened from grime, mildew, and bits of moss growing on it, claiming it for its own.

Beneath the floor. Renal had told me to look beneath the floor. I lift my right foot and bring it down upon the wooden floorboards over and over again and stop when I hear a hollow sound echo around me. The thrill of curiosity takes over and I smash my boot into the hollow spot, using my weight for added force, until I hear a crack. Dropping to my knees, I force my fingers into the cracked wood and pry one of the rotted boards up, revealing a hidden cache, but it is not the cache that excites me, but what it contains: three black fire explosives. Stealing from the armory is not allowed and black fire explosives are not standard issue: I have only seen one or two in my lifetime, but have never been allowed to handle them, and for them to be here in what I assume used to be Renal's former quarters makes me wonder what he had done to get these. I pull them out of the cache with care, knowing that old explosives of any kind can be volatile, but also useful. I yank the blanket off the cot in the room, coughing as clouds of dust fill the air, and wrap the black fire explosives in it and before carrying them out of the room with care as I head for the outdoors and for Bessy, knowing what to do with these.

As I stand outside, looking at what is left of this place, I consider my options. Molers will not come alone, of that I am certain, but there are enough materials here for me to even the odds, and that is what I intend to do.

"Time to get to work," I tell Bessy, who nods her head in agreement while blowing a tuft of air through her nostrils.

The afternoon passes as I plan where to set my traps, and I tear away the sides of the dilapidated buildings, carving the ends into spikes and setting them in a platform to hoist up high, with Bessy's help, and secure them with a rope, that when cut, will deliver a fatal surprise. One of the crates of supplies still holds wire, half-filled canisters of oil and gasoline, a belt with smoke bombs, and nails—all of which are useful—and I discover an exposed pipe near the entrance that still has water running through it from the well. As I work through the day, I glance at the trees beyond the gates of the outpost, knowing that I will need the advantage out there as well. The sun snakes across the sky—Bessy and I work, putting my plan into play, pausing on occasion to nibble on some of the food Perce left us or to get sleep—and disappears, allowing the night to have its time, and when daylight appears the next morning, marred by low hanging clouds filled with rain, I know the time has come.

Bessy nudges me with her nose as though to say that she is pleased with what we have done, and I pet her muzzle with affection, knowing that I need to send her away. I do not want her to get hurt.

"You need to go, girl," I whisper to her.

She snorts in protest, but I cannot have her here when Molers arrives: he will kill her.

"Go"—I turn her toward the entrance of the compound and urge her to go through it—"Go home!"

I slap her rump to make her leave.

As though she understands my reasoning for sending her away, she looks back at me and snorts again, swishing her tail in protest, before galloping off and disappearing in the thin veil of fog that hovers in the air.

Once she is gone, I walk over to the exposed pipe, pick up the wrench I had found and left there and undo the connector, allowing the water trapped in there to burst free and cover the flat surface in front of the gates, until the silt turns to mud. I drop the wrench and grab the bow and arrows Perce had left me, taking one last glance around the area, remembering all the little surprises I put in place before ripping the leather breastplate from around my thigh and toss it on the soupy ground before burying myself in the fresh mud where I wait.

Chapter 17

Predator

Soft drops of rain fall from the sky and plop in the mud around me as I wait, concealed from the world, knowing that my quarry will arrive, and as a thick-soled boot steps into the mud next to me, I know my patience has been rewarded. I wait as more boots ease their way into the mud as they move toward the abandoned leather breastplate on the ground, knowing that if one of them steps on me, it is over, but that is a risk worth taking. I will my heart to beat at a steady pace as the knowledge that this could be my last day on this earth threatens to make it panic, and as the boots continue by me, an inward smile appears when the last one lifts into the air and moves in front of me. I force myself from my muddy bed, looking like a creature from some tale as globs of mud drop from my body, and raise my bow with an arrow nocked, pleased that they are still unaware of my presence. I release the arrow and it plunges into the back of the neck of one of the arbiters sent to kill me. Before the others can react, I release a series of arrows, dropping them all, and dart away.

I race for the east end of the outpost to another of my traps and hunker in the shadows as another arbiter sneaks past me, having entered through one of the holes in the surrounding wall. His eyes look all around, except behind him, and I fling my bow over his head, wrapping it around his throat and pull as he struggles to break free, giving a quick twist, stopping his movements. His body drops to the ground.

"She's here!" shouts a female arbiter.

Giving her a grim smile, I run, hurrying down a narrow passage with her behind me. As I pass beneath a beam, I fling my bow out, tugging a rope free, releasing a wooden spear, and it flies through the air, catching her in the chest, causing her limbs to jerk before going limp. Before another can see me, I crawl through a hole in the foundation of the building next to me, forcing my way through sludge as I wriggle through the darkness and to the other part of the foundation that has crumbled away, stopping as boots pass by me, waiting for the last pair. I throw my bow out, tripping the arbiter they belong to, and drag her underneath the building as she tries to grab onto something, but the slick mud refuses to help her, and before she can scream, I grab my knife and run its blade across her throat.

Sparse raindrops strike the ground as I crawl out from underneath the foundation and into the open air. I watch as three arbiters pass underneath an archway and fire an arrow at the gas can I had rigged earlier, and it dumps it contents onto them, soaking them, and as they dance around, trying to figure out what is happening, I fire another arrow at the metal sheet I had placed near there, and its tip creates sparks, setting them ablaze. Anguished screams assualt my ears, but pity is denied them. The rumble of an engine causes me to turn around and spot a transport with a rotary cannon attached to it.

"Kill her!" says Molers, but his voice sounds electronic, and for the first time, I notice a short-wave radio in the hands of one of the arbiters. Of course. Leave it to Molers to put the odds in his favor by bringing a unit of arbiters with him and using an archaic form of communication to avoid being heard by Arel.

As the operator of the rotary cannon turns his sights on me, I charge for the radio in the hand of a dead arbiter, snatching it as the first series of bullets strike the ground around me. Seeking protection, I dart behind a wall, bending low as I run down another narrow passage while the rotary cannon rips holes through it, pelting me with bits of brick and dust. I head for where I stashed one of the black fire explosives. The narrow passage ends, and I burst into the open where an arbiter awaits. He raises his weapon at me, but I swing my bow and knock it from his hands before dropping to the ground and swiping at his leg, sweeping it out from under him, but instead of crashing to the ground, he somersaults and rams his fist into my cheek.

Stunned, I fall backward. The man charges me, but I lift my leg and kick him as another series of bullets fly, and they tear through him, shredding him. I bolt, diving behind a metal barrel and snatch the arrow I attached the explosive to as gunfire strikes the barrel, filling the air with its fury. It stops. The man has to reload. Seizing my chance, I spring to my feet, pull the pin to the explosive, take aim with my bow, and fire. The loaded arrow soars through the air, and as it reaches the transport with the rotary cannon, the explosive detonates, spewing black fire in every direction, covering the transport with its wrath. A door flings open as the driver jumps out, flailing his arms in a vain attempt to extinguish the flames, but black fire is almost impossible to put out, and the man drops to the ground, succumbing to a painful death, while the rotary cannon operator succumbs to the same fate.

Someone strikes me from behind, and I sprawl across the ground, losing my bow. An arbiter, more muscular than most, leers over me. He lifts his foot and I roll to the side as he brings it down, missing its crushing blow. He grabs one of my legs and drags me across the ground on my stomach. I throw mud at him, and he releases my leg. Rolling onto my back, I kick at him as he lunges for me, but it does not faze him. He lunges for me again, and I dodge out of the way, staying on my hands and knees as I wait for his next move. Again, he charges for me, and I dodge to the side, staying out of reach, knowing I cannot win through brute strength. I spot my bow, and I still have an arrow in the quiver on my back. Preparing to make my move, I spring across the ground as he lurches for me, seize my bow, and fire an arrow, striking him in the neck, unmerciful as blood seeps between his fingers while he clutches the wound and drops to the ground. I stalk over to him and rip the arrow out, allowing him to bleed to death.

A single shot pierces the air and a thump behind me forces me to whirl around in time to watch another arbiter, his weapon ready to fire at me, drop to the ground. Once again, Perce has saved me, and it seems he never left, but chose to hide where he could observe and lend a hand.

"East side of the compound," comes a crackled voice over the radio.

I ditch my bow and the empty quiver and dart through an open doorway and into what had been the mess hall, heading for where I stashed my rifle, the belt with smoke bombs, and the remaining black fire explosives, before hurrying back outside and to where a ladder leans against the side of a building missing half its roof, and climb up it. The rumble of engines resonates around me as more transports approach the outpost, causing the roof to vibrate as I race across it, jumping to the neighboring roof and speeding along it before stopping and hunkering next to another of my stashes as more arbiters step into the outpost through an opening I had made the day before. I watch as they sneak inside, holding their weapons up, ready to unleash hell should they see me, and I ease the hatchet out of the hole I had made for it on the side of the roof. Just a little bit closer.

With each step, they delve deeper into my trap as I watch and wait before raising the hatchet and slicing a rope that causes the boarded windows to burst open, releasing a hailstorm of rusted nails. Painful screams echo around me as the nails dig deep into their skin, making them look more like pin cushions than people, but I hurry off, knowing that I need to get away from this outpost as the engines of the transports grow louder. Parts of the roof sink beneath my weight, creaking as I race along it to where I fashioned a zipline, but I dare not think about it. I need to get away from here. Mortar shells strike the building behind me, sending shockwaves that cause me to stumble and fall to the side, rolling over the edge of the roof, but I manage to grab hold of it, stopping my descent as bits of tile crash onto the broken pavement below, shattering to pieces. My exhausted body rebels as I try to heave myself back onto the roof, and I pause for a moment, allowing my feet to dangle as I order my arms to obey me or I shall perish, and I have no desire to die before facing Molers.

A surge of energy courses through me as my arms agree to hoist me back onto the roof, and I crawl back to the center beam before charging down its length, ignoring the chaos around me as I head for the zipline, jumping on it as the roof collapses, creating a cloud of debris and particles that swirl around me before being carried off by the wind. Air flaps my braid behind me as I slide down the zipline over the outpost wall and to the ground below, letting go before I hit the rocky dirt, rolling across the ground when I land. The barrel of a weapon greets me as I look up and find an arbiter. I remain still, weighing my options, knowing that the slightest move will be the end of me.

The sound of hooves reaches my ears, and before I can comprehend what is happening, Bessy charges up behind the arbiter, rearing up on her hind legs, and she brings her front hooves down upon him, allowing me to scramble out of the way. The arbiter tries to flee, but Bessy is too fast and her powerful hooves stomp on him, until all movement ceases. Another arbiter appears, taking aim at the horse, but I spring to my feet and run for him while I unsling the rifle from my shoulder, take aim, and fire. He drops to the ground. Another arbiter charges from behind with a knife, and I whirl around, raising my rifle to block the attack, before hitting her in the face with it, aiming, and shooting her in the chest. Mercy escapes me as she drops to the ground with blood spurting from her wound. Bessy walks up to me, snorting, and nudges me with her nose. Though worried about her safety, I am glad she came back, and I pet her muzzle, whispering, "Thank you."

She shakes her head in response as though to say that I am welcome.

More transports approach the compound, standing between me and the tree line, causing me to chuckle: this looks familiar. Slinging my rifle back over my shoulder, I lift myself onto the horse, sitting in the saddle as I watch the line of armed transports approaching, wondering why all this is for me as a drone hovers nearby. Annoyed, I glance at it, but before I can do anything, Molers' voice comes over the radio.

"I want her dead!"

Unable to contain myself, and tiring of this cat and mouse game, I bring the radio up to my lips and say, "Come and get me yourself. Or are you not arbiter enough to do it?"

I check the remaining two black fire grenades and glance one last time at the drone, deciding to leave it be, before galloping away, heading for the transports, shoving all doubt and fear aside. Bessy breathes hard as she runs for the approaching transports, their heavy engines vibrating the air around me, causing my own body to resonate in tune with them the closer I get as my heart beats against my ribcage, warning me that this may be my last act and begging me to turn away, but I steel myself against its pleas, determined to end it here and now. The gun atop one of the transports takes aim at me, and I swerve to the side, dropping a smoke bomb, and hide in the cloud of smoke its detonation releases as it fills the air around me, knowing that my horse is more nimble than the clunky vehicles racing for me. I dodge around another transport as I unsling my rifle, take aim, and fire, taking out the operator of the mounted machine gun upon it, pleased when he drops to the ground below and is run over.

Again, I rear back on the reins and veer around another transport while throwing another smoke bomb, staying on the move, hoping that it makes me a more difficult target as I scan the vehicles surrounding me, determining the best place to set my secret weapons. A transport comes too close and Bessy darts to the right, avoiding it, while I take a shot at its driver. Amidst the smoke and the chaos, drowned by the noise of the transports, I move around them like a waltz, making them turn and follow me as I veer in every direction, using the clouds of smoke to my advantage, forcing the vehicles where I want them. I feel Bessy tire beneath me and know that she cannot keep this up for much longer. Grabbing one of the black fire explosives, I charge for a transport, pull the pin, and place it on there. Knowing I haven't much time, I pull the pin of the other and toss it inside another before kicking Bessy in the side and charging away for the trees, speeding away from the mass of transports as they try to turn around and chase after me.

The explosives detonate, their blasts dulled by the roar of the transports, but the screams pleading for relief as flailing creatures covered in black fire drop to the ground and wander in circles pierce my ears, but I refuse to turn back, keeping my focus on the wilderness in front of me. Once I reach the tree line, I stop and face the carnage littering the open field as a lone transport drives up and stops on its edge, allowing the driver to get out. Intuition tells me that it is Molers.

I raise the radio to my lips. "Come and get me," I say into it before dropping it on the wet ground and disappear into the trees. Once I am in far enough, I stop and jump off Bessy.

"I need you to go to Perce," I tell her as the sky opens, releasing a downpour. "I need you to be safe."

Bessy stares at me with her big, brown eyes, as if to say she does not want to leave, but I know what Molers will do to her if he finds her.

"Please," I plead.

She nuzzles her wet nose into my chest before galloping off, leaving me alone in the wilderness to wait for Molers.

I run deeper into the wilderness to where my traps are set, aware that Molers will not come alone; he always did get others to do his dirty work. A strange calm settles over the jungle as I place my back against the soggy trunk of a tree, listening for any breakage in the rhythmic repetition of the rain falling on the overbearing leaves as it picks up, drenching any unfortunate enough to be caught outside, listening for any telltale sign of not being alone. Nothing. Unsettled silence envelops me, broken only by my heart letting me know its nerves are on edge as it awaits another confrontation and prepares to fight. Where is he? Anger rises within me as the thought of Molers having given up fills my mind. He has cheated throughout this entire challenge; the least he can do is fight me in person—the coward.

A twig snaps.

I twist my head, pointing my left ear in the direction of the sound when another twig snaps. An unsurprised smile spreads across my lips: of course, Molers did not come alone. He never does. I remain still as drops of water stream down my face, waiting for one of the arbiters to get closer, glad for the reduced visibility the rain provides. The unsure step of one searching for prey settles next to me, unaware that here I am the predator. I jump out from behind the tree and grasp the weapon in his hands, pushing it forward into his face, causing him to stumble back. Dazed, he shakes his head, but I wrench the weapon from his hands before raising it and ramming the butt of it into his nose, forcing him to fall backward. He struggles to get to his feet, but I refuse to allow him the chance as I flip the weapon around and plunge the tip of its barrel into the man's throat until it gouges out his windpipe.

More footsteps move through the wilderness with care, creating soft slurping noises as the soaked ground is forced to release them, hoping to catch me by surprise, and I toss the weapon aside, knowing that it will be useless to me, since almost all the Arelian weapons I've encountered out here have been implemented with a biometric signature and can only be used by the arbiter it is assigned to. I slip into a tangled mesh of foliage, ignoring the splinters that tear into my clothing in an effort to impede my movements, as I wait for another arbiter to wander too close to my position. A vine brushes my shoulder, and I pull it free of its hold, wrapping its ends around my hands and squeezing the rainwater from it as another arbiter stalks into view, holding her weapon up, ready to fire should the need arise. I burst from the bushes and wrap the vine around the arbiter's neck, pulling as hard as I can as she drops her weapon and reaches for the make-shift cord in an effort to free it from her throat, but the more she struggles, the tighter it becomes. I kick the back of her knee, forcing her to the ground, before giving the vine a final twist, ending her life and dropping her into the soiled water pooling around us without bothering to remove the vine, leaving her body as a warning to any who find it.

Whispering catches my attention, and I find three arbiters standing a few yards away from me, unaware of my presence. I whistle at them. They all turn, looking at me with dumbfounded expressions, before chasing after me. I sprint through the wilderness, jumping over rocks buried underneath rotted leaves and brush as I lead them deeper into another of my traps, while pulling out the hatchet, readying it, and swiping it through the air as I run, cutting a rope. As I dive to the ground, a pole with spikes on it swings downward away from the branches of the trees and skewers the three arbiters, allowing them to hang in the air for a moment as they succumb to their mortal wounds. Before leaving, I pause in front of them, noting the spikes protruding from their bodies and the blood dripping on the ground, lamenting having to kill them in such a manner, but what choice do I have? They would have killed me.

Molers' voice comes through one of their short-wave radios,

demanding to know where everyone is, causing me to smirk: it seems that he is now alone. Good. I take my rifle and check it, noting that only a single round is left, before pointing it in the air and firing a single shot, hoping that not only will Molers hear it, but that he will come to investigate. I toss the empty weapon aside. Looking around, I spot a tree, perfect for climbing, and hurry over to it and shimmy up the trunk to one of the lower branches where I crouch and wait.

Time eludes me as I sit poised in the tree with the rain drumming on the leaves above me, before seeping down to strike me with their damp chill, but I ignore the discomfort as I wait for my enemy to appear. The gloomy day turns darker, and I imagine the sun sinking lower in the sky to rest, even though the clouds prevent me from viewing it, while at the same time imagining how I will make Molers pay for all that he has done. My knees threaten to spasm as they cramp and demand that I stretch, but I command them to remain still, knowing that any sort of movement will be my demise, so I remain still with rain dripping from the ends of my hair as it continues to saturate me all the way down to the bone.

A soft rustling sound catches my attention, but it is so slight that my mind passes it off as nothing more than a small animal, until another similar bit of rustling reaches my ears, causing me to glance in its direction in time to see the shape of a man skulk through the trees, heading toward me. I reach behind me and pull out the hatchet, waiting for him to come closer as he kneels on the ground, investigating one of my footprints, and I hold my breath in anticipation, hoping that he does not figure out my location. The rain picks up. Molers inches his way closer, studying the ground the entire time while also looking around him, wondering where I am. He is almost there. As Molers positions himself beneath me, a drone appears, its high pitch whine distracting both of us for a moment, but to avoid my plan being ruined, I jump from the tree and land on Molers' back, grabbing hold of his rifle and ripping it away from him and tossing it far away. Venom spews from his eyes as he glares at me.

"Where's your posse?" I taunt.

Enraged, he charges me, but I dive to the ground, roll on my back, and nick him in the shin with the edge of my hatchet. He howls in anger as I jump to my feet. Again, we eye one another, waiting for the other to move, but my desire to beat him gets the better of me and I attack, swinging my hatchet. Molers grabs my arm, wrenching it behind him, almost pulling my shoulder from its socket, as he rams the heel of his hand into my sternum, causing me to gasp and stumble backward. Once separated, I shift my shoulder, making certain it is okay, but small spasms of sharp pain strike it with each movement, and I force myself to ignore it while keeping my eyes on him.

Molers rushes for me with a fist raised. I block it and swing the hatchet at him, but he manages to avoid my blow and ram his heel into the back of my knee, forcing me to the ground, where I receive a kick to the stomach. My hatchet flies from my hand as another kick sends it skittering across the ground a few yards away. Molers' left foot rises into the air, and I roll out of the way, avoiding its blow, but before I can stand up, his other foot slams into my back, stopping me. I jut my foot out, catching him in the ankle, but he ignores what little discomfort I cause him and grabs my leg, lifting me off the soggy ground and throws me into the trunk of a tree. I try to cover my face as bark approaches, but the impact causes my head to spin as confusion takes hold after I crash into the soaked earth.

Mud encases me as I crawl across the ground, trying to regain my senses, while Molers approaches, convinced of his victory. He raises his foot again, but I scramble out of the way, causing him to strike the base of the tree as I get behind him and pull his other leg out from under him. Once he's on the ground, I leap for him, fist raised, but he rams his foot into my chest and forces me away from him, and I crash into the ground, wincing as a rock digs into my side. Lying still for a moment, I watch as Molers approaches, sneering, assured of his conquest, before rolling onto my hands and knees.

I lunge for him. Molers expects my attack and sidesteps, causing me to miss. Unable to regain my balance, I fall to the ground and sink into the mud, but before it can bury me, Molers lifts me up and smashes my face into the base of a tree, and sparks fly before my eyes for a split second from the impact as blood dribbles down my face and onto my shirt. Molers digs his fingers into my hair and yanks my head back so he can look into my eyes as he relishes his moment of victory before ramming his fist into my face and dropping me to the ground. My head flops as my mind struggles to remain focused, while warm liquid oozes past my lips and chin, pooling in the black slime that clings to me. I rub my swollen nose with the back of my hand and stare at the blood on it as rain mixes with it and washes it away, while the drone circles us, taking in every detail for those watching back in Arel to salivate over.

I try to get up, but my hands slip and I crash back into the muck, getting some of its filth in my mouth. Pain grips my stomach as Molers rams the steel toe of his boot into it, causing me to gasp for air, and before I have time to react, he kicks me again, and again, moving me across the ground as though I am nothing more than a toy. Coughing, I spit up blood, and the fear that I have lost overwhelms me as bloodied saliva drips from the corners of my cracked lips, forming a silky line from my mouth to the ground. Molers flips me onto my back, forcing me to look up at him and his triumphant smirk as he straddles me and leans close to my ear.

"What did you think you would accomplish out here?" he whispers.

A tiny glint of light catches my attention, and I glance at it, realizing that the hatchet isn't far, if I can get to it, but pain consumes me as my mind threatens to succumb to the torture my body has suffered.

"I guess I can let you have some peace," he continues. "I did set one of them free."

My fogged mind jerks its attention to Molers' words as it becomes alert once again, dreading what he will say next as a sinking feeling consumes the pit of my stomach.

"I will always cherish her screams as the dogs feasted that night, and your name was the last word upon her lips as she begged for help."

Sheila!

My mind grapples with his words, unwilling to believe that they are true, but as I look into his eyes, I know they are not lies, and that knowledge turns to anger and an insatiable desire for revenge. Fury erupts within me as my hand digs into the slime surrounding me and scoops up a handful of the mud, squeezing so hard that bits of it squirt between my fingers, but before I lose it all, I shove what remains of the muck into Molers' eyes, causing him to sit up as he rubs them, trying to clear them. Seizing my moment, I roll to the side, throwing him off me, and dive for the hatchet, wrapping my fingers around its smooth handle, and throw it at Molers, but my grip slips and the hatchet misses its mark, planting itself in his thigh instead. Molers roars in pain and frustration.

I charge him. He tries to dodge, but falters as the hatchet in his thigh shifts, causing him more pain, and I tackle him, ramming my elbow into his cheek before we fall to the ground. He tries to get up, but I plow my fist into his chin, rip the hatchet from his thigh, and swipe it across his face as he lunges for me, creating a bloodied line stretching from his forehead, past his eye, and to his nose. He staggers back, clutching his left eye as blood pours down his hand.

We both rise to our feet, but he falters when his right leg refuses to hold his weight. He swings at me, but it is wild and uncontrolled. I duck, missing it with ease, and deliver a blow of my own, forcing him to take two steps back. My eyes narrow as I watch him struggle to find his footing, determined to make him pay for what he did to Sheila; I want him to suffer. I place the hatchet in my waistband, pick up two rocks from the ground, placing one in each hand, and stalk over to him, and before he has a chance to realize what I plan, I ram my fists into his face, one after the other, in a repeated fashion, glad as his blood covers my hands while the whine of the drone intensifies as it moves closer. Molers drops to his knees and sways, and I spin around, kicking him in the chest and knocking him onto his back. Dropping the rocks, I pull out the hatchet, once again, and straddle him as I raise it high above my head, ready to strike, but before I can deliver the fatal blow, something stings as it hits me and an electric shock courses through my body, freezing my muscles and causing me to fall backward.

Arbiters approach.

Enraged, I force myself to ignore the agony of the electrical pulses engulfing my body, and crawl to Molers, raising my hatchet once again, preparing to strike. Another pellet hits me, sending another series of electrical shocks throughout my body, causing my muscles to freeze.

"No!" I scream, furious at being stopped.

As my body convulses, I force it to obey my command, determined to not let Molers escape my wrath, and I crawl through the mud, not caring as it seeps down my shirt as I force my way toward Molers, raising my hatchet a third time, receiving a third pellet in response and another series of electrical shocks rack my body, causing me to go into a mini seizure.

"Enough!" a familiar voice screams at the arbiters surrounding me.

Renal?

Ignoring the orders, an arbiter stands over me and raises his weapon, but Renal appears from behind him, rips the weapon from his hands and slams it into the arbiter's throat, causing him to choke and foam at the mouth until he stops breathing. He rounds on another arbiter that opens his mouth to speak.

"Are you challenging me?" he demands, and the arbiter backs down.

As my body convulses on the ground, I notice the flare gun that Perce had given me, laying not too far away. It must have fallen from its holster during the fight; I hope no one else sees it.

"Come to witness my victory?" Molers says.

Renal stalks over to him, speaking in a low voice that is still loud enough for the rest of us to hear. "Victory? All of Arel just saw you get your ass handed to you by one of your students, and you would be dead if it wasn't for your little arrangement."

He snatches a stun gun from one of the surrounding arbiters, shoots Molers with it, and stands over him as the electrical shocks force Molers' muscles to seize, causing him to collapse on the ground in a series of convulsions.

"Get her out of here!" Renal shouts at the arbiters.

Hands pick me off the ground and place me on a stretcher.

"If anything happens to her," Renal says to the arbiters in a low growl, "you'll answer to me."

The arbiters carry me to a helicopter—I wonder why I did not hear it—and as we disappear behind the brush, I notice Renal pick the flare gun up and shove it underneath his jacket when the others are not looking, but before I can ponder his actions, remembering the way he had hidden my makeshift wristband the night Commander Vye caught me out of bed after hours, I am shoved into the helicopter and it lifts off the ground. Wind brushes the tangled mess called my hair as my eyes glaze over and unconsciousness threatens to overtake me, but before it does, I crane my neck and look out in time to see Perce galloping away on his horse with Bessy trailing behind, and I smile, pleased that they are safe, before the bitter reminder of Sheila's fate overwhelms me, and I pass out.

Chapter 18

Sullenness

Darkness surrounds me, penetrating my body and consuming what is left of my soul as I stare at the small sliver of light poking through a tiny hole within the shade covering the window of my room as the sun tries to shed some light on my dismal world, but I prefer the darkness as the weight of Sheila's death tears away the last vestige of my humanity. I deserve the darkness. I wanted her to be free, to be able to live her own life, and to be safe from the constant fear of death, or worse, and now she is, but not in the way I intended.

Tears escape my eyes and ooze their way down my cheeks and over the curve of my chin before snaking a trail down my throat. I cannot stop them. The more I imagine her screams and the fear that must have plagued her as the dogs tore her apart, the more the tears come before morphing into unquenchable rage. I snatch a bedpan off a nearby table and throw it across the room, and it strikes a mirror, breaking it into five pieces that clatter to the floor, but it does little to ease my anger.

"You shouldn't do that," says Natalie—I never heard her enter the room—as she picks up the pieces and throws them in the trash. "Mirrors are not easy to replace."

Her movement allows a draft to weave its way through the room, causing something on the bedstand to shift, and the slight movement forces me to look at it: it's a tulip, but the petals (purple with a soft, white stripe going through its center, mirroring a brush-stroke) are dried and shriveled, meaning that it has been sitting on the bedstand for a day or two. I pick it up and twirl it between my index and middle finger, wondering who left it here and who would care enough to do so, knowing that Chase would not have been allowed to, so someone else left it there.

"Where's Chase," I say, wondering if he has met the same fate as Sheila.

"Who?"

"I've been locked in this room for a month, so don't bullshit me! Where is Chase and his sister?"

Natalie knows whom I speak of; she's met him before, but she shushes me, as though she is afraid to acknowledge him or the fact that I have been a prisoner for the last four weeks. Quarantine is what they call it, telling me that I may have brought in a contamination after having been in the wilds for so long, but something else is happening, something they don't want me to know. The bigger question is: why am I not dead?

"This dark room will not do," Natalie says, changing the subject and walks over to the shade, ripping it open and allowing the bright sunshine to fill the area, illuminating the pearl-colored walls and the pristine tables that reflect even the minutest details of the room, looking so immaculate that I wonder if they are ever used at all, or are mere decoration to give the appearance of perfection.

"So, there she is," comes a snide voice as a woman enters the room, who reminds me of one of the members of the arbiter tribunal during one of the many times I was questioned by them.

I place the dried tulip back on the bedstand while this intruder paces the room with an air of importance, as though all are supposed to bow before her, but her very presence angers me.

"What are you doing here?" demands Natalie. "No visitors are allowed."

The woman ignores her.

"You're not—"

"Test me again," says the woman, "and I'll throw you in the darkest hole I can find."

Natalie runs out of the room, leaving me alone with this woman, whom I have an instant dislike for.

"So, you're the young arbiter all of Arel speaks of," says the woman.

"What do you want?" I demand, my patience thin as I look for anything, or anyone, to plant my fist in.

"You should show me the respect I deserve."

"Which is none," I snap.

"You are a bold one." The woman's eyes darken, but I do not care; I am tired of pretending and of fearing for my well-being. "I see why Tapiwa took an interest in you. Pity her interest wore out."

"Cut the bullshit, bitch, and tell me why you are here," I hiss, preparing to pounce on her so as to ease the fury boiling within me.

The woman closes the distance between us, not liking my tone, but aware that I am ready for a fight with little concern for the consequences to myself.

"You are not the first arbiter to initiate the Challenge of the Fates," says the woman, "but you are the first to do it in order to save two plebeians. I find that to be of interest. As it is, Molers' victory—"

"Stolen victory," I say, my voice harsh and full of rage. "If it wasn't for his arbiters appearing when they did, he would have died by my hands."

"Are you accusing him of cheating?"

"We both know he did."

"I remember the first day you stood before us. You were defiant even then."

"What is it you want?" I demand, my voice low, almost a growl.

"To know how you slipped through the cracks. We have measures in place to rid ourselves of problems, such as yourself, and yet, here you are. Arel desires obedience from her people. Nothing less will do. But, somehow, your defiant nature survived."

I maneuver to the trash can where Natalie had dumped the broken pieces of the mirror, not liking the way this councilwoman speaks to me—something within her eyes tells me to be wary of her—and as I move away from her, she stalks over to the bedstand.

"Though it seems that your defiance is driven by some sort of emotional attachment."

"I have none," I reply, scooping one of the pieces of glass out of the trash, hiding it behind my back as I grip it, prepared to do what is necessary to survive so that I can learn what happened to Chase and Gwen.

"This"—the woman picks up the tulip by its yellowed stem and holds it up for me to see with a sneer on her face—"says otherwise."

The edge of the broken glass pricks my skin as I tighten my grip on it, but before either of us can make a move, Commander Vye storms into the room.

"What is the meaning of this?" she demands, her attention fixed on the councilwoman, who stops cold, irritated by the interruption.

"How dare you..." begins the councilwoman, but Commander Vye stops her.

"How dare you! You come in here and harass one of my arbiters. If you wish to speak with her, you will go through me."

"Always her protector."

"She is under my command. Your place is in the Command Division, not here!"

"You dare tell me where I belong?"

"I do! What business do you have here?"

The councilwoman looks at me before answering Commander Vye. "Seeking answers, and I think I found them."

She places the tulip back on the bedstand before leaving, while

Commander Vye stares after her with a murderous look I have only seen a few times since I've known her, and I drop the piece of broken mirror back into the trash as I await orders, but before anyone can say anything, we all stop and stare at a man standing in the doorway not expecting anyone else to be here, and he shoves something in his pocket: it's Luther.

"Who are you?" Commander Vye demands of him.

"My apologies, commander," says Luther. "I was told to talk to you about an escort to the rail station."

Commander Vye studies his face, recognizing him, and I hold my breath, knowing from where and when she has seen him before.

"Do I know you?" she asks, unable to place where the prior instance was.

"I've been here overseeing the reconstruction of the medical facility," Luther replies.

A doubtful expression crosses Commander Vye's face, but she lets it go, as worry also clouds her features, making me wonder what has happened in Arel since my absence.

"I will take him, ma'am," I volunteer.

She gives me a questioning look.

"Am I not still an arbiter?" I ask.

Commander Vye looks at Natalie.

"Doctor Sahir says she can be discharged," Natalie says.

"Please, commander," I plead. "I'm sick of this place."

"Very well," Commander Vye relents. "Afterward, go back to the manor."

"Yes, ma'am." I salute her and leave the room, waving Luther onward, wondering what he is doing here.

Neither of us say a word as we walk through the pristine hallways and the white lights that reflect off the floor as our steps send soft echoes around us, but as we walk, I notice something different about the plebeians cleaning the windows as we pass. Instead of averting their eyes like they have always done, they look right at us, unafraid of being punished. Stranger still, is when an orderly knocks a mop over by accident. Instead of yelling at the plebeian it belongs to, he picks it up and hands it to him with an apology. I stop, watching the proceeding, unsure of how to view it and wondering if I am in an alternate universe, but Luther urges me onward, and I allow him to lead me to the elevators. The reflective doors open before us, and Luther ushers me inside, waiting to speak until they close.

"I'm sorry about the girl," he says.

The moment the words leave his mouth, I break down, and tears burst from eyes, covering my face and making it look splotchy and red within seconds, but I cannot stop them from coming—I cannot pretend to be unemotional any longer—and Luther does something I never thought he would do: he places his arms around me, allowing me to cry on his bony shoulder, not caring that my tears soak through his sleeve as I turn into an emotional wreck, instead of being the hardened arbiter I am supposed to be.

"She was innocent! Because of me she is…" I wail, unable to finish my sentence.

"There. There," Luther says in a gentle voice, comforting me as best he can as he hits the red button, stopping the elevator. "One as young as you should not have to carry such burdens."

"I don't even know what has happened to Chase, or…"

"He's alive. He and his sister are both alive, but I do not know where they are."

"How…"

"I have my sources," Luther says. "Now, dry those tears."

He wipes a rough finger across my cheek, sweeping away the tears dotting it.

"Why did you come to my room?" I ask.

A sheepish grin takes over Luther's face as he pulls out a purple tulip with a white strip that mimics a brushstroke, and hands it to me. "I had come to give you this and wish you well. Mora always liked these flowers, and I thought that…" His voice trails off.

I take the tulip, remarking at how it looks like the one on the bedstand in my room. "You've been leaving these?"

"I might have snuck into your room and checked in on you from time to time."

"Luther, are you in danger of caring about an arbiter?"

"Don't let it go to your head."

He starts the elevator and it jerks as it continues its descent, stopping when we reach the lobby, and as the doors open, letting in the natural light that fills the entranceway, I gasp when I see Renal's face, and hide the tulip in my pants.

"Lieutenant," I say, "Commander Vye has ordered me to escort this man to the railcar station before returning to the manor."

"I will join you, then," he replies, and a part of me wonders if he has orders to escort me back to the manor, or is he afraid something will happen to me?

As though answering my question, two arbiters approach us, but stop the moment they see Renal, turning around and leaving, hoping to remain unnoticed by him, and again, I wonder what has happened in my absence as the thought that Renal is not here by accident touches my mind.

"This way," I tell Luther, acting every bit the professional and unemotional arbiter Arel expects me to be, hoping Renal does not suspect that Luther and I know each other outside of a chance meeting within the medical facility.

Luther follows my lead and we all leave the medical facility, stepping out onto the street, and I remark at how quiet it is. There are no people huddled together chatting; the trolley does not give the occasional toot of its horn as a greeting; and the people who are out remain silent and distant as though they are afraid to be seen together, with the exception of a group of seven children all in different uniforms—two wear red, two wear yellow, one wears white, one wears green, and one is a plebeian—kicking a ball to one another, playing a game in which only they know the rules. I pause, watching them, wondering how it is they are allowed to play together, considering that Arel forbids its citizens from associating outside the caste system in place, but no one admonishes the children for disobedience. The ball runs away from one, and she chases it, only to be stopped when an arbiter scoops up the gray sphere. At first, she recoils, afraid of what the consequence will be for her infraction, but the arbiter hands her the ball and smiles at her, not an evil smile, but warm like the one you would receive from a friend. He pats her wiry hair as she takes the ball and runs back to the other children, where they continue playing their game.

I feel eyes on me and realize I have been standing still in the middle of the street for over a minute as I watch the exchange between the children, unaware of a small crowd building around us from curious onlookers, but it's the looks on Renal's and Luther's faces that spur me to move. Both remain impassive, unwilling to share their innermost thoughts with the world and unsure if they can trust the other, but each concerned about my reaction.

The arbiter who handed the ball back to the child strolls past us and salutes me.

"Arbiter Noni," he says in a respectful tone.

Confused by his behavior—he outranks me, and no outranking arbiter has ever saluted me before—I return the greeting and continue toward the rail station before my company worries about my odd behavior.

As we walk the cracked pavement with the green stems of weeds poking through, trying to establish a foothold, we pass a store with a lopsided awning pulling away from its supports, shading a small table with green apples piled on it and a woman offering them to any who pass by, but when she spots us, she stops, picks through her apples, selecting her best one before running up to me, and places it in my palm.

"Thank you," she says as some of her brown curls escape the pins holding her hair.

She wraps my fingers around the apple and scurries back to her table.

Once again, I stand in the street, confused by her behavior, and she is not the only one to act this way toward me. My eyes survey the scenery surrounding me, seeing the strangeness for the first time: citizens respecting those outside their caste and plebeians being treated as equals. One man and his plebian carry bags of potatoes, but when he notices his plebeian struggling, the man takes the bag from him.

"Let me carry those," he says in a gentle voice. "You rest."

I force my feet to move, and as Renal, Luther, and I walk past him, he looks up at me with an amicable grin and warm greeting, "Arbiter."

The plebeian's step falters, and I throw my arms out to catch his scrawny arm, atrophied from age, and a grateful smile spreads across his pale and wrinkled face, making me wonder how he managed to live so long. The man swoops in and wraps the plebeian's arm around his shoulders, while holding the bags of potatoes with his free arm. That is when I notice it: on his arm where the sleeve slipped is a tattoo—crude, as though someone possessing no skills of finesse did it—and it matches the one I possess on the base of my neck—the first letter of my name and my serial number embedded in it.

"Lean on me," he tells the plebeian in a gentle voice, before turning toward me. "Thank you."

As we continue our trek to the rail station, oddities plague me as people act in a manner Arel deems unbecoming, and neither Luther or Renal say a word as they observe my reaction, while keeping a wary eye on the other, and soon, our silent walk ends.

"What brings you to the medical facility?" Renal asks Luther.

"I am an engineer."

"And do you often need the assistance of an arbiter?"

"After the attack on the medical facility, I considered it prudent."

I listen to their exchange, sensing a bit of mysteriousness from each, as though both are measuring the other and searching for his true intentions, but before they can continue, I notice an arbiter gluing a sign to the side of a building and walk toward it, curious as to what it says. Once in view of it, my eyebrows scrunch together as I stare at Tapiwa's pompous face as she stands erect and proud, looking to the sky as though seeking guidance, while her eyes appear to follow you, demanding your obedience. Next to her, in bold, silver print, is a new slogan for all Arelians to live by.

Together, we can build a sustainable future.

Another poster goes up, featuring Tapiwa smiling as she eats; I cannot make out what she is supposed to be eating as I study the gooey, sloppy mess on the porcelain plate she holds, and I imagine her spitting it out as soon as the picture is taken. I read the words beneath her image.

A better protein. A more sustainable
protein. The answer to the food crisis.

Food crisis? What food crisis? My mind races as I try to grasp this new development, wondering what has happened within Arel during my time in the wildlands and forced quarantine, while a long-forgotten memory ebbs at my mind. In my seventh year at the training facility, word spread of a blight that affected the agricultural sector, destroying crops and livestock, thus causing a food shortage. I remember the morning I reported for breakfast to find a dish with some sort of red goo in its center, releasing an odor that made me want to vomit. I refused to eat it. Within moments, a female instructor forced my face into it until I choked on it as I tried to breathe.

"Eat it or starve!" she snapped at me.

In the end, I ate it, only to throw it up later in the bathroom.

A few years later, rumors spread that the reason for the shortage was because Arel's president, with the backing of the council, had ordered healthy livestock and crops to be destroyed as part of some experiment. Many within Arel died that year, including recruits—the weak ones, we were told—and many more fell ill; and as I stare at the posters before me, I cannot help but wonder if history is repeating itself.

"She expects us to eat that crap?" says a voice behind me, pulling me from my memories, and I turn to find a man glaring at the posters with disgust, and again, I wonder what has happened while I was in the wildlands.

"How dare you question her!" says another, and I find myself trapped between two men intent on fighting one another, unsure of how the animosity between the two escalated so fast.

"Why not?" quips the first one. "I'm not eating that slop."

"Don't you want to do your part to save Arel?"

The first man laughs at such nonsense.

"Arel is in crisis and you're laughing!"

The two circle one another, each intent on forcing the other to agree, as their words turn more wrathful and their fists clench.

"Enough!" I shout at them as Luther and Renal approach. "You are both Arelians. Allies, not enemies!"

The second man looks at me in confusion. "President Tapiwa..."

"I do not care what she says," I reply, fantasizing about implanting my fist in her face.

I glance at the poster again, unsure of what she is supposed to be eating, or trying to convince others to consume as well, but it looks unappetizing, and I want nothing to do with it; so, I say as much. "If you want to eat that garbage, go ahead, but you've no right to force another to do the same."

"What is your name, arbiter?" demands the second man, no doubt wanting to report me for sedition. Citizens are encouraged to report anyone who appears to not adhere to Arel's dictates, and some will report arbiters if they believe it will garner them a massive reward. In most cases, they are sent to the crematoriums, along with the one they turned in.

I step closer, squaring my shoulders, readying myself for a fight. "Noni," I tell him, placing my face an inch away from his. "Go ahead and report me."

A small crowd gathers around us as the man steps back, unsure of what to do, while the other salutes me, even though he is not an arbiter.

"You shouldn't be here," the second man whispers. "You lost the challenge."

"No, she didn't," says someone within the crowd, and I notice a crude tattoo, similar to the one I've seen moments before, underneath the collar of his blue uniform. "We all saw it. It was stolen from her."

Murmurs flow through the crowd, growing with each second as people take sides, threatening to spill forth into a riot, and I step back, unsure of what to do, but Renal steps in.

"Back to your posts!" he shouts. "Or I'll have you all arrested for an unauthorized gathering!"

One man takes a swing at him, but he puts him down with ease.

"Anyone else wish to challenge me?"

Renal's imposing stature forces them all to disperse and fade away as they mingle with others walking along the street.

"Lieutenant," I say to him, "what happened while I was gone?"

Renal extends his arm in the direction of the rail station, refusing to answer me, and I obey his unspoken command, while Luther observes everything, but remains silent, choosing prudence over foolishness.

We reach the platform and worm our way into the crowd gathered there, waiting for the railcar. Plebeians stand next to their masters instead of behind them, and again, I feel Renal's and Luther's eyes upon me, and a question forces its way to my mouth, but I bite my tongue, suppressing it, unsure if it is safe to ask it. The sharp whine of the railcar rises in the distance, intensifying with each second as it nears and rushes past us, creating a whirlwind that sends small bits of litter and dried leaves spiraling into the air, circling around us, until it stops. The doors open with a hiss and people rush inside, desperate to get aboard before the railcar speeds away.

Once aboard, I hear the familiar cry of a woman, a plebeian, running to make it to the railcar in time, and for a moment, I find myself transported to my first day as a commissioned arbiter and how a plebeian woman pleaded, like this one does now, as she tried in vain to make it on board, but failed and was run over by the railcar because no one helped her, not even me. As this plebeian woman begs for the railcar to wait, squeezing the packages in her arms so that they will not fall, I push my way forward, unwilling to allow the past to repeat itself, but before I reach the doors, they start to close, and the fear that I have failed wafts over me. A man sticks his arm out, stopping the doors, and his muscles strain from the effort to hold them open for her. I push my way to the doors, joined by others, and together, we hold them open as the railcar starts to move and the woman dashes across the platform and leaps for the opening and our outstretched hands, grabbing hold of us as we pull her inside before allowing the doors to seal shut.

"Thank you," she says in a breathless voice, before seeing me and recognizing me, even though we have never met, and says to me, "Most of us know you were robbed of your victory."

Others around her see me for the time, nodding their heads in agreement and salute me, even though they are not arbiters.

Unsure of what to do, I stand amid plebeians and citizens from different castes as they stare at me, not with fear, but with respect.

The man who had first stuck his arm out to stop the doors from closing speaks so all can hear, "The child never should have suffered such a fate."

The others murmur their agreement as tears well in my eyes over the thought of Sheila's unfortunate demise and the terror she faced because I was not there to save her, to comfort her when she needed it most.

"Thank you," I whisper as my voice cracks from my efforts to not break down in front of them and show weakness.

A gentle hand rests on my shoulder, and I turn to find Luther's calm and intelligent eyes looking into mine as he guides me back, away from those gathered around me, and a quick glance reveals that Renal observes it all, but says nothing.

The railcar speeds along its track, forcing me to grab hold of one of the bars running along the ceiling as it arcs upward, allowing us all to see ourselves in the topmost windows of the pristine buildings as the sunlight spills through the glass surrounding us, breaking into its colors of red, blue, green, and purple, while orange light drapes across my face, highlighting my brown eyes. I watch as plebeians and citizens alike talk with one another, something that has never been done before, chatting as though they are old friends, as though they never once despised one another, but that is not what intrigues me: before today, I never observed citizens conversing among themselves in such an amicable manner, because in Arel, everyone distrusts one another, and Arel encourages it, but something has changed.

The railcar soars above the city, allowing me to see it in all its glory, but as I stare at the tops of the glass buildings, I find myself yearning for the ones made of stone that Perce had shown me, but it is not the structures I long for, but a place where I do not to have hide anymore, where I do not have to always be on my guard.

My body leans forward as the railcar descends into the shadows obscuring the sun from view, delving deep into the belly of the beast as we enter the center of the eastern sector, passing underneath another set of tracks as a shuttle passes overhead. Shattered windows pass by us as we continue our short journey through a sea of decayed buildings with awnings dangling from doorways at odd angles as though making a desperate attempt to escape the black mold climbing up the exterior walls.

The shuttle car banks to the left as it turns toward the platform, preparing to stop, and I tighten my grip on the bar as the brakes squeal—the efficiency of the railcars must always be maintained—and my body jerks when we come to a sudden stop. The doors slide open, but people do not scramble over one another to get off like they had done in the past, choosing to depart one by one, each nodding in my direction as they do, muttering, "Arbiter."

As they pass, I notice a man sitting in a far corner, watching, making no effort to get off the shuttle, but before I can dwell on it, Renal steers me to the open doors and we run into the man who first helped the plebeian woman get on the railcar.

"Arbiter," he says, not with fear, but with respect.

"Noni," I tell him, unsure of what prompted me to tell him my name.

"Noni," he muses. "That is a beautiful name."

He walks off, leaving me alone on the platform with Renal and Luther.

"Do you need us to escort you to your home?" Renal asks Luther.

"I shall be fine from here," he replies, before nodding his head in my direction as a way of saying farewell, for now.

"Come," Renal says to me.

I obey, knowing it is unwise to do otherwise at this moment, even though I want to ask him about the man in the corner of the railcar, but decide it prudent not to. As we hurry through the streets of the eastern sector, I notice the same behavior of those out and about as the ones near the medical facility and wonder why they avoid every arbiter they see, except me; with me, they issue a pleasant greeting, not one that is forced, but genuine. It is different with my fellow arbiters: some look upon me with respect, while others possess disdain. Their mannerisms are not the only thing that seems strange; many have crude tattoos on them, out in the open for all to see, matching the one at the base of my neck. One woman passes me and points at her tattoo with pride as she smiles. The eeriness of it all forces me to hold my tongue no longer.

"Lieutenant," I say, "what happened while I was away? The people here seem different."

"You are the youngest arbiter to issue a challenge for the Rite of Conquest. You are the youngest arbiter to receive the Arelian Medal of Honor."

And of all the recipients, I am the only one left alive. Though Renal does not say it, his tone implies it.

"Previous Rites of Conquest have been used as instruction videos for recruits at the training facility. This you know. But what you are not aware of is the fact that Tapiwa chose to stream your exploits in the Rite of Conquest live throughout all of Arel, hoping to capture your death and have it serve as a warning, but it did not go according to her plan." He turns his gaze toward me. "You were smart to destroy the drones."

"What?"

How does Renal know all this? Even as a marshal, he will not be privy to Tapiwa's innermost secrets or acts unless he is a party to them or has his own sources within her innermost circle keeping him informed. As always, more questions abound from Renal's actions than are answered.

Kumi had warned me about Tapiwa's ever-changing mood toward her playthings, but it never occurred to me that this would be part of it.

"Lieutenant," I say, even though I know the answer to what I am about to ask; I want to see if Renal sheds anymore light on it, "Commander Vye mentioned that I am the only Medal of Honor winner left alive. What happened to the others?"

"Arel is aware that heroes give people hope and pride in their own city, but heroes also have a way of gaining a following, which cannot be allowed. Think of all the Arelian heroes you were taught about at the training facility. How many are mentioned to have achieved any accomplishments after they were awarded their medal?"

"None."

They are all dead. During our lectures at the training facility, we learned about some within Arel who were deemed heroes and received a medal recognizing them for their achievement, and they died soon after: months, if not weeks, after.

"My assignment to the mines was never about increasing production," I say as we reach the driveway leading to the manor as its cracks and missing patches of asphalt, filled in with weeds, form a path for us to follow.

Renal's face remains unreadable.

"Were you ordered to ensure that I never made it back to Arel?"

He stops and looks at me, and I shrink under his gaze, wishing I had not asked such a question, but I need to know the answer.

"My orders were to take care of you," he says in a stern tone. "Clearly, their failure to clarify their meaning resulted in some miscommunication, a mistake that neither Commander Vye, nor I, intend to rectify."

"How..." I begin, but he interrupts me.

"It is best you do not know."

The door—the black mildew covering it makes me miss the murky green color of the original manor—to the quarters assigned to us in the eastern sector as a temporary replacement, until a more permanent settlement can be determined, opens as we approach. We step inside the dim interior, and I study the lit wall lamps and the anemic sunlight spilling through fogged glass windows that look as though they haven't been cleaned in weeks. Two arbiters greet us in the hallway, and one slips a small bundle in my hand as he passes. If Renal notices, he gives no indication of it.

"I suggest you go to your quarters," he says. "They are up those stairs and the second door on your right."

"Sir—"

"Now."

Knowing it best not to argue, I salute him before heading to the stairs, pausing when I reach the bottom step—it's corner having broken away—remembering my first day as an arbiter and how Sheila had been sweeping paint chips on the floor with a broom near a staircase just like this one, and I kicked her little pile with callous neglect, not caring that it meant more work for her, and now, as I stare at that spot, I want nothing more than to undo that act, wishing I could have protected her from being torn apart by the wild dogs. Renal clears his throat, and I hurry up the stairs and to my room, aware that my lingering garnered a few odd glances from some of the arbiters in one of the side rooms. The door to my assigned room slides open, allowing me inside, and I go in, heading straight for the window looking out at the wall surrounding the city (ever-present and unescapable), wishing I was beyond it because, despite the dangers the outside world held, I was free. Tears escape my eyes as Sheila's death weighs on my mind and my heart, and the knowledge that I failed both her and Chase tears away at the last vestiges of my soul.

"Noni," says a soft voice.

I turn, seeing Chase for the first time as he steps from a shadowed corner, and run to him, allowing him to wrap his arms around me as I cry on his shoulder, unable to contain my tumultuous emotions any longer. He says nothing, but allows me to bury my face into him as he comforts me in the only way he can. The sun lowers in the sky and sinks behind the wall, but despite the passage of time, the tears refuse to stop, and Chase never moves.

"I'm sorry, Noni," he says when the crying slows.

"For what?"

"I was unable to save her."

"There was nothing you could do. It is my fault."

"Don't say that. You made a bargain, and they chose not to honor it. Her death is on them, not you."

"Yes, it is. People die around me," I say.

Chase hushes me, urging me to push such sentiments from my mind, but I can't; all I can think about is the fact that I am the reason for Sheila's death.

"We're getting out of here," I say.

Chase pushes me away and stares into my eyes. "Where will we go?"

"I know a place."

"Noni..."

"We're leaving: you, me, and Gwen."

"Gwen isn't here."

"What?"

"When Renal brought me back here, other arbiters took her. He tried to stop them, but couldn't. Their orders came from higher up. I can't leave without her."

"You won't," I say, not sure what to do with this new development, but I will never ask him to abandon his sister. "We will find her, and we will all leave this place."

A soft knock interrupts us. Straightening my uniform, and wiping the last tears from my face, I stroll over to it, knowing that my blotchy eyes will be a giveaway of my emotional outburst, and open the door where a plebeian boy stands with a thin, rolled disc.

"Sorry to bother you, ma'am," he says in a soft voice, "but this was delivered for you."

"Thank you," I say, trying to keep my voice even as I take the disc before shutting the door.

"What is it?" asks Chase.

I unroll the disc and a message appears. "Commander Vye and I have been summoned to the home of Githinji."

"He's one of the most influential people within Arel," says Chase. "Why would he invite you to his home?"

A picture flashes to life at the bottom of the message with a man dressed in the finest silks, showing off his perfect smile, but it is the small plebeian girl with blonde hair that captures my attention.

"I think I know why," I say, pointing at Gwen.

I roll up the disc and tuck it away, while Chase struggles to keep his anger and worry contained so as not to alarm me.

I place my hand on his warm cheek and turn his face toward me, whispering, "It's okay. We are all leaving Arel. I promise you."

He wraps his arms around me again, pressing his face into my hair as he holds me close, and we stay that way long after the sun disappears below the horizon as my mind thinks of one possibility after another for how to escape, always settling on the same solution: Luther.

Chapter 19

Githinji

A soft, pale glow brightens the edges of the wall surrounding Arel, and I watch the arbiters stationed there walking along it as they wait to be relieved of duty. I woke before dawn, unable to sleep any longer as my mind dwells on the impossibility of escaping Arel, finding the flaw in every plan I devise. Security is tighter, and the feeling of always being watched shadows my waking hours as I ponder who is keeping an eye on me and why. As I stare at the wall, while the pale glow morphs into a vibrant red with tinges of orange, making it look as though fire overwhelms it, I think of Perce, hoping that he escaped Molers' little army, angered that I lost the flare gun he had given me. How shall I call for his help now?

Chase snorts as he rolls over, causing me to smile as the sun peeks over the wall, brightening the room with its warm glow and warning me that it is time to get dressed. I step to my closet and pull out a uniform, pulling the pants up over my toned rump and snapping the waistband in place, pausing when my hands reach the area of my lower abdomen where the scars are. My fingers roll the fabric of my undershirt up, exposing the scars of my forced hysterectomy, reminding me that I will never be able to bear children, an ability stolen from me by Arel because it decided that I should be an arbiter: emotionless and robotic. Anger fills me for a moment, and I yank my uniform jacket off its hangar, causing it to fall to the floor, but I ignore its clatter as I think about the jacket Perce had purchased for me—another thing Arel stole from me.

"Everything okay?" Chase moans from the bed, waking up.

"It's fine," I say, putting on my jacket.

He crawls out of bed and stands before me, brushing a strand of black hair from my cheek. "You do not need to protect me."

"But I do," I whisper back to him.

I rest my head against his chest and listen to his heartbeat.

"What if we never get out of here?" I say.

"We will," he replies. "I have faith in you."

His words bring a smile to my face.

"Your hair, however, does not look like an arbiter's," he says.

Chase leads me to a chair and picks up the brush, gliding it through my long hair, never pulling when he encounters a knot, but works it out with gentle strokes so as not to cause discomfort. Mesmerized by how well he treats my hair, I watch his reflection in the mirror as he finishes brushing it before braiding it and twisting it into a bun, pinning it into place, but being careful not to tug it as he does so.

"Now you look like an arbiter," he says, admiring his work.

"I still need my boots."

"Stay right there, my lady."

He grabs my boots and brings them to me, but instead of allowing me to slip them on myself, he holds one out, waiting for me to put my foot in it, and laces it up for me.

"You don't need to serve me," I say.

"I want to," Chase replies.

Once my boots are laced up and secured, Chase holds his hand out for me, and I take it, allowing him to help me stand up. A knock sounds at the door and I open it, finding a young plebeian there.

"Commander Vye is waiting for you, mistress," he says, before pointing at Chase, "and she wants you to bring him."

"Thank you," I reply, and as the boy hurries away, I stop him, noticing how scrawny he is. "Why don't you go to the kitchen and get something to eat? If anyone gives you trouble, tell them you are obeying my orders."

A hopeful gleam fills the boy's eyes, and he runs down the hallway and to the stairs, eager to get to the kitchen.

"We should go," I say.

Chase puts on his shirt and follows me down to the foyer where Commander Vye awaits us, both of us uncertain about her insistence that he comes along.

"For a moment, I thought you were going to sleep all day," she says in her usual curt manner.

"My apologies, commander," I reply, sneaking a quick peak into the kitchen—someone had left the door open—pleased to see the boy eating.

The viewscreen in the gathering area flashes to life as one of Arel's state-approved reporter's face fills the screen, taking me aback since I am not yet used to the layout of our new quarters after the destruction of the manor. The woman's serious demeanor draws my attention, and I turn toward the viewscreen as her yellow-tinted lips move and her tone remains somber so as to convey the seriousness of her message: or rather, Arel's pre-approved report.

"More uprisings take place as another processing plant goes up in flames, started by treacherous rebels within the city. In response to the impending food shortages, President Tapiwa has called for a new sustainable food source developed by Arelian scientists."

The camera cuts to a man in a gold-colored uniform with white around his collar and the cuffs of his sleeves as he holds up a petri dish with a spongy substance in it.

"In meeting this crisis," he says, "we have developed a better food product sourced from a combination of mealworms and synthesized proteins. It will meet all your dietary needs and consumes only a fourth of our resources to create. Agriculture will no longer be needed as we build a stronger and healthier Arel."

The camera fades from the scientist and Tapiwa appears on the screen, acting as though she is speaking before a crowd.

"There is nothing we cannot achieve together! We are a proud people who have overcome insurmountable odds. First, at the hands of the fair-skinned, and now this, brought upon us by our own kind—by traitors amongst us! Under my rule, Arel will always be strong. We will always prevail so long as we always maintain our collective unity!"

Cheers come through the speakers, but the camera never pans over the crowd, making me wonder if this entire video of hers is staged, and the cynical part of me believes it to be the truth as her lips curve into a small smirk before she catches herself and recomposes herself as someone concerned for her people.

"Strength in our kind! Strength in numbers! Strength over weakness! Weakness is failure! Failure is death!"

While Tapiwa repeats the mantra of Arel, a mantra instilled in us all since birth, the mouths around me repeat it as well, but I do not, and as others take notice of my blasphemy, they stop as well.

The camera focuses back on the reporter, who continues her pre-prepared story.

"Fueled by President Tapiwa's resolve to meet this crisis head on, Arelians band together in acceptance of the solution provided by Arelian wisdom."

Images of Arelian citizens enjoying the spongy slop appear on the screen, but their eyes, and the armed arbiters surrounding them, betray the falsity of their actions.

"We will keep you updated on this developing story."

The viewscreen goes blank while I glare at it, certain that the

Arelian News will keep us all up to date as and when Tapiwa and the Arelian Council see fit. I turn toward Commander Vye, but she refuses to indulge my questioning nature.

"We're late," she says, and I bow my head, knowing what is expected of me, while the feeling that there is more to this outing than a simple summons washes over me, but I shove it aside and follow her.

Commander Vye leads us to the driveway, where a transport awaits us and signals for us to get inside. Once again, I sit in the back, as is my place, while Commander Vye sits in the front, knowing that decorum must be maintained, but when Chase starts to sit in the footwell, I stop it. There is decorum, and there is abuse.

"No," I say, stopping him, and he shakes his head, warning me not to break the rules here, but he deserves a small amount of respect, even if it is allowing him the dignity of sitting in the seat instead of the footwell, "you'll sit in the seat."

An appalled expression crosses the driver's face and he opens his mouth to protest, but Commander Vye stops him.

"You heard her," she says in a stern voice.

Chase settles in the seat with unease, wondering if Commander Vye is toying with him, but she says nothing and closes her door, indicating to the driver that we are to leave. To avoid attracting unwanted attention, I resist the urge to grab hold of Chase's hand and stare out the tinted window instead as the sun's rays drape across my face only to disappear when we near the center of the eastern sector and its buildings tower over us. The wall of one crumbles away bit by bit, exposing metal rods that used to keep it intact, and I turn my head to get a better glimpse of it, knowing that it was not like that before I was forced into the wilds. As I do, I spot a replica of my tattoo—the one Arel gave me upon my birth on the base of my neck—painted on the crumbling exterior wall. More buildings, as damaged as the last, bearing the same replica of my tattoo, pass by us, making me wonder what took place within the city while I was gone.

"We had an incident while you were away," Commander Vye says, without turning her head to look at me. She knows me and my curiosity too well.

As we continue through the city, the dilapidated buildings of the eastern sector disperse before being no more as the well-constructed structures of the southern sector replace them, standing tall and proud, letting any who pass by them know that they are in a better and more affluent part of Arel. I stare at the windows with plant boxes on them and the assortment of flowers growing within them, surprised that such a thing is allowed, knowing that Arel does not like frivolity, but demands conformity, but my amazement vanishes the moment I realize that each box contains three marigolds, two irises, and four tulips: Tapiwa's favorite plants. A hand bursts out a window, where a box with five marigolds rests, and plucks two of them, leaving only three, and tosses the two unwanted flowers into the street, where they glide past my window before landing on the pavement to be trampled by those allowed outside.

Like the eastern sector, uniformed citizens, each wearing a specific color denoting their station, walk the streets, ignoring the transport as we drive past. Transfixed, I watch the ordered lines of colors as uniformed citizens stroll by, but my eyes flicker to a man in a green uniform—on his hand is a replica of my tattoo—picking up a tablet that a woman in a red uniform dropped, disobeying Arel's rule about the classes mixing, but what startles me is how no one takes notice of it and treats the incident as normal, including the arbiter passing by. I steal a quick glance at Commander Vye, who keeps her eyes focused straight ahead, refusing to acknowledge what I witnessed or that anything has changed, or maybe she is wise not to speak of it, making me wonder, once again, about what has happened within Arel during my time in the wilds. As though in answer to my question, the transport drives past the blackened, hollowed remains of what was once the office for the Ministry of Justice within the southern sector. A portion of the roof caves in and crashes on the ground, sending plumes of ashen dust into the air, blocking my view of it for a moment until the wind whisks it away, allowing me to see a familiar mark in red paint on the inner wall, one I have come to know well: the symbol of Arel crossed out.

The transport turns left onto a winding driveway made of black asphalt that reflects the bright sunlight almost as though it is made of glass, but it's the golden spikes up ahead with the naked bodies of men and women impaled upon them, forming a fenced perimeter around a building the size of a city block with three black spires stretching upward into the sky that command my attention and horrify me. The sunlight appears to form waves as it shines upon the exterior walls, making them sparkle as though they are made of thousands of jewels, while the curved windows remind me of eyes and give me the uneasy feeling of being watched. The gate opens, allowing us through, and my eyes wander to the men impaled on the golden spikes as their blood forms jagged, red streaks that ooze their way downward to the asphalt. The hand of one moves, causing me to gasp. How is this man allowed to get away with this? Before I know it, my mouth starts to ask this question.

"Commander…"

"Silence." Commander Vye's stern voice stills my tongue.

I have heard rumors of Githinji, but thought them to be more fiction than truth. Seeing the impaled bodies surrounding the manor turns that fiction into an all-too-real scenario. As we pass by them, Chase and I share a terrified look, but keep our mouths shut, knowing the consequences of speaking up. The dark asphalt makes me feel as though I am being led to the depths of the underworld to have my soul ripped from body before being buried for all eternity, never to see the sun again. Nerves cause my stomach to quake as the transport parks near an entranceway with a three-pointed arch supported by two gray columns and made of Vantablack with little specks of amber sprinkled throughout it, giving it the appearance of stars within a black hole. The moment the transport stops, Commander Vye steps out, and Chase and I do the same, only to be greeted by a man wearing silk as dark as his skin, making it difficult to distinguish the two, and a square-shaped hat covering his shaved head.

"Welcome," he says to us. "I hope you will enjoy your stay. This way, please."

Unsure of what to expect, we all follow him through the entranceway and into a world I do not recognize. Vines—fake ones made from a spongy material and painted green to look realistic—brush my shoulders as we pass through the opening and into the manor. I reach up and touch one, remarking at how lifelike it is, but stop the moment I notice the floor: blood red with darker shades of crimson mixed in, making it look as though I am walking through a recent massacre, and the pale light adds to the ominousness of this place as it forms a deep contrast with the pale green walls. I stop. Moaning reaches my ears, forcing me to study the shadows within the walls and step closer to them—they are people! Nails hold them to the wall, and some have been hung within the last hour as a bright red stream trickles from their wounds and to the floor below, disappearing in its matching color.

"Admiring my décor, I see," says a strong voice as a man steps out of another doorway and into the middle of the room.

"Githinji, I presume," says Commander Vye.

"At your service," he replies. "And you, my dear," he says to me, "what do you think of it?"

"It's repulsive," I reply before my mind is able to clamp my mouth shut.

Anger flashes across Githinji's eyes, but before he can say a word, Commander Vye's voice echoes off the walls.

"I'm sure you did not bring us here to admire the décor."

"So, I didn't," he says.

He motions for us to follow him and leads us through a darkened hallway with black lamps lit, casting deep shadows upon walls made of the deepest shade of green I have ever seen. Unable to help myself, I reach out and touch it, jerking my fingers back the moment something sharp pricks their tips, and as I inspect closer, I realize that the walls are not smooth like they are in other places within Arel, but made of tiny, copper needles, but aged so that it created a green hue. My foot trips on a rug. After steadying myself, I glance at the others, making certain they are too occupied to notice me lagging behind, before bending down on one knee and grabbing the edge of the rug, noting its leathery feel but remarking at how it seems different. This is no normal rug like what I've seen in the presidential palace. I hold it out to one of the lamps on the wall, trying to catch the light for a better glimpse, and jump back the moment I realize what is in my hands: human skin. I cover my mouth so as not to yell in outrage as I stand back, allowing myself a better glimpse of what I have been standing on, aghast at the humanoid shapes from the lightest to the darkest shade, all sewn together to form a runner rug for the corridor, with braids made from human hair serving as tassels to give it a finished appearance. I drop it in disgust and hurry after the others, wondering why this man is allowed to live in Arel.

"Your plebeian…" begins Githinji.

"Stays with us," Commander Vye finishes for him.

Annoyance flashes across his eyes, but he rids himself of it as he pastes a fake smile upon his lips, pretending to be the gracious host. "This way."

The corridor ends and a set of wooden doors, encased in steel edging with the faces of people in pure agony carved upon them, open before us, allowing torchlight to spill upon us as we enter a massive room with a curved table in its center, and within the hollow formed by the table rests a cart with covered trays upon them. Awed by the torchlight—no one in Arel uses such an archaic form of light—I stare at the dancing flames as bits of smoke wisp away from their edges. Plebeians appear to walk out of the walls, startling me, until I realize that their clothing is made to make them look like the wall itself, disguising them from guests so as to catch them off-guard. They pull out chairs for Githinji, Commander Vye, and me. Wary, but knowing that I have little choice, I sit in the chair, while Chase stands behind me like a dutiful servant, keeping my gaze upon the plebeians surrounding us as a bad feeling fills the deepest pit of my stomach, warning me that something is not as it seems. Bits of light dance around us as the plebeians each pick up a covered tray and place it in front of us, removing the lid and exposing our meal: steamed broccoli with dates, swimming in some sort of sauce that looks more like dried blood than anything edible.

"I must say," Githinji says to me, shoving a broccoli floret in his mouth after soaking it in the sauce, "that I am intrigued by your exploits."

"How so?" I ask, refusing to touch my food.

"It isn't often that a young arbiter issues the challenge to the Rite of Conquest and manages to—"

"—survive," I say, finishing his statement for him.

A sardonic smile crosses his lips. "You're not touching your food. Is it not to your liking?"

I glance at the meal, not trusting it. Even Commander Vye refuses to touch hers.

Chase walks up to both our plates, takes a piece of broccoli from them, and places them in his mouth, chewing in slow, rhythmic fashion, and nods when satisfied that nothing is wrong with it.

As Githinji's eyes study my every move, I cut off a piece of the broccoli not covered in sauce and place it in my mouth, aware that this is another test, and swallow the mushy vegetable, wondering if he had it overcooked on purpose. I place another piece of unsoaked broccoli in my mouth, making certain I do not touch the sauce, but it falls from my fork and lands on the table, forcing me to notice the details of the dining set for the first time. My fingers brush the smooth, black marble of the table's surface as I stare into its darkness as though being pulled into an abyss from which there is no escape. A torch flickers, making me gasp as ghostlike faces etched deep within the marble itself come to life—each one in agony and crying for help—and stare at me as though I am their only hope for release from the torturous prison trapping them in a never-ending agony. Feeling Githinji's eyes upon me, I pick up the fallen piece of broccoli and place it in my mouth, while keeping my face impassive so as not to give away any hint that the horridness of the table's artwork (Or are they real faces?) unnerved me in any way.

"I must say, Noni," Githinji says in a sweet tone that is about as honest as water telling you it isn't wet, "you have made quite the name for yourself here."

"I do not believe so," I reply, keeping my voice steady so as to mask the anxiety that has been coursing through me ever since I stepped foot in this wretched place.

"How so?" continues Githinji, while Commander Vye's gaze darts from him to the plebeians around us, wondering what else hides in the shadows, and I notice her grab the knife next to her plate and move it to her lap.

"I am an arbiter. That is all," I say.

"A bit more than that, I'm afraid," Githinji continues, and my eyes narrow as he speaks. "No arbiter has ever issued the Rite of Conquest for the sake of a plebeian."

"If you had done your research," I reply, "you would know that there is more to it than that. My challenge to Molers was a long time coming."

"Are you ready for the next course?" asks Githinji in an innocent tone.

Unease fills me when Githinji motions for the plebeians to bring in another round of dishes, each with a silver cover reflecting the dancing light of the torches—the archaic lighting makes me feel as though I am trapped in a tomb, buried alive—and I cringe when one is placed in front of me and its lid removed. It's moving. Disgust overwhelms me as I stare at the pile of mealworms as they wriggle around on the polished plate—some drop off the side and onto the table—trying to navigate their way around crickets that look as though they had been charred in a fire before being served as a meal. I swipe my plate off the table and its clatter bounces off the walls when it hits the floor, scattering the mealworms and crickets. A plebeian swoops in and sweeps them up before disappearing back into the shadows.

"Not to your liking?" Githinji motions for the plates to be removed. "It seems the rest of Arel shares your sentiments. Oh, I keep forgetting; you weren't here when Tapiwa made the announcement."

My eyes narrow, suspicious of Githinji's words and motives.

"I'm surprised that your commander hasn't told you about the food shortages. Processing plants have mysteriously gone up in flames, destroying months' worth of food. Not to mention the diseases spreading through our livestock, killing them. I must say that I find Tapiwa's solution ingenious. 'Let them eat crickets,' she said. I'm sure you arbiters will adapt, but as for the rest of Arel… a few deaths are always acceptable when keeping the population under control."

I bite my tongue as I clench my fists underneath the table, imagining what I would do to this man if allowed.

"You don't agree? How else does one find food during a shortage?"

"I hunt," I say, allowing my venomous tone to reverberate throughout the room, thus making my intentions clear as I stare at my chosen prey.

Commander Vye taps her index and middle finger of her right hand on the table, warning me to remain in control of my impulses. Why? What does she know that I do not?

Githinji locks his eyes on mine, but his face and fallacious, jovial tone never falters. "It seems we must all find a way to fill our stomachs."

I remain silent.

"Perhaps the main course will be more to your liking."

Both Commander Vye and I stare at Githinji as he waves his hand and what appears to be a covered tower on wheels is rolled into the room by two plebeians going through the opening of the curved table, stopping in its center. They rip the cover off, revealing a cage with a naked and terrified woman chained to it. Her whimpering cries infuriate me as I picture what I would do to Githinji himself if I could, but I push such thoughts from my mind, knowing that they are a distraction at a time when I need to remain focused. My fists clench as the desire to rescue her shoves its way to the forefront of my mind, but I will myself to remain still, knowing that there is nothing I can do as the ominous feeling that had overwhelmed me when I first entered this place is proven correct.

"What was her crime?" demands Commander Vye.

"Pardon?" says Githinji.

"This woman is no plebeian," Commander Vye replies. "What was her crime?"

A sadistic smile snakes across Githinji's face. "She fell in love with a plebeian."

He flicks his hand and a plebeian man stalks up to the crying woman, pulling out a curved knife and allowing the sharpened blade to glint in the torchlight as he reaches for her exposed breast with his other hand and stretches it out. My hand goes for my knife, but Commander Vye seizes my wrist, stopping me as the man cuts off the woman's breast amongst a torrid of screams and places it on a platter for another plebeian to set before me. I stare at the breast and the blood pooling beneath it as its nipple mocks my anger at such a terrible act, wishing to make Githinji pay as the woman's agonized screams echo around me, while blood pours from the gap on her chest: it is time for him to reap what he has sown. She shrieks even louder as the plebeian man raises his knife to her other breast and severs it from her body, not caring about the blood that sprays his arm, and places it on a tray to be set before Commander Vye. Transfixed by a rage desiring justice and the knowledge that such an act will warrant swift action, I continue to stare at the bloody breast, until my mind decides that it does not care about the consequences and, once again, my hand reaches for my knife only to be stopped by Commander Vye's firm grip.

"Is the food not to your liking?" says Githinji, and I am surprised that I can hear his words among the woman's screams.

I shove the platter away. "I've lost my appetite."

"The music has lost its ambience," Githinji sighs, and the man with the knife slices the blade across the woman's throat, silencing her. "Perhaps you would prefer something sweeter."

My eyes widen as a familiar person is dragged into the room with tears streaming down her bruised face—some are yellowed from trying to heal, while the others are fresh and swollen.

Gwen!

I thrust my hand back to stop Chase from reacting, knowing that Githinji wants him to. Besides, if anyone is going to punish this cannibalistic bastard, it will be me. A man forces her to the table and she looks at me with wide, terrified eyes as tears fill them, and I know what Githinji plans.

"They're so tender when they are young," he says, stroking her blonde curls as her lips quiver from fear.

The pit of my stomach grows larger as the realization of what he intends to do swamps my entire being.

He grabs her wrist and stretches her arm out on the table and raises his knife in the air, prepared to slice off her hand, but before he can make another move, I reach for my knife, shoving Commander Vye's hand out of the way, prepared for her reaction, seize it, and throw it. Githinji yelps as he drops his knife and stares at his hand with my blade poking though his palm as his blood drips from its edge.

"Touch her again and I will take your other," I growl at him.

Githinji jerks his head, but before he can do anything else, Commander Vye leaps from her seat, jumping over the table and lands next to him, placing her own blade at his throat.

"If anything happens to my arbiter, I'll spill your blood all over this table."

"You'll both be put to death for this," Githinji says in a low voice.

"Arbiters do not fear death," Commander Vye says, as armed men appear from the shadows, "but you... you're terrified of it. Go ahead. Tell your men to kill us. You'll be dead before they do."

I scold myself for not being aware of their presence, but my commander knew of them.

"We're leaving," says Commander Vye, before looking at Chase. "Grab her."

Chase rushes to his sister, who nestles into his arms, relieved to be with someone who cares for her, and he whispers something to her, comforting her.

"Let's go," commands Commander Vye as she lifts Githinji from his chair.

I get up from my seat and move toward Githinji and rip the knife from his hand, prepared to use it as more men surround us. The armed guards keep their distance as Commander Vye leads us through the room and to the corridor with the runner rug made from human skin, never taking her eyes off them or allowing her blade to leave Githinji's throat. As we reach the doorway, the guards disperse as though directed to do so, and one look at Githinji tells me that he never gave them that order, not even a silent one, and as I wonder who did, I spot a flicker of movement and zero in on the familiar shape as it tries to remain hidden: Tapiwa.

Before my mind can ponder about her presence and what she is up to, I force it to focus on the matter at hand: getting out of this chamber of horrors. We duck through the doorway and hurry through the corridor to the foyer, but no one stops us. Once we reach the outside world, Commander Vye throws Githinji aside, and he grunts as he hits one of the statues, but remains silent, too afraid to speak, or knows that he was never in control.

Commander Vye hurries to the transport and rips the driver's door open. "Get out!"

The driver stares at her, confused.

"Did I stutter?" she growls, placing her knife by his throat.

He jumps out of the transport and she takes his place, starting it up as I hop into the passenger seat and Chase and Gwen get in the back. She steers the transport down the long lane and to the street below, and I find myself wondering when she learned to drive, but shove the extraneous thought aside.

"We should hide," I say.

"No," replies Commander Vye.

"Commander," I say, "they will never let you get away with this."

"They want us to do one of two things: go underground, or head straight for the gate. Both will get us killed before the day is over."

"Commander..."

"Noni, you need to trust me."

I settle back into my seat, knowing I have little choice but to do as she says and take a quick glance toward the back where Chase comforts his sister and nods his head as though trying to tell me that they will be all right. Buildings whiz past us in a blur as we work our way back to the eastern sector, and before I know it, we pull into the driveway leading to our temporary quarters. Commander Vye parks the transport and orders us to get out, and we do so, hurrying through the entrance doors and into the manor itself.

"Commander"—Renal stalks up to her—"you need to see this."

He takes us to the main living area, where a monitor flashes to life as Arel's approved newscasters appear.

"We have breaking and disturbing news," one says. "Githinji, one of the most well-respected citizens of Arel, was found dead just moments ago inside his home."

"They work fast," Commander Vye mumbles, but I remain silent, knowing that she intended for no one to hear her as I ponder whether Tapiwa killed him soon after we left his residence.

The entrance door slides open as members of the palace guard hurry inside, causing my fellow arbiters to raise their weapons in defense, creating a standoff.

"Commander Vye," says one of the guards, and a patch on his arm tells me that he is a captain, "you are under arrest for the death of Githinji."

"Is that so?" Commander Vye challenges him. "Tell me, is it customary for arbiters to be arrested for enforcing the law?"

"You killed him..."

"I never harmed him," Commander Vye interrupts.

"Take her," the man orders, but before his subordinates can move, Commander Vye speaks.

"I would be very careful about your next move."

As her words sink in, the arbiters under her commander put their hands on their own weapons, ready to defend their commander even if it means their death.

"I think your superior will find this to be of interest," says Commander Vye as she pulls a small round button from her jacket. It's a camera. She knew Githinji's invitation was a setup. "In fact, I'm sure that all of Arel will find it of interest as well."

The captain makes a move for it, but Commander Vye jerks her hand back.

"I suggest we come to some sort of agreement," she says.

The captain listens to his earpiece a moment before replying, "What sort of agreement?"

"Githinji's unusual pastimes will come to light, one way or the other. Such secrets never remain hidden, and you know the outcome if citizens learn that you concealed it for years. So, which story are they going to hear: the one where two arbiters learned of his activities and punished him according to the law, or the other where Arel's own president knew of his misdeeds and hid it for her own gain?"

"What's to stop me from taking that camera from you?" the captain demands.

Commander Vye looks around the room at her arbiters.

Again, the captain listens to his earpiece before speaking. "Your terms are acceptable."

He holds out his hand and Commander Vye places the tiny camera in his palm, pleased when he closes his fist around it.

"And don't make the mistake of believing you have the only copy," she warns.

Scowling, the captain turns and orders those under his command to leave, and we watch as they file out of the manor and into their transports, listening to the engines as they fade away.

"Don't you all have duties to attend to?" Commander Vye barks, and everyone puts their weapons away and goes back to their activities. She turns to Chase. "Take her to her quarters. You'll be finishing her duties for today."

Chase refuses to argue as he leads his sister to the basement door and disappears through it, glad to have Gwen back as I remain behind, wondering why Commander Vye has done all this.

"Commander," I begin, but she stops me.

"Whatever you are going to do, do it soon." She starts for her office, but pauses a moment. "It's too bad you don't know someone with intimate knowledge of Arel's secrets."

Her door snaps shut behind her as she vanishes inside her office, leaving me alone in the manor's gathering area, plagued by questions for which I will never receive the answer. I turn for the stairs leading to my room and find Renal, who nods his head in a greeting before strolling past, heading for Commander Vye's office.

How did their friendship form? What makes them loyal to the other? It's not romantic. It's respect.

Determined to get Chase and Gwen out of Arel, I head up the stairs to my room to get some rest because I have a meeting with Luther tonight, even if he is unaware of it.

Chapter 20

A Request

A wisp of chilled air caresses my exposed cheek as I poke my head through the hole in the fence and stare at Luther's door as a single light glows in his covered window, broken by a crack in the grime-filled glass, another sign of the eastern sector's decay being allowed to happen despite Tapiwa's promise to remedy such neglect. I pull the covering—I had ripped a part of my blanket off and fashioned it into a hood so as to conceal my identity—a little further down my face and touch the bare spot on my wrist, reminding myself that my wristband is safe underneath my pillow as I debate my next act. I do not wish to get Luther into more trouble or to put his life in danger, but he knows secrets about Arel, secrets that were never on the city schematics recruits were forced to memorize at the training facility. I need that knowledge now.

A quick sweep of the space between me and Luther's door tells me that the coast is clear. It is now or never. If I do not risk this, I will never be able to get Chase and Gwen out of Arel. I dart from the shadows and up the stairs to Luther's door, but before I can raise my hand to knock, it flings open and a hand yanks me inside, closing the door behind me.

"I knew you would come," Luther says as I pull my makeshift hood off.

"You've been expecting me?" I reply.

"Ever since this appeared." Luther walks over to a monitor in the other room with the Arelian news playing.

"A most horrific scene was found at the home of Githinji today as arbiters swooped in amid a series of reports of cannibalism taking place there," says the anchor on the screen. "What they found has shocked us all. A respected man of Arelian society, Githinji has been keeping peop—plebeians for the sole purpose of... consuming them."

He says the last bit with a mixture of disgust and confusion before continuing.

"Led by Commander Vye, arbiters appeared at Githinji's house and discovered his horrific acts, executing him as he tried to escape Arelian law. A true testament to the swift justice Arel offers us all. I'm sure we can all sleep in peace now that this butcher is gone."

That was fast. They wasted no time in acting upon Commander Vye's words and spun the story to put Arel in a positive light.

"But the real tragedy," continues the news anchor, "is what influenced Githinji to commit his crimes. A plebeian that has been at Githinji's side since his birth filled his mind with hatred toward his fellow Arelian and influenced him to become the butcher. Plebeians by their nature are untrustworthy and filled with hatred toward all. It's in their DNA and systemic. Their vile nature corrupted Githinji and forced Arel to put down one of their own. Though we are pleased one evil has been eliminated, Arel will not be sleeping tonight so long as the scourge of the fair-skinned remains."

I watch the broadcast with incredulity, amazed at how the newscaster went from telling us that we can all sleep in safety to we cannot sleep at all in less than two minutes.

Luther shuts off the monitor and throws a blanket over it, covering it.

"Did they just make an excuse for that monster?" I say in astonishment.

"Did you really believe they would admit that a man like that was a product of their own making? Societies like Arel always need a scapegoat, and who better than those that have been forced into slavery and demonized because of their pigmentation?"

"Will people believe this nonsense?"

"You know they will."

I let out an exasperated sigh.

"When you live as long as I have," says Luther, "you will learn that some will always believe anything and everything they are told by a person in authority, while others will question what they hear. In Arel, the latter are eliminated, leaving only the former. Now, you did not come here to talk to me about this."

"I need to leave Arel."

"It seems you missed that opportunity when you were already outside the wall."

"You misunderstand me," I say. "I need to leave Arel with Chase and his sister. We cannot stay here, but I know that I cannot use the same method I used for the others."

Luther rubs his chin as he considers my request, and I watch the gears of his mind turn over, contemplating my request and whether he can meet the demands of it. He stalks over to a cabinet with a single, six-pointed star carved on it, its uneven lines indicating that it had been done by a child, and opens the left door, pulling out what looks more like a stack of napkins, but as he comes closer, I realize it is a map. Without a word, Luther clears a table and motions for me to approach as he unfolds a map and flattens it out in an attempt to undo the creases that time has etched in it.

"There is one weak point in the wall," Luther says, placing his finger on the map. "Unlike the eastern sector, the southern sector is not as well protected. Only half of the southern sector is covered by the wall, the rest is protected by the terrain that Arel is built into. The eastern sector has always been the only sector exposed to the wildlands, which is why the wall surrounds it in its entirety, and is why it always suffers attacks from barbarians.

"Think about it, Noni. This one section of the wall never suffers an attack. Never! In the entire history of Arel, it has never seen one barbarian attack. Not only is that an oddity, it is something that should be of interest to you. This one section is not well-guarded. There are not even wild dogs here."

I stare at Luther with a confused look. No wild dogs?

"Do you know how the barbarians get the weapons they use to attack us?"

"Arel gives it to them," I say, remembering what I had witnessed while outside the wall.

"Yes, but they have to be smuggled out in secret; otherwise, people might witness it and ask questions. This one area is where they do just that."

"How do you know this?" I ask.

"My position allows me a few privileges. Now, getting out that way is the easy part."

"Easy part? I'm sure there will be a few arbiters guarding it."

"Yes, but a few of them should be no problem for you. It's getting there that will be the hard part. You may have been able to sneak around the eastern sector after curfew, but our lack of surveillance due to the constant attacks played in your favor. In the southern sector, the cameras work quite well, and you know well that you cannot take a railcar there in the middle of the night, nor will you be able to sneak two plebeians to this one spot during the day without raising questions."

"So, how do I get there?"

Luther points to a section of the map and runs his finger along it, pointing out a path to follow. "There is an unfinished tunnel..."

"Another tunnel?" I ask.

"This one is different. It was supposed to be used as an underground railway to transport arbiters around the city to put down any protests. I'm sure you're familiar with such tunnels."

I nod my head.

"This one experienced unforeseen problems, and they decided to abandon it. It hasn't been used since. Now, I cannot tell you that you will be able to get through it for certain, but if you are desperate to get out of Arel, it may be your only option."

"Where is its entrance?"

Luther points at the map. "Here. It is disguised as a drain."

"They didn't seal it completely?"

"They saw no need. The entrance is in the middle of the public square in the southern sector and is patrolled by arbiters. You'll have to time it right."

"Are you saying people have been walking over this method of escape without realizing it?"

Luther nods his head.

I frown, not liking this plan, but I know I cannot walk out of Arel and bottle up my questions, choosing to focus on the task before me.

"And the exit?"

"Here, not far from the wall. It's been turned into a cache. There might be one or two arbiters there, but I'm certain it's nothing you can't handle. They change them every fifteen minutes."

"Are you telling me that they allowed an abandoned tunnel to be a secret entrance to a cache?" I ask, incredulous.

"Hubris knows no bounds," replies Luther. "The abandoned tunnel is the cache. Very few know about this tunnel, and fewer still are willing to risk such a venture to escape. Most attempt to slip through the obvious weak points."

"How do you know all this?" I ask.

"You are not the only one to consider leaving," replies Luther.

I stare at the map, considering Luther's plan. It is risky, but so is staying in Arel, so I commit the map to memory as I remember the flare gun Perce had given me to signal him for help and how I had lost it, wishing I had it now.

"What's wrong?" Luther asks, sensing a change in my demeanor.

I consider not telling him, but there is no point in keeping secrets from him. "There was a man outside the wall who helped me. He gave me a special flare gun to use as a way of signaling to him that I needed help. I could use it now."

"What happened to it?"

"I lost it after my encounter with Molers."

"That's unfortunate. I'm sure you'll find a way to contact him."

"It doesn't matter," I say in a weary tone. "The tunnel is the easy part. The trick will be getting to the southern sector unnoticed. I cannot take a main road, and as you've said before, railcars are out of the question."

Luther grins. "What divides the sectors?"

"Walls and massive hedges."

"Did you never ask why hedges were used as markers for the boundaries between the different sectors?"

No, I did not.

Luther continues. "If people believe they are in a prison, they will act on it, but if you disguise that prison with beauty and entertainment, they will willingly stay, hence the greenery and yearly gauntlet. The hedges themselves are made of thorny brush that have grown around barbed wire fences, disguising it from view. If you make it past the thorns, you have the other to deal with, but it is doable."

As I listen to him, I wonder if he has too much faith in my abilities, but I also realize that my opportunity for escaping Arel may soon vanish and this is my only hope.

"I would try to cross here"—Luther points at the map—"where it is thinnest, and it is close to the plaza. There are cameras here, here, and here."

I study the map but realize it is getting late, and I need to get back to the manor before anyone realizes I am missing.

As though reading my mind, Luther starts to fold the map.

"You should come with us," I say to him.

He stops and looks at me. "There was a time I considered leaving, but with Mora and my wife gone, I have no reason to..."

"Let me give you a reason. Two of them. We need your help and we need more than a map."

"Noni..."

"Please," I beg him, "don't ask me to lose another."

A small smile fills Luther's face. "So, the trained killer has a soft spot for an old man."

"Because the old man has a soft spot for an irredeemable killer."

Luther turns away and places the map back in its drawer, shutting it with a soft thump that fills the silent space between us.

"Come with us," I say again.

Luther doesn't answer.

"We leave in forty-eight hours. If that lamp in your window is lit, I'll know you've decided to stay."

I head for the door, but before I can open it, Luther stops me.

"Noni," he says with a note of concern, "be careful."

"Same to you," I reply as I slip outside and dart off into the night, hoping to make it back to the manor before sunrise.

Chapter 21

Snared

Air escapes my lungs as I lie on my cot and release a long, slow breath in an attempt to calm my nerves as the darkness settles around me, informing me that the time has come for me to get Chase and Gwen out of Arel. There will be no turning back. Another slow release of air forces its way through my parted lips when I turn toward the monitor in my room, remembering my last conversation with Faya. She had called me earlier in the day, an odd act considering her overt hatred for me after Joel's demise, not that I blame her since I am responsible for it, but she seemed different… a controlled rage, with concern sprinkled within it. In the end, I wished her well and ended the call.

I throw my blanket off and stand up, already clothed, and pull out a small pack containing two bottles of water and a day's worth of rations—I was unable to steal any more than that—before standing to my full height, and my eyes gravitate to the window and the wall beyond, gazing upon it one last time. The wall, a constant reminder of Arel's might and control, a barrier between us and the outside world. I tear myself away from it and replay the plan in my head, while tying my hair to contain it, as I glance at the mirror and my silhouette in the dark glass, remembering how Sheila would bring me food as her way of ensuring that I ate, and a tear escapes my eye as I think about it. I brush it away with the back of my hand. Now is not the time for regrets. Now is the time to make certain it does not happen again. I lift my wrist and stare at the band on it, remembering the first day I received it and my excitement at being commissioned as an arbiter and how that excitement turned to sadness and anger. Wrapping my index and middle finger around the thin bracelet—it lights up when I touch it—I remove it from my wrist and set it on the corner of the dresser in my room before turning away and walking out the door—a final farewell to my former self.

Once in the hallway, I scan it, making certain that no one is up, but the lights are out and welcomed silence ensues, allowing me to creep to the stairwell and go down them, being careful to not make any noise and alarm others to my disobedience. I do not need prying ears to know of my presence. Once at the bottom, I peek around the corner, assuring myself that no one is up, and hurry to the corridor leading to the plebeians' quarters—like the previous manor, this one has a basement where the plebeians are kept—darting past the door to the kitchen in case someone is helping themselves to a late-night snack, despite it being against regulations. Once I reach the door, I pull it open enough to slip through before shutting it behind me, remaining still for a few seconds to listen for sounds that someone noticed my presence. Nothing.

I turn toward the murky darkness obscuring the steps leading into the basement and start down them, keeping one hand on the rough railing to steady myself, but it shifts under my weight, reminding me of its deceptive sturdiness. The damp air chokes me, but I refuse to cough and alert anyone to my presence. A small puddle has formed at the bottom of the steps, reminding me of the other manor, and I step over it, wondering if it is water or sewage as I eye its inky substance, but push such thoughts from my mind. I need to remain focused on my task, or we will all perish. The lack of time weighs on me as I creep past rooms with sleeping plebeians in them, making my way to where Chase and Gwen are, hoping that they are ready to go, and when I reach the splintered door to their room, I pause for a moment as my mind reminds me of the consequences should we get caught, and an ominous feeling pulls me back, but I slough it off and open the door with care to find Chase holding his sister as they wait for me, while their bunkmate snores on the floor. I wave them forward, while keeping a wary eye on the other in the room, hoping he remains asleep and unaware of us.

Chase picks his sister up, who mumbles something, but he silences her and hurries into the corridor. Together, we make our way back to the steps and head to the main floor with me in the lead. Pleased that everyone is still in bed, I motion for Chase to follow me to one of the side rooms and to one of the few windows that open—I discovered it by accident my second day here—and lift it up, wincing as it makes a small sound and hoping that no one hears it, but it is too late to turn back. Cool air rushes in, and I take Gwen from Chase as he squeezes through, before turning around and reaching up for Gwen. When she hesitates, Chase gives her an encouraging nod, and she forces her way through the opening and into his arms. I face the window, take one last sweep of the room, and crawl through to the ally outside, shutting the glass behind me and on the only life I have ever known.

Damp air surrounds us as we hurry through the alley, doing our best to not make any noise so as not to wake anyone. Bits of thunder roll in the distance, soft and melodic as though trying to lull us to sleep with its lullaby, but I remain focused on the goal: leaving Arel. We sprint through the alley, dodging trash cans waiting to be picked up and ducking low each time we pass a window with a cracked shutter. Gwen murmurs again, but Chase soothes her with a whisper. I quicken my pace and he does the same with Gwen still in his arms as the still night remains unaware of our presence. I turn another corner, heading toward the alley that leads to the familiar fence with its broken board and smile when I find it before darting through it and turning back around to help Chase with Gwen. Neither say anything, trusting my judgement, and my stomach drops as the fear of misleading them strikes me for a moment, but I shake it off, unwilling to let it cloud my judgement or force me to turn back: I made a promise, and I must keep it.

Once through the fence, we hurry to the small clearing with two sets of steps and two doors, both sealed and covered in darkness, making it difficult to discern their edges, but it is not the doors I concern myself with, but the window with a lone lamp in it, shedding a soft, yellow glow on the ledge. Disappointed, but not surprised, I swallow back the emotions threatening to burst free and turn back to Chase as he calms Gwen and looks at me. There is no need for him to ask his question because my face displays the answer.

"We should go," I whisper.

"Confound it," comes a harsh whisper. "Are you going to stand here all night?"

Startled, I spin around and find Luther standing behind me with a pack strapped to his back, and my mouth opens to ask what he is doing, but his words force it shut.

"Lead the way, arbiter," Luther says.

As he looks at me with expectation, I realize why Luther placed the light in the window: in case anyone had been listening. I picture the map of the eastern sector in my mind as I remind myself of which path to take, knowing that we can go through the alleys, except for the last stretch to the southern sector if we wish to bypass the gate leading into it.

"This way," I whisper, as I take them back through the hole in the fence and down another alley before turning a corner and leading them down a narrow stretch.

Stone walls close in around us, squeezing together and forming a narrow passageway that forces us to walk sideways to get through, but conceals our presence. I turn and sidestep into the passage, letting out some air so that I can fit through as the rough stone catches on my clothes and frees a few threads from what was smooth fabric as every inch of my body is pressed against the stone. Chase puts Gwen down and urges her to follow me. She studies the narrow space and turns sideways too, stepping into the blackened space with tepid movements, but her hair catches on the stone and she releases a tiny squeal before silencing herself as Chase reaches in and frees the strands of her hair, while Luther takes up the rear. Musky air swells around us, strengthened by the two stone walls pinning us between them as they hold moisture and radiate heat, creating a cloud of unbreathable air, made worse by the sweat streaming down our faces, while our breaths form clouds of vapor before our faces, only to be inhaled. Time slips past us, evading us as we make our way through the narrow space between the two walls, but I urge them onward, trying to go faster, but the walls pinning us mar our progress, feeding my frustration, but I conceal it, not wanting to give them a reason to turn back.

Refreshing air brushes my face, drying the beads of sweat upon it when I burst free of the enclosed space. I turn around and help Gwen out of the narrow space before Chase's face appears as he crawls out, followed by Luther who seems to be as relieved as the rest of us to be rid of that part of our journey. We all lock eyes for a moment, sharing an unspoken hope, but know that this is not the time for conversation. Chase scoops up Gwen and we all race through another alley, taking care to not step into the holes with water pooled in them from the last rain, having never dried because they are always hidden from the sun. The less noise we make, the better. We reach a sidewalk and I stop, pointing at the causeway, it's belt no longer moving as they are shut down for the night, but it is the only way to the southern sector if we wish to avoid the gate. An arbiter strolls past, hindering our ability to reach the stairs going to the walkway. I study his movements, timing his steps and how many passes he makes, and no matter what scenario I play in my head, there is no way for us to sneak past him without being noticed, leaving me one choice.

I whistle. His head pops up, and he stares in my direction as I crouch even further into the shadows, hoping to remain unseen until the time is right as he steps toward my position with caution.

"Who's there?" he demands, and I cringe as his voice echoes around us, fearing that it will attract unwanted attention.

His boots clack on the pavement as he steps closer. I crouch, mimicking a praying mantis before it strikes its prey as I wait for the right moment. The toes of his boots are a foot away. I lunge for him, catching him around the knees, causing him to fall backward onto the pavement, pleased when he releases a grunt from the impact, but before he can regain his senses, I crawl atop him, lift his head and bash it into the pavement, rendering him unconscious. Chase gives Gwen to Luther and helps me drag the arbiter into the alley, where we cover him the best we can with the trash that has been piled in there; I hope no one notices him until we are far from this place.

Once done, we hurry to the stairs leading to the moving walkways above us and take them two at a time as we race for the first causeway, but I stop them, pulling them underneath an awning, when I notice a flicker of red, indicating that one of the cameras is operational. Most of the cameras within the eastern sector do not work due to the constant attacks on the wall and the failure of the Arelian government to ensure that repairs are made, but this lone camera is working, which makes me wonder what others are operational, and if repairs were made unbeknownst to the arbiters so that they could spy on us with better efficiency. I open my pack and pull out an infrared laser and scan the area, looking for more cameras but do not see any, aware that there might be more, but we will have to chance it. With a steady hand, I point the laser at the camera's lens and motion for Chase and Gwen to make their way to the other side, followed by Luther, and they do, running down the walkway and ducking in the shadows. Chase holds his hand out, and I slide the laser down the rubbery surface toward him, and he catches it and points it at the camera, allowing me to pass unnoticed as I hurry toward them.

Our feet leave soft thumps as we rush down the walkway and past a monitor screen and its light that casts out the immediate darkness as it recounts its propaganda, lamenting Kumi's demise, and ends with an image of Tapiwa standing tall and proud, ready to defend Arel from the evil within. I turn away from it in disgust. We reach another causeway, and I stop them, noticing another camera with a small red dot, indicating that it is recording. Before I can do anything, Luther snatches the infrared laser and points the slim, red beam at it, motioning us to cross. We do. Once on the other side, I turn back to Luther and catch the laser when he tosses it to me and point it at the camera, allowing him to cross to safety. Once we are gathered on the other side, I guide them to a set of stairs, knowing that we are not far from the barrier to the southern sector.

A soft whine fills the silent air, warning me of its approach. A drone. Cursing its existence, I pull all of them further into the shadows, placing my finger over my lips, indicating that they should remain silent. We still our breathing as we wait for the drone to approach, the ever-increasing pitch of its whine causing anxiety to course through me as I play every scenario in my head for how to address this situation, but hope that it will pass by us. The drone hovers before us, scanning the area for any rule breakers, and as it starts to move away, Chase's foot slips, causing a lone pebble to clack down the stairs. The drone stops and turns toward us as we push ourselves further into the darkened shadows, but it knows we are here and is sending data back to its central hub. Before it can come closer, I spring for it, wrap my hands around it, and throw it onto the metal grate where Luther stomps on it until sparks fly from it, indicating that it is no longer active.

I urge them to hurry down the stairs, knowing that arbiters will be here within moments to check the status of the drone and will search the area once they discover it; we must be as far away from here as possible and hope that they do not broaden their search. Once we reach the last step, I push them through another narrow alley, and we disappear into its depths as a pair of arbiters arrive and discover the broken drone and blow their whistle. Not daring to look back, I continue to push them onward, knowing we need to get away from here and am relieved when we reach the end of the alley and a small clearing with a wall of thorny bushes on the other side. Chase starts for it, but Luther's hand stops him and points at a watchtower and a beam of light forming a circle as it searches for anyone breaking curfew. Luther looks at me with worry, and as I think back to the schematics he had shown me earlier, I realize that this light is new, but determination sets in as the knowledge that there is no going back reminds me of the choice we all made.

I watch as the white beam of light circles the area, counting the seconds before it hits the expanse we must cross.

"Now!" I say to Chase, and he grabs Gwen and runs across the grass with her clinging to him, and they reach the bushes as the light touches the area again.

"Go!" I tell Luther who jumps to his feet and races across the muddy expanse, not bothering to look back, and dives into the bushes, missing the light's return.

Once darkness falls on us again, I spring from my position and sprint across the open area, kicking up mud as my feet fly over the ground, while keeping a watchful eye on the approaching light as it makes its circle. Fearing that it will reach me before I have cleared the area, I drop to my side and slide across the moist ground and into the brush, where thorns and waiting arms greet me, pulling me in as the light reaches us. Seconds pass while I wait and listen for any signs of having been noticed, but silence ensues, much to my relief.

Taking the lead, I crawl through the thorny brush and its deceptive beauty of green and purple, ignoring the barbs that push their way through the fibers of my shirt and prick my skin, causing droplets of blood to appear, willing myself through this sea of tiny needles thirsting for blood. A purple flower with specks of white on its petals cause me to stop for a moment and admire its beauty in this darkened place of spindles waiting to trap us all, and Luther's words about beautiful prisons forcing the inmates to forget where they are return to my mind, and I remember all the times I swelled with pride at the pristineness and elegance Arel pretended to offer, never realizing, never suspecting that I was a prisoner the entire time; but here in the dark, surrounded by tiny spikes doing their best to hinder my escape, I see Arel for what it is: a lie.

Gwen squawks as thorns snatch her hair and it entangles around the branches, causing her to stop. I turn around, receiving a cut on my chin in return, and help Chase free her, while Luther reminds us to be quiet, but the spindles refuse to let go of her hair, forcing me to pull out my knife and cut her free. Chase moves in front of her, breaking a few branches, but not so many as to alert others to our presence, in order to forge an easier path for Gwen to follow.

The deeper we go, the more vaporous the air becomes as claustrophobia wraps its tendrils around me, threatening to take its hold and whispers to me, telling me that we will never leave this place and will all die in this trap of barbs, while the flowers feast upon our corpses. I push such thoughts away from me, refusing to let them convince me to quit as everyone here depends upon me and trusts me to get them out. I refuse to fail them. I ram my way through the prison of spindles, breaking a few as I go, determined to reach its end. More barbs tear at my clothing and poke my skin with their sharpened ends, but I ignore their pricks, forging ahead, while the others follow the path I create for them, ignoring the increasing feeling of being trapped as the moisture from the soft ground swarms around me, forming its own sauna while sweat streams down my face, neck, and torso, unhindered by my already soaked shirt. A wisp of cool air touches my cheek. Almost there. I push harder, shoving branches out of my path, until metal greets me. I stop the others. We each look upon the fence before us with a mixture of relief and exhaustion, knowing that our night's journey is not over, but aware that we have overcome one hurdle. I pull out a pair of wire cutters from my bag and cut the fence, creating a small opening big enough for us to squeeze through. Once done, I push my way through the fence and into the brush beyond before turning back to help the others. Without a word, I continue onward, showing them the way through the brush on the other side, but this time, it does not seem like much of a hinderance as I crawl through it with them behind me, until we reach its edge. I stop them.

The southern sector. Unlike the eastern sector, the southern sector is more well-kept, with sturdy structures that shine and reflect any light that touches them, where all paved areas are surrounded by emerald grass that never grows beyond the height of two inches, and where all surveillance cameras work. As I plan a way to the plaza with the drain, I picture the map Luther had shown me, remembering where the cameras are and how there are some areas that even they do not reach.

I watch the light from the watchtower, timing it like before, waiting for the right moment…

"Go!" I hiss at Chase. He grabs Gwen, and charges for the shadows on the other side, reaching it before the light returns.

"Now!" I tell Luther, who jumps from his position and races across the paved squares (ground smooth, almost satin-like, to the point that they reflect the smallest specks of light), filling the space before us and jumps the last two feet to the shadows beyond before the light detects him.

Moments tick by as I inhale, filling my lungs to maximum capacity, preparing for the sprint of my life. The light passes. I bolt from the brush, shaking off the barbs that attempt to hold me prisoner, not caring that a hole forms in my sleeve as I run for the shadows, trying to not slip on the silky surface of the stones underneath my feet. I reach the shadow and hug the wall beyond it as the beam of light turns in my direction and hold my breath as I wait and listen for any sign of discovery, but when the bored murmurs of the arbiters on the tower reach my ears, I exhale, knowing that, for the moment, we are safe.

I motion for them to follow me as I move through the darkness, hugging the side of the building, remarking at the cool smoothness that greets my skin instead of the rough edges of brick I am accustomed to in the eastern sector. The alleys are few and far between in the southern sector as we navigate our way through the streets and the square-shaped structures that surround us, all spaced apart with a quad of greenery, edged with colorful flowers and each with a shaped juniper bush honoring a fallen hero of Arel in between them, giving the appearance of pleasantry and sereness, not the decay and misery of the eastern sector.

We reach the edge of the building screening us from detection, and with a quick scan of the green square before us, I spot a camera as it turns back and forth, sweeping the area with its mechanical gaze, and wait for the right moment. It turns away. Wasting no time, I motion for us all to cross, and we sprint across the grass, doing our best to keep our footfalls silent as we hurry to the other side and the protection of another building, reaching it before we are spotted. Again, we make our way along the exterior of a structure until we come to another green square, where we wait for the camera to turn away, and sprint across to the side of another building, zigzagging our way through the southern sector, and with each hurdle passed, the feeling that it is too quiet fills me, but I shove it aside, focusing on the immediate task before me: getting us all out of Arel.

We reach the plaza. I stop everyone and hunker behind the

edge of a stone wall, watching as a lone arbiter patrols the plaza, pacing back and forth, keeping his posture rigid as he lurks in the shadows. There is no camera in sight, but that does not mean there isn't one. The more I search for one, the more I realize that there are two possibilities: no camera was installed because of the arbiter stationed there, or it is well-hidden. Either way, we must risk it. There is no turning back.

I study the arbiter's movements, how long it takes him to cover the perimeter of the plaza, when he pauses, including the length of time he took to pick his nose, wiping his finger on his uniform afterward. He strolls past, releasing a long sigh, before moving away from us, and I count his steps, while formulating a plan.

"Stay here," I whisper to everyone, before placing my pack on the edge of the waist-high wall and moving into position to wait and listen.

The clomping of boots draw nearer, moving at an even pace before stopping, telling me that the arbiter has seen my pack. Slow steady steps approach as caution and curiosity brawl with one another, but curiosity wins in the end as the arbiter picks up my pack and examines it. I pounce on him from behind and wrap my arm around his throat, but he throws me off before I can cut off his airway. His hand goes for a whistle. I lunge for him, snatch his whistle and ram it into his eye, causing him to stagger backward in pain, but before he can recover himself, I ram my hand into his throat, forcing him to clutch it as he chokes and realize that I had hit him too hard. His widened eyes look into mine as he struggles for air, and for a moment, I believe he recognizes me as confusion clouds his face, and a pang of guilt strikes me for having been too forceful; he is a fellow arbiter. We trained together, only for me to deal out his fate in the end because we made opposing choices.

"I'm sorry," I whisper to him as I wrap my arm around his neck and jerk, until he goes limp,

Luther helps me hide the body, choosing to keep silence between us, knowing the remorse gripping my mind. I never wanted to kill anyone. I only wanted to free those I care about.

"Let's go," I say to them, spotting the drain before snatching my pack and heading for it.

Together, Luther and I lift the grate, allowing Chase to lower Gwen into the depths of the tunnels below, before following her. Luther climbs in next with me trailing behind, pulling the grate back over the opening so that everything looks as it should.

Strange silence surrounds us, broken by a single drop of water falling from the grate above us and splashing on the remnants of a metal rail stretching in both directions, disappearing into the darkness, into different unknowns. I pull a small flashlight from my bag and shine its light on the rails, half-buried underneath years of mud buildup as the earth attempts to take back what was hers to begin with, while I recall the map Luther had shown me and what direction we must head in, before motioning the others to follow. The quiet eats at me as we tread along the underground path and our feet step upon the rails, causing bits of metal to flake off, formed by years of neglect and decay and eaten away by rust. The further we go, the more the feeling of being encased in a tomb swarms over me, trapping me with its tendrils of fear and trepidation, filling me with unease as my thoughts lose focus, developing a will of their own and always ending up in the same destination, with a singular conclusion: much of this seems too easy. I shove it aside, not wanting paranoia to dictate my actions or cause me to fumble, knowing that being underground, away from the light and the fresh air, can cause even the sanest individual to lose his grasp on reality.

We continue moving through the abandoned tunnel, ignoring the mud that oozes over the tops of our feet in a feeble attempt to stop us, but determination spurs us onward as our desire to be free—free to live our lives—strengthens our resolve. A single light that was once built into the tunnel wall hangs loose and leans away from its support, as though torn between a desire to remain where it had always been or to break away and become what it was born to be. For a moment, I study it, feeling a bit like that light, and the desire to go back to a life I have always known forces its way into my thoughts, until I glance at Chase as he helps Gwen walk along the eroding track. Luther clears his throat, pulling me back to the present, and I continue, aiming the beam of light ahead of us to guide us.

My foot slips on the rusted rail, causing me to lose my balance, but Chase catches me, refusing to let me fall, and for a minute, I find myself thinking of the moment we were lost in the wilderness, climbing a cliffside, when he slipped and almost fell to his death, but I refused to let go. I smile at him, thanking him, and squeeze his arm in affection, determined to get us all out of here and to a place where our affection for one another is not forbidden, but respected. We continue onward, not daring to speak or break the silence surrounding us, fearing that such an act may draw unwanted attention.

A blockage stops us. Luther warned that such a thing may happen. I scan the debris with my light, noting how bits of the ceiling fell and caved in, closing off the tunnel, except for a tiny opening near the top. How long this has been here is a mystery, but I refuse to stop when we have come this far. I give Chase the flashlight and climb up the rubble, ignoring the bits of rock that fall downward as my feet slide on the lose debris beneath them while I claw my way to the hole. It's just big enough. I take my pack off and throw it through the opening before shoving my way through, ignoring the sharp edges of metal shards that dig into my shoulders and tear at my shirt as I pull the rest of me to the other side. As my torso escapes the small opening, I tumble downward to the ground, glad to be free of the hole. My pack sits a few inches from me. I grab it and stand up, facing the hole.

"I'm through!" I say, cringing when my voice echoes.

Gwen's head appears next, and I reach up and grab her, helping her through the opening and set her on the ground as she brushes dust from her pale face. Next appears Luther. He struggles to force his way to our side, and I grab his arm, giving it a tug as I help him, until his feet pop free, followed by Chase's head. Once we are all reunited on the other side, I spot a faint light up ahead.

"This way," I tell them.

We trek over small mounds of compacted mud and broken concrete, formed when parts of the tunnel wall broke away, moving as fast as possible without making any sounds as the light up ahead grows stronger. I turn off my flashlight. More water drips from the ceiling above us from the condescension that has formed, creating a watery film on the interior of the tunnel, but I remain focused on the light up ahead, stopping when I realize that it comes from a vent leading to an enclosed room, where soft voices emanate. I put my finger to my lips, warning the others to remain silent as I peek through the slits within the vent and count two arbiters stationed within, both looking bored and tired, as though they would rather be anywhere but where they are. Studying the vent, I notice two of the screws are loose and halfway out, giving me an advantage.

We're almost there. Freedom is within our grasp. The only thing between us and the outside world are these two arbiters.

I hand Luther my pack as I calculate my next move. A single kick to the vent covering should force it free, but I will have to be quick in order to prevent them from raising the alarm. I peek through the vent again, memorizing the layout of the room and the location of its contents. The cases holding the weapons are locked, but below the vent is a table with a paperweight on it, securing a stack of forms, and a plan forms in my mind. I take a deep breath, position myself, and ram my feet into the vent covering, forcing it to fly across the room. Before the arbiters inside can register what has happened, I jump out, snatch the paperweight, and throw it at the closest arbiter, catching him in the face. He rears back and holds his head, stunned.

I jump for the second arbiter and grab his weapon, wrestling it away from him. The first arbiter regains his senses. I kick him in the face while still clinging to the second arbiter's weapon, before flinging him to the ground and freeing it from his grasp. He tries to grab my foot, but I ram the butt of his weapon into his face, until he lies still. The first arbiter charges. Knowing that I cannot fire the weapon without warning everyone to my presence, I swing it around and strike him with it, ramming it into his stomach, and as he doubles over, I drop it, grab the man's head, and ram his face into the sharp point of my knee, allowing him to drop to the ground.

"Come on!" I hiss, and Chase lowers Gwen into the room as I turn for the exit, wasting no time to clear the way.

The door slides open, and I peek outside, my heart pounding the closer we get to our goal, but relieved when silent darkness greets me. I see no one. Knowing that it is now or never, I take the plunge and step through the doorway with Chase and Gwen behind me.

Bright lights flare to life, blinding me as my unaccustomed eyes struggle to adjust, and I raise my hand to shield them, while my feet slide on the pavement beneath them from my sudden effort to stop. Someone charges from the side. I twist around, blocking his attack, while driving the heel of my palm into his face, but his helmet blocks the force of my impact, so I grab his head and force him to the ground, snatching the knife in my boot and plunging it into his chest. Another comes for me. I pull my knife free from the first one's chest cavity and swing it, allowing the blade to scrape across the visor of the other's helmet, before twisting around and catching him in the leg. He drops to his knee, and I pounce on him, stabbing him in the shoulder.

"Run!" I yell to the others.

Chase and Gwen try to flee, but are surrounded within seconds.

Hands seize my arm. I try to throw them off when more hands grab me, surrounding me, and I turn into a madman, stabbing anything that comes near. A blunt force strikes me between my shoulder blades, forcing me onto my stomach as they wrench the knife free from my grasp, allowing it to clatter on the pavement. I try to look around, and spot Chase and Gwen, having been separated from each other, but as my mind grasps the futility of our situation, only one thought enters my mind: where is Luther? He is nowhere to be found.

"You should have seen this coming, recruit," says a familiar voice: Molers. "You never did learn one of my most invaluable lessons. Trust no one, and always expect the worst."

I struggle against my captors, but their hold on me remains firm. The single clacking of heels on stone pavement stops my efforts to break free as purple shoes with diamonds embedded in them appear before me, followed by the silky, yet arrogant, voice of Tapiwa.

"I had high hopes for you, Noni," she says. "An arbiter so young achieving the Arelian Medal of Honor was promising. You proved capable in so many areas, but you failed in one."

She scoops up my knife, weighing it in her hand, admiring its potential to do harm if one wishes it, before stalking over to Chase and stroking his chin as though admiring a piece of property while disappointed in its lost potential.

"It appears your toy is much more than that." She turns her attention to Gwen. "Now this one… she has promise."

Tapiwa faces Chase. "Such a pity."

She plunges the blade of the knife deep into the space underneath Chase's ribcage, causing him to double over as blood spurts from his mouth, and I scream in a rage.

I'm released.

I scramble to my feet, racing for Chase as he falls to the ground, and catch him before he hits the pavement, while his blood, his life force, pools around him and soaks into my sleeve as I hold him, trying to save him, knowing it is futile. Tears fill my eyes, but I blink them away, trying to remain strong for him, while Gwen's cries remain distant to my ears.

"Stay with me," I tell him. "I love…"

"Gwen." The word floats off his mouth as he struggles to say it, his final thought about her and how he will be unable to protect her.

"I promise," I whisper to him, knowing that I am the only one who can be her guardian now.

Chase coughs and more blood spurts from his mouth as his pleading eyes look deep into mine, reminding me of the first instance I stared into them, telling me that he knows the reality of his situation as thoughts of what could have been rush through his mind. His bloodied hand reaches for my face as time seems to stop, as though we are alone, despite the arbiters surrounding us, and wipes the tears crawling down my cheeks as I try in vain to save him, knowing that I cannot.

"Do what… you have… to…" he struggles to say before his hand drops to his side and his eyes turn vacant.

With a shaky hand, I run it over his face, closing his eyes so that he appears to be sleeping, and so he doesn't have to witness what happens next as tears drip from the edge of my chin and dot his pale face. Tapiwa bends low until her face is close to mine, while I cling to Chase's body, wishing that I could undo this night's events, wishing I could bring him back.

"They say you should guard your actions, for you may create your worst enemy," Tapiwa whispers to me. "Tell me, have I created an enemy?"

My head turns toward her and that sardonic smile upon her face, and I glare at her, my anger boring into her brown, confident eyes, and for a moment, her smile wavers, replaced by fear, and that fear strengthens me. I snatch the knife from her hand and swing it at her face, but Tapiwa proves to be quick on her feet, yet not quick enough as the blade slices her cheek, but before I can go for the kill, five arbiters tackle me, pinning me to the ground and rip the knife from me.

"Get her out of here!" screams Tapiwa.

"You should kill her now," warns Molers.

"No!" Tapiwa says. "I have other plans."

Her voice fades when someone rams a bag over my head and everything goes black as hands seize my arms and haul me away, not caring if my feet drag on the ground and scrape against the concrete, while Gwen's terrified screams pierce my ears, growing fainter the further away I am taken. My shoulders twist and turn as my feet flop about in a vain attempt to fight back, but more hands seize me, lifting me into the air as something blunt rams into my stomach, forcing the air out of my lungs and causing me to gag, allowing my captors to subdue me and secure my hands and feet, preventing me from causing more trouble. I crash onto a hard metal surface as they throw me into a transport and slam the door shut, while the engine roars to life and takes me away. I kick the door with my bound feet, screaming in rage, but to no avail as the driver of the transport ignores my cries and carts me away, wondering why they have not put me in a detainment box.

The transport stops. I pull back my legs, preparing for what is next as voices filter through the sides of the vehicle before the door opens, and I kick at any fool enough to try and grab me, but my bound feet prove a hinderance. Strong hands yank me from the back of the transport and throw me to the ground. Grunting, I take in a sharp breath when I land on razor-edged stones that cut through my skin, but before I have time to consider where I am, the heel of someone's boot slams into my face, causing my nose to bleed and soak into the canvas bag on my head. More hardened soles of military boots drive themselves into me, leaving my body battered and bruised, despite my attempts to protect myself, and the more I endure, the more I give up, hoping, wishing for death to take me as I dwell on Chase's gray eyes and the lifelessness that overtook them.

The beating stops, and I am left, still alive, with my guilt, and my shame.

Once again, hands seize me and toss me into the transport,

slamming the door shut before it bounces down the road, turning a corner as needed, while I lie on the cold, metallic surface, resigning myself to my fate while wishing my heart would stop and end its pain. We turn another corner, and my body rocks back and forth in motion with the vehicle as my willpower leaves me. Chase. His very memory blasts through the dam holding back my emotions as I desire to join him. He is dead because of me. I failed him. My very existence is a curse to those around me. As the transport continues its trek, I curl into a fetal position, wishing I would wake from this nightmare, but deep down, I know it is no dream, but my new reality.

A loud pop bursts through my melancholy and the transport comes to a sudden stop. Before I have time to grasp what has happened, the door opens, allowing a set of hands to grab my legs and drag me out of the back. My legs buckle when my feet touch the ground, refusing to carry my weight, but the arbiters dragging me do not care.

"The tire is flat," says one of the arbiters. "Put her over there!"

My feet scrape the ground as the other arbiter forces me to a spot away from the transport and out of sight before throwing me to the ground, laughing at the fact that my bound hands and feet prevent me from stopping my fall, and I crash onto my side.

"Don't move," a voice commands me.

As the clinking of tools and cursing voices rise in the distance, gentle hands lift the bag off my head, and Renal's face comes into focus.

"I haven't much time," he says. "I need you to tell me where you got this." He holds out the flare gun that Perce had given me. I thought I had lost it during my confrontation with Molers in the wildlands.

"Why should I trust you?" I hiss.

A somber look crosses his face, expecting my answer and unspoken accusation. "Numerous times I could have turned you in or executed you myself. A man of my position needs no excuse..."

So, he is a marshal.

"...but I never did. I've known of your nocturnal activities for some time, Noni." He holds the flare gun before me. "Where did you get this?"

I think back to all the times Renal seemed to have covered for me: the wristband, stopping Molers' snooping, and even the flare gun. During any one of those instances, he could have turned me in, but refused. Why? More cursing ensues when the tire refuses to budge.

"What does it matter?" I say, my voice choking with tears as I think about Tapiwa thrusting the knife into Chase. Another one killed because of me, like Sheila, leaving me to wonder if I am more of a curse to those around me.

"And what of the girl?" Renal says.

Gwen. I had forgotten about her, yet had promised to protect her moments before. How could I have abandoned her so soon? How could I have done that to Chase? I cannot abandon her, not now, but how do I help her? Ashamed of having forgotten her plight, and her own torment at having been forced to watch her brother—her only family—be murdered wafts over me, forcing me to go limp, as I look into Renal's strong but merciful eyes as he does the one thing he can think of to help us both.

The sounds of tools being put away warns me that there is no time for questions. I either trust Renal now and take a chance, knowing that my fate cannot be any worse than it is at this moment, or I refuse and accept my end.

"A man gave it to me," I reply. "I had help outside the wall. His name is Perce. There is one shot—one flare left in that—and only he can see it. He'll be waiting outside the wall on the eastern side of the reservoir."

Before the two men finish putting their tools away, Renal places the bag back over my head and sneaks away, whispering, "Survive."

He leaves, and doubt creeps into my mind, like it always does, forcing me to wonder if I made the right choice in trusting him.

One of the arbiters yanks me off the ground and drags me back to the transport, throwing me in the back before it takes off again. The longer I am trapped there, the more I wonder why they have not taken me to a detainment box. The grooves in the floor of the vehicle dig into my back as the transport hurries down the road, refusing to slow down even for the sharpest of turns, tossing me around as though I am mere garbage. The transport stops for the third time, and the doors fling open as rough hands yank me out and onto the ground, but before I have time to consider where I am, they drag me across the ground, allowing the pavement to tear into my clothing, and my bottom scrapes across the threshold of a doorway before I am dropped on the floor. Something warm and viscous coats my arms as I roll on the floor, trying to regain some sense of control, but a foot presses into my chest, pinning me while someone rips the bag from my head.

"Arbiter Noni, welcome back," says the same arbiter that had ordered me to be thrown into a chute with Amal the last time I was here at the detainment facility, making me realize that the arbiters' orders were to deliver me like a gift-wrapped package. He leans in close, sneering, "How do you plead? Guilty? Or not guilty?"

I spit in his face, and he backhands me in response.

"Take her away!" he shouts at the arbiters around him.

They lift me by the shoulders and haul me down a tunnel, leaving the bag off my head, allowing me to see the yellowed lights with small halos around them connected by cables left exposed to the dampness within the air, doing little to expunge the darkness from this foul place. A long pipe coated in rust trails on the ceiling behind us, following the winding corridor with ease, as though mocking my efforts to keep some sense of direction in this place. My heels hit a small rise as they drag me further downward into the depths of my new hell before a door opens, exposing a dark interior, matching the hollowness within my heart.

I am thrown inside and roll across the damp floor as the door slams shut and the locks click into place, while the arbiter's footsteps fade. I twist and turn, forcing my bound hands past my rump and my legs, until they pass under my feet and are no longer behind my back, but in front of me, allowing me to focus as I work the bindings loose and free my hands and feet. I toss them aside, screaming in a rage as the memories of the last few hours plague me, until I lay down, exhausted. Unable to fight it any longer, I curl into a ball and release the tears that had built up within me, weeping alone in the darkness, surrounded by concrete walls and the melodic, hollow drips of water.

Chapter 22

Survival

Darkness surrounds me, except for a single pinpoint of light that forces its way through a small crack in the ceiling, telling me that daylight has come in a vain attempt to comfort me in my despondency as I lie on a moldy mattress that sits flat on the floor, wondering what will be in store for me today. I've no idea how many days have passed—how long I have been imprisoned here. For a while, I marked the wall, but stopped when my days turned into a blur of dolor and survival, each battling the other, hoping to come out as the victor, but neither has succeeded in suppressing the other.

Chase is dead, and his death is my fault. I never should have tried to escape or believed that we would be able to have a life outside of Arel. No one ever does. Arel always wins. Its will is to be obeyed, and yours crushed. I want to feel Chase's hand again, his warmth, and his strength, but all I'm left with is the cold darkness of this cell as I wait for what my captors have in store me next (hoping that it will be my last) and the reality that he is gone, and that

Gwen is trapped as Tapiwa's prisoner. Rage boils within me as the memory of Tapiwa stabbing Chase with a knife fills my mind, making me wish I could exact my vengeance on her, and I grip the filthy, tattered edge of my mattress, pretending that it is her throat as I envision myself squeezing the life out of her, before remembering where I am, and I release my grip as a series of silent sobs overtake me, alone in my solitude and sadness, until they come for me.

When my captors grow bored, they take me to an arena where my audience consists of other arbiters, more prominent members of Arelian society, and promising recruits. My opponents are undesirables or recruits who made one mistake too many. Kill or be killed: that is the only rule. There, I am nothing more than entertainment, and a warning, as I am forced to fight another to the death: the winner is rewarded with a meal and lives to fight the next day. In that arena, I release my rage and do as Chase begged me to do with his last words: I do what I have to, to survive, forcing my days to pass with the repetition of a simple routine: fight, eat, sleep.

Each day is the same.

Fight.

Eat.

Sleep.

Fight.

Eat.

Sleep.

Fight.

Eat.

Sleep.

Fight.

Eat.

Sleep.

Each day, I am dragged from my cell.

Fight.

Eat.

Sleep.

Fight.

Eat.

Sleep.

Fight.

Eat.

Sleep.

Each day, I am forced to fight another to the death.

Fight.

Eat.

Sleep.

Fight.

Eat.

Sleep.

Each day, I imagine myself in the arena with Tapiwa.

Fight.

Eat.

Sleep.

But the desire for retribution only carries one so far, and as I lie here with nothing but my somber memories, I wish for it to end, to be freed from my lugubriousness before I lose myself to the animal inside that craves the blood of innocents as it tries to quench its thirst for revenge.

The door opens, allowing the cloudy light from the hallway to fill my sordid cell, forcing me to open my eyes and pull myself from my atrabiliousness.

"Up," says a stern voice as an arbiter with a baton storms in.

I refuse to move.

He hurries over to me and strikes me in the back, screaming, "Up!"

More arbiters enter the chamber, forcing me to my feet and secure shackles around my wrists, restricting my movement before they rush out, while a familiar shadow appears in the doorway, and I recognize the wiry hair, the stance, and the hesitation.

"Five minutes," says the arbiter as he leaves.

"Noni?" Faya's trepid voice echoes around me, sounding as hollow as my heart. "Noni, please look at me."

"Why are you here?" I demand, my voice sharp and filled with venom.

"I know we haven't seen eye to eye lately, but..."

"Why are you here?" I demand again, and the forcefulness of my tone causes her to pause for a moment as it echoes around us.

"I never should have been angry at you for Joel," she says in a quivering voice, making me wonder what secret she holds that wants to be revealed, and what she bribed the guards with to be allowed in here.

"What do you know?" I ask, looking up into her guilt-ridden eyes.

"Noni, please..."

"What did you do?" My harsh voice forces her to take a step back.

"Molers came to me after Mandi had confessed her treachery, and after Joel had died. I was angry and sick with grief! I wanted the pain to go away and for someone to pay the price and—"

"What did you do?" I scream at her.

Tears stream down her face as she struggles with telling me the truth.

"Molers prides himself on being able to read people, but he is not as knowledgeable as he thinks. I told him the best way to manipulate you—how easy it would be because of your sudden soft spot for plebeians, and how you always stepped in to save the same one or two, not because you pitied them, but because you cared about them. I saw it in your eyes the day you stopped Grelyn from striking that plebeian."

I remember that day. Grelyn had raised her hand to hit Chase, but I had stopped her.

"How could..." I began.

"Molers never forgot the humiliation he suffered the night Mandi confessed. It cost him. You know the lengths he will go to salvage and protect his reputation and to get what he wants."

"So, you gave him what he wanted," I spit at her.

"I didn't mean for it—I wanted my own pain to end, but I never meant for any of this to happen! I feared for you when you made your challenge, and I never thought you would try to leave Arel. It wasn't supposed to end like this!"

"Like what?"

"With you trapped down here as nothing more than a spectacle!"

"And how did you expect it to end?"

"Not like this."

"What did he promise you?"

Faya's lip trembles as she struggles to stay silent.

"What did he promise you!" My rage-filled voice fills the atmosphere around us, and even I am surprised by its fury.

"A seat on the council, where I can do as I wish and be awarded special privileges, and…"

"And not have to worry about having a forbidden love affair. Joel's fate was an unforeseen consequence of an act I have wished I could undo each day, but you knowingly and willingly stole mine!"

"Noni, I know I don't deserve your forgiveness…" she says though tears.

"And you'll never have it," I reply.

Guilt obliterates what control she has left on her emotions as tears stream down her face and her body shakes in remorse, but I do not care as we both stare at one another in the darkness: Faya pleading for forgiveness, while I contemplate a just end for her. She glances around and pulls a small vial out of her pocket, and for a moment, I wonder how she got it and what favors she had to promise to obtain it.

"Take this."

I stare at it. I do not need to ask what it is.

"She says it is like going to sleep. You'll feel nothing."

I remain silent, wondering whom she refers to, though I can wager a guess.

"Please, Noni! I can't—they make me watch the fights, and I can't bear to watch you suffer anymore!"

"It's always about you, isn't it?" I say in a quiet voice. "You're not here because of me."

"Noni, please," Faya pleads through tears as she holds the vial out to me. "We both know this only ends one way."

I consider her request, ending it here and now and no longer suffering from the loss of Chase, and of Sheila before him, no longer being reminded of how I failed them both, of how they were murdered despite my efforts to save them is welcome, but I remember Gwen. Who will help her now?

"What about Gwen?" I say.

"Who?" asks Faya, confused.

"The plebeian's sister," I say. "She has been taken by Tapiwa. What about her? Are you going to spare her from her suffering the way you are trying to spare me?"

Faya says nothing as her hand with the vial remains extended.

"Keep it," I say. "Use it on yourself."

Before more words can pass between us, the guard bursts into the cell, forcing Faya to hide the vial of poison.

"Time's up," he growls at her.

As she leaves the chamber, Faya pauses, taking one last glance at me, saying, "I'm sorry."

"So am I," I whisper, but do not know if she heard me as the door closes behind her and locks into place.

Moments pass before the door opens again, allowing arbiters inside carrying a metal pole with a collar attached to it. They snap it around my neck, unshackling my hands as they haul me to my feet and drag me from my cell and down the familiar sordid hallway to the arena for me to prove if I should be allowed to live another day. The noise grows louder, its intensity deafening when the arbiters force me to pause before the copper door—turned green from years of oxidation—and detach the pole from my collar before shoving me through. For a moment, my senses suffer from overload as those gathered in the stands fill the area with a mixture of cheers and jeers, making me wonder what bets have been placed on me today: the former Arelian hero turned into a spectacle for others' entertainment. I refuse to acknowledge them as I move to the center where a man wearing a similar collar to mine awaits me, flexing his muscles and bouncing from one foot to the next in anticipation, and judging from his cocky demeanor, he must be another arbiter.

"Why did they pick you?" I ask, letting my curiosity govern me.

The man flexes his chest muscles and cracks his neck. "I volunteered."

A slight smile appears on my face before vanishing. Another hopeful wishes to make a name for himself, by ridding the world of me.

Two trap doors open and spears appear before our feet. Spears. Arel loves its entertainment, and the bloodier the better. The man reaches for his weapon, but an electrical jolt shoots through his collar, forcing me to step back—a painful reminder to wait for the buzzer.

"Welcome! Welcome!" greets the announcer as I scan the crowd, spotting both Tapiwa and Molers sitting side by side in the shadows, watching with neither joy nor amusement as their interest rests with the actions of the crowd, not me.

"In one corner, we have our champion"—the announcer waves his hand in my direction, while a mixture of boos and applause fill the air—"while in the other, is our challenger!"

A series of cheers emanate from the stands as my opponent raises his arms and shouts at the crowd while beating his chest with his fists. Rolling my eyes, I spot Faya positioned between two arbiters, making me wonder if she is as much a prisoner as I am, to which my subconscious scolds me, telling me that I already know the answer: we are all prisoners here, even if no one realizes it because it is filled with pretty things, like Luther warned.

"Let the games begin!" yells the announcer over a loudspeaker and the buzzer sounds.

My opponent and I dive for our spears. He grabs his first and thrusts it at me as I reach the floor, forcing me to roll to the side while I swing my spear to block. He stabs at me a second time, and I roll to the side again, until I am out of range. I jump to my feet. He does the same. Seconds pass as we circle one another, waiting for the other to move. I charge him, swinging my spear at his right foot, but he steps backward, forcing me to stab the concrete floor instead. Before I can react, his fist rears downward, plowing into the side of my face, stunning me long enough for him to jab the blunt end of his spear into my stomach. I stagger backward, gasping for air. He lunges for me, and I plant the end of my spear into the floor, using it as a support while swinging both my feet into the air, kicking him in the face, and the moment my feet touch the floor, I bring my spear up and strike him in the neck.

Enraged, he charges me, thrusting his spear at me. I block him, but he still barrels into me, knocking me to the ground with the full force of his impact. Knowing that momentum is on his side, he jabs his spear at me, and sparks fly as its point strikes the floor near my head, forcing me to roll from one side to the next in an attempt to avoid his blows. Again, he aims his spear for me, and I hold mine in front of me, blocking his attack, but a jolt of electricity bursts through my collar, causing my muscles to seize and allowing him to rip my spear from my hands, and it clatters on the floor several feet away. The electrical shock stops, and I try to catch my breath as I lie on the frigid floor.

Knowing I am defenseless, my opponent sneers, bringing his spear up for a fatal blow, but I sit up in time to avoid it and lunge for his leg, knocking him to the floor only for him to slam his heavy-soled boot into my back, causing me to flop onto the floor once again. Another electrical shock bursts from my collar and courses through my body as my opponent lunges for me only to have his collar release a burst of electricity, stunning him long enough for me to kick him in the face and force him back onto the floor. He scrambles to his feet and tries to kick me, but I block his attack only to receive another blow to the side of my face from his powerful fist. Rage fills him as he bears down upon me, and sweat glistens off his dark skin. Again, he jabs his spear at me, but I somersault away, diving for my own spear, but my efforts stop as he seizes my left ankle and jerks me backward, tossing me aside as though I am nothing more than a piece of unwanted furniture.

Dazed, I stare at the lights above me and spot Molers, and the memory of what he did to Sheila and how he cheated during the Challenge of the Fates enrages me, but then I spot Tapiwa, and the memory of her knife plunging into Chase infuriates me further, giving me the motivation needed to end this. Fueled by this anger, I rise to my feet, while my opponent prances around, beating his chest, playing to the crowd's thirst for blood, but their enthused shouts dwindle as I stand, and my opponent turns around, noticing my newfound will to survive. Unfazed, he faces me, twirling his spear, pleased that the fight is not over. He races for me with his spear extended, but I turn on my feet, forcing him to miss, but before he can react, I snatch his spear and slam my head into his face, breaking his nose and causing him to take a step backward as I wrench the spear from his hands. He wipes the blood trickling from his nose and grunts in anger, while I laugh and motion for him to pick up my abandoned spear.

He takes a step toward it. Without warning, jolts of electricity stem from his collar, causing him to drop to his knees in pain after it stops, allowing me to attack from behind as I drop the spear, seize his collar, and plow my fist into his face over and over again as blood coats my fist with each strike, giving in to my anger and the desire to force others to suffer from the pain I feel. As my fist goes in for a final strike, electricity surges from my collar and throughout my body, forcing me to release him, and I drop to the floor, waiting for the pain to stop. The electrical shocks cease. For a few moments, we both kneel on the floor, recovering our senses, until I crawl to one of the spears on the ground and force myself to my feet, waiting for him to do the same. He does so. I motion for him to attack. Furious, he rushes toward me, but I stand my ground, waiting for the precise moment, not caring if this is my last, so long as I take him with me. When he is almost upon me, I turn away, sweeping the blunt end of my spear across the floor, tripping him, before dropping to one knee and planting my spear on the floor with its pointed end up as he falls into it, and it plunges its way through the bottom of his chin, into his skull, and out the back of his head. His spear falls from his grip and clatters on the floor to stunned silence.

I turn my gaze toward Tapiwa and Molers while my opponent's body hangs in the air, supported by the spear poking out of his skull.

"How about a real challenge?" I scream at them. "Do you not have the courage to fight me yourself! Is your courage dependent upon whether the odds are in your favor?"

I raise my foot and kick the dead man to the ground before picking up the spear that fell from his hand.

"You are weak!" I shout at them. "Weakness leads to failure, and failure leads to—"

I throw the spear in the direction of Molers and Tapiwa, but a protective barrier stops it, put in place for such a moment.

"Noni!" someone within the crowd cheers, and others join him. "Noni! Noni! Noni!"

As the crowd shouts my name with praise, more electrical shocks spur from my collar, causing me to drop to the floor in pain, helpless, as arbiters burst into the arena and attach a pole to it before dragging me away. As my feet scrape across the concrete, the cheers turn to boos and hisses that fade when I pass through the door, but before it can shut out their ire, I notice a man watching me—not cheering, not booing—only to vanish when the door closes, making me wonder what will happen to me next.

Chapter 23

Mercy

Lines mark the wall in front of me, displaying how many days I have been kept in this dark hole. Sixty; I count 60. It is an approximate number. After one of my last triumphs in the arena, I resumed keeping track of my time here, though the moisture clinging to the wall threatens to wash them away, and may have already caused a few marks to vanish. Sixty days of the same routine (fight, eat, sleep); 60 days alone in this hole with only my anger to comfort me as I spend every minute envisioning myself exacting my revenge for the deaths of Chase and Sheila; 60 days of pure hell. A soft, honey-colored glow appears on the bricks behind me as the tiniest bit of light pokes through the small crack in the ceiling, growing bolder and brighter with each passing second, transforming into fire before morphing into a more subdued marigold yellow, and it greets me as the light passes over my face, warning me that another day has come.

I pick up a piece of chipped stone that has nestled itself within the crack that formed between the bottom of the wall and the floor and mark another line, thus marking another day spent here. Sixty-one. It has now been about 61 days since my incarceration.

Heavy-soled boots pound the floor of the corridor outside my cell, and judging by the force behind them, they must belong to a heavyset man. I drop the small piece of stone and scoot away from the wall, knowing that the footsteps come for me. The door opens, and in rushes arbiters with cattle prods. I back away, but there is nowhere for me to go, and they corner me, ramming their cattle prods into me, forcing me to my knees as another collar snaps around my neck before hands force me to my feet and drag me from my prison. Every resistance is met with a shock from one of the cattle prods. One guard rams his prod into my face and receives a fist to his own in response.

"You know your orders!" shouts his supervisor.

Steamed at being reprimanded, he rams his cattle prod into my stomach to relieve his anger, causing me to double over and retch, and he smiles, until my bile covers his boots. Distant cheers rumble in the background, growing louder with each step, telling me that, once again, I am to be put in the arena, as has been my life since they imprisoned me here. I dig my heels into the floor, knowing that it is useless to do so, but I have no intention of making life easy for my captors. A jolt from a cattle prod reminds me of who is in charge here: and it is not me. We pause before a set of steel doors, waiting for them to open as a series of gears grind together, warning me that this could be my last day here—a moment I welcome. When the doors open, pain bursts from my ears as the roar of the crowd in the stands pounds them with endless fury while hands shove me through, and I walk to the center of the arena, knowing what is expected of me, and what will happen if I fail to comply.

Three people wait for me: all of them female recruits, each with a weapon, and none wear a collar. I eye them, focusing my attention on the two who look as though they will run their gauntlet soon, noting the bloodlust within their eyes as they glare at me, planning their attack, and I return their scowls with my own while remembering Chase's words before he breathed his last. I scan the repugnant crowd as they cheer and salivate at the chance to see more carnage and witness my demise. Damn them all.

The buzzer sounds.

My focus remains on the two older recruits (one holds a machete and the other a chain) while the third seems to have disappeared, and we circle each other, waiting for someone to make the first move as we eye one another, each desiring blood: they want mine, and I want revenge. The one with the machete makes a move and I back away, avoiding her blow as she swipes her blade through the air, hoping to strike me with it. As I dodge her attack, a jolt of electricity bursts from the collar around my neck, causing my muscles to seize. I force them to move, to do as I will as she charges me with her teeth bared, but the pain refuses to release me, so I go limp, falling to the ground, forcing her to strike air. The electrical shocks cease. Before I can catch my breath, my opponent turns on me with her machete, while the other takes aim with her chain, whirling it in the air as she plans her attack. I kick the ankle of the one with the machete and roll out of the way as the chain crashes onto the floor, creating sparks as it strikes the concrete. I snatch the chain and yank its owner off her feet, but am forced to let go when the blade of the machete crashes into the links of the chain.

Once again, we circle each other, with them desiring my death and the glory they will receive should they succeed, while I see nothing but the system that murdered Chase and Sheila, and I will settle for nothing less than retribution. One flings her chain at me, catching me around the ankle and jerks me off my feet, while the other dives for me with her machete, forcing me to roll out of the way as the blade strikes the floor with a clink. My fingers work in vain to get the chain off my ankle while they both move toward me, ready to strike me down, but before they reach me, my third opponent stabs one of the others in the ankle with a wooden staff, making me wonder why she would choose such a weapon, while the other backhands her, knocking her to the ground. I free my ankle and spot the recruit on the ground with her staff laying next to her and calculate my next move. The other two charge for me, but I somersault across the floor in between them and lunge for the abandoned staff, scooping it up in time to block an attack from the machete and jab its wielder in the chest. As she stumbles backward, the other whips her chain at me and I dive downward, forcing her to miss, as I swing the staff and hit her in the face, before swiping her feet out from under her.

I spring to my feet in time to block an attack from the one with the machete. She swings at me in rapid succession, and each time, I block her attack while being forced to skip backwards in an effort to avoid her blows. She feigns an attack, and I fall for it, allowing her to slice me below my left shoulder. She moves in for the kill, but I duck and step around her before bringing the staff up and ramming it into her back between her shoulder blades, followed by another blow to the back of her knees. Before I can attack again, electricity shoots from my collar, forcing me to drop the staff and fall to my knees in agony. The one with the chain wraps one end around my torso and yanks me to the ground, forgetting that metal is a conduit, and she drops the chain as an electrical shock reaches her hand. Undeterred, she snatches her chain when the electrical shocks cease and smacks me in the chest with her end before kicking me in the stomach, while the other recovers from the blows I had given her. Another kick heads for me. I roll out of the way and free myself from the chain as she races for me in a rage, but I block her attack and kick her in the abdomen, forcing her to double over before wrapping the cable around her neck and giving it a good twist. I drop her body, pleased when it thuds on the floor.

Rage spills from the one with the machete when she sees her fellow recruit lying motionless, and she races for me, her machete ready to strike me down, but I am ready for her. I pick up the chain and wrap both ends around my hands, waiting. She swings her machete at me, but I stretch out the chain and block, remarking at the sparks that hover around us after metal meets metal. She strikes again, and I block her attack with the chain as we move around the arena with her expending all her energy into trying to hack me with her blade, while I wait for the right moment. She swings at me a third time, and I wrap the chain around the blade of her machete before ramming each of my fists into her face, stunning her. I release her weapon and toss it to her before motioning for her to come at me. She takes another look at her fellow recruit and tightens her grip on her weapon as she lunges for me. She strikes with the machete, but I wrap the chain around her wrist and twist, forcing the blade into her chest, and horrified shock appears on her face before she falls to the floor.

Something shifts behind me. With lightning movements, I whirl around and knock the person to the floor, jumping on her and pinning her as I raise my fist, when a frightened squeal reaches my ears and stops me. I stare at the girl beneath me—the third recruit. She cannot be more than eight years old. I glance at the abandoned staff and realize that it was not her chosen weapon, but one assigned to her because she was setup to fail, making me wonder what she did to be placed here as punishment. Her frightened eyes stare into mine and all the rage that has consumed me dissipates. She never murdered Sheila—Molers did. She never murdered Chase—Tapiwa did. I lower my fist and stand up, extending my hand to her, and after a moment's hesitation, she takes it as the crowd falls silent and their bloodthirsty cheers vanish.

"Go," I tell the girl, and she hurries away, while I turn toward the door that I had entered the arena through.

Another door slides open, allowing a man with a spiked ball on a three-foot chain to enter. He plows the spiked ball into the girl's face, shattering her skull, forcing me to watch in horror as her limp body slumps to the floor surrounded by a pool of her own blood.

She had no warning—no time to react—and all I can do is stand statuesque as the pooling blood around her grows larger, reflecting more of the lights above us as it covers her black hair. She never should have been here; they sentenced her to death regardless. Stunned silence hovers over us, refusing to believe the reality of the girl's fate. I face this newcomer as he turns toward me; my eyes turn to slits as I devote my attention to him, while my simmering rage returns to a rolling boil, ravenous for my sort of justice. Since the day I received my commission, people have died around me—people I tried to help, people I took mercy on because they did not deserve life's injustices (the plebeian girl, the infant, Sheila, Chase, and now this recruit), but Arel overruled me and murdered them—but no more.

I sprint for him as the crowd remains silent—no cheers, no shouts, just hushed silence—and the man raises his flail, swinging it around his head, lengthening the chain as he frees the wrapped end from around his gloved hands, letting what I thought was a three-foot chain become a ten-footer, preparing to strike me with it. The spiked ball crashes into the floor, cracking the concrete as I dive to the side, avoiding its blow. He jerks the chain, lifting the spiked ball into the air and swings it at me again, but I jump out of the way and lunge for him, catching him around the legs and forcing him to fall to the floor. Enraged, he plows one of his gloved hands into my face, followed by an elbow to the stomach, stunning me.

As I gasp for air and try to regain my feet, my opponent jumps to his and widens the gap between us as he jerks the spiked ball into the air and swings it above his head, preparing to strike me, while I watch, evaluating his movements, trying to guess the precise moment he will release it. He makes his move. The ball whooshes through the air as it heads for me, and I jump out of the way at the last moment. The man howls in a rage and jerks the ball into the air again before flailing it at me, but I dodge to the side, avoiding its blow, but the moment my hands touch the floor, electrical shocks shoot from my collar and course through my body, causing my muscles to seize once again. I try to ignore the pain, but these jolts are more intense than the previous ones, making me wonder just who controls this collar. Or is it on a timer? While I lie on the ground, unable to move, the man rips his spiked ball from the floor and swings it above his head again, grinning in triumph as he prepares for another strike. The electrical shocks cease, and I lie still for several moments, forcing my lungs to take in air as I flex my fingers in an attempt to get my muscles back under my control. I need to get this cursed collar off. My eyes look up in time to see the spiked ball coming for me, and I roll out of the way, cringing when it strikes the floor and sends a series of cracks zigzagging through the concrete. An idea forms in my mind.

Jumping to my feet, I charge for the abandoned chain, dropping to the ground and sliding across the floor as the spiked ball careens for me again, avoiding its blow as bits of concrete fly into the air and nick my exposed skin. I ignore it. I reach the chain and snatch it, wrapping one end around the dead recruit's body. The spiked ball crashes into the floor next to me, forcing me to lunge to the side with the chain in hand. Again, he jerks the chain, and the ball rises into the air. He swings it around his head, building momentum as I scan the floor and spot an area that has been damaged. I race for the other end of the arena, stretching the chain out so that it sits between my opponent and the damaged area of the floor before dumping it and racing to where the cement has cracked as he prepares to attack. He flings the spiked ball at me, and I jump out of the way in time to avoid another blow, hoping that my plan works. It does. The spike ball crashes into the already cracked cement and sticks. Confused, my opponent tries freeing it by jerking on the flail's chain, and I use those precious seconds to ease a spike underneath the collar where its locking mechanism is, ignoring the bits of blood that drop to the floor as it cuts my skin, and tug as hard as I can, until…

The collar falls off.

Freed, I run to the chain I had stretched out on the floor as my opponent realizes something is amiss and charges for me, reaching me at the exact moment I raise the chain and trip him. He crashes to the floor, and I wrap part of the chain around my fist before plunging it into his face. He rears back in pain, juts his foot out, and kicks me in the chest. Ignoring the pain, I unwrap the chain from around my fist and throw it at him, forcing him to bring his hands up in a defensive posture as I wrap another part of the chain around his ankle. He kicks at me again, and I jump back, avoiding it. We eye each other, trying to read the other's thoughts. He lunges at me, but I take my collar and wrap it around the chain I had attached to his ankle and step back as another electrical shock is released from it. His body seizes and convulses on the floor as electricity rushes through him, but I know it will not last long, so I jump to my feet and head for the spiked ball stuck in the floor, kneeling before it when my opponent stops convulsing.

Enraged, he rips the chain from around his ankle and stands to his full height, narrowing his eyes as he focuses on me, preparing to go for the kill. He races for me, picking up speed with each step as he draws nearer, while I brace myself, listening to his feet pound on the concrete as everyone within the arena remains silent, unwilling to intrude upon our fight, while they wait with bated breath to see how it ends. When my opponent is a few feet away, I tackle him, catching him around the knees and force him to fall forward into the spiked ball embedded on the floor, pleased when a spear goes through his skull and pokes out the other end with bits of his brain matter decorating its tip.

An astonished hush surrounds me as I force myself to my feet and look around at the crowd watching me. Not once did they make a sound during our fight, and even now, they remain still as their initial shock morphs into respect, as though they themselves believe they owe some measure of deference for what has happened. I turn away from the man with the flail and step toward the girl—she never deserved what life dealt her—and kneel beside her before turning her over and folding her delicate hands on her chest, doing my best to hold back the tears that desire to break free, when a pair of black boots step beside me. I jump to my feet, ready to fight, but stop when a pair of hands stretch out a folded blanket for me to take, and I look into the respectful eyes of the man handing it to me, and sweat streams down his dark skin as he nods his head in the direction of the girl. My fingers wrap themselves in the coarse and grimy fibers of the roughhewn blanket and take it from him, unfolding it. He takes one end, and together, we place it over the girl, covering her, giving her a small tribute. It isn't much, but it is all we have. Once finished, the guard salutes me, and as I glance around the arena, people, one by one, including Faya, salute me, except for Tapiwa, except for Molers, and except for a man who is very interested in this turn of events, the same man I saw before.

A door opens and the guard signals for me to pass through it. I do so, but as I trek through the corridor, none of the guards come for me. They step to the side, allowing me to pass unhindered as I walk back to my cell, knowing that there is no other place for me to go. Each one nods approval in my direction, some salute me, and a few whisper the word arbiter with a note of respect, telling me that, for now, we have reached some level of agreement: the young recruit—the girl—did not deserve what happened to her. I, for all my sins, belong here; the others chose to come here for glory; she did not and deserved far better.

When I reach my cell, a guard opens it for me, but instead of shoving me inside like has happened so many times in the past, he steps aside, his apologetic eyes indicating that he wishes he could do more for me. I give him a wry smile, unsure of what else to do, and step into my cell as the door seals behind me and locks into place.

A single voice breaks the quiet surrounding me.

"I see you have survived another day."

Commander Vye? What is she doing here?

Her eyes burn through me like they did the first day I met her, as though she can see through me and into the innermost depths of my soul and knows my darkest secrets, but unlike that day, there is empathy and warmth mixed with sorrow and determination.

"Commander," I say, confused, "how did you get in here?"

"I've been around for a long time," she replies, "long enough to curry favors."

"But..."

"Shh! I haven't much time." She pulls a small vial out of her pocket, and I recoil from her, remembering how, earlier, Faya had done the same.

"What is that?" I demand.

"I haven't time to explain," she says as heavy boots stomp down the corridor, drawing nearer, indicating that her allotted time nears its end.

I stare at the vial in her hand, unsure of what to believe.

"I need you to trust me, Noni."

"I don't know who to trust," I say, remembering how Luther had left Gwen, Chase, and me when Molers and Tapiwa sprung their trap. Was he in on it and led us there?

"Noni," Commander Vye says in a gentle voice, a tone I have never heard her use before, and it seems foreign to her very nature, about as foreign as a fish swimming in sand, that it captures my attention and forces me to silence my doubts and listen to her, "I once said that you were a lot like me, but I was wrong. You are far better than I ever was. You kept your soul, whereas I abandoned mine long ago."

Silence passes between us as I digest her words.

"That is what Arel does. It beats every essence of humanity from you, until you submit to its will, and its will alone, without question. I saw you the day you ran the gauntlet; saw how you risked your own life to help another; how you could have ended the life of another recruit, but showed mercy instead; how, somehow, despite all their efforts, they remained unable to squelch that last spark of humanity within you. I knew that if they had sent you to their first choice, that spark would be extinguished."

"Where?" I ask, allowing my curiosity to have its triumph.

"The borderlands," Commander Vye's voice echoes around us, forcing me to remember pieces of my past.

Beyond the barren wasteland, beyond the outposts, are the borderlands. None ever speak of them, and we all pretend that they do not exist. The crematoriums may be a standard punishment for arbiters who fail to always obey, but the borderlands are an eternal sentence into Hell, where the most resistant to Arel's rule are dumped as a warning to others. Isolated, away from any ounce of civilization and forgotten, no one, except for the rare exception, lasts long out there. It is said that the borderlands harbor the most vicious and beastlike of creatures. They once resembled men, but are now nothing more than ravenous beasts who hunger for human flesh. Even the barbarians refuse to enter that place.

How many of these stories are true? I don't know.

Perhaps Arel started them so as to keep people compliant by making them fear the world outside the wall. I once thought they were told to us to keep us afraid, until a former recruit returned from there during my ninth year at the training facility. How he managed it, no one knows. But six months after being left in the borderlands for a simple infraction, he appeared at the gate, holding a severed head in his hand. The head itself looked to be that of a monster, probably due to decay and rot. The council allowed him inside, believing that they could use this as a tale about the greatness of their arbiters and their ability to survive insurmountable odds in the protection of Arel and her citizens. They transported him to the training facility and lined us up in the courtyard, so that we could bear witness to a great hero, but he snapped. He tackled one of the instructors and ripped her throat out with his teeth, and before anyone could react, he lunged for the recruits with the instructor's flesh hanging from his lips and dripping blood as he killed any in his way, but that is not what I remember most.

The crazed look in his eyes and the inhuman features of his face burned themselves into my memory and gave me nightmares for weeks afterward. Thinking about it now makes me shiver in terror. They put him down, riddled him with so many bullets that his body resembled a mangled rag more than a corpse. Reports of the incident spread, and the stories about mad, flesh-eating animals that inhabit the borderlands grew. Could this former recruit have been a tool of Arel, drugged to act insane? It is possible, but no one will ever know the truth of the incident, only the stories that grew out of it, and how, for a while, there were no incidents of rebellion within the city.

As I remember that fateful day, I realize that Commander Vye has never betrayed me in the past, and even when she could have turned me in for disobedience to the will of Arel, she never did.

"Please"—she holds the vial out to me—"trust me once more. Don't let the harshness of the past embitter your heart."

I snatch the vial from her hand as the door opens and a different guard's gruff voice fills the cell.

"Time's up!"

Commander Vye stalks past the guard with her head held high, exhibiting that commanding stature that I have always admired and hoped to one day possess, leaving me alone in the dark and the damp as the door slams behind her, sealing me inside once more.

I study the vial in my hand and the clear liquid within it. If she had wanted me dead, she could have done it the moment I stepped into my cell. She is planning something. I do not know what, nor do I know how, but this unusual behavior of hers tells me that she has made a choice, much like I did when I tried to get those I cared for out of Arel.

I pull the cap off the vial and bring it to my cracked lips, whispering, "Bottom's up," and drink the contents, grimacing as the bitter liquid touches my tongue before plunging down my throat and to my stomach, hoping that her plan works and is worth it.

Chapter 24

Sacrifice

A foot in my stomach jerks me from a deep slumber as a guard jostles me until I roll into the slimy wall. Instinct forces me to grab his foot and prepare to yank it out from under him, but he expects my actions and whips me with his baton, forcing me to bring my arms up to block his attack.

"Go!" he yells at me as he hauls me to my feet and shoves me out into the corridor without bothering to place a bag over my head.

Looking around, I do not see my usual guard, and wonder what is going on. Something is different. The point of a baton presses into the space between my shoulder blades as the force behind it pushes me down the hallway and past plastic bulges within the corroded wall, allowing yellow light to peek through tiny holes in the years of accumulated dust and grime, thus adding to the ominous feeling of dread that fills me with each step I take. We turn a corner and another corner before stopping before a massive door with sludge covering it, forming ripples as it stretches downward from the top, reflecting the murky light, forming the illusion of a flowing river, albeit one that resembles sewage more than a serene piece of scenery as it opens, revealing the arena within. Another stab by a baton in my back urges me to walk through the doorway and into the chamber where, once again, I must fight another for the privilege of breathing. Muffled cheers greet me as my sluggish feet carry me into the enclosed arena filled with a crowd gathered to watch me battle another, but there is a change in the atmosphere: gone are the exuberant cheers from before, replaced by half-hearted shouts as the crowd goes through the motions of appearing enthused, while always keeping their eyes on the armed arbiters surrounding them, while drones dart about, recording everything. My suspicions that there is more going on here than a simple test of wills and strength are confirmed when I spot Commander Vye in nothing more than her uniform pants and undershirt, waiting for me in the arena's center.

Fury rises within me as I remember her visit and her pleas to trust her.

Trust her?

Trust her!

What was in that vial she gave me?

I stop before her, scowling at her as the feeling of betrayal wafts over me and wraps its tendrils around me, mocking the trust I had in my commander as the idea that I am nothing more than a pawn in everyone's game mocks my naivety and desperation to have even the smallest amount of faith in someone. She glances in my direction, unsurprised by the venomous look on my face as I circle her, flexing my muscles, ready to eliminate another enemy.

"Arbiter Noni, once a hero to Arel, now reduced to a disgraced traitor!" comes a voice over a loudspeaker. "Let's see how your skills measure up to your former commander. Place your bets!"

No one speaks. No one shouts. No one offers any coins.

"I said place your bets!" shouts the announcer in ire, but no one accommodates him.

A flicker of movement in the shadows shows Tapiwa waving her hand, indicating that the fight should begin, regardless, and next to her sits Faya, cloaked in worry and sadness, and for a moment, my anger toward her dissipates and is replaced by pity. Like me, she is a product of Arel's dominance and desire to eliminate any essence of individuality, by forcing all to conform to its will.

I turn my attention to Commander Vye, focusing all my anger on her, not bothering to wait until the buzzer sounds before pouncing on her and landing a fist into her face, forcing her to step backward, but my arm feels heavy, weighed down. She stares at me, unsurprised by my actions, refusing to rub the welt forming as she takes a step sideways, allowing the light to dance upon her shaved head as she measures me and decides her next move. Fueled by my anger, I charge her, but she blocks my attack and throws me to the floor. I roll onto my back and wrap my legs around her left ankle, twist, and force her off her feet. She crashes onto the floor, and I spring for her, but Commander Vye expects my attack and brings her legs up, ramming her feet into my stomach and sending me flying backward. Once again, we face one another as we stand up, waiting for the other to make their next move.

"Noni," she says, "it's not what you think."

"You said to trust you!" I spit at her.

"And you must!" she hisses at me, frustrated but unsurprised by my reaction toward seeing her here.

Rage overpowers my judgement, and I lunge for her. Together, we struggle to get the better of the other, locked in a battle of wills as I try to ram my fists into her, while she blocks my every move and my limbs begin to feel numb.

"You still leave your left side open!" she says as she plows her fist into it, forcing me to cringe in pain before I whirl around and elbow her in the chest.

As our fight continues, the crowd remains silent, and the only noise I hear is the whine of the drones as they hover around us, capturing every moment of our battle. I snatch one from the air and fling it at her, aiming for her face, but Commander Vye brings her arms up, crosses them, and blocks. Enraged, I charge her, twist, and drop to one knee when I reach her before grabbing her by the shoulders and flipping her over me, allowing her to crash onto the floor. She rolls out of the way before my fist touches her face, and it strikes the concrete instead.

"What was in that vial?" I demand, as I breathe heavy, wondering why my body feels as though it has weights strapped to it.

"Necessity," she answers.

I lunge for her again, catching her around the middle, and we both fall to the floor, rolling around, fists flying, until we break apart and stare at one another with me full of rage, while Commander Vye possesses understanding. Another drone hovers past, and I snatch it from the air, smashing it into the floor, reveling in the sound of it breaking as sparks fly from it, before flinging it at her, but my arm refuses to work and she blocks it with ease.

"This is the only way to save Gwen!"

Blood drains from my face as her words hit me, cutting me to the core, and memories of Chase and Gwen that last night I saw them thrust themselves to the forefront of my mind, consuming my thoughts and blocking out my current situation. All I see is Chase's empty eyes as he stares back at me, devoid of life, devoid of hope after telling me to do what I had to, to survive, while echoes of Gwen's anguished screams fill my ears. My sudden lack of awareness is all Commander Vye needs to get the upper hand. She jumps on me, pinning my arms behind me as she presses me into the concrete floor, while wrapping her other arm around my neck, and places her lips against my ear.

"I'm sorry," she whispers as a small prick tickles my neck and my mind turns hazy, while the world before me blurs before everything goes black.

My eyelids close and seal themselves shut, while my breathing shallows and my muscles seize and refuse to obey my commands as she allows me to drop to the floor, and though a slight bit of pain jabs itself into my side, I am unable to utter a single word as my jaw clenches itself. I cannot move. No matter what I do, I cannot move. Panic grips my mind as the feeling of being trapped in my body washes over me, and the fear of spending the remainder of my existence in a body that won't allow me to communicate or even open my eyes takes hold, leaving the torture of being able to hear what happens around me, mocked by the whine of a drone hovering close, taking in every moment of my torment.

Before anything else happens, screams fill the arena as gunfire echoes around me, while people trample one another in a desperate attempt to get out. Was this Tapiwa's plan all along: to force people to watch my demise before slaughtering them, or did they not act according to her wishes and saluted me like they did before? I will never know. I only know their fate in the end. The thought of Faya being forced to watch all this in horror enters my mind, assuming she even survived Tapiwa's latest burst of anger.

"Fools!" screams Tapiwa in disgust. "Get them out of here!"

"Wait!" Commander Vye's voice breaks through the panicked barrier within my mind. "We had an agreement!"

"I've changed the terms of our agreement," replies Tapiwa's cold and calculating voice.

Hands lift me from the floor in unceremonious fashion and cart me away. I try to move, but my body refuses to obey, forcing me to endure this agonizing uncertainty of what will become of me. The hollow sounds of heavy boots stomping along the grime encrusted grate that covers the floor of the corridor fill my ears as my mind ponders every possible outcome, each ending with me stuck in this nightmarish scenario. How much time passes I do not know, as this prison seems to last an eternity before a thump sounds behind me. I crash onto the grated floor as those carrying me release their hold to deal with this new and uninvited threat. A man grunts as items are knocked to the floor and scatter in several directions before being drowned out by the sounds of fists finding their way into the soft underbelly of another's stomach before…

Silence.

Once again, I will myself to move, a finger, a toe—anything!—but nothing happens. I am trapped, appearing dead before the world when I am very much alive. Gentle hands lift me before another prick tickles my neck.

"Come on, Noni," comes Commander's Vye's voice, filled with a worried tone that I have never heard from her before, but I still cannot move and my breathing remains shallow.

A fist slams into my sternum, prompting my lungs to open up, causing me to breathe in all the sudden before coughing up wads of spit as my heavy eyelids open, allowing me to see the dingy confines of the hallway and the still bodies lying among broken glass and scattered utensils. I try to lift my arm, but it feels heavy and sluggish, as though it hasn't been used in ages and protests my insistence that it work. Someone bursts into our little area, and Commander Vye snatches a shard of glass off the floor and throws it at the man, striking him in the throat where he clutches it, surprised by the deadliness of her aim, before collapsing in a pool of his own blood.

"Come on," says Commander Vye as she helps me to my feet, but they flop about, causing me to wobble as I try to stand. "The effects will wear off in a few minutes."

"What did you do to me?" I ask, my voice sounding harsh, like it hasn't been used in years.

"What I had to," Commander Vye replies as she leads me through the hallway, supporting me as I try to regain my balance, but I still feel groggy from whatever drug she had given me.

We hobble through the corridor, past the streams of brown water snaking their way down the walls, channeled through the moss that dares to grow as I try to make my torpid feet work, but they still feel heavy, as though they are encased in giant blocks of concrete. Noise echoes from ahead, and she leans me against the wall for support and creeps onward, peering around the doorway and into the small room where muffled, anguished screams escape. Someone spots her. Commander Vye leaps into the room and tackles one of the arbiters, and as the sounds of scuffling fill the area, I inch my way closer for a better look, forcing my legs and arms to obey me, despite their protests, and demand they ignore the effects of the drug, and I enter the room as an arbiter pins her against the wall. I try to help her, but my leg falters and I stumble, causing the arbiter to glance in my direction, allowing Commander Vye to use his distracted mind to throw him off her, before snatching a rod from a table and slamming it into his face.

Another arbiter approaches her from behind.

"Commander!" I scream.

She whirls around and throws the rod at him, causing him to block, before lunging for him and knocking him to the ground, where she rams her fist into his throat until he stops moving. As she searches the body and grabs his sidearm, I notice a man strapped to a chair with a muzzle over his face, riddled with open wounds on his bare chest: he's the guard that had shown kindness to me yesterday. Such an act is never tolerated. I walk up to him—my unsteady legs force me to lean on a nearby table—feeling pity for him, and undo the straps to his muzzle before untying him, while Commander Vye watches, unsure of my actions. He lifts his hands and removes the muzzle, while I take a step back, hoping my judgement is correct, and Commander Vye tightens her grip on the sidearm she had taken from one of the arbiters.

An alarm sounds. Our escape has been noticed.

"Noni!" Commander Vye motions for me to follow her when the arbiter I freed stops her.

"Wait! Not that way!"

"We need to get to the tunnels," Commander Vye says.

"That route will be watched," says the man. "A previous prisoner tried escaping that way."

"The tunnels are the only way out of here," protests Commander Vye.

"There's a better option," the man says to me.

"Take us to them," I say, trusting him.

The man crawls out of the chair, grimacing as his open wounds tear, causing more blood to ooze from them, contrasting against his dark and sweat-soaked skin, before heading in the opposite direction of the approaching guards, with Commander Vye bringing up the rear, while I remain between them, unsure of my willingness to trust this man but knowing I have no choice. He leads us down another dark corridor, stopping us whenever an arbiter or two runs by before continuing. We reach a doorway leading to another hallway. After waiting several seconds, he motions us through, and we chance upon a guard, but before the guard can speak, the man grabs him by the face and shoves him into the wall before dropping his lifeless body.

A shot rings out and grazes the man's arm. Undeterred, he picks up the dead guard and throws the body at the approaching arbiters before grabbing me and pushing me down another hallway, while Commander Vye fires the pistol at them. Bullets riddle the wall protecting us as we charge down the hallway, with me still wobbling as I struggle with the effects of the drug Commander Vye had used on me. The man I freed grabs my shirt and yanks me back before I pass the threshold to what seems to be an abandoned room, and jumps in front of me when two arbiters appear. He seizes the arm of one and bends it backward, snapping the bone at the elbow before shoving the arbiter into the other one. The second arbiter goes for her gun, but the man snatches it from her and fires two rounds into her chest before rounding on the other and emptying the magazine. Feeling useless, I watch as he strips them of their weapons and hands one to Commander Vye before helping me hurry down the corridor, where we round a corner and come face to face with a hatch.

"What is this?" demands Commander Vye.

The man opens the hatch, releasing a foul, decayed stench that makes my stomach churn until I retch, spewing bile onto my boots and the floor.

"This is where we keep the bodies, until they are taken to the crematorium. Follow the chute and drop into the water when you reach it. Dive, until the current catches you. It will take you to the tunnels."

Placated, and knowing she has no other options, Commander Vye shoves her way into the tunnel. Shouts draw closer as arbiters close in on us.

"Go!" he says to me, and when I hesitate, he adds, "I'm right behind you."

I force my way into the chute, ignoring the urge to vomit a second time as the stench of rotted flesh and putrefied blood overwhelms my senses before turning around to help the man when the hatch seals shut behind me, followed by a spray of gunfire, telling me what his fate is. The only thing I know about him is that he showed me kindness, and I'll never know why he sacrificed himself for me. Aware there is nothing I can do for him now, I turn and follow Commander Vye, crawling over mangled and rotting corpses, knowing that, at any moment, I may become one of them. My hand slips into the open stomach of one, and I cringe as the slime of their intestines wraps around my arm before I am able to pull myself free. Seconds crawl by as I worm my way over the bodies, clenching my throat in an effort to not throw up, hoping that my nose will accustom itself to the stench, but the further we go, the worse it becomes. At one point, I taste death and know that I have gone where even the Devil would not dare tread.

A hollow sound pricks my ears as we reach an open chamber with stagnant water (black from decayed blood), telling us that we have reached our end in this nightmarish tomb. I stare at the still water, noting how its spoiled essence reflects nothing but absorbs every speck of light that dares enter this place, thus giving it a ghoulish life, and the thought of diving into it sickens me. I steal a quick glance at Commander Vye and the regal stance she maintains, refusing to show disgust at what she must endure next, making me wish that I shared her iron will.

"Remember your underwater training?" she asks.

I do, and I wish I didn't. I despised that part of my training, and I despise what I must do now.

She dives into the water, and I do the same, recoiling as the viscous liquid, made so by the bodies within it, envelops me, impeding my efforts to move through it to get beneath its prison. I refuse to open my eyes in this filth and point myself downward, kicking as hard as I can, while holding onto the precious air within my lungs, even if it had been fouled by the miasma of death. Swim until you feel the current, and allow it to carry you, that is what the man said, and that is what I will do. My lungs burn from the desire to release the air within them and replace it with something fresher, but I command them to remain shut as I push my way through the black water and past the bloated limbs of the bodies that have fallen in, hoping that the current finds me soon. A wisp of bubbles flips a strand of my hair. I must be close. I kick harder and pull myself with my arms in an effort to propel myself further through the water when...

Bubbles escape from my lips as a force slams into me and carts me way, tossing me around as though I am nothing more than a rag doll, meant to be abused rather than treated with any sort of care. My body flops around in the current as it carries me away, causing me to lose my bearings and not know which way is up or down, and the more it tosses me around, the more my stomach churns and the more air bursts from my lips. I force myself to swallow in an attempt to not gasp as bubbles rush past my ears, tickling them while my body spins as it moves with increasing speed, making me fear that I will splatter into the side of a metal wall, never to be seen or heard from again. Another force crashes into me, whipping me into another direction, and despite my efforts to stabilize myself, my arms and legs flail around in chaotic fashion as the current reminds me who is in charge. Fire engulfs my lungs as an intense pulse pounds in my head and neck from my efforts to hold onto my breath, and I know that I cannot hold it for much longer. Another flip from the current and my lungs win out, allowing the air contained within them to explode from my mouth, and before I can stop it, the natural reaction to inhale takes hold, causing me to cough and sputter, while the current whips me around until…

Weightlessness takes hold for a moment before I plummet downward and crash into a pool of water, plunging deep beneath its surface, until I am able to move my arms and legs and push myself upward. A hand grabs my arm and yanks me free, pulling me onto a solid surface as I gasp and cough, spitting water from my mouth in a desperate attempt to clear my lungs, thankful to be able to breathe once again, even if it is stale air.

"We've made it to the tunnels," Commander Vye says, not bothering to ask if I'm all right, though the fact I am still breathing answers that question for her. "Come on. They'll learn where we are soon."

"Where do these tunnels lead?" I ask, still coughing.

"To the reservoir."

The reservoir. That's where this all began, in a way, when I ran the gauntlet and had to swim across the reservoir in order to complete it, and afterward, I received my commission and was assigned to the eastern sector to be under the command of Commander Vye, never knowing the two of us would end up here. Such is the way life is.

Still coughing, I force myself to my feet, while Commander Vye checks the weapons she took from the arbiters who tried to stop us, frowning at what the decayed water did to them. Greenish water flows past us, wrapping itself around my legs, forming ripples as it continues its journey through the tunnel, not caring about us or why we are here, only that it does not wish to be slowed in its desire to keep going. We follow the current, jogging through the knee-high water as best we can, doing our best to not fall when shouts reverberate off the concrete walls, drowning the soft roar of the water, warning us that we are no longer alone down here. For a split second, we glance at each other, each thinking the same thought: they found us. The sharp barking of dogs pierces our ears adding to the terror we face, and we both bolt down the tunnels, splashing through the water, not caring about its filth as we try to escape, knowing what will happen if the dogs catch us.

Metal bars stop us from going further, but as I study them, I realize that they have corroded from all the moisture, allowing the bottom to tilt upward and break away, thus forming a small opening. Before I can point it out to Commander Vye, a low growl rumbles behind us, and the hairs rise on the back of my neck as a wave of cooled heat washes over me, and my stomach drops because I know what I will find when I turn around. Keeping my movements slow, I face the dog behind me, only to find that, instead of one, there are three. One charges Commander Vye, while another runs for me, teeth barred and snarling as it jumps for me. I throw my arm up to block it, while clenching my jaw to keep from shouting in pain when its teeth sink into my flesh, while it growls around the saliva dripping over my arm. I punch it in the eye, and it jumps back, yelping, but before I can react, another jumps for me, forcing me to duck in order to miss its attack, only to have the first one lunge for me a second time.

Again, I throw my arm up and its teeth pierce my skin as it snarls around the warm blood coloring its yellowed fangs, and I face the gate blocking the tunnel and ram it into one of exposed spikes, relieved when its grip loosens the moment its side is pierced. I drop it in the water. The other dog leaps for me, forcing me to fall backward into the water, and as I struggle to get it off so that I can breathe again, a shot fills the tunnel and, the dog goes limp. Flinging it off me, I sit up, coughing, while Commander Vye remains poised with steam escaping off the barrel of the pistol in her hand. More shouts enter the tunnel and draw closer, telling us that they've heard us and we haven't much time. Sucking in a lungful of air, I dive into the water and swim underneath the rusted bars, cringing as warmth mixed with a sharp pain scrapes my back from having been caught by one before coming out the other side. My head bursts through the surface as I gasp for air before checking the blood oozing from my new gash. It isn't deep; more painful than mortal.

Commander Vye bursts from the water next to me, breathing deep, but neither of us waste time continuing on as we both push ourselves through the water, following the current to where it leads, hoping that it will take us to our salvation. The irate voices of arbiters behind us grow closer, their echoes surrounding us and mocking our efforts to escape their clutches. A tremendous explosion rips through the tunnels, deafening us with its shockwave, telling us that they wasted no time in destroying the corroded gate. We pick up our pace, lifting our knees high so as to move faster through the water, welcoming the roar of a waterfall as light fills the tunnel, and water spills from its open mouth and to the reservoir below, creating clouds of vapor that swirl into the sky, producing tiny rainbows, unconcerned about our predicament. Arbiters close in on us as their shapes appear at the end, morphing from shadows into clear images of armed guards intent on killing us.

I peer over the edge. "It's too far down!"

"Remember your training!" Commander Vye screams over the noise, checking the number of rounds she has left.

My heart beats faster, not because arbiters are closing in on us, but because the thought of jumping from this height frightens me; it always has, but I know I have only two choices: risk it or face the arbiters.

"I once told you that you were a lot like me," Commander Vye says for a second time as she cocks her pistol, "but I was wrong. You're better."

I glance at her, unsure of what to think about this newfound parental affection she has toward me, and a sinking feeling grips my stomach.

"Save the girl. Trust only Renal."

As her words hit my ears, I realize that she is saying good-bye, that she has made her final choice in this life.

"Comman—"

Before I can finish, her heavy-soled boot rams into the center of my chest and shoves me over the side and into the falling water, where its mixture of gaseous and liquid forms overtake me as I plummet downward, unable to stop, rendered helpless as flashes of gunfire escape the tunnel before falling silent, ended by drops of fresh blood mingling with the waterfall. Commander Vye is no more. Water slaps my back as I plunge into it, forcing the air out of my lungs and disorienting me as the current twists me around, trying to keep me under. I kick and thrust my arms out, trying to make my way to the surface, but with each effort, water pulls me back under, determined to drown me. A hand grabs my arm, yanks me free of the water's hold, and pulls me onto the bank of the reservoir, where others wait for us with clothes to conceal my mangled uniform.

"Breathe, Noni," says a gentle voice.

Renal?

He carries me away from the bank and to two people I do not recognize, while gunfire rains down upon us from the tunnel, only to be met by single shots, whose origins are hidden above us. I know of only one person able to do such a feat: Perce. The world fades around me as my body shuts down, and before it goes black, Renal and I are thrown into the back of an unmarked transport before it speeds away, taking us with it.

Chapter 25

Forgiveness

Metal confines my wrist, refusing to let it move as my mind reenters the realm of conscious thought, trying to grasp my new reality. Commander Vye is dead. I never gave much consideration to the possibility of being in a world where she no longer existed, nor did I realize how much I relied on her strength. She pushed me, forced me to become tougher than I thought possible, and at times, her methods seemed harsh, but there was always something else there as well, a sort of kindness, and above all, she was fair. When others tried to harm me, she was the first to stop them, even if it meant her death, and in the end, she paid that price.

Trust only Renal. That is what she told me. As I think about her last words, I realize that I know nothing about her past, or what happened to make her believe that Renal is the only one she could trust, but I do know that they had a mutual respect for each other and always looked out for the other: a strong bond—not intimate… platonic. Or, at the very least, they never allowed it to move past that stage.

Gwen!

Her name bursts into my muddled mind as I consider lying on the bed and surrendering to the demands of my battered body, but the memories of her horrified face as Chase died in my arms forces me awake. I am her only hope now, and I will not abandon her to a fate worse than death. I failed Sheila. I failed Chase. I will not fail her.

Metal springs poke my back from the mattress I lie on, squeaking from the slightest of movements. Part of me wishes to remain numb and unaware of the world around me, but the other half insists on waking up, and its insistence grows louder by the second, until my heavy eyes pry themselves open, allowing me to see the drab and gloomy room I am in: my new prison. I stare at the mismatched wallpaper as it forms an abstract puzzle (bits of it peel away, exposing the metallic wall behind it), as though someone placed scraps of it wherever they could to try and bring some humanity to this place but gave up, an act for which I do not blame them.

I tug at the handcuff holding me to the bedpost—if one can call a mattress with springs poking from it set between four metal posts a bed—wishing to be free from the confines of this room. Pressing my other hand against the bedpost, I push it, taking note of its weakness. Twisting, I stretch out my handcuffed arm as I turn so that I can place my feet on the post, ignoring the protest of my muscles as the smallest of movements causes me to ache, and kick it. It screeches, not liking my actions, and I hope no one hears it as I kick it again and again, until it pops free of its base, allowing me to slide the handcuff from it. Freed, I jump up and go to the door. Locked. I expected no different, but… The hinges. They are on the inside of the room. Perfect. I rummage through the room, searching the floor with its mangled carpet—it feels heavy as though it holds decades of grime, having never been cleaned—frowning as bits of it flick away from the slightest of movements. Nothing. I scan the dim chamber, but there isn't much in it, except the bed and a small dresser.

I hurry for the dresser, yanking open drawers, coughing as each one releases a musty smell, but their emptiness mocks my failure to escape this room and mingles with the anger already germinating within my heart, causing it to grow stronger until nothing will stop it. As each drawer proves useless, my anger festers and rumbles until it explodes, and I rip out one of the drawers and throw it across the room at the bed, breaking it, stopped only by the clatter of the pieces crashing on the floor and the distinct sound of something small and metallic breaking free.

Calmed by my curiosity, I approach the broken pieces of the drawer and rifle through them until I find a small screw. Picking it up, I study its pointed tip and turn back to the door: it might do. Fueled by a renewed sense of purpose and feeling a sort of energy I have not felt in a long time, I rush for the door and pry at the hinges with the screw, pleased when they loosen even more, proving the faultiness of their construction and the complete lack of maintenance in this place. My sweaty palms cause me to drop the screw a few times, followed by a series of curses as my handcuff clinks against the wall, but determination sets in, convincing me to continue as thoughts of Gwen trapped in a personal hell fill my mind. Concentrating on the task at hand, I pry away at the hinges, working them loose, doing my best not to allow my elation at my small success to cause me to falter now, but instead, remain focused as I pick at the bottom hinge, until it pops free, allowing the door to lean at an odd angle, thus giving me enough space to squeeze through.

I enter a corridor with a strip of light stretching from one end to the next, creating a lone aisle of illumination, while the edges remain in mysterious shadow, harboring any number of threats, and like a thief that wishes to go unnoticed, I steer clear of the light, choosing the darkness and its concealing cloak, and the anonymity it provides. With a ginger step, I press down on my left foot, testing the floor in case it creaks, but what lies underneath the sticky and grime infested carpet (green at one point, but now brown) sounds more metallic than wood, so I hurry down the hallway, pleased that the carpet muffles my footsteps, allowing me to move in silence before being forced to stop and cling to the wall for support as my breathing becomes rapid and pain grips my side, reminding me that I am not well. The least bit of physical exertion is excruciating and forces me to stop as I try to catch my breath and ignore the stabbing pain that causes my body to beg me to go back to my cell and the bed within it, but I refuse its pleas. I push myself away from the wall, forcing myself to hobble down the corridor and to light spilling from a doorway, hoping that it will lead me from this place. Voices emanate from the opening, and I start to turn, looking for another way out so as to avoid detection, when the familiarity of one stops me cold.

Luther.

Memories of the night when Chase was taken from me, when I was cursed to hold him as he breathed his last, and of how Luther had abandoned us, flood my mind, bringing with it all the rage that such betrayal builds. My skin turns hot as righteous anger rises within me, building by the second and funneling itself to my desire to exact vengeance, until its eruption dwarfs any awakening volcano. Blinded by my longing for revenge, I abandon reason and burst into the room, finding two men: one I do not recognize, and Luther. Surprise stuns them for a few seconds, but the other man regains himself and goes for a weapon. I lunge for him, knocking him to the floor, but my body rebels as a severe pain in my side grips me, forcing me to falter and to fall back onto the part of my training that taught me to ignore it.

The man sees my weakness and uses it against me, punching me in my injured side, forcing me to stop. Gritting my teeth, I push through it, and grip his weapon, wrestling it away from him, and before he can retaliate, I strike him in the head with it, rendering him unconscious. I turn toward Luther and lunge for him, astonished that he makes no move to escape or stop me as I pin him against the wall with my forearm against his throat, while sweat drips down the sides of my face as I use all the strength I have to keep from collapsing, determined to get some measure of justice for those I've lost. My eyes focus on his, intent on letting him know why this is happening, but instead of defiance or fear, all I find is sympathy and remorse.

"I won't stop you," he whispers, knowing why I want him to suffer.

Taken aback by his willingness to allow me to exact my sense of justice, I loosen my grip on him, and the weakness of my body overcomes my will, forcing me to fall to the floor, but before I reach it, Luther catches me and helps me to a chair.

"Noni, you're not well. You need to—"

"You left us!"

"And I have suffered from it each day."

"How?" I demand. "How have you suffered?"

"Guilt is a terrible punishment," Luther says, but my anger refuses to take notice of the agony within his voice.

"Have you ever watched the ones you love die?" I hiss at him.

Luther's lower lip trembles as he kneels in front of me and looks me in the eyes. "I never told you the truth about what happened to my wife."

Curiosity forces my anger to subside as Luther tells his tale, allowing me to learn more about his mysterious past.

"Ysla. My beloved Ysla. We were both older when we met, but we both felt as though we had always known each other. I loved her strong will, amazed that Arel had failed to stamp it out of her, and neither of us could have been happier when our permit to live together as husband and wife was approved. After a few years, we decided it was time for an addition to our family.

"As you know, Arel permits some couples to have a child, and such a child is provided by the breeders. My wife and I were one of the lucky few, and when Mora was delivered to us by representatives of the maternity ward, we couldn't have been more thrilled. And so, the years passed, and Mora grew, but Ysla's strong passions could not be quelled. She spoke out against the iron will of Arel and how the most minor infractions warranted the harshest punishments. I begged her to stop, but she refused, saying that silence in the face of tyranny is the worst of all evils. One day, she criticized the sitting president, who, at the time, was the father of Tapiwa and Kumi. That night, the arbiters came. They didn't waste their time with an arrest. They judged her there in our home and carried out the execution against the wishes of their commanding officer. He tried to stop them, but they overpowered him and knocked him out. By the time he came to, the deed had been done. The one thing I'll never forget is how he apologized and the genuineness behind it. Before Ysla died, she made me promise to care for our child, who had just entered her eighth year. That night burned itself into my memory, and when alone, it's all I think about."

Ashamed of believing that I was the only one who has suffered, I hang my head, unable to say anything, except for the two words that manage to make themselves known. "I'm sorry."

"Mora never forgot that night either, and she was so much like her mother. I couldn't stop her, any more than I could stop her mother, and knew what had happened when she never returned. I had made a decision to leave Arel that night, but not in the way you think. I had my books, my favorite drink, and then you appeared on my doorstep, as though fate herself had placed you there.

"I failed you that night. I know I did. And if it is what you wish, and I know I deserve it"—Luther pulls a knife out from under his shirt and places it in my right hand, curling my fingers around the smooth hilt—"take what you will."

I stare at the knife for a moment, remembering the first night I met him and how he saved me from the arbiters chasing me, and as I ponder the chance of such a meeting, all anger toward him dissipates, leaving me my shame. I release the knife, allowing it to drop to the floor with a clunk, unable to carry out what I had wanted moments before. More death is not the answer. Helping Gwen is all that matters now.

"I guess I should thank the commanding officer that night, for sparing you."

"It won't be hard. He's the one who brought you here."

Renal?

"The night you were arrested, he was waiting for me when I managed to make my way back to my home. I told him about the tunnels that led to the reservoir. He did the rest and is the reason we are all here now."

It seems there is no end to Renal's secrets, but before I can ask any of the multitude of questions yearning to break free, my injuries prove too much for me, and I slump over in an effort to ease the pain in my side.

"You need rest."

"Gwen!" I say as Luther helps me up and carries me back to my room.

"You cannot help her in your current condition."

I glance at the man I had knocked out earlier, and as though reading my mind, Luther says, "Just leave him. He'll be fine. Though he may have a headache when he wakes."

He has me lean on him as he helps me down the corridor to the room I awoke in, noting the broken hinges of the door as it hangs off-kilter, and smiles to himself, unsurprised. He lays me on the bed, and I grimace as more pain grips my side.

"But..." I start to say, but Luther interrupts me.

"Rest. I'll stay here while you sleep."

He sits on the corner of my bed in a manner I always imagined a father would when caring for his child as I stretch out on the lumpy mattress and exhaustion overtakes me, despite my efforts to remain awake, and before another second passes, my eyes close, and I pass out.

Chapter 26

New Faces

My slumbering mind receives a small spark alerting it that I must wake up, and it grows with each second as the lumps within the mattress I lie on poke my back, moving as I move, determined to remind me that I am in a strange place. I do not want to wake. Doing so reminds me of all that has happened the last several weeks, and of all I lost, but the more insistent that first spark becomes, the more I realize that I cannot lie here forever. My crusted eyes refuse to open, preferring their stickiness that forces me to blink as I try to clear them. As the room around me comes into focus, I look around at the metallic walls and the haphazard wall paper of every color (pink, puke green, yellow, orange, and brown, to name a few) dotting it while peeling away in places as the adhesive loses its effectiveness.

Gwen!

I bolt upright and wish I hadn't, as pain grips my head, and it spins for a few moments before my equilibrium resettles itself, followed by sharp pain within my side.

"I see you are awake."

I turn toward the voice and find Renal sitting in a chair, wondering where Luther has gone.

He steps toward me and holds out his hand with two white tablets in it. "Here. It will help with the pain."

I stare at the tablets, remembering how, as a recruit, I was forced to endure pain so as to build strength.

"Weakness is failure," I whisper, still remembering the mantra that had been drilled into my head since birth.

"Bullshit."

Renal's sharp response causes me to look at him as I have never heard him speak against Arel before, and though I do not wish to appear weak, my ribs are killing me; so I snatch the two tablets and pop them in my mouth, swallowing them.

"Come," he says. "It's time you meet who owns this place."

I get out of bed and follow Renal as he leads me into the dingy hallway with its dim lights and notice a spider in a corner, weaving its web underneath one of the wall lamps, unconcerned about our presence as it works with diligence while we pass. Renal's pace remains steady, but I can tell that he has slowed it for my sake because each step causes me to pause before continuing, yet I do not lag behind. I do my best to not show weakness: I do not know who may be watching.

The corridor ends when we reach a dark doorway and enter a stairwell beyond that is darker and more foreboding, or perhaps it is my apprehensiveness giving way to imagining possible terrors that do not exist. The steps sound hollow as I trudge up them, trailing after Renal's erect form as he takes them with ease, while I try to not show any sign of pain, but the more I climb, the harder I breathe, and the harder I breathe, the more my ribs hurt, but I refuse to give in and grit my teeth as I keep pace. Renal pauses and looks back at me, a dark silhouette against the shadowed stairs behind him, almost like a mysterious guardian keeping an eye on his charge as I continue up the stairs, forcing myself to reach the step he stands on and stare at him as though asking why we have stopped.

He snorts before continuing, unsurprised by my defiance, and I follow him with questions growing in my mind as I ponder the people who live in this place and who they are. As we move up the dark stairwell, light appears above us, growing brighter the further we go, until we step through another doorway and into a massive domed interior with chandeliers hanging above us, dispersing the shadows as they try to brighten the path before us. As I enter their domain, I blink from the influx of light, having grown used to the darkness.

Unable to help myself, I stop and crane head backward as I try to look straight up at the dome above us, and despite the paint covering the glass panels so as to keep nosy eyes from peeking in, bits of it has flaked away, allowing the sunlight to spill through and add a golden glow to the already lit chandeliers, highlighting the spiral staircase leading to the top balcony. Mesmerized by the hidden glamor of this place, I fail to see the years of neglect at first, but as I walk across a frayed rug, I notice a screw hanging out of an unused light fixture, unable to decide if it wants to fall or remain where it is. My feet sink into the purple carpeting that runs up the spiral staircase—its once vibrant essence dulled from time's collection of grime and dirt—but its plushness surprises me as I climb upward, while Renal watches me with amusement.

"What is this place?" I ask, unable to keep my curiosity inside.

"This was once a place where dignitaries from across the world would meet for entertainment before it was abandoned."

"Entertainment?"

"Or so I'm told."

"And no comes here?" I ask with skepticism.

"As you know, condemned buildings in Arel are often off limits to all, including arbiters, until they have been given new purpose by the Arelian government. This one has a certain member of the Arelian Council seeing to it that it is never repurposed, thus making it a good place to hide."

I notice a small hole in the painted panel of glass next to me as I climb the stairs and move closer to it and peer out at the world beyond, remarking at the busy streets below as people in their different colored uniforms hurry along, oblivious to our presence and ignoring the building we are in like they were trained to do.

"Welcome to the northern sector," says Renal.

He waves me onward and I pull myself away from the window and follow him to the balcony, unable to stop myself from touching the tarnished railing, not caring about the specks of rust that stick to my fingers. Renal continues down another corridor to a room, where inaudible voices seep through the cracked door. He pauses before it and holds his hand out, waving me inside.

"They're waiting for us," he says.

Unsure of what I will find, I step inside and the voices cease.

Strange faces, each regarding me as nothing more than an unwelcome guest whom they must tolerate for the moment, turn toward me. My eyes roam the room, scanning their faces as they sit at a round table, darker than my hair, with a single, bulb-shaped lamp shining harsh white light on us all, making us look more like specters instead of people, until I spot a familiar one: the councilwoman from the Command Division who had visited me while I recuperated in the medical center. Her harsh eyes send stabbing pricks of venom, and I return the favor, knowing that I am as welcome as a parasitic infection.

"Please," says a man with gray around his temples, accentuating his dark skin, and dressed in robes of the Arelian Council, "sit."

He gestures to an empty seat, and I take it, knowing that, for now, I have little choice, while Renal sits beside me.

"You may go," he says to Renal with dismissiveness, but Renal remains seated, refusing to acknowledge the man's words. Perturbed, the man allows Renal's defiance to go unheeded. "I'm sure you all know who Arbiter Noni is. We..."

"Why am I here?" I demand, my lack of patience rising.

"Such rudeness," scoffs the councilwoman.

"I'll show you rudeness," I mutter, my anger rising, but Renal places a light hand on my knee, warning me to keep my emotions in check and have the stoic posture that every arbiter is expected to possess.

"Ha'ya, please," says the man from the Arelian council.

The councilwoman snorts, but remains silent.

"Arbiter Non—"

"Just Noni will do," I interrupt him. "Who are you and what is this place?"

The man from the Arelian council gives a wry smile, doing his best to ignore my rudeness, before answering. "I am Councilman Anshu and this is where those of us who wish to rebel against Arel and what it has become reside."

A marking on the shadowed wall behind the man stands out for the first time as my eyes adjust to the light and focus on it: the symbol of Arel with a slash through it. I jump from my seat, causing my chair to fall backward and crash on the floor. "You're terrorists!"

"Noni..."

"It's you! You are the ones responsible for the bombings!"

"Those were meant to get Arel's attention and to weaken the Arelian government's hold on all of us," says Anshu.

"Innocent people died!" I continue.

"There are no innocents," mutters another man at the table, but before I can react, Anshu silences us all.

"No one was to get hurt. That has always been my policy."

"Tell that to the ones who suffered."

"The man responsible for that has been dealt with," Anshu says, and it hits me: I know why his voice sounds familiar.

"The railcar," I whisper. "You were the voice on the railcar!"

"Yes, that was me. I wanted to spur the people into action, and at the time, you were a symbol of Arel's oppression."

"You've been toying with us, using us," I say.

"I am not proud of it," Anshu says, sounding regretful, "and I know you have no reason to trust us, but I am not asking for your trust, only your help, since our goals seem to be aligned."

"And what would that be?" I ask.

"Bringing down Tapiwa. Now, please, sit."

I glance at Renal, who nods his head, and I pick up my chair, righting it, before sitting down.

"I know that our previous actions deserve to be judged, but we do want the same thing: a free Arel where people decide the course of their own lives, and where they no longer live in fear of a government that intends to control them. You are here because he"—Anshu points at Renal—"made a deal with us to get you out of the detention center, and because you have become a symbol for justice to the people of Arel."

I laugh at that notion. How can I be a symbol for anything?

"Are you so ignorant," Ha'ya says, "that you do not know what is happening within your own city?"

"Considering where she has been for the last few months, how could she?" Renal says, coming to my defense.

"Ha'ya," Anshu says with a silent warning in his voice before turning toward me. "I'm not surprised you do not know. Your actions have initiated a change within Arel. The people are standing up to the tyranny that has plagued us for so long. They are no longer cowering in fear. Tapiwa had your exploits in the wilderness during your challenge transmitted throughout Arel, when you weren't busy destroying the drones, no doubt hoping to capture the moment of your death. But you refused to give up, and when arbiters stopped you from finishing Molers, people gathered in the streets and cried out in anger."

I look at Renal.

"It's true," he says. "When your face appeared on the screens throughout the city, people cheered. Every time you destroyed a drone, they cheered, seeing it as a symbol of you standing up to the Arelian government. And when I returned with you to the city, I saw the aftermath of a protest and Arel's way of dealing with it."

"The point is, Noni, you are a Medal of Honor recipient who has defied a dictator again and again, and whether you meant to or not, you have become a beacon of hope to the people of Arel. And that is why, when he"—again, Anshu points at Renal—"came to us with a deal, we accepted it, and helped him get you out of the detention center. We need you as a..."

"A pawn," I say.

"An ally," Anshu corrects me. "We have a plan, and it hangs upon your cooperation."

"Wait a minute," Renal says, "the deal was with me. Leave her be."

"No," Anshu says. "We risked everything to get her out. It's time to keep your end of the bargain."

"And have I not fulfilled my end?" Renal's tone darkens.

"You have. She has not."

"One condition: you help me get Gwen," I say, knowing that there is no way to get out of this.

"The plebeian," laughs Ha'ya. "You'll never get close enough."

"You all seem to be very resourceful," I say. "That's the deal. I'm not helping any of you, unless I get Gwen out of her prison, and so help me, I will go in there alone if I have to!"

"You won't be alone."

Perce steps into the light, and we all stare at him, wondering how he managed to enter the room unnoticed, and how long he had been standing there in the darkness.

"Who let you in here?" demands Anshu.

"Me, myself, and I," replies Perce, saying each word with precision, mocking Anshu's irate demeanor before looking at me.

"We cannot..." begins Anshu, but Perce ignores him and closes the distance between us—Renal starts to move to protect me, but I raise my hand, stopping him—speaking so that all can hear his words.

"I will go with you. I owe them nothing," Perce says, referring to the others, "but I owe you everything for saving my people. I know the hurt of not being able to help the ones you love. If you wish to save the girl, I will be by your side."

"Noni," says Anshu, trying to get me to see reason, but I want none of it, "it's too risky to save just one plebeian."

"Girl!" I scream at him. "She is a girl—a child who has lost everything because of me! Now, I'm going in there to get her, whether you like it or not!"

"Noni—"

"Your deal was with him!" I shout, pointing at Renal, "Not me! You want my help? Then prove to me you are a man to be trusted."

Before Anshu can speak, another voice cuts him off, silencing everyone. "I'll go too."

"Joseph," begins Anshu before being cut off.

"I have not always agreed with your methods, Anshu, but you assured me, after the incident with the train, that we were fighting for all Arelians, including the plebeians. Was that a lie?"

The rising tension within the room warns me that whatever alliance these people have, it is an uneasy one.

Anshu's face contorts before his mouth sets in a firm, thin line. "No, it was not. But you are a part of this council. We cannot risk…"

"All the more reason for me to go. We've given her no reason to trust us. Perhaps this will."

I watch this exchange between the two, unsure of what to make of this Joseph; he seems honest, but I hope his actions prove that to be true.

"We should put it to a vote," Joseph says.

Anshu gives a stiff nod of his head in agreement.

"All those in favor of rescuing this Gwen, should Arbiter Noni help us in our plans, raise your hands."

Hands around the room go up, including Perce's.

"You are not a member of this council," Anshu tells Perce.

"Consider me an honorary one," Perce replies.

"With eight in favor and five opposed," says Joseph, "the motion passes."

"Very well," Anshu says. "If you agree to help us, then we will help you."

"Agreed," I say. "So, what's the plan?"

"The only way to free Arel, is to rid it of Tapiwa's corruption, and of the current council," says Anshu, "but the presidential palace is well guarded. We need to draw them out. To do this, we will be infiltrating the aerodrome and disabling their aircraft. As you know, Arel's might depends heavily upon the aircraft they use to put down rebellions and any sort of discontent that rises up."

I remember. Too many times I have witnessed the aftermath of an unrest that was shut down by the bombs dropped by the Arelian aircraft. Too many times I have seen the charred remains of what was once living people as smoldering fires continued to ravage them in the hopes of extinguishing any memory of their existence.

"We must disable those aircraft," Anshu continues, "before we can hope to take the presidential palace. Once that is achieved..."

"Perhaps both should be done at the same time," Renal says, interrupting Anshu.

"Impossible," says Ha'ya.

Anshu raises his hand to silence her.

"If you wait to go after Tapiwa, until after you disable of the aircraft, they will tighten the guard and be waiting. The key to winning any war, is to attack from all fronts at once. Keep your enemy confused, while allowing them to bask in their arrogance."

"What are you suggesting?"

"Bring in Luther," says Renal.

Perturbed, Anshu agrees, and a man leaves the room, returning a few moments later with Luther in tow. He glances around the chamber, spotting me in an instant, but diverts his eyes back to Anshu, having an inkling of why he is here.

"So?" says Anshu.

"It would help," replies Luther, "if you asked a question or told me why I am here."

"You are one of one of Arel's top architects and engineers," says Anshu, "Renal, here, believes you can be of some help."

"Tell them the best way into the presidential palace," Renal says.

Luther raises an eyebrow and takes in a deep breath as he considers his answer.

"The presidential palace is well-guarded. The architects accounted for every possible point of entry that would allow any with nefarious purposes to sneak inside, and made certain that they remain closed, except one: the front gate."

"Are you saying we should just go through the front door?" mocks Ha'ya.

"Precisely," answers Luther.

"This is insane!" Ha'ya shouts.

"To defeat your enemy, you must always do the unexpected," Renal says. "No one will be expecting us to even attempt to enter the palace, much less to try coming in through the front gate, but it can be done."

Ha'ya starts to open her mouth, but Anshu silences her.

"And how do you expect to get through there?"

I know. The oldest trick in the book. Tapiwa will not be happy about my escape, and no doubt, has issued orders that I be found no matter the cost. Give her something she desires most and the gate will open.

"Bait," I say, understanding Renal's plan.

"Bait?" Anshu repeats.

"Me," I reply as understanding washes over his face.

"I propose," says Renal, "that we use Noni to enter the presidential palace at the same time your men infiltrate the aerodrome. While they disable the Arelian aircraft, we will keep them focused on us, which will also allow us to rid ourselves of Tapiwa. We will need uniforms so that your men can disguise themselves as arbiters, a transport, and a little bit of theater."

"Theater?" asks Joseph.

"We will stage an arrest of Noni. Tapiwa will want her brought to the presidential palace, which will allow us entrance. Once inside, we will neutralize the guards and help her locate the girl. Two purposes will be served here."

"How do you know that Tapiwa will have her brought there?"

"I have my sources," replies Renal.

"And how do you know the girl is there?"

"I have my sources," Renal says again.

"I see."

"To do this, you will have to sacrifice some of your people."

"Sacrifice is part of the game," Anshu says. "Very well. We'll finalize the plans over the next few weeks."

"We should go now," I say, not liking the thought of Gwen spending one more night in Tapiwa's clutches.

"You are not well enough," Anshu says, "and we need you at your full strength."

"But..." I begin.

"Noni," Renal's firm voice stops me from continuing my outburst, and I sit back in my seat, hunching my shoulders in disappointment. "He is right. You are of no use in your current state."

"Yes, Lieutenant," I reply.

Perce places a reassuring hand on my shoulder and gives me a warm smile, the only bit of comfort in this foreign environment.

"In the meantime," Anshu says to me, "you will record a message, saying that you support us."

I nod my head, knowing that I have only one choice: agreement.

Anshu looks around at those seated at the table before speaking, "This meeting is adjourned."

Chairs screech across the floor as they are pushed back and people filter out the room, but Renal remains seated, so I do the same, along with Luther and Perce.

Anshu is the last to leave and glances at us with a questioning look.

"I'll help her to her room," Renal says with finality.

An awkward pause fills the space between them before Anshu steps through the doorway and disappears into the corridor beyond. Several moments pass before anyone dares to speak.

"Do you trust them?" Perce asks; his tone indicates that he already knows the answer.

"No," Renal replies.

I share his sentiment.

"How do you know Gwen is at the palace?" I ask.

"The most current report I have indicates she is," Renal replies, but his voice seems worried, as though something has happened, but he refuses to tell me about it. "We have to act on that."

Before anyone else can speak, my stomach grumbles loud enough to wake the dead, forcing Perce and Renal to look at me with surprise.

"Perhaps we should get you something to eat," Renal says.

"I will get her something," says Perce, "and you can keep an eye on our hosts."

Renal nods in agreement before looking in my direction. "Food. Then, rest."

"Come," Perce says, leading me out of the room. "You should eat and get some more rest, and"—he pauses for dramatic effect, piquing my curiosity—"there's a surprise for you in the kitchen."

Though ravenous, I do not wish to leave Renal, so I stop and glance back at him, and though he remains rigid, his eyes are soft, full of understanding, and he gives a slight incline of his head, as though to tell me that it will be all right. I acquiesce and allow Perce to lead me away, unsure of how much time I will be forced to spend in this place and curious about this surprise of his.

Chapter 27

New Surroundings

The lumps within the mattress form their own mountain range beneath me as I move to smooth them out, hoping to go back to sleep, but another lump prods the middle of my side, interrupting my half-dream, half-awake state, causing me to turn once again. Sleep evades me. I turn on my back and stare at the ceiling and the tiles that hang loose, threatening to fall on top of me, desiring to forget everything, and wanting nothing more than to be in Chase's comforting arms as he tried to wash my worries away with his strength, or to see Gwen's eyes light up when her brother entered the room with a small gift—most times it was a scrap of food he saved for her—and Sheila's smile when I gave her a piece of Sigal's pie. The corner of my eyes grow damp as tears form and force their way into the world, trickling down my temple and into my hairline before I wipe them away. I cannot weep. Not here. Not in this place full of strangers looking to me to be the symbol of their little rebellion or looking for any reason to toss me out with the garbage, having never wanted me here in the first place. Weakness is not allowed, only strength.

A peculiar, yet familiar aroma tickles my nose, causing my mouth to salivate and a memory to pop up. It is familiar, but... it can't be! I sit up and place my feet on the hard floor, reaching over to grab my boots and put them on, lacing them up tight. I head for the door, with its hinges fixed, pausing when I reach for the handle, remembering when I first came through here. How long ago was that? Four weeks? I shake my head, unsure of the exact amount of time I've spent here, and as I ponder it, the sweet aroma, with a hint of paprika and chili spice to it, strikes my nose again, tantalizing me, urging me to leave my room, an act I've refused to do for a while now, having allowed myself to succumb to my sadness.

The moment I open the door and step into the corridor, the aroma grows stronger, causing my stomach to gurgle as it beckons me forth, and I follow the smell, unable to stop myself, wanting to know what it is while remembering a meal I had once with a similar redolence, and the man who created it. My mouth waters as I move through the corridor and its dim lighting before stepping into an open area with the spiraling staircase and the dome up above, and... people. It's been some time since I have been in a small area surrounded by people, and truth be told, I had forgotten that others, besides the leaders of the rebellion, live here. Most are soldiers, if one can call them that, awaiting their orders, but a few are average citizens and plebeians in hiding, waiting for a day when they do not have to live in fear any longer.

As I step out into the light, some stop and stare at me as though I am a novelty to them, while others look at me with caution, unsure of what I will do, having heard the stories surrounding me, but some give me looks of praise, and a few even salute me. Unsure of how to react, I return the gesture, hoping that they will take it as a sign of respect. They do. As I make my way to the stairs, one man bumps into me, knocking me off-balance, and when I pause, he turns and glares at me; words are not needed for me to know that he despises me, but why, I do not know, and in the end, it does not matter. As we stare at one another, more arrive, pushing any of my admirers out of the way as they surround me, flexing their muscles. I am not welcome, in their mind, and they intend to let me know. Bracing myself for a fight, I start to raise my fists, when a shadow swoops in by my side and causes the others to back up.

"Is there a problem?" Renal's voice echoes around the room, daring any present to challenge him.

One man rears his fist back and prepares to throw a punch at Renal when something tiny strikes him on the cheek. In the shadows stands Perce, watching and waiting, and the man reconsiders his actions, choosing to walk away instead of spitting at me, while the others fade away, leaving a mesmerized crowd.

"Noni!" comes an exuberant voice, and Joseph rushes up to us. "I'm glad to see you have decided to join us."

"Maybe I should go back to my room," I say. "My presence seems to be causing a disturbance."

"Nonsense," replies Joseph. "Anshu has made plain the situation to them."

"Not plain enough," mutters Renal, but Joseph ignores him.

"You mustn't blame them," Joseph says. "Many here have suffered under the might of Arel and her arbiters."

"And the arbiters don't suffer?" I snap, tired of being told how I should accept people's ire toward me because they suffered injustices at the hands of others.

I have tried to be fair, even stopped fellow arbiters from abusing their authority, yet I am treated as though I am the unjust one. Every child in Arel is ripped from its mother's arms and placed in the caste it will be a part of, arbiters included, but unlike some castes, arbiters are beaten into submission and into shape. I have watched fellow recruits die because they failed. Forced to kill, forced to rob ourselves of any sense of compassion or mercy, we arbiters become machinelike in how we carry out our duties, because if we do not, we are dead. How many others in Arel can say that they were splattered with the brains of a fellow recruit who failed to duck during a live fire training exercise? We have all suffered.

"I know," replies Joseph, and his eyes hold no malice or animosity toward me, but pity. "I've seen the cruelty arbiters suffer. I was born a plebeian, cursed to always work under the yoke of those who claimed to be my betters, but there was one man who did not share the beliefs of his superiors, and it cost him. I had committed an infraction and was to suffer a severe punishment, but one arbiter stopped it, believing that the punishment did not fit the crime. For that, he was punished, and as though to make a point, I was forced to watch as he suffered the Long Knives."

The Long Knives—I know that punishment well. The one receiving it is bound to a post, unable to use his hands or legs as five other arbiters use knives to administer deep cuts into his flesh, enough to cause pain and make him bleed, but not enough to kill. It can go on for hours until the one being punished dies from eventual blood loss, but not after suffering the harshest of pains. Such a punishment is meant to discourage future disobedience.

In my thirteenth year as a recruit, the commandant ordered us all to the courtyard to witness justice being carried out. An instructor had helped an Arelian citizen escape beyond the wall, for which immediate execution is the usual punishment, but the Commandant believed making an example of him would be best, and the tribunal agreed. So, we gathered and watched as other arbiters stripped our former instructor of his clothes and tied his wrists and legs to four posts, securing him and ensuring that he could not move. He did his best to maintain a proud posture, but I saw fear take hold of him as five arbiters approached with knives—their steel glinted in the faint sunlight—ready to carry out their duty and to admonish the one who dared challenge Arel's authority. One by one, they cut into him. At first, he gripped his tongue and remained silent, except for a moan or two, but by the twentieth cut, the pain proved too much, and he could hold his screams in no longer. Eight agonizing hours passed as we watched. Any who collapsed from exhaustion or fainted from watching this horror found themselves thrown to the wild dogs, and their screams from being ripped apart mingled with those of our former instructor. I had tried to look away, but Molers' hand seized my chin and forced me to watch.

"Watch! This is what happens to those who disobey. Learn your place and stay there," Molers whispered into my ears, enjoying every minute of this spectacle, and his words burrowed themselves deep into my mind.

Hours passed, and Faya, who stood next to me, wavered on her feet, having grown tired from standing to the point where her legs could bear her weight no longer, and I caught her, allowing her to lean on me as I supported her, whispering to her to remain standing and hoping that no one noticed or would report us. When night fell, only a hanging carcass remained, looking as though it had been put through a shredder as blood dripped from it and melded into the pool of blood turning brown from oxidation. Arid silence surrounded us as we remained standing, staring at the consequence of disobedience, while I continued to support Faya, relieved when an instructor issued orders to go back inside. This is the Long Knives, and if Joseph suffered through watching its execution, then he knows what arbiters face for the infraction known as failure.

"You must be hungry," Joseph says to me, changing the subject and pulling me back to the present. "I have to admit, we were unsure if your friends would fit in here, but one of them must have been heaven sent. Before, we ate what we could get, and though that is still the case, he has a way of turning a plain dish into a delicacy."

Joseph leads us up the winding staircase, and I try to ignore the looks I receive from others, a mixture of hatred and admiration, as we climb to the second floor, allowing the dome to overshadow us with its faint light. For a moment, I pause and glance at those below us as they go about their business, having duties to attend to, wondering why they are here, or how they were brought here, and how it is no one seems to know of this place, though, having a man on the Arelian Council who can divert attention elsewhere does help in maintaining secrecy.

"What was this place?" I ask, looking at the ornate mounted lights, thinking that their shape and structure is too un-Arelian.

"It was once an opera house," Joseph says.

"A what?" I ask.

"A long time ago, people used to come to places like this to listen to stories told in song, but with more elegance, or so I'm told," replies Joseph. "It has been repurposed over the years to be an arbiter manor, a brothel that served the elite here in Arel, an education center, and a rehabilitation center, before being abandoned entirely."

"Why is that?" Perce asks.

"Well, when the leader of your movement sits on the committee for repurposing old buildings, it is easy to ensure that the one you use is indefinitely condemned."

"And no one bothers sneaking in here?" Perce asks.

"Anyone caught entering a condemned building is immediately executed, or worse," I reply. "Arelian law declares them off limits. Disobedience is not allowed."

"Which is why we are able to use it. However, the windows are boarded, no one leaves without permission and must use the approved points of entry, and we are all to remain silent."

"So, no one speaks of this place?" Perce asks.

Joseph turns toward him, two steps away from the top of the staircase. "Anshu has spies everywhere. Any who give the slightest hint that they will not remain silent are dealt with."

"Total obedience," Perce says with disdain.

"If you like. We must take measures to protect ourselves," replies Joseph, but there is something to his voice, something that betrays him, that sets him apart from the others in this place, something that indicates he is not happy with this rule.

"But you don't agree with them all," I say, and Joseph shushes me the moment the words leave my mouth, telling me that my initial suspicions about him might be correct.

"The kitchen is this way," he says, pointing us to the left and forgetting that I have been here long enough to know its location, even if I've chosen to stay in my room.

Perce opens his mouth to speak, but Renal stops him, knowing the value of silence, and understanding that we are outnumbered here. For now, we must comply.

Joseph leads us down another hallway, and I glance at the various lights illuminating it; some triangular, with diamond-shaped metalwork forming a border along their edges, give off a soft, amber glow that invites one to stay and rest, making me think that they were left over from the days when this place was an opera house, and others are more square, industrial-looking, and give off a garish, white light that makes anyone caught in its glow appear to be ashen. Though apprehensive about this place and its residents, I find myself unable to look away from the left-over woodwork decorating the walls and carvings within it, portraying what I assume to be great performers surrounded by eight-pointed stars and half-moons as they sing their tale to any who would listen, while trying to not be overshadowed by the few slabs of metal that had been erected to conceal them and wipe their existence from the people's memory.

As we walk, our footsteps echo around us, drawing my attention to the floor, and I realize that what I thought was a thin piece of floor covering, is tile, designed to look like gold carpeting—it's more brown and gray from years of residue and neglect—and I stop, kneeling down to feel the tile, amazed at the intricacy that went into it and the amount of hours a person must have spent creating such a thing so as to give the illusion that one walked on carpet.

"Even now, it's construction is remarkable, isn't it?" comments Joseph. "Despite the attempts of Arel to destroy any ounce of a society that existed before, vestiges of it manage to seep through for young eyes to see. I sometimes walk this corridor, imagining what it must have been like in the days before, and there are times when I believe I can hear them shout, 'We were once here.'"

Joseph's appreciation for a bygone era, and a time most of us know nothing about, gives me a newfound appreciation for Luther, and people like him, who try to preserve the past so that we all can learn from it. History should never be forgotten, erased, or ignored; such actions are what led to Arel. I remember hearing once that those who refuse to learn from history are doomed to repeat it, making me wonder: how many Arels existed before?

Joseph continues down the hallway, while I try my best not to become distracted by the original construction trying to peek through the repurposing of the building and all attempts to conceal its memory. He turns a corner, and we all follow in silence, while others stroll past us, some with interested looks, while the rest ignore us, hoping that by doing so, we will disappear. He stops in front of a set of double doors that flap from the slightest draft and beckons us to go in. I walk through first, unwilling to wait for someone else to make the first move and unwilling to be left behind, only to be greeted by a person I never grow tired of seeing.

"No, no, no," says the familiar, jovial voice as he instructs a young boy on how to prepare a specific dish. "A little basil goes a long way."

"Sigal?" I say with excitement, while still disbelieving that he is here, even though Perce brought me to him my first day in this place.

Unable to help myself, I run to him and wrap my arms around him, giving him the biggest hug I can, and he wraps his gentle arms around me, coating me in flour as it flies off his sleeves.

"When... how..." I begin.

"I've already answered these questions of yours!"

"And I want to hear you tell it again."

"You have Renal to thank for that."

Moments of silence pass before he continues as I give him a pleading look.

"Oh, very well, child. Not too long after you left us, Perce traveled here to await your signal should you choose to ask for his help, and I insisted on coming along. Imagine both of our surprise when it was Renal who sent the signal."

"And why is it you haven't visited me more often?"

"We thought it best to let you recover," Sigal says with a note to his voice, indicating that there is more to the story—a secret everyone is afraid to reveal—but as eyes turn toward him, he changes to a more jovial tone. "And why is it you haven't visited me?"

"I'm glad you're here," I say, giving him another embrace.

"Oh," says Sigal as he reaches for a plate with a slice of pecan pie on it and places it in front of me, "I almost forgot! I remember you have a particular fondness for it."

He sticks a fork in my hand, but I hesitate, unsure about eating in front of the others.

"Go ahead," encourages Sigal. "They already had theirs."

"I didn't have mine," jokes Perce.

"No one cares," quips Sigal with a dismissive wave of his hand, causing more flour to fall from his sleeve and dust the countertop, and Perce laughs before Sigal turns around and catches someone trying to smash dough into a pie pan and rushes off to demonstrate how it is done. "No! No! No! Not like that! You must be gentle with it."

"Some things never change," Renal whispers to me as I shove a bite of pecan pie into my mouth, savoring the burst of nutty sweetness as it touches my tongue and mixes with the buttery crust.

Someone rushes into the kitchen and whispers into Joseph's ear; a worried expression crosses his face before he mutters something back to the messenger.

"I must leave you," he says to us, stepping closer to the door. "Please, help yourself to anything in the kitchen."

He disappears, but before I have time to wonder why he was called away, or what it is that concerns him, Renal breaks the silence.

"Sigal," he says, indicating that he wishes to speak with us in private, and Sigal abandons his futile attempt at teaching another how to create a proper pie crust.

As I continue to shove bits of pecan pie into my mouth, relishing the sweetness of the custard, Renal leads me and the others from the kitchen and into another room, away from prying eyes and ears. Once secured in the chamber, I place my empty plate on a lone table, settling it in a half inch layer of dust, making me wonder the last time it was used, and as I wait for Renal to speak, I glance around at the musty drapes covering boarded up windows, forcing me to concentrate in order to make out the molding that forms swirled patterns on the dull-yellow wall, its once vibrant red wood now cracked and faded. I amble over to it, placing my left palm on it, saddened by the splinters that now form its edges, instead of the smooth finish it once possessed, picturing what it might have looked like back in a time when it shone with splendor and pride.

A light rap at the door jerks me away from my reverie, and I whirl around, waiting with bated breath as Renal opens the door, revealing Luther. He lets him inside before poking his head out, making certain that Luther was not followed. Once the door seals shut, Perce lights a single lamp, allowing a flaxen light to touch a tiny corner of the room, and Renal motions us to come to him.

"What have you found out?" Renal asks Luther.

"Not much," he replies. "I suspect that Joseph isn't too keen on Anshu's ambitions, but I do not think he will break away from him."

"Out of loyalty?" Renal asks.

"No," says Luther, "it's something else."

"What are you talking about?" I say, not liking the feeling that they have all been conspiring without me.

"While you were recuperating," Perce says, "Renal has been making plans."

"What sort of plans?" I ask.

"We are going to need outside help," Renal says. "I know a captain within the Arelian fleet who owes me a favor."

"In the aerodrome?"

"No," replies Renal. "The aerodrome contains the bulk of Arel's fleet, but there are those who are stationed at one of the many outposts."

That explains how Arelian aircraft managed to arrive at the mine in such a short time-frame to put down the uprising there.

"That is where the captain is stationed. Never mind why," Renal says, when I open my mouth to ask. "But I know she will help us."

"You do not believe that Anshu will keep his word," I say.

"Neither do you."

"There is the matter of Anshu's plan," Luther says. "From what I can gather, he may be persuaded to allow Noni to not be a part of it."

"No!" I say, my voice sharp.

"Noni..." begins Renal.

"No!" I say again. "I'm not leaving Gwen."

"Noni," says Perce, "no one is asking you to."

"While you were imprisoned in the detention center," Renal says, his voice tight as he struggles to hold in his emotions, and I do not recall ever seeing him in such a state of despair and inner turmoil, "I promised Commander Vye that I would ensure your survival and escape from Arel."

Unsure of what to do—for the first time, I see Renal as a man who feels and cares for those around him, but is unable to show it because of the world we live in—I move over to him and place my hand on his, hoping to calm him and make known to him that I understand the vow he made, because I made similar one to Chase regarding his sister.

"I know you have all made plans," I say, "but I have created some of my own. Don't ask me to abandon Gwen."

"Never," Renal replies in a soft voice.

I turn toward the others.

"We have to follow Anshu's plan as discussed earlier; however, we can tailor it. When I was out in the wilds, I witnessed Arelian arbiters give Arelian weapons to barbarians. During one of the attacks on the wall, I noticed that the attackers were not just barbarians, but plebeians as well. This makes me wonder what we are not being told. And when Anshu speaks, I wonder the same thing. You are right, Lieutenant, we need outside help. Can you get word to this captain?"

"Leave that to me," Renal says. "Luther found a way out of this place, one that even Anshu's men are unaware of."

"Are you certain?"

"Yes."

"But won't arbiters arrest you when they see you?"

Renal shakes his head. "None will question me."

I study Renal, wondering, once again, if he is a marshal. Why else would no one question his strange acts. Annoyed that he will not tell me how he plans to get word to this captain that he knows, much less who this person is, I decide to let it rest, knowing that Renal is a man of many secrets, and he is alive because he knows how to keep them.

"Is there any way to get communicators?" I ask.

"I can help with that," replies Luther. "Joseph loves showing me the architectural design of this place, and I know where they keep the communication devices."

"Very well," I say. "I want you, the lieutenant, and Perce to stay in contact. I cannot have a communication device because that is the first thing they will scan for when I enter the presidential palace. If Gwen is there, I will get her out. Lieutenant, you and Luther will have to find a way to get away from Anshu's men before they destroy the aerodrome. When you do, come find me."

"Perce," I turn toward him, "do you think your people will help us?"

"My grandmother will. I can…"

"No," I reply. "Lieutenant, you said that you know how to sneak out of this place. I'm assuming you know a way to get in and out of the city unnoticed."

"What are you planning?" asks Perce.

"I want Sigal to take your message to your grandmother. Give him whatever he needs to do that, so that she will believe him, and convince her to come here with an army. I believe we will need it in order to escape this city. They can provide a distraction for us, but I need to know that he can get past the wall."

"It is best to avoid using the same way too often," Renal says, "but transports to the outposts have increased, and there is a way to hide him among them."

"Won't they be searched?" asks Luther.

"Not these," says Renal. "These particular ones carry supplies, and the Arelian council do not want anyone to know what is being stored at these outposts. Sigal can hide on the one making up the rear of the convoy and make his escape from there."

"Do you agree to this?" I ask Sigal.

"You helped save my family," he replies. "It is only right that I do the same."

"This is what I propose," I say, using my index finger to draw a quick, but crude, map of Arel in the dust on the table the lamp sits on. "Luther, stay on friendly terms with Joseph and get the communicators, one for you and Renal, and one for Perce. Warn us if they suspect we're up to anything. Renal, get your message to your captain, after which, you will get Sigal out of Arel and return here. Can you do it tonight?"

He nods.

"Make sure no one notices your absence. I will go with Anshu's men and abide by their plan to get into the presidential palace. Luther and Renal, you will go with the rest of Anshu's men to the aerodrome. Find a way to get away from them before they detonate their explosives. Once I have Gwen, I will meet you all here"—I point at the map—"Sigal will go to Croatia and give Perce's message to his grandmother. If she refuses to send help, he will stay where he is, and the rest of us will be on our own."

"And what about me?" asks Perce.

"Sneak out of here with Renal and find the high ground," I say. "And keep Tapiwa's guards off me."

He nods. "In that case, I want you to have this."

He hands me a wristband.

"I've noticed you all wear these things and discovered that they are used as a way to track your movements. I swiped this from someone—do not ask me how—and modified it."

He hands it to me.

"Keep it with you."

I twirl the thin wristband in my fingers and smile, until Luther breaks the silence.

"I guess the plan sounds simple enough," he says. "One question: what if something goes wrong?"

"Let's hope it doesn't," Renal replies.

Luther's question weighs on me. There is no backup plan if things go awry. I can only hope that, somehow, we all make it through alive, but one thing is certain: I am getting Gwen, one way or another.

"We should get back before they wonder where we are," Renal says.

One by one, we leave the room and head back to our respective areas, doing our best to not attract attention, and after the others leave, I turn toward Renal, saying, "Be careful."

"You do the same," he replies before hurrying down the corridor and disappearing into the shadows, leaving me alone to wonder if any of us will see each other again.

Chapter 28

Retribution

My fingers pinch the semi-smooth, black fabric as they rub together, remembering the uniform I used to wear, that I was once proud to possess, until I realized its true nature and meaning, as I sit in my room, doing my best to calm myself for what lies ahead, knowing that there can be no mistakes. Not this time. Failure is not an option. As I pull off the clothes lent to me and put this arbiter's outfit on—the jacket has a crude hood handstitched on, telling me it was a last-minute addition—I wonder whom they stole it from, or whom they killed so as to achieve their goal, and why they insisted I wear it. Perhaps it does not matter, but an arbiter did wear this uniform—the sweat stains still marking the armpits of the jacket are a testament to that—and a part of me knows that I was once like this person: a follower, a person who obeyed orders, until something changed. I snatch the boots, checking the heel to make sure the wristband, or better yet, the tracking device Perce gave me is secure, and put them on before lifting myself off the bed.

I stand in front of a mirror—it is more of a cracked piece of glass than a mirror, but it has to do—staring at my worn face and the forlornness, mixed with determination, that consumes it as I remember the day of my commission—the day excitement filled me at the thought of being an arbiter and embarking on my first assignment. It seems like decades ago, but it was only two years ago at most. I slip my arms into the jacket, wishing it fit more like the ones that had been tailored for me when I was still at the manor, but I shove such frivolous thoughts aside as I zip it up before looking up at the shadow that fills the glass, not recognizing the woman staring back at me. She appears older beyond her years as crow's feet begin to form near her eyes, faint for now, and the slight scar that adorns her right cheek—a gift from Molers—void of happiness, having suffered the ordeal of having joy ripped away from her. It would be better if this woman was a stranger, but she is not; she is me. Her eyes burn into mine and determination sets in, ironing my will to do what must be done, to fulfill a promise to a love I lost.

I'm coming for you, Gwen.

A hard knock rattles the door, pulling me away from my thoughts.

"Enter," I say.

Renal steps inside. I had not expected to see him. He is to accompany the others to the aerodrome.

"It's time," he says to me.

I scoop up my long hair and twist it around before tying it into a secure knot and moving toward the door, when he stops me, holding a knife in the air.

"Take this."

I remain still.

"It belonged to Commander Vye. She wanted you to have it."

Renal's voice cracks when he says her name, and though he keeps his emotions in check, refusing to let any witness them, this small bit of humanity escapes his control, allowing me to confirm a recent suspicion. This is the sole explanation for why, despite her actions, he never reported her, but risked everything for her.

"Commander Vye said I should trust only you. At the time, I never questioned it or pondered why she would put all her trust in a single individual."

Renal remains silent.

"You loved her, didn't you?" Once the words leave my mouth, I regret saying them when emotional pain crosses his face. Even if they loved one another, it was a love that could never be, and they knew it, and to my knowledge, they never acted upon it.

"Take the knife," he insists, refusing to answer my question.

I grab it and place the knife inside my boot before starting to leave, but Renal forces me to pause, showcasing a characteristic I never thought he possessed.

"Arel forbids the notion of family, but I do not share their view."

Intrigued, I ask the obvious question. "Who is your family?"

"One is dead. The other is in this room."

His words stun me into silence, and I am unable to think of a proper response, having never considered the idea that Renal would think of others as his family, but it makes sense. In a way, the caste we are forced into becomes our family, because they are the only ones we are allowed to associate with. I follow Renal into the corridor and to the main room, where the others wait, with Anshu shifting from one foot to the other, and I spot Luther pinned between two of Anshu's men, but he remains calm and unsurprised.

"I thought you weren't coming," Anshu snaps.

My eyes narrow in response.

"Your friends…" he begins, "the outsiders have disappeared."

"I wouldn't worry about them," I reply, hoping that Sigal and Perce made it.

"You will go with them," he says, pointing at two of his men. "They will…"

"I know the plan," I interrupt.

A scowl crosses his face. "Very well."

He turns to the others. "Today is the day we end the tyranny of Arel and get justice! Today we rise as one!"

Two of Anshu's men turn toward me when he finishes speaking, while others cheer his words, and I know what they want: they want me to follow them, and as I take one last glance at both Luther and Renal, a sinking feeling fills my stomach, but I shove it aside. I need to focus on Gwen. She is what matters most now. Within moments, I find myself outside and shoved into a transport that Anshu's men must have stolen earlier, but instead of being allowed to sit in the backseat, they force me into the footwell, as though I am nothing more than refuse, something to be ashamed of and discarded at the first opportunity. Now I know how Chase felt when he was forced to do the same the first time I went outside the wall.

The movement of the transport rocks me back and forth, but not in a pleasant way as though I am in a hammock, but more like the jerking of a ship lost at sea as a storm rages around it, causing my stomach to churn as nausea sets in. I close my eyes, and one of the men with me laughs at my discomfort. I am a pawn to him—a means to an end—and he tolerates me because he must. That much is clear. The transport jerks again, causing me to bump my head against the side of the footwell and forcing me to open my eyes to a day of gray sunlight as a mist hovers in the air, leftover from last night's rain. The shadows of buildings pass over us as we move through the city, claw-like in their makeup as they reach out to snatch us and prevent us from fulfilling our mission, while the windows glare at us, mumbling curses at us, hoping that we fail. I take in a long, slow breath in an effort to calm the anxiety threatening to overtake me as we draw closer to our objective.

The transport stops.

"Out," says one of the men with me.

We lock eyes a moment, his disdain for me evident. I am a tool to him and nothing more. The door opens, and I stretch my legs as I place my arms on the backseat, lifting myself up, and ignoring the tingling discomfort that grips my cramped muscles as I haul myself out of the transport and step onto solid pavement. Hands shove me the rest of the way, eager to be rid of me.

"You know what to do," he says, slamming the door as the vehicle speeds away.

I know what to do. I'm the distraction for the others on their way to the aerodrome. I hope Luther and Renal fare better than me.

Looking around at the narrow space between the sleek, metallic buildings that reflect their surroundings with precision, I realize that I am in the northern sector: higher-class than the eastern sector, but not as elegant or luxurious as the business district. I pull the hood up, covering my head for now, until the time is right. Muffled noises penetrate my ears, attracting my attention to the bustling of activity, but not the ambient, joyful activity that comes from people enjoying a day within the city, but the sort that indicates distress and a clash between authoritarians and a disgruntled citizenry.

I rush for it, not caring if I was to go in the other direction toward the piazza, and race down the narrow alleyway until I burst out from between the towering structures and into a small clearing, where a man lies face down on the ground, while an arbiter plants his foot in the man's back and aims his pistol at his head, ignoring the screams of onlookers as they try to outmaneuver the two arbiters holding them back. Unable to contain myself, I charge for the one with the weapon, tackling him before he can fire, forcing him to crash onto the ground. He lies stunned, and I swing my leg around, kicking the pistol from his hand before ramming my foot into his head, sending it flying back at an odd angle, and his limbs go limp. I stand up, facing the remaining arbiters and remove my hood, revealing my identity, while the high-pitched hum of a drone echoes nearby.

The two remaining arbiters abandon the people in their custody and charge for me. I dodge to the left, avoiding one, but the other manages to catch me in the chest, causing me to stagger back. Coughing, I eye them, waiting for them to make their next move. They do. Both rush for me. I duck downward, grabbing hold of the arm of one, before twisting it around his back and ramming my foot into the stomach of the other. He attacks. I turn around, placing the arbiter in my grasp between me and my attacker, allowing him to take the full impact, before letting go and kicking him in the back. I dive for the legs of one, sweeping him off his feet, but before I can attack, the other rams his fist into the side of my head, dazing me and allowing his partner to wrap his arm around my neck and squeeze. Blood pulses in my head as he constricts my airway. The arbiter who struck me pulls out his weapon and takes aim, but before he can fire, two of the onlookers tackle him and wrestle the weapon from him, but not before it goes off, striking one of them. The one choking me loosens his hold, allowing me to sink my teeth into his arm.

Freed, I turn around and plow my fists into his face before ramming my heel into his left knee, dislocating it. He screams in agony, but before I can finish him, a force knocks me to the ground, and I find myself face first on the pavement as hands wrench my arms behind my back and snap binders on them, while others put down the gathering crowd. More arbiters arrive. My head spins when an arbiter jerks me to my feet, drags me to a detainment box, and slaps my palm on the screen. It flashes to life, scanning my palm before turning red, warning the arbiters detaining me that I am dangerous and should be treated with extreme caution, but instead of putting me in the detainment box, he pauses and glances at his commanding officer in confusion.

The commanding officer yanks my arm up and presses my palm on the screen, causing my fingers to turn white from the pressure of his grip. Once again, the same words appear on the screen as a drone hovers around us: Priority Red-Code 17. But it is not the words on the screen that concerns the commanding officer the most, it's my face filling the view screens surrounding us and the reaction of some of the arbiters under his command when they see it. Some, release the people they have pinned to the ground as they stare at the screens before turning toward me, and place their fists against their chest in salute, while the remaining arbiters look at their commander for orders.

Light glints off the blade of a knife as one of the arbiters holding me prepares to stab me with it. I jump to the side, ramming my shoulder into his knife hand, pressing it against the side of the detainment box until he drops the blade. Chaos ensues as arbiter fights arbiter and onlookers join in the fray, tired of suffering at the hands of Arel's elite. A force crashes into my back, knocking me to the damp ground, and I cringe when pain grips my shoulder, but refuse to give in to it as I kick my feet out, catching my opponent in the calf and his leg buckles underneath him, forcing him to drop to his knees. I ram my foot into his face and roll onto my back, while scooching my bound hands past my rump and lifting my legs as I do so, bringing them under my feet until my hands are no longer behind my back. The butt of a rifle jabs me in the stomach, causing me to curl into a fetal position as gloved hands shove a gag in my mouth before placing a black hood over my head as a transport speeds into the center of the plaza, striking any—arbiter and civilian alike—who gets in its way, until it comes to a screeching halt in front of me.

I struggle against the hands lifting me off the ground as they throw me in the back of the vehicle. I manage to kick one in the face and receive a fist to the stomach in response before the doors to the transport close with me pinned between two arbiters, and as the driver speeds away with us inside, gunfire echoes behind us, growing fainter the further away we get. Incensed, I grip my fists together and strike the arbiter on my right before diving for the door, guessing where the handle is as the canvas bag molds around my face, sticking to the vapor clinging to my skin. The arbiter snatches the waistband of my pants, yanking me back, so I bring my legs up and push against the floor of the transport, forcing my entire weight into him before lunging for the door again, but as I do, the transport swerves as the driver cranks the wheel to avoid hitting something, followed by a concussive force that knocks the vehicle into the air, flipping it on its side, while a flash of white light fills the area around us, seeping through the black canvass around my head.

My body smashes into the ceiling of the transport as it rolls, and I try to cling to something to stop myself from being thrown about like a rag doll. It stops. High-pitched whistling fills my ears, subsiding with each second as the sounds of the world around me return. Nothing moves. I try to pull the hood off my head, but before I can, the doors fling open and arms reach in, seizing me around my legs and yanking me out of the transport and onto rough pavement, not caring that my elbows slam into it and blood soaks the sleeves of my shirt as the skin is scraped off. Two more sets of hands seize my shoulders and lift me into the air, dragging me across the ground before shoving me into another transport, while scuffling noises surround me, followed by gunshots and silence. The arbiters in the transport with me must have met an unfortunate end. Despite my kicking, despite flailing my arms about, I am no match for my new captors as the doors close behind me and the engine of the vehicle roars around us, blowing smoke out the exhaust, as the driver punches the accelerator.

"Fool!" says a masculine voice to me.

I rip the bag off my head and find myself face to face with Anshu's men, the same men who had dropped me off near the piazza.

"You were supposed to provide a distraction!"

"I did," I hiss at him.

"By almost getting yourself and others killed!"

"What do we do now?" asks one of the others.

"Take me to the presidential palace," I say, remembering the words on the screen when my palm had been scanned.

"Are you insane!"

"Tapiwa is expecting me," I snap. "Besides, she is the only one who can tell me where Gwen is, and did you all not promise to help me get her?"

No one says anything.

"One of you may even get the chance to rid us of her," I add.

"Very well," says the first man. "We are arbiters bringing the president a dangerous fugitive."

The driver turns the wheel, taking a side street before turning onto the main road leading to the executive district and the presidential palace, while I settle into the back seat between the other two in the vehicle, watching as the shadows of buildings pass over us, each more ominous than the last, warning me of my doom. Before I know it, the presidential palace looms before us, and I am thrust back into the memory of the first time I had been here so as to receive the Arelian Medal of Honor and the excitement and pride I had then. Now, only hatred and loathing remain. Tapiwa will suffer for what she has done, and I will bring justice for the deaths and the misery of those I love. The driver pauses before the gate, the same gate I have been through on prior occasions, and the guards point their weapons at us, ready to fire should we prove untrustworthy.

One approaches the driver's window.

"Say you are here in accordance with code seventeen," I tell him, remembering the words on the screen of the detainment box.

"State your…" begins the guard when he reaches the window before the driver interrupts him.

"I am here in accordance with Code Seventeen."

The guard pauses and looks at the others, unnerved by the driver's statement. Code 17. I do not remember a time when it was ever used, since it is reserved for the most special of criminals, the kind the president of Arel wishes to meet in person and execute herself.

"Let them through," the guard at the window says, not wanting to be on the receiving end of Tapiwa's wrath for refusing to enforce Code 17.

The gate swings inward, allowing us entrance, and the driver lets out a slow breath as he puts the transport in gear and drives forward toward the giant double doors of the palace, while more guards line the steps with Kaleb waiting at the top for us, his loose-fitting pants whipping in the wind as the satiny fabric reflects the light around us, with a tepid expression on his face. The transport stops.

"Here we go," I whisper to myself, when the doors open and

Anshu's men get out, yanking me out of the transport, not caring if my head hits the side. Annoyed, I keep my mouth shut and my head down, doing my best to act like a defeated prisoner, as something deep down warns me that their actions are far more than trying to sell our deception. They drag me across the paved pavilion and to the marble steps leading to the entranceway and past Kaleb, the bronze-colored fabric of his pants matching the mood of Arel, dark and brooding, and a part of me misses the more flamboyant colors I have seen him wear on past occasions, but when I glance at his eyes, I see what I've seen in so many others: a mixture of sadness, anger, and fear.

"This way," he says, as though he longs to tell me something, something forbidden, but he maintains tight control over his impulses as they struggle for dominance.

Anshu's men shove me past the columns, almost causing me to trip over the top of a marbled step, and I glare at them, wondering why the harshness, but they look past me, as though I am not there, and the hairs on the back of my neck rise while dread creeps up on me. We pass through the entrance, and I find myself admiring the floor as each tile meets another, forming an invisible seam, and the soft lights dotting the walls reflect off it, forming a golden bubble around us; it's warmth almost forces me to forget the harsh realities that brought me to this place. Kaleb leads us toward the wide staircase, and the memory of seeing Tapiwa and Kumi on them on my first visit here remind me of a different time, but it is stripped away the moment we go past the bottom steps and underneath the stairs themselves to a narrow corridor I never noticed before. With each step, the uncanny feeling of unwanted eyes watching me cause my skin to grow cold, and as I scan the area, I notice the palace guards as they stand rigid, blending in with the background, ready to strike should they need to, but there does not seem to be many of them, or so I can see.

The walls light up, casting a harsh, fluorescent light upon us, making us look more ghoulish than human as we tread after Kaleb, wondering where he is taking us. I had expected to be taken to the second floor where I was taken when Tapiwa had summoned me here, not into a cave within the palace, but the further we go, the more I wonder if that is where Kaleb leads us. An unexpected hand rams itself into my back, causing me to stumble forward, and my anger flares, but I clamp my mouth shut, knowing that now is not the time, though my mind ponders the use of force by those who are supposed to be allies, unless...

"Enough!" Kaleb says to the one who shoved me.

He glowers at him, but Kaleb, in a rare instance of courage, does not back down, making me wonder what has happened to him in my absence.

"You are here in accordance with your orders, but those orders do not include your current, bullish actions. Is that understood?"

Anshu's men glance from one to the other before one of them mutters, "Yes, sir."

The further we walk, the more I wonder why Anshu's men have not loosened the binders clamping my wrists, and as each second passes, thoughts, each darker than the last, cross my mind. I hope the others fare better.

A final light illumines the hallway, and Kaleb stops before what appears to be a solid wall. He types in a code and a panel opens, revealing a room beyond, and ushers us inside.

"Kaleb?" comes a confused voice.

Tapiwa. Anger rises within me at the thought of her still being alive, and it takes every ounce of my will to not jump for her and wrap my fingers around the throat of the woman who murdered Chase.

"I told you to take them to the atrium and wait for me," she says with irritation.

"I thought this more suitable," replies Kaleb, and again, this unusual and forceful nature of his strikes me as odd, making me wonder what happened to him since the last time we met.

"You have been bold of late," Tapiwa scolds as she takes a step toward him, allowing the vibrancy of her mint green tunic to contrast against the ebony walls and the guards dressed to match them.

"My apologies, Madam President," Kaleb says, but the sarcasm within his tone is unmistakable. "I thought you would like to deal with her yourself and as quick as possible—without prying eyes."

Kaleb grabs me from Anshu's men and pushes me to the center of the room, but before he lets go, his hand sweeps past the binders around my wrists and loosens them. Though confused by his actions, I keep my face unreadable, except for the anger within me and the vengeance I wish to take.

Tapiwa looks at me and her marigold-colored lips curve into a wry smile as she picks up a curved blade from a nearby table with a slim light running along its edge, causing me to look around the room for the first time, while scolding myself for not doing so the moment I first stepped in here. Glass cases line the room, each filled with an array of weapons, the likes of which I have never seen, and some, only pictures of during my studies at the training facility. Each sharp, bold, and archaic.

"They say," Tapiwa says while picking at her oval-shaped nail (painted blue with flecks of yellow dotting them) with the tip of the blade, "that our ancestors understood how to cause pain, and understood the best way to fight one's enemy. Some weapons are too impersonal, but this allows one to feel the life of their enemy leave their body."

My face flushes with rage as her words enter my ears, and I am thrust back to the night Chase died and how I held him while he breathed his last.

Do what you have to, to survive. That is what he told me.

I intend to. And more.

"I found you intriguing at first," Tapiwa continues. "Pity that you turned out to be such a disappointment."

I twist my hands, trying to loosen the binders even more as she talks.

"You are an enigma, Noni," says Tapiwa. "I saw it the day of the banquet when you received your commission and again during the ceremonial dinner when you received your medal. At first, I thought I could use someone like you to quell the growing discontent within this city. Harsh measures and punishments are no longer enough to contain it, but Molers warned me to be careful. Perhaps I should have listened, but now"—Tapiwa holds her knife in front of her, admiring the pristine blade as the light reflects off it, accentuating its sharp edges—"we get to hash out our differences in a more preferred way."

Molers?

"You were working with him?" I ask, confused as Molers steps out of the shadows.

"He works for me," Tapiwa says, emphasizing the word "for", and an irritated expression crosses Molers' face; he must have had a different view of the nature of their relationship. "Didn't you wonder why he was at the ceremonial dinner when he should have been in the factory, as you had ordered?"

Tapiwa studies my face, pleased with what she finds.

"Of course you did, and now you know. You see, ambition—blind, relentless ambition—is useful, and it helped me achieve what I wanted most. And his knowledge of your weaknesses proved useful as well as his willingness to do anything to achieve what he desires most."

Tapiwa steps over to Molers and rubs the back of her fingers down his cheek, mocking the affectionate nature of it. "But every object's usefulness comes to an end."

Guards appear from the doorway behind her and grab Molers. He struggles to break free, but it seems like a half-hearted effort, and before I can ponder it, he is dragged from the room, leaving Tapiwa and me alone with Anshu's men, while four more guards enter the chamber.

"I must admit," Tapiwa continues, "the dynamic between you two, how you each try to outwit the other, is intriguing. I do not know how you managed to get under his skin, but I must commend you. It made manipulating him easier."

"Kumi warned me about you," I say.

"I'm sure he did. He never had much ambition, and yet, everything was laid before his feet for the taking! Ruling Arel was always my birthright, but because I was born second, it would never be given to me. It mattered little. First, my mother died in an accident, if you can call a knife to her throat an accident, and with my father so distraught, it was easy to slip a little something into his drink while pretending to comfort him. I played the part of the mourning daughter well, but Kumi wasn't fooled. Not that it mattered. Kumi could never deny himself the pleasures of the flesh, including his sister's, and until you showed up, he did whatever I told him to. A nice little puppet with his master to lead him, but you… your actions made him question the nature of our unagreed upon arrangement, but death has a way of solving certain problems."

Kumi's mysterious illness and the bombing… not that it surprises me. He tried to warn me, before the end. He was nothing more than a plaything to her, like me, and for a moment, I pity him, a man who was never able to have his own mind, but always found himself manipulated by the people around him.

"Why are you telling me all this?" I demand, continuing to loosen the binders even more.

"Well," Tapiwa scoffs at my question, "I guess, sometimes, I like to brag. You were an interesting toy, but you became an annoyance in the end, and Molers informed me of one way I could break you. I could not dispatch you like others in the past; you had become a symbol to the people of Arel, especially to those who seek to supplant me and remove me from my birthright! So, I had to destroy you and the symbol you have become."

"Didn't go as planned, did it?" I say, mocking her.

"I've overcome bigger obstacles. You are one person. I control Arel's arbiters."

My hand slips free of its constraint.

"You were a worthy opponent," Tapiwa says to me, "but your usefulness has come to an end."

She stabs at me with her knife, but I jump back, bringing my freed hand forward and grab her wrist, squeezing as hard as I can, as she stares at me in surprise, but her surprise is short-lived as she pushes me away and swipes at me again, forcing me to dodge to the side. I grab a cup off the table and smash her in the face with it, forcing her to turn away, while I rip the binder from my other wrist. A guard tackles me, slamming me into the side of the table, causing it to scoot across the floor as one of the legs crack. I ram my elbow into the guard's face and glance around at Anshu's men, each of whom is locked in a fight of their own, and notice that Kaleb has left. The guard brings his weapon up, but I grab hold of it, putting all my weight on it before he can take aim, ripping it from his hands and pointing it at him. Nothing happens. A quick glance tells me why: biometric sensors. He charges me, but I jump back and ram the point of his weapon into his neck, stopping him and forcing him to clutch his throat as he gags for breath.

A blade slashes the top of my arm, forcing me to recoil as blood seeps from the wound and down my arm. Tapiwa stands before me with a knife in each hand, smiling at me. She swings at me. I raise the guard's weapon, blocking her attack as metal strikes metal and sparks fly past my nose. She attacks again, and again I raise the weapon in my hands, blocking her knife before it reaches its target, and it slides down the barrel of the rifle, before she kicks me in the leg, forcing me off-balance, and as I teeter, she rams her knee into my chin, causing my teeth to clack together. I jump forward, forcing her to stumble backward, breaking our weapons free before swinging mine across the floor and knocking her feet out from under her. One of Anshu's men jumps on me, plowing his fist into my back, and Tapiwa laughs in response, using the distraction to flee the room. He grabs my hair and lifts my head before ramming my face into the floor as the table next to us breaks under the impact of another being thrown on it, sending knife-like pieces of wood my way.

The man lifts my head again, but I seize one of the pieces of wood and stab him in the leg, causing him to howl in pain as he loosens his grip on my hair, and I push myself off the floor, forcing him off me. He rips the wooden stake out of his leg and dives for me, and a clink sounds as he misses my neck and strikes the floor instead. He lifts the piece of wood again and brings it down upon me, and I cross my arms in front of me, blocking him. My lungs cease their function as I struggle to keep him from stabbing me as he places all his weight upon the stake, grinning in triumph. Shadows appear on the edges of my vision as the pointed tip of the stave drops lower, and my focus remains on stopping it. My arms tire. The sharp piece of wood inches closer.

A crash sounds next to us, and a guard slams into my opponent, knocking him to the ground and freeing me from his clutches. I spring to all fours, releasing the breath trapped in my lungs and sweep my leg across the floor, knocking the man down. He rolls onto his stomach and lifts himself. We eye each other a moment, while confusion clouds my mind, wondering why one of Anshu's men has attacked me, until the obvious truth hits me: I am the distraction in the plan, but also a liability that needs to be dealt with because they have no intention of rescuing Gwen; their only goal is taking over Arel. A part of me suspected this would happen when the plan was first formulated, while another part had hoped that Anshu spoke the truth. The man lunges for me—I jump out of the way—going still after hitting the floor, and I roll him over, finding the stake poking out of his diaphragm.

The guard that had saved me by accident notices me. He grabs a spear from the wall and thrusts it at me, forcing me to duck in order to avoid it. He jabs at me again, and once more, I duck out of the way, trying not to trip as I do so, while the man continues to step toward me, forcing me to walk backward. Another of Anshu's men sees my predicament, but instead of helping me, he pulls out his pistol and fires, causing me to dive to the floor as bullets whiz through the room, pelting the far wall. When I look up, Anshu's man stands limp with a spear through his chest as blood oozes around the metal tip, running down his front and pooling on the floor, turning the ivory color crimson, and his pistol falls from his grip before he collapses. The guard glances in my direction, and as he yanks his spear free, I snatch a metal rod from the tile and strike him in the shin with it before swinging it a second time, hitting him in the crotch. When he doubles over, I swing it a third time, striking him in the head. He falls to the floor.

I reach for the pistol, but yank my hand back the moment bullets strike the tile near me, rolling to the side and seeking cover. More gunfire pelts the wall behind me, leaving small, round holes in it as I cover my head in an attempt to shield myself from the flying debris, while bits of the wall chip away from the assault. Risking a small peek, I crane my neck to see over the table I hide behind and find the last of Anshu's men reloading his pistol. Seizing my chance, I dart from behind the table and rush for a cabinet full of archaic weapons, grabbing the first thing I can—a mace—and duck low as he points his weapon at me, darting behind a case.

While he searches for me, I slink through the room, working my way around him, crawling over the body of a guard, wincing when my hand presses against her wound, squirting bits of blood onto my sleeve, as Anshu's man searches for me, his pistol raised and ready to fire. His foot kicks something, sending it skittering across the room, telling me where he is. Staying as quiet as I can, I inch my way to the other side until I am behind him, and I pick up a piece of debris and chuck it across the room. When he turns in its direction, I spring from my hiding spot and swing the mace at him, catching his shoulder with one of its barbs and tearing into his skin. He whirls around, aiming his pistol at me, but I swipe the mace through the air and knock it out of his hands before ramming it into his chest, and he staggers backward from the impact.

"Why?" I ask him as he catches his breath.

He glares at me. "You're just a means to an end, and you couldn't even accomplish that."

Raising the mace, I charge him and...

A tremendous force shatters the window, surrounding us in a storm of glittering shrapnel and knocking us off our feet, forcing me to drop the mace and place my arms in front of my face in a vain attempt to shield it from the glass swirling around me, until I crash on the floor, sliding across the razor-edged shards as they cut through my clothing and into me. Stunned, my head pounds as I force myself onto my knees, trying to not cut myself on the glass littering the floor, and wincing whenever one cuts my palms. Air rushes into the room blowing bits of my hair around my face until it sticks to the skin, and I glance up, looking out at the aerodrome, or the gaping hole that used to be the aerodrome. How many explosives did they use? Which explosives did they use? The full weight of what just happened hits me and confusion turns to panic as I picture Renal and the others lying dead, or what is left of their bodies in the aftermath of the blast.

The click of a pistol being cocked snaps me back to my present situation. I look up into the bloodied face of my would-be assassin, but before he can squeeze the trigger, something strikes him in the head, blowing half of it away. He drops to the floor, landing face first in a bed of glass as something falls out of his pocket and rolls across the floor before settling next to the toe of my boot: a flash bomb.

Perce.

I rip the pistol from his frozen grip, hoping it does not have a biometric sensor, pick up the flash bomb, and run for the door, darting back into the room the moment gunfire tears into the doorframe. My body presses into the wall until the gunfire stops, and I peek around the corner, trying to get a glimpse of what awaits me in the corridor, spotting a nook. Two palace guards stand on the other end, weapons raised, waiting for me to allow one strand of my hair to become visible in the light above me. I shoot the light. As the sparks fall around me, dissipating with each passing second, I picture my next move, envisioning it in my mind as one of my instructors taught me to do, in what seems like eons ago, and ready myself for what is to come. I wait, letting them sweat and wonder what will happen next—why I haven't acted. The small clicking of a weapon as the owner checks its magazine tells me that impatience has set in.

Perfect.

I dive from the doorway and into the nook, taking note of the flashes of light when the guards fire at me, detonate the flash bomb, and throw it in their direction, turning away before it goes off. With them stunned, I charge down the hallway before dropping to my knees and sliding down the tile until I reach them, falling on my back the moment I do, and swing my legs, knocking one to the floor. I point my pistol at his head and fire. Before I can turn my attention to the other, a boot comes for my head, and I roll to the side as it strikes the floor, leaving a hollow echo. I get up, but the same boot slams into my chest, hitting me over and over again, forcing me to drop my pistol and stagger back until I am pressed against the wall. His fist flies toward me and I duck, dodging around him before throwing my entire weight into him, forcing him into the wall. He swings his elbow back, and I jump away, not expecting his counterattack when his gloved fist strikes me in the face, followed by another. I kick at his knee, but he blocks it and elbows me in the stomach before punching me in the middle of my back as I stand doubled over and drop to the floor. Stunned, I remain still, letting him believe that he has won as he stalks around me, gloating in his perceived triumph. I spot my pistol and form a plan. As he nears, readying the final blow, I kick my left foot out, breaking his kneecap, and as his screams of pain echo around me, I dive for my pistol, aim, and fire, silencing him for good.

Sore, I push myself to my feet, rubbing the bruise forming on my face as I calculate my next move, when a single gunshot shatters the tense calm surrounding me, forcing me to whirl around and raise my weapon: a guard stands behind me, weapon in hand, and drops to the tile floor in a pool of her own blood, revealing Kaleb poised behind her with smoke coming out of his own pistol. I point mine at him.

"There is no need for that," he says, his tone controlled, unlike previous occasions when he spoke to me, and he lowers his weapon. "I'll not stop you."

"Why?" I demand, wanting to know why he has helped me.

"I have witnessed many horrors in this place, since the days of their father's death," Kaleb says, understanding my question, "and went along with it, pretending to be the bumbling servant that will do anything to remain in the presidents' good graces. Then you showed up. The defiance in your mannerism. You didn't even know you possessed it or exhibited it, but Tapiwa saw it. It was I who convinced her to use you. She always did like her playthings."

"You—"

"If I saw it, others have as well, not tribunals or the council, but others within Arel—average people!"

"So, you're part of the underground?"

"No! I'll have no part of them. I just want to end the killing."

"And Chase! You're respon—"

"No! I had hoped we could have been allies, but with the increased attacks on the city, I never got the chance to speak with you, nor did I foresee Tapiwa's amusement turning into obsession."

"Why should I trust you?"

"How do you think your commander and lieutenant knew where you would be, and at what time, when they got you out of the detention facility?"

My index finger trembles on the trigger of my pistol as I struggle with disposing of him or allowing him to live, wondering if he speaks the truth, unsure of which course of action to choose.

"Shoot me, if you must," Kaleb says. "I'll not stop you. But if you want Tapiwa, and to save the girl, you'll need this."

He tosses his wristband to me and I catch it, twisting it in my fingers before lowering my weapon.

"There is one place she always goes when she feels threatened. Go down this hallway, turn left. When you find some stairs, go down two floors, until you come to a door with a keypad."

"What of the guards?" I ask, but Kaleb shakes his head.

"Only three people have access to that part of the palace: her and me."

"And the third?"

"He's dead."

Keeping my eyes glued to Kaleb, I step past him, walking backward for a minute, refusing to be taken by surprise, before turning and racing down the corridor as gunfire rages outside the palace walls.

Lights flicker as I hurry to the other end of the hallway, while the echoes of distant explosions reach my ears, muffled by the walls surrounding me, wondering what has gripped Arel. It seems that the resistance, as they call themselves, was less than truthful about how much artillery they had or the extent of their reach, much less their trustworthiness. Why did Anshu's men turn on me? I doubt it was of their own accord. Curiosity about their betrayal pillages my mind as I continue my trek through the hallway, hoping to find Tapiwa and to free Gwen from this place.

A palace guard appears before me and charges the moment he sees me. I do not stop. I do not slow down. We run toward one another, playing a fatal game of chicken. When I reach him, I duck low and fling him over my back, and he crashes onto the floor, but before he can get back up, I ram my foot into his throat, crushing his windpipe and continue on. I reach the end of the hallway and veer left as Kaleb instructed, but before I get far, a group of palace guards burst into the corridor, firing at one another, forcing me to dive to the floor to avoid the crossfire. Are they fighting each other?

I stay pinned to the cold tile floor as they stab, shoot, and kick one another, mutilating and maiming each other before dealing the final blow, reminding myself that I haven't time to wonder about their actions. As the fight rages around me, I crawl across the floor, doing my best to go unnoticed.

A body crashes beside me, and blood pours from her gaping wound, but I continue my trek, pulling myself through her pooling blood as it sticks to my skin and clothes. A raging yell forces me to look up. I've been spotted. I roll onto my back and kick at a female guard as she lunges for me, hitting her in the stomach. She staggers back before lunging again. I raise my pistol and fire, stopping her, and she collapses in front of me. Not wanting to stay here, I jump to my feet and charge through the fray, shoving anyone in my way to the side, and firing at any who try to stop me, leaving my own trail of carnage until I am free from the chaos. I hurry down the corridor as the sound of the fight dims with each step I take, until I come to a solid door with a scanner. This must be the stairwell Kaleb told me about. I pull out his wristband and hold it against the scanner, pleased when it flashes green and the door's lock clicks as it slides open, allowing me through. Once on the other side, the door closes and the lock clicks into place, sealing me in darkness and silence, separating me from the madness overtaking the presidential palace and trapping me between two choices: go up or down.

Remembering Kaleb's instructions, I hurry down the steps, taking them two at a time, determined to find Tapiwa and exact my revenge, while forcing her to give me Gwen. I reach the first floor and continue on, rounding the corner in the railing, not bothering to glance at the door there beckoning me to go through, but I refuse to be sidetracked. Low, thundering vibrations migrate through the steps and the railing, shaking them as I rush down them to my goal, while dull roars echo above me, telling me that the aerodrome was not the only target of Anshu's men. Something else is taking place. I hope Renal and the others are all right. The stomping of my boots fills my ears, while the staircase turns into a never- ending trek, where each step becomes a marker of my failure, but I push such negativity aside, quickening my pace, before hopping over a rail, skipping the last seven steps, and landing in front of a locked door with a tiny keypad nestled within it. This must be the door Kaleb told me about.

Another low rumble reverberates around me, filling the entire stairwell with a soft roar that causes my eardrums to itch as I stand before the door with trepidation and determination, knowing that this is the moment I exact justice for Chase's death and prevent Gwen from suffering the same fate. The keypad releases a tiny, high-pitched note when I hold Kaleb's wristband to it before releasing the locks on the door and allowing it to slide open, granting me entrance. I step through and the door slides shut, locking into place. Instead of another hallway, I enter a room, but one of unspeakable horrors. Pale green light emanates from the walls as I tiptoe through a maze of poles stretching from floor to ceiling with beams attached to them covered in spikes. My shoulder brushes one as I tread past, and I jerk it back as the razor-edged barb cuts through my shirt and into my skin, drawing blood. Curious, I grab it in one of the spaces between the spikes and move it, noting how it is designed to spin in a circle, in varying patterns. Is this some sort of training room?

Unsure of what sort of place this is, and not liking the silence surrounding me, I continue moving my way through the room, trying not to touch the blades attached to the spinning beams. The further I go, the more I wonder if Kaleb sent me into a trap, or did Tapiwa not come here like he thought? I reach the center of the room, where a table with old blood stains on it, browned and oxidized from time, and empty shackles hang limp, unable to fulfill their desire to hold someone prisoner. I pick at one, noting the worn edges, wondering how often it had been used and frightened of the answer as I imagine a poor soul pinned to this table and tortured for someone's own entertainment. Tapiwa loves her toys, or so seems to be the consensus. Is this where I was meant to end up?

A small creak—subtle, as though someone does not wish to be heard—catches my attention. I move away from the table and back into the maze of spinning, barbed beams, oozing my way through them in search of the creak, my mind alert. Another low rumble echoes throughout the building, indicating that all is not well outside these walls, while uneasy silence reigns supreme within, making me more anxious the longer it drags on. One of the beams flies for my head, forcing me to duck and dive over another before impaling myself on it. As my chest heaves from the sudden excitement and exertion, I look back at the spinning beam, wondering what, or who, moved it, aware that I already know the answer.

"You're quick. I'll give you that."

Tapiwa's voice echoes around me, making me believe that she is everywhere and nowhere at the same time. I twist around, wondering where she is, and how her voice is able to come from every direction, when I notice tiny speakers within the ceiling and walls. Another beam heads straight for me and I duck low, avoiding its blow. It creaks as it spins above me, mocking me.

"I've trained in this room since I was girl," Tapiwa's voice spills from the speakers.

I stay low, crawling among the spinning beams as I search for her. Another soft creak reaches my ears. I pause. It happens again. I scoot back into the maze of beams and use my foot to turn one, while I wait behind another for my prey to show itself. A wisp of movement appears before me, and I spot her as she approaches the spinning beam, making little noise, with a curved knife in each hand. The moment she is before me, I kick at the beam in front of me, sending it spiraling toward her, but she hears it and swings one of her knives down, blocking it, before jumping out of the way and darting back into the sea of spiked planks. I jump to my feet and follow her, but I do not know this place as well as she does, and I lose her among the barbed terror before me, but continue on, knowing she will not remain hidden forever.

Tapiwa jumps out at me, knife raised, and I knock one of the beams at her, blocking her attack, but not before she manages to knock the pistol from my hand, sending it flying even deeper into the spinning pillars of death. She tries punching me, knife in hand, but I dodge behind a pole and over one of the spiked beams, circling around her, but before I can attack, she twists around and blocks me. She kicks at me over and over, and I block her each time as she pushes me through the spiked maze, determined to make me pay. She kicks again, and I dodge to the side, allowing her momentum to propel her forward and into one the spiked beams, but Tapiwa manages to catch herself, suffering a cut to her arm instead of impalement.

She swings both knives at me, and I jump back, pushing beam after beam between me and her, wincing as the curved blades strike the spikes, sending a deathlike note into the air, telling me that each one could well be my last. Another beam swings for me, and I dive to the floor, avoiding its fatal blow as I ram my foot into Tapiwa's stomach. Stunned, she staggers back, but gets control of her senses and charges for me, knocking a series of barbed beams in my direction, forcing my attention on blocking and avoiding their attack, allowing her to forge a path toward me, and she rips my shirt with one of her curved blades. I catch her wrist, stopping the second knife from reaching me, while she brings the other blade up, and I twist her arm, turning her away from me, before planting my foot in her back and forcing her into a set of barbs. Blood trickles from her right arm as they pierce her skin, fueling her rage. She turns toward me. I meet her venomous gaze as she rips her tunic apart, exposing her yellow undershirt, and wraps the scrap of material around the wound on her arm.

She tightens her grip on her knives while her eyes narrow on me.

I spot the pistol on the floor.

"Where's Gwen?" I demand in a soft voice.

Tapiwa smirks.

She races for me, bringing her blades up, but I dive over a spinning beam as the knife strikes it and lunge for the pistol, grab it, aim, and fire. Tapiwa pauses, touching the spot where the bullet grazed her shoulder, and stares at the blood on her fingers. She attacks, and I squeeze the trigger again, receiving a click in response: empty. I jump to my feet and face her as she runs for me, knives raised, and use the pistol as a barrier, blocking each of her attempts to impale me with her blades, and sparks fly each time metal meets metal. She swings at me again, and I raise the pistol, my only line of defense, and the two meet, locking together, forcing us into a deadlock, until I use my other hand to wrench one of the knives from her grasp, and it clatters on the floor as it skips across it. Enraged, she swipes her curved dagger at me again and I jump back, continuing the series of attacks, dodges, and counterattacks as we move through the labyrinth of twirling, spiked beams in a sort of death waltz, until she sweeps her foot and knocks mine out from under me, causing me to falter. She pounces on me, using my moment of weakness to place me in a headlock, and presses the tip of her knife against my cheek.

"All this for a plebeian?" she hisses at me. "Maybe I should have kept him alive. The perfect leash for an untamed mutt."

The very mention of Chase causes something within me to rage to a rolling boil until it erupts into unbridled fury, and I drop to my knees and twist, surprising her, and flip her over me, causing her feet to fly through the air, until she crashes onto her back. For the first time, I see fear on her face. She scrambles to her feet and rushes past the spinning beams, avoiding their blows, until she finds a panel in the wall with a keypad embedded in it, and it opens for her. Refusing to lose her, I hurry after her, reaching the panel as it closes. I rip out Kaleb's wristband and hold it to the scanner. It flashes green, and the panel opens. I charge through and into a corridor, jumping to the side as Tapiwa throws her knife at me, and it strikes the wall behind me.

"Where is she!" I scream at her, shoving the wristband in my pocket.

I lunge for Tapiwa and catch her around the middle, slamming her into the opal floor, and she winces from the impact, but before I can pin her down, she uses her legs to push me off her and kicks me in the face, forcing me to fall backward. Tapiwa kicks me again before scrambling to her feet and running to the other end, with me right behind her, and slams her fist into the wall as another door opens, allowing her through, but before I can reach it, a piece of the floor drops away beneath me, causing me to fall.

My hands throw themselves in every direction, grasping for anything to stop my descent, while also refusing to let go of Kaleb's wristband, and my fingers screech against the smooth floor until I come to a stop. My heart pounding and threatening to jump out of my throat, I glance down as my feet dangle above the shiny spikes below me, reminded of a portion of the gauntlet and how I almost did not escape it. My muscles burn as I haul myself up and onto a solid surface, pausing for breath once the threat of being skewered is no longer present. I focus on the door Tapiwa escaped through, determined to make her tell me where Gwen is, and race for it, pressing Kaleb's wristband against the keypad embedded in it. It flashes green, allowing me entrance, and I charge through into a room full of incessant barking.

Nunchucks fly toward my head. I dive out of the way, allowing them to crash into the door as it slides shut behind me. I glance around the room, noting the cages full of wild dogs, snarling at me as drool falls from their mouths, pooling around their paws, all while they bark and bite at the bars confining them, and spot a lever controlling the locks. Tapiwa jumps out at me, swinging a machete, and I roll out of its way, forcing the blade to strike the floor, creating an icy clink that sends sparks into the air. She strikes again, and again, I roll to the side, and the blade slices off bits of my hair as it rushes past my head. I take a quick look at the black strands on the glowing white tile, fearing that the next assault could be my last. I spot the nunchucks. Tapiwa raises the machete a third time. As she swings at me again, I roll across the floor and seize the nunchucks, and jump to my feet, forcing her to miss me a third time.

Enraged, she swings at me again. I stretch the nunchucks in front of me, and its chain bends under the force of the blade burrowing into it, while my knees buckle from the force as it inches its way to my face. I dive to the side, lowering my weapon, and whirl around her as her machete clinks the floor. Her lips curl and her eyes narrow on me as she turns and swings at me again, forcing me to jump backward a couple of times amid an incessant chorus of salivating, barking dogs. In a burst of anger, Tapiwa releases a blood curdling battle cry and charges for me, but I stretch out the nunchucks and wrap its chain around her machete's blade, ripping it from her hands, and it flies across the room, striking the far wall. Thinking I have the advantage, I whip the nunchucks at her, but Tapiwa proves more adept than I anticipated, and catches it with her left hand before ripping it out of mine, and swings it at me, catching me in the face. I fall to the floor, dazed. Stars cross before me as I close my eyes, trying to capture my bearings and make my mind focus, but it refuses to, preferring the unknown darkness, but I cannot pass out now. I shake my head and blink, forcing myself to focus. I think of Gwen. If I die, what becomes of her? If I die, she dies. I failed Sheila. I failed Chase. I will not fail her.

Steady footfalls echo around me, sounding distant to my confused mind as I lie on the floor, battling wills with the limits of my physical form. She continues pacing around me, reveling in her moment of triumph as she strikes me with the nunchucks, causing bursts of intense pain to surge throughout my body before concentrating in welts that form on my back, taunting me with words.

"You thought you could come here"—she strikes me again—"and make me bow to your will!"

My hands grip the cold tile of the floor as their pristine color darkens beneath me and my struggle to break free of Tapiwa's wrath.

Faint sounds rumble through the walls of the palace, but they are insignificant compared to the tribulation I face here, in this room, as she flings the nunchucks at me for a… I've lost count. Pain ripples through me, begging me to cease, to give in and let her kill me, but Gwen's frightened face fills my mind and I think of the night I first saw her, of the day she and Chase first came to the manor, of her anger when I sentenced him to the mines, and her grief when she watched him die in my arms. Such thoughts morph into rage, a rage that I kept caged for a long time, but no more. She brings the nunchucks down upon me for a final time, but I roll onto my back and kick them out of her hand before ramming my foot into her stomach, forcing her to stagger back. As she struggles for breath, I rise to my feet, prepared to end it here and now.

Our eyes lock before I lunge for her, griping her around the middle and forcing her to crash into one of the cages, while the dog inside growls and bites at the bars. She swings a fist at me, but I block it and thrust my elbow into her chin, before gripping the back of her head and forcing her face into my right knee, crushing the cartilage in her nose. Blood pools past the corners of her mouth as she looks up at me, ready for revenge. She pushes me off her and rams her foot into my chest, but I refuse to give in to the pain it causes me and lunge for her again. We crash onto the floor and roll across it, each one trying to get the upper hand until we stop, with me atop her, plowing my fists into her face, until it is no longer recognizable.

"Where is she?" I scream at her, continuing to hit her as her blood covers my knuckles and sprays my clothes.

She laughs.

"WHERE IS SHE?" I scream even louder, my uncontrolled rage refusing to be satiated with each strike to her face.

"Where is who?" Tapiwa says as she spits blood from her mouth into my face.

"Where is Gwen!"

A maniacal laugh escapes Tapiwa's mouth. "You thought she was here?"

"Tell me where she is!" I grip her tunic by the collar.

"I had her moved." Tapiwa's laughter circles around us, mocking me and my desire to save Gwen. "She's in the detention center. Try and save the plebeian bitch if you want. You'll die!"

My stomach drops down the largest pit imaginable as Tapiwa's words repeat themselves in my mind. Gwen is not here. The thought taunts me, reminding me that I have failed again, but… I know where she is now.

I get off Tapiwa and stretch to my full height as she lies on the once pristine tiles, coated in her own blood, her face resembling a slab of meat instead of a person.

"Coward! You can't kill me!" She laughs, sputtering cruor as she mocks me and the fact that she still breathes, unconcerned about the blood soaking her clothing.

"I'm not going to kill you," I say, walking over to the lever that controls the locks on the cages, "but I cannot say the same for them."

I pull it, releasing the locks, and the dogs burst form their cages, converging on Tapiwa as she lies helpless on the floor, choosing the easier prey, while her screams fill the room as they tear her apart, and I step out the door, letting it slide shut behind me, sealing what's left of her with the fate she deserves.

Chapter 29

Unexpected Turn

Muffled explosions and gunfire fill the stairwell around me—a testament to the structure of the walls—as my feet pound the steps as I charge up them, heading for the floor I had first entered them from, knowing that I must get out of here. With each passing second, the muffled sounds intensify, rattling the walls, causing them to shake the stairs as I hurry up them, making me wonder what is happening outside, and what Anshu's real plans were. My thoughts drift to Renal, Luther, Perce, and the others, but I shake them from my mind, keeping my focus on Gwen and the horrors she must have suffered at the hands of Tapiwa, and how frightened she must be now, trapped in the detention center, locked in a cell, never to be freed. The others can take care of themselves. Gwen is my priority now.

A rumble stretches from the top of the stairwell, past me, and to the levels below, reverberating through the massive walls, causing vibrations in my chest as it passes by me in waves. More follow, pulses that grow stronger, causing my stomach to churn with each series of rumbles. Exposed on the stairwell, the vulnerability of my precarious situation strikes me, and I charge up the stairs, knowing that I must get out before I find myself trapped, and with each step I take, the fear of this place becoming my tomb grows stronger, threatening to overtake my senses. I push onward before a sudden silence makes me stop and look up. Fire and smoke fall from above, coming straight for me. I look at the door I had come through in my search for Tapiwa. If I hurry, I can make it.

I start for it, but something crashes into the presidential palace, sending a jolt throughout the building that slams my body into the railing, and it gives way from the force of the impact and the sensation of falling takes its hold. Desperate, I fling my arms in every direction, grasping at anything, and snatch what's left of the railing, gripping the metal rods as tight as I can, but my sweaty palms cause me to slip. Metal and wood crash around me as the raging inferno above plummets, assisted by gravity, and with me in its sights. I glance down at my dangling feet and the stairs not far below, knowing I have two choices. I let go. I crash onto the steps and roll down them amidst a cascade of falling debris, unable to stop as bits of steel, concrete, wood, glass, and smoldering embers crash around me, cursing their failure at striking their target, until my body slams into a wall. Each breath pains me as my chest struggles to expand, allowing me to fill my lungs, only to cough from the exertion.

A chunk of the ceiling slams into the floor next to me, still aflame, forcing me to cover my head. The stairwell shakes again as I pull myself to my feet, wincing as my body cries out in pain, but I force my mind to focus on getting out and saving Gwen as I trudge down the stairs, taking them one at a time at first, until necessity forces me to hasten my pace as more debris crashes around me, singeing my clothes with burning embers. I turn a corner and slide down the rail before hopping over a series of steps, running as fast as I can without tripping as the walls cave in around me, surrounding me with a chaotic storm of metal plating and rods as the building crumbles around me. I am almost to the bottom. Desperate, I jump over the railing, skipping the last set of stairs, and crash onto the copper floor below, grunting as my knees buckle beneath me and I drop to the ground. Despite the sharp pain filling my legs, I roll across the floor underneath the steps next to me, allowing them to take the full impact as the ceiling and walls crash.

Smoke and dust fill the atmosphere, causing me to choke as I try to breathe, threatening to suffocate me if I do not get out. I peek out from under the steps as the stairs and the railing above me buckle underneath the destabilization of the structure around them, forming an earsplitting noise that drowns the thunderous roars above, spilling in from the cavity that used to be the top of the building. My eyes search the foggy darkness, hoping to find a way out, when I spot a doorway with a keypad in its center and my hands fumble through my pockets, until they pull out Kaleb's wristband. More metal panels crash around me, warning me that I must chance it. I burst from underneath the stairs and race for the doorway, holding my arms up to protect my face as the world around me is obliterated, and I shove the wristband into the keypad, pressing it against it, until the metal band bends. It flashes green, but I do not wait for the door to open all the way as I shove my way through as the stairwell collapses, creating a massive force that propels me across a room and into a massive window before everything falls silent with only a plume of dust as evidence of the terror I escaped.

For a few moments, I remain where I am, pressed against a massive window, not wanting to open my eyes or move, but my mind reminds me of what matters most right now: Gwen. I press my palms against the floor, ignoring the bits of rubble that cut into them as my shaky elbows threaten to give way beneath my weight, and I force myself to my knees before standing up. My legs wobble and

I lean against the cracked glass for support, surprised that it did not break from the concussive force that burst from the stairwell moments before, willing my body to endure the abuse, reminding it that remaining here is a death sentence. I take an unsteady step, clinging to the glass as my mind clears itself. I take another and another, forcing my legs to carry my weight, until I am able to stand. I need to get out of here, but which way should I go? I circle around, trying to determine which direction to go in, unsure of where I am; I have never been in the presidential palace without a guide before. I spot a corridor and head for it. It's as good as any. I run for it, pausing when my body argues with me, but I will it to obey my commands and force myself down the hallway, picking up speed as I go, knowing that I must keep moving. Muffled chaos surrounds me, growing stronger the further I go, leaving me to hope that I am able to bypass it. I turn a corner, and another, picking up my pace, and for a moment, I believe that I have escaped the worst until…

A baton slams into my stomach when I turn a third corner, forcing me to drop backward and collapse to the floor, rolling on the linoleum and clutching my stomach as I struggle to breathe. My head turns so that I can look at my attacker: Grelyn. She towers over me, swinging her baton, daring me to fight back as her unnatural blue eyes glower at me, telling me, without the need for words, the animosity, the anger, and the hatred she feels toward me. She has always loathed me. Perhaps she thought me a weak-minded fool. Perhaps she is correct.

"Grelyn," I say, breathless.

Murder fills her eyes as she glares at me. She brings her baton down upon me, and I roll out of the way as it strikes the floor with a sickening thump. She swings a second time, and again, I roll out of the way, missing the baton by inches as it smacks the floor. I stand up and face her, watching her, waiting for her next move, wishing I knew why she wants me dead, and how she found me. She swings her baton at me, swiping the air with it as she charges me, forcing me to jump back to avoid each blow until a wall stops me. She swings again, and I dodge to the side, but not before her baton hits my elbow, causing a burning sensation to tingle through my arm. Once again, we face each other. Vengeance fills her eyes. Whistles fill the air around us, mingling with the sound of distant explosions as she swings her baton at me, and I jump out of the way.

"Trevors is in the detention center because of you!" she says as she charges me.

She swings at me again, and I catch her arm, elbowing her in the face and punching her twice in the chest, but as I try to dodge one of her fists, she trips me, giving her the advantage as she rams her knee into my stomach, causing me to double over, before kneeing me in the face. I stumble back, dazed, trying to regain my senses as Grelyn charges me with her baton. I dodge out of the way. She charges again, and I catch her arm and kick her in the stomach before wrenching the baton from her grip and swinging it at her. She blocks my attack, and it flies from my hand, stopping only when it strikes a wall. An elbow flies for my head, but I duck, twist around, and slam my fist into her side.

Unfazed, Grelyn rounds on me with a backward swing, catching me off-guard before swiping my leg out from underneath me and forcing me to crash onto the floor. As I lie there, confused, the sole of her boot comes for my face and I roll to the side, twisting and turning as needed to avoid her blows, until I manage to wrap my feet around her ankle and knock her off-balance. Once on the floor, I pounce on her, but Grelyn is ready. She raises her foot and throws me off her, and I slam into a wall, while the walls tremble from the chaos outside. Grelyn lunges for me. I kick at her, but she grabs my foot and punches me in the thigh before I manage to roll away and get to my feet. Crouched—her murderous look could crumble stone as she glowers at me, sizing up her prey and planning the next stage of her attack—she lunges for me. I twist my body, grab her arm, and flip her over me, allowing her to slam into the floor with a grunt, but that only angers her more, and she jumps to her feet, swinging her fists, forcing me to raise my arms to block her series of attacks until she tires of this unending battle of wills, and we both pause, wondering what to do, and who will make the next move.

"Grelyn," I begin, but she cuts me off.

"He refused to fight you," Grelyn spits at me.

"What?"

"Those fights—they aired it throughout Arel, and Trevors refused to be a part of it, so they threw him in a cell!"

"Grelyn..."

"And forced me to be here to be a plaything for Tapiwa! Just like Faya! And all because of you! Everywhere you go, destruction follows! The mines! Arel!"

Grelyn is right. It seems that no matter where I go, chaos and destruction follow. There is no denying this.

"I never meant for any of this to happen."

"You never do! But look around you!"

"Please," I plead with her, "I don't—"

Grelyn lunges for me. I swerve out of the way, but Grelyn is quick and counters my move, grabbing me around the waist and flinging me across the room until I crash onto the floor, rolling across it as though I am nothing more than a mere piece of refuse. Before I can regain my feet, Grelyn grabs her baton and pounces on me, pinning me to the floor as she presses the baton against my throat. I grab the club, trying to push it off me, but she has the advantage, and darkness seeps in as I struggle to breathe. I go limp. Surprised, Grelyn releases her hold on the baton and stares at me in confusion.

"I won't stop you," I say, coughing as I speak.

Whatever rage she feels toward me dissipates in that one instant as I never once allowed her to have her way before.

"You're right. Most everyone I've cared about is dead because of me. I never meant for this to happen. I never wanted Arel to fall apart. I just wanted to save the ones I love. I just want to save Gwen."

Grelyn stares at me, struggling with the desire of what she wants to do and with the morality of her wishes, and the baton shakes in her hands as the two opposing forces battling within her mind struggle for dominance, before…

She tosses the baton aside and it skitters across the floor.

"I always thought you were a fool for falling in love with that plebeian," she says as she helps me up, "but you shouldn't have had to watch him die. The truth is: Arel was falling apart long before you."

"What did you see outside the wall?" I ask, remembering one of our previous encounters and what she told me then.

"Too much."

Silence ensues as we each come to an understanding and a delicate truce.

"I need to get to the detention center," I say. "That is where they are keeping Gwen. I'll help you get Trevors…"

"…if I help you get her," Grelyn finishes my thought for me. "If you betray me…"

"I know. You'll kick my ass."

She holds out her arm and I clasp it, agreeing to her terms. In all the years we've known each other, I never thought we would become allies, even if it is temporary.

"I guess we'll have to get rid of the bitch," Grelyn says, referring to Tapiwa.

"She's dead," I say without emotion, and Grelyn laughs, unsurprised, as the walls tremble again from the war raging outside the presidential palace.

"This way," she says to me.

I chase after her, allowing her to lead me through a maze of corridors as the lights embedded in the walls flicker, threatening to darken forever, but Grelyn pushes forward with confidence, making me wonder how often she has walked these halls, and how long she has been trapped in this place as Tapiwa's prisoner. We turn a corner and come to what appears to be a dead end, but Grelyn swipes her wristband and a door opens, revealing an elevator, confirming my suspicions about her having been trapped here for a while. We get inside the elevator and she pushes a button, and it surges upward, taking us up several floors, making me wonder how many floors the palace has, and how far beneath the surface I have gone. Uneasy silence fills the space between us as we stand on opposite ends of the elevator, waiting for it to reach its destination, while I think about the times she tormented me while at the training facility; though, in truth, I was no better. She glances in my direction, and I wonder if she is thinking about our past encounters as well, but before either of us can say a word to break up the monotonous silence choking us, a dull explosion vibrates through the elevator shaft and rattles the walls imprisoning us, and we glance around with unease.

The elevator lurches. Grelyn and I cling to the rail within the elevator as our tepid expressions mirror each other's. It lurches again with a force that knocks Grelyn and me to the floor. We cannot stay here. As though reading my mind, Grelyn hurries to the center of the elevator and motions for me to lift her and support her as she tears away at a panel in the ceiling, prying it away. My muscles shake from supporting her weight and threaten to let go, until a cable snaps and the elevator drops, giving me the strength to hold her so she can complete her task. The panel clatters on the floor, landing near my feet, revealing a hatch concealed behind it. Grelyn opens it and crawls through before reaching back down with her hand extended, and I clasp it, allowing her to pull me up. She points at a series of rungs bult into the side of the elevator shaft, heads for one, and starts to climb them, but after she scrambles up a ways, some of them break off the side of the elevator shaft, and she crashes onto the top of the elevator with a sickening crunch. I start to help her, but she throws me off.

"I'm fine," she says, but the tightness in her voice tells a different story.

I let it go, knowing that weakness is never to be displayed to others, and Grelyn prides herself on her ability to appear strong.

The elevator drops an inch beneath our feet, and we both know that we need to leave if we are to survive. As I study the rungs and the gap above us, the daunting task of climbing upward starts to overwhelm me, but I push it aside, forcing it from my mind as I think of Gwen and the fear she must be experiencing as her world goes to hell. I'm not dying here. A long, thin piece of metal the length of my hand catches my eye, and an idea forms in my mind.

"I don't think..." begins Grelyn, but I ignore her, picking up the thin metal strip and clamping my teeth around it as I place it in my mouth, before backing up to the far end of the elevator and taking a running leap at the rungs embedded in the shaft.

I wrap my fingers around one as I grip it, refusing to let go as I lift myself up and start the climb. When I reach the gap where the rungs broke free, I press my feet against the side of the shaft and push off. For a moment, I believe I've misjudged the distance, until my hands touch the rung above me and I cling to it, refusing to let go as I pull myself up, until I am able to climb the built in ladder. Grelyn rolls her eyes but follows suit. More thunder rumbles through the sides of the elevator shaft as we climb upward, hoping to reach a door before it is too late. The sweltering interior of the shaft suffocates me as I climb, threatening to cut off my air with each rung I reach for, as sweat coats my arms and my neck, making me wonder why it is so hot in here. I glance at Grelyn as she climbs behind me, noticing that it proves to be a struggle for her as well. Eternal seconds pass as we haul ourselves up toward the first door, while my teeth remain clamped around the metal strip and saliva forms around it, dripping down the corners of my mouth.

Almost there.

As I near the door, I reach out for it, but pull my hand back and turn away from the door, clinging to the rungs, as it bursts from its hold, followed by tongues of fire that shoots across the shaft, slamming into the far wall before plummeting downward and crashing onto the top of the elevator. An ominous creak echoes around us as a thin cable snaps and the elevator drops even more, leaving the main one. Judging by the sounds surrounding us, I do not think it will hold for much longer. After the initial shock of the exploding elevator door wears off, I continue upward to the one above it, remembering Gwen and keeping my focus on her, as the heat from the fire that has engulfed this floor, wafts over me, threatening to roast me in this elongated oven.

"We can't be here when that cable snaps!" Grelyn yells at me, urging me to go faster.

I pick up the pace, going up as fast as I can, but my hand slips, and I drop down a rung before I manage to break my fall as Grelyn covers her head, fearing the worst. Relieved, I plant my feet on a rung and push myself upward, climbing past the inferno on the floor we are level with, heading for the door above us. Another series of rumbles, each louder than the first, travel through the walls, reverberating around us, filling us with dread and curiosity about what is happening within Arel, while we are locked in here. More creaking emanates from the cable, pushing me onward, forcing me to go faster as my boots pound each of the rungs they step on, creating a sort of musical sound that stands out among the dread surrounding us.

I reach the second door and press the back of my hand against it, testing it, pleased that cool metal touches my skin, before ripping the metal strip from my mouth, relieved to no longer have it in there as my teeth ache from holding onto it, and jab it into the crack where the doors meet, working its way between them until they pop apart. I grip the rungs with my legs as I lean over and force the doors open, my muscles straining from the effort, burning and aching the more I push the doors apart, creating an opening large enough for us to squeeze through. My arms press against the ledge of the door, relieved by the coolness of the steel covering it, as I haul myself upward and through the door, thankful to be on a solid floor, but that relief is short-lived when I hear Grelyn struggling to climb up. I throw my arm through the opening and hold it out to her. She looks at it for a moment, debating whether to accept or reject my assistance, before clasping my arm and allowing me to pull her through the opening, where we both lie on the floor and catch our breath.

Gunfire forces us to stand up, and Grelyn points at a corridor on the other side of the room. I follow her as she runs for it, charging through the hallway and into a giant room with a glass wall looking out at a giant garden, and I recognize it from my first visit when I received my Medal of Honor, but instead of a peaceful place full of greenery, flowering bushes, and flowing fountains, it is more hellish, resembling a battlefield as guards and rebels clash and bodies litter the ground, while the fountains that remain intact produce blood. A palace guard charges us. Grelyn closes the distance between them, grabs his weapon, and flipping him onto his back before killing him. More enter the chamber—guards and rebels alike—each looking at us as the enemy, while fighting themselves. A rebel heads for me. I jab him in the throat before tossing him aside, where a guard swings his weapon at me, catching me in the chest. Gasping, I watch as he swings at me again, grasp his weapon, headbutting him and sweeping his foot out from under him, and force him toward Grelyn, allowing her to finish him. More come for us. Grelyn tears a knife out of the hand of one and jabs it in his throat before stabbing another in the chest.

"Grelyn!" I yell at her when I notice someone approaching from behind.

She rips her knife free of the second man's chest and sticks it in the face of the third. Someone grabs me from behind, while another attacks from the front. I lift my feet and kick the one in front of me before diving for the floor and flip the one behind me over my back. He slams into the linoleum and remains still for a moment, stunned from the impact, and I use that moment to jam my foot into his throat and twist.

"Duck!" Grelyn screams at me, having managed to wrestle an automatic weapon free from a guard.

I dive for the floor, pressing myself against it and covering my head as Grelyn unleashes a spray of bullets at a group of guards heading for us, emptying the magazine, but before either one of us can think of what to do next, something lands on the floor nearby.

"Grenade!" Grelyn screams, running for cover.

I jump to my feet, hurrying away as fast as I can, refusing to stop, and spot a group of corpses on the floor. I race for them, dropping to the floor and sliding across the linoleum, until I reach them, piling them on top of me and hoping for the best when an earsplitting explosion fills the area, shattering the glass wall to the garden as its force scoots me across the floor, while debris pelts the bodies around me. Stillness reins for a moment as I push one of the bodies off me, dazed and confused, unable to gather my senses. Hands shaking my shoulder break the factitious calm, jerking me to my feet and turning me around, until I face Grelyn.

"Noni!"

Her voice sounds distant, muffled through layers of soundproofing and drowned by an intense ringing as my ears struggle to hear her, and my mind struggles to comprehend her actions.

"NONI!"

The fierceness of her voice breaks through the fog, forcing my mind to focus on her, though her words are still muffled, even as the ringing dissipates.

"This way!"

"How did you get past the biometric sensors?" I ask, still groggy and unable to contain my curiosity.

"I was assigned here, remember?" Grelyn replies.

She jumps through what is left of the shattered glass and into the garden, where rebels and palace guards war with one another, each struggling for the upper hand, and I chase after her, unsteady at first, but I refuse to be beaten, and compel my legs to carry me. We duck behind a topiary shaped like the crest of Arel, gauging the scene around us.

"There's a vent over there," she says to me, pointing to the other end of the garden, "which leads to an aqueduct that will take us out of the palace."

Before I can say anything, Grelyn runs off, charging through the fray, throwing anyone who tries to tackle her to the side. I go after her. A rebel lunges for me, but I jump back, allowing her to crash into a water fountain, before hurrying off, keeping Grelyn in my sights. A rebel points a rifle at her, but I lunge for him, gripping the barrel and ripping it from his hands before bashing him in the face with it and firing at another that jumps for her. Another charges me, going for the rifle, but I twist my body, throwing him to the ground before firing rounds into him.

The vent.

I race for it, ignoring the chaos around me as guards and rebels fight one another, some with firearms and others with more ancient weapons, spilling blood over what was once luscious emerald grass that is now matted and soaked in entrails and corpses. A body lands in front of me, but I jump over it, refusing to stop as I chase after Grelyn, heading for our only way out of here, as agonizing screams mixed with wrathful yells surround me. A guard spots me and tries to grab me, but I pivot to the left, avoiding him, forcing him to land in the midst of a few rebels who finish him off. My feet stumble over shattered stone and slip on squishy tufts of grass as I run for the vent, watching as Grelyn dodges out of the way of two rebels who try to pin her down, killing one in the process. The closer I get to the vent, the faster I go, ignoring everything around me and remaining focused on my goal, hoping to make it unscathed.

We both crouch by the vent and kick at it, forcing the panel to bend around the screws holding it together, until it pops free and is washed away by the water inside. Grelyn jumps in first and a bullet strikes the wall near me just as I dive through the hole and splash into the water below before being swept away by the current. My head bursts through the surface of the water as I cough from some of it trickling down my throat, and I glance around in the darkness, splashing my arms in an effort to remain afloat amidst the current, yelling Grelyn's name before I spot her faint form ahead of me. The water twists and turns me around, disorienting me as I am tossed up and down, failing in my attempt to not swallow it, while thoughts of perishing here fill my mind and doubts about Grelyn's knowledge of this place take over, but I shove them aside. There is nothing I can do about it now.

The channel veers to the right and the water propels me into the side before carting me further downstream, reminding me how powerless I am against its wishes. A low-bearing ledge looms ahead, and as I study it, I realize that I will have to dive beneath the surface or be killed. Grelyn disappears beneath it. Momentary panic grips me, but I remind myself why I am here, and as the ledge draws near, I face it, counting the seconds until I reach it before gulping air and plunging beneath the water, passing underneath it. The current tosses me around as it carries me away, and my lungs cry out for air, but I keep my mouth shut, even pinching my nose, until I burst out the other end of the tunnel and kick for the surface, relieved when cold air hits my wet face.

Cold air?

I'm outside!

I splash about in the water, looking out at the city of Arel as Grelyn and I travel above it, carried away by the current of the aqueduct, reminded of years past and the days I spent staring at it, marveling at its engineering, before discovering that a civilization long since dead built the first aqueduct. I turn myself so that I face forward and can get a better glimpse of Grelyn as we veer downward into a lower part of the city, and the water rushes past me, threatening to drown me. Grelyn yells something, but I cannot make it out as the water drowns her words, so I keep my eyes on her, waiting to see what she does next, surprised when she grabs the side of the wall and hoists herself over it, dropping to the ground below. My mind struggles to grasp the result of her actions, believing that we are higher off the ground, while knowing that I cannot stay here. Mustering my courage, I swim to the wall and grip the side, fighting the current as it tries to cart me away, unhappy with my actions, and heave myself upward until I roll over the other side and let go. Air rushes past me as I plunge downward, until branches catch me, breaking my fall, and I slam into grass, grunting from the force of the impact. Sharp pain rips through me, subsiding with each passing second as Grelyn lifts me to my feet, unsympathetic to my suffering.

"There's a detainment box not far from here," Grelyn says.

I study my surroundings, trying to place where I am in the city, before recognizing the western sector. Peacefulness ensues, unaware of the turmoil elsewhere in the city, or perhaps it hasn't reached this part yet. As though reveling in dashing my hopes, an explosion shakes the ground, ricocheting off the supports of the aqueduct, forcing us to cover ourselves from falling debris. Grelyn grabs me and shoves me away from this place, pushing me toward the center of the sector as more explosions shake the ground, kicking up dirt, and shrapnel flies in every direction as we try to avoid its fury, followed by the yells of people intent on murdering anyone who gets in their way.

I spot the detainment box and hurry for it with Grelyn by my side. Bullets litter the ground, forcing us to dodge to the side in an effort to avoid them, remaining focused on our goal, while people, desperate to escape what they want no part of, scream in fear and run in any direction, hoping to find safety. A group of teachers direct students to a building, hoping to get them out of the line of fire, when three rebels fire on them, killing them all, and they fall into a crumbled heap with bright red stains soiling their yellow uniforms. Enraged, I ditch Grelyn and charge for the three rebels, crashing into one and knocking her to the ground, while I round on the two men. One tries to aim his weapon at me, but I shove the barrel upward and kick his knee, pleased when it bends in an awkward direction, and he squeals in pain. The other man takes a swing at me, but I block it, bringing my elbow down on his before jabbing him in the face until he staggers backward. The woman slams into me, catching me off-guard, but I throw her off me, twist around, and ram my fist into her face before grabbing her by the head and flinging her to the ground, breaking her neck. Motion catches my attention, and I whirl around to deal with the two men, only to find that Grelyn already has.

"The detainment box is this way," she says in a bored tone.

We race for it, dodging around those within the square as arbiters fight rebels, and others attempt to flee what we are charging into. When we reach the detainment box, we notice the door is ajar and the panel on the side is blank, having suffered the wrath of the chaos surrounding it. Grelyn stares at it, unsure of what to do, wondering if it will work, but I decide to risk it.

"In!" I say, screaming so that I can be heard over the melee, and push my way into the dark interior of the box.

Grelyn opens her mouth to question my actions, but the shouts of arbiters preparing to fire on us propels her to follow me, and we squeeze inside the tiny box, struggling to pull the door shut as it catches on the foot of a man's dead body. She kicks the foot out of the way, and the door slams shut, sealing us inside. A few seconds pass, and I fear that I have trapped us inside this box to die of suffocation when the bottom drops out from beneath our feet and we plunge downward.

Chapter 30

Reckoning

Darkness surrounds both Grelyn and me as we fall, surrounded by metal walls that encase us in a slippery cell, and the fear that I will crash and be transformed into a mushy pile of skin and bones fills my mind as air swarms over me from toe to head, causing my hair to whip around my face, while sucking away the oxygen around me, making it difficult to breathe. I try to look at Grelyn, but cannot make her out, except for a faint form against the backdrop of a darkened metallic shine. The chute bends, like before, and we both crash into it, almost hitting each other as our feet and arms fly in odd directions, and neither of us knows what to expect in this maze of confusion. We slide downward, unable to stop ourselves, despite the screeching of our palms against metal in a vain attempt to do so, and my hands burn from the futile effort. A part of me wonders what Grelyn thinks of this ordeal, if she experiences the same fear of being trapped in a never-ending chute, sliding further and further into hell, but I remind myself to remain focused on my goal while noting her refusal to make any vocal indications of fear, inspiring me to do the same. We are arbiters, after all. Our downward plunge comes to an abrupt end as Grelyn and I both land in the waiting transport beneath us, slamming into its single, metallic seat, void of cushioning, with a grunt, each gasping for relief from this madness, but before we can react, the glass casing slides shut, sealing us inside, and takes off, careening down the twisting rail as it carries us through the tunnel and to the detention center.

No lights mark our way, except for the console lights of the transport, as we speed down the tunnel, following the track up the sides of the enclosure, while it carries us through, obeying its own orders, forcing Grelyn and me to bump into one another as we try to keep from be flung around in this tiny space that is meant to hold one occupant. The transport picks up speed as it travels further up the side of the tunnel, and I remember my last experience in here and grip one of the handles of the seat as I try to peer into the darkness.

"Hang on!" I say to her, before remembering that Grelyn's unnatural blue eyes have the ability to see in the dark, and she has already tightened her grip on the other armrest as we flip upside down and both of our feet smack into the glass covering, while our arms burn from the effort of stopping ourselves from being flung about and beaten into submission.

My head spins from the twisting and turning as confusion envelops my mind, like the builders of this tunnel intended, unable to comprehend where I am as the transport speeds onward, swerving up and down the tunnel walls before righting itself, forcing Grelyn and me to be pushed into the single seat again, grimacing as its sharp edges cut into our skin, leaving lasting impressions and drawing small bits of blood. I wrap one of my feet around the bottom of the seat and Grelyn follows suit as the transport goes vertical, plunging further downward in a corkscrew motion and dizziness threatens to take hold, but I close my eyes, doing my best to not give in, knowing that this moment of torment will end soon.

The transport comes an abrupt halt, forcing us both to be squished into the glass covering as we are ripped out of the seat, unable to hold onto it any longer, knocking the air out of our lungs and fogging up the glass as it disappears, allowing us to spill out of the interior and crash onto the metallic grating below. We remain still for a few moments, trying to recapture our bearings and our equilibrium, waiting for the world around us to stop moving.

"Let's never do that again," Grelyn says, sounding out of breath.

I share her sentiment.

Boots stomp around us as arbiters approach and jerk us off the floor, wrenching our hands behind our backs as they try to put binders on us, but we both refuse to be stopped. I press my feet into the floor and jump backward, catching the ones behind me off-guard as we all crash onto the grating. I roll away from them, twisting around in time to deliver a kick to the head of one, but before I can finish the other, she tackles me, and we roll across the floor until we slam into the rails. I throw her off me, spring to my feet, and lunge for her before ripping her mask off and beating her in the face with it until she no longer moves. I hear Grelyn struggling against her own opponents, but have no time to think about it as more hands come for me, and I dive for the floor, breaking free of their hold, and sweep my feet across the grating, knocking one arbiter off his and roll away before the other has a chance to stick me with his cattle prod.

I jump up and tackle the other arbiter, ripping the cattle prod from his hands before ramming it into his side, showing no mercy as his body seizes and he drops to his knees, frozen from the electrical shocks coursing through his body until he collapses. The first arbiter gets to his feet and charges me. I raise the cattle prod, blocking his attack, before countering with well-timed strikes to his face, pushing forward as he allows himself to be backed into a corner, before jamming the cattle prod into his stomach until he foams at the mouth and vomits.

Three arbiters pounce on Grelyn on the other side of the room.

I run for her, leaping over the front of the transport and swing the cattle prod, striking one in the head, not caring as a few teeth fly from his mouth and blood splatters his uniform as he crumples to the floor. One grabs me from behind, pinning my arms to my body, but I throw my head back, hitting him in the face before flinging him over me and ramming the cattle prod into his chest, and finishing him off by planting the sole of my boot into his face and twisting. The third arbiter hits Grelyn in the face with brass knuckles, stunning her, allowing him to secure her in a choke hold, but I lunge for him and plow the cattle prod into his neck, forcing him to release her as his muscles seize, and he collapses to the floor in a series of erratic convulsions that are short-lived as Grelyn presses her foot against his windpipe, until his movements cease.

She looks at me as she catches her breath, but no words pass between us as none are necessary, and I point at a set of steps leading to a door before saying, "We need to find a console."

One of the arbiters on the ground groans, having managed to avoid being killed, as he holds his stomach, still pained by the electrical shocks my cattle prod gave him. Grelyn pounces on him, grabbing him by the collar of his jacket and raising his head so that she can look him in the eyes.

"Where is a console?" she demands.

He groans in response.

"A monitor!" she screams at him, shaking him. "Where do we find one!"

"Through those doors"—he points at a set of doors behind the stairs I spotted earlier—"is a hallway that will take you to the mainframe."

After he finishes speaking, Grelyn slams his face into a post, shattering his jaw, before allowing him to drop to the floor.

We both run for the doorway, but it refuses to open, and we know why. Together, we grab one of the bodies and drag it to the exit, slapping her hand on the pad embedded within it, and it slides open, allowing us through. We charge through it, dropping the body in the middle of the doorway, and it acts like a barrier as the panel tries to slide shut, but we do not care as we remain focused on our mission. Lights flicker on as we sprint through the corridor, and I notice a line of cables running along the walls, connecting boxes dispersed at even intervals; as I study them, I realize that they are electrical cables. Sticky, moist air envelopes the area around us, making me want to cough as it fills my lungs, but I mustn't show weakness or allow it to slow me down, and as I glance at Grelyn, I notice she struggles with it too, but like me, she refuses to display any weaknesses.

We turn a corner and something glints, catching my eye, forcing me to focus on it: a camera. Of course. I should have remembered. I point it out to Grelyn, who grimaces, but there is little we can do about it as we hurry through the hallway, hoping to get to the end before being discovered. A door lays up ahead. Surprise greets me when it opens upon our arrival, but perhaps the architects decided that no prisoner would ever get out of their cells, much less get this far. Once through the door, we stop. Arbiters wait for us. Grelyn and I pause for a moment, studying the arbiters before us, counting the number and the weapons in their hands as they prepare to strike. I grip the cattle prod, ready to defend myself, when I notice more cables running the length of the wall and get an idea. I jump for the cables and ram the cattle prod into it, creating a series of electric shocks as sparks burst from it, encasing me in a charged cloud of lightning, forcing me to close my eyes, until the lights burst and go dark, plunging us all in blackness. A sly grin crosses my face: Grelyn is in her element.

Gunfire rattles the walls, creating streaks of light as one of the arbiters screams before going silent. Not wanting to be an unintentional target, I dive for the floor and hug the base of the wall while covering my head as I allow Grelyn to do as she wills. Another arbiter yelps before being silenced, while a third fires in every direction, striking one of his own before being yanked off his feet, and I hear two shots go off in succession, telling me that Grelyn has dispatched another. A boot stomps on my hand and jerks, surprised that I am there. I grab it and pull, but the person it belongs to manages to reach down and seize my shoulders, lifts me off the ground, and throws me to the other wall, where I crash into it before collapsing to the floor. Wincing from the pain, I struggle to get to my feet as boots stomp in my direction before stopping, followed by a scuffle as two people battle for the upper hand.

Darkness surrounds me, and I know I am of little use here, so I limp to the other end of the hallway—I hope it's the other end—keeping one hand on the wall to help me navigate as the last remaining arbiter struggles against someone he cannot see. A thud sounds as someone slams into the wall, filling the room, while I try to avoid the fight amidst the sounds of someone being punched without mercy before a single gunshot goes off. Stillness fills the atmosphere, and the nagging fear that Grelyn lost, leaving me alone in this black hole, creeps in on me, intensifying with each second, until light spills from ahead, small at first, until it fills the area and lands upon me, causing me to squint from its intensity as my eyes adjust.

"Come on!" says an impatient Grelyn, and I chuckle, relieved that she is not dead, even though I know that, at some point, our truce will come to end; but for now, I need her.

I hurry to the opening and jump through, entering a room with wall-to-wall monitors (some with images of the Detention Center's interior, others with a series of letters and numbers on them that I do not understand, while the rest are black, as though the feed has stopped), stretching from floor to ceiling, surrounding a massive U-shaped desk covered in transparent keyboards, electronic pads, and two surprised arbiters. The thought that there should be more arbiters in this room enters my mind, only to scurry away when the two jump from their seats and run for Grelyn and me.

We split up—she takes the one on the right, while I take the one on the left—and meet our attackers head on. I duck, avoiding a blow from my opponent, and maneuver behind him before kicking him in the middle of his back, forcing him to crash onto the table. Infuriated, he throws his arm backwards, but I bring mine up, blocking him. He swings at me again, and I catch his arm, yanking him downward as I ram my knee into his elbow, breaking it, and his cries of pain torture my ears. For a moment, we eye each other as his arm hangs limp at his side. Enraged, he charges me, swinging with his other fist, but I jump out of the way and thrust my cattle prod into his chest, causing him to convulse from the electrical shocks sent through his body. As he staggers backward, I lunge for him, grabbing his head and ramming it into my knee before letting go, allowing his limp body to fall to the floor with a thud. I turn toward Grelyn as she slams the face of her opponent into the edge of the table and discards him in the same manner one disposes of garbage.

I run to her as she hits a button, and a monitor rises up out of the table, but a message appears, demanding a retinal scan of an authorized user. Annoyed, Grelyn grabs the arbiter on the floor near her feet and holds him up, using her index and middle finger to hold his eye open, allowing the scanner to capture it. She drops the body the moment the message flashes green, while I keep watch on the three open doors leading into this room, afraid that anyone might come in at any moment. I watch as Grelyn punches keys, bringing up the manifest of the prisoners kept here, and her face lights up when she finds Trevors' name.

"Here!" she says, pointing at the translucent monitor, and the number to his cell A-17.

"Now find Gwen," I say.

Grelyn's elation dissipates when I remind her of the reason I am here, and I clench my fist, ready to fight her if I must, but she punches a few keys and scrolls through the list of prisoners before bringing up camera feeds, until she finds one focused on a girl with pale skin and messy blonde hair that sticks to her face as she huddles in her cell. The normal punishment for problematic plebeians is death, making Gwen's presence easier to find, and making Grelyn's idea of searching the feeds lucrative. I check the cell number: B-6. Eager to get Gwen, I tap a few keys and bring up a map of the detention center, noting where she is, and start for the door, but Grelyn stops me.

"Where are you going?"

"To get Gwen," I reply as though it should be obvious, and the unsurprised look on her face tells me that she expected this reaction from me.

"Trevors is closer."

I hesitate, unsurprised that she wants to get Trevors first, though she is correct about one thing: he is closer.

"It makes sense," Grelyn continues. "We get him, then we get the plebe—"

"Gwen." My harsh voice stops her, and Grelyn takes a breath before continuing.

"Gwen," she says with deliberation. "Use your head, Noni."

We stare at one another, me clutching my cattle prod, while Grelyn's right hand curls into a fist as our mini-standoff causes a terse silence to fall between us, followed by a series of explosions outside the detention center, telling me that our time here grows short and our window of opportunity has shrunk. I loosen my grip on the cattle prod, acquiescing to her unspoken demand, admitting, with reluctance, that it is logical.

"How many arbiters are between us and him?" I ask.

Grelyn checks the monitor before replying, "Nothing we can't handle."

A shout rises from one of the open doorways as arbiters rush for us, and Grelyn and I prepare to fight when it seals shut, preventing the arbiters from entering. Confused, we glance at each other, unsure of what just happened, but a part of me wonders if there is someone watching us who remains unseen, but is determined to lead us in a certain direction. A series of bangs echo off the metal door as the arbiters on the other side fire upon it, and I shove my suspicions aside, reminding myself of why I am here, while Grelyn rechecks the schematics of the detention center and points at one of the other doors, using her other hand to show me the path to our desired goal on the map.

We run through the door and head for section A of the detention center, hurrying through the murky and humid corridors as the harsh white lights turn yellow from the moisture in the air, forming waves of illumination that make me believe I am bobbing on water. Our footfalls echo throughout the enclosed hallway as we charge through it, hoping to reach Trevors before others notice our presence and realize that something has gone awry. Sweat streams down my neck and back, going past my shoulders and down my arm, threatening to make my hand lose its grip on the cattle prod, but I clutch it even tighter, refusing to let it go as Grelyn and I rush through the hallway to where Trevors is.

Two guards appear. At first, they stop, surprised to see us before going for their weapons, but Grelyn and I pounce on them, taking their weapons and aim for them only to realize that both are imbued with biometric sensors, rendering them useless to us. Frowning, we flip them around, using them as clubs. One guard jumps for me, but I step back and jab him in the larynx with the butt of his weapon before ramming the cattle prod into him, forcing him to stagger back, clutching his throat as he gasps for air. I ram his weapon into his head and knock him to the floor. I glance at Grelyn as she finishes her opponent and tosses her weapon aside, and I start to run down the hallway, stopping when I notice her pause and grab something from the guard's vest, rolling it in her palm before closing her fingers over it and shoving it in her pocket.

"What is it?" I ask her, curious.

"Nothing," she replies, but I place my arm out, stopping her when she tries to walk past me.

Perturbed, Grelyn pulls out the small item she took from the guard and holds it out for me to see: a black fire grenade. They are illegal to have, and very few arbiters are allowed them due to their volatility when detonated and their tendency to harm the wielder as well as the intended target, so why does a guard in the detention center have one?

"Where did he get one of these?" I voice my question out loud without meaning to.

"Doesn't matter," replies Grelyn, shoving it back in her pocket. "It's contraband."

"And you've never had contraband?"

She has a point. We have all broken the rules in Arel. Most of what Faya and I possessed in our bunkroom at the training facility was contraband, and so did the other recruits.

"Let's go," Grelyn says, pushing her way past me and heading for section A.

I want to say something, but know it will do little good—Gwen is what matters—and I follow her, clutching my cattle prod as we hurry through the maze of hallways, following their twists and turns, while getting rid of any arbiters who get in our way, until we come to the entrance to A-block. I peek through the doorway and spot five arbiters, but they seem distracted and fail to keep an eye on the entrance to their section. I motion for Grelyn to go in, taking advantage of their inattention. Grelyn rushes through the doorway and rams her fist into the back of the skull of one arbiter, while I tackle a second one, and we roll across the floor until we crash into the wall, but before he can get up, I jam my cattle prod into him, forcing him to seize and convulse as electrical shocks run rampant through his body as I stand up. Another arbiter slams into me, knocking me down, and my cattle prod flies from my hand, landing several feet away, releasing a few sparks. A boot kicks me in the stomach, causing me to curl into a fetal position in an effort to protect myself as it continues its assault until…

A massive explosion rocks the detention center, causing the floor to jerk, forcing my attacker to fall over mid-kick as ear-splitting roars course through the building, causing the walls, supports, and floors to shake as bits of the ceiling crash around us, and I cover my head to protect myself. The lights go out. Unnerved, I glance around, trying to peer through the darkness, afraid to move, not knowing what attacked the building, but the fear dissipates the moment the emergency lights flicker on, turning everything into a reddish glow.

I spot the man who kicked me. Scrambling to my knees, I lunge for him, landing a punch in his face. He throws me off him and jumps for me, but I lift my legs and plant both feet into his chest, pushing hard so that he flies backward and slams into a wall. I spot my cattle prod. As the man comes for me, I roll onto my stomach and crawl for it, hurrying across the floor, avoiding the feet of Grelyn and her attackers as I charge for my only weapon, determined to get to it before the arbiter reaches me. I'm close. An animalistic yell erupts from my attacker as he races for me, and I reach for the cattle prod one last time, pleased when my fingers touch it. I grab it, flinging it upward until it is between me and my attacker, and jab him in the leg with it, forcing him to halt as his muscles seize from the electrical shocks. I pull the cattle prod away, but he continues to convulse while I rise to my full height and finish him off by plunging my cattle prod into his throat, watching as he foams at the mouth and his eyes roll into the back of his head before he drops to the ground.

I turn toward Grelyn, locked in battle with an arbiter, while one lies at her feet with her head at an odd angle, and notice another creeping up behind her. I charge across the room, leaping over the only desk in there—translucent, paper-thin tablets fly off it as my feet strike them—and land on her back, causing her to stagger to the side while my fist plunges into the arbiter's nose. She glowers at me and wipes the blood oozing from her nostrils. She attacks, swinging her fists before trying to land a kick on me, but I jump backward, blocking and dodging her attacks as her fury takes over and all her anger is poured into them. She swings again, catching me in the shoulder, but I bring my cattle prod up, aiming for her side. As though she reads my mind, she thrusts her arm downward, blocking the cattle prod before twisting around and elbowing me in the chest, causing me to stumble backward.

She lunges for me. I twist to the side, allowing her to miss, while I strike her with my cattle prod, and her body seizes until I release her. Turning so she can face me, the fury on her face tells me what she wishes to do, I remain still, waiting for her next move. She charges, but I lift my cattle prod, blocking her attack, and she counters by hooking her foot around my ankle and pulling, causing me to fall sideways. While I recenter myself, she rams her elbow into the small of my back, causing me to yelp, but I shove the pain aside, choosing to ignore it as I face her. Our eyes burn in each other's, each wishing the other dead and waiting for the other to act. I start for her, feigning an attack to her left, and as she moves to counter, I change direction and ram my shoulder into her, knocking her off her feet. As she falls, I plow my cattle prod into her, ignoring the blue sparks that jump from it, refusing to remove it until she stops moving. I turn toward Grelyn in time to watch her plant her elbow into her opponent's throat and his eyes go wide, clouding over as he falls.

Wasting no time, we grab one of the dead arbiters and drag her over to cell A-17, slapping the arm with her wristband on the keypad, and the door slides open, revealing a dark interior with a shirtless Trevors, and fresh marks on his back, poised and ready to fight anyone fool enough to challenge him.

"Trevors," Grelyn whispers as we drop the body, and the gentleness in her voice confuses me; I have never heard her use this tone before.

"Grelyn?"

Again, I find myself confused when Trevors answers with the same tenderness. She rushes into the cell and embraces him while their lips lock, neither caring about the chaos around them, and I look on in awkward silence, wishing I was somewhere else. I clear my throat, forcing them to recognize my presence.

"We should go," Grelyn tells him, and they step out of the cell, while the walls tremble around us and more of the ceiling crashes to the floor, sending small particles through the holes in the metal grating. As Grelyn leads Trevors through the entrance we came through, I hurry to the opposite doorway, the one that continues to section B.

"Gwen is this way!" I say, trying to hide the desperation in my voice.

For a moment, an apologetic expression crosses Grelyn's face, proving that she does possess a small bit of humanity, before it disappears as she struggles to tell me what I already guessed.

"I'm sorry, Noni," her voice cracks as she speaks, and she keeps a hand on Trevors, not wanting to let him go.

"I kept my promise," I tell her, trying to keep my anger in check. "It's time for you to keep yours."

Grelyn shakes her head, struggling with the action she is about to take, and I resign myself to reality as a part of me knew she had no intention of keeping her word, and knows that, if in her position, I would do the same.

"Good luck to you," I tell her with sincerity, and start through the doorway, but Trevors' overbearing voice stops me.

"Wait!" he calls to me before turning to Grelyn. "You gave her your word?"

She nods, while pleading with him to run off with her. He takes her left hand and kisses it in such a tender manner that, for a moment, I find it difficult to believe that this is Trevors, my enemy from the training facility when we were all recruits.

"When we were in the mines, she risked her own life to save yours," he reminds her.

After planting a gentle kiss on Grelyn's lips, Trevors faces me. "Lead the way."

I swallow back the lump forming in my throat as it threatens to make me turn into a crumpled heap of unmitigated emotions and turn to the hallway beyond the door as red lights flash around us, warning us to get out before the building collapses, and take off. We race through the corridor, and the blaring alarms torture our ears as we navigate our way through another maze of corridors amidst a constant red glow that dims and brightens in the same intervals, ignoring its warnings to evacuate the building. A guard appears from a doorway, but Trevors sees him first and elbows the man in the jaw before gripping him by the head, flipping him over, and dealing the final blow, while Grelyn and I continue to section B.

The hallway diverges, and we stop, unsure of which way to go. I close my eyes, trying to remember the schematics of the detention center Grelyn and I had looked at, and point to the right, hoping that my memory is correct, but before either of them can ask me if I am certain, a guard heads for us in a panicked run, throwing his weapon behind him in a desperate attempt to stop his pursuers. Trevors starts to put his arm out to capture the man, but Grelyn stops him, and he rushes past us, unaware of our presence, and disappears behind a cloud of red mist as the floor and walls tremble again, warning us that time is our enemy. We charge down the corridor—the doorway behind us seals shut, making my neck hairs stand up, but I push suspicion aside—in the direction the man came from and stop when four shapes appear in the murky darkness, all of them armed, and none of them arbiters.

Grelyn steps on a fallen rod the length of my leg and points at it. I nod my head, having an idea of what she wants to do; it was part of our training, but the timing must be perfect. I grab one end, while she grasps the other and signals to Trevors which two he should focus on, before locking eyes with me. I give the signal. Seconds pass as we match the other's breathing before taking off, our steps mirroring the other's as we match our speed, heading for one of the rebels in the center. As we charge, I glance at Grelyn, awaiting her signal.

She gives it.

Together, in perfect step, as though we are of one mind, we drop to the floor, sliding across it as we hold the bar between us, and ram it into one of the rebel's lower legs, causing him to crash face first into the metal grates. I release the bar, allowing Grelyn to have it, as I twist and jump to my feet, delivering a kick to another rebel's back, while Grelyn deals with the one on the floor by striking him in the back, the side, and finishing him by ramming the rod into the side of his head. She tosses me the metal bar, and I catch it in time to block an attack by the rebel I had kicked. He attacks again, and I swipe the bar upward, catching him in the jaw before hitting him in the head with it, knocking him to the side and ramming it into his throat. He drops to the floor and his weapon falls from his hands. I pick it up, but frown. It's empty. I hear a thud and turn in its direction, finding Trevors with the bodies of two rebels at his feet, and take off again with them close behind.

My stomach turns into a whirling mass of nerves as the never-ending corridor stretches out before me, mocking my efforts and threatening to never allow me to see Gwen again, much less free her, and I curse the horrible thoughts that plague my mind as I push myself onward. Three arbiters appear in front of us, but before Grelyn and I can react, Trevors races ahead, his powerful legs giving him an advantage, and picks one of the arbiters off the floor with ease before using him like a battering ram against the other two. They crumple to the floor when Grelyn and I catch up, and Trevors follows us.

We reach the entrance to section B and pause, unnerved by the eerie stillness within, and hunker outside, unsure of what we will find. As the seconds tick by, my desire to find Gwen overrules the sensible part of my mind, warning me to be cautious, and I charge into the room only to stop, aghast at what I find. Grelyn and Trevors appear behind me, ready to scold me for my recklessness, but they also stop, unsure of what to make of the scene before us. Bodies, some bloodied, some mangled, as though they have taken a beating, are strewn about throughout the room with arms, legs, and heads at odd angles—all of them arbiters—but this is not what surprises me; it's the table in the center. I walk up to it and touch one of the two arbiters seated there, slumped over as though they have had too much drink, but their blue lips and unresponsiveness tells me that death is what attacked them. But how? As I examine them, I find no bruising, no signs of a struggle. It is as though they laid their heads down for the last time and accepted death's specter without argument, but not before one managed to push the alarm.

A pitcher of water sits near one's hand, almost like he had been reaching for it, and two cups (one upright and the other on its side in a pool of water) sit before both. Curious, I pick up the one standing upright and glance at the water still left in it, bringing it to my nose, detecting no odor before setting it back on the rusty table and taking a step back, but as I do, the side of my boot touches something, and it cracks underneath my weight. I pick it up—it's a tube, smaller than my hand—and note the fresh crack from my carelessness, but this isn't what strikes me as odd: I recognize this vial—Faya had tried giving it to me earlier, while I was imprisoned in this place. Was she here? Did she give these two the poison, but one managed to push the alarm before he died, summoning others and forcing her to fight them? As I look around at the room, it's the only conclusion I can come up with. But whom did she come for? My heart skips when Gwen's name bursts into my mind and all my thoughts turn to her.

"Gwen!" I yell, running to the cell she is supposed to be in, but it is empty.

"Gwen!" I continue yelling, darting about the room like a madwoman, unable to keep my fears in check and unwilling to accept the possibility that she might be dead.

Grelyn tries to stop me, but I throw her off as my stomach churns and my heart pounds from my frantic movements, afraid of the truth. I need to find her.

"Faya!" I shout, remembering the vial.

She has to be here. She has to be the reason for this.

My shoulder slams into a doorway as I continue my frenetic search, screaming Gwen's name, not caring if it brings more arbiters; they will all face my wrath if the worst has happened to her.

"GWEN!"

Trevors seizes me around the middle and slams me into a wall, forcing me to stop, and to think.

"Noni!" he yells at me, getting me to hold still.

"She can't be dead," I whisper through tears as all hope leaves me, threatening to turn me into a deflated shell of my former self. "I made a promise."

"We will find her," he says to me, and I stop struggling, having never seen this side of him, but before either of us can say more, Grelyn spots a trail of blood and motions us over.

Trevors lets me go, and I step over to the blood stains, kneeling down to inspect them closer, noting the freshness of it—it hasn't congealed yet—but before I can say anything, two gunshots echo from another hallway, entering the chamber. I spring to my feet and chase after the sound, charging down another corridor, with Grelyn and Trevors on my heels, pushing myself as hard as I can and clutching my cattle prod until it hurts, when a scream pierces my ears: Gwen's screams. The terrified nature of her voice spurs me onward, propelling me forward as I pick up my pace, unwilling to lose her. The closer I get, the louder the sounds of a struggle become, and I increase my speed, allowing my feet to fly over the floor, unwilling to allow this place to beat me.

I burst into another chamber and find Gwen trying to flee from an arbiter, while Faya battles two more, favoring her left side, and blood soaks that part of her jacket. I spin on my feet and head for Gwen, tackling the arbiter chasing her, and we roll across the floor, but I manage to stop myself and crouch, facing my opponent. She recoils from my venomous stare, but only her death will satisfy my hunger for vengeance. She tries to flee, but I lunge for her, catching her around the middle, and force her to crash into the wall, satisfied when I hear her grunt. She tries elbowing me, but I grip her arm and bend it backward, pleased when I feel her bone break and she cries in agony, before jamming my cattle prod into her side. I pull my cattle prod away and wait for her to gather her senses. She tries taking a swing at me with her good arm, while the other hangs at her side, but I jump out of the way, pivot around her, and force her to the floor, before placing my knee on the back of her neck and putting all my weight on it, causing her to stop moving. I jerk my head in the direction of Faya and find that Trevors and Grelyn have eliminated her attackers before turning toward Gwen.

I hold my arms out to her and she runs to me, burying herself in my chest as she cries, and I hold her, trying to comfort her, but knowing that we cannot stay here as the floor and walls tremble once more from the war raging outside.

"Come on," I whisper to her and guide her over to Faya, who looks as though she is about to collapse as she clutches her side.

"Faya," I say, not believing what I see, "what are you..."

"I owed it to you," she replies, her voice strained.

"How..." I begin, but she holds up a presidential pass, which explains how she was not only allowed into the detention center, but able to get to Gwen's cell.

"Where did you get one of those?" asks Trevors.

"There's more to Tapiwa's servant than meets the eye," Faya replies, and I assume she means Kaleb, because no one else would be able to smuggle a presidential pass out of the palace, and he also told me how to access her most secretive room within the palace.

"I ran into a little bit of trouble," Faya jokes before falling over.

Trevors catches her, prying her hand away from her left side, revealing a gunshot wound as blood spurts from it, coating her uniform.

I place her arm around my shoulder, while Gwen gets on the other side, doing what she can to help support Faya.

"We need to go," I say.

"There should be an exit this way," Faya points in a direction, and we all follow it with Trevors and Grelyn in the lead, while Gwen and I support her.

Our snail-paced trek through the detention center worries me, as every second spent here is another second closer to our own deaths if we do not escape. We turn a corner and head down another corridor, glad of the dim, red lighting, making us look more like demons escaping hell as its shadows conceal us, while the alarm continues to blare around us. Faya points where we should go and we obey, trusting her, but the further we go, the weaker she becomes. As we hurry through the hallway, a massive explosion rips the path behind us apart, forcing us to duck for cover as shrapnel flies for us, overwhelming our senses with a series of clicks as they stab the walls around us. Once the chaos settles, I lift Faya to her feet, and we all continue onward, knowing that there is no going back.

"Hang on," I whisper to her, not wanting to lose another, as her sins of the past fade away from my memory, eradicated by her one act of redemption: she risked everything to save Gwen.

"There!" Grelyn points ahead at a massive doorway that leads out into the streets of Arel.

We all quicken our pace, while I keep my hold on Faya, urging her to continue, but before we can reach our exit, it seals shut, and the grinding of the gears sound more like maniacal laughter, reveling in our misfortune. Trevors pounds his fist against the steel door, angered at having been tricked, but stops when another door opens, giving me the feeling that we are rats in a maze. But whose maze? An ominous feeling wafts over me as I stare at the open door, warning me that this is a trap, but I know that we have no choice as our only other exits have been blocked, so I carry Faya through.

"Noni," says Grelyn.

"What choice do we have?" I ask.

Grelyn frowns. She knows we have no other choice, but she likes it less than me.

We all follow the hallway beyond and continue down the path someone is directing us down, but Faya goes limp, and falls from my grasp, unable to continue, and she pulls me to the floor with her.

"Faya…" I begin, worry scars my voice, and the slow realization that I have lost the only true friend I have had in this world weighs down my heart, causing me to go limp.

"Leave me," she says, her voice weak as her usual dark-skinned face turns ashen and her lips turn blue, while blood drips from her uniform jacket after saturating it. "Go."

"No," I say, unwilling to abandon a friend.

"You can't save me this time, Noni," Faya says.

"Faya..." I begin.

"I never should have told Molers what he wanted to know."

Tears blur my vision as her voice weakens, and I press my hand to her wound, trying to stop what refuses to be quelled.

"I know you loved him," she continues, referring to Chase. "I know you made a promise to him. It's who you are. There is no redemption for what I've done, but I thought I could at least help you keep your oath."

"Faya, please," I continue, my voice cracking at the thought of losing my very first friend in this world of senseless death. "I never should have said what I did."

"You were right."

I shake my head, refusing to accept this reality, but death creeps in on her, drawing nearer, unwilling to let her go, and Faya breaks the silence shrouding all of us.

"I am proud to have called you my friend."

"And you mine," I say through tears.

Faya looks at Trevors and Grelyn and releases a strained laugh. "I never thought I would see you three working together."

Unsure of what else to do, but knowing that Faya deserves some amount of respect before her last breath, they salute her, casting aside old rivalries.

"Go," Faya says to me, before taking one last glance at Gwen's tear-stained face. "Take care of her."

Before the last word touches her lips, Faya's head rolls to the side and her chest ceases to rise. I place her on the floor with care, doing my best to not show grief, knowing that I can do nothing for her now, and we still have to escape this place. There will be a time for mourning, but this is not it. I have Gwen to look after and a promise to keep to Chase, so I stand up, and walk forward, refusing to look back at the one person who befriended me when we were both recruits and afraid of what life at the training facility would force us to endure.

I take Gwen by the hand and continue through the corridor, while Grelyn and Trevors follow behind us, leaving Faya's body alone on the cold, metallic floor, soaked in a pool of her own blood, reminding myself that there is no helping the dead, only the living. We charge down the hallway as the sounds of the war raging outside find their way into the detention center, warning us that we are about to be caught in the middle of it. I spot a doorway and hurry for it, only to have it close before I get there, so I pick up Gwen and continue. Trevors spots another doorway, and we head for it, hoping to get through it before...

It closes.

Frustrated, I slam my fist against it, screaming in anger, and stop when the low hiss of a door opening reaches my ears, forcing me to turn in its direction, taking note of the stairs behind it, not liking the feeling of being led to slaughter. As we remain still, unwilling to follow this marked path, a bullet whizzes past my head and strikes the wall behind me, diverting my attention to the murky darkness filling the hallway behind us. As I concentrate on it, I make out shapes of people, armed and ready to kill, but as they draw closer, I realize they are not arbiters, but rebels who have managed to break into the facility. We cannot fight them all. I take Gwen and race for the open doorway—my only option—and charge up the steps, taking them two at a time, ignoring my strained breathing as I climb higher, heading for the roof. The maniacal sounds of people lusting for blood fill the atmosphere around us as they enter the stairwell, deafening us with their weapons and endless shouts for revenge, not caring that their leader had enlisted my help in the first place: they want blood—ours. My foot slips on the edge of a step and I fall forward, grimacing when my shoulder takes the impact, and Trevors takes Gwen from me, shoving her into Grelyn's arms, stopping her from reaching into her pocket for the black fire grenade.

"Go!" he says, pushing her up the stairs before turning back and hauling me to my feet with ease.

I tap his shoulder, indicating that I'm fine, and he releases me, urging me to hurry after Grelyn as she runs up the steps with Gwen.

One of the rebels reaches us, but Trevors whirls around and punches the man in the jaw, dazing him. He lifts him up and throws him at a group of rebels in the stairwell, causing them to tumble down the steps when their compatriot's body slams into them. Having bought us some time, he follows after us, hopping over the railing as he climbs, until we reach the door at the top, and it opens for us, allowing us through. Cool, moist air slaps us in the face as we charge outside and stop, not recognizing the city of Arel as buildings in all sectors are in flames, burning until nothing is left, not even smoldering embers.

Bulbous clouds of thick, black smoke rise into the air and hover over the city, blanketing it and blocking out the sun, making it appear to be night, while bodies litter the street—innocent and guilty alike—covered in rubble, charred from incessant bombing, and riddled with holes from indiscriminate gunfire. A series of shouts fill the streets as more rebels engage arbiters, while citizens and plebeians, hoping to not get caught in the middle, flee only to be stopped. The horrific scene freezes my legs, and I find myself unable to move as my eyes remain transfixed on it.

"What have I done?" I whisper to myself, but Trevors pushes me onward as fire pokes through the roof of the detention center, having worked its way up, still ravenous for more, refusing to stop until it has consumed everything in its wake.

"This was a long time coming," he says, having overheard me.

I allow him to make me move as the rebels reach the top of the stairs.

"There!" yells Grelyn, still holding onto Gwen, pointing at a walkway leading to another part of the roof with a short tower encased in stairs, while swirls of barbed wire line its edges.

We head for it, hoping it provides a means of escape. Grelyn puts Gwen down once we reach the causeway, and we form a single file line as we cross, while the fury of the rebels behind us close in. Some get on the walkway, hoping to follow us to the other side. A sharp explosion sounds, and the one in the lead falls over the side after being struck in the chest, causing a small amount of relief to flood over me: Perce has found us, making me glad that he put a tracker in my boot, though a part of me wonders what he went through to get here. Another rebel slumps over and drops to the side, having taken a shot to the head. Fearing for their lives, the rebels stop their pursuit and face the building closest to the detention center, firing in every direction, not caring whom they hit, so long as they rid themselves of this silent killer.

Another falls to his death. None of us look back as we continue across the walkway, nearing the end, knowing that more rebels are behind us as they scramble onto the causeway. The building trembles, causing me to teeter as I threaten to lose my balance, and Trevors catches me, but not before I drop my cattle prod and it falls to the ground, swallowed by the smoke encasing us. More rebels swarm the causeway, and a grenade flies over us and lands behind us, detonating as we reach the other side, blowing it into pieces, while the rebels plunge to their deaths. Our moment of relief never comes when a familiar face—one I had hoped to never see again—emerges from the trails of smoke that encompass the roof.

"Hello, Noni," says Molers, dropping a tablet.

His voice sends chills throughout my body, while my heart tries to escape my chest, and fear grips me, but I force myself to remain still, not wanting to give him the satisfaction of seeing me tremble before him.

"I believe I owe you something."

He points at his clouded eye.

No mysterious shot flies through the air. No mysterious savior appears, making the fear surrounding me intensify: where is Perce? He was here. Did arbiters or rebels find him? My mind races through every possible scenario, but I shove it all aside, knowing that, if something has happened to him, there is nothing I can do but hope that he makes it through unscathed.

Grelyn takes Gwen and runs to a secluded part of the roof, placing her in a shadowed corner and whispers something to her. Trevors rises to his full height, flexing his muscles as he envisions what to do to Molers in retaliation for what Molers did to him while we were still recruits, and a sardonic grin crosses Molers' face as he awaits Trevors' first move.

Trevors rushes Molers, feigning an attack, and when Molers goes to block it, he counters with a punch to the jaw, but instead of fazing Molers, it enrages him, and he throws his elbow back, ramming it into the side of Trevors' face with such force that he suffers whiplash and staggers, unable to focus. Molers goes for the kill, and I lunge for him, ramming my shoulder into his side, while Grelyn jumps on his back and slams her fist into his ear, causing him to sway. Before she can land another blow, he throws her off him and in my direction. She crashes into me, knocking me over. I shake my head to clear it and watch as Trevors attacks again. Molers swings a fist at him. Trevors blocks it and brings his own into the underside of Molers' chin, but before he can attack again, Molers knees him in the stomach, bringing both his elbows down onto his back before ramming his knee into Trevors' face. Stunned, Trevors never sees Molers' boot coming for him, and it strikes him in the face as Molers spins around and swings his other foot at him as well. I watch in horror as Trevors spins and teeters before regaining his focus. He spits out blood, holds his fists in front of him, and glares at Molers who goads him into attacking again.

Grelyn gets off me and struggles to stand, still dazed from being thrown, but I cannot wait for her. I charge for Molers, dropping low when I reach him, and I sweep his leg out from under him as Trevors' body slams into him, and Molers lands on the rooftop with a thud. Spotting Grelyn coming for him, he scoops up some dirt and flings it into her eyes, stopping her as she rubs them in an effort to clear them. He swings his foot in my direction, kicking me in the face, forcing me to roll backward. Trevors tries to bring his foot down upon Molers' face, but he jerks to the side, avoiding it before plowing his foot into Trevors' leg. I hear him howl in pain, and he hobbles as Molers stands up. Angered, Grelyn jumps on Molers, slamming her fists into him, each more furious than the last. She kicks at him, but he grabs her leg and brings his elbow down upon her knee, and a sickening crack fills the air before he tosses her aside toward the roof's edge. Trevors tries to attack, but Molers throws him off with ease, laughing as he does. While he is distracted, I lunge for him, but he grabs me by the shoulders, flips me onto my back, and jams his foot into my stomach, twisting as he presses it into me, reveling in my torture as I writhe on the rooftop unable to breathe. He stops.

"Leave her alone!" yells Gwen as she beats him with her flimsy fists.

Molers backhands her, knocking her over. I try to go for her, but receive a kick to the face in response, followed by Gwen's screams when he picks her up by her shirt and carries her toward the ledge and the raging fire below.

"Shall we see if you can fly," Molers says, throwing her to the ledge.

Gwen lands on the roof, leaving me powerless to do anything but watch as she rolls to the edge and goes over the side as I scream her name in terror, but before she vanishes, Grelyn appears and snatches her arm, stopping her from falling to her death. My eyes remain fixed on them, ignoring all else, as Grelyn lifts Gwen back onto the roof amidst the dancing flames that cast shadows upon them, while releasing black smoke that swirls around them, but Grelyn refuses to cough or loosen her grip. As she sets Gwen back on a solid surface, Molers rips a knife out from his belt and plunges it deep into her back, piercing one of her lungs.

Her eyes widen as she gasps for air, unable to breathe, and blood gurgles around the blade piercing her, drowned by the anguished screams of Trevors as he watches, unable to stop his worst fear from coming true. Molers rips his knife free, not bothering to wipe the blood off it, but stands back, allowing Trevors to go to Grelyn and lift her into his arms, cradling her while she struggles to say his name. She pulls the black fire grenade from her pocket, but it falls from her weak grip as her life leaves her. I run for it and scoop it up, but Molers is ready for me, and he kicks it from my hand before kicking me twice in the chest and forcing me off my feet.

"Hide!" I yell at Gwen as I roll around on the roof.

Molers lifts his foot to finish me, but he stops when my eyes focus on Trevors' distraught face as he holds Grelyn, begging her not to leave him, his face wet with tears—I've never seen him cry before—and his voice cracks with each word. Molers lowers his foot, relishing in our loss, and the emotional torment of Trevors. Grelyn continues to try to speak, but her breaths grow shorter, and as a final farewell, she lifts her hand and touches Trevors' cheek before it flops to the concrete rooftop, and she is no more. Time slows, hiding the number of seconds that pass as Trevors continues to cling to Grelyn's lifeless body, while I remain still, clutching my chest, both of us tormented by the brutality of Molers' actions, while he feeds off our anguish.

"Weakness is failure," he shouts at the smoke-filled sky and the red sun that hides behind it. "Failure is death!"

Giving her one last kiss, Trevors lowers Grelyn to the concrete surface, closing her eyes and placing her arms by her side, so that she appears to be sleeping, before rising to his feet, glaring at

Molers, preparing to release his unbridled rage. Molers stands ready for him. Trevors rushes toward him, releasing a fury of fists and kicks, forcing Molers to move backward in an effort to avoid being hit. Trevors' ruthlessness breaks through Molers' defenses, and he plows his fists into our old instructor's face, until…

The building trembles and the roof bends, weakened by the fire engulfing the detention center, causing Trevors to miss his mark. Molers counters, landing several blows of his own on Trevors before they part and circle one another, waiting. Molers lunges for Trevors, but he drops to the ground and wraps his feet around Molers' left ankle and twists, forcing him to fall, and before Molers can recover, Trevors rams his elbow into Molers' knee, receiving a kick in response. All the chaos outside this place freezes as I remain where I am, my eyes locked on the battle between Trevors and Molers, unable to look away from their dance with death, until a single bullet strikes the ground near me, forcing me to look at the building next to us where I spot someone waving at me to get my attention.

Perce!

He points at the tower above me and the cables dangling from it, giving me an idea. I can use those to get Gwen and me out of here, but a cry of pain from Trevors jerks my attention back to the fight between him and Molers in time to watch Molers stab him twice in the side, before bringing his knee into Trevors' face. Trevors falls backward, unable to defend himself when Molers plants his boot into his face and twists, pleased when Trevors ceases moving.

This ends now.

I spot the black fire grenade, pleased that it sits in a clear area, free from obstacles, and I point at it, hoping Perce gets my message, and judging by his reaction, he does. My foot bumps something, and I pick it up, chucking it at Molers.

"Come and get me! Coward!" I scream at him, taunting him, and judging by the enraged expression on his face, I succeeded.

As the sounds of the rebels and arbiters fighting reach us,

Molers chuckles. "Listen to that," he says as he approaches. "Where do you think they got the weapons?"

Confusion crosses my face as I remain silent.

"Listen! What did their leader tell you? That he wants peace? That he wants a free Arel?"

Why is Molers telling me this?

"Do you honestly believe that the barbarians are the only ones who have been bribed to attack the city?"

What?

"Why do you think the rebels have never been captured?"

I keep my mouth shut, but my suspicions about Anshu burst into my mind, pounding my head to the point where it aches.

"I know you wondered why I was at that ceremonial dinner when I should have been where you sentenced me. I have my informants. I made sure she could not silence me the way she has silenced so many others."

I stand transfixed by his words as my mind struggles with this new revelation, not wanting to believe it, yet a part of me wonders if it is true.

"It's not enough to control people with an iron fist. You have to convince them that they need you. Attacks from within are as effective, if not more so as those from without. She never counted on his ambition to overrule his ability to reason."

I remain silent, refusing to give Molers the satisfaction of knowing that his words pierce the very core of my being as I realize that the lies of Arel are even bigger than I first thought.

"I want you to die, knowing that you have been nothing more than a tool."

He comes for me, hobbling, telling me that Trevors did injure him, and I brace myself, ready to rid the world of him once and for all.

Use your size to your advantage.

Mandi's instructions echo in my mind, and I am thankful for the reminder.

Molers takes a swing at me, but I duck, avoiding it, while ramming my fist into his side. He turns and tries to strike me in the back, but I duck again and dance around him, kicking him in the back of his injured knee, forcing him to drop to the ground. Seizing my chance, I land two punches into his head before darting away, keeping out of reach, using my size and agility to my advantage. Enraged, he forces himself to his feet and comes after me, while I continue backing away, leading him to an area free of obstacles, taunting him. He throws a fist at me, but I catch it and jab my elbow into his stomach, jumping away before he can strike again, taking advantage of his injured knee.

He swings at me again, and I go to catch it, but Molers pulls back and uses his other fist to hit me in the cheek before ramming his knee into my stomach. Gasping, I stagger back, continuing to lead him to the clearing while throwing insults, angering him even more. He lunges, but I drop to all fours, twist around, and kick him in the groin, before ducking around him and planting my foot in his back, forcing him into the clearing. He faces me, and I dance around him, making him turn in circles, hoping to keep his focus on me as we move across the roof, while bits of it crumble away and flames burst through the holes, relishing in our conflict and doing their part to add to the atmosphere.

Molers charges me, and I dodge to the side, kicking his bad knee, but before I can dart away, he twists around and grabs me by the throat, lifting me so that the toes of my boots brush the ground before tossing me away from him. I crash into the rooftop, wincing as the concrete tears at my clothing and scrapes my skin. Coughing, I forget to keep my distance from him, and he leers over me, pleased with his victory, comforted in his belief that he has won, but as he glorifies in his own sense of self-righteousness, a red dot appears in the center of his chest.

"You should have known better than to fight me alone," he says. "Remember last time."

I do, and as I recall, I would have won if his arbiters hadn't stopped me.

"I'm not alone," I reply.

A massive explosion rocks the building, and Molers' shoulder is jerked back as Perce's shot strikes him—the detonation must have forced him to miss his target—but as Molers stands stunned, unable to fathom that his shoulder is now nothing more than shredded flesh, I am glad he is not dead… yet. I reach for the black fire grenade.

"Weakness is failure," I say as I hold it in front of me, letting Molers see what I intend to do, and for the first time, I see fear in his eyes. "And failure is death."

I detonate it and throw it at him, diving behind cover before it goes off and showers Molers in its fiery fury of never-ending torture. Anguished screams escape his mouth as he cries out in torment, unable to stop the flames from eating away at his flesh, melting it away from his bones, and he staggers, unable to find relief as his body disintegrates. I come out from my place of hiding and stand before him, unmoved by his torment, but I do not relish it either; it is righteous punishment for all the pain he caused.

"This is for Sheila!" I shout, kicking him toward the edge of the roof.

His tortured cries fill my ears, but I ignore them as I pace before him, determined to see to it that he does not survive—not this time.

"This is for Gwen!"

I kick him again, pushing him closer to the ledge, while his screams drown the roars of the fire below us.

"This is for Chase!"

I kick him a third time, and he staggers back, teetering on the edge.

"And this is for me."

With a final kick, I shove him off the roof, and he falls to the fires below, his anguished cries fading the further he goes, until the flames swallow his body and silence falls.

More holes appear in the roof as it falls inward and the fire promises to overtake the entire building, regardless of who is fool enough to remain. I need to find Gwen.

"Gwen!" I shout, hoping she can hear me over the thunderous

roar of the flames as they grow higher, and their heat sears my skin, despite the protection of my jacket.

"GWEN!"

"Noni!"

I turn in time to watch as Gwen comes out from between a set of pipes, thrilled at seeing her, and rush to her, embracing her, squeezing her so tight that she reminds me she cannot breathe, but I do not want to let her go and risk losing her. More of the roof crumbles away and jerks me back to our present predicament, and I take her by the hand and head for the stairs leading up to the tower as the flames leap higher, lighting the darkened world around us, while the smoke blocks the sun even more. Wind whips around me when we reach the top, and Gwen holds back, frightened of how high we are, but I urge her onward, comforting her, and reminding her of her bravery when she attacked Molers to protect me. She steels her nerves, looking at me with those gray eyes as strands of her hair cover her face, reminding me of the night I first saw her, never knowing that we would end up here.

A whistle prickles my ears, and I turn to see Perce on the roof of the next building, waving at me, reminding me to hurry up. I jump at one of the cables swinging in the wind, pulling it away from its hold, and throw one end to the roof Perce is on. It misses. Frustrated, but trying to remain calm for Gwen, I pull it back, tie a knot in it to give it some weight, and throw it at Perce. He jumps for it and catches it, securing it, while I tie it on my end. Sweat falls from my brow and covers my eyes, making it difficult to see, but I swipe at it, refusing to allow it to stop me. I need a harness. I grab the other cable and rip it free from the tower, twisting it and tying it, until I create a harness, and wrap it around Gwen before securing it to the line connecting the two buildings. The moment Gwen puts her weight on it, the cable slips from where I tied it and she panics, jumping back onto the platform and squeezing my arm until it tingles, unwilling to let go.

"Gwen," I say in a gentle voice, even though fear tries to overwhelm my mind each time fire spurts from the roof and bits of it fall away, causing the tower to lean and threaten to collapse, but I need to be calm and confident for her sake, "I need you to be strong. This line will not drop you. I promise."

I push her to the edge after double checking her harness, and grip the cable, bracing myself so that my hold will not falter, and nod my head at her.

She jumps off. Her terrified screams fill my ears as she speeds to the other rooftop where Perce waits for her, while my heart refuses to beat as my muscles tighten and burn as I cling to the cable, and my hands grow numb from it digging into them. The line slips. Fearing I will lose her, I tighten my grip until blood trickles between my fingers, refusing to let her fall. It slips again, proving to be too much for me, and Gwen's fearful screams tear at my heart, and all I can think about is how I have failed another. The cable continues to pull away from me, despite my attempts to stop it, but if she falls, so do I, and just when I believe that there is no hope for either of us, Trevors' strong hands snatch the line and yank it back, providing the extra bit of strength I need to fulfil a promise. I keep my eyes on Gwen, unwilling to look away until I know she is safe, and relief wafts over me the moment Perce catches her and takes her out of her harness.

I release the cable and turn toward Trevors, having never been so grateful to see him before, elated that he is here.

"Trevors, I thought you were..." I cut myself off before I finish, but he guesses what I was about to say. "If we can secure this cable, we can both..."

"Go," he says, his voice soft and respectful.

"Trevors..."

"I won't leave her." He glances at Grelyn's body, before turning back to me. "It will hold," he says, wrapping the cable around his arms and tightening his grip as he braces his legs. "Go!"

I rip off my jacket and wrap one of the sleeves around my right hand as I position myself in front of the line, taking one last look at a man who had been my sworn enemy and is now my savior. I push myself off the ledge and fling my jacket over the cable, snatching the other sleeve, and cling to it as air rushes over me, pounding my ears and stinging my eyes as I sail over the fires below. I choke on the smoke engulfing me but refuse to cough or allow it to distract me from my goal as Perce and Gwen grow larger. The line jerks. Just a little bit longer. It jerks again as Trevors' hold on it weakens, and the roof of the detention center withers away, but I refuse to allow the fear of falling grip me. Fear is weakness, or so I've always believed, but at this moment, fear is to be conquered. Perce reaches out for me as I near the end.

The cable goes slack, and I release my jacket as I plunge downward, throwing my hands out to Perce, and he catches me, stopping my descent, and hauls me onto the roof where Gwen wraps her arms around my neck, thankful that I did not perish. Unable to contain myself, I look at what is left of the detention center as its walls crumble inward, replaced by an insatiable fire that desires more in order to satisfy its ravenous hunger, noting that the tower and the roof are gone, and a pang of sadness strikes me, tugging at my heart for two people I had called my enemy, until today. A part of me wonders what Grelyn, Trevors, and I could have accomplished if we had realized that we had more in common than differences—petty hate will destroy us all.

Perce taps my shoulder, reminding me that we are not out of danger as the sounds of the melee beyond reach our ears. I jump to my feet, take Gwen's hand, and follow him, allowing him to lead me away from this place of misery.

Chapter 31

A Lie Exposed

The sounds of an endless battle rage around us, swamping us with their never-ending anger as we race across the rooftop, desperate to get out of here. Perce takes the lead, urging us to hurry, and our feet fly over the concrete surface as we follow him until he stops at the edge. Gwen clings to me, afraid of going over it and falling to her death, and I squeeze her shoulder to comfort her as Perce slings his weapon over his shoulder and climbs over the ledge. He gives me a look that tells me to hurry, and I peer over the edge, spotting a fire escape. I pick up Gwen and hand her to Perce, who takes her and sets her on the first level of the fire escape, while I climb over the ledge beside him. Wasting no time, we hurry down the steps, following them as they corkscrew downward, while he remains in the lead, ready to stop anyone or anything that might harm us. As a bolt pops free of its hold, it seems that our saving grace has become our enemy.

We pick up the pace, tromping downward so fast that my feet tangle, and I trip over them falling forward. I throw my hands out, gripping the metallic rail as its smooth surface burns my hands during my desperate attempt to stop my fall, until Perce catches me. I shake my head at him as a way of telling him that I am fine, and continue downward when another bolt springs from its hold and the fire escape leans away from the building. I grab Gwen and push her in front of me, determined not to lose her as we hurry down the stairwell, rounding each corner as our feet pound the steps, doing our best to outrun gravity as the fire escape lurches again, causing my stomach to jump into my throat.

It drops again.

Knowing we have no time, Perce leaps over the side, jumping past the final twist in the fire escape, and I lift Gwen up and toss her over the side into Perce's waiting arms, relieved when he catches her and sets her on the ground with care. The top of the fire escape pulls away from the building and throws me into the railing, and I grunt as my stomach takes the brunt of the impact and double over, reminding myself to breathe, but danger refuses to give me respite as the fire escape drops even more, promising to take me with it. With little choice, I climb onto the rail, swing my feet over, and jump. My legs buckle beneath me when I land and I drop to the ground, rolling, wincing as bits of rubble dig into my arms, burying themselves beneath the surface of my skin, burning as they do so, but the final creak of a falling fire escape distracts me from the pain. I look up, powerless to stop death's grasp as it comes for me, but Perce snatches me and lifts me up with his free hand as he drags Gwen with his other. I scramble to my feet as we run, desperate to get away. The fire escape crashes into the ground behind us, sending clouds of dust into the air, and we turn back, watching the dust as it mingles with the smoke, becoming one.

"We need to find Luther and Renal," I say, "and get out of here."

Perce's face falls.

"Perce, what's wrong?" I ask, concerned, knowing that he was the only one able to stay in contact with them.

"Things at the aerodrome did not go well," he says, trying to phrase his words with care.

"Perce."

"I lost contact with them. Before they went dark, Renal said something about them having Luther and about going to the media center."

I face the fires surrounding us as worry eats away at me and the thought of having failed again creeps in on me.

"You should have..." I begin, my voice loud and harsh, but I stop myself; it isn't Perce's fault that any of this happened, but his next words indicate that he knows what I was about to say and forgives me for my outburst.

"The last thing Renal told me was that, if anything happened to you, he would filet me alive."

I press my lips together, biting them with my teeth as I contain my reeling emotions—anger, fear, and sadness—each battling with the other to be free from the cage I must keep them locked in. Besides, what Perce told me sounds like Renal, and he never makes a promise he cannot keep.

"Have you heard from Sigal?" I ask.

"No."

Worry fills Perce's voice, but we cannot worry ourselves over Sigal's silence; we have more pressing matters.

"We need to get to the media center."

Perce pauses for a moment. "That place is going to be filled with Anshu's men."

"And I just escaped a detention center filled with arbiters," I reply, while Gwen remains silent, watching us bicker as the city burns around us.

Perce rolls his eyes and nods his head as though he has suffered from a momentary bout of forgetfulness. "Well, it's a good thing I came prepared."

He hands me a knife and a pistol.

"Do you have another magazine?" I ask him, checking the amount of ammo left.

"I might have had to use it, and that's what's left."

I shake my head and place the pistol back in its holster before tying it around my waist.

"Are you both going to stand here all day?" quips Gwen, breaking up our bit of verbal humor, and we both laugh.

"I want you to stay close to Perce," I tell her, knowing that I cannot leave her here.

He bends down to one knee and holds out a pair of brass knuckles, and she takes them, unsure of what to do with them, until he shows her how to hold them. "If anyone comes at you, hit them with this. Go for the face and the throat—any place that is soft."

She nods, clutching the brass knuckles, while I hope she never has to use them, but aware that she might.

We charge through the alley, getting as far away from the detention center as we can as we navigate our way to the media center, surprised that it is void of people, and I remain wary of our sudden seclusion, wondering where everyone is. The alley comes to a dead end, and I curse myself for allowing us to end up here. I know better and I know the city, but in my rush to get to the media center, I forgot to turn when the alley forked. I motion for them to turn back, and we hurry through the labyrinth of towering buildings and walls of stone as I race back to the where the alley diverges. When I reach it, I veer to my left, remembering that the media center is closer to the middle of the city. All my movements from the pounding of my boots on the cracked and uneven pavement to the distant sounds of a few stragglers fighting converge around us, surrounding us in an amphitheater of never-ending noise, amplified by the solid walls closing in on us. I push harder, desperate to get out of this prisonous maze, and when I see light ahead, I sprint faster, unable to take this enclosure anymore, and the closer I get, the faster I run, pushing and pushing, until...

I stop.

Carnage awaits me outside the alley with bodies scattered about in the courtyard beyond, while blood runs down the cracks between the paved stones, forming crimson rivers of death that coat the edges of my boots, warning me to go no further: I'll not like what I find. Metallic particles hover in the air, twisting and turning as they reflect what light the smoke covering the city allows through as I step between limbs torn from their bodies and torsos that have been separated from their legs. Perce and Gwen arrive, and I whirl around, desperate to keep her from witnessing this carnage, but it is too late as her eyes widen in horror at the sight of the corpses filling the square from edge to edge, some of them covered by the rubble of an exterior wall that fell away from its hold and crashed onto the ground, crushing any unlucky enough to be near it. Still fingers touch my boot as I tread through carnage, unable to believe it, and shaking from the cruelty of what surrounds me. I lift my feet, doing my best to not step on any of the people here, while Perce carries Gwen, trying to shield her from this, and for a moment, I am reminded of the times Chase tried to protect his sister.

My foot touches something as I bring it down, and I lift it, startled, and look down to see what I have stepped on. Curled fingers belonging to a soft hand that has never seen a day of hard work point upward, stiffened from the lack of blood flow, but it is not the fingers themselves that attract my attention, but the sleeve covering the hand they are attached to. I know that sleeve. Perce stops when I bend low and pick up pieces of rubble the size of small boulders, tossing them aside and allowing them to thump on the ground while I try to clear the debris and expose the person the hand belongs to. I know I need to move—that I should not linger here—but I must know if my suspicions are correct. I remove the final piece and drop it the moment I see the face.

Kaleb.

Movement spurs me from my frozen state, and I whip out my pistol and point it in the direction it came from and stop when I see a woman and an older man, their dark skin having darkened even more from the soot.

"Please," she pleads with me, and I lower my weapon.

"What happened here?" I demand.

"They came," she replies, "and pulled us from our homes. The arbiters came, but could not fend off the monsters who tried to kill us."

She glances at Kaleb's still form. "I remember a deafening roar and blinding light before the building fell, and he pushed us out of the way, but could not escape it himself."

I stare at Kaleb. Cunning as he proved to be, he deserved a better end. It seems, in his own way, he tried to save Arel and, in the end, gave his life for these two strangers.

"Where are the arbiters?" I ask.

"When the aircraft never came, and when the screens turned on and his face appeared, they fled."

"Where is everyone?" asks Perce.

The woman stares at him, inspecting his strange clothes, but chooses to keep her questions to herself and answer his instead. "To the screens. The ones that are left, anyway."

"Go," I tell her. "Find someplace to hide and stay there."

She takes the hand of the man and leads him away without argument.

Crackling fills the air around us as static brings the untouched speakers to life and a voice echoes around us.

"People of Arel," it says, "in a few moments, I will address what has happened. Your liberation is at hand."

The last words Molers spoke to me enter my mind, and the cloud of suspicion grows stronger, solidifying into the weight of a potential falsehood being exposed. Molers may have been cruel, but he never lied. I need to get to the media center.

"Are you able to get ahold of Renal?" I ask Perce.

He fiddles with the communicator strapped to his wrist and shakes his head.

I motion for Perce to follow me, and he grabs Gwen's hand and chases after me as I head for a set of steps leading to one of the causeways above us. We charge up them, stepping around the bodies of those unfortunate enough to not escape the uprising, and I dare not look at them for fear of being incapacitated by the horror surrounding me. My feet plop on the belt as I stomp onto the moving walkway, but it is frozen, and upon closer inspection, I realize that the gears have ground together, causing the conveyor belt to stop. Refusing to be outwitted by a broken piece of machinery, I hurry down the causeway, not caring that my boots thump on the belt as it sinks beneath my weight, wary of the silence surrounding us as we run to the other side until it is broken by a low creaking that causes knots to form within my stomach as the eerie creak morphs into a screech. I stop. Glancing around, I search for the source, and the tiny hairs on my arms rise the moment I find it: one of the main support beams has broken away, causing the walkway above us to sag and press into the remaining supports, sagging lower the more gravity weighs it down. Horrified, I scan the entire underbelly of the causeway above us, noticing its continual sagging, cursing myself for not seeing it earlier.

"Run!" I scream.

I take Gwen's hand and charge down the causeway as the supports surrounding us groan underneath the pressure of the walkways above, determined to break free. A piece of metal drops from above and lands near my right foot as we run, while my grip on Gwen's hand tightens, causing her to whimper, but I refuse to let go. I'll not lose her here. One of the supports surrounding us crumples, mimicking a crushed can, and the structure drops lower, while the feeling of being trapped closes in on me, threatening to crush me with its fearful promise to bury us alive. I pick up the pace as more debris crashes around us, tripping over a piece of metal plating. Gwen cries out as I stumble, but I catch myself and continue, dragging her behind me, while Perce takes up the rear. We're close to the end. Only a little further.

Before we reach the other side, some of the supports break and a portion of the walkway above us plows into the causeway we are on, forcing us to stop, and I turn around, kneeling on one knee as

I cover Gwen with my body, while Perce tries to protect us both from the shards of shrapnel flying around us. More groaning reverberates around us in mesmerizing waves of intensity and softness, unsure of which support it wants to break next as it circles around us, taunting us. Once the dust clears, I lift my head, noticing that the way ahead is blocked, and as fear rises within me, whispering to me to give up and accept the inevitable, I spot the causeway across from us and the clear path it provides. I pick up Gwen and head for the railing, studying the space between the other walkway and us: it's not far, but is a bit of a jump.

Perce notices my actions, straps his weapon behind his back, and leaps across, landing on the other side with a thud, dropping to one knee before recovering. He turns toward me and reaches his hands out for Gwen. I lift her onto the rail as the walkway above sags even more, and though her eyes widen when she glances downward, she remains quiet, knowing that there is little choice. I steady her as she reaches out for Perce, their fingers touching the others', but only the tips. More groaning echoes around us as more supports bend to the point of breaking. Risking it all, I shove Gwen toward Perce and she squeals, but he catches her, lifts her over the rail on his side, and sets her on the conveyor belt.

Metal bars drop around me as I step onto the railing, balancing myself, before sticking my left leg out and leaping across, but I miss my mark and my chest crashes into the railing on the other side, while my hands scramble to find a good hold and stop me from falling. I cling to it, but my sweaty palms cause me to slip, and my grip falters. My stomach lurches as I start to fall, and my mind grapples with the realization that this is my last act, but before I can close my eyes and accept my fate, Perce snatches my arm, stopping me, and heaves me over the railing, allowing me to tumble onto the soft belt as Gwen slams into me, wrapping her skinny arms around my neck, but the moment of relieve comes to an abrupt end as the causeway above us falls away.

"Go!" I scream at them and jump to my feet.

Perce and I stretch our legs to their fullest length, matching the other's stride as we charge down the walkway, with me clinging to Gwen, while the supports holding the causeway above break free of their hold, shooting out in multiple directions with us as the unnamed targets. I hold my left arm in front of my face, while keeping my hold on Gwen as we all race to the other side, desperate to stay ahead of the turmoil crashing behind us. We reach the end, but celebrations have to wait as the walkway we are on bends beneath the weight of debris crashing into it, and its supports snap.

"There!" I yell, pointing at the stairs.

We run for them, and I'm unable to breathe as my sides ache from the exertion, but I refuse to let any of us slow down, and push the others onward. We reach the stairs and take them two at a time, not caring if we almost fall, so long as we get away from the moving walkways before we are buried beneath them. With one final push, we jump the last steps at the bottom and hurry away as the entire walkway caves inward, and disintegrates behind us, leaving nothing more than a pile of rubble, veiled by billowing clouds of metallic dust that hover in the air before settling around us, coating our skin and making it glitter in the bits of sunlight that manage to break through the smoke covering Arel, until it is barred from shining on us once more.

"Well," says Perce, trying to catch his breath, "we are closer to the media center. I hope."

I direct his attention ahead of us.

He laughs as he gets off the ground, but before I can move, the barrel of a pistol appears near my head with one of Anshu's men on the other end, while another appears next to Perce. They motion for me to stand, but before I can, Gwen points behind them and screams, "Look!"

Using the distraction, I knock the pistol from the hand of the one closest to me—Perce goes for the other—and sweep his feet out from under him, before placing him in a wrestler's hold with his left arm between my knees, while my legs pin him to the ground. He struggles to break free, but I jerk his arm downward, breaking his collarbone, and as he screams in pain, I wrap my legs around his neck and twist. Gwen screams, and I look up in time to see a third rebel lift her into the air by her shirt, but she pulls out the brass knuckles Perce had given her and hits him in the face with them, drawing blood. Angered, he raises his hand to slap her, but Perce tackles him, forcing him to release her as he puts the man in a headlock and squeezes until the man's movements cease. Silence falls around us as we wait to see if any more of Anshu's men will appear, and we jump when Perce's communicator crackles with life.

"Perce," comes Renal's voice, desperate, as though he had been calling him for a long while, "where are you?"

"How's Luther?" Perce says.

"I have him. Where are you?"

"I'm with Noni and the girl. We are outside the media center."

A series of cursing spills from the communicator—Perce mouths the words, "Told you so"—when I notice a drone trying to get off the ground, but unable to. Curious, I pick it up and inspect it: its camera works, but it is unable to fly, not that I need it to. I rip off the back paneling, revealing the drone's serial number, and a plan forms in my mind.

I snatch Perce's wrist with the communicator attached to it and yank it toward me.

"Is Anshu in there?" I demand.

An irritating pause fills the air before Renal replies. "Yes."

"Where is he?"

"In the main camera room on the second floor."

"Where are you?" I ask.

"Luther and I are in the main control room on the third floor."

"Do they know you are in there?"

"No. I stopped them before they could raise the alarm, but I do not know how long we have."

"Do the wireless communications in there still work?"

"Yes." Renal pauses for a moment. "Noni, what are you…"

"I need you to tap into the signal of this drone and broadcast it throughout Arel."

"Noni..."

"Renal, please," I plead with him. "We have to stop Anshu."

Another irritating pause comes from the communicator.

"What is your plan?'

I think about it, wishing I had more time for planning, knowing that what I have at this moment is all I got. "How many rebels are in there?"

"Not many, but enough to prove a nuisance. I do not have an exact count."

"Perce is coming to you with Gwen. I need you to override the signal for this drone, serial number: A89Y65GFX9R2. Broadcast its signal throughout Arel. I'm going after Anshu."

Renal protests, but I ignore him and place the drone in my pocket, while the pistol remains in my waistband before facing Perce.

"How good are you at remaining unseen?"

"I followed you for days in the wilderness before you learned of my presence," he replies.

I turn toward Gwen. "Stay close to Perce."

She shakes her head as tears stream down her soil encrusted cheeks, leaving uneven patterns on her pale face, causing strands of her yellow hair to stick to it.

I drop to one knee and look her in the eyes. "I have to stop him," I tell her, "before he harms more people."

She hugs me in response.

"Stay close to him," I tell her.

Gwen nods, and I grab Perce by the shirt, whispering to him, "If anything happens to her..."

"I know," he interrupts. "You'll gut me."

I release him and check the entrance to the media center, wondering why there are not many rebels posted to guard it, unless Anshu is too confident in his victory, and as I plan my next course of action, Perce mumbles, "But you won't have to."

I do not respond, knowing that he never meant for anyone to hear his silent vow, and run off as his speaks into his communicator—I hear Renal's curses when Perce tells him the plan—saying that Renal could kill him when he gets there, before following me with Gwen by his side. As I creep up on the three rebels posted at the entrance, I pick up two stones, placing one in each hand, being careful not to allow my steps to make a sound as I move across the ground, sticking to the shadows, glad that the smoke from the fires blocks the sun. I point at the one I intend to take. Perce nods and motions for Gwen to hide. I veer toward the rebel and toss one of the rocks, allowing it to land near his feet. As he bends low to examine it, I swoop in, wrapping my leg around both of his, and yank them out from under him, forcing him onto the ground.

Before he can cry out for help, I smash the other stone into his face until his skull caves in. A scuffle sounds behind me, and I whirl around, but stop when I see Perce grab a rebel around the neck before yanking out his knife and throwing it at the third, striking him in the throat. When all are dead, he whistles for Gwen, who appears from her hiding place and runs to him as he places a protective arm around her. He glances at me, and I head for the door, remaining alert as it slides open and we step inside.

Unease fills me as I walk across the teal-colored tiles with amber circles spaced throughout the room as it reflects the lights above, all enclosed by ivory walls—some parts of the walls are sunken in, creating what looks like a tiny nook—with the seal of Arel etched in gold in them. I tiptoe to the center where a giant desk is—my mind remains alert—wondering where everyone is. I find my answer when I spot a smeared bloodstain on the edge of the desk. Perce moves around to the other side with Gwen and places his hand over her eyes, causing me to lean over the surface, hoisting myself up so that I can get a better view, finding the bodies of the two who were stationed here before the rebels arrived.

A door closes. Perce drops behind the desk with Gwen, while I hurry to the edge of a corridor, pressing myself into the wall as the methodic sounds of someone walking echo from a distance, growing louder with each step. When the shadow of a man appears on the floor, I throw my arm out, ramming it into his throat. He goes for his weapon, but I grab his arm and bend it around the corner of the wall. He cries in pain, but I grab his mouth with my hand, trying to silence his cries, before ramming his head into the wall until his blood stains it.

Another rebel appears and sees me standing over the body of his comrade. Perce pulls two knives from his boot and rushes past me, catching the rebel off-guard, and stabs him until he drops to the floor, turning the teal-colored tiles red. Not wanting to run into any more of them, I motion for Gwen to go to Perce. We hurry down the hallway, being careful to not make a sound, wanting to keep all present unaware of our presence. Perce spots an elevator and heads for it, but I stop him, pointing at the stairs instead; elevators warn others of your arrival, and I want ours to be a surprise. He abandons his original plan and follows me as I step through the door and into a stairwell, wary of being in another one after my experience in the presidential palace, but I swallow back my unease, knowing that I can sneak into the second floor far easier this way. We hurry up them as our ears remain alert and our eyes keep watch on the doors above and below us, hoping that no one walks through them, and I let out a slow breath when I reach the door to the second floor, relieved to have gone unnoticed so far.

Perce pushes his way past me with Gwen, but I grab his arm and whisper, "Remember, no one can know we are here. Not until I reach Anshu."

Perce taps my arm, indicating that he understands, and I remind myself that I needn't worry; he did follow me for days in the wilderness before I learned of his presence, indicating that silent movement is one of his attributes. I wait by the door to the second floor until he and Gwen reach the third, and together, we open our respective doors and cross through them, with me hoping that he succeeds and that Gwen remains unharmed.

Muted darkness greets me as I step into a world I do not know—no hallways, no hidden offices, except for a single doorway on the far side—a massive room filled with wires, cords, cameras on tripods (all placed at various intervals around the chamber), a giant viewscreen making up one wall, and a table at the far end underneath five massive spotlights, each striking it from a different angle. No one notices me as I creep through the room, spotting a door tucked away with a sign in red above it, indicating that it is an emergency exit, taking great care to not trip on a wire while making certain that the drone remains in my pocket.

My foot presses down upon something hard and soft, causing me to look down and find the body of one of those who worked here, discarded as though she was nothing more than a piece of refuse and unworthy of proper disposal, and the frightened look on her dark face, frozen in time, moves me with pity, causing me to bend low and close her eyes, so she appears to be slumbering. Anshu's incessant demands rip me back to my mission, and I continue moving through the room, inching my way to the front, ready to fight any who get in my way, but thankful that their backs remain toward me. A foot reaches out for mine, and I turn in its direction, spotting an arbiter with his hands and feet tied and a gag in his mouth. Though curious as to why he is not dead, I place my index finger over my mouth, signaling for him to remain quiet before inching away from him.

"Get on with it you fool!"

Anshu's voice cuts through the mundane sounds of the room, and I turn in its direction, narrowing my eyes when I spot him as one of his men runs off. Joseph stands next to him, but his face betrays his concern as he watches Anshu's temperament grow worse, spiraling downward into uncontrolled rage, while I remain in the shadows, creeping closer to him, noting the questioning looks on the faces of those surrounding him. Someone turns in my direction. I freeze, hoping he does not see me, unsure if he does and chooses not to speak. When he turns away, relief swarms over me as my tense muscles relax. I am too close to fail now. The light is inches from me, and I pause, calming myself and preparing for what I must face before I stretch my foot out and put my weight onto it, thus stepping into the light and allowing everyone to know I am here.

Some of the rebels jerk in my direction and go for their weapons, but Joseph stops them.

"Noni?" says Anshu as he tries to conceal his surprise, and a fake smile crosses his lips as he places his hand over his chest, mocking the salute arbiters give one another. "I didn't expect to see you here."

"We have matters to discuss," I say.

"I'm sure it can wait," Anshu replies, before holding his arms out in a gesture of friendship. "Come. Celebrate with us. Tapiwa's reign has ended. The tyranny that has plagued Arel is no more."

"Or has been replaced with another," I say, remembering how his men had turned on me.

"I don't know what you mean."

Movement catches my eye, and I jerk my head in its direction, spotting Ha'ya as she works her way toward me, and I clench my fists, ready to fight my way out of here.

"Call your dog off," I say, keeping my eyes on Ha'ya, and Anshu whistles at her, forcing her to stop.

"Noni," he says, "I can tell that you have a lot of questions. Perhaps we should speak in private."

He motions toward a somewhat hidden doorway leading into a side room that looks as though it is used more for storage than anything else, and I allow myself to be directed to it and go inside with him following behind. While he paces the room, searching for a place that gives him the upper hand, I pull the drone from my pocket and stick it on the shelf next to me between two pieces of filming equipment, making certain that the camera focuses on

Anshu, while hoping that Renal succeeds in tapping into its signal and relaying it throughout the city.

"No one knew what had happened to you Noni. We received no word from..."

"They're all dead," I say.

Anshu's lips press into a single line as he contemplates his next words. "Noni, I understand that you are upset."

"Your men turned on me once we got to the presidential palace."

"I never believed... If I had known that they had been working with Tapiwa all this time, I never would have sent them with you."

"Cut the bullshit."

"Tapiwa corrupts many," he says, changing tactics. "We will have to deal..."

"She's dead, as promised."

"Then, after we are done here, we will need to find Molers..."

"He's also dead," I say, noting how he mentions Molers when neither of us have spoken of him to the other, meaning that there is no reason for Anshu to be worried about him at all, but the relief on his face is evident.

"Then, we have succeeded."

"You know, before he died, Molers mentioned something that I found intriguing. He implied that the attacks within the city, the ones your men participated in, were at the discretion of Tapiwa herself."

"Noni..."

"Don't lie to me! We are alone, and we both know that I won't be leaving here alive."

"I assure you..."

"You may have used me, but don't play me for a fool."

Anshu closes his mouth, and his expression changes, transforming from one of feigned innocence and incredulity to callousness, malevolence, and cruelty.

"Very well," he says, his voice full of spite, "enough of this façade."

I move away from the drone, allowing it to get a good view of Anshu as he paces in front of me, his robes swaying with each movement as his smugness takes over.

"People are sheep. You know this, but Tapiwa's father had the dangerous idea that they should be allowed to govern themselves and live their lives as they saw fit. He planned on relinquishing his power and holding elections. That's what allowed the fair-skinned to rule over us in the past! We are better than them! More deserving of riches and ownership than they will ever be. But he wanted them to be treated equally. It never occurred to me that Tapiwa would murder him, but such ambition can be useful."

"So, you used her."

"We used each other. It was Ha'ya's plan, and it was a good one."

"And Kumi?"

"Kumi was always weak, but Tapiwa convinced me to let her deal with him, having outserved his usefulness. His lust always overruled his sensibilities, but in the end, even she knew she had to dispose of him."

"And Molers?"

"Molers has an uncanny ability to gather information. His ambition knew no bounds, and he convinced us that we needed him; besides, we needed the loyalty of the arbiters, and with Molers at the training facility, he could supply us with ones who would swear allegiance to us and no other. His obsession with you is what ended him."

"Is that why you tried to be rid of me when you turned those on the railcar against me?"

"You were proving to be a nuisance. Tapiwa's insistence on toying with you—she always liked her playthings—and Molers' growing obsession over your ability to defy the odds was getting in the way. I needed you gone, but then you challenged him to the Fates, and the people started to look upon you as some sort of hero. And Tapiwa—the fool—broadcasted your exploits throughout the city. She believed she would be showing them your death. She should have had you killed the moment you were dumped in the wilderness."

As I listen to Anshu speak, much that seemed unknown becomes clear. Molers' constant rejection for another assignment, his uncanny ability to know everything and to always be in a position of power, Kumi's warning to me, the incident on the railcar—all of it comes together, a puzzle, once jumbled, now forms a clear image.

"So, what was this arrangement?" I demand, hoping to keep him talking.

"You already know about the barbarian attacks and how the Arelian government supplies them with weapons and people. You see, it is not enough to rule over these despicable masses with an iron fist, through a series of harsh punishments for the most minor of infractions. You must keep them in a state of constant anxiety and desperation while always providing the solution to ending what they fear most. You must keep them agitated and scared. Keep them divided. Keep them fighting amongst themselves. Never give them a moment's peace, because if you do, they might get ideas and talk with one another. So, we made a deal with one of the barbarian clans to attack the city at certain intervals, while allowing us to appear stronger by proving our superiority."

"They willingly sacrificed their people?"

"Only those who were useless. They sent prisoners captured from other clans or neighboring city states, promising them riches; undesirables from Arel; and plebeians who were promised their freedom if they killed a few arbiters, which they were more than willing to do—all of them were ones whose usefulness had come to an end and were a drain on resources. It's not difficult to find people willing to die for a lie. Why do you think our detention center always has room for more?

"But the staged attacks on the wall proved to not be enough in the end. People started asking questions; some arbiters were too skilled in protecting the city from barbarians, and we realized that we needed another way of keeping the people in a constant state of fear, hence, the attacks by rebels. I knew I could use my theatrical performances in the council, where I pretended to care about the destitute and impoverished people of Arel to my advantage, and formed a group of people who wanted to free Arel from the tyranny of Tapiwa and her brother, while never realizing that they were puppets in a grander scheme. Attack an educational center, a medical center, and the people quiver in fear, begging their rulers to protect them, to save their children, and we, the benevolent leaders, did; all they had to do was give up more of their freedom. It was so simple. All I had to do to get people to destroy these areas of Arel was convince them that they were symbols of Arelian imperialism and aggression, which didn't take much. It is easy to fuel hatred and animosity."

I quell the rage growing within me as I listen to Anshu bragging now that he has an audience.

"It's quite comical," he continues. "The people of Arel, even the plebeians, demanded that we protect them from those trying to kill them, willing to do anything for such protection, never realizing that it was us doing it the whole time. Sheep. Easily controlled through fear. Easily convinced of a lie. Easily convinced to despise one another.

"But fear isn't always enough. Certain people in the past realized early on that the best way to control a population is to control the food, the water, the infrastructure, and their beliefs. Every once in a while, you allow them a period of plenty so that they become fat, apathic, and lazy, but after a time, a culling must take place, especially when the masses start to become restless and get dangerous ideas about choosing the course of their own lives."

"The shortages," I interject.

"The periodic shortages. You probably witnessed one or two yourself. Imagine my surprise when people willingly ate insects during this last one, and all because Tapiwa told them to as a way of saving Arel. You can imagine her amusement at such docility and compliance, while she ate a rib roast. Keep people in a constant state of survival and they will never notice when you enslave them through a slow erosion of their liberties. They will fight one another—even accuse one another of despicable crimes—all while you pretend to be their salvation, playing the part so that they can have the illusion of having been liberated when fear and control of their activities no longer work.

"And now, I'll be known as the one who freed them from tyranny—their savior. I outgrew Tapiwa and Molers, and though I thought they would do me a favor and kill you and all that you stand for, in the end, it was you who ridded me of my biggest threats; but your usefulness has come to an end."

"What of the council?"

"I am the council. Arel is mine. Its people are mine to do with as I will; their only function is to serve their better."

Anshu reaches into the sleeve of his robe and pulls out a knife. "And now, my dear, the truth will die with you."

I scoop up the drone, hoping that Renal was able to do as I asked, and gambling that he did, I hold it out to Anshu.

"I always found these drones annoying and invasive. Always spying on you and showing up unannounced, and at the most inopportune moments, but sometimes… sometimes, they have their uses. They never stop recording, or broadcasting."

Anshu's eyes widen in fear, before narrowing in anger as his face turns red with rage when he realizes that, for the first time, the people of Arel know who have been ruling over them: three people who lusted only for power and ruled through a series of lies and deceptions that cost the lives of many, until one decided that he had to have it all. I smile at him and wink.

Infuriated, Anshu charges me, but I throw the drone at him, and he turns, covering his head, preventing it from hitting him. He charges me, swinging his knife, cutting the air with it, while flinging his other fist at me, forcing me to jump back and hold my arms up in an effort to block each of his attacks. My back presses against the shelves on the wall. Thinking he has me cornered, Anshu stabs at me, but I cross my arms in front of me and push against his knife hand before ducking low and circling around him. He swings his knife backward, but I jump out of the way. He swings again, and again, I jump back, but Anshu is ready, and he dives low, swiping the knife's blade across my calf, causing me to falter. He kicks at me, but I fall to the floor, landing on my back, wrap my feet around his left ankle, and twist, causing him to crash onto the hard surface of the grungy tiles. He rolls onto his stomach and faces me before lunging in my direction, but I kick him in the face.

While he lies stunned, I try to get up, but Anshu jumps on my back and pins me to the floor, crushing me, while the tip of his blade strikes the tile with a sickening clink. He goes for the pistol in my waistband, but I throw my head back, ramming him in the face with it, and his blood drips into my hair when his nose breaks. He loosens his grip, and I push myself off the floor—my pistol falls from my waistband and clatters on the tile—rolling onto my back and throwing him off me. While he clutches his nose, I jump for him, but Anshu is ready and kicks me in the chest, knocking me backward. He gets to his feet and kicks me again, sending me flying into the door, and it cracks from the impact. Before I can gather my senses, he rams his foot into my chest again with such force that I crash through the weakened door, and its splintered pieces scatter around me when I slam into the floor and roll onto my side, stunned from the impact.

Anshu jumps through the doorway and into the media room, his knife ready. One of the onlookers goes for his weapon, but Joseph grabs his arm, stopping him.

"Kill her!" Anshu screams.

Joseph shakes his head, and for the first time, Anshu notices the viewscreen within the room and how it is broadcasting what the drone records.

"She's betrayed us all!" he shouts.

Anshu goes for the weapon of one of the rebels, but the man points it at him, stopping him.

"This is your fight, Anshu," says Joseph. "We are your pawns no longer."

I rise to my full height, readying my stance, prepared for whatever he brings me. "What's the matter, Anshu? Not man enough to kill me yourself?"

Anshu faces me, the venom in his eyes willing me to die where I stand as he studies me, eyeing me up and down, gauging how to respond to my taunting.

"Fool," he says, his voice nothing more than a growl, "I've been trained in the same manner as you arbiters."

"Someone else said the same, and she's dead."

Renal and Perce burst into the room with Gwen, but I hold my hand up when Perce goes for his weapon, and Renal stops him while using his other hand to grab Gwen's shoulder. This is my fight, and he understands that.

Anshu lunges for me, but I step to the side and swing one of the cameras at him, bashing him in the face with it before it topples over and crashes onto the floor. Still clutching his knife, he races for me, swinging it at me, but I block it and fling a fist at him, but he manages to stop it and kick me in the stomach. I stagger backward but refuse to allow the pain gripping me to show on my face. He charges for me again, but I jump into his attack and elbow him in the chest before ducking underneath his arm, and wrenching it behind his back. He manages to twist his foot, catching mine, causing me to fall backward. Seizing his chance, he whirls around and brings his foot down upon me, but I jerk out of the way as it slams into the tile, missing me by a couple of inches. I kick at him, but he blocks it and continues to try and bring his foot down upon me as I roll across the floor, avoiding his wrath, until I manage to trip him, and he crashes into a tripod. I jump to my feet, standing near the edge of the light, and prepare to face him when he stands.

Ha'ya jumps me from behind, wrapping her arms around my throat and squeezes, crushing my windpipe as I struggle to breathe. Anshu grins when he sees my predicament and raises his knife as he approaches and stabs at me, but I turn around, placing Ha'ya between us, and her eyes widen as she gasps for air when his blade goes into her back. She goes limp. I throw her off me and at Anshu, who stares at her still form in disbelief before rage takes over. He jumps for me, swinging like a wild man, determined to make me pay for her death, and I back up, blocking each attack before grabbing his arm and jamming my elbow into it, and he cries in pain as he pulls away.

We pace the room, circling, staring at one another, predators determined to destroy our prey. I attack. He dodges, but I expect it and bring my knee up, catching him in the stomach before slamming both my elbows on his back. Enraged, he kicks at me, striking me in the side, and I gasp for air, but before I can retaliate, his fist strikes me in the face, dazing me. I wobble, but refuse to give in, willing my mind to focus as I remind myself of what he has done: the puppet master tugging at people's strings, not caring if they perished. He runs for me and kicks, but I bring my hands up and block before grabbing his leg and using it to stabilize me as I perform a cartwheel and flip him over, pleased by the grunts escaping him as he crashes onto the floor.

I spot the knife poking out of Ha'ya's back as Anshu tries to get up. I run for it as Anshu jumps for me, howling in fury at my refusal to die, and I rip the knife from her body, ramming the hilt into his face before rolling between his feet. I plunge it into his thigh, twisting the blade, ignoring his screams as his flesh tears from his bone. Before he can react, I push my foot into the back of his knee, forcing him to the ground, and kick him in the back of the head, sending him flying forward. Struggling to breathe, his fingernails screech as he claws at the tile, trying to lift himself up, while I walk over and pick up my pistol and carry it back to where he is. Anshu pushes against the floor, but I place my foot in the middle of his back and pin him to the floor.

"Councilman Anshu," I say, my voice cold and devoid of emotion, except righteous anger, as I think about how his actions cost many innocent people their lives, "by your own admission, you are guilty of trying to overthrow the Arelian government, of conspiring with our enemies, of selling weapons to our enemies, of murdering innocent civilians, and of acts of terror within the city of Arel for which the punishment is death; and I, Arbiter Noni, am charged with its enforcement."

I squeeze the trigger, and he collapses to the ground with a hole in his head in a pool of his own blood. No one speaks when I turn to Joseph and hold the pistol out to him.

"If any of you wish to punish me for killing your leader, I'll not stop you," I say.

Joseph refuses to take the weapon. "He is no leader of ours."

Gwen plows into me, squeezing me tight, thrilled that I am not dead, and I return the embrace, not wanting to let go, while Perce, Renal, and Luther gather around me.

"Are you all right?" I ask Luther, noting the blood-soaked scarf around his leg.

"I will live," he replies, "as unfortunate as that may be."

My euphoria at seeing them dissipates the moment an alarm blares throughout the city, one that I've heard before, but not for a long while: the wall is under attack.

"It appears," says Luther, "that someone else has spotted an opportunity."

I bolt to the emergency exit and burst through the door into a world of death and decay, veiled by clouds of lingering smoke as tendrils of it caress my skin as though to apologize for its unsuccessful attempt at concealing this tragedy. My fists clench the railing of the balcony as I look out at the bodies in the streets, mourned by those still left. A ball of fire lights up the darkened sky in the distance and sails over the wall, striking the center of the eastern sector, and I envision the suffering that has been wrought on the people there.

"We can leave," says Perce, appearing by my side.

I face him, unsure of what to do. Arel has always been my

home; its people used and abused by their own government and now wolves are at the gates, salivating at the chance of tearing us all apart, the final trek to the crematoriums.

"You do not need to stay here," continues Perce.

The screams of desperate people reach my ears as more balls of fire fly over the wall and crash into the buildings closest to them, covering them in their fiery wrath. The thought of taking Gwen and leaving all this behind fills my mind, beckoning me to accept Perce's proposal, reminding me of what I have suffered at the hands of Arel's rigid rules; but the more it urges me to flee, the more I resist. The people here do not deserve to be left to their fate. They never asked for any of this.

"I am an arbiter of Arel," I say to Perce. "Who will protect these people if I do not?"

Perce readjusts his weapon over his shoulder, nodding his head in the direction of the eastern sector, saying, "I'll go find the high ground."

He climbs over the railing and jumps to the stairs below, disappearing behind the clouds of smoke.

I need to get a message out to Arel's arbiters. But how?

The cameras!

I hurry back inside and stop next to the cameras.

"Do these work?" I ask.

"Yes," replies someone within the room.

"Are they on now and broadcasting throughout the city?"

She checks the equipment and replies, "Yes, but I do not know if all the viewscreens will receive the signal."

That is a chance worth taking. I stand in front of one and the woman gives me a thumbs up sign, indicating that I may speak.

"I am Arbiter Noni. I know what you have suffered. I know that a group pretending to free us from the prison we have allowed ourselves to be forced into have burned our city. This infighting stops now. We are all Arelians, from the highest member of the council to the lowest plebeian. Barbarians have attacked the wall, and they do not care who you are. To them, we are all their enemy. This is my… our home. I refuse to stand by as they take it from us. Therefore, I ask that every able-bodied person prepare to defend this city and report to the wall in the eastern and southern sectors."

I pause, not sure what else to say, except, "I know you're afraid. I know you're angry. But right now, I am asking you to set that aside. I will stand against this threat, even if I stand alone."

I step out of range of the camera and say to Luther, "Is there any place you can go that is safe?"

"I know of a place," he replies.

"Take Gwen and go there."

"No," Gwen says, clinging to me, and I bend low so that I can look her in the eye.

"Gwen, I need you to go with him."

"But…"

"I'll be fine. Take care of him for me."

Though reluctant, she lets go and nods in agreement as she struggles to conceal her worry that she may never see me again, but Luther takes her by the shoulder and leads her away.

"Joseph,"—I turn toward him—"take who you can and go to the southern sector. The wall there is not as strong as we have been led to believe."

He salutes me and leaves with his people.

"And where are you going?" asks Renal.

"To the eastern sector," I reply, "to see if anyone has answered my plea."

A knowing smile crosses his face, as though he expected no less of me.

"I hope Sigal and your messengers made it through," I say.

"We will know soon enough."

I shove my pistol into my waistband and head for the stairwell, unsure if we will survive this latest threat but determined to meet it regardless.

Chapter 32

Arel's Protector

Panic fills the streets of the eastern sector as people dart in every direction, desperate to get away, but pausing long enough to give Renal and me confused and worried glances as we run for the wall. The more people hurry past us, the more dread fills me as I picture us arriving to find that no one bothered to answer my plea for help, not that it would surprise me; they are not soldiers. The wall looms before us as we rush for it, and the faster I run, the more I focus on getting there, while the distant sounds of mortar shells being launched intensify. Renal and I jump out of the way as a trolley races down the tracks, carrying people away from the center of the eastern sector, avoiding it with the slightest of margins, but I refuse to stop, and continue racing for the wall.

Another trolley speeds toward us as a ball of fire flies through the air and smashes into one of the tall buildings, obliterating the top three floors. Chunks of brick, wood, and metal fall away from it and crash into the trolley, knocking it off the tracks, and sparks form around it, creating a glittering globe of orange and yellow as it crashes on its side and careens down the pavement, carried by its own momentum. Renal thrusts me out of the way as it crashes into another building and turns into an insatiable inferno, killing everyone inside. Infuriated, but unable to do anything for them, much less mourn them, I continue on with Renal by my side.

The towering wall grows larger the closer we approach, while the battle cries of those on the other side blend with distant explosions and the sounds of metal upon metal, followed by gunfire, fill my ears, but I refuse to stop. Once there, I skid to a stop and look around, disheartened by the lack of people present, finding only the arbiters stationed there, looking out at the barbarian forces beyond with horror. One turns and flees, jumping over the side of the wall and scaling down a supporting post, and as I watch him try to escape, disgust fills me at the sight of such cowardice. Unwilling to let him run away—we are arbiters and protecting Arel from outside invasion is one of our sworn oaths—I jump in front of him and rip his weapon from his grasp before whacking him in the face with it, cracking the visor of his helmet. He falls back, stunned, while I leer over him, angered by his actions.

"Get back to your post!" I yell at him.

"There is too many of them!" he pleads, but I refuse to back down.

"And where are you going to run?" I look up at the other arbiters watching the exchange. "There is nowhere to go! This is our home!"

"But we'll die," says the arbiter I knocked to the ground.

"Death is certain," I reply, reminded of Molers and how he had tried to teach the same lesson when I was a recruit, making me realize that, despite all the horrible acts he committed in his lifetime, he was correct about this one basic fact: death is certain for all of us. "Look out there! They intend to kill us all! I will die on my feet before I show them my back! You are an arbiter! Get back to your post or I'll kill you like the coward you are."

I point his weapon at him.

The fear leaves his face, and he stands up, taking his weapon, while I keep my eyes fixed on him.

"Go back to your post."

He does.

Unable to wait any longer for people to arrive, I go to the armory with Renal, and he opens it by holding his wristband up, and we step inside. I go to the glass doors holding the body armor and yank it out, putting it on, not caring if the fit is not right as it slips over my sweaty skin, clinging to me in places as I reach for a helmet, before pulling my hand back, refusing to grab it. No more hiding. No more anonymity. I move to the cabinet with the automatic rifles and yank it open, grabbing the first one, pleased that no biometric lock has been put on it. Renal knocks something over as he fills two belts with magazines and explosives before handing one to me, pleased about my choice in weaponry, and we head back out, ready to do our duty to defend those within Arel. The moment I step outside, I stop, taken aback by the faces greeting me—arbiters, citizens, and plebeians alike—all looking to me for orders.

Unable to fathom how they got here, I stare at them, wondering where they came from as they seem to have appeared from nowhere, yet pleased to see them.

"Arbiter Noni," one of the arbiters present salutes me. "Your orders?"

"The southern sector?" I ask.

"Many have gone there as ordered," the same arbiter says.

I look out at the crowd before me, wondering if we will be able to defend this city, knowing that we have no choice.

"There is armor, ammunition, and arms," I say. "Grab what you can carry."

Some move into the armory, while I continue.

"You"—I point at a group—"go to station three."

When they leave, I continue pointing at groups and telling them which station to go to while naming an arbiter to lead them until only Renal and me are left, and for a moment, I think I see pride on his face, but it disappears, leaving me to wonder if it ever existed in the first place.

Shouts from beyond the wall jerk my attention to the present, and I race to the stairwell leading to the upper level, taking the steps three at a time, ignoring the musty darkness that threatens to choke me, remembering the time Commander Vye first made me walk through here, but that is in the past now. I burst through the other end and hurry across a causeway to the outer wall looking out at the field beyond and the barbarians before it as they prepare another attack, recognizing some of the weapons they have and fuming over the reason why they possess them—they are Arelian.

"Listen up!" I shout to any who can hear me. "If you have breath, you fight!"

"Man the black fire cannons!" Renal yells, appearing by my side, having chased after me, and arbiters move to them, awaiting his command, while others grip their weapons, ready to defend themselves.

A low rumble vibrates through the ground and up the wall, causing my feet to tingle as it touches them and works its way through my legs, and an ominous feeling wafts over me, warning me of a weapon I never considered they would have. I turn in the direction. Barbarians step to the side, forming a wave among a sea of people as they allow a transport with a massive machine gun anchored on it to move through, until it parks in line with the gate.

"Get down!" I shout, and others repeat my warning as I dive for the ground as the barbarians release hell, sending a barrage of bullets at the wall, targeting the gate and weakening it.

Chunks of stone rain down upon me, covering me as I cover my head with my hands trying to protect myself from the onslaught of gunfire, while the intense noise bombards my ears, causing my head to ache while a ball of pressure forms around it, making me think it will explode if no release happens soon.

It stops.

Moments pass, but curiosity gets the better of me, forcing me to get up and peek over the wall in time to watch the barbarian using the machine gun sway before falling over and crashing into the dirt.

A single shot rings in the air, striking the driver of the transport. Enraged, a barbarian jumps atop the transport, going for the machine gun, but drops to the ground when another single shot echoes around us, followed by a third striking the gas tank, detonating an explosion that consumes it, rendering it useless, while those closest to it catch fire and run in terror, desperate to escape their pain.

Perce.

The barbarians point at where they believe the shot came from and send a ball of fire flying toward it, pleased when it crashes into a tall building, ripping through it as it engulfs it in flames until it no longer exists. My thoughts turn toward Perce, but as shouts among the barbarians rise, morphing into a chant, I refocus my attention on them, knowing that there is nothing I can do for him, other than hope he survives. The barbarians regroup, aiming their weapons at us, while their commanders give instructions, and I know what comes next.

"Ready!" I shout at those around me. "Fire!"

Everyone along the wall aims their weapons where I point and fires, releasing a barrage of bullets, striking any unfortunate enough to be in their path, and I watch as a line of barbarians fall prey to their wrath. Another line of barbarians, carrying shields, rush forward, replacing their fallen comrades, and kneel down with their shields in front of them, providing a line of protection as more gunfire comes their way, while those behind prepare for another assault. Before I realize what is happening, Renal throws me to the ground, screaming at everyone to duck for cover while massive rounds tear into the wall, chipping at and creating holes big enough to allow light through while the enraged battle cries of our enemy reach our ears, warning us that they are far from finished. Grappling hooks fly over the wall and embed themselves into it, pulling ladders with them.

"Cut the lines!" Renal yells.

People run to undo the grappling hooks, some succeeding while others are struck by gunfire, but there are too many, allowing ladders to smack against the side of the wall, carrying barbarians into our midst. A woman rushes to a grappling hook, trying to undo it before falling dead. Unable to sit by any longer, I burst from my position and run for the grappling hook, forcing the woman's body out of the way, while I yank my knife out and cut the line, pleased when the ladder it holds teeters before falling away, taking barbarians with it. Another grappling hook attaches itself to the wall next to me, but before I can cut its line, a barbarian jumps over the ledge and kicks me in the face, forcing me to fall to the ground. Stunned, I shake my head, trying to refocus my attention, but the barbarian sees me struggle and charges for me, raising his weapon and prepares to fire.

Renal pounces on him, knocking him to the side as he grabs the man's weapon and wrings it from his hands before ramming his shoulder into the man, causing him to stagger backwards, and turns the barbarian's weapon on him and fires. More appear on the wall. With quick reflexes, Renal rounds on them, unleashing a hailstorm of gunfire as he yells at me to get up, while my mind struggles to focus on what I need to do. I grip the edge of the wall and haul myself to my unsteady feet, swaying to the side as I take a few steps, until I am able to walk a straight line.

A barbarian appears beside me, and I dodge out of the way, avoiding his blow. He kicks at me, and I cross my arms, blocking it, but he counters with a second kick, striking me in the abdomen, sending me staggering back. He charges me, and I run toward him. Surprised by my aggressive reaction, he pauses, allowing me to bring up my weapon and fire it in his face. More come over the wall. Refusing to allow them entrance into Arel, I lean over the side, taking aim at those below me, and empty my magazine, pleased as barbarians fall underneath my spray of bullets. It stops. I check the magazine, realizing it's empty, and toss it at a barbarian climbing one of the ladders before replacing it. Again, I lean over the wall and release a hailstorm of bullets. Others follow suit, emptying their weapons as they take out as many of the enemy as possible, crying out in triumph whenever a barbarian falls from a ladder and crashes onto the ones below.

A flurry of movement catches my attention, and I notice Renal struggling against a barbarian twice his size. Unwilling to lose another, I pull someone over, ordering him to continue firing upon the attackers, before sprinting over to where Renal is. The barbarian has him in a chokehold. I push harder, refusing to fail, holding my rifle out like a club and bashing the barbarian in the face with it, causing him to loosen his hold, giving Renal the advantage. He pulls free and kicks the man's foot out from under him, forcing him to fall over. Before he can regain his feet, both Renal and I put rounds into his chest.

More barbarians swarm around us, and Renal and I stand back-to-back, each of us firing as we create a circle until our ammunition runs out. I go for another magazine, but as I unhook it from my belt, a barbarian knocks it from my hands and it skitters across the stone, over the side, and into the space where the wild dogs are kept. The barbarian lunges for me, but I duck and roll underneath her arm as she swings at me, before twisting around, rolling onto my back, wrapping my legs around her right calf, and yanking it out from under her. She crashes face first into the stone. For a moment, she seems dazed, and I pounce on her, but she recovers and jumps for me, reaching for my arm, but I jerk it away from her, delivering a blow to her face. Before she can counterattack my movement, I latch onto her and flip her to the ground, scrambling to straddle her, and ram my fists into her throat, until she gasps, unable to breathe. Her fearful eyes look into mine, aware that she is about to die, forcing me to provide the only mercy I can, while ensuring she is unable to harm another. I place my hand over her nose and mouth and cut off her air supply until her hands go limp.

A force plows into my back as I reach for my weapon, propelling me forward until I hit the stone with my face, losing my grip on it and grimacing as a stinging burn overwhelms my left check, while the stone scrapes the skin away. Ignoring the pain engulfing my cheek, I roll onto my back in time to jerk to the side as a boot comes for me. Enraged, the barbarian kicks at me, and I roll to the side again, avoiding the blow, while reaching for my rifle. He kicks at me again, and I swing my weapon in front of me, blocking it, but the force of the impact forces it out of my hands. I dive for it. Predicting my actions, the barbarian kicks it away, far from my reach before ramming his fist into my face, striking the wound on my cheek, causing my eyes to water from the impact, and as the pain overwhelms me, I slump to the ground. I hear Renal call my name, but as I peer in his direction, two barbarians impede his efforts to get to me. I try to get up, but my opponent leers over me, relishing the fact that he is much taller and stronger than me, and kicks me in the back, forcing me onto my stomach as he leans into me, putting all of his weight onto me.

The pressure lessens.

Again, I try to get up, and my arms shake as I force them to lift me off the ground, but before I can get to my knees, the barbarian wraps his arms around my middle, lifts me off the ground, and tosses me aside with ease. Pain grips my right shoulder as I crash into the ground, and I flop onto my back, trying to get my bearings as my mind threatens to black out, but the frenzied sounds of battle as people struggle to survive, only to fall silent, force me to get up. The man stalks toward me, confident in his victory as I shake my head, commanding myself to stay conscious, while pretending to have given up. He reaches for me, but I rip my knife free of its hold and plunge it into his left calf, and he howls in pain while throwing a fist in my direction. I tear the knife out of his leg and block his punch with it, allowing the blade to go through his palm until it sticks out the other side. Infuriated, he swings his other fist at me and punches me in the side, causing me to double over from the force of his impact, but I refuse to allow the pain to cripple me and use it as a way to fuel my efforts to survive as I yank my knife free of his hand.

Once again, I hear Renal call my name, but I refuse to take my eyes off my opponent, knowing that such an act will mean my end. Hatred fills his eyes as he glowers at me, and I brace myself for another attack, noting the bulging muscles beneath his clothing. Fear rises within me when a sneer crosses his lips and he pulls out a machete, clenching it in his hand while blood drips from his wound and forms crimson spots on the gray stone, warning me of what is to come. I sneak a quick glance in Renal's direction, and worry fills me when I notice him facing four opponents after having dispatched the previous two, but that glance almost proves to be my undoing.

The barbarian uses my distraction to his advantage and charges me, swiping the air with his machete as he closes the distance between us. I jump back, doing my best to not let his blade touch me. He pushes forward, forcing me to back up as he swings his weapon at me, until my bottom presses against the edge of the wall, and I lean backward, avoiding a final blow. He swings at me again and I duck underneath his blade, cringing as the air from its momentum causes strands of my hair to dance. He whirls around and lunges for me, but I twist to the side, slashing his upper arm with my knife, forcing him to pause as he places his hand over it before looking at the blood and fixing his venomous eyes on me. He lunges to my right, and I dodge it, only to realize that he faked the move when he jumps to my left and slams the hilt of his machete into my face, causing me to stumble backward, dazed.

Using my confusion to his advantage, he stabs at me with his machete, but I trip over my own feet and fall backward, avoiding his fatal blow. He howls in anger as he charges me, bringing his weapon down upon me, and I roll from side to side, avoiding the sharp edge of his blade as it clinks against the stone, creating sparks with each strike. I try dodging around him, but he predicts my movement and brings his knee into my face, causing me to fly backwards as he swipes his machete across my side, cutting into my body armor, but not deep enough to pierce my flesh. I get on my hands and knees, gripping my knife, awaiting his next move, noting that his grip on his machete falters as more blood pours from the hole in his hand and down the edge of his blade. Hoping to end this, he lunges for me, but I jump to my feet and swing my leg at him, kicking the machete from his hand, pleased when it flies over the edge of the wall, and before he can recover, I dive for him and plunge my knife into the side of his torso three times before jumping out of reach.

He gasps, telling me that I punctured a lung, but his determination to end me wins out. Releasing a furious battle cry, he rushes for me. I try to dodge out of the way, but he is too quick and rams his shoulder into my ribcage, knocking the air out of me as I fall backwards, and before I can get up, he places a heavy foot on my chest, bends low, and jerks my knife free of my grasp, tossing it over the wall. I struggle to break free, but his weight pins me down, and the barbarian laughs at my futile efforts. He notices a boulder-sized piece of rubble and picks it up, holding it high above his head as he prepares to throw it at me and finish me. For a third time, Renal screams my name as he attempts to push his way through a crowd of barbarians, kicking and punching as he goes, not caring whose limbs he breaks or whom he throws over the side of the wall, but more crowd in on him, and his desperation turns to fear.

I turn my head back to the barbarian standing on my chest as he revels in my efforts to free myself from him, knowing I cannot defeat him. Before he releases his hold on the massive stone, shock covers his face, while blood pours from a single spot in his chest. Perce. Excitement fills me with its warmth when I realize that he did not die after all, and as that knowledge comforts me, the barbarian's body twitches again when another sniper's bullet strikes him, and he falls backward, tumbling over the wall.

I jerk my head in Renal's direction in time to see two of the people blocking him fall, each a victim of Perce's skills as a sniper. Shouts attract my attention as people pause, and all look to one area. I rush to the edge of the wall, leaning over to see what has mesmerized them, only for all hope to fall the moment I see barbarian after barbarian push their way through the black fire aimed at them and place block after block of explosives at the base of the wall.

"Stop them!" I shout, pointing at them, as more arrive, while another transport with a machine gun mounted atop it rolls through the horde of barbarians and takes aim.

"Stop them!" I scream again, knowing what is coming.

I search for a rifle I can use to put them down, but before I can find one, the machine gun fires, detonating the explosives as Renal appears behind me and wraps his arms around my stomach, jerking me away from the wall, using himself as a shield between me and certain death. Parts of the wall crumble beneath our feet, and my stomach lurches into my throat as we start to fall, while the fear of being buried alive takes hold before the force of the explosion stops our descent and propels us away, until the side of a tower stops us and we drop downward. Air shoots out of my lungs the moment I slam into the hard surface of the wall, while chunks crash around us and shimmering dust buries us. Pressure imprisons my head, causing it to spin, while the feeling of clamps tightening on my temple grows until I believe my skull will burst, unable to contain it anymore. I close my eyes, while I wait for the pressure to dissipate, and muffled sounds surround me, but my fogged mind refuses to process it.

A menacing growl, followed by warm vapor coating my cheek, forces its way through my fogged mind as my ears clear, though some noises further away remain difficult to make out, and I open my eyes, disbelieving what I see. The growl continues as I focus on a wild dog bearing down upon me, warning me not to move, while looking at me with ravenous hunger. I stretch out my fingers, careful to keep my movements slow, noting the rock my fingernails scrape, while keeping my gaze fixed on the dog's barred teeth as drool pours from the corners of its mouth, pooling before me. Something shifts nearby. The wild dog jerks its head in the direction of the movement, barking with ferocity, and I grab the rock and smash it into the dog's head. It turns on me. I push myself off the ground and strike the dog in the head again, while clumps of dust fall from my body and form a choking cloud of ash. The dog yelps and runs off, while I lean against what remains of the ledge on the wall, using it to support me as my legs threaten to give out, and I stumble to the side.

As the edges of stone press into my body, I force my legs to support me, while panicked cries draw my attention to a gaping hole in what remains of the outer and inner walls as the wild dogs that had been contained there spring from it, going in every direction, attacking Arelian and barbarian alike. Shouts of triumph rise from the barbarians beyond the wall as they charge for the hole, weapons raised, but before they get far, four mortar shells detonate among them, stopping them. Curious, I look out at the open field and past the tendrils of thick, gray smoke hovering over the grass, and my eyes widen the moment I make out shapes coming out of the tree line, and after a minute, I realize they are people walking next to armed transports, followed by horses with riders. Sigal made it through after all. Perce's people have arrived.

One of them issues a command and the armed transports fire upon the barbarians. Some run for the hole in the wall only to be stopped by their commander as he forces them to face this new threat, while hope builds within me: perhaps we will survive this day. I turn toward the hole, taking note of the people gathered there.

"No one gets through!" I scream, while those at the black fire cannons fire upon any fool enough to try and breach it, but judging by the strength of the flames, their fuel reserves are running low.

"Noni," a weak voice calls to me.

Renal!

Scolding myself for having forgotten about him, I run to the mound of rubble and dig into it, brushing the dust away, revealing Renal's limp form. He reaches for me, and I grasp his arm, yanking him free of the debris before leaning him against the side of the tower, concerned about the shallowness of his breathing.

"Report on the situation," he says.

"You're hurt," I say, worried about his labored breathing. I press my fingers on his side below the breastbone, and he jerks away, doing his best to not scream in pain. "You might have a broken rib—"

"Report," he says again followed by a gurgled cough as a few bloody bubbles form on his lips.

"—and possibly a punctured lung."

"Report!"

I pull my fingers away from his side and drop them by my own, somewhat hurt by the harsh tone of his voice, but more worried about the paleness of his face as his dark skin turns ashen, making me fear that he has internal bleeding as well, and without immediate medical care, I'll lose him.

"Noni, you are an arbiter. Now, report the situation."

Swallowing back the lumps building in my throat, I look him in the eyes, and tell him what he wants to know.

"The barbarians have breached the wall, but the majority of their numbers still remain outside, distracted by our reinforcements."

He gives me a confused look.

"Sigal made it through."

A smile crosses his face. "We need to close that breach."

"How? We don't..."

I stop, allowing my voice to trail off as I look at the watchtower towering over us, which Renal leans against, and an idea forms in my mind. I sprint over to the ledge and study the distance to the hole in the wall before looking at the tower once more. It is a gamble, but it could work.

"How many explosives do you have?" I ask him, while remembering the number I had with me.

Renal follows my gaze, reading my mind. "Enough."

A single bullet strikes the stone near my feet, forcing me to look in the direction it might have come from.

Perce.

Hoping he understands me, I point at the watchtower and the hole in the wall, trying to show him my intention through various arm signals. Please understand my message, Perce, please! Desperate to make sure he realizes my intention, I lean over the ledge, screaming at any who can hear me, "Fall back! Get away from that hole!"

More explosions beyond the city echo around us, and a quick glance tells me that the barbarians are distracted by Perce's people, and I hope it gives us enough time. Having no way of knowing if Perce comprehended my message, I hurry back to Renal as he pulls the last explosive from his bandolier, and I place the ones I have in the pile.

"Take this wire," Renal says to me. "Place one here… here… and here." He points where each explosive should be placed.

"I'll work on these," he finishes.

I do as instructed and place an explosive on each side of the tower before placing a third in the back, attaching the wires to them and stretching them back around to the front where Renal arranges the rest. He takes the wire from me, his hands shaking as he struggles to not show the agony that grips him, and finishes rigging our makeshift bomb.

"I'll be fine," he says, feeling my worried eyes on him.

"Maybe I should…"

"It's finished."

"What about the detonator?"

"Right here," he says, holding it in his fist, but he refuses to allow me to have it.

I start to help him up, but Renal stops me.

"Get me to the tower's control room."

"What?" I say, taken aback.

We need to abandon this place before more barbarians flood through the opening their explosion caused. For a moment, we both stare at one another, willing the other to understand our unique viewpoint and to be persuaded to our bidding, while bits of sunlight break through the swirling smoke surrounding us, warning us of our predicament, and that our time has drawn to a close.

"There is something I must do."

"Lieutenant..."

"Noni," Renal says in a gentle voice as he tucks a lose strand of my black hair behind my ear in much the same way a father would, "I need you to trust me. It is the only way to end this."

For a moment, the feeling that I will never see him again grips me, paralyzing me and forbidding me to move, but the more I look upon Renal's pleading expression, I know that I must abide by his request. Relenting, I place his arm over my shoulder and haul him to his feet, almost stopping the moment a strangled cry of pain escapes him against his will, but he urges me to keep going. He places all his weight on me, and though I almost cave underneath it, I refuse to falter, to deny him this request, or to show weakness when he needs my strength the most. Renal has always been my anchor when I needed it; now it is my turn to be his. I lead him to the narrow steps carved into the stones of the watchtower, and when he places his left foot on the first step, it slips and falls back to the bottom, causing him to lean to the right, but I retain my hold on him and pull him back until he is balanced once more.

"Take your time," I tell him. "I won't let you fall."

He smiles, remembering a time when he told me the same, and he places his left foot on the first step again, while I join him, and together, we haul ourselves upward. With one hand, I cling to the side of the stairs, while with the other, I cling to him, steadying him as we climb upward, taking one step at a time. The cacophonous sounds of gunfire, mortar shells, metal clinking against metal, and the agonized cries of those suffering unspeakable injuries surround us, enveloping us in a prison of chaos that attacks our senses, mocking our efforts to climb the narrow stairs to the control room within the tower, while its edges cast a dark shadow over us, forbidding the sun to shine its light upon our path and guide us. Renal's foot slips again. My arms and fingers ache as I grip him, refusing to let go as I yank him back before he falls to the bottom.

"We're almost there," I tell him, encouraging him.

He places his hand on the side of the stairwell, trying his best to stabilize himself and push himself upward as we continue the almost vertical climb. I go higher and lift him as he pushes with his legs, struggling with each step, while his breaths become shorter and shorter. An unspeakable worry nudges the edge of my mind, but I shove it aside, refusing to allow it any attention, fearing that it may be true. He looks up. Only three more steps left. Again, I go to the next step—the wind whips my lose bits of hair, pelting me in the face as a way of trying to convince me to quit, but if it believes this will deter me, then it is mistaken—and heave him upward while he tries to push with his legs. My muscles burn and threaten to give out on me because of the exertion, but I command them to remain strong, telling them that today is not the day for weakness or failure, but a day for extraordinary strength, where one's will overpowers the body. One more step. I haul Renal to it, and he latches his hand around what can be construed as a makeshift rail, while I reach up, open the hatch, and crawl inside before reaching down for him. He clasps my arm and I yank him into the control tower, and we both roll onto the floor heaving from the exertion.

Silence.

Where is the guard?

Though exhausted, I force myself to my feet and look around, spotting the answer to my question: outside, leaning on the railing, is the guard with his limp arms swaying in the wind, while blood drips from a wound in his neck where a piece of shrapnel had struck him. Pitying him, but knowing there is nothing I can do for him, I grab Renal's arm and lift him up, half-carrying, half-dragging him to the console, where the transparent screen flashes to life the moment we approach. I release his arm when he motions for me to and watch as he types, leaning further and further over the console as his weakened state proves unable to support him, but before I can do anything, a woman's face appears on the viewscreen, and judging by the pins on the collar of her uniform, she is a pilot for the Arelian fleet.

"Lieutenant," she says, "I told you that I cannot..."

"Captain Soryn, listen," Renal says, struggling to get the words out as his breathing becomes more labored, while sweat drenches his face and drips from the point of his chin.

"Renal," her tone full of worry, "what's wrong?"

"I need you to heed my request."

"If the council or Tapiwa learn..."

"Tapiwa is dead."

I try to melt into the background, not wanting to interrupt Renal's plea for help, while I wonder who this woman is, knowing that she is another part of a mysterious past I will never know, and wishing we had the time for him to tell me.

"What?" the woman says, surprised.

"Captain," Renal's labored words force her to listen, "Arel has been attacked by barbarians."

"These attacks have always been..."

"Not this time. This time, they mean to annihilate us all. We will not survive the day unless your fleet abandon your orders and help us."

The captain purses her lips, unsure of what to say or do.

"Please, captain. You swore an oath to protect the people of Arel—to protect the innocent. Will you abandon them now?"

"Renal..."

"Your oath supersedes your orders."

Unable to stand by any longer, I step forward, uttering the only words I can think of. "Please, captain, help us."

The woman looks at me before returning her gaze to Renal's weakened form and whatever reservations she had about his request dissipate. "Your orders?" she says to him.

"Execute Operation Niner."

"Understood."

The moment the screen goes blank, Renal collapses to the floor, unable to stand any longer, and I rush to him, wrapping his arm around my shoulders as I try to lift him up.

"Noni," he says, stopping me, "leave me."

"I can carry you," I say, trying to lift him up again, but his weight proves too much for me, and he flops back down to the floor, taking me with him.

"You need to go," he says in a whisper and pulls out the detonator.

"You never planned on leaving the tower," my voice cracks as I realize the finality of the situation and Renal's decision.

"Go."

Shaking my head, protests escape my mouth as my refusal to leave him sets in. "I won't leave you! You can't… I can't leave another!"

"I'm already dead."

Tears fill my eyes as my arbiter façade vanishes, and I crumble before him in an emotional mess of denial.

"There is a cable over there. Take this," he says, pulling off his belt and handing it to me. "Get to the black fire canon and hold out until Captain Soryn arrives."

Fear etches itself on my face as I remember the last time I used a black fire canon and the images of my stony face as I murdered any who got in my way.

"You are not that person anymore," says Renal, reading my thoughts.

"Please," I whisper as a tear falls from the corner of my jaw and dots my arm.

"Some of us are called to protect those who will guide others and preserve our civilization. You have a chance to rebuild Arel for the better. Use it."

I shake my head, unable to accept the inevitability of the situation. I know he is dying, but I refuse to accept it. "I don't want to."

"Life isn't always about we want. Sometimes, you have to learn to live with your choices and the outcomes given to you. This, I can live with, if you survive."

More tears fill my eyes.

"Gwen needs you," he says, using the one thing that will make me see reason.

Still unwilling to leave him, but realizing I have no choice as the cries of battle draw closer and a mortar shell detonates near the tower, shaking it, telling me that its foundation is weakened, I push myself to my feet, taking his belt and wiping my tears. As a final act of respect, I salute him.

"Go," he says.

I head to the door leading to the walkway circling around the control room. It slides open the moment I step in front of it and wind rushes in, drying the tears on my face as strands of my hair form a wild dance around my head. Wasting no time, I go to the cable Renal spoke of, and study it, noting how it stretches down to the far side of the wall, near where a black canon sits—the arbiter using it falls over after taking a round in the chest—and I climb on the ledge surrounding the walkway and place the belt over the cable. My heart aches at the thought of leaving another behind. Doubt creeps in, causing me to pause and think of myself as incapable, and when I believe I will be unable to do what I must, I think of Gwen and my promise to her. Stealing one last glance at Renal as he watches, I jump off the ledge.

Wind whips around my body, causing goosebumps to form along my arms, while I careen down the line, and my knuckles turn white from clinging to the belt as I refuse to let go, unsure if I will be able to stop. The far side of the wall approaches faster than anticipated. As I brace myself for the impending impact, the explosives Renal and I placed around the base of the watchtower detonate, causing a massive explosion that rattles my body as I speed away from it as pieces of brick sail past me, while clouds of a fiery inferno illuminate my silhouette. The cable slackens. I jerk my head in time to see the tower lean toward the hole in the wall as it starts to topple over. Almost there. Just a few more seconds.

The cable slackens even more, and I focus on my goal, refusing to give in to the rising fear within me that this could be my end, determined to survive for Gwen's sake. The top of the wall rushes for me, and as the line goes limp, I let go of the belt and drop the remaining four feet, crashing into the top of the wall, unable to stop as the momentum causes me to roll onward until I go over the inner edge. I throw my hands out and grip the edge of the wall, refusing to fall over the side. My body jerks to a stop, and I cry out as my shoulders are almost torn from their sockets. Mustering what strength I have left, I heave myself over the edge and onto a flat surface, but I have no time to rest.

Barbarians approach. I force myself to my feet and stumble over to the black fire canon where its original user remains slumped over it, and shove him off, allowing him to drop to the side as I take charge of the weapon. A group of barbarians break away from the rest and head for the breach in the wall. Once they are close enough, I release a fury of black fire on them, and they turn in every direction as their skin melts from their bodies, warning others to stay away. Before I can see if more come my way, the sounds of Arelian aircraft approach, soft at first, but growing stronger with each passing second.

"Get down!" I yell at any who can hear me.

Arelian aircraft appear from the mountain, flying over the city and to the field beyond the wall where the barbarians are, and before they can react, bombs fall from the sky, striking the earth. A fiery wall bursts from the ground, covering the field and engulfing any who get in its way, as a hellish inferno consumes the area, producing an intense heat that singes my skin. Unable to look away, I watch as the barbarians disappear beneath the fury of the bombs as more aircraft fly overhead. One misses his mark, and drops his explosive too close to the city. I dive for cover, hoping to avoid its wrath, but when I hit the ground, debris crashes around me, burying me as it attempts to erase my existence, and the world becomes a blur.

Shouts, cheers, and explosions meld together as I remain underneath the rubble, unable to free myself and unsure of how long I have been confined here. A muffled voice calls my name, but I do not respond, unsure if I am dreaming or not. Hands remove pieces of stone from me, but my mind remains dazed and confused. Is my name still being called? I cannot tell as all sounds blend together, forming a chaotic mess in my mind, until hands pull me free of the debris.

"Noni?" says a familiar voice.

I should know that voice.

"Noni!"

The same hands give me a gentle shake before smacking me in the face, not hard, but soft, in an attempt to get me to wake up. A part of me does not want to wake. It would be easier to remain as I am, detached from the world, until eternal slumber takes hold, but memories of why I am here flood my mind as Renal's last words about Gwen take root, and I open my eyes to find Perce's relieved face above mine.

"Perce?" I say as he sits me up. "How did you find me?"

"I gave you a tracker, remember?"

That's right. He did.

I grin at him, pleased that he found me, and rub my face, aching all over. "The barbarians… are they…"

"Gone," he answers. "Those still alive scattered when your aircraft came back for another pass."

"And your people?"

"Fine."

"And the others?"

"They're all fine. Your city still stands, as do her people. It's you I'm worried about."

"I'll be all right," I say.

"I'll believe that after you've seen a doctor."

Perce helps me to my feet and leads me across one of the walkways leading to a stairwell. When we reach the bottom, I almost gasp from amazement as plebeians, arbiters, and citizens embrace one another, thrilled at having survived this ordeal, while welcoming Perce's people.

"How long..." I start to ask.

"It took me a while to get to you."

Perce leads me away from the opening within the wall, making certain that I do not collapse from any injuries I may have sustained, while my mind jumps in and out of a fog, desiring rest, but I must know what has happened to the others. Perce must have read my mind because he pushes his way through the sea of people with me in tow, refusing to let go of my arm, leading me to a lone bench—how it escaped destruction is a mystery—where Sigal, Luther, and Gwen are. Gwen sees me first and rushes for me, grasping me around the waist as she hugs me, refusing to let go. Perce reminds her that they should get me to a doctor, but I wrap my arms around her, thrilled that she and the others are okay.

"Where's Renal?" Perce asks, and I shake my head, causing him to frown in response.

Some surrounding us recognize me and salute me, signifying their respect, and I return the gesture. It is the least I can do.

"Where is she?" demands a woman as she pushes her way through the crowd with two others behind her until she finds me. "I need to speak with Arbiter Noni."

The moment the woman appears, I recognize her from the viewscreen in the watchtower; she is the one Renal referred to as Captain Soryn.

"What do you want with me?" I demand, doing my best to appear strong.

"Arbiter Noni?" she asks.

"Yes," I reply.

"The barbarians have abandoned their attack and fled for the jungle. What are your orders?"

"What?" The word is out of my mouth before I have a chance to stop it.

"Lieutenant Renal was very specific. If Operation Niner was ever executed, we were to follow your orders, and only your orders."

As I think back to his call to her, I realize that he must have set this up a long time ago in case something like this happened. Did he suspect Anshu and his men would commit a coup? Did he suspect the complete collapse of Arel would happen? The more I think about it, the more I wonder how much Renal knew and how much he had been privy to. The suspicion that he was a marshal fills my mind one last time, and I allow myself to believe that he was, even though I will never know for certain, because it is the only thing that makes sense.

Joseph appears from the crowd, pleased to see me, but upon noticing Captain Soryn, he backs away, choosing anonymity.

"Arbiter Noni?" the captain says with impatience. "Should we pursue the barbarians?"

"Let them be," I reply. "They know we are strong, let them also know our mercy. Convene the Arelian Council. They will need to elect a new president. See to it that all the wounded receive medical attention, and begin repairs on the wall."

The captain starts to walk away, but my curiosity stops her.

"How do you know Renal? Why risk everything for him?" I ask.

Captain Soryn purses her lips as she considers answering me. "He saved my life once. Perhaps I'll tell you about it someday."

"I'd like that."

Captain Soryn salutes me and hurries off to carry out my instructions, disappearing into the crowd as she picks out volunteers to assist her.

I teeter on my feet, and Perce catches me. "You need a doctor."

I try to wave him off, but his insistence wins the argument, and I allow him to sit me down. While he runs off to seek help, Gwen nestles into my arms as the others keep an eye on me.

"What do we do we do now?" she asks.

"We rebuild," I tell her.

"Rebuild what?"

I look at all the people clapping each other on the back or

helping one another get the care they need, unconcerned about their station, but seeing another human being instead. The more I watch them, the more that little spark of hope grows, until it consumes me with its optimism that we can, and will, build a better future for all.

Chapter 33

A Final Farewell

The pointed tips of the blades of grass brush my elbows as I stand in the meadow outside the wall, the one portion untouched by the battle, looking out at the field beyond with Arel behind me, tucked away in the mountain and watching my final farewell to those I loved and will never see again, while Gwen, Luther, Sigal, and Perce stand nearby, respecting my wishes. Seven stones, each matching the length of my arm in width, stare up at me as they lay in a bed of flattened grass, while the dawn's sun shines upon them, exposing the names carved on each of them, one for each of those I've lost: Chase, Sheila, Faya, Commander Vye, Renal, Trevors, and Grelyn. Though Trevors, Grelyn, and I may have had our differences, they chose to sacrifice themselves in the end so Gwen and I could survive and deserve to be remembered for their final act. The wind caresses my long hair, convincing it to dance around me as my hand grips seven distinct flowers: a purple orchid, two Gladiolas, a white lily, an Alstroemeria, and two pink carnations.

I glance at Luther as he stands next to the others, respecting my need to say a final farewell. It was his idea to perform this sort of ritual, and I had asked him how he knew any of this. He said he had read it in a book, in one of the many forbidden volumes he possessed. He gives me a weak smile, encouraging me to do what I must, but my feet remain frozen, unable to carry out this task as my heart remains unwilling to admit that the time has come to move forward. A gentle hand places itself on mine, forcing me to glance at its owner, and Gwen looks up at me with her gray eyes, encouraging me at a time when I should be comforting her.

Taking a deep breath, I step toward the stones and, one by one, I place the flowers before them, allowing their vibrant colors to contrast against the green blades of grass and the muted neutral tones of the stones themselves. Before each of the stones with Grelyn's and Trevors' names, I place a pink carnation in remembrance of their sacrifice. In front of Faya's, I set the Alstroemeria, memorializing our deep-rooted friendship. Before Commander Vye's and Renal's stones, I place a Gladioli in remembrance of their strength of character. A tear escapes my eye when I step in front of Sheila's, wishing that she had not suffered the fate Molers dealt her, and I set a white lily in front of it, signifying her innocence. Only one stone left. Lumps form in my throat as it seizes from my efforts to stop myself from weeping, wishing that I could feel his comforting arms around me once more as he tries to shield me from the world's cruelty, and I kneel before his stone, allowing the grass to dig into my knees, leaving chaotic impressions in my skin as I place the purple orchid before it, vowing to never forget him.

"I love you," I whisper, hoping the wind carries my message to him.

Moments pass, but the others remain silent, giving me the time I need to say good-bye, but I know I cannot remain here. The world is for the living, and the time for mourning has passed. I rise to my feet and face Arel, noting all the new construction as dark and fair-skinned alike work together to rebuild our home, and I hope, make it better.

"Let's go," I say, and Gwen hurries to my side, placing her hand in mine as we walk back to the city, leaving the past where it belongs because we have the future to consider. I hope it is far better than what we left behind.

Chapter 34

Noni's Peace

The unified shouts of new recruits responding to my instructions reach my ears as I pace before the latest batch of individuals hoping to become arbiters, never thinking I would see the day when individuals from every background chose to work together. I spot Gwen's form among them as she stands at attention in her new uniform, with her blonde hair pulled into a bun, ready to do what is asked of her for the good of Arel, amazed at how fast she has matured in the last 12 years. I avoid smiling at her, not wanting to show favoritism, while deep down, my heart bursts with pride.

Twelve years. The events of the past seem like a lifetime ago. By unanimous vote by the people and the council, I was made Arel's president following Tapiwa's death, Anshu's coup, and the final attack of the barbarians. I didn't want it, but Luther convinced me to accept the honor bestowed upon me, fearing what would happen if I didn't and reminding me that I was the one thing uniting all of Arel. I accepted on one condition: that he serve as my advisor in addition to his other duties. Luther frowned but gave in, and we shook hands as a symbol of our agreement. After a long, hard battle, certain changes have been made. The caste system is ended. There are no more plebeians because we are all citizens. The breeding centers have been destroyed. Infants are no longer ripped from the arms of their mothers. There are no more sterilization chemicals in the water supply or forced hysterectomies and vasectomies. People are allowed to decide their own fate instead of having their position within Arel chosen for them. The gate to the wall, though still there for our protection from the outside world, is open to any who wish to come here, so long as they respect our laws, and to my surprise, many barbarians have chosen to become Arelian citizens, bringing with them their knowledge of certain trades. For the ones who have not, a peace treaty has been negotiated, and they are no longer given our arms and ammunition. Other cities have been found, and we have sent ambassadors to them, hoping to trade with them.

Doctor Sahir runs a school of medicine with Natalie by his side, open to all. Sigal and his family returned to Arel, and he now owns three cafés, which my stomach is most happy about. And Luther? Through his knowledge of architecture, Arel's infrastructure has been rebuilt, and he has taken on apprentices. Sometimes, I have caught him acting as though it is an imposition to train them, but I do not believe he would have it any other way. I make sure to visit him from time to time—he still hides treats for Gwen, despite the fact she has grown—and he always acts annoyed, but behind that stern expression lies a grin. Yes, some good changes have been made, and though the echoes of the past sometimes try to undo it, so far, it has been ignored, and I believe, that with time, those echoes will fade and disappear, so long as we remember who we are and remember that we are one people.

After eight years as Arel's president, I resigned. Eight years is enough, and if Tapiwa's example is any indication, no one person should hold power for too long. Heeding my plea, the council agreed and issued an edict, declaring that eight years is a sufficient term for serving as president, and that no individual may serve more than one term in their lifetime, adding that one must be a minimum of 30 years of age—at my insistence because I always felt too young and inexperienced—and members of the council must follow the same law: serving one term in a single lifetime, spanning eight years, after which, they retire, and a new individual, who is a minimum of 30 years of age, fills their seat, chosen by those living in their district.

I returned to my life as an arbiter, and it is my job to prepare the next generation of arbiters to become the protectors of Arel, a task I embrace with enthusiasm, having forbidden many of the methods used to train me.

"Listen up!" I shout over the recruits. "You have chosen to become arbiters of Arel. You have sworn an oath to protect the people and to protect their rights. You are not above the law, and you will not exert your authority to terrorize them. The oath you swear today is not an oath to be taken lightly. It requires sacrifice, diligence, and fortitude. Any who feel unable to fulfill this obligation may leave at any time, but for those of you who stay, I expect you to give one hundred and ten percent, and you will be held to the highest of standards. The job of an arbiter is a sacred duty, a calling, and it will have its challenges, but let me assure you, it also has its rewards. Understood?"

"Yes, commander!" a multitude of voices reply, and my eyes settle upon Gwen as she stands in formation.

A slight smile crosses my face as amusement takes hold; Commander Vye got her wish after all: I am the commander of the eastern sector.

"Commander,"—an arbiter approaches me—"the ambassador of Croatia is here."

I glance in the direction he points, and Perce waves at me.

"Take over," I say.

"Yes, commander," the arbiter replies, saluting me as I walk in Perce's direction.

Whenever he visits on official business, Perce always makes certain to stop by—I have come to look forward to such occasions—and as I approach him, a warm grin fills my face, causing Perce to return the gesture.

On cold nights, I still feel sorrow for Chase and the others, but I have come to terms with it. Renal once told me that life isn't always about getting what we want, but being able to live with the choices we have made and the outcome that is given us, and as I take one last look at Gwen embarking on a new future—her future—I turn back toward Perce, knowing the time has come for me to do the same.

Some of you may wonder why I have chosen to stay in Arel. The answer is simple: I am Noni—an arbiter of Arel, and a protector of my people.

The
End

Read the Entire Series

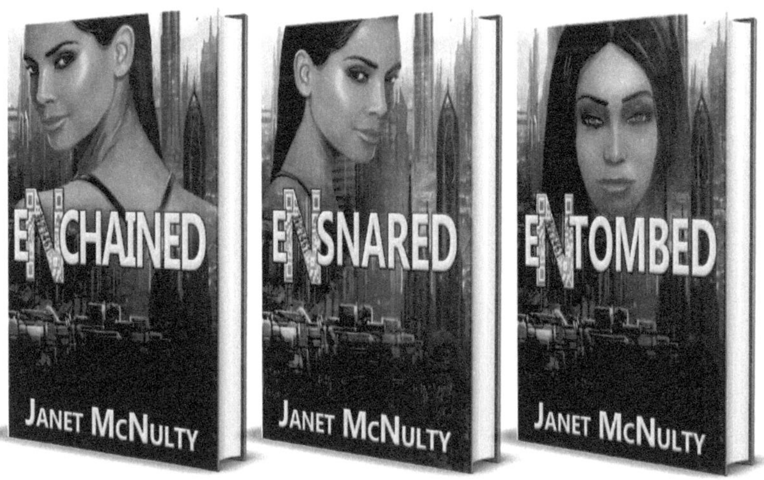

Having spent her entire life secluded in the Martial Diplomatic Corps, Noni passes the final test, achieving the coveted position as arbiter of Arel. Placed under the tutelage of a seasoned veteran, Noni will see her city for the first time and learn that not everything is as she had been taught to believe.

About the Author

Janet McNulty is an independent author, practicing what she calls the most expensive hobby one can engage in, and a former candidate to the West Virginia House of Delegates.

In 2011, she released Legends Lost Amborese, which was published under the pen name of Nova Rose. Ms. McNulty has since published three novels in the Legends Lost series: Tesnayr and Galdin.

Ms. McNulty has gone on to publish four more fiction series in the last seven years: The Mellow Summers Series, The Dystopia Trilogy, The Solaris Saga, and The Enchained Trilogy.

More books by Janet McNulty

The Solaris Saga

Solaris Seethes
Solaris Seeks
Solaris Strays
Solaris Soars

Also available in audio.

Every myth has a beginning.

After escaping the destruction of her home planet, Lanyr, with the help of the mysterious Solaris, Rynah must put her faith in an ancient legend. Never one to believe in stories and legends, she is forced to follow the ancient tales of her people: tales that also seem to predict her current situation.

Forced to unite with four unlikely heroes from an unknown planet (the philosopher, the warrior, the lover, the inventor) in order to save the Lanyran people, Rynah and Solaris embark on an adventure that will shatter everything Rynah once believed.

The Mellow Summers Series

Sugar And Spice And Not So Nice
Frogs, Snails, And A Lot Of Wails
An Apple A Day Keeps Murder Away
Three Little Ghosts
Oh Holy Ghost
Where Trouble Roams
Two Ghosts Haunt A Grove
Trick Or Treat Or Murder
Roses Are Red…He's Dead
Double, Double Nothing But Trouble
Ring Around The Rosy Not Another Ghosty
Hickory Dickory Dock The Ghost In The Clock
Violet Are Blue More Trouble Brews
Hey Diddle Diddle The Zombie In The Middle
Easy as Pie Until Someone Dies

Mellow Summers moves to Vermont to attend college, accompanied by her friend Jackie. They soon find themselves running into ghosts and one mystery after another.

The Dystopia Trilogy

Dystopia (Book 1)
Tempered Steel (Book 2)
Liberty's Torch (Book 3)

Imagine living in a world where everything you do is controlled.

Dana Ginary lives in a world where every aspect of her life is controlled by the Dystopian Government. Forced to work in Waste Management, her life becomes a nightmare with hunger and survival is her only constant. Before she knows it, she is caught up in a resistance movement and exiled from Dystopia, forced to find her way in the barren wastelands. While there, she must learn to live independently and discover how far she is willing to go to live and achieve freedom.

The Legends Lost Series

Published under Nova Rose

Tesnayr
Amborese
Galdin

Enter the Lands of Tesnayr and join on an epic fantasy adventure that spans over 1,500 years.

Begin with Tesnayr, the first king of the five lands as he unites the against a savage foe bent on their destruction.

Next, Join Amborese as she fights reclaim the throne after her family was forced to flee from it.

Thinking peace has finally entered the land, follow Galdin as he returns to Tesnayr to find it greatly hanged. Barbarians, led by a mysterious sorcerer, burn and destroy as they go. And only Galdin can stop them if he chooses to accept his fate.

Grandpa's Stories

My grandfather grew up in Arizona during the 1920s and 1930s. One week after the attack on Pearl Harbor he joined the Navy. During the summer of 2012, my mother visited him and recorded his stories about growing up, World War II, and his time as an employee at the Pacific Bell Telephone Company. This is the history of the 20th century as he lived it. These recordings make up this book. These are his words.

www.ingramcontent.com/pod-product-compliance
Lightning Source LLC
Chambersburg PA
CBHW020602310726
48979CB00008B/1307/J

* 9 7 8 1 9 4 1 4 8 8 9 8 0 *